BOOKS BY ELLIOTT ARNOLD

The Time of the Gringo   1953

Walk with the Devil   1950

These are BORZOI BOOKS
Published in New York by Alfred A. Knopf

THE
TIME
OF THE
GRINGO

THE

TIME

OF THE

GRINGO

01389

BY

Elliott Arnold

1 9 5 3

ALFRED A. KNOPF
NEW YORK

L. C. catalog card number: 52–6402

THIS IS A BORZOI BOOK,
PUBLISHED BY ALFRED A. KNOPF, INC.

FIRST AND SECOND PRINTINGS BEFORE PUBLICATION

THIS BOOK IS FOR

Tommy

AND FOR

Mary.

NOTE

Gringo (green-go): (coll.) Unintelligible, gibberish: applied to a language. (vulg.) A nickname given to one who speaks a foreign language.

VELAZQUEZ: *A New Pronouncing Dictionary of the Spanish and English Languages.*

T HIS WORD, "gringo," so popular among the Spanish-speaking natives of the Southwest and Latin America, has long beguiled etymologists, who have tried valiantly, but thus far without success, to run down its origin. It is believed by many that the word is a corruption of the Spanish *"griego,"* meaning Greek. The Spaniards use *"griego"* as slang for any incomprehensible language, and have an expression: "To speak in Greek," which corresponds to our "It's Greek to me."

A naïve but persistent legend has the word "gringo" originating from the popularity of the song, based on Burns's poem "Green Grow the Rushes, Oh!" which American cowboys in Texas and American soldiers of that time are supposed never to have stopped singing as they went about their business. According to this fairy tale, the Mexicans themselves invented the word out of the first two words of the tune.

Dr. Frank H. Vizetelly, however, has traced "gringo" as far back at least as 1787, to P. Esteban de Terreros y Pando's *Diccionario Castellano,* published in Madrid, where "gringo" is defined as "The name given in Málaga to those foreigners who have a certain accent which prevents them from speaking Spanish fluently and naturally; and in Madrid the same term is used for the same reason, especially with reference to the Irish." The word also appears in a French-Spanish dictionary issued in Paris in 1838 with the same meaning.

Dr. Vizetelly adds: "This serves to show that some 'Spanish' was as so much Greek to the Hidalgos long before the Mexicans heard 'Green Grow the Leaves on the Hawthorne Tree' or 'Green Grow the Rushes, Oh!' "

Whatever its origin, it would appear that the word was brought to New Spain by men from old Spain and was used, always with some degree of contempt, as a perfect expression of their feelings toward American usurpers who too "had a certain accent which prevented them from speaking Spanish fluently and naturally."

E. A.

THE
TIME
OF THE
GRINGO

THE TIME OF THE GRINGO   PART I

1

Iᴛ ᴡᴀs ʟᴀᴛᴇ ɪɴ ᴛʜᴇ ᴅᴀʏ and Don Manuel's shadow was long on the land. The six riders strung out behind him on the Taos Road waited for him to order the halt, but he remained hunched over his great bay horse, and the hot miles and the hours in the harsh Spanish saddle seemed without meaning to him.

One of the riders twisted in the saddle and creaked the muscles in his back. "By the nails of Christ, and does he intend to reach there tonight?" he muttered.

The rider nearest him said: "Until now it was the heat, Emilio. Now you tire. It is that you are soft."

Emilio spat. "I am not soft. That is the trouble. God gave to Don Manuel the cushioned rump. I have not lived in the palace and I have no hacienda and I am thin and bony. I feel as though I ride on thorns."

"That is good for your soul," the other man said.

Emilio spat again. "I urinate on my soul."

The trail above the Rio Grande narrowed in a canyon. Beyond the lean hill the sun dropped away. The empty air chilled instantly. The light was less than before, but vision cleared. The New Mexican mountains assembled, their spines littered with stones. The knuckled trees emerged into isolated focus. Sound filled in the vanished heat: hoofs on the flinty earth, aching saddles, the icy jingle of spurs. Now the river rippled almost delicately. An evening breeze was freed. A mountain wolf sobbed and the horses' ears twitched and the men touched their guns.

The road descended until it came to the bank of the river. Don Manuel raised his head for the first time. He lifted his hand in a peremptory gesture. "Give the horses to drink, hombres," he ordered. His voice was rich and resonant as the deep sound from a guitar. "If there be those among you roosters who still taste it,

3

give yourselves to drink as well. If the horses do not make objection."

Emilio dismounted painfully. "The flesh hangs in strings from my buttocks, and Don Manuel makes the jokes!"

His friend looked frightened. "Close your beak!" he said.

"Don Manuel no longer is Governor," Emilio said angrily. "He is nothing now."

"He will be Governor again," his friend said. "He will be everything. That one is designed for the power."

Don Manuel lowered himself from his stirrup and, limping, led his horse to the river. The animal dipped its muzzle eagerly into the cold mountain water. Don Manuel removed a silver flask from his saddlebag and swallowed a mouthful of brandy.

He was a man well over six feet and in New Mexico he was a man of great size. He was big even when he stood among the traders from the United States. He was not yet forty. His strong face was cleanly shaven, in a country where men grew beards and mustaches to show their Spanish blood before Indians, who could seldom grow either. His mouth was wide and full-lipped. His eyes were dark and set widely apart from the large, straight nose, and they rested deep in sockets above the high cheekbones. Now they stared broodingly across the river at the gray mountains lying against the darkening sky.

He took another draught from the flask. He wiped his lips with the back of his hand and removed his black, flat-crowned, wide-brimmed hat and ran his fingers through his thick hair. He filled his chest with the high, taut air so that the buttons on his embroidered jacket strained.

Now there was no sound save the sucking of the horses and the quiet murmuring of the men.

Don Manuel raised a finger. "Señor Caballero," he said. A young man with a careless, cheerful face left the group and came to him immediately, touching the brim of his hat. Don Manuel pointed to the northeast. "That light, Don Esquipulas, there in the cleft of the hill."

"Indians, señor," Caballero said indifferently. "I have watched them signal to each other all day. I do not believe they will trouble us. We are too well armed."

Don Manuel nodded. He held out the flask. "Brandy, amigo?"

4

"Many thanks, Don Manuel. You are more than kind. Do we rest here for the night?"

"We go on to Taos."

"We shall arrive late."

"It is necessary that we arrive late."

"I will give the order to the men whenever you are ready."

Don Manuel replaced the flask in the saddlebag. He smiled with great charm. "I am ready now, but first, for favor, help me with my serape."

"Willingly," Caballero said. He unstrapped a finely woven blanket from the saddle and opened the center slit so Don Manuel could slip it over his head.

"And now, querido amigo, if you would be good enough to help me into the saddle," Don Manuel said.

Caballero made a stirrup of his hands. Don Manuel mounted. "You may now give the order, Don Esquipulas," he said. "And then ride with me. Your company pleasures me."

Emilio, kneading his bruised hams, was the last to climb into the saddle as the caballada resumed. "Host with vinegar! Do we ride through half the night?"

"Now you fear the night," his friend mocked.

"I fear nothing, hombrecito," Emilio said angrily. "Bravery has nothing to do with a chafed rump."

"Don Manuel has ridden as long and as hard, and he has twice your years."

"He is as tireless as a rock, Ernesto," Emilio admitted.

"Do you begin to find that out? I remember him from the old days when he was in power, when you were yet a child with a snotty nose. He was like a boulder rolling down a hill. Those who did not scamper away were injured."

"In Santa Fe it is said his day has passed."

Ernesto looked at him scornfully. "That is why he rides to Taos in secret, fool. That is why Capitán Caballero gave to him six men with his own son in command."

"Why does Don Manuel have to go to Taos to see Padre Martínez? Why did he not send for the priest? It is not fitting that a man like Manuel Armijo should journey from Santa Fe to Taos to see a plain priest." Emilio crossed himself. "It is not to show lack of respect to the cloth that I speak, only that it seems to me

5

unfitting. Don Manuel once was Governor and had all the power. Padre Martínez is a country priest."

Ernesto snorted. "You are supreme in your stupidity! In Taos Padre Martínez is the leader, and not only in church. If Don Manuel has chosen to come up to see him, he has a good reason and there is something big in the wind."

"The reason is not difficult to imagine," Emilio said, winking craftily.

"You talk too much. We were not sworn to secrecy for nothing. Be silent, your head was not created for thinking. Obey orders and ask no questions and you will find that perhaps you have been attached to good fortune."

Riding in front again, with Caballero a few paces to the rear, Don Manuel kept his eyes on the hills. He saw a second fire. Apache? Navajo? He wrapped the blanket more tightly around him. "There is little danger," he thought. "Seven armed men rarely are attacked on the road between Santa Fe and Taos. Wild Indians do not move at night. My friends assured me of this before I started out. They told me a larger escort would call too much attention to itself and would start rumors that would reach the Governor. It is true that I must not be seen in the company of men who formerly were presidial soldiers. But was there treachery? Did they allow me to go inadequately protected to see the priest, so that I might be destroyed? I would not put it beyond them," he thought, "even those who call themselves my friends. I do not believe in friends."

He looked again at the signal fires and then he turned his eyes upward. The stars were cold and hard in the night sky. The land was empty and big and seven men were nothing in it. His stomach tightened and he felt a sudden twinge in the old bullet wound in his right thigh. Then he relaxed. Esquipulas Caballero was with him. The old captain would not have sent along his only son if there were treachery, he assured himself.

The canyon opened into a valley and Don Manuel smelled the odor of piñon fires still slumbering on hearths. The weary horses raised their heads and shivered with excitement. The smell was harsh and acrid, like the country, and yet nothing smelled better. The smell got stronger. A dog barked. He was answered

by others. A mule brayed. In the night the adobe houses of Taos
seemed to have grown from the earth.

Don Manuel led the party to a house that bulked larger than
others. He dismounted, soothing his thigh. "Find a tavern, Don
Esquipulas," he ordered. "Allow your men some wine or brandy
and then find lodging. I will send for you. Remember, above all,
there must be no disturbance."

"We should remain on guard, Don Manuel," Caballero said.

"Ah, Dios," Emillio groaned. Ernesto jabbed at him.

"A guard will attract attention," Don Manuel said. "Take
yourselves off and do nothing to make yourselves conspicuous."

"Señor," Caballero protested.

"I order it so," Don Manuel said. He crossed the patio and
rapped lightly on the door. It was opened and a face looked out
over a flickering taper. "*Ave María purísima, padre*," Don Manuel
said.

"*Para siempre bendito sea Dios y la siempre Virgen María*,"
the priest said. "Come in, Don Manuel, my house is yours."

2

PADRE ANTONIO JOSÉ MARTÍNEZ, holding the candle aloft,
led Armijo to a small room. The priest fixed the tallow in a sconce,
and the yellow light twitched over walls lined with cases of books,
over a crude, handmade desk littered with papers. The priest
seated himself in a stiff, high-backed chair in front of the desk. The
gesture was charged with so much natural energy it became almost
an act of violence.

There was one other chair in the room, as uncomfortable as
the priest's. Don Manuel lowered himself stiffly into it. He sighed
heavily and stretched his long legs. The shuffling of the chairs
raised dust from the dirt floor. There was an old, familiar smell in
the room: the stale odor of punche, the weed the peasants used
for tobacco. The smell brought back memories to Don Manuel.
He took a silver cigar case from his pocket. He offered the case to
the priest and selected a cigar for himself.

Martínez removed the candle from the sconce and held it out. Don Manuel pulled at the flame. The taste of the fine imported leaf made him forget the aura of punche and the memories. He glanced around the room. "So many books, Don Antonio. Do you read them all?"

The priest tilted a decanter over two cups. "You must have a thirst, Don Manuel," he said.

Armijo was surprised to find the wine excellent. He looked up to see Martínez smiling with amusement.

"It is better than you expected," the priest said. "You should not forget that the French trappers work north of here and that even in a wilderness a Frenchman never finds himself without his wine."

Over the thick rim of the cup Manuel Armijo surveyed the gaunt, cragged face of the priest. It was a face he knew well and for many years, but now that he had to ask the priest for help it seemed a new face.

He had to find in it the clues he needed. They were there, in the brown eyes that were so dark they were almost black, that were now without expression but which could smolder and flare into black flame when the priest was in ecstasy of temper; the clues were all there, in the lofty forehead, in the beaked, arrogant nose, in the thin lips and sunken cheeks which gave asceticism to the somber face, asceticism called fraudulent by the priest's enemies because of the girls who came to live in his house and share his bed and bear his children. And yet Don Manuel knew there was no true deception there; Martínez's austerity was a concept of the intellect. He indulged in his body almost as an act of charity as though the flesh and its needs belonged to someone else.

The former Governor held out his empty cup and the priest refilled it. Don Manuel looked penetratingly at the grim face, which was long and lined and appeared to be even longer because of the shining baldness of the skull. Don Manuel thought that the word "calvatrueno" might have been invented for Martínez because the word meant baldness of the whole skull and it also meant wildness of the spirit, as though there were a natural association between the two things. On the large bony head there was only a narrow horseshoe of sparse hair.

The room was blue with the smoke from the cigars, and the

8

decanter had been raised over the cups four times, before Manuel Armijo spoke. "Don Antonio, when Governor Pérez removed me from the post of customs collector two weeks ago and turned me out of his government, of all the deputies to the Assembly you alone objected."

"I have no love for Pérez."

"Why, padre?"

Martínez rose to his feet and began to stride up and down the confining room as though he could not contain the energy that bubbled within him. He turned, the skirt of his black cassock whirling like the flaring dress of a ballet dancer. "Don Manuel, you have come here to ask me to help you make a revolution," he said bluntly.

"I have not said that yet."

"Nothing else would bring you here. We must understand each other completely so that if we work together we will know exactly what we are working for." The priest's voice was harsh, imposing a grating roughness upon the liquid words of Spanish. His speech was a scourge. And yet Armijo knew that no one in New Mexico, not even himself, whose voice was an instrument from which he summoned music, could talk to people as Padre Martínez could.

The priest stopped his pacing so abruptly that a bullet of ash toppled from his cigar and dropped to the floor in silent explosion. "Let us review the past years, Don Manuel. Better still, *you* review them. I should like to listen to the gospel of New Mexico according to Manuel Armijo."

Don Manuel concealed his irritation at the sarcasm in the priest's tones. He smiled affably. "I will do so with much pleasure, mi compañero."

He was pleased and a little amused to see the priest's eyes under their flaring brows flicker at the word "compañero." Don Manuel had chosen it deliberately. It meant comrade, companion, battle-friend, but above all else it was used only between equals. Since at one time or another Manuel Armijo had held all the important positions in New Mexico, since he bore one of the good names of the country, had been married to a Chaves, which was a great name, and now was married to a Gabaldon, which was a name of wealth, the compliment he paid to the priest was a

9

considerable one, for despite his influence among the people of
the Rio Arriba, or upriver country, and his political position as
deputy in the Junta, Martínez was peasant-born.

Don Manuel puffed slowly on his cigar. "It was just fifteen
years ago, padre, that our country made its great revolution against
Spain and became a free nation among nations," he said. "What
great happiness there was! I was just beginning to serve my country. I held the unimportant post of census taker in my own village
of Albuquerque. It was necessary for me to visit family after family,
and among our people I found nothing but happiness. Among the
wealthy estate-owners there were many who were bitter at the success of our revolt, but among the paisanos there was nothing but
joy that the ancient halter of tyranny had at last been lifted from
the neck of our motherland.

"In the years that followed we had to make our own way up
here in New Mexico. We are so distant from the City of Mexico,
communications are so delayed, we won more than we at first
realized. We found ourselves almost an independent nation, with
problems unlike those of any other state in Mexico. Although we
officially were a territory of the Republic, we were virtually self-
governing. It is true that our governors were appointed by the
central authorities, but they were chosen always from a list we ourselves sent down to the City of Mexico, and this list contained only
names of our own New Mexicans, men who understood our
peculiar problems: the American traders who beset us, the vexa-
tions with the foreign trappers, our exposed position in a world of
wild Indians, our financial troubles."

He sipped from the wine cup. As always, the sound of his own
voice gave him assurance. Other men found confidence in weapons. All he needed was the opportunity to use words.

"When I was appointed Governor in 1827, ten years ago, we
had come a long way in five years. We had developed as a free
country. True, we made mistakes. I personally made many mistakes. I am not a professional politician. I am a simple man, concerned only with the welfare of our country. But we were learning.
I resigned as Governor after the first year, but there were some
things accomplished." He looked carefully at the priest. "It was
said that I appropriated government funds and that I resigned

when it appeared there would be an investigation by the authorities from the City of Mexico. Of course I appropriated funds. I took all I could get. Who in government does not appropriate funds?" He leaned forward. "At least I produced results."

Martínez exhaled softly. He rubbed his hands. The room seemed suddenly cold. He arranged a few pieces of piñon wood on the hearth and lit a sliver from the taper. The fire cast a pleasant glow. Martínez turned, his hands held out behind his back to the blaze, and he looked at Don Manuel, at the magnificent short jacket with its rows of intricate embroidery, at the tightly fitted trousers gusseted below the knees so they flared out at the ankles like inverted flowers, at the soft glove-leather boots that had never been made in Mexico. There was, he admitted to himself, a certain grandeur in that frank confession of larceny.

"Yes, padre, I produced results," Don Manuel repeated. "In the short year that I was Governor I raised the business on the Santa Fe Trail to one hundred and fifty thousand dollars, almost double what it was the year before. I raised the customs duties as high as the sky. The yanquis had to pay to bring their goods into New Mexico! I did more. I sent troops to our borders and prevented the Americans from finding other routes to Chihuahua—routes that would have passed by our country, that would have taken the gringo dollars down to Mexico before we could get our hands on them. There was fighting, por Dios, and there were deaths and there are bones bleaching under the sun, but the trade still comes to Santa Fe. Although it is against Mexican law, I permitted foreigners to trap in the north. Why? They paid for the privilege. I took money for myself. I do not deny it. But more was brought into our treasury."

It was true enough, the priest admitted. Money stuck to the hands of Armijo and his cronies, but the country had benefited. And the New Mexicans, far from criticizing Don Manuel for his personal graft, were proud that there was one among them clever enough to beat the Americans at their own game. Oddly, the Americans themselves did not protest too much. Their attitude was that Manuel Armijo was at least a man with whom they could do business.

But all this, the priest thought, belonged to Manuel Armijo's

11

days of power and now he was in total eclipse. The post of head of customs was the second highest in New Mexico, and Governor Pérez had dismissed him as though he were a clerk.

Martínez lifted his head and said raspingly: "Stop speaking of trade and tariffs and foreign gold, Don Manuel. Por amor de Dios and you know that I would not help you raise a rebellion in behalf of the Santa Fe traders. I grant your business acumen. Now speak to me of what you would do and why you would do it and which way you intend to go when it is done."

Armijo sat up straight and nodded brusquely. "Two years ago there was a constitutional change made in the City of Mexico. New Mexico was reduced in status from a territory with autonomy to a department with no more independence than a provincial colony."

"It is part of the backward trend throughout all of Mexico," the priest said quickly. He opened and closed his big hands. "The crushing is on again. All over, the army and the clergy have linked hands to drive out what little wisp of freedom has drifted into the land. Too many men were lifting their heads to the sun. They must be driven down until they are animals again."

"For certain, padre!" Don Manuel's eyes flashed. "We are in agreement. First we are made into department and then this Albino Pérez is sent to govern us, a foreigner, an outsider, to rule us like the viceroy of a conqueror. He brings all the abominable things we thought we banished forever when we drove out the Spaniards. He creates a court filled with pomp and show and French manners and surrounds himself with others of his kind, people from the City of Mexico, from Chihuahua and Sonora, who have been here scarcely long enough to warm the insides of their houses, dainty lace-cuffed scum, mincing and bowing as though they were in Madrid, filling the air with their foul Castilian lisping. But for our country? Nothing! For our people? Nothing! Nothing, that is, except this new law of direct taxation. For the first time in our history of the government goes to the people for money, and when there is no money to give the government dogs, they take the sheep and the cows and the grain. And all of these taxes will come from the poor, padre. Because you know as well as I do that the ricos will find ways of avoiding payment. This is close to your heart, Don Antonio. I have not forgotten how, two years ago, you led a successful fight in the Chamber of Deputies to repeal the ancient law that empowered the Church to call upon civilian authorities to assist it in collecting its tithe. That was close to heresy and might have unfrocked you. But you fought on. And yet how small is that taxation compared to what is before us now!"

The priest's eyes were blazing. "How honest are you about the poor of our land?"

"I grew up as one of them."

"You are an Armijo."

"I bear the name. There are those among the ricos who say that it is not mine to bear. They say that my mother was not Señora Armijo or that my father was not an Armijo, and since both are dead there is no one to prove or disprove it. But I grew up a paisano, padre, more wretchedly than you yourself did perhaps, and there can be no doubt of that. The earliest memories in my life are those of tending sheep. Not my own sheep. Not Armijo sheep. There were eleven children, and by the time anything reached me there was very little of it left. I worked for old Chaves like an Indian in the field. It was an education, padre. They say that I stole sheep. I stole sheep! I do not deny it! I took Chaves's sheep and sold them back to him. Once I sold the same ewe to the old fool fourteen times—and I had stolen it from him in the beginning. I was hungry and I was penniless and he had thousands of sheep and he got them by buying them from the peasants at prices he himself had set, knowing they could not sell them elsewhere. And if they did not sell them to him at his price, something happened to the sheep. You know all this, padre."

The priest nodded. Only Manuel Armijo could make sheep-stealing into something heroic.

"I taught myself to read and to write," Armijo said. "I used a church primer. Alone I did it, padre. Do you think I can forget those days? Do you believe I can forget the years I spent on the bare hills with no one to talk to except sheep, no matter where I go or what I become? My first friends were shepherds and I lived with them and ate with them and starved with them and froze with them. I am of the land, padre, as you yourself are of the land. The earth of our country is my body. Can a man forget the people whose blood thinned with his when he was young and filled with

13

hunger and around him everywhere was food he could not eat? The fat sheep and the thin people, padre. The label of our country! The plump healthy animals and the peasants whose skin hangs from their bones like damp cloth. I spent many hours with my thoughts in those days. It is the only comfort when the belly tightens its own teeth and there is nothing to grind between them. I vowed that one day I would be wealthy and that when that happened I would never again allow myself to be poor. I have stolen for myself every chance I could—but always from those who could afford it. And I made another vow. I swore to myself that if ever it came within my power I would help my people. I have been true to the first vow. And, con el favor de Dios, I will be true to the second!"

"If I could believe you," Martínez whispered, writhing his hands. "If you are speaking the truth."

Don Manuel rose to his feet and he filled the room. The priest sat down slowly, his eyes fixed. "Hear me, vicario!" Armijo said sternly. "As I lay in the lonely places listening to the bleating of sheep that belonged to one sick old man while thousands of men and women and little children were hungry, as I lay there I was one with the rocks and the stones and the trees and the hills and the sky above me."

The priest reared his head. Through the blue haze he saw Don Manuel's face, remote as the peak of a mountain. The note had been sounded and the priest felt his blood churn.

"I am of the land," Armijo said harshly, wearing it as a hair shirt, as flagellation, as the Penitente fanatics wore their thorns. "The earth, padre, the earth, the mountains and the valleys and the rivers and the little mud towns and the people, the people, padre, indomitable, enduring, all in me, flowing with my blood, drunk and breathed in the solitary hours." He held out his hands. "I carry it all there, the past and the present and what will come." He paused. He said slowly: "And what I am down below, so you are in Taos."

The priest's face jerked upward. The cords of his neck stood out. He raised his hand and shielded his eyes as though there was suddenly too much light in the room. The words remained in the air. He could reach out and touch them. The old dream, Taos, an independent republic, with Antonio Martínez at its head. In the

14

quiet of the room it had led to now, and he asked: "What is it that you want of me, Don Manuel?"

"I need all your people." Armijo's voice grated with a kind of joy. "When the time comes it must seem that the uprising comes from the people. That is the only way an insurrection can have validity. Most of all I need your Indians. They will burst from their pueblos for you alone."

"The Indians too."

"The Indians more than anyone, padre."

The priest thought of the men of the pueblos, living at peace with the Mexicans they hated as they would live with incurable disease, the frozen men who collected in their hearts, from father to son, the accumulation of execration that was passed on as a holy legacy, as tribal cult; whose faces were of stone to contain the hatred, who allowed themselves to be called Christian, and tame, and who took out the rage and the bitterness and the black memories, and the dreams which lived with the flame that never was extinguished, in the secret and terrible rites in the kivas where the pueblo man made his peace and opened his soul to his true gods.

"The Indians," Martínez said, knowing that he should have known and that now it was too late because he had listened too much. Then he said in a voice that was emptied and exhausted so that the words seemed to have to struggle to penetrate the smoke: "Rest yourself, Don Manuel." It was past the point and in the same drained voice he said: "Later I will take you to the pueblo."

3

THE PUEBLO of San Gerónimo de Taos was rosy in the sun as Don Manuel and Padre Martínez approached it from the south, Armijo astride his charger, the priest riding bareback on a burro so small his sandled feet scraped the ground when he allowed his legs to dangle.

"Tell me more about this Indian Gonzales," Armijo said. "Why is it better to deal with him than with the cacique?"

"The chief is very old and already halfway into the next

world," the priest said. "He appears only for the ceremonies of the kiva. José Gonzales is a young man. He is not even a subchief."

Don Manuel frowned. "Can such a man serve our purpose? One without standing among his people?"

Martínez shrugged. "It is difficult to hunt buffalo these days. The foreigners destroy them all." There was a small smile on his lips. "A man who is the greatest buffalo-hunter in his tribe is held in very great respect."

"Por amor de Dios!" Armijo said with irritation. "It is not a hunting expedition I plan. Is there no young leader, a man in line to become cacique, perhaps?"

"There are several such, Don Manuel. The question is would such a leader be content to return to obscurity when the change is made. The younger men in the tribe will follow Gonzales. Also he is not a clever man. He will cause you no trouble later on."

Now they entered upon the wide plaza that separated the two sections of the pueblo. Don Manuel looked around curiously. On the left was an apartment dwelling four stories high, on the right one of five stories. Through the plaza a creek flowed even now in July. A felled tree made a footwalk across the stream. The buildings dominated the landscape, and on all the outer sides were broad, painstakingly irrigated fields where now the corn swayed silkily in the bright morning light.

"It is an impressive thing, is it not?" Martínez asked, sliding off the burro.

"It is a pueblo," Don Manuel said.

"Each time I see it I think that in this land it is as though the pygmy ruled the giant," the priest said musingly. "A stranger come into our country for the first time would think that it is in the pueblo that the rulers of New Mexico must live and that in our squat mud buildings could be only the conquered."

"I do not find that conception amusing, padre."

They tied up their animals, and the priest led Don Manuel across the pine log, past the old mission, now rapidly going to ruin, to the left section of the pueblo. The Indians were at work everywhere, hauling water, fashioning the large brown clay containers which served them as cooking and eating utensils, tanning leather, weaving woolen strands into cloth, making arrows and lances and boots and leather cloaks.

The men were tall, spare, and erect; the women were smaller and moved with a controlled grace. The children were quiet. As the priest neared them, men and women rose and touched their foreheads. It was, Don Manuel knew, a very great compliment to the priest. The Indians of the pueblos pretended to Catholicism and some of them truly accepted the Christ of the conquerors, but only as a supplement to their more familiar and reliable deities. It was, an Indian once said, like having an extra arrow along on a buffalo hunt. Padre Martínez accepted the gestures of respect without fuss, calling many by name, Indian or Spanish. The Indians appeared not to notice Don Manuel.

Finally the two men reached the building, laced with ladders. Here and there the ladders emerged from the ground itself, leading down to the underground kivas. The priest walked without hesitation to one of the ladders and clambered up, his skirt billowing. Don Manuel followed more slowly, feeling the strain in his thigh, wondering whether the slender struts would hold his weight. On the first terrace more Indians were at work, and if the priest and his companion did not pass directly by them they merely glanced up, quietly, incuriously, and then resumed their labors.

The two men moved upward in this silence and tranquillity to the second and then the third tier and the land opened before them: Taos was clear to their eyes and the hills were rich with the blood of the sun.

The priest moved rapidly along the level of the third tier until he came to a hatchway over one of the apartments and there he squatted on his haunches and motioned for Don Manuel to do the same. The former Governor followed suit, his irritation rising again. It would have been more fitting, he thought, for the priest to have arranged this meeting in his own home so that the Indian would have been in the position of having come to him.

They waited for more than thirty minutes. The rising sun bleached the blood on the hills. The heat seared Don Manuel's back. Sweat trickled down his neck, and his back and his legs grew stiff. Padre Martínez sat quietly, his head lowered almost to his knees, his hands clasped around his thighs; his face had drifted into meditation, content, it appeared, to remain so forever. His patience almost at an end, feeling that half the Indians must

17

be staring up at him, Don Manuel was about to ask the priest how much longer he would have to remain in this ridiculous position when a head appeared through the opening in front of them.

It was a large head, the black hair hanging to the shoulders, a band, covered with symbolic markings, around the brow. For several moments the head said nothing and then the mouth opened and spoke and said in good Spanish: "Hail Mary Immaculate, padre."

The priest did not move. "Forever blessed be God and the Holy Virgin Mary."

The familiar greeting and reply, prescribed by Mexican mores and said so often and for so long that the words almost had lost meaning, sounded strange to Don Manuel in the heart of the pueblo. For the first time in very long he was conscious of each word. He found the eyes of the Indian upon him. The eyes were black and they had contradictory qualities of abstraction and intenseness. Don Manuel felt the eyes upon him as though the Indian had laid a hand on his shoulder and yet they were hooded and remote.

"Is this one your friend, padre?" the Indian asked.

"Yes, my son."

"Enter my house. You both are welcome."

The head disappeared. Martínez got up and descended the ladder into the hatchway. Armijo, his legs almost numbed, followed him slowly. The apartment was small and contained nothing but a few eating dishes and a colchón, a mattress rolled up during the day and used for a seat. The room was windowless and, Don Manuel thought, smelled of Indian. The only light was that from a tallow candle. As Don Manuel reached the bottom of the ladder he saw that both the priest and the Indian were already on their haunches, their hands clasped, their heads lowered. He groaned silently and took his place with them. He noticed that the Indian had positioned himself so that the candle was behind him, leaving his face almost in darkness.

The three men sat silently for another quarter of an hour. Padre Martínez again appeared lost in thought. Gonzales seemed beyond thought. He was turned inward, as though for him time had no existence. Don Manuel knew the manners of Indians and understood that this preliminary period of silence was customary and yet he found himself resenting it. He resented particularly the fact that Martínez was able to give himself to it so naturally. Somehow, he thought, the priest should have indicated to him how foolish he thought it was. He felt that in some obscure way the two men had joined against him.

Gonzales raised his head. "I will listen, padre."

The priest did not reply immediately; it was as though he too had to return from a distance. When he spoke, it was in a low voice that filled the cubicle. "José Gonzales, this is Don Manuel Armijo, a great leader of his people. He comes to see you from the capital in Santa Fe. He has been chief of New Mexico and has held other important offices but he is a man from the people. He has a big name and one that is very old, but before he made himself into a leader he worked in the fields among the peasants."

José Gonzales, listening, did not take his eyes from the priest. His face, in profile, outlined against the candlelight, was without living expression, so that the high cheeks, the bulging forehead, the thick chin, could all have been part of the adobe wall behind him. The face, Don Manuel thought, could have been made as the pueblo had been made, mud slapped on and shaped by palm, hardening into the flat, enduring, unreflecting quality of adobe, which could turn away an ax blow.

"This Don Manuel has been watching for many months the direction his country is going and he is unhappy," the priest continued. "He sees oppression and tyranny returning. He is a man of courage and with a good heart and he has within him at all times a concern for the welfare of his people. He wants to do something about the evil that he sees developing. He thinks perhaps this may lie in your heart as well, my son, and if this is so, that you may join your hands to bring a change for the better."

When Padre Martínez finished, Gonzales turned his head slowly, like a beacon, until his eyes were on Don Manuel. In the darkness of his face his eyes were only darker places. The candlelight made a yellow nimbus around the huge skull. Looking at Armijo, Gonzales spoke to the priest. "Do you believe in this man, padre?"

"Yes."

"Do you trust him?"

"Yes," the priest whispered.

Again Don Manuel felt anger. He calmed himself, and knowing his features were full in the light, he arranged them into an expression of quiet simplicity.

"Do you support these plans of his, padre?" Gonzales asked.

"Yes." The priest's voice was almost inaudible.

José Gonzales reached out and his fingers bit into the flesh of Don Manuel's shoulder. "Then you are welcome in your own right, Don Manuel. Speak to me and I will listen."

Armijo now was grateful for the Indian custom of long pauses between speech. The interview was following a different course from that he had envisioned. He had expected to treat with a mestizo, an Indian half-breed, who would be awed by the appearance of a former Governor of New Mexico in his miserable pueblo and not with a man who gave commands with the air of a Spanish grandee.

"The good priest has spoken well for me," Don Manuel said at last. "He has told you how my heart grieves for the sorrows that are come on our people. We are now ruled by a foreigner, a man sent up from Mexico, and this man has filled his government with other men like him, men fresh from below the border, almost fresh from the despotism of Spain. Everywhere the people are groaning. And now come the new taxes, which will sneak like rattlesnakes into every home."

He cursed the Indian for sitting so that he could not read his face. It was as though he were talking to a statue. The air was closer than ever. The sweat again was running down his back. He had lost all feeling in his legs.

"What is it you want of me?" he heard the Indian ask suddenly.

"There was once a mighty leader among the pueblo people. His name was Popé. More than one hundred and fifty years ago he rose in wrath and drove the Spaniards from the land. It lies within the power of your people today to do the same and the name of José Gonzales can forever be linked with that of Popé."

Don Manuel heard the Indian inhale sharply.

"Popé?" Gonzales said with quiet ecstasy. "Do you name Popé to me, Don Manuel? Is your understanding of history the

same as mine is? Did not Popé drive *all* the Spaniards from New
Mexico? Are you asking me to lead the Indians in another such
war? Popé saw no difference between one Spaniard and another."

Padre Martínez held his hands clasped tightly together. It
was strong and dangerous medicine. The Indians outnumbered
the Mexicans many times over. United, they could easily drive
the usurpers from the land. It could start, catching like fire on a
dry prairie, exploding among the tribes, from the smoldering
pueblos to the adamant Apaches, the wild Navajos, the Pawnees,
Commanches, Caws. To ask Gonzales for help to rid New Mexico
of Pérez was one thing. To talk of a holy war in the name of the
legendary Popé was another. The priest lifted his eyes and waited.

Don Manuel smiled. "You are quite right, Don José. Your
understanding of the tragic history of our country is accurate. But
in those days there were two peoples, the natives and the invaders.
And that is not true today. Today we New Mexicans are no
different from the Indians of the pueblos. We who have lived
here, whose fathers have lived here, have become one with you.
Today the poor New Mexican is no different from the poor Indian.
He suffers. He is hungry. He is oppressed. In the veins of New
Mexicans flows of the blood of the conquistadores, it is true, but
there also is the blood of the Indian there. We have intermarried
with you. There are none of us any more in whose bodies the red
streams of both peoples have not mingled again and again. It is
known that the ricos who boast of the Spanish purity of their
blood do not regard me entirely as one of them. It is because they
know that in me is the true blood of New Mexico. You yourself,
Don José, have in you the blood of the Spaniard. In that com-
mingling we have created a new race, and we of that new race
must stand together. We must stand side by side against this new
invasion, against new conquerors who come not honestly with
weapons but who sneak in behind a rigmarole of politics and laws,
who bleed us not with lances and swords but with taxes and persecution." He laid his hand on the Indian's arm; it was a stronger
gesture than it would have been with a Mexican. "We are brothers, mi compañero," he said, and in his voice now was the same
note of ecstasy that had trembled in the voice of Gonzales. "The
padre is one of us. We all share blood. There are others. We

21

now must form our battalions. The time is now. Before long we shall be beaten down so that we can never rise again. All of us, all of us of the land!"

Martínez felt a dull pounding in his head. There was, the priest now understood, no limits to which Manuel Armijo was not prepared to go. In this land where the well-born would kill at a hint that his heritage was not all Spanish, he had heard Don Manuel Armijo tell an Indian mestizo that he too was a half-breed. He thought of the sensation a repetition of those words would create in the Chamber of Deputies in Santa Fe. He thought that Armijo must be very certain of him to give him such a dangerous weapon, only he knew too it was a weapon too lethal for him to use. He knew if he ever repeated what he had just heard he would be signing a warrant for his own destruction.

"Our country is greater than any individual," Armijo said. His voice filled the room, echoed from wall to wall with the insistency of drums. "Now we have a true native people, and the sum is more than any individual among us—more than you, Don José, or I. We are men of spirit and heart, mi compañero, and we know that our existences are nothing compared with the fate of those we love. That is why I have come to you, a natural leader among your own great people, a leader in spirit even if you do not have the rank of chief, to ask your aid. Your people will follow you. Others will follow the padre. Still others will follow me. Together we can drive out the tyrant and his court of foreigners from our country."

"Your words have the sound of truth to me," Gonzales said. Then he added: "Mi compañero."

Martínez knew now that Armijo had won. He had used the name of Popé, wielding it like a naked sword, and then he had gathered the emotion he had aroused and had placed it behind himself. He had spoken of his own Indian blood, whether it was true he had it or not. He had called Gonzales his equal and had prevailed upon the rigid Indian to unbend enough to use the word too. And he had not forgotten to remind Gonzales that among his own people his leadership was not recognized. He had omitted nothing. There would be no one to stop him. His kind of elemental ferocity was almost lost from the land. The priest thought of the ricos, fat, soft, living like kings in their vast estates, removed entirely from the people who supported them. Who among them in all the land could stand against this ruthless energy? It was good that he had pledged himself. In what was to come there would be no middle ground.

"I am happy that what I have said has found its way to your heart, Don José," Armijo said quietly. "I knew in God's light when Padre Martínez described to me your wisdom and humanity that the truth would make itself clear to you."

Gonzales stood up. He turned his back to the two men and faced the wall. He held hands flat against his sides, so tensely his arms vibrated. He was a big man. His legs were like the trunks of young trees. He was silent as he held communion with him who lived behind his eyes. He turned and looked down. "Lead and I will follow, Don Manuel."

Armijo rose and embraced him. "We will go far, mi compañero."

The gaunt, fissured face of the priest turned upward toward the men, held enclasped. He lowered his eyes again to the floor.

4

IN THE LATE AFTERNOON in the little study in the priest's house Martínez sipped scalding chocolate and asked: "When do you return to Santa Fe, Don Manuel?"

"Immediately."

"And what is the next step?"

Armijo felt large and filled with himself. In the daylight the small room was mean and undistinguished. The house was filled with the sounds of children and babies and smelled of urine. He had seen a girl, no more than fifteen, her belly swollen with child. The priest himself was reduced. What was he, after all, but a village curate? A little mad and with influence, but still a provincial village priest. With great ambition. To be president of a country called Taos. Don Manuel asked: "Padre, there are no doubts in your mind?"

"I am pledged to you."

"There are no reservations?"

"There are none."

"In the name of Christ?"

For a moment the priest's eyes flashed. Then he said: "*En el nombre de Cristo.*"

Don Manuel nodded. "I have in Santa Fe a great number of muskets. They are American, of the newest type, brought in from the east by my business partner, Don Alberto Speyer. These weapons are for Gonzales and the men he recruits."

Martínez looked at him in astonishment. "But Pérez must know about these muskets. What of the law that requires the registration of all weapons entering New Mexico?"

Armijo looked at him with pity. "Dear padre," he said gently, "I have not been head of the customs for nothing. There is no record anywhere of these muskets having been brought across the border. Pérez knows nothing."

"When will they arrive here?"

"I will send them by mule train as soon as I return to Santa Fe."

"And meanwhile?"

"You will talk again to Gonzales. Give him a day or two to reflect and react. Study him when you speak to him. If you feel there is the slightest doubt of his reliability notify me immediately. I will give orders to the commandant of the mule train to turn back if you intercept him with such a message."

"And if Gonzales has not changed?"

Armijo's mouth tightened. "Distribute the muskets, padre."

"All to Gonzales?"

"No. I have other agents here in the Rio Arriba working among the peasants. They will require some of the muskets."

"How will I know them?"

"By the password, 'For God and Liberty.'"

"You are a man of humor, Don Manuel, to use the motto of the President of Mexico in this revolt against his own appointee."

Don Manuel smiled thinly. "Have no fear, padre. In the end it will work out that the insurrection will be acceptable to General Santa Anna."

A furrow appeared on the priest's brow. "Don Manuel, these peasants and the pueblo Indians—they are unused to the handling of modern muskets. Will they have time to train themselves?"

"The muskets must not be displayed until the revolt begins."

"They will be slaughtered. Governor Pérez will turn the presidial troop on them. Those men are trained soldiers."

"The presidial troop? You forget, padre, that it has been disestablished for lack of funds. Its commandant, Capitán José Caballero, is in this with us."

"But surely Pérez will call the men together again when the trouble starts."

Armijo shook his head. "I do not believe he will. It would cost money. Pérez says there is no money to pay soldiers."

"But at such a time."

"And Pérez is proud, padre. He will consider it beneath his dignity to call upon the disbanded army to put down a peasant revolt in the Rio Arriba. He will call for volunteers, as usual, and the volunteers will be as inexperienced as the insurrectionists—but with the single difference that our men will have modern guns and his men will be armed with bows and arrows and pointed sticks."

"The government armory has plenty of guns."

"He will not issue them, padre. He would be afraid they would never be returned when the fighting was over. No, he will call for volunteers and, as he does when he makes his expeditions against the wild Indians, he will ask the volunteers to bring their own weapons. Do not forget that Pérez will not have the slightest knowledge of how our own men are armed. He will believe that they too are carrying pieces of wood. Besides, the man believes that his own person at the head of a band of men is worth more than guns."

The priest's face was grim. "You gamble a great deal on the arrogance of Pérez, Don Manuel."

"I know my man, padre," Armijo said equably.

"May God give you right," Martínez said quietly.

"Before I depart, are there any last questions?"

"Just one—what starts the revolt?"

"It will start of its own accord. The peasants and the Indians have suffered enough to have started a revolution before this. They lacked only weapons and leadership. There are, all the time, little events that stir up a small commotion and then fade away. Once the guns are in the hands of the people, we will await the next event, and that time it will not fade away. It will happen soon enough, padre. That is how the time is now. If necessary, a situation can always be contrived, but it will be far better if something occurs naturally."

The priest said with respect: "You have forgotten nothing."

"One small thing more, padre. It will be bruited about that I have been up here. My story is that, having been retired from politics, I have been up here to make certain arrangements, trade agreements, with the gringos at Bent's Fort. I have come up here with only a small escort and it will not be questioned." He held out his arms and smiled. *"Adiós, Don Antonio, por Dios y Libertad!"* He lifted the silver cross that hung from the priest's neck and kissed it. He took the priest by the shoulders and squeezed powerfully. "Always remember the old proverb, padre: *'Al hombre osado la fortuna le de la mano.'*" He released his grip and held out his large hands. "These hands, padre," he said. "My own."

5

ON THE RETURN TO SANTA FE, Don Manuel turned morose. He had been filled with confidence when he bade farewell to the priest and he had believed in the proverb he had quoted, that the bold man held his fortune in his hands, but the village was hardly out of sight before a reaction set in, the fears and doubts. His leg ached again and he felt as though he had spent the last twenty-four hours with an insatiable woman. So many things could go wrong, and his initial success in aligning Martínez and Gonzales now appeared only to portend failure in the end. He doubted everything there; he was apart from his men, alone in the empty country. He trusted no one. Loyalty was bought as a whore was bought. He accepted this, but it made for no ease.

He looked around him. There was harshness everywhere. The land was graceless and unyielding. There was nothing on it of the men who tried to possess it. The men and the little buildings of mud they lived in had made no true union with the earth. The men could leave and the mud would wash away and nothing would be left. The land suffered them to abide on it, and though men had lived there for centuries, they were still transients.

He needed to speak to someone, to build again on the sound of his own voice. There was no one to speak to. Esquipulas Caballero? The fancy rico? His lip curled. This was the lineal descendant of the conquistadores. This dandy was the blood and the pride and the glory of the land. This was what the Spaniard had become in New Mexico. The men who had fought and hungered and thirsted through the hundreds of years must be turned down with shame in their graves. He laughed with sudden satisfaction that the purebloods now were such men. Their weakness was his strength. He glanced back at the chiseled face of Caballero. It was his fortune that he had to deal with men of such faces.

Santa Fe was silent in the early morning hour. Don Manuel thanked Caballero and the men and again cautioned them, and then he dismissed them and hurried to his house. He looked at the long, low, darkened Palace of the Governors, which occupied one entire side of the plaza. It had been his house for a brief time and it would be his house again. Don Manuel Armijo, Jefe Militar y Político. El Gobernador Armijo.

His wife, Doña María Trinidad, was awake, awaiting him as he knew she would though this was the third hour after midnight and she could not have been certain this would be the morning he would return. She was dressed elaborately as for a formal reception, and on each hand she wore large rings. Her pudgy, ugly face with its dark shadow of hair on the upper lip, on which a small mole rose like a butte, took on its only quality of beauty when he entered the large sala: her eyes, smoky, enormous, filled with light. She asked immediately in her deep, unwomanly voice, "How did it go, Manuelito?"

"It went well, señora." Her eyes glowed with even more intensity and he thought how he had waited through all the bare miles from Taos to see that.

"There is chocolate. Or perhaps you would prefer wine or brandy. There is also meat."

"Only a little wine, Mariquita, for favor."

He sat down heavily in a large, hand-carved chair and held

27

his hands extended before the wood coals smoldering on the hearth. It was his favorite chair, brought up from the City of Mexico. A royal governor from Madrid had once used it. It was so uncomfortable that to sit in it for any length of time was almost to do penance, but it had authority.

Doña María Trinidad poured some vino de Jerez from a square cut-glass decanter imported from St. Louis in the United States into a silver goblet that came from Spain. She saw the content in his face as she handled these things of luxury. She knew how he needed these evidences of wealth for his peace.

He accepted the goblet with the amber wine and looked at her uncomely face and thought how they were bound together, how, not loving her, a stranger to her physically, he yet was closer to her than to any other person alive. She had nothing for him as a woman. No woman would ever truly have that for him again. That was gone with Doña Rafaela, his first wife, whom he had loved as a man could love a woman if he were very lucky, an isolated emotion unrelated to ambition, coming from a heart that had died when she had died and had been buried when she was buried. With Doña Rafaela there had been nothing more in the world than the glory of making her a woman. But that was long ago and she was dead and the husband of Doña Rafaela Armijo de Chaves was dead too.

But somehow in the circuitous windings of this second marriage, undertaken by both as a simple business arrangement, he wanting the support of the great merchant family she came from, she an unsought woman needing a husband even if only in appearance, somehow they had reached another point. It was a common ground, unique, a site that belonged alone to them. It was as though she were a sister who had become, as the years passed, an extension of himself.

He sipped the wine, savoring its quality. He was part of the room now, assured on all sides, protected from the outside. "Before I tell you of Taos, do you tell me of Santa Fe. Was my absence noticed?"

"It was spoken of, here and there. I said you went to the Rio Arriba to arrange for the purchase of peltries. There was all the usual excitement when the yanqui caravan arrived, so that it was forgotten quickly."

"What did the americanos say when they heard I had been removed from the customs?"

"They were not unhappy. They do not love you, Manuel."

"Has Don Alberto disposed of our merchandise here?"

"Yes."

"Were there difficulties?"

"Nothing to faze Don Alberto. There was a small conspiracy on the part of your usual customers to make Don Alberto sell the goods at lower prices. They said that it was one thing to pay such prices when you were in charge of the customs and in a position to bestow favors, but quite another now that you were only another business man with nothing left but your post as alcalde of Albuquerque." She smiled. "They made little progress with that argument with Don Alberto. There is too much Jew and too much Prussian in that one. He did not debate the matter. He left the goods in the wagons and said he would take it all down to Chihuahua and sell it there at even higher prices. The conspiracy collapsed immediately."

Don Manuel laughed delightedly. "The dogs!"

"Don Alberto told me he was more than satisfied. He is in a great haste to have an accounting with you so that he may depart as soon as possible with the merchandise you have committed to Chihuahua."

"I will see him later today. We too will leave Santa Fe for Albuquerque, immediately."

Her eyes sparkled. "It went that well, Manuel?"

He told her rapidly of his success in Taos. "The powder barrel has been set, woman," he said, his voice rising. "The fuse now is attached. It now awaits only the flame to be touched to it." The ends of his mouth pulled down. "They thought they had written Manuel Armijo from the books. They have put him in the past." He banged the goblet on the arm of the chair. The knuckles of his fingers showed white around it. "They will see how wrong they were. The day of Armijo just dawns. There is still history to be written. It will burst like the sun from the clouds. They will hide their eyes, Pérez, the dancing master, his cabinet of Abreus, all of them. First I will blind them and then I will destroy them."

She felt her heart pounding rapidly and she knew that she

alone had this from him, that this nakedness was greater than any nakedness of the body, that now during such a moment he gave more of himself to her than he could give to any other woman. She stood up, her shapeless, stocky figure tense with rapture, and she said in the voice of a woman who has had her climax in love: "And now you must retire, Manuelito. You must be weary and there will not be enough hours in the day for you."

He felt the union with her. He nodded.

"Do you desire a girl?"

"Yes."

"I have kept one ready. I will send her to your bed." She leaned against his shoulder for a moment and touched his cheek with the tips of her fingers. Then she walked without grace from the room.

He refilled the goblet and drained it. He rose to his feet. He again was filled with his strength. He could feel his muscles, in his arms, his legs, his torso. He flexed his hands. He no longer had fears.

Slowly he walked to his bedroom, his blood warm with wine. A candle flickered in a sconce. He did not look at the bed. He undressed silently, letting his clothing remain where it fell. Naked, he swelled his chest and pulled in his belly. He blew out the candle and climbed into the bed. He felt the sheets on his skin. They were the finest in Santa Fe. There were ricos in the Rio Abajo who had never heard of sheets. He turned to the girl. He did not know who she was and he had no desire to know. Before dawn she would be gone. He knew only that she must be very young. Doña María Trinidad was painstaking about that. He fell upon her with hunger.

She cried out: "Don Manuel, you hurt! Madre María, you hurt!" Then she tore at the skin of his back and sobbed: "*Con fuerza, con fuerza, Dios mío*, but you are a bull!"

When he fell away from her at last and lay panting at her side, he thought as he always thought that the sequence was wrong. It should be the girl first and then the greater emotion with Doña María Trinidad.

6

Don Manuel made his way slowly through the plaza, which was always crowded in the hours before noon and which now during the time of the caravan was packed with a milling mob of townspeople, ranchers, beggars, priests, merchants, whores, and, mingling among them, their shouts raucous over the soft speech of the New Mexicans, the big gringos who had just completed the eight-hundred-mile crossing from Independence, Missouri, in the United States. In the vast field called plaza by courtesy, now laden with dust, which turned into a morass in the infrequent but violent rains, were wagons of all kinds, from the simple carros of the natives, made entirely of wood and wooden pegs, the wheels cut from single sections of tree trunks, to the beautiful large vehicles of the American merchants.

All men, all women, all children, all equipment were jammed into the plaza as though there were no other place for them in Santa Fe. Cooks had fires going not a dozen yards from the palace; horses, burros, mules were tethered everywhere; pigs and sheep and goats were enclosed in pens; dogs ran in all directions. The smells, the old familiar smells, rose in Don Manuel's nostrils. A peasant called out: "Hola, Don Manuel, and when are you going back to the palace?" Don Manuel laughed. He tossed the man a copper. The man shouted: "*Válgate Dios*, Don Manuel!" Armijo wagged his hand. "To you, my countryman!"

He filled his head with the smells. They were the smells of his country—people, animals, beans, tortillas and burning meat, piñon and brandy and cheap wine, the smells of perfumed whores and sweating Indians and punche—together with all the sounds, of talking, laughter, cursing, whispering, singing, of braying, neighing, barking, grunting, stamping, and the sounds of creaking leather and ungreased wheels, of the shouts of the monte dealers in all the gambling stalls, of dice clicking, of roulette wheels turning, of crackling flames and of guitars, of bells and fiddles, all of them, the smells and the sounds, woven into a life. He was a large, confident, handsome figure, dressed with flare and swagger and this was his city and these were his people, and he loved them

31

as people, as ones he could laugh with and throw coins to, as children with all the joy and sorrow and strength and weakness of children.

In all this sprawling noise there was only one sour note for him: the gringos, whom he hated and on whose money New Mexico depended for existence. As he moved toward the palace, he saw native women from good families, driven by inexplicable impulses, offer themselves to the laughing, boisterous, light-haired Americans, who were hungry for the flesh of women after the weeks on the lonely and dangerous trail. There would be trinkets and baubles given but it was not for them that the women sought out the Americans, and Don Manuel wondered, as every other New Mexican man wondered, what it was that drew the women to the strangers. He glanced at a man lounging somberly under a huge sombrero and saw the death in his eyes as the women pursued their flirtation.

As he came out of the crowd and stepped under the portal that extended the length of the street in front of the palace, he saw a woman block the path of a tall American trader, who laughed and shook his head. The woman slapped her groin and wiggled her buttocks. The American pushed her away. She ran around in front of him, pleading, posturing, touching him with her hands. He pushed her away again. The New Mexican that Don Manuel had just looked at could bear it no longer. He rushed up to the pair and slapped the American and drew his knife. The American roared with laughter, and when the native closed in on him, the death still in his eyes, his blade glinting, he sidestepped neatly and easily and caught the native from one side and twisted his arm so that the knife fell to the dust and he lifted him bodily and hurled him through the air onto a small fire burning under an iron tripod.

Above all the clamor, Don Manuel could hear the scream of the New Mexican as the pot under the tripod, filled with boiling stew, spilled over him and the fire caught his white cotton shirt and trousers. The American picked up a water jug and dumped it on the blazing man, extinguishing the flame, and then he turned him around and booted him away. Now the cook whose fire had been disturbed began to argue with the American. The trader tossed some coins at the cook, who scrambled in the dust to get them, and strode away. A moment later the woman accosted another American. He did not refuse her.

Don Manuel's mouth tightened as he entered the palace.

Don Albino Pérez, lieutenant colonel in the cavalry of the Mexican army, at present serving as Governor of New Mexico, was not alone in his office when his secretary, Jesús María Alaria, announced that Manuel Armijo sought an audience. With the Governor was Santiago Abreu, former Governor and now highest judge in New Mexico and considered by many to be the most brilliant mind in the land, eldest of the three brothers who were the chief supporters of the Pérez administration. Another brother, Don Ramón, was prefect of the North District, an area that included Taos, and the youngest, Don Marcelino, had been in charge of the public school that Don Albino had started soon after he took office. This school had to be abandoned because the wealthy citizens of Santa Fe refused to support any such foolish institution, agreeing with the clergy that education was necessary only for those boys who planned to enter the priesthood, and there were priests enough to teach them.

An expression of annoyance appeared on the Governor's face, fine and slim as that of a greyhound, when he heard the name. "Armijo? I suppose we will have to see him." When Abreu made a move to rise, Pérez said: "Please remain, Don Santiago, for favor. Perhaps he will make his visit briefer if he thinks we are in conference."

Don Manuel, limping slightly, walked to the Governor's desk and greeted him warmly. Pérez, touching his lips with a cambric kerchief, murmured with automatic politeness: "My house is yours, Don Manuel."

After bowing courteously to Abreu, who had been his secretary when he was Governor, Don Manuel said, "I am on my way to visit my estate in Albuquerque, excelencia. I have come to pay my respects to your excellency and to bid you farewell."

Pérez brought a frosty smile to his lips. "We shall undoubtedly experience great loss in Santa Fe, Don Manuel. I wish there was some post in my government worthy of your many talents. It grieves us to think you will sequester yourself in the Rio Abajo. However, you will be no stranger to the capital and meanwhile our loss is the gain of your abajeños. I know the people of the south will benefit greatly with you as their alcalde."

"Many thanks, excelencia," Don Manuel said gravely.

"You will do me the honor to share a glass of wine with me before you go, Don Manuel." He poured three glasses and then raised his own and spoke the common toast: "Health and money and time to spend it, Don Manuel!"

"I have a more amusing version," Armijo said. "Health and money and girls with good breasts!" He grinned at the slow flush that spread over the Governor's cheeks. "Do you know, Don Albino, that when I proposed my version of the toast at a baile not long ago, a most charming woman had something to reply to that. She said, without blinking an eye: 'Health and money and a man with force!' "

Pérez averted his head with distaste. "I have no liking for vulgarities, Don Manuel."

"Your pardon, excelencia," Armijo said contritely. "It is just that I keep forgetting that there is a difference between us and the Mexicans below the border."

"There is no difference in good taste, Don Manuel," Pérez said stiffly.

"Perhaps it is just the difference in what is considered good taste, excelencia."

Abreu spoke for the first time. "You have just returned from Taos, I am informed, Don Manuel."

"Yes. I went to the Rio Arriba to arrange for the purchase of skins from the trappers." He smiled gently. "Now that I am only a private citizen I must expand my business."

"What was your impression of conditions up there?"

Armijo shrugged. "The same. People grumble, there is discontent. But people have always grumbled and have always been discontented."

"What particular thing makes them grumble now, Don Manuel?" Pérez asked in bored tones.

"The new taxes."

"Money has to be raised to support the Republic."

"There are different ways to raise money."

"The central authorities specified this precise way."

"Forgive me, excelencia, if I say I believe they have made a

34

mistake. Not even in the worst days of Spanish rule were the people of New Mexico taxed directly."

"Times change."

"But the nature of the people does not change. Taxes can be added to anything—the price of goods, food, to ceremonies, to gambling, to anything, even the operation licenses for brothels. So long as they are hidden they will be paid. But it is another thing to order a man to hand over hard money for nothing that he can see. He will pay ten dollars in taxes on goods but fight like a cornered bear against handing over one cent directly."

"Nevertheless it has been decreed in the City of Mexico and it will be done," Pérez said indifferently.

Don Manuel put down his empty glass. "I must depart, excelencia. I want to say only that I am always wholly at your service."

Pérez held out his hand. "We appreciate your loyalty, Don Manuel."

7

Don Manuel now was almost ready to leave Santa Fe. He had had his final conferences with his fellow conspirators, Juan Bautista Vigil, the old postmaster; Juan Estevan Pino, and the others, and now there was but one more person to whom he had to give final instructions before he departed for Albuquerque to await the fruition of his planning. He turned in the direction of the home of Captain José Caballero.

He turned into the Calle de la Muralla at the end of the palace and walked until he came to the outer door marked Number 23. He entered the patio behind the wall. The house was built in the usual way around a smaller inner placita. A servant admitted him to the long sala that ran the length of the building on the street side and then went to notify his master. Armijo looked around. It was the first time he had ever been in the casa of the old presidial commander. The sala was plain, sparsely furnished, and yet it possessed quality. It was in the air, he thought,

35

the years of money and breeding and easy living. It was something he always felt in the homes of the ricos. It was a quality that was not yet present in his own establishments, not even the great one near Albuquerque, which was furnished with the finest of everything.

He looked around more carefully. Was it something he could put his finger on? There were the usual straight-backed chairs, some entirely of wood, some with leather seats; there was a long, simple table bearing two large silver candle-holders. There was nothing unusual, nothing rare, nothing, as far as he could determine, of any value. The chest of drawers that stood in a corner was carved, but not particularly well. There were, he knew, single pieces of furniture in his house in Albuquerque which were worth more than all the furniture in this place put together. Even the cloth tacked to the lower part of the walls to protect clothing from the whitewash that rubbed off was plain and inexpensive.

He frowned with irritation. It was something he could not define, and it was necessary that he discover eventually what it was so that he could bring it to his own house.

"Good day to him of God, Don Manuel," a voice said.

Don Manuel turned with a start. He did not like to be surprised. He said quickly: "May God give many good ones to you."

"Welcome to my home. Everything in it is yours. Please sit down. Would you like some brandy? Wine? Chocolate?"

"A small brandy, for favor."

"Pablo!" The servant who had admitted Armijo emerged from a shadow. Captain Caballero gave the order, and when the brandy was brought in on a silver tray in thin, delicate glasses, Armijo lifted his and expressed the hope that the presidial troop soon would be reorganized.

The old man was moved. "A thousand thanks, Don Manuel," he said. "As you know, there are but two loves in my life. The first is my son and the second is my troop."

Unlike his son, Esquipulas, the elder Caballero was below medium height. His face was small, each feature finely cut, with something of the decadent elegance of a cameo. His hair, dead white, was worn overly long and, Armijo suspected, probably was powdered. There was something archaic about him, and Armijo thought with the bitterness that never was far removed from him that in a very literal way Caballero did belong to another time. He was all the ancestors who had preceded him. It was that that the gente de razón had, the bond with the past. Such men never were wholly alone. Not as he could be alone. But there was one way to substitute for a lack of past, and that was to create a future.

The old man was lost for a moment in the fumes of the brandy, which was French and superb. It was the third thing he loved, Don Manuel thought, after his son and the troop, and perhaps before either.

Caballero recalled himself. "How did my son behave?"

"Very well, Don José. You should be proud of him."

"He lacks experience. My son has been trained to be a professional officer, but how can an officer gain experience without soldiers? It will be different when the company is revived." He looked at Armijo. "He worships you, Don Manuel. You will find him to be a right arm."

"I have no doubt of that, my dear capitán," Armijo said warmly.

"He is frivolous, but that is because he is young. In time, with proper experience—he has good blood, Don Manuel, good blood." He refilled the glasses. For a moment his eyes went away.

It was only a little after noon and he already was half drunk, Armijo thought with contempt. These ricos!

"Did it go well up north?" Captain Caballero asked.

"It is time to send off the cases."

"Santa Madre!"

"Vigil has everything ready. All that was lacking was one to command the mule train."

"My son," Caballero said instantly.

"Precisely the one I have decided upon."

Tears came in Caballero's eyes. "He will be honored, Don Manuel."

"The time is exactly right. Santa Fe is filled with gringos. Everybody is drunk or will be by nightfall. Caravans are moving out to the north and the south. The departure of the mule train will never be noticed. Tell Don Esquipulas to go to Vigil's house after the sun sets. Don Juan Bautista will give him his final orders." He lifted himself to his feet. "I leave for Albuquerque immediately. You can reach me at my estate at any time. Keep me informed. I regard you as my eyes and my ears in Santa Fe." His looked at Caballero with affection. "I will not forget your part in all this, Don José."

Captain Caballero stood up, swaying slightly. "I am a loyal New Mexican," he said in his old voice of command. "And I believe in you, Don Manuel."

"With patriots such as you and Don Esquipulas ready to draw your swords for freedom, there can be no doubt of our success," Armijo said. He embraced the old man. He could feel the trembling in the frail body and he smelled the stale alcohol, alcohol that had entered the blood and now seeped out from every pore. "Adiós, for the moment." He walked to the door and raised his right arm. *"Por Dios y Libertad!"*

Captain Caballero beamed. *"Por Dios y Libertad!"*

As Don Manuel's carriage left the city later in the afternoon, he heard in the distance behind him the church bells start the tolling of the Angelus. He could sense, over the beating hoofs of the horses, over the creaking of the wheels, the hush he knew was descending upon Santa Fe, quieting with a blanket of soft command Catholic and gringo heretic alike. He tossed away his cigar and leaned back. He smiled contentedly at Doña María Trinidad. He accepted the rich tolling as a good omen.

THE TIME OF THE GRINGO PART II

1

Don Esquipulas Caballero tossed some coins to the beggars collected in the street and then he joyfully entered the building where the baile was being held. He exchanged brief greetings with his host, James Magoffin, the American merchant who had just arrived with his wagons over the Santa Fe Trail and then went to the wine table and accepted a glass of champagne. He looked around. Smiling, he made his way through the crowded room to a small young man with a homely, candid face. "Hola, Ramón, what passes? Why do you stand alone?"

Ramón Baca, his best friend and fellow ensign in the presidial troop before it was disbanded, said: "I am observing the breasts of women."

"Have they changed in some way?"

"Only in quantity."

"You mean there are some women here tonight who have more or less than two?"

"I mean that now that so many of the women are wearing American-style clothing, the breasts are all disappearing. Somehow it makes those which still peep out so much the more intriguing."

"And the ones that have disappeared become more interesting still."

"It is true," Baca said. "But I wonder about one thing. How does a yanqui know what he is getting in a woman? I am told a respectable lady in the United States remains a stranger to her man until she is married to him. If they all wrap themselves up like some of the women here tonight, how does the man know what is underneath?"

"He gambles."

"It is the one thing I would not care to gamble on. I have read somewhere that in Oriental countries a man does not see

39

his wife at all until they are married, and I begin to believe the custom is the same in the States."

Don Esquipulas drank the last of the cold sparkling wine and exchanged his glass for a full one as a servant passed. He felt very good. There was nothing he liked better than a baile, and the bailes given by Magoffin were legendary. He tapped his foot to the music and he felt the glow of the champagne and he breathed in the perfume of the women.

"What made you so late tonight?" Baca asked. "You are usually the first one in when the doors open."

Don Esquipulas grinned. He was about to tell Baca how, until a very short while before, he had thought he would not be able to attend the baile at all. He had protested when his father had given him Don Manuel's instructions, and he had gone to the house of Don Juan Bautista Vigil depressed at having to leave for Taos on this night of all nights when everybody of any importance in Santa Fe would be at the party that traditionally started the fall social season. He had been overjoyed when Vigil decided that he would be conspicuous by his absence and that he should go to the baile and not leave until after midnight, when, if anyone saw him go, it would be thought he was on some affair of the heart.

Then he remembered he was pledged to secrecy and the words died in his mouth. It made a sudden unpleasant impression upon him. He and Baca had never before kept anything hidden from each other. He drank more of the wine to cover his uneasiness. Fortunately Baca was still craning his neck, looking at the ladies. Don Esquipulas saw that Baca was not drinking. "Your hand is empty, little monkey. Why?"

Baca made a mysterious gesture and screwed up his face. "I am on my good behavior tonight, chiquito. I have heard a rumor that the Governor plans to bring the troop back to life. When he arrives tonight I want him to see me as judicious, temperate, and wise. I should like him to see in me a future lieutenant."

Don Esquipulas felt a chill again as though a door had been opened to the dark outside. He gestured toward the dancers. "Your little niece Soledad is becoming quite the young lady."

Baca nodded. His features were suddenly grim. "She is."

"You say that in a strange manner."

"Not strangely, but with a little sickness. Manuel Armijo has come to the same conclusion."

"What do you mean?" Caballero asked, knowing.

"I mean that that pig has looked upon that little flower and he has found her good."

Caballero felt suddenly tired. It was Armijo everywhere, in all directions. "But she is a child," he said feebly, hoping that perhaps it was a joke, knowing it was no joke and that she was not a child because a girl of sixteen was not a child, even when one has known her since she was eight and has not been able to stop remembering her as a child.

Baca smiled painfully. "You make foolish words, amigo. Look again. She is far from being a child, to anyone, and to Armijo least of all."

Caballero felt his stomach contract. "You cannot be serious."

"I am serious. The dung in human form who pollutes the air wherever he is saw her at a reception. He got the light in his eyes. You know how Don Manuel reacts when he sees a woman who excites him. He arranged to be introduced to Soledad, which did not make her father happy since Santiago Abreu has knowledge of Don Manuel from old. It was something, I have heard, Manuel Armijo, the bull, simpering. For Soledad it must have been like wallowing in a pigsty."

It was going in wider circles, Caballero thought. First the feeling of dishonesty and dissimulation with his friend and now, because he was committed, the inability to permit himself the outrage he should feel.

"It is too bad that Don Manuel is not in power," Baca said cynically. "The star of Santiago Abreu would rise."

"Stop!"

Baca took his arm. "I know how you must think of this, chiquito, you who love the girl as I do. But this Armijo is a disease."

Caballero looked across the dance floor at the girl, the youngest daughter of Santiago Abreu. She was whirling in a waltz. It seemed he could not find his way out of the woods. He had brought up her name to change the subject from Pérez and Armijo and he had brought in the former Governor more. He could feel himself being tied to the man, string by string. He shook himself. "Let us get some wine, monito. The devil with your trying to make the impression on Pérez."

Baca stared at the dancers for a moment and his impish face broke into a grin. "Why not?" He clapped his friend on the back and they started for the wine table. Then Baca stopped. "A little moment—there he is, speaking to Señor Magoffin. No, amigo, you guzzle. I shall be model officer material. I am a career man."

2

"I AM GREATLY HONORED, excelencia," Magoffin said in his perfect Spanish.

"You know I would not miss one of your parties, Don Santiago," Pérez said. The governor was in uniform. His decorations blazed on his chest. "One has only to attend one of your bailes to understand why you are called the most beloved American in all Mexico."

"You are very kind, excelencia."

"It is even in your speech. Unlike most of your countrymen you speak our language as though the words tasted pleasant to you."

"It is the language of my wife and children, excelencia. It could not be otherwise."

"When you return to your home, convey to Señora Magoffin my felicitations."

"I shall, excelencia. I plan to leave for Chihuahua next week."

Pérez glanced around the room. "Your guests smile, Don Santiago. There are not many social occasions where men of Mexico and men of the United States smile at one another."

"That is true, unfortunately."

"But here there is nothing but an atmosphere of courtesy. I have been told that your state of Kentucky breeds courtesy. It is easy for me to believe."

Magoffin, a tall, keen man with brilliantly clear blue eyes, smiled. "Do not forget the Irish blood that is in me, excelencia. That counts too."

"Ladies and gentlemen conversing in pleasure," Pérez mused. "It gives one hope. I like too to see how our different styles of clothing blend. On an evening such as this I feel as though the great wall that has surrounded this country for so long is lowering a little and that fresh air is coming in." He looked up almost shyly at the American who towered over him. "But I keep you from your other guests, Don Santiago."

"May I order some wine for you, excelencia?"

"Do not disturb yourself. I will look at the wine table. It is not very often in this country that I can view so many exquisite bottles."

The Governor bowed and left. Magoffin thought that while Albino Pérez might have failed utterly to win the hearts of his subjects, he was a gentleman.

At the refreshment table the Governor encountered Esquipulas Caballero. Pérez bowed and Caballero returned the gesture with his own innate good manners. It took a few seconds for Caballero's thoughts to catch up with him and again he felt the chill.

"How are you this evening, Don Esquipulas?" Pérez asked in his Castilian accent, which offended so many New Mexicans.

"Very well, thank you, excelencia."

"And how is your father? I have heard he is ailing."

"He is somewhat better, excelencia."

"But not well enough to attend the baile tonight?"

"No, excelencia." His father's illness was only an illness of the bottle and would not be wholly cured until once again he could sit on a horse in front of soldiers. He had to remember that this small man standing before him, glittering like a chandelier, lisping like a Spaniard, was evil for New Mexico. He was a man of charm and breeding, but he was a bad Governor. His father believed that and his father could not be wrong. It would be better when Pérez was sent back to Mexico and New Mexico again was in the hands of a man who understood her and the needs of her people. It was unpleasant that it had to be done in violence, but in the Republic that was how things were done, in the City of Mexico and everywhere else.

He held out the glass he had just picked up. "May I have the honor to offer this glass of champagne to you, excelencia?"

43

"A thousand thanks," Pérez said, though he had not intended to drink champagne. He took the glass and waited politely until another glass had been poured for the younger man and then he said: "In good health, Don Esquipulas."

"To you, excelencia," Caballero said. He found it difficult to swallow the wine. He excused himself, knowing that he was being somewhat rude, and he looked again for Ramón. But that was no good either, he remembered. The music ended at that moment and the dancers broke up their ranks. He saw Soledad and walked toward her. "Hola, hola, mi princesa," he said. "Do not hurry so."

"Don Esquipulas," she said happily, "I was wondering when your eyes would fall upon me."

"That dress. I have never seen it before."

She held out her arms and whirled with exquisite grace. "Papa had it sent up from the City of Mexico. It is beautiful, is it not?"

Caballero stuck out his lower lip. "It is very beautiful, mi chula, but it is a dress for a woman."

Her eyes snapped. "I am a woman. I am seventeen."

"Sixteen."

"Seventeen!"

He touched her chin. "Sixteen, little friend of my soul. That locket that hangs around your neck was a present from me on your birthday."

She touched the locket and lowered her head and looked up at him from under her brows. "Of course, mi caballero, you are right. I lack eight full months of being seventeen." She asked slyly: "Have you heard that Lucía Mendoza is but three months older than I and she already is engaged to be married."

He snapped his fingers. "Ea, pues, it is well known the Mendoza women ripen early." He pretended to study her critically.

She stamped her foot. "I hate you when you tease me this way, Esquipulas! Whatever the Mendoza has, I have more."

"I would not say that."

Her eyes snapped again and then she smiled and tilted her head. "There are others who do not agree with you."

"Like Don Manuel?" He regretted it immediately. He had meant it for a joke, but when he heard it on his lips he knew it was no joke. Her face saddened so quickly he felt his heart tighten. "Pardon, corazón, I could cut my tongue," he said.

44

"It is true then, is it not?" Two lines embraced her mouth.
"What is true?"

"That everyone speaks of Don Manuel and me?"

As she spoke, it burst upon him again in full obscenity. "No
one, mi bonita, no one. I would run steel through the heart of
anyone who spoke so." There was a tear in each of her eyes and
he felt the knife was in his own heart.

"But you heard enough about it to make a joke," she insisted.
Her voice was changed and now was that of a child.

"It is so funny, chiquita," he said helplessly. "To think of
you and Manuel Armijo in one thought."

"Papa does not think it is funny."

"Of course he would not. And it is not funny. I say it only
to bring the laughter back to your eyes."

She slumped and her dress was suddenly the dress of a woman
on a child, as a child might wear something belonging to her
mother, for a masquerade. There was destruction taking place
before him and he was unable to do anything to stop it.

"My father must be right, Esquipulas. I should not have
doubted him," she said listlessly. "He is sending me away."

"Sending you away? Away to where?"

"Papa says I must go to the City of Mexico to visit for a
while with relatives."

"Because of Armijo?" he asked incredulously. "Because
Manuel Armijo wanted to meet you?"

Her voice was dead. "Papa does not admit that it is wholly
because of that. He had spoken of it before, from time to time,
since my mother has been ill and staying with my sister in
Chihuahua, but now he is firm." As she spoke she slipped uncon-
sciously into an attitude of supplication, clasping her hands together at her breast, leaning forward slightly as though to ask in
gesture what she would not permit herself to ask in words.

"But it is ridiculous," he said, knowing with the recurred
sickness that it was not ridiculous at all. "Your father cannot be
serious."

"He is serious. Don Santiago Magoffin leaves for Chihuahua
sometime next week. I am to journey with him."

Listening to her, it was as though there were no one else in
the room. He thought how she was in some way apart from every-

45

one else, had always been apart, even as a leggy child he had once taught to ride a horse and throw a lazo. The Abreus came originally from France, it was said, and perhaps that was it, the Gallic strain together with the Baca blood, born centuries before in Navarre in the northernmost part of Spain, combining into a subtle refinement that belonged alone to her. It was in her face, in the wide, full mouth, in the clear, honest, frank eyes that never in the years that he had known her were afraid to look upon anything. She was tall among Mexican women, and perhaps that was the French part too; now, waisted slim as an arrow, full and sweet-breasted, in a dress that was not intended to fit around the curveless body of a child and that showed, even to the eyes of one who loved her with nostalgic tenderness as a rare flower, that she no longer was a child; wearing a high jeweled comb in her hair, draped over which was a lace mantilla that had been worn how many years before by what ancestor, perhaps the one who knelt before the great King, Enrique de Navarra, at the time the name Cabeza de Vaca was given in honor to the family. Now, even now, the difference was there, so that, next to her, other women seemed coarse.

She waited as she might before an altar, patiently, imploringly, and he thought that until that moment there were things he might have said, a calling to that which they had saved together so long; but now he could say none of these things. The quality of their belonging to each other had undergone a tenuous mutation as it inevitably had to do, but the direction of the new course was linked with Manuel Armijo and with the way Manuel Armijo had looked upon her. The purity between them was tainted. The pollution beclouded more than her, he thought, for lost in it was his own time of youth.

"Hermanita," he whispered, calling her that, "little sister," to try somehow to salvage something, as though the taint could be lessened. "You should be filled with joy to go to the capital of the country. The City of Mexico is a place of gaiety and filled with handsome officers who will adore you."

She was able to open her hands and raise her chin. "It will be exciting, Esquipulas, will it not?"

46

3

Esquipulas Caballero scooped up the last of the frijoles with the last piece of tortilla and deposited them in his mouth. He took a final swallow of wine and wiped his mouth with the back of his hand. He rolled a cigarette and lay back on the saddle and stared at the sky. Here, in the clarity of the country and the night and the stars, his confusions vanished.

They had been on the trail four days, and from the beginning, listening to the relaxing creaking of leather, the cursing of the muleros, the grunts of the animals, smelling the clean ammonia smells of the horses, feeling the weight of the heavy pistol in his belt and the cutting of the musket strap across his chest, his mind cleared. The vapors and the smoke and the music and the perfume which had filled his head at the baile were gone. There was the simple harshness of the trail, the danger of Indians, nothing else.

The night had in it only its own sounds. The rich smell of the silently burning mesquite was the perfume now. The music was in the low voices of the men around the fire, in the distance where the predators made their own sounds. His cigarette tasted good. His doubts were gone.

It was better for Soledad to go to Mexico for a little while. There would be disturbances and there was no reason for her to have to witness them. It soon would be over, as all political disturbances soon were over, with few if any hurt, with the victor in power and the defeated in flight, uninjured, except perhaps for his pride. He knew from his military studies that in some countries insurrections were accompanied by a great deal of bloodshed, but in Mexico a small revolt was only a requisite prelude to change and the bloodletting always was restricted. What the devil! A little blood spilled was good anyway. Life was dull enough, particularly since the troop had been disbanded. He had received no instructions beyond bringing the muskets up to Padre Martínez, but he had already resolved to remain in the Rio Arriba until the insurrection started. There would be some excitement.

Poor Ramón, acting like an acolyte in front of Pérez when

anyone with sense—his father, Don José, for example—knew that under Pérez there was no possibility of any reorganization of the presidial companies! When Don Manuel was again in command and the soldiery resuscitated, Ramón would take a different attitude altogether. The Baca was a man of arms, by inclination and heredity, and only under Don Manuel could he find an outlet for his ambitions. All the others, even Santiago Abreu, would find out how much better it would be. Only Manuel Armijo was strong enough to defy the central government on the matter of taxes, and only he was strong enough to squeeze money out of the gringos.

He frowned for a moment, thinking again of Don Manuel lusting for Soledad, and then he thought Don Manuel was a man and Soledad was opening like a rose. Armijo would have to be a maricón not to have noticed her. It was no sin that he did what nature impelled him to do. Jesucristo, he had not knocked her down to rape her! He did only what any man might do. But with any other man Santiago Abreu would have not made an issue. It was an open insult for him to send her out of the country because Don Manuel looked upon her. Caballero hoped that when Don Manuel again was in power he would have the charity to look upon it all as only the extreme concern of a father for a young daughter. But of course he would. Don Manuel was a man of honor. His father, Captain Caballero, who owned the proudest sense of honor in New Mexico, could not support him otherwise.

He heard footsteps. A bulk loomed between him and the fire. "Hola, Fernando, do you not sleep?"

The man kneeled. "Is there anything you desire, Don Esquipulas?"

"Nothing. Is all well, amigo?"

"Yes. The mules are cared for. The men now go to sleep. I shall take the first watch."

"Then remain here for a little moment and smoke a cigarette with me. Sleep eludes me." Fernando crossed his legs and sat down. He made a cigarette. Caballero said: "This is our last night. This time tomorrow, with the favor of God, should find us in Taos and our responsibilities discharged."

"Yes," Fernando said quietly.

Caballero raised himself on his elbow. "What has been the matter with you these last days, Fernando?"

Fernando did not answer. The blanket around his shoulders had covered the human outlines so that now, still, solid, he was like a rock. His hat shielded his profile from the firelight. Caballero could see no more than the round, motionless mass and the glow of the cigarette, brightening with each puff, illuminating the strong mouth and the square jaw.

"Speak out," Caballero ordered. "It is a long time since the time you might act as a stranger to me, and yet your face has not been a familiar one since we left Santa Fe."

There was no response from Fernando, and Caballero thought the Indian was coming out again and that there would be something but it would take time.

Fernando had entered the Caballero household seventeen years before with his mother, a peasant woman from Tomé whose husband had been killed in a Navajo raid. Fernando was seven, Esquipulas six. The boys grew up friends, and as they became older the peasant child adjusted himself slowly into his status as personal servant. He was not yet ten when he understood it was his responsibility to watch over the son of the family. It had matured him early. With a somberness that came naturally from his Indian blood he had stopped being a child long before his master. He grew into a large and powerful man. His face was set in flat planes. His eyes were watchful. The Indian part of him, as Esquipulas had understood a long time ago, gave him a sense of timelessness. His speech, when it came, came like a plant, emerging from the earth.

Fernando seemed to settle down harder against the ground. He said without removing the cigarette from his mouth: "It is not for me to say, Don Esquipulas."

"What is not for you to say?" Caballero asked impatiently. There was a catechism that had to be gone through.

"It is my duty to serve you and ask no questions."

"That is true. But I ask you now to speak."

Fernando took the infinitesimal remains of the cigarette from between his lips and ground it slowly between his thumb and forefinger. He made another cigarette. "Why are we delivering muskets?"

49

"For freedom," Caballero said instantly.

"Freedom?" Fernando struck flint. "Bought with guns?"

"It frequently is bought with guns. Pérez is a dictator, sent up from Mexico. He leads the country back to darkness." When Fernando made no reply, Caballero said: "The new Constitution and the new taxes will make slaves of our people."

"Governor Pérez did not invent peonage," Fernando said in his deep voice. "Governor Pérez obeys orders. He is a soldier. He did not invent the new Constitution either."

"He enforces it," Caballero said, an angry note rising in his voice. "That is enough for me."

"Then it is enough for me, señor." Fernando pulled farther into himself, as though he considered the conversation at an end.

"But I want you to understand it yourself," Caballero insisted. "You are not an ordinary peasant. You have been educated, almost as well as I. We have read from the same books. It is something you should understand from within yourself."

Presently Fernando asked: "Where are the Governor's muskets? Where are his soldiers? Against whom are the muskets we bring to Taos to be leveled?"

"The guns are to show force. Few will be fired."

"Is that understood by those to whom they will be issued?"

Caballero shook his head. The argument was escaping him. It was so clear to him and yet it appeared it could not be put into words Fernando could understand. Of course, Fernando did not know Don Manuel. "It goes deep, amigo," he said. "The central authorities would take away our rights as free men. It is necessary to make a stand now for those rights or lose them forever."

"Then this is an insurrection against the central government and not against Governor Pérez."

"It is not to be an insurrection *against* anything. It is to be an insurrection *for* liberty. We demonstrate to those below who regard us as children, ready to submit to any tyrannical law, that we are free men. We will send Pérez back to Mexico, his tail between his legs, with that message. Then perhaps we will be treated as equals by those who make the laws for the Republic." He now was warmed to his argument. "We must be strong here in New Mexico, and Don Manuel alone understands that. We are surrounded on all sides by enemies. The gringos swarm over us."

"Are the americanos enemies?"

"They are enemies as a people. They are heretics."

"They show no enmity to our priests."

"They cannot do otherwise in New Mexico."

"Don Santiago Magoffin is a Catholic. I have seen him attend Mass."

"There may be believers among them, but most of them are heretics and if they had their way they would do harm to our priests. We are isolated, separated from the motherland by desert and mountain, and Pérez allows us to grow so weak we cannot protest against persecution or infestation."

Fernando made his third cigarette. "The Indians are true enemies."

"Yes, for certain!"

"Then why do we arm Indians?"

"The men of the pueblos are not Indians in that sense. They are not Navajos or Apaches or Utes. They are Catholics. They hate the wild Indians as much as we do."

"My father was murdered by Indians."

"By Navajos—wild Indians."

"All Indians are Indians."

"You have Indian blood in yourself."

"I am a Mexican."

"My father and I believe that Don Manuel can save the country before it is too late," Caballero said. "When you come to know Don Manuel as we do, your doubts will leave you."

A patronizing note had crept into Caballero's voice. It was detected immediately by Fernando. It was the old thing. It said peasants were children and incapable of adult thought. It said leave the thinking and the planning to those who were born to rule the country. Fernando drew his blanket more closely around him and pulled his hat farther down over his face. He now was withdrawn entirely. He stood up. "I will look again at the mules, señor, if there is nothing else."

It had not ended right, Caballero thought, but there was nothing more he could say. A peasant remained a peasant. No matter how much education was given to them, their minds remained closed. "I will try to sleep, Fernando."

"Good night."

"Good night, Fernando." He watched his servant move away, his bulk large in the night. He closed his eyes and tried to sleep. He was tired from the long day in the saddle, and his stomach was pleasantly filled with food and wine and his mind was at peace, but sleep would not come to him. He thought about Fernando and his intractability. Ah, Dios, but there was nothing like a stubborn peasant! Still, Fernando was a better man than that and certain truths should be evident to him.

4

ON THE WAY to the inn after they had turned the muskets over to the priest, Caballero said: "You curse like a Spaniard, Emilio."

Emilio beamed. "Many thanks, Don Esquipulas."

"It has a positive sound, soldier, and it does not offend me. But you are not in the capital now and mine are not the only ears in Taos. Here there is a great hatred for the Spaniards and for all things in the Spanish style. Much more than there is in Santa Fe. Save your varied defecations for another place, and while you are here curse like a Mexican."

Emilio looked abashed and then he jutted his chin. "But, señor comandante, my veins are filled with the blood of Spain. It is natural to me to use the profanity of my ancestors."

"It is more necessary for you to keep that blood inside your veins, dolt," one of the other men said. "The comandante speaks true. Let these savages here suspect you consider yourself as anything but native and they will have a look at your Spanish blood." He spat. "Spanish blood!"

"The blood is Spanish, ass," Emilio said angrily. "The father of my father—"

"Enough!" Caballero ordered curtly. "Here you will keep the filth of your defecation from the face of God, from Christ, from the milk of the Negro, from the prong, and from anything else. And you will avoid all reference to the genitals of the saints."

"It is *my* life, Don Esquipulas."

"For the moment it belongs to Don Manuel. When it is returned to you, you may dispose of it as you please. That is the end of it."

The conversation affirmed Caballero's decision to keep the men in the Rio Arriba. It would not be safe to allow any of them to return to Santa Fe before the insurrection started. Although they had all taken solemn oaths to silence, one or another of them might talk. The wheels were turning now. The priest had the muskets and soon it would begin. He felt excitement. There would be changes when it was over and all good. He remembered how, some years before, because of political intrigue his father had been superseded as commander of the presidial companies by an officer sent up from Mexico and how, when this officer was killed in 1835 in a battle with the Navajos, Don Manuel had manipulated things so that Captain Caballero was restored to command. Armijo had not enough power at the time to make the appointment permanent, and a few months later another officer had arrived from Mexico to take over the troops and had remained in command until Pérez disbanded the army entirely. But this time it would be different. The word of Don Manuel, as political and military chief of New Mexico, in this matter would be law.

Caballero thought how good it would be again with the army in being and his father in command. Captain Caballero had said often that more than any other man Don Manuel understood the army. In that he was like the great Santa Anna.

They reached the inn and dismounted and Caballero handed the reins of his horse to Fernando. "Drink and rest yourselves, hombres. But do not get drunk. The Governor has spies everywhere. Keep to yourselves and remain quiet."

He entered the posada. As it had been the last time he was there, the air was thick with smoke and the smell of unwashed bodies and cheap brandy and wine. Low talk hovered over the tables, constant as the smoke. Somewhere two men were singing gitano music over guitars. Caballero sniffed, wrinkled his brow, and took an unoccupied table in a corner, conscious that eyes were raised to look at his good clothing. Talk ended temporarily in his wake as though his passage blotted speech, but he took no notice. The peasants used the same language he did, but he paid as little attention to it as he would to the barking of mongrels. He seated himself so that he could keep an eye on the table where his men had gathered. The room was crowded. Some of the natives played at monte or rolled dice, but most of them huddled over small cups and talked. There was no ventilation anywhere and in a few moments the atmosphere seemed to become bearable. He removed his hat, made a cigarette, and lit it from the tallow lamp on the table. He stretched his long legs as far as they could go. A peasant girl appeared before him. So thick was the smoke, it was as though she had materialized from it.

"What do you drink, señor?" she asked.

He looked at her, appreciating the flimsy chemise through which he could see the small breasts on the thin body. She remained motionless, inert, fixed as the table. There was nothing on her face, no coquetry, no impatience.

He said: "Brandy, muchacha. I do not suppose you have that of El Paso?"

"Just the local, señor."

"Bring it. The best of the local."

"It is all the same, señor." She walked away.

She was not unpleasing to look at, he thought. Her chemise was draped low over her shoulders, and her breasts as she moved made attractive shadows. Except that she would be sweaty. When she returned with a cup of brandy, he pushed some silver across the table and pointed to where his men were seated. "Tell those hombres that I buy them their first drink, muchacha, and that I drink to their health."

The girl took the money and left. He tasted the brandy. It was that called Taos Lightning, raw and hot. The second swallow was more palatable. He leaned back against the adobe wall and puffed on his cigarette and looked again around the room. He felt pleasantly superior to the other people. His eye was caught by some men at a table not far from him. There were five of them, their bowed heads like the closed-in petals of a flower. One of the men, scrawny and pinch-faced, with a small hump on his back, was talking vehemently. The other four listened, nodding. One of the four was a giant of a man. Every time the speaker made what appeared to be a telling point, the giant lifted his huge head and looked around belligerently as though defying anyone to contradict the speaker.

At first Caballero could not make out what was being said, but he would wager it was about politics. Politics was the life of these people. It was more important than their religion or their wives or their children. Then he caught some of the words:

"Your chickens, every time they lay an egg, it will be taxed. . . ."

Caballero swallowed another mouthful of brandy and shook his head indulgently. The new taxes—everywhere the people talked of nothing else. Even his own friends, who had so many more interesting things to discuss. Although their talk was centered mainly on ways to avoid paying them.

The giant glared fiercely around the room, and the hunchback continued: "When a sheep drops a lamb the owner is taxed. If there is no money for taxes the lamb itself must serve. It is worse than it was in the days of the Spaniards."

The waitress placed the drinks Caballero had bought on the table where his men were seated. The men lifted the cups and gestured their thanks to Caballero, and then Emilio swallowed some of the fiery brandy and snarled immediately. "By the nails of Christ! This tastes like horse piss!" Several men at near-by tables looked up angrily. Caballero's face darkened with annoyance. Emilio waved his hand to him placatingly.

When the girl returned with the change, Caballero said: "Keep it, chulita."

"A thousand thanks, señor. You are generous."

"What do you do when not serving drinks? I am a stranger and alone."

She looked at him closely for the first time. "I may join you. It is not done usually." There was a faint smile on her lips.

"But you will do it this time in courtesy to a stranger. Refill my cup, bonita, and fill one for yourself." Then he said: "Smile again; it brings the light of the sun to your face."

The girl left and returned with two cups of brandy. She set them on the table and started to sit down in the chair facing him. He made room against the wall. "No, here, muchacha, next to me."

She walked around the table, sat down, and found his arm outstretched. He closed it around her indifferently, his hand on her breast. She looked at him quickly. His eyes were on the table where the thin man again was talking. His fingers stroked idly. She shook herself away. "I am not a goat, señor. My udder is not for milking." He let his hand fall away. She kept her eyes on him as she drank her brandy. It is not the touching of the breast, she wanted to tell him. That and more has been done before, and it always is pleasant and you are a rico and very handsome. But it must not be done inattentively. She opened her small sack of punche and made a cigarette. The guitar-players were singing of a hopeless love, and in the silence that followed the lament the voice of the hunchback carried across the room.

"When you take your wife to bed, then the next day you report to the alcalde and pay a tax for the pleasure."

The room filled with laughter. The giant half rose from his seat, his face enraged. The hunchback touched his arm lightly and he sat down again, and then the thin man spoke again, more loudly this time because he knew the room was listening to him. "Laugh, pobrecitos," he said. "You think that it is all a joke. But unhappily it is true. Everything now is to be taxed. I have studied the new laws and it is true that each time you bed your wife it will be your duty to pay a tax."

The giant opened his mouth. "My brother speaks the truth." He spoke with the solid assurance of a powerful man. "He has been to Santa Fe and he has had the new laws explained to him. Nothing, not the wine you drink, the corn you grow, nothing is to escape the new taxes. The taxes have a thousand eyes, watching everything you do, all the hours of the day and night, and when you fall upon your pallet with your woman at night to find the only ease that cannot be taken from the poor, even then the eyes are on you."

There was another silence and then the room broke out with angry murmuring. Caballero fondled the girl's breast again. She was concentrating on the talk in the room and for a moment was unaware of what he was doing. Then she turned to him, her face furious.

"Such lovely breasts," he said. "Not at all like that of the goat, not even the beautiful wild mountain goat." He pulled her closer to him. The noise rose in the room. "Tell me, querida, do the men here have nothing to interest them but politics and taxes?"

She removed herself from him again. "The problems of taxes do not bother ricos, señor. They are real to us. The hunger is here now, and how will it be later when they come to collect for the taxes?"

"Who are the men who talk?"

"They are the Montoya brothers. The large one is called Desiderio. The one with the hump is Antonio. He is a thinker."

"It is evident. But there are ways to get around things, one way or another." He was bored with the subject.

"Don José Esquibel, the alcalde of La Cañada, is a paisano. We looked to him to help us."

"There you are." He brought her to him.

"But that was foreseen by the Governor. The new prefect of the north has been given powers greater than those of the alcalde. It is said that this new prefect has been sent up here for no purpose other than to enforce the taxes. The alcalde is left without authority."

A voice called out: "What does Padre Martínez say about the new taxes?"

Antonio Montoya said: "There is but one thing the good padre can say. He is a friend of the poor."

"I will wait to hear it from his own mouth." Other men agreed.

With an oath Desiderio Montoya lurched toward the first man who had expressed doubt. Several men tried to block him. He shook them off as a horse might shake off flies.

Then Antonio Montoya said: "Sit down, mi hermano." The giant's shoulders sagged and he returned to his seat. "There is no reason to quarrel among ourselves, countrymen," Antonio said in the same quiet voice. "For us it is necessary that we stand together so that we make a wall of ourselves, one shoulder against the next. I have not spoken to Padre Martínez, so I cannot say what is in the heart of the priest. Since he loves us, there can be but one thing there. I have spoken to our true friend, Don José Esquibel, the alcalde of the people. The new prefect, Ramón Abreu, has taken over complete control of the Rio Arriba. Don José now has no more to say than a clerk in his office." He emptied his cup and

57

stood up, bent under his hump. "It becomes more and more clear that the day soon arrives when we have to make the decision. If we quarrel we will fall, one by one, and when the halter is fastened around our necks again, it will not say 'Made in Spain,' but it will feel as though it came direct from Madrid." He touched his brother on the shoulder and the two men left.

"Well, now that the little sermon is ended, perhaps we can resume our drinking," Caballero said. "Fill our cups again, chula." When she again was seated next to him, he asked: "How are you called?"

"Morena."

" 'Dark one.' It is a fitting name."

"I have no shame for my Indian blood, señor."

"I was not speaking of the darkness of your skin. It is an old name and it is beautiful."

"I do not know your name, señor."

"Don Esquipulas Caballero, Morenacita."

"Caballero? Knight? I did not know it was a name too. It is fitting for you as well, Don Esquipulas."

"Thank you, little friend."

At the table where his men were seated he heard a commotion and looked up. A number of native men were standing around the table, shouting hoarsely. Then he heard Emilio's voice, thick with drinking. "I am not drunk, and no one of you is my superior officer. By the mast of San Antonio, I am a free man and will speak as I please."

"*Español*," one of the natives spat.

"Yes!" Emilio shouted. "My father's father was born within sight of the Escorial. Host with vinegar! Do you ask that I show shame for my blood?"

"Son of a whore!" the native shouted. "I defecate on your Spanish blood!"

Caballero pushed the girl aside and got up swiftly. He pushed his way to the table. The natives were closed in, cursing. He heard Emilio cry in pain, and then he saw the other soldiers and Fernando on their feet and in the dim light the gleam of their knives. He reached the table and thrust aside two of the natives. "Enough! Enough!" he ordered. He turned his back on the soldiers and faced the natives. "The man is filled with strong drink, amigos. He speaks, but he knows not what he says."

The faces in front of him were contorted with fury, the wildness of raw brandy on stomachs that never held enough food. Caballero said over his shoulder: "Take the drunken fool out of here. Hold your hand over his mouth."

He heard Fernando say quietly: "There is no need for that now, Don Esquipulas. He is dead."

Caballero twisted his head. Emilio was slumped over the table, blood oozing from his chest. He smelled the blood, through the smoke and the brandy fumes, and he heard the voices rise again. Again he faced the natives. The smell had reached them too, and their mouths were pulled back like those of wolves. He drew his knife and made a wide sweep with the point, and when the natives crouched back he said: "You have killed a man, brutes, and one who was such as yourselves."

"Kill them all!" one of the natives screamed.

The soldiers behind Caballero pushed over the table as they moved forward. Caballero, not turning his head, said: "All of you get out of here. Pronto!"

"Emilio is dead!" Emilio's friend of the trail said.

"Leave him. Get out of here. Fernando, take command." Caballero swept his knife in an arc again. "Stay where you are, hombres."

The natives remained motionless, the rage arrested on their faces as though carved there. Their eyes wavered. The instinct was to obey. It was in the voice, the ancient command, the tone that forbade disobedience, the inflection that bore the weight of the centuries.

Caballero snapped his fingers and he heard the chairs scrape behind him and knew the soldiers were backing toward the door. He waited until he felt a draft of cool air; then he sheathed his knife and with cold arrogance turned his back to the natives and followed his men out. There was no sound except the stamping of his own boots until he was almost at the door, and then he heard a strangled cry, the sound of an animal tearing itself loose from a trap. The cry was repeated by others and he knew it had not held long enough. He pulled his knife free again as he passed through the door. He heard the clatter of chairs and the scrape of feet and a low snarling, a sound less than human. Outside, the soldiers were already mounted.

"Do not command us to fly like frightened grandmothers, Don Esquipulas!" one of the soldiers pleaded. "We can make these dogs bark different sounds."

"We get out of the village."

"What of Emilio? What of his killing and the body that lies within the filthy inn? Does it remain unavenged?"

"He is dead and cannot be returned to life." Caballero leaped upon his horse. "Vamos!"

"Do not order us to be cowards!" the soldier begged. "Not before peasants and a dead comrade to avenge."

"Save your vengeance. You are a soldier and on duty. Move!"

The natives burst from the inn. They stood in front of it, sniffing, looking in all directions. Caballero felt a tug at his leg and looked down, gripping his knife. He said: "You, querida, what do you do here?"

"Let your men go, Don Esquipulas, and follow me."

She was gone, moving like a wraith. The soldiers spurred their horses and clattered off. Caballero reined to follow them and then he looked again at the girl, laughed, and turned the horse in her direction. He looked back at the inn. The natives were still standing there, already cooled by the night air. It had been a kind of purge and now they would return to their drinking and look shamefaced at the corpse, and soon they would drink in respect to the dead, and by the next day the slaying would not live even in memory, since Emilio was only a man and all that had happened to him was that he had been killed.

"Here, Don Esquipulas." She was standing in front of an adobe hut. He dismounted. "There is a corral in the back," she said. He led the horse into the corral and removed the saddle, then entered the one-room building. In the room was a wooden chest, a colchón rolled up for the day, a crucifix on the wall. In the corner on the floor were some cooking utensils. The girl faced him, her arms folded against her stomach. "My house is yours, Don Esquipulas." She opened the mattress and spread out an Indian blanket inside of it. She said: "Let me remove your boots, Don Esquipulas."

He held out one foot and she pulled off the boot and then the other. She straightened up. "Make yourself comfortable, Don Esquipulas. Sleep, and with the protection of God."

"And yourself, Morena? Where do you go?"

"I sleep on the floor next to you."

"You shall sleep with me."

"Would I please you?"

"Yes."

"A mestiza, such as I?"

"Remove your blouse and your skirt, querida, and join me."

"There was an Anglo from the north here in the spring, a gringo trapper."

"Ca! Quia!" His voice hardened.

"I tell it to you only that you may know I am not untutored."

"I did not expect ignorance," he said harshly.

She stood quietly, her hands against her stomach. "Now you are angry, and that is good. Now it has a little meaning for you, and that will leave something between us."

5

EsquIPULAS CABALLERO signaled to Padre Martínez, and the two men stepped away from the campfire. "What the devil is the matter with that man, padre? The battle will take place at any time and he will make no plans. He will not even listen to anyone."

The priest looked over to the Indian, José Gonzales, seated cross-legged at the fire on a hill above the black mesa of San Ildefonso. Gonzales was staring into the flames. His features were as still as a mask of death. "He is taking his counsel from voices he alone can hear," the priest thought. But he could not tell this to Caballero because it would only puzzle the young man more.

"He seems to be in a trance," Caballero said. "He has not spoken five words since we started out. If we are to defeat Pérez's army, plans must be made."

Martínez shrugged. "He is the commander. He will do it his way."

"How big is the Governor's force? How are the men armed? Where are they at the moment? These are important questions, but he is making no attempt to find answers."

"He is the commander," Martínez repeated.

"He is a fool. He will ruin everything Don Manuel has planned." Caballero walked angrily into the darkness.

Martínez went back to the fire and sat down next to the Indian. He did not think Gonzales was a fool. Whether the Indian would ruin Armijo's planning remained to be seen, but the priest did not think that either. From the beginning it had worked out as Don Manuel had predicted.

The incident that had started the insurrection had taken place exactly as Don Manuel had said it would. It was an unimportant affair, something that happened all the time among the peasants. A moneylender had lent a poor farmer some money the year before, and when the note fell due, the farmer had been unable to meet his obligation. The matter was brought before the alcalde of La Cañada, and the farmer gave as his reason for defaulting the fact that livestock he had set aside for sale to satisfy the debt had been confiscated by the Governor's agents in lieu of money under the drastic terms of the new tax laws. Don José Esquibel, the alcalde, considered the excuse valid and extended the time of the payment of the debt for another twelve months. The decision pleased all the other peasants greatly, and ordinarily the case would have ended there.

The moneylender, however, appealed to the new prefect, Don Ramón Abreu. Don Ramón reversed the decision of the alcalde, authorized the creditor to appropriate the farmer's remaining livestock, and as that satisfied only the amount of the loan and not the interest also due, Don Ramón ordered the farmer imprisoned until the additional amount was paid. Don Ramón also arrested the alcalde for failure to administer justice.

On that same night Antonio Montoya called a mass meeting of peasants in front of the jail where the two men were being held, and after a fiery speech the hunchback led the peasants in breaking into the jail and freeing the prisoners. The farmer and Esquibel were carried around the plaza of La Cañada in triumph on the shoulders of the peasants, and after another speech Montoya and his brother issued muskets and then the aroused peasants cried for

the blood of Ramón Abreu. The prefect fled for his life to Santa
Fe, and the revolt was on.

Throughout the Rio Arriba the men gathered—peasants from
the hills and Indians from the pueblos, men who believed in
freedom and men who hated taxation; men who had been taught
to hate Pérez and the Abreus; men who loved excitement; men
who would have fought against God to get new muskets free; men
who loved the priest, Antonio José Martínez; men who believed in
the buffalo-hunter, José Gonzales; men whose friends believed in
any of those things and who wanted to be with their friends; men
who had nothing else to do. The Indians from the Taos pueblo
were joined by Indians from the pueblos of San Juan and Santo
Domingo and Cochiti and San Felipe. The army of revolt strengthened as a river tumefies from little streams pouring into it, and the
men looked upon one another with delight because they had not
known until then how many they were.

And José Gonzales remembered how Popé had been a true
sorcerer and how Popé, though he had been a San Juan Indian, had
received his instructions from the three infernal spirits of the kiva
of Taos. Gonzales remained away from the growing horde and
even from Padre Martínez and he communicated with his spirits
in the small holy estufa below the pueblo. He said the name Popé
again and again so that all the years were erased and what he was
about to do was only continuing what Popé had done and the
century and a half that lay between belonged to the reckoning of
the Spaniards and had no existence. He sat alone in the chamber,
which was filled with the stale stink of sweat and the heavy smell
of incense, and he extended his long arms and he linked his hands
with those of Popé, and as he remained there bound to the past,
the spirits came to him and he understood himself as a sorcerer
too.

The Mexican peasants had come first to enlist in the army of
insurrection. The Indians had followed more slowly, but in the
end, as more than two thousand men started south toward Santa
Fe carrying muskets so new that even in the night the light from
the stars was reflected on shining barrels, there were more in the
army who were Indians than Mexicans.

The peasants had leaders of their own, and the Indians from
the other pueblos had arrived with chiefs, but from the beginning

all men accepted José Gonzales as the supreme commander of the army. When Esquipulas Caballero offered himself and his men, Gonzales nodded silently, and on the march down from Taos the Indian did not speak, not to Caballero nor to the priest nor to anyone else.

Don Esquipulas returned to the campfire in great excitement. He crouched before the seated Indian. "Don José, deserters are coming up from Governor Pérez's army. Indians from the pueblos of San Juan and San Ildefonso. They say the Governor is encamped at Pojoaque, only a few hours from here." Gonzales looked up indifferently. "These men should be questioned," Caballero said. "We should find out everything we can about Pérez's forces."

"Question them," Gonzales said.

Caballero ordered one of the deserters brought before him. He questioned the man, a squat, flat-faced Indian. "How big is the Governor's army?"

"Thirty Mexicans. There were two hundred Indians," the Indian deserter said in Spanish, the tongue used by the pueblo Indians as a second language common to all tribes.

"*Thirty* Mexicans?"

"And in the beginning two hundred Indians, no more."

Caballero believed the Indian must be making a mistake with the language. He held up his hands and opened and closed the fingers three times. "Thirty? Thirty?"

"Yes. Maybe a few less."

"Santa Madre de Dios! Only thirty Mexican soldiers."

"Not soldiers, señor—volunteers. The Governor would not call soldiers," the Indian said.

Padre Martínez held his hands before the fire. He could hear the voice of Manuel Armijo as though he were sitting next to him.

"How are they armed?" Caballero asked.

"Some of the Mexicans have old guns," the Indian said.

"And the others have wooden lances," Martínez said.

The Indian looked at him. "That is right, padre."

"And the Indians carry sharpened sticks as well and a few of them have bows and arrows," the priest said.

"How do you know that, padre?" the Indian asked.

"I know," the priest said.

"They also have with them a small cannon," the Indian said.

"That should be helpful."

"But what of the weapons in the government armory?" Caballero demanded. "The armory is filled with modern muskets."

"The Governor ordered the volunteers to bring their own weapons. It is all I know. He said the insurrection would not be serious," the Indian said.

Padre Martínez turned his eyes toward José Gonzales, who was still gazing into the fire. It was as though he had heard nothing of what had been said.

6

AT DAWN the deserters were counted and it was found they numbered more than seventy which meant Pérez had little more than one hundred and fifty men remaining under his command. Gonzales now roused himself. He became brisk and curt. He deployed his men with skill. Caballero watched him with astonishment. Gonzales was another man. The ambush was set with the proficiency of a trained officer.

Shortly after noon, with the sun hot and high in the clear sky, the army of Governor Pérez marched on to the dark mesa of San Ildefonso. Riding in advance was a small company of men. Caballero, lying prone, focused his glass and recognized as the commander of the vanguard Francisco Sarracino, a close friend to Pérez, whom the Governor had appointed to replace Manuel Armijo when he dismissed Armijo from his post as head of the customs. Caballero frowned in bewilderment. Although the Indian deserter had said there was none but volunteers among the Mexicans with Pérez, it was still difficult for him to believe that the Governor, a professional soldier, would entrust the important command of the reconnaissance company to a business man.

Sarracino's military ignorance was apparent. Instead of being scattered and alert, his men were riding together in a compact group, making a perfect target. Caballero could see them laughing and talking to one another as though they were out for sport. Less than a third of them carried firing pieces, he could see, and most of those pieces were escopetas, firelocks that were obsolescent two centuries before and dangerous only to those who fired them.

José Gonzales waited patiently until the advance party was well within range and then he gave the signal to open fire. Caballero saw half a dozen men in Sarracino's platoon fall at the first volley. The survivors, led by Sarracino, turned and galloped back wildly to the main force.

The insurrectos fired a second barrage, and Caballero saw a few of the Mexicans fire back aimlessly into the hills and Pérez trying to bring the midget cannon into position, and the Indians who had not abandoned Pérez the night before now running off to join the insurrectos in the hills. Then he saw that the army of Governor Pérez was now less than twenty men grouped around the polished brass fieldpiece.

He lowered his glass and wiped the sweat from his face. Fernando crawled next to him. "Do you see who is with Pérez, Don Esquipulas?"

"There is almost nobody with Pérez."

"There, the man talking to him now."

Caballero looked and then jerked the glass to his eye again. "Madre de Dios! It is Don Santiago Abreu!" He looked down at the man whose house had been as familiar to him as his own for almost ten years. "En el nombre de Dios, what is he doing here! He is no soldier."

"He is a soldier now," Fernando said. "And his brothers with him."

Caballero moved the glasses. He saw the plump, soft figure of Ramón Abreu and then Marcelino Abreu, dwarfed by the big horse he was on. "Sound retreat," Caballero whispered. "You are lost. God in heaven! Sound retreat." The glass slid around in his sweaty fingers.

He could see Santiago Abreu arguing with the Governor, and Pérez shaking his head. Then Abreu waved his arm and Pérez looked around, and then Caballero saw the Governor sag limply in his saddle and his lips moved and the bugled notes of retreat filled the mesa. Caballero breathed a prayer of thanks. The men below left the cannon and fled from the field.

The smell of powder disappeared, the air cleared, and there was silence. For a moment the land again was untouched save for the bodies lying on it, and then, screaming their victory, the insurrectos poured down from the hills. Gonzales, his face transfixed with his mission, ordered the men who had horses to follow him in pursuit of Governor Pérez.

After the riders were gone, the men on foot discovered fourteen of the enemy in a small clump of mesquite trees. These men, eight of them Mexicans, the others San Juan Indians, had become separated from the others when the battle began. The Indians among them joined the insurrectos, and the Mexicans were tied to trees and killed slowly with lances.

7

THE TRIUMPHANT INSURRECTOS swarmed into Santa Fe chanting deliriously. By now they were almost entirely pueblo Indians, most of the Mexican peasants having returned to the Rio Arriba, their appetite for battle sated. The citizens of Santa Fe barricaded their doors and climbed to the rooftops behind the ramparts built there and prepared to defend themselves against the expected pillage.

Esquipulas Caballero kept his men with him and began a search for Santiago Abreu to give him protection. He thanked the Holy Virgin that Soledad had left the city the week before with James Magoffin. He learned Pérez and the Abreus and other remnants of Pérez's forces had fled through the city to the south, accompanied by the jeers and curses of the natives. He led his men off on the road to Chihuahua in an effort to pick up the trail of Soledad's father.

In the plaza the Indians built fires and commenced the religious rites of victory, a ceremony they had not practiced for a very long time. José Gonzales, in the center of the celebrants, lifted his face to the sky and called upon his brother and teacher, Popé, to look down upon his success. But then Gonzales left the path of his preceptor, who in his victory led his people to the waters of the Bravo, the mother river, and there commanded them to wash themselves with soap made from amole to cleanse their bodies of the stain of Christianity. Now, in his triumph, José Gonzales left his people and made his way to the military chapel, La Castrense, across the plaza from the palace, and there in the empty building he knelt before the altar and gave his thanks to Jesus Christ.

When he crossed himself and rose, it was to find Padre Martínez standing there. "This is a great moment for you, my son, the greatest."

"Yes, padre."

"It must not be tarnished, not for you nor your people. There must be no war upon the innocent here, no pillage, no rape, no killings."

"There will be no disorder, padre, unless it is started by the Mexicans."

"They will start nothing."

"Nor will I against the peaceful. I am not a bandit, padre." Gonzales gripped the priest's arm. "I must find Governor Pérez."

"Why? The battle is ended."

"It is only the battle that is ended, padre."

The priest looked at him strangely. "What more do you want with him?" he asked.

Gonzales's fingers tightened. "I am the victor and I must treat in honor and dignity with the man I have defeated. Until Governor Pérez gives me formal surrender my insurrection has no meaning."

Martínez watched him stride out of the church and he wondered where this fell in Don Manuel's design of conspiracy.

8

GOVERNOR PÉREZ tasted bile as he whipped his flagging horse southward. Everyone had scattered. He was alone, with nothing to distract his memories of how people had spat upon him and had called him coward. When he thought it was safe he drew rein to give the animal rest. Almost immediately he heard the pounding of hoofbeats behind him. He spurred the horse. It would not move. He whipped it. The horse staggered on for a few paces and then stopped. Pérez dug his spurs into the animal's sides again, hearing the hoofbeats more loudly now. The horse strained forward, its great eyes bulging, buckled, fell on its forelegs, and toppled over.

Pérez almost fainted with the pain as the hard saddle pinned down his left leg. He cried: "Madre María, help me," and he attempted to pull his leg free, biting his lip with the pain. The whole weight of the horse was on the leg. He lifted his right foot and jabbed the rowel points into the horse. The animal heaved convulsively and Pérez was able to extricate his leg. He attempted to stand. His ankle would not support him and he fell over. He got on his knees. He knew there was a ranch, El Alamo, not far away and the ranchero was a man who had once shown him friendship. He might be able to hide if he could reach there.

He pulled himself along on his hands and knees, tearing himself on the stones and the cactus, and then he fell again and now the sounds of the horses were very close. He attempted to draw his sword and fell unconscious.

Not far from where he lay Gonzales passed.

When Pérez opened his eyes again, the sun was high. It was quiet. He rested peacefully for a little while, tasting the silence. He was aware of the throbbing in his ankle. He realized he had slept through the night and that his pursuers had somehow missed him, and he crossed himself and whispered a prayer of thankfulness to the Blessed Virgin. He raised his head. It was past noon. His throat was parched. He had not eaten for more than twenty-four hours but felt no hunger. He had to return to the capital. Somewhere in the capital there must be someone who would hide him. It was necessary to find someone who had belief in him. He might even be able to present his sword to the leader of the insurrectos and surrender honorably.

He began to crawl back to Santa Fe. Presently he knew he must get up. It was not the estate of man to crawl. He stood erect. His ankle felt as though it were aflame. He straightened his torn clothing and adjusted his hat. He drew his saber and gained strength from that familiar act. He rested his weight for a moment on the saber. Then, using it for support, he started back for the capital. If it were necessary for him to die, the place was the Palace of the Governors.

Word of the success of the Gonzales revolution spread to the pueblos, and by the evening of the 9th day of August, the day after Pérez was routed on the mesa, more than two thousand Indians had come to Santa Fe. They overflowed the plaza. They spread to the hills around the city and there their families made camp and built cook fires. There was no opposition to the Indians from any source. Only a few government employees remained in the city, and they cowered in houses. The palace was empty.

The Indians continued to drift into the capital. The chanting and dancing went on in the plaza without end, but there was no attempt to resume the fighting. The civilians were not molested. There were Indians who took no part in the victory celebration. These men prowled through the streets with cold purposefulness, ignoring New Mexicans, who fled from them like rabbits. The Indians searched houses. They were almost polite. Their eyes were quick and keen but without animosity. They went through the rooms, opening cabinets and chests, carrying torches into darkened corners. They left the houses as silently as they entered.

It became understood after a while that the Indians planned no outrage against civilians and were looking only for certain high government officials. Now the natives opened their doors and besought passing Indians to come inside and look around and verify that they were not giving sanctuary to anyone who was wanted.

Ramón Abreu and Jesús María Alaria, secretary to Governor Pérez, were captured hiding together in a ranch house a short distance from the outskirts of Santa Fe. They were dragged from the house and stripped and their naked bodies were bound to posts. The Indians began the dance for the ceremony of death by lancing. They wove around the men for some time, working up their emotions, and then the man who had discovered the fat prefect and the secretary made the initial lance thrust into the right foot of Don Ramón. The prefect screamed and begged for mercy. The unmanly sounds increased the passion of the Indians.

Alaria behaved better; he kept his gaze fixed upward and prayed.

The art of muerte á lanzadas consisted in inflicting the maximum number of lance wounds before the victim died. It was, in its way, as much a test of the skill of the Indians as of the resistance of the victim. The thrusts started at the extremities and worked closer to the vital places. The excitement was in the need for each Indian to hold himself in restraint and not deliver the mortal thrust too early.

Soon after the Indians began their torture a small crowd of New Mexicans collected around them, at first in a wide perimeter. After a while the victims ceased to be men of their race. The affinity for death that was contained in every drop of their Spanish blood made the New Mexican spectators part of the ceremony and they felt as much contempt for Ramón Abreu's screaming as did the Indians.

The death blows were given more than an hour later and by that time Ramón Abreu and Alaria each had more than one hundred lance wounds. Abreu died badly. He never quit his pleas for mercy and toward the end he added prayer, only his praying was hysterical and lacked dignity. Alaria died very well. His head fell over early and it was possible that he was dead before the last thrust was made into his heart.

When the two men were dead and hung limply from their bonds in what in the night seemed to be a weird distortion of the Crucifixion, the New Mexicans who had looked on felt hollow and purged as though they had undergone a religious experience. It was better in some ways than even the flagellations of the Penitentes. Long after the Indians departed, the New Mexicans remained there and stared at the bodies.

9

IT WAS EARLY AFTERNOON when Albino Pérez reached Santa Fe. He was almost dead of thirst. His ankle was swollen badly and the pain was throughout his body. He could hear the sounds of the celebrants in the plaza. He squared his shoulders and lifted his head and held his body correctly, as an officer and hidalgo. He held the saber firmly, no longer as a crutch, but extended.

He rapped on the first door he came to. The door was opened by a New Mexican, who thought it was the Indians again. His face was set in a smile and there were words of welcome ready on his lips. When he saw it was Pérez, he spat upon him and called him a diseased dog and slammed the door. At the next door Pérez was called a despot and a coward and the door was slammed in his face. The third door was opened by a woman. She said: "Pobrecito."

"Water," Governor Pérez said. "Water, señora, for favor."

The woman's eyes filled with tears. A man appeared behind her and looked over her shoulder. "Go to the devil, bag of evil!" he screamed. "Go! Go! You will bring death to all of us!" He pulled the woman inside and shut the door.

No one answered his knocking at the next two houses. At the house after that a girl opened the door, and when she saw him she turned white.

"*Agua, señorita, por amor de Cristo,*" the Governor said.

The girl looked up and down the street in fright and then extended her hand to the Governor, her fingers spread wide, and she whispered: "A little moment, excelencia." She disappeared into the house and returned with an olla, which she handed to him, her eyes fluttering like startled birds. He tilted the jug to his mouth and drank deeply. He handed back the olla.

"Now go, Don Albino," the girl said.

The Governor bowed in a curiously archaic manner. "Many mercies, señorita. *Válgate Dios.*"

"It is you who need the help of God," the girl said.

She closed the door. It was done gently. The Governor smiled and bowed again and said: "God bless you, bonita," and his face became serene. He walked down the street and turned toward the palace and he was surrounded by Indians. He lifted his saber. Before he could use it a dozen lances were thrust into him. His hat was torn off and an Indian seized his hair and jerked back his head. The last thing he smelled was the grease on the Indian who cut his head from his body.

The head rolled into the street. An Indian impaled it on his lance and held it aloft. The other Indians stripped and mutilated the body. They trotted to the plaza, following the Indian who bore the head on his spear. He pushed his way to the center of the crowded square and held the head high. He shouted: "The tyrant is dead!"

He swung the lance with a powerful motion and the head flew through the air. It was caught by an Indian who tossed it to a friend. It was thrown again. This was not unlike the game the Indians played in the pueblos, a game in which a leather ball filled with grass was tossed and kicked from one man to another.

They were playing this game of football with the head of Pérez when José Gonzales returned late that night.

10

SANTIAGO ABREU was found by Santo Domingo Indians near Los Cerrillos, just south of Sante Fe. He was fettered and taken to the pueblo, which was not far away. He knew that his luck had run out all the way because the Santo Domingo Indians had regarded him as their particular enemy from the time he had handed down decisions adversely affecting their sheep-grazing rights.

The father of Soledad was stripped and locked into a stock in the plaza in front of the pueblo, and the Santo Domingo men danced around him and accused him of crimes against their people. One of the Indians suddenly drew his knife and severed Abreu's right hand at the wrist. He threw the hand into the judge's face. "That hand will sign no more papers against us!"

Don Santiago knew there was no hope. It was necessary only to die as well as he could. He compressed his lips in his tired, scholar's face and began to pray silently.

An Indian cut off his left hand and waved it in his face. An old Indian knelt before him and asked: "How many innocent people from our pueblo have you put into prisons?" He cut off Abreu's right foot and threw it in his face. One by one the Indians stepped up to the judge and charged him with crimes, going back as far as the time when he was Governor of New Mexico, and each accuser hacked off a part of an arm or leg.

73

"Nuestra Señora, help me," Abreu prayed. "Give me strength and keep me from crying out. Jesucristo, forgive me my sins."

An Indian pried open his mouth and cut out his tongue. Others gouged out his eyes and cut his ears from his head. The Indians were still listing his crimes against them when one man plunged a knife into his heart and Santiago Abreu found relief.

THE TIME OF THE GRINGO   PART III

1

As the carriage rolled swiftly toward Santa Fe, Manuel Armijo said: "You are silent, Don Esquipulas."

"Forgive me, señor."

"What is the matter? Do you not share my happiness?"

"I am happy for you, Don Manuel."

"For me? For me alone? But this is a success for both of us. It could not have been done without you." He placed his hand on Caballero's knee. "Was it the killings?"

Caballero nodded. "Yes, Don Manuel."

Armijo pulled away his hand angrily. "Did you believe we could unseat the dog Pérez without a few deaths? You are an officer. Have you ever seen a battlefield without bodies?"

"It was not the deaths in battle," Caballero said.

"Yesterday I was proud of you," Armijo said sternly. "When your father ordered you to come to me and report on all that had taken place, you spared neither yourself nor the horses and when you arrived you were exhausted, but your speech was clear and your information was factual. And now look at you! Concerning yourself with a few deaths, and you an officer in the presidial troop!"

"None of it bothers me, Don Manuel, except that which happened to Don Santiago Abreu."

"Abreu!" Armijo said harshly.

"I have eaten food at his house and have drunk his wine."

"And have read fairy tales to his daughter, Soledad."

"I have not mentioned her name, señor."

"But I have. And may I not?" Armijo drew in his lips. "What are you, man or child, señor? Do you think evil removes easily, as one washes dirt from one's hands? Do you not believe ridding New Mexico of tyranny is worth a few deaths?"

"I am sorry, Don Manuel, but I cannot regard Don Santiago as evil."

75

"Because he had charm? Because he was of your own caste? He was no better than Pérez. He gave Pérez advice for years, and when Pérez went out to fight he and the other Abreus were standing at Pérez's side." Don Manuel's voice altered and he again patted Caballero on the knee. "But I know how you must feel, dear Don Esquipulas. You did as much as you could. You looked for him for days. It was not intended that you find him alive."

Don Manuel took his cigar case from his pocket and offered it to Caballero. The young man shook his head and stared at the passing countryside. Don Manuel shrugged and selected a cigar for himself.

He spoke to Don Esquipulas no more. He dismissed him from his mind and remembered instead with satisfaction how the news of the revolt had brought panic to the aristocrats in the Rio Abajo. They had gathered in the Armijo hacienda, which they normally, on one pretext or another, declined to do, and had listened to Esquipulas Caballero, and at first they had found in their numbers an imitation of strength. They ignored Don Manuel and spoke to Caballero and began to make bold noises, sounding like the ancestors whose name they bore. They formulated one brave plan after another, and when Don Manuel finally asked if he might speak they made no attempt to conceal their disdain.

"It is good to know that this courage exists in you, señores," Armijo said. "An idea has occurred to me. Under the new Constitution the prefects of the north and the south are next in authority only to the Governor of New Mexico. Pérez is dead. Don Ramón Abreu, the prefect of the north, is dead. That leaves only Don Antonio Sandoval, the prefect of the south." He smiled sweetly at the white-haired, pompous Sandoval. "You are the highest government officer alive in all of New Mexico, Don Antonio. In effect, you are the Governor. Why do you not then journey to Santa Fe and assert your authority to this Indian leader José Gonzales and order the insurrectos to leave the capital?"

There was silence as he finished and sat back. He looked at Sandoval. It was amusing that it should be Sandoval. Until that moment the chief interest in the life of Don Antonio Sandoval had been the Castilian roses that he grew on his estate. He watched a slow flush of pride creep up on the flabby, jowled face of the prefect and he watched him stick out his chin, the weakness of

76

which was almost concealed by a carefully tended imperial. Then he saw the smirk suddenly freeze on Sandoval's lips. Sandoval's cheeks twitched and his body trembled and he looked at his friends in terror.

"What do you say, Don Antonio?" Armijo asked. "You have the legal authority and you have bold and fearless supporters. Form an army of order and place yourself at its head and wrest the capital from the insurrectos."

Sandoval at last found speech. "They will kill me! They killed Pérez and Ramón Abreu and now they will kill me!"

Armijo shrugged. "Men have died before, fighting for what they believed. You have an old and hallowed name, Don Antonio." He stood up and now his words flicked around the room as though he were delicately cracking a whip. "Caballeros of the Rio Abajo! You have muskets and you have fine Toledo blades that you have inherited from your ancestors, and on your walls are hanging saddles, waiting only to be thrown over your horses. You are all blue-bloods and descendants of conquistadores, and you have just proclaimed your courage was no less than theirs. Perhaps you will find you do not even need swords and muskets. Perhaps your names, your names alone, will make the insurrectos fly when you approach. Form yourselves behind Prefecto Sandoval and put down the revolt."

He moved slowly through the room and peered into their faces. Each man lowered his eyes at his approach. Never before, he knew, was he so hated as at that moment when he removed the thin skin of their courage and revealed the emptiness that lay beneath. He said nothing for a few minutes, letting them look well upon themselves, and then he said: "Rest yourselves easily, caballeros." He weighted the last word just enough to make men writhe. "I will go to Santa Fe."

2

LONG BEFORE THEY REACHED SANTA FE they could see the smoke from the Indian cook fires, so dense in the clear atmosphere that it appeared almost that the city had been put to flame and still smoldered; but when the carriage entered the streets, Don Manuel thought things looked almost normal. There were more pueblo Indians to be seen, of course, and the men, removed from their ordinary busy existence, already were showing the debilitating effects of their prolonged contact with the Mexican civilization. Drunk and sober, the Indians wandered aimlessly in the narrow streets, unlearned in the art of wasting time with grace. But apart from the excess of Indians very little seemed changed.

Don Manuel, who had leaned forward in his seat from the moment the carriage had come into the city, fell back. He felt sweat on his back. He had been tenser than he had realized and now he sighed in relief. The first thing he would do when he assumed power, he resolved, would be to order the stinking savages back to their pueblos.

The plaza still showed the signs of the lengthy celebrations. Before the Indians returned to their villages, Don Manuel vowed grimly, they would clean up the mess they had made.

He ordered the carriage to draw up in front of the house of Don Juan Bautista Vigil, one of the fine establishments facing the plaza, and he thanked Caballero warmly. He went directly to the postmaster's office. Vigil was crouched behind his desk and with him was Juan Estevan Pino. Vigil looked at Armijo sourly. "So you are here at last."

"Of course I am here. What is the matter with you?"

The postmaster was an emaciated man in his fifties, with a large nose and a prolonged, upturned chin. His speech was rapid, jerky, and nasal and when he became excited his chin and nose became a pair of choppers, snapping at the words that passed between them. He wore steel-rimmed glasses, behind which his eyes gleamed with ferocious intelligence. He had been in government since the Revolution, and with the instinct of a chameleon he had managed to weather all changes.

Now Vigil lifted himself from his chair and waved his hands in mock greeting. "Welcome, Don Manuel, welcome to the Indian capital of the world. Does that greeting please you better?"

"You speak in riddles, amigo. I have hastened here without pause from Albuquerque for the final step in our planning." Armijo sat down slowly. "I am tired. Speak plainly."

Vigil was seized with a fit of uncontrollable laughter. "Our planning?" he croaked. "He, he, he, he, he!" His eyes ran with tears. "And did you plan for the mestizo José Gonzales to be Governor of New Mexico?"

Armijo leaped from his chair. He grasped Vigil by the shoulders and shook him violently. "Body of God! What are you saying?"

Vigil tore himself free and pounded the desk with both fists. "Keep your hands from me!" he screamed. "New Mexico has a new Governor and his name is José Gonzales, buffalo-hunter from the Taos pueblo. Do you understand now?"

Pino, a short, fat, wealthy merchant with a broad, good-natured face, spoke for the first time. "Señores, calm yourselves. You waste time and strength. We gain nothing fighting among ourselves. Sit down, sit down and let us discuss this quietly."

Armijo sat down again. He said through his teeth: "Tell me what happened, and quickly."

"I will tell you," Vigil shouted, still bent over his desk. "I will be happy to tell you, Don Manuel Armijo, planner, intriguer, plotter. We had a revolution in the north and the government was overthrown, and while you were sunning yourself in Albuquerque there was an election and an Indian was chosen for Governor. And now at last you have found the time to leave the soft bellies of your abajeñitas and return here, and what will you do about it?"

Don Manuel looked at Pino. The merchant nodded. "It is as he says, Don Manuel, neither more nor less. Last week, on the 10th day of August, just after Don Esquipulas was sent down to you, Gonzales called together what he called the General Assembly. He summoned many alcaldes from the north but his assembly consisted mainly of Indians. They met in the Chamber of Deputies and legalized the insurrection and elected Gonzales Governor of New Mexico."

"Temporarily," Don Manuel said in a still voice. "Until my return."

"I am afraid that it is not intended as temporary," Pino said. "Gonzales sits in the palace, Jefe Militar y Político, and he issues decrees and has an army to back them up."

"Decrees?"

"Yes, yes, decrees!" Vigil cried out. "Have you left your hearing in Albuquerque? He has ordered the confiscation of all prop-

79

erty belonging to Pérez and all the Abreus. He has taken the property of half the business men in Santa Fe. What he confiscates he gives away with the generosity of a drunken emperor, some to his filthy Indians and some he has sent north to be distributed to the proletariat of the Rio Arriba, so that now he is worshipped and men would like to kiss his feet and preserve his sweat. And we sit here waiting, waiting for the knock on the door and the gang of Indians come to take what belongs to us." He fell back into his seat and buried his head in his hands and sobbed.

"How can these Indians form a government?" Armijo asked. "They can neither read nor write."

"They can kill," Pino said. "And so long as they can kill they find Mexicans who will read or write for them. Already half of the Pérez government is returned to work for Gonzales and they recognize his authority without question."

Armijo stood up. "I will visit Gonzales."

Vigil raised his head. "Go, go, yes, go!" He wiped his eyes. "Only perhaps you will have some difficulty. Have you an appointment with Governor Gonzales?"

"Yes."

3

WHEN HE RE-ENTERED THE PLAZA the city no longer appeared almost normal. The Indians, drifting about without purpose, now seemed to have a sinister air. On the thick, deep dust in the plaza he saw a punctured drum, a split lance, broken arrows, and he paused and looked at the palace and for the first time thought of José Gonzales in fear.

Many years before he had coined an expression: "It is better to be thought a brave man than actually to be one." This motto had been quoted often to label him coward. If a disinclination to die uselessly, for whatever purpose, were cowardice, then he was that kind of coward, he admitted. Blind courage he left for other men. His ambition was too great for him to be able to do other than avoid an unnecessary end to his existence.

But there were times when it was required that a risk be taken. And he could not believe truly that Gonzales was a threat. Gonzales was an ignorant, superstitious savage. It was only that in the reaction to the outrages committed against Pérez and the Abreus and the others no one would take a stand against him. Manuel Armijo would take that stand.

He quickened his steps and entered the palace. Squatting under the portal, on either side of the door, were two Taos Indians, muskets across their knees. His muskets. He was not displeased to see that the guns were dirty and showed no care and that one, even in the dry climate, was beginning to rust. The Indians did not look up as he passed.

In the entrance to the office used by the secretary of the Governor, through which it was necessary to pass to reach the Governor's office, several Indians were seated around the desk last used by Jesús María Alaria, playing a game of cards with a battered deck. They glanced at Armijo and returned to their game.

"I am Don Manuel Armijo. It is my wish to see Don José Gonzales." He found himself unable to say Governor Gonzales.

The Indians, deep in their game, paid no attention to him. He waited for a couple of moments and then repeated his name and his request. When he continued to be ignored he made a move toward the door of the Governor's office. One of the Indians, without raising his eyes, pushed a lance across the door. "Sit down," the Indian said.

Don Manuel sat down on a bench, digging his nails into his hands. It was at least five minutes before one of the players yawned, rose, and entered the Governor's office. When the Indian stepped out he said indifferently: "Wait here. The Governor will see you."

Another five minutes passed before he heard the deep voice of José Gonzales ordering him to enter. Don Manuel was struck immediately by the smell as he walked into the familiar room. The pig Gonzales, he thought, has made the chamber of the Governor of New Mexico stink like his pueblo! He gazed across the room. Gonzales was alone, sprawled in the Governor's chair, one naked leg draped over an arm. He was naked from the waist up. His long black hair was tied in a knot with red flannel. His broad chest was streaked with dirt. His face was as Don Manuel had remembered it last, except that there was something new in the

81

eyes. Armijo walked slowly toward him. *"Hola, compañero,"* he said.

"Excelencia," Gonzales said. "The Governor of New Mexico is called 'excelencia.'"

"It is true. Congratulations, excelencia."

"I have been waiting for you."

"Have you? Ea, here I am."

A faint smile appeared on the Indian's cold face, but it did not remove the look from his eyes. "Here you are, Don Manuel. When the fighting is over. When the danger is passed." He lifted his leg from the arm of the chair. "Sit down."

"I was somewhat surprised, Don José, when I arrived here today and my friends told me of the developments."

"Were you?"

"I await an explanation."

"Would you like some wine, Don Manuel?"

"Thank you, no."

"Some brandy then? Pérez had a taste for it."

"So you have proclaimed yourself Governor, Don José."

The muscles swelled in the Indian's cheeks. "I have not proclaimed myself Governor. I was elected Governor."

"Have you gone mad, Gonzales?" Armijo asked quietly.

The Indian jumped to his feet. He picked up a lance lying on the floor and hurled it against the wall. The lance quivered there and the plaster splattered onto the floor. "Don José!" the Indian shouted. "Don José or excelencia. You address the Governor of New Mexico."

"Pardon, excelencia." After the first shock the outburst pleased Armijo. "May I ask Don José how long he plans to *remain* Governor of New Mexico?"

"I will make a full report to the authorities in the City of Mexico," Gonzales said harshly. "I will tell them everything that has taken place. I will include all the grievances, the years of suppression and persecution, the corruption of the government and the courts here, the impossible taxation, the starvation among the people while the ricos live in luxury. I will send all of this, in detail, direct to the President of Mexico and I will await his reply. Until then I remain Governor."

Now Armijo too stood up. "All, Don José?" he asked courteously. "And will you include how Governor Pérez was beheaded by your Indians and his skull used as a football? Will you tell General Santa Anna how the Abreu brothers and the others were tortured and slain by your Indians? And you think that will win you support from the City of Mexico?"

The expression in Gonzales eyes now spread to the rest of his face, and Don Manuel understood it at last. "I did not want them killed," Gonzales said. He clenched his fists. "I would have saved them. This was no revolt of savages."

"Do you believe you can make that clear to the President of Mexico?"

"You will help me."

"I? I, Don José?"

Gonzales strode up to him. "My people are untutored in Mexican ways, Don Manuel. It is not their fault. They are wise in their own things and know many things unknown to you. But they have no knowledge of writing. I know what is in their hearts. I know the secret torments and the shame that broke loose and made them do what they did. I will tell you of these things and you will put them down on paper. You know of our years of humiliation. You told me of them yourself when you came to the pueblo. That is what caused me to lead my people forth. You will help me."

Armijo turned his back with studied deliberateness and walked to the table with the bottles. He made a show of inspecting them and then selected a sherry. He filled a small glass. "Why will I help you, Don José?"

The Indian's eyes blazed. He rushed to Armijo and knocked the glass from his hand. "Because you made the revolution!" He brought himself under control with a powerful effort. "You yourself have just named the names of those who were executed," he said quietly, and the haunted look reappeared in his eyes. "They are dead through your doing. The words that inflamed the people were your words. The muskets that won the insurrection were your muskets. You will help me!"

"So, it is blackmail?"

Gonzales shook his head. "I do not want to fight with you, Don Manuel," he said tiredly. "We use the wrong words to each other." He clasped his hands. "I am the first man of my race to be

83

Governor of New Mexico. For the first time my people have for governor one who thinks of them. And not only of them. I have not forgotten the Mexican peasants. You told me we were all the same, that in your heart you were not one of the ricos. I wish to do only what you told me should be done. The taxes must go. The Indians must live as equals with the New Mexicans. I will be fair to all, Indian and New Mexican alike. The people will not complain of me." There was fever in his eyes now. "Mexico is no longer part of Spain, Don Manuel. You said that yourself. It is a government for the people who live here. I want only to give those people a voice."

Don Manuel walked to a window and gazed for a time on the plaza. He turned back to Gonzales. "If I should deny all connection with the insurrection, do you believe the authorities in the City of Mexico will take your word against mine?"

Gonzales stared at him for a long time. "Then what I have said means nothing to you, and what you said to me in Taos meant nothing to you." He walked back to his chair and sat down. His face became fixed and his voice cold and impersonal. "So be it. It is necessary only to remind you that it would not be my word alone. There are the Montoya brothers, who were your agents, and the alcalde, Esquibel, and Padre Martínez and others. More than anything else there are the muskets. Each musket has a mouth, and each mouth says Manuel Armijo."

Armijo rushed to the desk. "I will go beyond you, to your people. They will choose a man of experience in preference to one such as you."

Gonzales smiled faintly. "I do not believe they will. Before the Spaniards came we were a nation of warriors. My people still prefer courage to cowardice." He draped his leg negligently over the chair arm again and his eyes became mystic. Don Manuel understood he was dismissed. As he left the room Gonzales called after him, as though from a great distance: "You will remain in Santa Fe, Don Manuel. I will summon you when I need you."

4

THERE WAS A CERTAIN HUMOR in this, Don Manuel thought: the Chamber of Deputies, to which Pérez had tried to give so much style, now filled with Indians from the pueblos. The odd thing was that the Indians did not seem at all ill at ease. Some in ceremonial dress, some naked except for breechclouts, they entered the hall, shouldering their way past New Mexicans, and they took all the seats and, when the seats were occupied, squatted on the floor. They smoked pipes and cigarettes and talked to one another in low tones as though they had spent half their lives in the legislative hall of New Mexico. There were many New Mexicans present, alcaldes from a score of towns and villages, members of Pérez's defunct Junta, government employes, business men, and priests, but these men might have been visitors, gathering in one part of the room in a group.

Don Manuel had been ordered by Gonzales to take a chair in the front of the chamber, directly under the dais on which the Indian Governor himself sat. Don Manuel was aware of the cleverness of that move by Gonzales and of the effect his appearance would have on the New Mexicans in the hall. He was calm. He sat placidly, his hands folded in his lap, and watched the thick smoke blanketing the upper part of the hall, remembering how Pérez had forbidden smoking during the sessions of his Junta. Don Manuel's first rage was gone. "Anger without purpose is a waste," he had said to Vigil when he returned to the postmaster's house after his initial meeting with Gonzales in the palace. He had quieted Vigil's alarm. "We are both old hands at this, Don Juan Bautista. Gonzales will make mistakes." When Gonzales had ordered Armijo to attend a meeting of his assembly on August 27 and Vigil had asked him if he would obey, Armijo had said: "Of course I will obey. I cannot destroy this mestizo if I am dead."

For the time being, Gonzales seemed to be doing very well. If he had no training in politics, which Don Manuel considered a complex profession, his instincts were sure and so far they had guided him. The Indian, wearing a heavy buffalo robe despite the heat, sat in the Governor's chair with majesty, his powerful presence reaching out, touching everyone in the hall. Any remaining doubts Don Manuel had had about public acceptance of Gonzales as a true governor had long since vanished.

Padre Martínez slipped into the chair next to Armijo. It was the first time Don Manuel had seen the priest since he left him in Taos. He thought Martínez's face was more lined than ever and he saw in his eyes the same look he had noticed in the eyes of the Indian. Who had learned it from whom, he wondered, and, knowing the priest, he guessed Gonzales had been a good pupil. "This is something, is it not, padre?" Don Manuel asked. "Not what we planned, but something." He looked ironically at the priest.

Martínez showed no discomfort. "*Sea como Dios quiera,*" he said.

"It may have been the will of God," Armijo said dryly, "but He was given some small assistance by one of His vicars on earth."

"You should rejoice with us all, Don Manuel." The priest's hands writhed. "You brought on the dream. The dream now is being made into reality."

"Do you believe that, padre?"

"Eternal truths come from the mouth of this Indian who last month was a simple hunter."

"Without ambition, padre. Do not forget that."

Martínez's lips moved in prayer and Don Manuel wondered if he possibly could be sincere. He could understand a man changing sides for personal gain, but to lose oneself to this mongrel with his insane delusions!

Gonzales pounded his desk with his war club and called for order. The chamber quieted instantly. Then, acting with celerity and assurance that made Don Manuel lift his brows, Gonzales entered into the business of the day. His first move was to have himself again validated as governor. The presence of almost all the alcaldes in New Mexico gave the action dimension. For the second item of business Gonzales ordered the confirmation by the deputies of his appropriation of the property of the assassinated officials and the business men. This was voted without demur.

Now Don Manuel sat more attentively. He knew Gonzales had made a major mistake. No one could protest on behalf of Pérez and few could make a plea for the Abreus, but the merchants of the capital were still very much alive. Now the Gonzales administration took official responsibility for the confiscation of their money and goods.

Don Manuel twisted his neck as Gonzales stood up. The Indian, monumental in his stiff robe, surveyed the chamber silently for several moments and then began to speak of the many years of suppression suffered by the Indians and the impoverished New Mexicans. He spoke slowly and well. "Words pass through the air as birds in flight and soon are lost," he said. "But these words will not be lost. I have ordered three famous New Mexicans to put down on paper what I have told you today. These men are Don Manuel Armijo, a former Governor; Don Antonio José Martínez, the priest of the people; and Don José Esquibel, the alcalde of La Cañada, who rightly has been called the judge of the people. Tonight these three men will prepare for me a document to be dispatched to the central government. The paper will be read to you tomorrow."

Gonzales adjourned the meeting and ordered the three men he had named to follow him to the Governor's office, and there he dictated his petition of grievance, having each sentence as it was put down reread to him by the priest. The words acted on the Indian as strong drink, and when the document was completed he was in a state of exaltation. Don Manuel, working without protest, wondered how long the brain that lay in the great skull could sustain the powers that had come so suddenly.

On the second day of the session the hall was even more crowded. It was hotter than the day before and the chamber was dark with smoke and smelled of grease and sweat and rancid oil. When Gonzales took his place, the talking dropped off. Don Manuel sensed how the Mexicans present, inclined by tradition and training to gravitate toward power, were sucked to the Indian as iron filings are pulled toward a magnet. Presently the Indian Governor of New Mexico crashed down his war club.

"The New Mexican uses many words," he said. "He has words to say things in different ways, so many words that he can always twist things around like the reins of a horse, to make the words go in whatever direction he wants them to go." He paused and was silent for a long time. Armijo, who regarded himself as a masterful orator, thought he would never have dared to hold the silence so long. "There was a war with Spain to make this country

87

free," Gonzales said at last, his Indian-hard Spanish giving his words a pounding force. "It says on paper in the City of Mexico that this country is free. It says on paper that the Indians and the New Mexicans, that rich people and poor people, are all the same. That is what it says. It says that everybody can make a living. But the words must have other meanings, because up here nothing was changed from the old days. That is the way it was. It is not that way now. There has been a change. Men have been killed and there is a change." Don Manuel felt a chill. He looked at the enrapt face of the priest and lowered his eyes.

"I spoke yesterday of a petition," Gonzales said. "It has been prepared. I have ordered the words carefully. Don Manuel Armijo will read the paper to you now."

Armijo did not show his surprise at this maneuver. He accepted the paper from Don Donanciano Vigil, a relative of the postmaster who had fought alongside Pérez and who now was serving as secretary to Governor Gonzales. He cleared his throat and read it clearly, aware that each word added to the glory of José Gonzales. When he finished, the deputies broke into cheers. Then Gonzales produced a final surprise.

"Present the paper to me, Don Donanciano," he said.

His secretary gave him the document and before the assembled people Gonzales signed his name to it, finishing with the ornate rubric so beloved by New Mexicans. It was, Don Manuel admitted, a superb conclusion. Not half the ricos in New Mexico could have done the same.

"There is one thing more," Gonzales said. "While we await a reply to our just demands, it must be known without question that we have a true and legal government in New Mexico."

The secretary read from another sheet of paper: "We again affirm the fact that José Gonzales is legally elected Governor of New Mexico and we each of us, in the name of the Holy Trinity, the Father, the Son, and the Holy Ghost, swear personal fealty to Governor José Gonzales, and swear to retain this fealty until a resolution of our demands is made by the supreme government in the City of Mexico."

For the third time Gonzales had himself confirmed. His face without expression, Manuel Armijo rose with the others and joined in the oath of allegiance.

Don Manuel had to leave Santa Fe. The longer he remained, the more he associated himself with the Indian's administration. He explained to Gonzales that his personal business and his official duties as alcalde of Albuquerque required his return to the south. Gonzales, lost in visions, granted him leave.

Before he departed, Don Manuel conferred with Captain Caballero and ascertained that Gonzales was unaware of the weapons in the presidial armory. He arranged with the captain to move the arms and ammunition secretly to a warehouse Armijo owned in Bernalillo, a town just to the north of Albuquerque.

1

Don Manuel strode up and down the sala of his hacienda. "It is the priest! It is the damned priest!" He glared at Doña María Trinidad, his eyes bulging. "No ambition! Martínez chose him because he had no ambition! Santa Madre de Dios!" He held out his clenched hands as though they were manacled. "And I can make no move. I cannot stir unless I am positive there can be no failure. I have given my oath to the mongrel, and if I move against him, then *I* become the insurrectionist and that lump of insanity would think nothing of sending his Indians down here to put a bullet in my neck."

"You must wait, Manuel," she said calmly.

"Wait! Wait! I do nothing but wait. I go insane with waiting."

"The mestizo will destroy himself."

He stared down at her. "Do you believe that? Do you truly believe that?"

"Yes, Manuel, I believe."

"Swear it."

"I swear."

"Swear it, María," he said hoarsely. "Swear it on the Virgin that you believe that he will destroy himself and that you do not say it just for me."

"I swear it, Manuel, as I believe in Nuestra Señora, whose namesake I am. The mongrel will destroy himself."

It was what he had told the postmaster, Vigil, but that was because Vigil was more frightened than he. He fell on his knees and buried his head in her lap. "When, María, when?" he asked in the voice of a child.

"Patience," she said tranquilly. "It will come, husband. He will make mistakes."

Don Manuel writhed with the knowledge that he was ridiculous in the Rio Abajo. The news of his conspicuous failure to oust the Indian from the palace had preceded him home. The ricos he had so pointedly humiliated were now having their revenge. José Gonzales had become a popular governor among the purebloods if only because he had outplayed Manuel Armijo at his own game.

When he had returned to his estate, Don Manuel was numb. There were business affairs to be taken care of. He had decisions to make in his capacity as alcalde. He could not bring his mind to bear on any of these matters. During the day he talked endlessly to his wife and drew comfort from the compassion in her luminous eyes. At night he took out his furies and his frustrations on one or another of the peasant girls Doña María Trinidad supplied for his bed.

He vented everything upon them, conjuring up delirium, winning oblivion for a moment, and then always loathing them afterward, thinking of them as filthy mestizas. He needed more than physical victory in bed. For him dignity, pride, breeding had to be broken and crushed, and how could this be done with those who had none of those things?

He heard a quiet cough. He snapped his head. A servant stood in the room. Armijo leaped to his feet. "Get out of here! A thousand times I have told you never to come upon me by surprise!"

"A little moment, Don Manuel," Doña María Trinidad said softly, extending her hand. "What is it that you want, Luis?"

The servant, shaking, said: "Two gentlemen to see Don Manuel."

"I see nobody!" Armijo waved his arms.

"With permission, Don Manuel," his wife said in the same gentle voice. "Who are the gentlemen, Luis?"

"Don Mariano Chaves and Don Antonio Sandoval, señora."

"I am not at home!" Armijo shouted.

Her hand went to her throat. "I believe you should see them, Don Manuel."

"Not for a Christ!"

"Don Manuel, my heart tells me they bring news. Admit them, I beg you."

He bit his lip and cracked his knuckles. Then he said: "Admit them."

Chaves, an attractive man in his early thirties, son of the Chaves for whom Don Manuel once worked as shepherd, and of all the ricos in the Rio Abajo the only man friendly to Armijo, entered the room swiftly, followed by Sandoval, whose wattles were quivering with excitement. The men bowed courteously to Doña María Trinidad, and Armijo said, automatically: "My house is at the disposition of you both."

"Don Antonio has just received a communication from Santa Fe," Chaves said.

"Ea?"

"Yes, yes," Sandoval said. His hands opened and closed convulsively. "It is an order from Governor Gonzales to me in my capacity as prefect of the south. Governor Gonzales has decreed that anyone in New Mexico who does not recognize his authority completely, without question, in all things, shall be instantly slain and all his property confiscated."

"Madre mía," Doña María Trinidad whispered.

"The order is directed specifically against the ricos," Chaves said. "Already there have been protests in the north."

"And?" Armijo asked.

"Those who raised their voices were executed and their estates taken by the government."

Armijo turned his back to the two men. "Why have you come to me?"

"We are having a meeting," Sandoval said. "You know this mestizo, Gonzales. You have dealt with him."

"And we have things in common?" Don Manuel asked.

"Yes! No! Pardon, Don Manuel, my mind is in a scramble."

"Your friends and your neighbors of the Rio Abajo ask that you attend this meeting and give them counsel," Chaves said.

Sandoval wrung his hands. "What can we do?"

"Obey," Don Manuel said.

"Gonzales is insane," Sandoval said.

Armijo turned and faced them. "I can give you no assistance, señores. I have sworn a solemn oath of allegiance to Governor Gonzales."

"An oath taken under duress," Sandoval cried. "You must

have had reservations. Such an oath has no validity, legally or morally."

"The oath of a gentleman, Don Antonio?" Armijo asked with a thin smile. "Would you so regard an oath of your own?"

"Por el amor de Dios, Don Manuel, stop speaking of oaths, this is more important than oaths!"

"And exactly what do you intend to accomplish at this meeting? Do you plan to form an army and march north?"

Sandoval shrank back at the sound of the word "army." "We want to talk it over. We want your advice."

"Talk?" Armijo smiled with great sweetness. "Then I can send my advice to the honorable señores from here."

"What is your advice, Don Manuel?" Sandoval begged. "What is the message? Give us the word."

"The word is obey."

"Señor!"

"Obey," Armijo said, his voice rising. He felt confidence returning to him. "You have received an order from the Governor of New Mexico. You are his deputy in the south. You have no choice. Do not waste time in meetings. Obey!"

Sandoval looked at Chaves in bewilderment. "I do not understand, Don Manuel. Obey? Obey this infamous decree? Order the execution of my friends who violate it?"

Don Manuel lit a cigar. "Don Antonio, as I had the honor to remind you once before, under the Departmental Constitution, a prefect is virtually a lieutenant governor. You are a confused man, señor. You are the voice of Governor Gonzales in the Rio Abajo, charged by law with implementing his commands. Instead you seek methods to circumvent them." He looked steadily at Sandoval. "That is open treason, Don Antonio."

"Treason!" Sandoval shuddered. "Ah, Dios mío, do not mention that word! Not treason, Don Manuel."

There now crept upon the face of Mariano Chaves a glimmering of new understanding. He exchanged glances with Don Manuel, and a smile played on his lips. "Vamanos, Don Antonio," he said briskly. "Don Manuel has expressed himself."

"But obey!" The prefect held out his hands helplessly. "What does he mean, obey? How can hidalgos of the Rio Abajo obey such commands from a half-breed Indian?"

Chaves bowed. "Many thanks, Don Manuel. I will see to it that the caballeros are informed of your attitude." He bowed again to Doña María Trinidad, and he took the arm of the trembling Sandoval. "*Vamanos*, Don Antonio," he repeated gently.

"Not treason, dear Don Mariano," Sandoval muttered. "Santo Dios, not treason."

When they were gone, Doña María Trinidad rose to her feet and pressed her hands against her breast. "Manuelito, my soul, you were magnificent."

Armijo's eyes glittered. "Your heart spoke truly, wife. He makes mistakes."

"But perhaps you should have gone to them when they called to you."

He patted her hand gently. "They will call me again. And the next time will not be to talk."

2

A LOUD CLATTER of hoofbeats aroused Don Manuel from dalliance with the latest fruit from Doña María Trinidad's inexhaustible orchard. He pushed the girl aside roughly. He wrapped a burgundy-colored velvet robe around him, and when he reached the sala he found Don Esquipulas Caballero. His heart pounded as he embraced him. "You are my fortune, Don Esquipulas. You bring news?"

"Gonzales has gone insane," the young man said, breathing hard.

"In what way, chico, in what way insane?" Armijo gripped Caballero's arms. "Speak! Tell me!"

"He has declared New Mexico independent of Mexico."

"Santa Madre de Dios!"

"He went further. He sent a commission to the President of Texas asking him to send Texan troops to New Mexico to support the secession."

"*Texans!*"

"For days he remained alone, locked in his office. He would

94

see no one. Then without warning he issued the decree. Texas had won its freedom from Mexico and now so would New Mexico. Then he sent his couriers to the heretics in Austin."

"A thousand Jesuses! It is the beginning of the end."

Neither man had heard Doña María Trinidad enter the room. "The boy is wounded."

Don Manuel saw for the first time how pale Caballero had become. He caught him in his arms. He felt the wet on the side of his jacket. "Nombre de Dios! You bleed, amiguito."

"An arrow, señor. We were attacked by a party of Indians, Fernando and I, soon after we left Santa Fe. I do not know whether they were wild Indians or those sent by Gonzales. We split just below Bernalillo, and Fernando led them away."

Armijo picked him up. "Woman, order water, cloths! The boy's blood runs from his body."

Caballero shook his head sleepily. "There is more to tell you, Don Manuel, news from my father. He is in Bernalillo."

"Not now, *mi héroe*, not now," Armijo said with deep emotion. "It will wait."

"He has moved all the weapons and ammunition from the armory. Everything is in Bernalillo. He has notified all his old soldiers. At a word from you he can raise and equip an army of six hundred men."

"It is enough for now," Armijo commanded. "All else can wait. Now you must rest." He held Caballero tightly against him and felt his blood on his hand. "You are my fortune, my true caballero," he said. "Our lives are joined."

When he returned to the sala, Doña María Trinidad was still there. "It is but a wound in the flesh," he said. "He is young and healthy. He will be good as new." He clapped his hands and lifted his eyes to the vigas on the ceiling. "Cuerpo de Cristo, marida! What could this Gonzales have done that would have been better for me?"

Her fingers shook as she made a cigarette. "Do you believe the Texans will come, Manuel?"

"It is not impossible."

Tobacco spilled on the floor. "The priests say they are all heretics and that they burn churches and rape women."

"They are heretics and they have done those things."

95

"Manuel, you must stop them from coming!"

"And they will be tempted." He poured some brandy. "Now that Texas calls itself an independent republic, it would be happy to break off another limb from the tree. Only the Texans would not come here to help José Gonzales."

"What do you mean?"

"The Indian apparently has forgotten an important fact. In announcing its independence the Texan government also defined the boundaries of the country. They included all of New Mexico east of the Bravo. According to the Texans we are part of Texas now."

"I have heard that ridiculous story. Nobody takes the Texans seriously."

"No one, querida, except perhaps Texans. The government of Texas would like nothing better than to send an army up here, an army that does not have to fight its way, but one summoned in friendship. An army, in truth, of liberation. And once the soldiers were here, they would never get out. And from the start Texas would have the Americans supporting them all the way."

"But Mexico would declare war."

"Against Texas and the United States together? Yes, we probably would." He smiled sadly. "But it would be a useless war, lost to us before it started."

"We would have God and right on our side."

"Neither wins wars. No, Mariquita, it is not the time for Mexico. Our history lives only in books. We showed ourselves no match for the Texans alone. We certainly could not defeat the Americans. Against both of them together—" He shrugged. "A few battles for the sake of glory, many deaths, and then the war is over. The hidalgo on horseback belongs to another day. This is the time of the gringo."

"But you will stop it all, Manuel. With your people behind you, you will keep the unbelievers out of the land."

"I will stop it." He emptied the goblet. "And it is interesting to think that in order to accomplish my own plans I shall have to be a patriot. Por Dios, I am forced almost to believe in myself!"

3

Manuel Armijo rode to Tome on the 8th day of September to pronounce against the Indian Governor, José Gonzales. When he arrived in the little Rio Abajo village, ready to be hailed as liberator by his fellow citizens who had summoned him, he had in his pocket the formal pronunciamiento, prepared earlier in the day after conferences with the leading men of the district. The plaza in Tome was packed with people of all classes drawn together by a common and very real dread of the Texans, who, according to rumor, were already halfway on their march to Santa Fe.

The people, Don Manuel noted with satisfaction, were in a suitable state of dismay, ready to commit their souls and their possessions to anyone who indicated he had the strength to lead them. No one could feel a crowd better than he. It was almost as though he extended his hand and touched them. When he stepped down from his carriage, however, it was to discover that people in the plaza were chanting a name, but it was not his name. They were calling for Mariano Chaves. He began to climb angrily back into the carriage. Doña María Trinidad touched his arm. "Listen carefully, Manuel. There are voices shouting for Chaves, but the voices are few. The call does not come from the people."

He turned his head and listened. She was right. The name Chaves was being repeated but the voices, despite their insistence, were few, and then his lips curled with contempt as he detected in the cries the lisping Castilian accent that made the name into Chaveth. "The ricos are still hoping to head the counter-revolution with one of their own," he said with bitterness. "They think perhaps I will be content to serve as Don Mariano's assistant." The tactics had been wonderfully simple. They had got him to the meeting. There was a state of panic, and decisions would be made quickly and emotionally. If they could shout Chaves into command, there would be nothing left for Armijo to do but acknowledge him and then accept whatever job was given to him. He had been seen by many persons. He could not ride away like a sulky child if he was not named leader.

At that moment Mariano Chaves stepped forward on the roof

97

of the house of the alcalde of Tome and held out his hands for silence. Armijo, a fixed smile on his face for the benefit of all who happened to look at him, gripped the pronunciamiento in his pocket. In that document he had been named commander, with Chaves his second in command. The ricos had gone that far in their intrigue to betray him. He wondered whether Chaves was part of the treachery.

"Dear friends," Chaves was saying in his melodious voice, "the enthusiasm so manifest in this assemblage in behalf of the lives, houses, and property of our people impels us to act promptly and concertedly against the enemy that now threatens us." There were some cheers. Armijo felt Doña María Trinidad's hand touch his shoulder reassuringly. "The army we contemplate raising now and in the next few days should be sufficiently strong for every purpose the occasion demands," Chaves continued. "It ought to be under the command of some person abundantly able to lead it to certain victory, a victory that will carry with itself into the ranks of the insurgents such a degree of consternation and fear as will forever quiet this bloody uprising."

Again he paused and Armijo sensed the beginning of the drumbeats, and then, as though he too understood what might happen, Chaves went on swiftly, his voice becoming stronger: "I know of no one better qualified to lead our army than Manuel Armijo. Therefore I ask this assemblage to declare him to be our leader! With the help of our Lord Jesus Christ and the support of his people he will lead us to victory!"

He stopped abruptly. The plaza was silent and Manuel Armijo could hear each beat of his heart. Then the plaza broke into new cheers and now it was the name Armijo that was shouted, and as the name rose louder and louder, he could hear the deep, rich, solid voices of the peasants.

"Go, Manuel," Doña María Trinidad said. "Go, your people call to you."

4

ON THE FOLLOWING DAY, in Bernalillo, Captain Caballero issued muskets and ammunition to six hundred men and declared the presidial companies again officially in being. The captain ordered the soldiers drawn up in formation and, drawing his saber, he too pronounced against the mestizo Governor Gonzales.

His officers immediately pressed him, the ranking officer, to assume supreme military command of the country. Captain Caballero was almost overcome by this expression of affection and respect. "For the present I command nothing more than my troop," he said. "In turn I consider myself under the orders of Don Manuel Armijo. It is through his efforts, and his efforts alone, that you once again wear your old uniforms. Until our present task is completed and our beloved capital is liberated, you will acknowledge him and no other as your chief."

Reservations the officers may have had as to Manuel Armijo's qualifications to lead an army were largely dissipated three days later when Don Manuel arrived in Bernalillo at the head of a force of one thousand armed men, trailing behind which were half the families of the ricos of the Rio Abajo.

The army was made up almost wholly of sturdy peasants whose friendship Don Manuel had won as long before as the days when he counted the census in the southland. He had come then to understand that the hidalgos were no more than the frosting on the cake. It was a revolutionary concept. He had listened to the stories of the hardships of the peasants, squatting like one of them on the dirt floors of single-room adobe houses in which lived families of ten and twelve, and had let them speak of their always increasing debts to the dons.

He had always felt secure among the people. When he was formally proclaimed leader at the mass meeting in Tome, his first act was to order the ricos to surrender to him all their weapons, and when he had these weapons he gave them to the peasants.

For years the dons had built their haciendas as bastions of defense against marauding savages, and the peasants had done the fighting for them. The ricos now found themselves unarmed and helpless not only against the expected Texans, but against the Indians who were already there. They packed hastily and loaded wagons and carriages and mules, and when Don Manuel started north with his army, they followed him for safety as sheep follow a shepherd.

Informed of the approach of Armijo, Captain Caballero had his troops formed and ready in the plaza of Bernalillo. Don Manuel rode majestically into the square. Caballero cantered up to him, saluted, and said in his piercing cavalryman's voice: "Don Manuel, the presidial troops await your command."

Armijo returned the salute with intense solemnity and then, though he had never before commanded so much as a corporal's squad, he said: "I proclaim myself colonel of the army of liberation."

Far from being amused, the regular officers thought Don Manuel was showing exemplary modesty, for rarely in the disordered history of Mexico had a revolutionary leader given himself rank less than a general's.

With his authority as colonel Don Manuel appointed Mariano Chaves lieutenant colonel and his next in command, and, aware as ever that the powerful rhythm must not be broken, he cried out: "And now, patriots and lovers of liberty, the moment is at hand! On to Santa Fe and liberation! For God and Liberty!"

5

CAPTAIN CABALLERO rode up abreast of Don Manuel. "Before the day is out you will be in Santa Fe, mi coronel."

Armijo nodded. Ahead of him in the distance he could see the low buildings of the capital. It was the morning of the 14th of September, a clear, brisk day. All the way up from Bernalillo Armijo had tried to imagine what reception he would receive when he tried to enter the city. He knew his sixteen hundred men constituted a powerful force and that in a battle with Gonzales his chances were more than good. He knew exactly how many muskets had originally been issued to the insurrectionists and how many rounds of ammunition had gone with them. He knew the predilection of Indians for firing guns wastefully in celebration.

He knew too that the nature of Indians was in his favor. They could be whipped up to incredible acts of courage and recklessness and ferocity, but when action ended they lost interest. It was quite possible there would be no resistance. He was tempted to remain at the head of his troops and enter the city as true liberator.

But he could not know definitely that Gonzales would not put up a fight and that he would not have enough men to make a strong defense. The Indian had captured the imagination of his people as no one had since Popé. And all that was needed was for a single Indian with a single well-aimed musket ball or arrow to change Manuel Armijo from a conquering hero into a dead martyr, which was absurd.

He looked steadily at Captain Caballero riding serenely at his side. "My dear capitán, I have not had the opportunity to thank you for the brilliant things you have done. No one else in all of New Mexico could have raised the presidial troops from the shadows as did you."

"You praise me too much, Don Manuel."

"Not enough, not enough. And you should be most proud of your son. He was almost dead with the loss of blood, but he did not falter until he reached me in Albuquerque."

"He is a Caballero, mi coronel. And he loves you."

"For certain, and there is as yet no way I can sufficiently show my gratitude. But it lies within my power to bestow some privilege. I assign to the presidial troops the honor of being the first to liberate the capital."

Captain Caballero could reply only in a choked voice: "Mi coronel, we will not fail you!"

The captain gave the command to advance, and through his spyglass Don Manuel watched the troops approach the city, their muskets at the ready, led by officers with drawn sabers. He saw them disappear into the city without a shot being fired. He waited for the sounds of fighting and heard none. Wild with impatience, he gave the glass to Chaves and jumped from his horse. He paced up and down nervously, gnawing at his lips. He heard Chaves shout: "Don Manuel, a rider comes from the city!"

He tore the glass from Chaves's hand, beginning to feel a

sickness. He watched the rider approach. In a few moments one of the ensigns from the presidial troop galloped up. "Señor Coronel Armijo, the compliments of Capitán Caballero and the report that the Indian Gonzales has abandoned Santa Fe."

The sickness spread.

"He departed at the first dawn when he received word of the approach of your army. The city was left undefended. The presidial troops are in occupation and Capitán Caballero salutes you and says that he awaits your arrival in the plaza."

Armijo limped to his horse, his thigh aching, and he said in a low voice: "Teniente Coronel Chaves, give the order to advance."

As he neared the city, his head lowered on his collar, cursing himself for not having followed his hunch to lead the troops himself, he heard the first cheers in the distance and looked up eagerly. But he could see no one and he knew that the cheers, which were within the city itself, were not for him. His face was ugly as he led his peasant army into the capital. He knew how ridiculous it was for him to arrive in this manner, and ridicule was something he hated more than anything else. More of it seemed reserved for him than was his due. As he got closer to the plaza he could make out the cries: "Viva Capitán Caballero!"

He ordered Chaves to halt the soldiers and place them at rest, and, accompanied by Chaves and Don Antonio Sandoval, whom he had brought along as the ranking political survivor of the Pérez administration, he rode to the plaza. The presidial companies were lined up in formation and at their head, his saber still drawn, was Captain Caballero, a man Armijo hated at that moment more than any other person in the world.

With a strong effort, Don Manuel removed the anger from his face and arranged his features into a smile. On all sides of the plaza the citizens were gathered. They hushed their cheering as Don Manuel rode toward Captain Caballero. Caballero raised his sword in salute and said: "Here is your city, Don Manuel. Viva Coronel Armijo, chief of the liberating army!"

The people cheered again, but Armijo knew it was not the same thing. He raised his hand for silence. In his mind he had framed a dramatic speech for his first arrival in the plaza, but the words stuck in his throat. The sweet edge of his triumph was gone and for good, and he merely said: "Greetings, my good friends. The insurrecto bandit Gonzales is gone. Peace and order are restored. I appeal to you, good citizens, to return quietly to your houses and your affairs."

He dismounted and handed the reins to a soldier. With his shoulders held back and his eyes straight ahead he entered the Palace of the Governors.

Captain Caballero found Armijo at the Governor's desk when he entered the office an hour later. "You sent for me, Don Manuel?"

"Yes, Don José."

Caballero looked around the room, shocked. Papers, empty bottles, broken glassware, littered the floor. Chairs were overturned. The desk top was scarred with burns. "The place is filthy, Don Manuel," he said. "The whole palace is a disgrace. I will order soldiers to clean up everything thoroughly."

"Good," Armijo said listlessly. He sat up in his chair. "It is necessary, señor capitán, to make a report immediately to the authorities in the City of Mexico, informing them of everything that has occurred. Do you then assemble the officers of your companies and obtain from them a formal statement of their preference for commander-in-chief so that that preference may be included in my report to the central government."

"There is no question of preference, Don Manuel," Caballero said immediately. "You are the chief of the army."

"If that is the case, it still is necessary to have it stated in formal election. Quickly then, so that my report will not be delayed, summon your officers from their celebration and hold a meeting only long enough to certify this fact."

"It shall be done as you command, Don Manuel."

When Caballero reached the door, Armijo said quietly: "I believe, Don José, that it is your duty to inform the officers of the action taken by the people in Tome."

Armijo waited. If the officers elected Captain Caballero as their chief commander, Armijo might still claim the political command of New Mexico, but then he would collide with Antonio Sandoval, and Sandoval would have the support of the ricos. Sandoval had a far greater claim to the office of chief executive than he himself had, and it could still work out that he would be given the power at least until clarification came up from the City of Mexico.

And if Sandoval and Caballero jointly prepared the report that would have to be sent to the central authorities, as they would be entitled to do if they held the political and military offices, then he knew he was through. The army would be behind Caballero, and the ricos would be behind Sandoval with all their connections in the City of Mexico, and behind Manuel Armijo would be nobody. It still might be that he had failed.

It was late in the afternoon, and the Governor's office was in semidarkness when he heard the knock on the door. He remembered at just that moment how he had been informed the officers in Bernalillo had begged Caballero to take command.

Caballero marched up to the desk. "I have the paper, Don Manuel."

Armijo fought to keep his hand from shaking. He took the paper, walked to a window, and held it to the light. ". . . They said unanimously: that with all heartiness they acquiesced in what had been done in the furtherance of order, of the laws, and of the supreme government, pledging themselves to give full obedience in accord with the military ordinances, and that they recognize the Señores Coronel Don Manuel Armijo and Teniente Coronel Don Mariano Chaves in their positions."

6

IN THE EVENING the office was thronged with merchants and politicians and priests who came to offer their congratulations and ask for favors. A squad of soldiers had cleared up the room. The visitors brought wines and brandies. The air was thick with cigar and cigarette smoke and the fumes of the liquors and the familiar mirth of political success.

It had been, all agreed, a month of hell, with a lunatic Indian brooding alone in the palace and no man able to imagine what insane decree next would be issued. Not that Gonzales had permitted outrage; oddly, the Indians had behaved themselves well.

But it was the uncertainty, the quality of the unknown in the fanatical Indian. There was nothing about Gonzales a sane business man could understand.

Armijo listened to the reports and nodded judiciously. It was a scene in which he felt thoroughly at home, and his tensions left him and his mind again was working. It was the old reassuring political atmosphere, the polite approaches, the bows, the smiles, the fulsome flatteries, the title "excelencia," and, with furtive glances in all directions, the inclinations of the heads and the whisperings. Don Antonio Sandoval was politely ignored.

The most insistent claimants were the wealthy Sante Fe merchants whose goods Gonzales had confiscated. These men appealed to Don Manuel to petition the central government to make restitution, as the losses were the direct result of the failure of the lawful government of New Mexico, headed by Albino Pérez, to protect its citizens.

As he listened to these complaints, in which he recognized a legitimacy, Don Manuel felt something was lacking. Then it came to him. He gestured to Don Juan Bautista Vigil, who was a more cheerful man than when Armijo last had seen him. "Tell me, why are not the American merchants demanding that I seek compensation for their losses?"

"They have already done so, Don Manuel."

"Not to me."

"No, they have drawn up a memorial setting forth their claims and have sent it through their own channels to the American Minister in Mexico."

"Their own channels," Armijo repeated. His eyes got hard. "They did not wait very long to go over my head. These gringos think they are greater than the government." An idea occurred to him. "Come closer, amigo, but turn away your mouth. The brandy from your breath puts me to sleep." He continued quietly in Vigil's ear: "I believe that all New Mexicans who lost property to Gonzales stand a good chance of collecting. But I do not believe this American Minister will be able to collect for the gringos and I do not believe they think so either."

"You are right, Don Manuel," Vigil cackled. "I have heard the yanquis say that the New Mexicans will get all that is due them but that they will never see a dollar."

"Some of the Americans have notes signed by Pérez for credits they extended to him to run his government. Those notes can be made worth their face value, but only by me."

Vigil pinched his lips, and his eyes sparkled shrewdly. "I think I understand, Don Manuel."

"Buy up as many of these notes as you can at whatever discount you can squeeze out of the gringos. They will sell them for next to nothing. They are still shaken from this Gonzales. Even a small amount of hard money will look better to them than a piece of paper signed by a dead Mexican." He lit a cigar. "Leave my name out of it. Bring Pino into the deal. We shall share the cost three ways."

"And the profits, Don Manuel?"

"I shall take half the profits for my firm, and you and Pino will divide the other half." He added coldly: "Save your protests. I alone can change those pieces of paper into money."

It was after midnight before Don Manuel was left alone. He had refused all invitations to attend parties of celebration. He could not leave the office of the Governor in the Palace of the Governors. He had waited ten years to occupy that room. He needed to sit longer and see the four walls around him and know that so far it had worked out as he had planned it and that if his luck held he soon would be confirmed officially as Governor of New Mexico.

He sat alone for almost two hours, sipping brandy, his mind rich with plans. He was startled by the sudden appearance of the sergeant of the palace guard with the news that two men sought an audience. "At this hour? Who are they?"

"Two brothers, excelencia. They gave their names as Montoya."

"Search them for weapons, sargento, and admit them, and then hold yourself just outside the door in the event I need you." He removed his pistol from its holster, examined it carefully, and then placed it in his lap.

The brothers, unshaved, their clothing dirty and torn, entered the room. "What brings you here, traitors?" he asked harshly. "When last I saw you, you were high officers in the government of José Gonzales. Why are you not with your elected chief?"

Antonio Montoya, his face more pinched than ever, said humbly: "We come to confess our errors."

"Confess your errors?" Armijo echoed scornfully. "The rains have washed away your adobe and now you do but seek new shelter."

Antonio straightened with some dignity. "We did not fight for a man, Don Manuel, neither for you nor for Gonzales. We pledged ourselves to a cause. We believed in Gonzales. We were mistaken. We confess our errors."

"There are priests to listen to confessions."

"You are right, Don Manuel. But we do not come with confession alone. We bring information."

"What information?"

The giant Desiderio stepped forward eagerly. "We know—"

"Silence," Antonio said. "I have said we fought for a cause, Don Manuel. Is the cause still your cause?"

"Do you dare question me, son of a whore!" Armijo shouted. "A word from me and each of you has a bullet in his neck."

"We know we risked death when we came to see you," Antonio said unemotionally. "It is not a new danger for us. We have walked with death from the day we pledged our lives to help the people of our country. Give your command, señor. We are ready to face Him who created us."

Armijo shivered. The men were true fanáticos and as dangerous as poisonous snakes. And yet they could be put to use. "What is your information? Is it good enough to buy back your lives?"

"What lies now in your heart, Don Manuel?" Antonio asked.

"There are cells in the palace!" Armijo snarled, gripping his pistol. "There are ways to pull words from your mouths."

"Torture will not make us speak. Where does your heart lie, Don Manuel?"

Armijo fell back in his chair. "I have never changed in my feelings to our people."

"Swear it, Don Manuel."

"I swear it, en el nombre de Cristo."

Antonio stepped closer to the desk. "Gonzales is at Pojoaque."

"There is no news in that."

"His warriors are disorganized. He no longer has an army. His men are almost without ammunition. They are little better

107

than a helpless mob. They wander aimlessly in the hills, filled with confusion."

"And Gonzales himself?"

"Gonzales is insane. He stays alone and broods and talks to his gods. His mind runs over with visions. He raves about armies from Texas and the restoration of New Mexico to the Indians and a great confederation of Indian tribes, with himself as supreme chief. He would now make slaves of New Mexicans. No one may disagree with him. If a man raises his voice in dissent, Gonzales orders him shot. Even his own people are afraid of him and would assassinate him except that the Indians think that a crazy man is holy."

"The priest," Armijo said, "what of the priest? What of Martínez?"

"Padre Martínez no longer is at his side."

"Where is he? Where is Martínez?"

Antonio looked at his brother.

"Where is Martínez?" Armijo asked.

Antonio said in a low voice: "He is here, Don Manuel."

Armijo leaped to his feet. "Here? In Santa Fe?"

"Yes, Don Manuel."

"Bring him here."

"Now?"

"Bring him here. Your other information means nothing to me." He leaned hard on the desk. "Bring the priest to me."

7

AND NOW the day that had started for him at dawn so long before and was now reaching for a new dawn had led to this, to the priest and him alone in the room. He rocked on his heels, his hands gripped behind his back, and he looked down at the priest in the chair, the shining bald head sunk so low in the folds of his collar that it looked like a distant moon settling into black hills.

"The good priest," Armijo said. "Hola, padre. Again we confer by candlelight in the small morning hours. All that is needed is the wail of one of your brats and I might believe I was in Taos again."

"What do you intend to do with me, Don Manuel? Is it to be a bullet in the neck? It would be kind to tell me. I must make my peace."

"Why did you desert Gonzales?"

"Our paths separated."

"How did they separate? How could you abandon your man of eternal truths?"

Martínez raised his head. His face, Armijo thought, was the classic face of the Spanish priest, knobbed with bones, surrounding eyes that seemed to begin in the back of his head. It was a face that would have taken its place among other such faces at sessions of the Holy Inquisition. Did the Church make the face, he asked himself, or did such faces go automatically to the Church? There was no other place such a face could be. Now the sunken eyes were glowing and the voice came from the earth: "He became deranged."

"Do you mean by that that he would no longer take your advice?"

Martínez sank more deeply into his cassock. His face filled with agony. "I am the guilty one, not that poor innocent. I did it to him. I selected him. At that moment I pronounced his doom, God forgive me. I filled his ears with great dreams, and his head could not hold them. I shined a light before his eyes, and his eyes were blinded."

"You are not entirely guilty," Armijo said dryly. "I had some small part in it. I will share your burden, padre."

Martínez ignored the sarcasm. "You spoke intoxicating words, Don Manuel, but he believed them only because I told him to believe. Without me your words would have fallen upon barren ground. It is I and I alone who am guilty."

"Say rather that you were unbelievably foolish," Don Manuel said. "Come, padre, save this face of the artless priest for others. You and I have passed the point of mutual deception. You selected your fighting cock carefully but not wisely." He snorted. "Por amor de Cristo, padre, and how could you believe this simpleton could be the leader of his country?"

Martínez jumped up. "There was Another who was an Innocent," he rasped. "His leadership has lasted through the ages."

"And do you speak of this mongrel in the same breath with Nuestro Señor Jesucristo?"

"Gonzales heard voices," Martínez shouted hoarsely. "He told me of his voices. I believed in them. I remembered there was another who heard voices, a maiden in France."

"And now you name the dog an Indian Juana de Arco? And yet believing that he might be a new Messiah or at least a vessel chosen by God, you forsook him? Why, padre, why?"

Martínez sank again into the chair and huddled in his robe. His bony hands twisted. "The vessel was too fragile. The visions were too bright. The voices were too loud. He passed from ecstasy into delirium. Gonzales is now a raving lunatic."

Armijo shook his head to clear it. He refused to believe Martínez was so deluded. It was a trick, conceived by the priest to exculpate himself for his betrayal of Armijo. And he was so tired from the fullness of the day that for a little while he had almost been deceived into giving him credence. "And the moment of his lunacy became apparent doubtlessly when he discharged you from your position as teacher," he said.

Martínez rocked his head back and forth. "It is all in the past. What have you planned for me? If I am to die I must know."

"What good would you be to me dead?"

"Good to you?" Martínez raised his eyes. They were suddenly clear. "Do you still talk of my being good to you, Don Manuel?"

"I do not permit myself the luxury of personal revenge, padre," Armijo said quietly. "At least not while you may still be useful. Such pointless vengeance is for children and fools. You can still serve me."

"How do you know that I will consent to serve you?"

"You have no choice."

"Death does not terrify me."

"Possibly not. But ridicule does."

"Ridicule?" Martínez repeated angrily. "Who speaks of ridicule?"

"I do." Armijo sat down. "You are proud, padre, and you are ambitious, as we both know. You attached yourself to Gonzales because you thought you could go farther with him than you could with me. You lost. Tell others about visions and voices and beliefs. To me only admit ambition. Serve me or not, padre, I would not order you killed. I would only tell all of New Mexico of the idiocies you have related to me tonight. How would you like yourself, Don Antonio, as the lunatic priest of New Mexico?"

Armijo leaned forward on the desk. "All the little people of the north who believe so sincerely in you, to whom *you* are religion, not the Book you read from, not the cross that hangs around your neck, but you, yourself. What would be it for them to discover their holy man was nothing but a madman? It would be so easy. First with Gonzales, who truly is mad. Then with the Montoyas, Esquibel. I could label them all madmen. And you, padre, as the chief maniac of them all. The insane pastor of Taos! The priest who believes in the 'voices' heard by an Indian mestizo! All your teachings through the years, padre, all for nothing. The little children who study with you would mock you when you passed and throw dirt in your face." He shook his head slowly. "No, my old friend, death would be relief. I would rather condemn you to life."

"*Es de la piel del diablo!*" Martínez clutched his cross.

Armijo picked up a cigar. "I may wear the devil's skin, Don Antonio," he agreed equably, "but do not forget that you invented Gonzales and that his crimes are on your head."

"What do you ask that I do?"

"Nothing unseemly. I respect your cloth. I have decided to appoint you chaplain to my troops."

The priest twisted the cross in his fingers. "It is a good price."

"There are many encouraging things you can say to men who go forth to fight José Gonzales."

1

With Padre Martínez riding a burro at his side. Don Manuel led his peasant army to the north to join battle with the insurrectos. He was not happy about the job, and its sole justification was its necessity. The Indian technically could still be considered the legitimate Governor of New Mexico, and Armijo, despite his maneuverings, the insurgent.

So long as fear remained that the Indian might counterattack and retake the capital, Armijo was aware he would never have the support of either the New Mexicans or the Americans who had the funds he must borrow to operate his government and pay his soldiers. And it was necessary to destroy the legend of Gonzales's invincibility for still another reason. The idea of a powerful leader in the remote New Mexico Department was always appealing to the harassed officials in the City of Mexico, and if it appeared to them that Gonzales was strong enough to maintain order and control the Americans, the central authorities would probably swallow him wholeheartedly, despite his proclamation of independence and his seeking Texan aid. They would accept that as a political gambit and bargain around it.

Much as Armijo disliked the idea, it also was necessary that he lead his troops personally. He could not entrust the expedition to Captain Caballero, who already was too popular in Santa Fe, or to Mariano Chaves, who still was the hope of the ricos in the south.

The two Montoya brothers guided the army to where the insurrectos were encamped at Pojoaque, where, just five weeks earlier, Governor Pérez had made his camp. It was obvious even to Armijo that Gonzales was in no condition to put up any fight and, drawing his saber and waving it heroically in the air, he gave the command to open fire. The Indians fled at this first volley

112

without returning the fire. Don Manuel gave the command to charge and his troops moved forward unchecked until they arrived in the canton of La Cañada in the heartland of the insurrection. There he drew up his soldiers and announced a great victory.

"It will be recorded forever in the glorious pages of Mexican history," he proclaimed. "And the favor of Almighty God and the Blessed Virgin has been shown plainly in that not a single drop of New Mexican blood has been shed!"

He ordered Padre Martínez to celebrate a victory Mass, and when it was over he sent Antonio Montoya on a secret mission. When the hunchback returned he had with him the alcalde, José Esquibel, and a man named Juan Vigil, a peasant from Taos, no relation to the postmaster. The Montoya brothers and the two newcomers were ranked directly under Gonzales himself in the Indian's government.

Don Manuel sent the quartet back to Santa Fe under guard.

2

RETURNING TO THE CAPITAL at the head of his victorious army, Don Manuel received a tumultuous welcome. To the rejoicing people of Santa Fe he was the true hero. Even the Americans, watching developments, admitted he had apparently restored order at last.

He was now almost ready to send his report to the central authorities, detailing every step from the time he was called upon by his fellow citizens in Tome to liberate the country. There was but one more thing to do, the climax that would make his report irresistible.

He summoned all available deputies from both the Pérez and the Gonzales government, all alcaldes, all military officers, and all prominent citizens of Santa Fe and other towns, to a meeting in the Chamber of Deputies. He permitted Don Antonio Sandoval to sit in the Governor's seat and open the meeting, which took place on the 21st day of September, and after asking leave to address the august gathering he limped to the podium and his deep voice filled the hall.

"Don Antonio Sandoval, honored citizens, victorious military commanders, deputies, I have called you together to inform you that with the help of God the army of liberation has rid Santa Fe of the Indians. I cannot express to you the sorrow that filled my heart when I was forced to stand in this hall, together with many of you, and pledge my oath of allegiance to José Gonzales. I held my grief in my heart and retired to my estate in Albuquerque and there prayed to our beloved Virgin of Guadalupe that the supreme authorities in the City of Mexico would afford speedy relief to our tragic land. Before that could happen the horrors conceived by Gonzales, which included a treacherous separation from the motherland and an appeal to the vile government in Texas to send an army of heretics up here, became so numerous that I was called upon to lead loyal New Mexicans in a war against him. We have been victorious! Once again you may sleep without fear that at any moment a brutal Indian will break into your house and murder you."

He bowed his head to the applause. "Gonzales has not remained unscathed," he continued. "God has punished him. He now is insane. It is impossible to make with him a formal peace. His sins have driven him to the black world of delirium." He paused and prepared to play his highest card, the idea that had occurred to him on the morning when the Montoya brothers visited him in the palace. "Since José Gonzales no longer is capable of reasonable dealings, my friends, I have been forced to go beyond him, and I have brought here his four chief lieutenants, who represent the highest lucid leadership in the Gonzales government. These four officials now are prepared to recognize the army of liberation as the sole lawful power in New Mexico and to conclude a formal treaty of peace ending the insurrection forever." As voices rose in surprise, Don Manuel said imperiously: "Capitán Caballero, bring before these honorable gentlemen the present heads of the insurrection!"

Caballero led the Montoya brothers, Esquibel, and Vigil into the chamber. The four men were dressed and barbered for the occasion. They walked to the front of the room, the eyes of everyone upon them.

"Gentlemen, I have informed this gathering that you are prepared to sign a solemn treaty of surrender to the forces of law and order," Armijo boomed. "Is that correct?"

The four men nodded.

"I have had the treaty prepared. Teniente Coronel Mariano Chaves, bring forth the document," Don Manuel ordered.

Chaves stepped forth and unrolled a sheet of paper. It was laid on the desk before Sandoval, and each of the four men signed it, Vigil and Desiderio Montoya with large crosses. When they were finished, Sandoval reached for the pen to sign for forces of law and order. As though he were not present, Armijo picked up the quill and signed.

Don Manuel laid down the pen and again faced the gathering. "I have been recognized as chief of the liberating army by the District of Rio Abajo in the Plan of Tome," he said slowly. "I have been recognized as the supreme chief of the presidial companies by the Military Act signed by all presidial officers. And now, by virtue of this treaty, I have been recognized as chief of the Rio Arriba and the insurrectos. The people of New Mexico have spoken." He filled his chest. "I now find myself called upon to take full responsibility for the government of New Mexico and I therefore assume, under God and the Holy Virgin, the hallowed and traditional title of Superior Political and Military Chief of New Mexico."

He turned slowly until he faced Antonio Sandoval fully. The old prefect, his flaccid cheeks puckered in bewilderment, stared back at him and then looked frantically around the room for assistance. At last he rose painfully to his feet and stepped down. Armijo, who had not removed his gaze from him, climbed to the dais and walked behind the desk. Looking calmly at the faces massed before him, he lifted his arms and cried: "*Por Dios y Libertad!*"

For a moment there was no response and standing there, his arms extended, Don Manuel felt fear. Then to a man the deputies and the officers and the civilians leaped to their feet and held out their right hands and thundered back: "*Por Dios y Libertad!*"

3

Don Juan Bautista Vigil placed some letters on Don Manuel's desk. "The gringo mail," he said. "To Texas and the United States."

"What is in it?" Armijo asked.

"The usual things." The postmaster shrugged. "They wonder whether you will be confirmed officially as governor. Shall I have translations made?"

"If there is nothing of importance, reseal them and send them on."

Vigil gathered up the letters. "Have you heard anything yet, Don Manuel?"

"It is too soon."

"The business men are beginning to have doubts."

"How can they have doubts?" Armijo asked angrily. "It is less than a month. They know how long it takes for word to come up from the City of Mexico."

"They know and yet they doubt."

"Let them doubt. Santa Anna will confirm me."

"The gringos doubt more than the rest."

"Damn the gringos!"

"But not their money. Have you managed to get any money from them?"

Armijo breathed out heavily. "No. I go to them like a beggar and they say they will consider, but it is always no."

"Then the soldiers are still discontented?"

"It is not my fault Gonzales robbed the treasury to the last penny. The soldiers will remain loyal. They have no other place to go."

"Soldiers who do not get paid find other places to go."

"I can always call back my peasants."

"Perhaps you should have kept your peasant army together longer."

"I had to send them back to the south. All the wild Indians in New Mexico were raiding in the Rio Abajo."

"How much longer do you believe it will take to get word from below?"

Armijo leaped to his feet and threw up his hands. "I do not know, nombre de Dios, I do not know! It takes time. Every one knows it takes time. They will have to confirm me. They know down there I could start a civil war that would open the country to the gringos. Who else could they name as governor?"

"Some say Gonzales."

"Gonzales!"

"There are rumors that he has gathered his warriors together again."

Armijo smiled grimly. "It is more than a rumor, Don Juan Bautista."

"Then the talk is not so crazy. Gonzales could attack Santa Fe."

"He could and he would if I did not hold him off."

"And how do you hold him off, Don Manuel?"

"He sends messages to me every day telling me that if I agree to his terms he will consider a peace. *His* terms! The departmental system must be abolished and the territorial system restored. The taxes must be canceled. The Indians must have equality. Madre de Dios, the man still looks upon himself as Governor of New Mexico! And on top of all else he threatens to tell the world that I made possible his revolution."

"What do you do about all this?"

"What do I do? Por Dios, I reply to all his messages, and I involve him in complicated problems. What else can I do? I must keep him quiet until my appointment is confirmed."

"Does that satisfy him?

"It satisfies him. It pleases him to discuss these affairs as one governor to another. The latest thing is that he wants me to send him his four lieutenants."

"Do you still have them in prison?"

"Yes, Don Juan Bautista. And every day Martínez also comes to me and demands that I turn them loose. God in heaven! Can you imagine those men walking free in Santa Fe?"

"You cannot keep them imprisoned forever, Don Manuel."

"They should be executed. It is the only safe thing to do.

And yet I cannot order that either. I raised the dogs to the status of diplomats and they fulfilled their function publicly." He laughed harshly. "It is amusing, is it not, Don Juan Bautista? They are the four most dangerous men in the world to me and I must give them my protection."

Don Manuel, who now was wearing the uniform of a Mexican general, a rank to which he promoted himself after his victory at Pojoaque, covered his tired face with his hands. Vigil slipped the opened letters into his pocket and left.

4

In October Armijo received information that he considered relieved him of responsibility to the four prisoners. The new alcalde of La Cañada sent down a frantic report that the insurrectos had rioted at Las Truchas. Don Manuel summoned Captain Caballero and, declaring that the treaty had been violated by this uprising, ordered the four men hanged.

Then, in order not to have to listen to appeals for clemency, chiefly from Padre Martínez, Don Manuel left the capital, saying he had to take care of business affairs in Albuquerque. He waited in his hacienda for word that his orders had been carried out. A week later he received a message from Captain Caballero to the effect that the rioting in Las Truchas had proved to be of minor importance and that he, Caballero, in his capacity as military commandant of New Mexico in the absence of Don Manuel, had decided to call together his officers and let them vote on the action to be taken with the prisoners.

The officers had decided that the execution of the four men might provoke a major attack from Gonzales and that the presidial companies were not in themselves strong enough to risk that danger. He reminded Don Manuel that though a request for troops to reinforce the presidial companies had been made some time before to the Department of Chihuahua, which had nominal military jurisdiction over New Mexico, those troops had not arrived. The four men would be kept as prisoners, and if the trouble at Las

Truchas showed any signs of developing into another general up-rising, they would be put to death immediately and then, if neces-sary, the presidial companies would defend Santa Fe with their lives.

The report was written with considerable subtlety. It pointed out in a number of ways that the presidial troops were all Armijo had to protect his government against Gonzales. The writing be-tween the lines was far too artful for the simple soldierly mind of Caballero, and Armijo saw throughout the skillful hand of Padre Martínez.

He knew he could not order Caballero to obey his original instructions. In their present frame of mind the presidial troops might easily be inflamed to revolt by the priest. Instead, Don Manuel composed a sorrowful reply in which he deplored "an exceedingly unhappy decision which has been made to relax the discipline of a respectable garrison."

He concluded, sadly: "The situation in which this finds me for the present compels me to overlook a fault which derogates greatly from the commendations of that body of officers made to the supreme government and which does small honor to their fine profession."

Although he managed a dignified answer, this act of outright disobedience had a stunning effect upon him. It exposed the true fragility of his position. All his life, it seemed to him, he had had to be dependent upon others. Would the time ever come when he would be free of need for the Caballeros, the Martínezes, the gringos.

The blow marked the climax of all the worries and tensions that had beleaguered him since he had come to power. He was chained by lethargy. He moved about morosely, almost in a trance, indifferent to the girls Doña María Trinidad produced for his pleasure.

He received ominous letters from the capital warning him about the increasing restlessness of the troops, who had not re-ceived payment of any kind since they had been reorganized in Bernalillo. He ignored the letters until, at the urging of Doña María Trinidad, he replied suggesting that the troops be paid in wheat, of which there was a quantity in the government ware-house. As though determined to bring about his own ruin, he set the rate of pay at four dollars a fanega, which was about a bushel and a half, more than three times the price of wheat on the open market, which meant the soldiers not only were to be paid in produce but were to be given less than a third of their salaries.

The letters from Santa Fe continued. The soldiers accepted the payment, but under protest. Government officials were quarreling and there was a growing anxiety that his administration would fall apart from neglect, bringing about the return of Gonzales.

None of the disquieting news could restore his energy. He grew shabby in his appearance. He let his general's uniform hang untouched in a cabinet and wore the clothes of a simple peasant. He wandered about, visiting the scenes of his childhood. He went to almost forgotten places where once he had watched over sheep and had dreamed of greatness. He spent hours on the bank of the Rio Bravo, staring into the muddy stream, remembering the times he had spent there laboriously picking his way through the primer lent to him by the parish priest. He visited the grave of Rafaela. Even there he could feel nothing.

He was seated one day near the summit of a hill. It was a cold afternoon in December. He gazed across the vast space before him. It was a scene he loved: the sand-colored hills, the green of the far-off trees reduced by distance to shrubs, the immaculate, cold sky. These were the unchanging things. His horse nuzzled him and he stroked its velvet nose abstractedly.

In the valley below the hill he saw a horseman and looked down at him idly. The rider waved and Don Manuel lifted his hand. Then he made out that it was Esquipulas Caballero and, feeling an old excitement, he stood up quickly as he watched Caballero spur the horse up the rise.

Caballero's face was reddened from the wind. "Doña María Trinidad said that you might be here," he said. "Word has just been received from Mexico. You have been appointed Governor of New Mexico for a term of eight years."

5

THE BAILES AND RECEPTIONS given in honor of the new Governor of New Mexico coincided that year with the festivities for the Christmas holidays and mixed with them to such a degree that presently many weary persons hardly knew whether they were celebrating the Natividad or the appointment of Don Manuel Armijo to the highest office in the land.

The presence of the Americans over the years had altered the purely religious nature of the holidays and had added secular gaieties to the church ceremonies. The yanqui custom of giving parties and exchanging gifts seemed more appropriate this year than ever before. Even the Americans themselves seemed satisfied at last. They knew Don Manuel for a hard man and had no great love for him but they agreed it was better to deal with a comprehensible politician than with a fanatic, and Don Manuel would be there for a long time. Before the year was out they advanced him the funds he needed, the money to be paid back as usual from revenues collected when the caravans arrived over the Santa Fe Trail in the summer. Governor Armijo paid off his soldiers, giving each man a bonus, inspiring new loyalty.

It was a happy season. The confirmation of Don Manuel had removed from José Gonzales whatever legality had still clung to him and had relieved the deputies of their oath of allegiance to the Indian. It was known that Gonzales still held an army together in the north, but it was assumed he would now return to his pueblo and again take up his life as a hunter of buffalo.

On the 12th day of January a squadron of soldiers under the command of Lieutenant Colonel Calletano Justiniani arrived in Santa Fe from Vera Cruz. The capital awaited the next development with interest. Justiniani's rank was high enough for him to take military control of New Mexico. It appeared, however, that he was under instructions to subordinate himself to General Armijo, and that Don Manuel was considered in Chihuahua to be military as well as political chief. The capital was vastly impressed. The arrangement suited Don Manuel perfectly. He could enjoy

121

the rank of general and military leader with a skilled officer under him to perform the duties.

On the 17th day of January Governor Armijo called his deputies into session and formally proclaimed the re-establishment of New Mexico as a department. The Chamber of Deputies was filled with brilliantly uniformed officers. The deputies were subdued by this display of force. They had received no salaries for more than a year. They had to pay their own expenses traveling from their villages and to take time away from their personal affairs to attend the sessions of the Junta. They made this session brief. They granted Don Manuel power to act thenceforth "as should appear to him to be convenient" and then voted to stand adjourned indefinitely.

6

GOVERNOR ARMIJO studied the newest proclamation of the insurrectos. The rebels had reacted immediately to the resuscitation of the detested departmental system. Within four days after the Junta voted dictatorial power to Armijo and then dissolved itself, the insurgent leaders called for a new uprising, claiming that José Gonzales was the true governor by reason of the "harmonious vote from the bosom of this peaceful Territory" and that Armijo had taken power "not through popular unanimity but purely by force and violence."

Armijo handed the Plan to Lieutenant Colonel Justiniani. The officer read through the paper, his slender, aristocratic face set in a sneer. He stroked his narrow mustache and looked up. "Why do we not take the field and put an end to this business once and for all, excelencia?" he asked languidly. "My soldiers need the exercise."

Don Manuel relit his cigar. "Do you believe we are strong enough?" He tried to keep the concern from his voice. "My spies tell me Gonzales has thirteen hundred warriors still loyal to him. I must keep part of the presidial companies in Santa Fe to protect the capital. Together with your soldiers we can call upon no more than six hundred men."

"Six hundred soldiers, excelencia. The mestizo has nothing but numbers. It will be like shooting buffalo."

Nothing but numbers and American muskets, Armijo thought. He looked at the officer. Justiniani exuded a contagious confidence. Don Manuel blew out a great mouthful of smoke. He felt suddenly brave. "Por Dios, my dear teniente coronel, I agree with all my heart. Let us go, and quickly and put a muzzle on the dog. I need some exercise myself."

Justiniani stood up lazily. "With your permission, excelencia, I will give the necessary orders."

Don Manuel summoned Captain Caballero. "I take the troops to the north immediately, Don José. You will remain here with half your soldiers and guard the capital."

Caballero's face showed his disappointment at being left behind. "I have a favor to ask of your excellency. My son took no part in the first battle with the insurrectos. Do not deny him this second opportunity."

"I will take him along, and willingly. One thing more, Don José. This new uprising makes forfeit the lives of the four prisoners. I leave at the first sun tomorrow. Before I depart they will be put to death."

"I obey, excelencia."

"I will be merciful," Armijo said. "Instead of being hanged as they deserve, they may be executed by firing squad. And they may each make last confession to Padre Martínez."

7

THE JANUARY WEATHER was bitter cold as the troops marched north. Scouts reported the insurrectos were again encamped at Pojoaque, and Don Manuel, operating now on a level of high policy as a governor and general might do with no dishonor, permitted Justiniani to work out the details of the attack. The Indians were caught by surprise. The engagement was ended in less than ten minutes. The insurrectos fled to the north.

"We have lost but one dragoon, excelencia, and but six others are wounded," Justiniani reported. "It was as I said, like the hunting of wild game."

"And the insurrectos?" Armijo asked.

"Six dead and a score wounded."

"Was Gonzales among them?"

"No, excelencia."

The victorious New Mexican officers gathered around a campfire and complimented one another. Armijo was filled with exhilaration. The smell of gunpowder was still in his nostrils. The icy air, the stern military sounds, the comradeship of men in arms under his supreme command, the laughter, the joking, together with the almost entire lack of danger, made the blood stir in his veins. Por Dios, this was how war should be fought! All the good things and none of the bad.

He saw Padre Martínez moving about, giving comfort to wounded men, and called to him. The priest, who had joined the troops after the prisoners were executed in the Spanish garita on the hill overlooking Santa Fe, came to the fire. His face was red from the freezing wind, and his breath leaped in white puffs from his mouth. He held his hands to the blaze.

"Padre, you perform your priestly functions well," Don Manuel said. "But you confine yourself to New Mexicans. Out there on the hard ground lie many Indians who call you their priest. Go to them, en el nombre de Dios, and give them the benefit of your religious office."

"You are considerate, excelencia."

"Comfort them, padre. Give to those who need it the final sacrament. And when you speak to them, perhaps you can learn where their comrades went and what are their plans."

Martínez's lips tightened. "I am a priest, excelencia, not a spy."

"I speak to you as priest. Gonzales's cause is doomed. If you can learn anything that will save the lives of your poor parishioners you will be performing the finest of your religious functions. What is nobler, in the sight of God, than the preservation of Catholic lives?"

Without replying, Martínez departed. It was almost dawn before he returned. Don Manuel rose from his pallet. The priest crouched at his side. "Gonzales has taken his men to La Cañada."

"How many men?"

"He has more than a thousand still, excelencia. They are prepared to fight to the death."

Don Manuel lowered himself slowly to the pallet. "Thank you, padre." He did not close his eyes again.

The government troops reached La Cañada early the following morning. Justiniani studied the situation through his glasses. "They are in excellent positions, Don Manuel. This Gonzales is not without skill."

Armijo shifted in his saddle. The campaign had lost all its attractiveness for him. Justiniani waited politely for him to give the order to attack. Don Manuel wrapped his poncho more tightly around him, grateful for the cold that served as an excuse for his trembling. His nerves cried for him to order retreat. He could settle with Gonzales later in ways more suited to his talents. "But you cannot retreat now," he said to himself.

His eyes fell upon the priest and he knew that the true conflict was between only them. The air might blacken with powder smoke and deafen with explosion, but there was only one battle being fought that day. Even Gonzales no longer was important. "It is you and I," Don Manuel thought, "alone on our eyrie. The thing that we started in Taos now comes to its conclusion. There is nothing for me to say, padre, it will be said."

Don Esquipulas Caballero, in his old uniform of ensign in the presidial troop, rode up. "With your permission, excelencia, I will oust that rabble with my company alone." Armijo continued to stare at the priest, and Caballero mistook the hesitation. "As a favor, excelencia. Let me show the soldiers from Vera Cruz what men from New Mexico can do."

Don Manuel touched Caballero on the arm. "Do you go, Don Esquipulas. May God bless your endeavor."

Caballero drew his saber and gave his company the order to charge. For a little while Don Manuel could see nothing but dust. Then, holding his glass to his eyes, he saw the hills sparkling with gunfire and three or four of Caballero's men topple from their horses. "Now, now, return the fire now," he said, and the flashes again illuminated the hills, and he said "Santa Madre, why do you wait? Return the fire, break the charge, break the charge." He saw the sparkle of the Indian fire for the third time and, lowering the glass, he watched the still charging men lift their own muskets. "It is too late, you have gone too close," he said, and he heard the cracking of their guns. "It is too late," he said, "they will destroy you and, after you, us," and in his mind he was in his carriage racing south from Santa Fe. Then he heard Justiniani say without excitement: "The young man was as good as his word, excelencia. The enemy is in full retreat."

Don Manuel jerked his glass upward. The Indians were scurrying into the hills.

"He is a gallant officer," Justiniani said.

8

DON MANUEL'S OFFICERS were all drunk in the Franciscan convento in La Cañada. Don Manuel emptied his glass as often as any of the others, but he could feel nothing from the brandy. The final reports were in. Three of Caballero's men had been killed and eight or nine wounded. The bodies of more than twenty Indians had been found, together with more than thirty-five wounded. When the reports were given to him Don Manuel asked one question: "Have you found Gonzales?" Each time the answer was no.

It was late that night when Padre Martínez made his first appearance. The black cassock of the priest was covered with dust, his face streaked with channels of grime. His eyes were somber. He took in the revelry in the building consecrated to holiness and went immediately to Don Manuel. "With permission, excelencia. A word with you."

"Come with me, padre." Armijo led him to a smaller room. "It is of Gonzales you wish to speak."

"He would treat with you."

"Where is he, padre?"

The priest ground his hands. "There are conditions."

"Where is he? I command you to answer." He gripped the priest by the shoulders. Martínez turned his face half away. Armijo released him and wiped his brow. "Speak, vicario. Where is Gonzales?"

"He wants to discuss terms with you, Don Manuel."

"Terms?" Armijo said scornfully. "He is defeated."

"He is the leader of his people," Martínez said in a monotone, as though reciting a litany. "He would speak to you as equal, as one governor to another. He no longer has personal ambition. He wants assurances only that the taxes will not be enforced and that his people will not be punished and so he will keep the peace."

Armijo turned his back to the priest. When he faced him again, he was composed. "Bring José Gonzales here, padre."

"I have advised him not to come."

"For certain. But he will come."

Martínez returned an hour later with the Indian. In the small room now were Armijo, Justiniani, Caballero, and six soldiers. Gonzales's buffalo robe was covered with snow. There was no sound but the wind.

Gonzales walked directly to Don Manuel. "*Saludes, compañero*," he said.

"*Saludes, compañero*." Don Manuel said to the priest: "Confess my compañero."

Gonzales's face was without expression save for his eyes, which focused instantly on Armijo and then became depthless. Two soldiers walked up behind the Indian and knocked him down to his knees. They drew their pistols and cocked them and held them at the back of his head.

Gonzales turned away his head so that he could not see the priest. Raising his eyes, he said: "Father, forgive me my sins."

Martínez stared at Armijo. The priest raised his hand, made the sign of the cross, and said: "*Ego te absolvo omnibus censuris et peccatis tuis, in nomine Patris et Filii et Spiritus Sancti.*" Looking upon the averted head of the Indian, he said: "Amen."

"Execute my compañero," Armijo said.

1

Jₐₘₑₛ Mₐɢₒғғɪɴ rose in his stirrups and held his spyglass
to his eyes. The dust in the distance was so thick and the air between so transparent that under the magnification the cloud
seemed to envelop him. Then, through the wall of alkali, he made
out a company of cavalry and behind it the buildings of San Miguel
and behind the low adobe structures the silver of the Rio Pecos.

He held up his arm, and the wagons in the caravan rumbled
to a stop. Other American traders rode up and gathered around
him. The soldiers from San Miguel galloped up as though they
were attacking and at the last moment pulled back on the reins
so their horses whinnied wildly and reared. Magoffin smiled and
thought it was a splendid show. The Mexicans were superb horsemen.

The leader was a man Magoffin had never seen before. He
was uniformed with extravagant splendor. His boots were soft and
fine and, where the dust had not coated them, highly polished. He
was a man in his middle thirties, with dark brown eyes set close
together. His nose was thin and Spanish, his color swarthy. It was
his mouth that interested Magoffin more than anything else. The
mouth, under a narrow, black, carefully tended mustache, was
without lips and ran like a jagged seam across his face. He was
stockily built, with broad shoulders made wider by gilt epaulets.

The officer saluted. "Greetings to him of God," he said.
When he spoke, his inner lips showed wet and red through the
dust on his face and it was as though he had exposed a wound.

"That God may give good days to you," Magoffin replied.

"May I have the honor to introduce myself, señor. I am
Teniente Damasio Salazar, in command of the San Miguel com-
pany of militia. I welcome you in the name of his excellency the
Governor."

"I am James Magoffin, Don Damasio."

Salazar smiled, revealing teeth that were yellow and long. "I should have recognized you by your speech, Don Santiago."

One of the traders, a man by the name of Carson, asked in bad Spanish: "Who *is* the governor these days, amigo?"

For a moment Salazar was not affable. He brought the smile back to his face. "Don Manuel Armijo is Governor of New Mexico, señor, may God give to him long years."

"Armijo, hey?" Carson grinned at Magoffin. "That's kind of surprising, hey, Jamie? Looks like the big greaser's staying in the saddle."

Magoffin watched Salazar's face as the Mexican tried to follow Carson's English. He saw the puzzlement and then a flash of hatred as he caught the word "greaser." It was the one American word every Mexican understood. Magoffin cursed Carson silently. He could not understand why so many of his countrymen went out of their way to be offensive to Mexicans. "Where is his excellency?" he asked Salazar in a friendly manner. "It will be a good thing to see Don Manuel once more."

Salazar's mouth was a razor line. He stared at Carson as though he wanted never to forget his face. "He awaits you in San Miguel, Don Santiago. My company was sent out to serve as an escort for the caravan."

"We are honored, Don Damasio, and we are ready to follow."

Salazar wheeled his horse and gave an order. The soldiers formed themselves and started back toward San Miguel, followed by the line of wagons. When he was able to engage Salazar's attention, Magoffin asked him to ride alongside one of his wagons. He reached inside and took out a silver-inlaid gun belt, from which hung a holster, pistol inside. "You would do me great honor to accept this, Don Damasio," he said.

Salazar's eyes hardened for a moment and Magoffin knew he was not fooling him. Then Salazar brought an expression of ingenuousness to his face, to play the part of a simple Mexican who has been given an unexpected gift. "Thousand thanks, Don Santiago. The stories of your generosity are already like folk tales in our land." He buckled on the belt, crossing it over the belt already there. Then he waved his hand and rode to the head of his company.

As they approached San Miguel, another cavalcade of horsemen appeared. Riding in the front was Don Manuel. Magoffin spurred his horse and greeted the Governor warmly.

"My eyes are happy to see you again, Don Santiago," Armijo said. He looked beyond Magoffin and frowned. "Was your journey good?"

"Neither better nor worse than usual, excelencia, just long. I love your country and my own. It is a pity that they are separated by so many hundreds of miles of difficult land." Magoffin looked at the Governor keenly as he spoke. He thought Don Manuel was putting on weight. His cheeks were fuller and the sash around his waist did not hide a developing paunch. "How is señora la gobernadora, may I ask, excelencia?"

"She is well and awaits your arrival with pleasure." Armijo again gazed over Magoffin's shoulder. His voice altered. "The caravan is a small one this year, Don Santiago."

"That is true, excelencia."

"Is there more to come?"

"I do not believe so, excelencia."

Don Manuel's face became briefly unpleasant. Then he recovered and swung his arm in a wide gesture. "Welcome to your second home, Don Santiago. Everything here is yours. Santa Fe will be a happier place now that you have returned. Come, amigo, I have had a small repast prepared for all of you in our little village. The people are gathered to give you welcome."

In the weeks required to make the crossing of the prairies, La Villa Real de la Santa Fe de San Francisco had become more than a city to the travelers. It was journey's end, a haven to dream on during endless days and nights. It was comfort and food and drink and women.

No city could match the feverish images created lovingly by old trailsmen around the endless campfires en route, and the men who had made the crossing for the first time were disappointed when they first saw the city. Just below Santa Fe on the road from San Miguel the trail rose to a ridge and opened upon a plain. To the northwest was a long valley broken by small growths of timber and occasional small block buildings. The valley was edged with fields of corn and wheat. Farther to the north the blocks were set more closely together and the initial impression of newcomers was that the buildings were kilns for the making of bricks for Santa Fe. The old-timers took pleasure in correcting this impression. The buildings *were* Santa Fe.

If the tyros were disappointed, the veterans were not. The night before in the village of Pecos halfway up from San Miguel they had labored to shine themselves up. By now they were bathed and cleaned and dressed in their finest clothing, still wrinkled from weeks of being packed away, and their beards were combed and their hair was plastered down with grease, and their boots glistened, from the same grease. They knew that Santa Fe would be no disappointment.

On the journey from San Miguel, Governor Armijo had appeared preoccupied. He had presided with inborn courtesy at the reception in San Miguel, but after that Magoffin sensed that the Governor desired to be left alone and he avoided him. Magoffin was not surprised upon waking in Pecos to learn that the Governor had risen much earlier and had already departed for the capital.

With consummate skill, abetted by bottles of wine and whisky distributed with his renowned generosity, Magoffin made inquiries of the officers to bring himself up to date. He learned that the months that had passed had not been altogether good ones for Don Manuel. There was no open challenge to his position and he was strong in his support from Mexico, but there was unrest, due primarily to the lack of money and to a silent and stubborn intractableness of many of the prominent men in the country, particularly the ricos of the Rio Abajo. His answer to the latter challenge was the palace prison, which now held more political prisoners than criminals. The money problems were not so easily solved. Although Don Manuel piously maintained his role as defender of the people by refusing to tax them directly, as the departmental system empowered him to do, his agents were making increasing demands on the peasants for livestock and produce, causing bitter resentment among many who had been his stanchest supporters. There was unrest among the soldiers, who again were being paid entirely in wheat.

There had been trouble again in the north. The followers of the slain Gonzales had staged another uprising in Taos, which had to be put down forcibly by Colonel Justiniani. After returning to Santa Fe, Colonel Justiniani had gone back to Mexico with half his squadron because Armijo had no funds to maintain them.

This information, which was uncovered bit by bit under Magoffin's masterful prodding, caused the trader considerable perturbation. He knew from experience that when things went badly with the government, they went equally badly with the foreign merchants. Armijo, he knew, was no man to tolerate financial troubles when there was a way to get money, and the only source of income lay in the wagons strung out on the road to Santa Fe.

The people showed no sign of this discontent as the wagons rolled into the city at last. They filled the streets, shouting: "The Americans! The wagons! The entrance of the caravan!" The drivers responded to their cries by cracking their whips like rifleshots. Thronging the streets with the citizens of the capital were farmers from the countryside, ranchers, shepherds from the hills. Miners from the mountains of Sandia and Abiquiu, from Picuris and Embudo, carrying the savings of twelve months, jostled against workers from the salt lakes who had put aside bits of their wages of thirty or forty cents a day to save enough to buy a few varas of calico or muslin to last them for the next year. The people were ecstatic. There might be discontent throughout the country, but nothing could interfere with this annual event.

The summer day was perfect. The goods were unloaded from the wagons and carted to the customhouse for inspection and taxing. The long journey truly was ended. The riders, with leisure on their hands while the merchandise was assessed, made their first stop at La Fonda. And then, after many drinks, could come all the rewards of their labor.

2

HIS HANDS gripped behind his back, Don Manuel watched the unloading of the wagons from a window in his office. Seated in the room, regarding him nervously, were Juan Estevan Pino, his plump body now encased in the uniform of a lieutenant colonel in the militia, a rank Armijo had given him when Mariano Chaves retired temporarily to attend to his business in the Rio Abajo; Juan Bautista Vigil, who now considered himself an elder states- man of the Armijo administration; and Armijo's business partner, Albert Speyer, who had arrived in Santa Fe with his wagons a few days earlier.

Don Manuel swung around. "This country is cursed! To have a whole people depend upon a dozen gringo dogs. Where else is there such a shameful situation? We are prisoners to the gringos! They own us, our bodies and our souls. The whole year we wait for them, a country, a people, a government holding its breath. And now they arrive! Less than fifty wagons. En el nombre de Cristo, how can a country have pride when it dangles like a pup- pet, jerked up and down by a few foreign traders?" He glared at the men. "We are a joke. We are comical. We are not a nation of men; we are beggars who survive on the garbage of gringos."

Pino and Vigil shifted uneasily. Don Manuel had been in foul temper since his return from San Miguel. What was this talk about pride? Why was he so concerned with pride?

"What are they trying to do to me?" Armijo demanded. "Did they not have enough of the mestizo Gonzales? Do they want another revolution?"

Vigil opened and closed his mouth several times. That was another thing. Why did Don Manuel take everything so person- ally? Nothing happened any more but the Governor thought it was being done against him. And now this. Now the falling off of the Santa Fe trade was a personal affair, as though it were some- thing between Don Manuel and the Americans. "What did Ma- goffin say?" Vigil asked at last.

"That one speaks with a tongue of silver. It is almost reason- able as he explains it. He said the gringos were frightened because they lost so much money to Gonzales. He has excuses enough."

"You may call them excuses, Don Manuel," Vigil said pla- catingly, "but they are not without justification. Most of the traders lost everything they had here to Gonzales."

"And to Pérez," Speyer said in his Spanish with its heavy Prussian accent. "Not everybody had your foresight, Don Manuel."

Vigil shuddered. The notes Armijo had had bought up from the merchants had been redeemed recently at face value by the central authorities.

"I have ordered that that subject remain unmentioned," Armijo said furiously.

Speyer lit a cigar. He was tall, bald, and bleak-looking. "I thought we were among friends. Your pardon."

"But the walls have ears," Pino said. "Don Manuel has remarked on that before."

"And you received your share, Don Alberto," Armijo said. He walked rapidly toward his partner. "For nothing! For nothing! Only because I am honest with you."

"We are partners," Speyer said.

"You are a foreigner like the rest of them! How can you be expected to understand the problems of this country?" He clenched his fists over the seated Prussian. "You are like all the other visitors who think this country is filled with buffoons."

Speyer smoked his cigar placidly. Depending on Don Manuel's mood, he was his intimate friend and counselor, a foreigner, a Prussian, a Jew. It mattered very little to him. His partnership with Don Manuel gave him unequaled advantages.

Armijo limped back to his desk and sat down. "What are they trying to do to me? I try to make it as favorable as possible for them. I have devoted all my efforts to aiding their trade. We need them, Madre mía, we need them, but they need us as well. Are they trying to destroy me? Are they trying to bring about another insurrection so that this time the country can be taken over by Americans?"

"Calm yourself, Don Manuel," Vigil said. He looked again at Pino, and Pino lifted his shoulders slightly. It was another obsession with the Governor. He was convinced that Gonzales had sought the aid of the Texans at the urging of the Americans.

There was a knock on the door and Vigil sighed in relief. Guadalupe Miranda, a little schoolteacher from Albuquerque who had tutored Don Manuel years before and who now was his secretary, poked in his head. "Your pardon, excelencia," he said in a precise, dry voice. "Don Santiago Magoffin asks an audience."

"Magoffin? Good. I want to see him too. Send him in, Don Guadalupe." Armijo held up his hands as his friends made motions to leave. "Remain here, amigos. It is something all of you should hear."

Magoffin strode in, his genial face smiling. He exchanged greetings with the other men and was diplomat enough to hide his surprise at Pino's new military status and to greet him by his title.

"To what do I owe the honor of this visit?" Armijo asked curtly.

"I have just come from the customs, excelencia," Magoffin said. "I am greatly disturbed."

"And for what reason, Don Santiago?" ·

"We have always paid a high tariff to bring our merchandise into Santa Fe, Don Manuel. But this year the taxes are beyond reason. The duty has gone to fifteen cents a yard on all goods. That brings it to one hundred per cent of the cost in the United States. Excelencia, this is exorbitant."

Armijo sat back in his chair. He selected a cigar and permitted Pino to light it for him. His eyes never left Magoffin. "I have ordered that the customs be increased this year, Don Santiago. There are only fifty wagons. Last year the number of wagons was almost double and the value of the merchandise brought into Santa Fe exceeded one hundred and fifty thousand dollars. This year the trade will come to less than one hundred thousand dollars. The business may rise and fall at the whim of you traders, but the government expenses do not adjust themselves so accommodatingly. Expenses must be paid, por Dios, no matter how few gringos decide to cross the prairies."

"Why should we be penalized for the timidity of others, excelencia?" Magoffin asked. "We who have risked the crossing this year have done so as an act of faith in you. Why punish us?"

"I punish nobody, Don Santiago. It is not a question of punishment. The money must be raised. Expenses cannot be tailored to the moods of traders. Unfortunately, it is the other way round, the value of the taxes must be tailored to the expenses."

"Why should the Americans have to pay virtually all the expenses of the government?" Magoffin said, knowing he was treading on dangerous ground. The objections would undoubtedly prove useless, but it was necessary to make a stand. "I have spoken to my countryman Señor Josias Gregg, who, as you know, remained here all winter. He informs me that you have abolished all taxation for native-born merchants."

135

"It is true," Armijo said. "There is no money among our poor people. They cannot pay taxes. They barely subsist as it is."

"There are New Mexicans who are not so poor," Magoffin said quietly. "There are countrymen of yours who have stores, gambling halls, dancing places. There are others who live in great haciendas and are wealthy. It is not just that they should be absolved of most of the responsibility in supporting the government while Americans, even those who have become Mexican citizens, have their taxes doubled."

"I am not interested in justice!" Armijo shouted. "Not in what you call justice, Don Santiago. I am interested in my people. They are poor. They hunger. They are sick. They are unable to pay taxes. I will not demand money where there is no money. I will not squeeze them so that blood comes from their eyes. Do not speak to me of justice." He puffed silently on his cigar and then said, more quietly: "I am a business man too, Don Santiago. I know that even with all the taxes you still make greater profits here than you could anywhere else. You know this as well as I do." Suddenly his face flamed. "You dare come to me and speak this way only because you lent me money last year to fight Gonzales. You believe that gives you the right to come here and insult me."

Magoffin ignored the last part of Armijo's remarks. "It is true, Don Manuel, that we make greater profits than we could selling our merchandise in the United States. But we also risk our lives every time we cross the prairies to come here."

"That is your concern, Don Santiago—your concern and the concern of the other Americans. No one asks you to risk your lives. No one asks you to cross the prairies. You have the privilege to remain in your own country and make your living there." He stood up and said with dignity: "This is a sovereign country, Don Santiago, as free and as independent as your own. You are my friend and you have been loyal and helpful to me and your presence brings pleasure to my heart, but when you come here and protest against taxes, you are not protesting against the casual whim of an amusing Mexican. I know what your people think of my people. But this is our country. I am the Governor of New Mexico. And you are a guest in a foreign land. You will obey the laws or you will leave."

Magoffin flushed slightly and lowered his head. He had thought he and Armijo were beyond this.

Don Manuel remained standing. Suddenly he smiled with charm. He walked around the desk and put his hand on Magoffin's shoulder. "Forgive me for speaking in such a manner to an old compadre. My mind is heavy with worries. It is better that old friends do not quarrel."

The Governor's face was warm and friendly. Magoffin sighed. Armijo was a complicated man, he thought, a man who never entirely meant anything he said, who always meant a little of everything he said. Armijo was aware of one thing, however: none of them, having tasted the wine of the Santa Fe trade, could ever do anything else. The trader returned the smile. "There is nothing to forgive, excelencia. You do what you must do."

Before he departed he invited them all to attend the baile he was giving several nights hence.

3

ESQUIPULAS CABALLERO shouldered his way through the teeming streets. There could be no doubt that the gringos were here. He looked around with distaste. The whole town was drunk.

People already were arriving at the house Santiago Magoffin had hired for his baile. Don Esquipulas wished he could go there directly. His throat was dry for some of Magoffin's champagne. He wondered why Ramón Baca had asked him to stop by at his house first. It was a request he could not refuse. Since Don Ramón had got married several months before, something in their friendship was lost and he did not want to offend him.

On his way to the Casa Baca he passed a religious procession, led by a priest, followed by chanting men and women. There was an epidemic of a typhoidal nature in the city, and the priest and the people were seeking divine aid. Caballero crossed himself. The procession moved on, making bizarre contrast to the drunks.

Ramón greeted him cordially as he entered the house. "Hey, chico, you are late. Do you want all of Don Santiago's fine wine to be drunk before we can get a taste of it?"

Caballero grinned. "The streets are as filled as a jungle. One has to fight one's way through."

Ramón's wife, Lupe, a short, bright-eyed girl, hugged Caballero. He kissed her on the lips. She pretended to swoon. "Dios mío," she sighed, "why do you not teach your good friend Ramón to kiss in such a manner?"

"It is nothing, woman," Baca said indifferently. "Every man has a special talent for kissing the wife of a friend."

Lupe put her hands on her hips. Her eyes sparkled dangerously. "Is that true? And do you have this special talent also, hombrecito?"

"For certain."

"I have warned you before, chiquito. I will remove it from you."

"The kiss, mi amor?" Baca asked blandly.

"Not the kiss." Lupe leaned forward from her waist. "You have insufficient for your own bed, husband. Let me not find that you burn the lips of anyone else. You will wake one morning and find yourself a capon!"

"The curse of a jealous woman," Baca sighed.

Baca and Lupe looked at each other. She crinkled her nose, Baca jutted his lower lip, and Caballero felt suddenly apart. He wondered again why Baca had asked him to call.

"You did not tell me that a handsome officer was coming," a woman's voice said.

Caballero looked toward the door. "Soledad!"

"Who is this strange man, Don Ramón?" Soledad asked.

"An army officer, mi chula."

"If one can call an ensign an officer," Lupe sniffed.

"Silence, woman," Baca said sternly. "Your husband holds that rank."

"I know that," Lupe said.

"Do you recognize this creature?" Baca asked Caballero.

"It is a familiar face."

"The body is not so familiar?" Baca took the girl by the hand and led her toward Caballero. "It arrived from the City of Mexico with a little label. The identification was Soledad María Concepción Abreu." He turned to her. "Smile, bonita. This one is called Esquipulas Caballero. Behind the uniform is a man."

"So it is rumored," Lupe said.

"Soledad, little light of my life!" Caballero felt a warmth flow through him. His loneliness vanished, like a damp place under the glow of the sun. His impulse was to throw his arms around her and kiss her and yet he could not bring himself to do it. He said, feebly: "Welcome to Santa Fe."

"Thousand thanks, señor," Soledad said gravely. "It is a greeting filled with wild passion."

"You are not the wife of a dear friend," Lupe explained. "There is a particular greeting for such."

"I noticed that," Soledad said.

"How does one greet a visitor from the capital of the country?" Caballero asked.

"The hand may be kissed," Soledad said. She extended her hand.

"Poof," Lupe said.

Caballero took the hand and made a leg. He kissed the fingers. He felt them tighten around his own.

"Walk around it," Baca suggested. "It looks equally good from all sides. Observe it, amigo, from this position if you will. From here it looks particularly good." He tilted his head at her bosom.

"Ramón," Lupe said warningly.

"Be tranquil," said Baca. "It is only that for the moment my dearest friend appears to be bewildered. I wish only to guide his eyes to where they belong."

"Come with me," Lupe said. "Leave them alone for a few minutes. His eyes will guide themselves."

When they were gone, Caballero stared at Soledad, conscious of behaving like a gawking peasant. He could not understand the hesitancy he felt before this girl he had known for so many years. He tried to recall his feelings of the year before when he had last spoken to her at Magoffin's baile. There was no faltering then.

And she was unchanged. Her face was as before and her eyes were as before, clear and candid, and yet there was a difference. She held her head with a kind of imperiousness he did not remember and there were a brightness and a gloss that were new. The months in the City of Mexico had given these to her and he knew that he felt truly provincial before her.

She was dressed in the style favored by foreigners, and though it did not look unattractive on her, neither did it help him. Her dress fitted snugly at the waist, and the sleeves and shoulders were puffed, but the neckline was cut lower than he had seen before and her breasts were squeezed upward.

"You look long, Don Esquipulas," she said.

"There are many months of not looking to make up."

"Does what you see please you, señor?"

The voice was the same as he had remembered it and yet there was something else there too, a secret amusement. He felt the wall between them and he broke through it angrily and kissed her violently on the lips. He felt her mouth open and she did not move away.

She said, demurely: "Thanks to God, hombre, that it is not restricted altogether to the wives of good friends."

"That was not the kiss from a little friend."

"It was not."

"You have been well tutored."

"You are right, señor. There are men in the City of Mexico."

He was furious for a moment. Then he shook his head and smiled. "Soledad, mi princesa, we say all the wrong things to each other. We have not seen each other for a long year and we begin with quarreling. Truly, mi corazón, I am filled with happiness at the sight of you. Truly, welcome to Santa Fe, and the city is more beautiful for your return."

She inclined her head. "You get better and better, mi caballero."

"You are back to stay?"

"No."

"Why not? Where do you go?"

"I have come up with a lawyer from Chihuahua to see whether there is anything left of my father's estate. Then I return to Chihuahua, where my mother stays with my sister. It was something my mother should have done, more properly, come here with the lawyer, but she is ill. She has not yet recovered from the assassination of my father." Her voice broke.

He felt the coldness again. For a moment or two it had been as it was before, but now the chill closed in.

She touched a lace kerchief to her lips. "It was very bad at the beginning when I first heard what had happened, but I thought I had grown used to it." She shook her head. "It is strange and difficult to be here without him."

He took her hand, wondering that she did not feel the coldness. "I cannot tell you, preciosa, how deeply I grieved for you."

Her eyes looked away. "For three days he remained, butchered like a sheep, before someone found the Christian charity to collect him and give him burial." She lifted her head and said proudly: "But it was said he died well. Others whimpered like wounded dogs but he died well. The barbarians wanted screams of agony, but he gave them none. His brother, Ramón, died as a coward, but the other one, my uncle Marcelino, and my father, they died as Abreus. Those two had no fear to face the Abreus who went before them."

He stirred with her pride. There was nobility in it, a clarion call that he could respond to and share. He had a name that was as old as hers and it was language that was in his blood. He held her hand tightly and looked upon her with love and thought how much they shared, and then he remembered.

Truth had many faces, he thought. He believed in what he had done, and when he listened to Don Manuel there were few doubts; and when he was with his father, there were no doubts and his father had honor. But there could be no final truth. Because to her it would be only that he had assisted in the slaying of her father. The wall was there again, but it was not the same wall. He could not break through this wall. He thought bitterly that he could not love her, either for herself or for her pride, that it had been taken from him.

He forced himself to remember how she had opened her mouth to him when he kissed her, how expert she was in that, and he made himself think of how many others had kissed her to give her such skill. He thought beyond that, looking at her womanliness.

Her eyes were wet. She shook her head with annoyance. She opened her large bag and began to fumble inside. She took out her guagito filled with tobacco and a small packet of hojas. She separated one leaf from the rest and sprinkled some tobacco on it and rolled a cigarette swiftly. She took out little gold tongs and snapped them over the cigarette. When she spoke, her voice was calmer.

"Only how did it happen so quickly, Don Esquipulas? How did Governor Pérez lose so swiftly and so completely? There were merely Indians up there, mongrels, savages, untrained. How did they organize so well and defeat Pérez and take over the capital, and no one to stop them?"

He made a cigarette for himself. He needed time to answer. "It has happened before," he said slowly. "Pérez made many mistakes. He was not loved. No one would fight for him. He had broken up the presidial companies, and only the troops could have saved him."

She nodded slowly. "It was the single thing that no one in the City of Mexico could comprehend. The news came down in little pieces. It was many weeks before I learned the truth of what had happened to my father and my uncles. My mother was in Chihuahua at the time or surely she would have shared his fate." She held the tongs to her lips, but she did not draw on the cigarette. "I tried to believe it was not true. My father had been filled with so much life and so many plans when he bade me farewell. I could not see him as dead." Her face hardened and he thought then she looked like Santiago Abreu. "The story is not yet told. The truth will come forth. God will not permit such sin to remain forever in the dark."

"It is ended now, muchachita," he said, wondering how much longer he could listen.

"It is ended. And it was ended well. I spent a day on my knees in church giving thanks to Don Manuel Armijo for making it end well."

"Don Manuel?"

"I was told it was a sin to give prayers of thankfulness for vengeance. I was told that Nuestro Señor Jesucristo taught that vengeance was evil. I was told it was not Christian to glory in revenge. But there is something older than the teachings of Christ!"

"Soledad!"

"It is written: 'An eye for an eye, and a tooth for a tooth.' Don Manuel understood that. The dead could not be brought to life, but their honor could be avenged. I remember very little about Don Manuel except that he is supposed to have looked upon me in a manner that displeased my father and so was I sent away. It is said Don Manuel is a brute and that his nights are filled with lecheries and that his blood is not pure. That may all be true. But it also is true that he is a man and that there was none other in New Mexico to unsheathe his sword. No one rose but this one who is himself called mestizo. Don Manuel made vengeance for me. I never understood my blood before, but when I heard how he shot Gonzales and the other mongrels I danced with joy. It was said he was too cruel and that he put too many to death, but it appeared to me only that he understood the words 'eye for eye, tooth for tooth.'" Her voice grated. "If only I could have been there, por amor de la Virgen Santísima, if only I could have been there! If only I could have fired the bullet that killed the Indian dog!"

He could listen no longer. "You torment yourself with things that are past, querida. You are young and you are very beautiful and you must not poison your heart with these memories."

"You were there when he was executed, were you not, Don Esquipulas?"

"Yes."

"You must tell me about it. You must tell me everything. You must tell it to me so that I can see it as though I had been there too."

"Not now, Soledad."

She smiled wanly. "You are right. This is not the time."

"What have you found out with your lawyer? Does anything still remain?"

She shook her head, and when she spoke, her voice was as he had remembered it and he could believe now she was not yet eighteen. "Nothing, Esquipulas, nothing. Everything in the house was stolen or destroyed. The house itself is in ruins, as you must have seen. There is nothing left here."

"What do you plan to do now?"

"There is nothing to do. I return to Chihuahua."

"Why do you go away?"

She closed her eyes again and her face, too, was again as he remembered it and there was in it all the years of their lives. He felt himself move toward her in his heart and then she opened her eyes and he could not look at them. "There are still many of my father's affairs to be settled in the City of Mexico," she said. "My sister has four children and a fifth is on the way and my mother is not able to do anything. There is only I. I must bring the disappointing news to them of what I found here and then go again to the City of Mexico until everything is settled."

"And then, chiquita? Then do you return to Santa Fe?"

"To what end? What is there in this hateful place to bring me back to it?" Her eyes filled with tears again and she blinked them furiously. "Wherever I walk I can see only the places where my father walked. His shadow is on all the buildings. His voice is everywhere. I cannot look at the palace without thinking that he is somewhere inside at work and that soon he will finish and come home and cup his hand under my chin and crinkle his eyes and ask me what important things I have done since he saw me last." She shook her head slowly. "Why should I return to Santa Fe, Don Esquipulas?"

His hands moved and he stopped them. "There are many here who love you."

She turned to him, a faint smile on her lips. "Many? Can one be loved by many?" She took his hand and pressed it to her cheek. "Thanks, little brother," she said. "I understand the feelings you have for me. They give my heart warmth."

4

AT THE BAILE, after they were greeted by Magoffin, who made much of Soledad's return, the women excused themselves to make their toilet, and Baca cast his eye about for the refreshment table. Caballero said he would join him presently. Baca cocked his eye shrewdly and said: "You want a few minutes to yourself to absorb this thing of Soledad."

Caballero made himself smile and nod and he strolled out to the patio, where he sat down on a secluded bench. Baca was right, he thought, but not as he had meant it. Caballero felt himself shaking as though he had contracted the fever that was running through the city, but it was for a reason Baca could not know. He thought he had long ago worked out the conflicts connected with Gonzales and the Abreus, but the few minutes with Soledad had

exposed them all again. He had to re-establish a pattern of thinking before he could listen to her again.

He rolled a cigarette and tried to collect his thoughts. For him,
all his life, the sole arbiter of honor was his father, who also was
his commanding officer. "There is nothing for which I must condemn myself," he said with anger. And yet he knew that the load
of it in his heart had lessened his intimacy with Ramón Baca and
that it had just been an evasion to lay the blame for it on his
friend's marriage.

And now this with Soledad, with the exquisite child who was
so much a part of the innocent days. Between them there had always been a sweetness he cherished as he would a jewel. The
thought of dishonesty between Soledad Abreu and himself was
incredible, and yet it was there and now it would always be there.
He could not tell her what was locked in himself. The beginning
was right and the end was right, and if the middle parts were
harsh, they too were essentially right and yet they added up to
the fact that he had had a hand in the slaying of her father and
uncles. He could never tell her that. Even if he could summon the
strength for it the secret was not his to tell. It belonged to his
father and Manuel Armijo.

It was necessary to make some resolution. The devil! Men
died. Men had always died. What was there in death? Everyone
lived close to it always. He threw away his cigarette and walked
back into the house. He accepted a glass of wine from a servant
and drank it rapidly. He took another and then looked for Ramón.
He saw him standing in front of one of the monte tables. He
asked, lightly: "Hola, monito, do you make your fortune?"

"I just watch."

"Where are the ladies?"

Baca screwed up his face. "They are doing something called
making up. You will find out all about it one day. A woman
spends half the day preparing her face for a baile, and as soon as
she arrives at the baile she must go somewhere to prepare her
face." He shook his head. "It is very puzzling and one of the
mysteries no married man ever solves. Speaking of marriage, chico,
why do you not speak for the Abreu?"

"Soledad?"

"She is the only Abreu present, unfortunately, so I can be

speaking of none other. She is not without beauty, as you have already noticed, and you both know each other well so there would be no surprises."

Caballero lifted his glass quickly to his lips. "Surprises?" He laughed.

"The most dangerous things in marriage, I assure you."

"What kind of surprises, little fool?"

Baca shook his head. "Those are secrets of the trade, señor. You are not of the brotherhood."

"Secrets from me?"

Baca pretended to reconsider. "I will tell you of a little one because you are a true friend. Would you believe that Lupe smokes three cigarettes in the morning before she does anything else? Always three. She makes three of them at once and smokes them and then, but only then, can there be any thought of anything else. Now, that was a great shock to me and on occasion it has proved difficult. You would not believe how long it can seem sometimes for a woman to finish three cigarettes. There are other things, far worse, but they are not for your innocent ears. But this Abreu. The two of you grew up almost in each other's pockets, so to speak. A curious conception, but true. There is very little with which you could surprise each other. It is a rare opportunity, amigo. No surprises and a woman with the face of an angel and the body of—ea, pues, let us say she is lacking in nothing. Take her quickly, hombrecito, before someone else snatches her."

"You are prejudiced because she is of your blood."

"There is nothing the matter with the blood. There is none better. Your children would hold their heads high."

"One marriage between the two of us is enough. You are like the fox in the fable who lost his tail. You want everyone to share your misery."

"Here they come," Baca said. "Look at the Abreu, big fool! Would you truly call it misery?"

Caballero saw men and women pause in their conversation and turn their eyes to look at her as she strode across the room with almost mannish briskness. She held herself with the air of a duchess, Caballero thought, and he felt the pride for her again. Her dress was of blue taffeta shot with undertones of silver, and in the brilliantly lighted room it brought out the whiteness of her skin. He knew what must be going through the minds of women who spent days with clay and alegría on their faces to lighten their swarthy complexions. At that moment, he thought, she would grace the court at Madrid.

"What have you two been doing?" Baca asked. "You have been gone half the evening and nothing about you is changed."

"Hush, talking bird," Lupe said. "Fetch us some champagne."

Soledad surveyed the room with bright expectancy. It was, Caballero thought instantly, her party expression, developed at how many affairs in Mexico? "How does it look to you, querida, your first baile in Santa Fe?"

She shook her head, puzzled. "I seem to see the strangest faces. Who are these curious people, and where are the people I used to know?"

Baca, returning with two glasses of wine, said: "In the calabozo."

"Quiet, fool!" Lupe said. "Your swollen tongue will lead you to a cell marked Baca."

"I am a Baca," he agreed impassively. "I speak. It is a trait of my family. One named Baca was Governor of New Mexico when Manuel Armijo was stealing sheep. The faces my niece seeks are no farther away than in the jail across the plaza." He handed each of the ladies a glass. "It is a manner Don Manuel favors to terminate all arguments. When anyone opposes him he simply orders him arrested. Presto! No more opposition."

"And you will be next," Lupe said angrily.

"Madre mía!" Soledad said suddenly. "There is the blacksmith to whom my father used to bring our horses."

"It is the same man," Baca said. "He now owns the largest stable in Santa Fe. The yanquis patronize him exclusively. They have heard it said Don Manuel himself has an interest in the stable, which is something I can easily accept. The blacksmith now is an important man in Santa Fe." He emptied his glass. "Pérez would not have remained for two minutes in the same room with him."

"I think my father would not have either," Soledad said. "But it is the new way of treating people. This might almost be a baile in the City of Mexico. There the shopkeepers are to be seen everywhere too. I did not think the infection had spread here."

"Here is more infection," Baca said. "Behold, El General Manuel Armijo."

The Governor, with Doña María Trinidad on his arm, was just entering the room. The music did not lessen and the guests still conversed and yet a kind of tenseness seemed to pervade the room. The women standing nearest the door curtsied deeply and then drew their rebozos more tightly around their shoulders. The men bowed and then resumed their conversation instantly as though to show they had no fear of speaking.

"He is bigger than I remembered him," Soledad said.

Esquipulas Caballero looked at her sharply. Her face startled him. There was on it a curious expression of judiciousness.

"He is a man," Lupe said.

"How do you know that, woman?" Baca asked, suddenly furious. "Has he spread your legs?"

"No one but you has done that," Lupe said quietly. "But I can recognize a man."

Armijo was in the uniform he now wore almost exclusively. A brilliant red sash bound his waist, and another cut diagonally across his chest. The gilded pommel of his dress sword glittered. His high, black boots were like polished glass. Doña María Trinidad, wearing a white low-cut, native blouse and a dark, red skirt, looked almost drab next to her husband, despite the large diamond pendant that hung from her neck and the rings and bracelets on her fingers and arms.

They watched Magoffin step up instantly and kiss Doña María Trinidad's hand.

"El Don has a strong stomach," Baca said.

"Is that witch his wife?" Soledad asked.

"None other. For her I could almost sympathize with Armijo."

Magoffin was bowing deeply to the Governor. He gestured to the refreshment table, and Don Manuel nodded amiably. The Governor murmured something to his wife and bowed to her and then he accompanied Magoffin to the table. Doña María Trinidad was immediately surrounded by half a dozen young men.

"Observe the roosters around the aged hen," Baca said. "They can see their careers resting at the junction of her legs."

"Enough," Caballero said.

"It is the stepladder for unmarried men. It is the next best thing to having a complaisant wife or daughter."

"Silence," Caballero said. "You speak of your commanding officer, and of his lady."

"But only before my wife and my niece and my friend," Baca said. He swayed slightly.

"You are drunk," Caballero said.

"No, amigo, I am not drunk," Baca said tiredly. "It is a sickness of the heart that I feel, and that is quite a different thing."

"Perhaps we had better go for a little walk outside."

Baca took his arm and squeezed it. "It is not necessary. Do not worry for me, chico. It is a poison that lies within me, and now and then I must rid myself of it. I shall behave from now on. I shall be the perfect ensign." His homely face twisted painfully. "I should play the part without fault. I have held the rank longer than any officer in the army."

Lupe seized his hand. "I love you, husband, even though you die an ensign."

He kissed her fingers tenderly. "I thank you, mi alma. And with Don Manuel's policy to promote only peasants I probably shall."

"I would have it no other way," she said fiercely. "Your pride is my pride."

"We have that, Lupe." He added in a very low voice: "There is little of it around here, and it grows less."

Soledad had not taken her eyes from Doña María Trinidad. "How can he bear to live with that lump?"

Baca shook his head solemnly and raised his hand. "I will not answer that. I am reformed."

"And now you too, Soledad?" Caballero asked harshly.

"He is a handsome man and she is an ugly old woman." Soledad tossed her head.

"I remain silent," Baca said. "You may interpret my silence as indicating accord."

"And that chemise! How does she dare so to expose those enormous breasts?"

"They are her advertisement," Baca murmured. "For a lieutenancy I could not bring myself to come within a dozen feet of them."

Soledad giggled. Caballero turned on her irritably. Her face was flushed. "I think that is enough, señorita," he said.

She whirled, her eyes snapping. He regarded her quietly for several moments and then she lowered her head. "You are right, Don Esquipulas. My uncle's attitude is contagious."

"But only for the wife."

The light came into her eyes again. "I have asked forgiveness, señor. It is enough."

"There is nothing to forgive," he said stiffly.

She held her hands crossed on her breast. "Look at him, Lupe. El caballero is jealous. Lupe, Lupe, there is some small chance for me."

"Ah, diablo!" Caballero said.

"And now the temper rises," Soledad said, her body weaving slightly from side to side. "He is truly jealous." The mockery left her face, and when she spoke again, there was wonder in her voice. "It is true, querido, is it not? Suddenly I have ceased to be your little sister."

He looked away.

"I am serious," she said. She touched his cheek. "There is no need to say anything. This has now become a large night."

He looked at her to see if she was still laughing at him and, seeing she was not, he felt himself open to her; and then there was the wall and it was so plain to him, so solid and thick, that he could not understand why it was not apparent to her, why she remained as she was, her face filled with wonder. He held up his hand. "Our glasses are empty," he said shortly.

"Let us go to the wine table," Soledad said instantly. Her voice became crisp. "I desire to be introduced to Governor Armijo."

Lupe shook her head sadly.

5

Don Manuel raised his head as they approached him. He frowned when he saw Caballero. The burden of his gratitude to the Caballeros, father and son, had grown heavy. Don Manuel had on several occasions been on the point of moving the young man up a rank, and each time he had held back. It was as though a reward, somehow, would underline his debt, increase his obligation rather than relieve him of it.

He recognized Baca and his wife. The face of the other young woman was vaguely familiar.

The officers stood at attention when they reached the Governor. The ladies curtsied. Caballero said: "Excelencia, may I have the honor to present Señorita Soledad Abreu. Her father was Don Santiago Abreu."

Don Manuel's eyes narrowed. Then he smiled. "You have been long from Santa Fe, señorita." He recalled now how, because he had found her attractive, her father had sent her south. She looked familiar to him for another reason he could not understand.

"I have been gone for twelve months, excelencia," she said.

"If I remember correctly, you have been in the City of Mexico."

"You honor me in remembering, excelencia."

"But you were little more than a child when you left. You have blossomed like a rose in Castile. You must have bathed in the warmth of compliments down there."

"Thousand thanks, excelencia." Her eyes twinkled. "Then your excellency does not disapprove of my appearance?"

"Disapprove? How disapprove?"

"My dress, excelencia. I have been informed that your excellency frowns on other than the native style and that I risk your excellency's wrath in wearing this dress from France."

He laughed. "But you took the risk! It is true, señorita, I believe New Mexico should remain Mexican. I have made it a firm policy—Mexican speech, Mexican manners, Mexican dress."

"And your policy is being obeyed, excelencia. I believe I am the only native lady present in alien dress."

"I should be stern with you, señorita," he said with pretended gruffness. "But I find that difficult. I will excuse you because in a sense you are a visitor. Additionally, you make too lovely a picture to be condemned."

Baca made a slight move and Caballero looked at him warningly.

"Thank you, excelencia," Soledad said.

"May we have permission to fill our glasses, excelencia?" Caballero asked.

"Of course, please," Armijo said. The meaning of her face continued to evade him.

Caballero pushed Baca ahead of him. "Control yourself, fool. I find it as disgusting as you do."

"Do you?" Baca asked. He gave his glass to a servant. He glared at Lupe as she joined them. "Did you have to leave them alone?"

Don Manuel said to Soledad: "In return for my leniency, señorita, I will beg a favor."

"Of me, excelencia?"

"You are recently returned from the capital of the country. There are questions I would ask of you. This is not the proper place. Would you honor me by calling at my office?"

"Willingly, excelencia. I was going to ask your excellency for the same favor. I have things to say, too, and I find a baile an inappropriate place to say them. May I call tomorrow, or would that be too soon?"

"The moment you are announced is the moment I shall be free of all other duties."

"You are kind, excelencia. I was hoping to gain the favor of an audience quickly."

"You do not mean you plan to leave Santa Fe again?"

"Yes, excelencia, within the next few days."

"But you have just arrived."

She told him of her reason for coming.

"I have said nothing about your father, señorita," he said quietly. "I did not want to bring unhappiness to your beautiful face. I will say it very quickly and then you must forget and amuse yourself with the pleasures here. Accept my sympathies and my grief that at your birth you were named too prophetically."

"I was well named," she said in a low voice. "Since I have returned to Santa Fe I have felt a solitude that almost is unbearable."

"The death of Don Santiago was tragic. But we will talk of it no longer at this time. That is an order from your Governor." He stared at her.

"You seem to look at me very strangely, excelencia. Is there something about me that displeases your excellency?"

"Nombre de Dios, but no!" Then it came to him and he stiffened. "Forgive me, señorita. Since I first saw you tonight I have had the feeling your face was familiar to me. I have just come to understand why. You look not unlike my first wife, God give rest to her soul."

"I did not know your excellency was married before."

"She died giving birth to our child," he said with extreme gentleness. "Both Doña Rafaela and the child went together."

She touched his hand instinctively. "It is as God wills, excelencia."

"God's will must be accepted." He looked down at her fingers on his wrist. "It is in more than your appearance, señorita. Now that I know, I can see it in many things—in your mannerisms, in the expressions on your face, even in the sound of your speech. She too was bold, as a woman may be bold, as you are bold."

"I meant no boldness toward your excellency."

"Please, please, señorita. I have been bemused listening to you and watching you and I did not know why. It was as though the years were falling away."

"What was her name, excelencia?"

"She was a Chaves. Her mother was a Sarracino."

"Then we were not unrelated, excelencia. The mother of my mother was a Sarracino."

At that moment two young, laughing girls tiptoed up to them. One of the girls threw an eggshell at the head of the Governor. The shell burst and he was covered with scented liquid. The girls, giggling, ran off. He said, laughing: "I am allowed by custom to chase the young lady who did that before she regains her seat. Then I would be entitled to a kiss in payment for her audacity." He sighed humorously. "Unfortunately the old wound in my leg does not permit me to play my part in the game."

The girl who had thrown the shell returned immediately. "In that case, excelencia," she said with merriment, "the rules of the game should be relaxed in your behalf." She inclined her head demurely. "I count myself fairly caught."

Don Manuel swept her into his arms and kissed her on the

lips. When he released her she pretended to swoon. "Excelencia, you take the game most seriously." She fluttered her eyes. "I need a stimulant to recover."

Don Manuel, his face beaming, snapped his fingers. "A servant handed him a glass of champagne. "If my infirmity did not forbid, señorita, I would command that you be my partner for the next fandango."

The girl walked off, blushing with pleasure, her hips swinging provocatively under her loose skirt. And then he remembered what Soledad had said to him and he turned to her eagerly. He was astonished at the anger on her face.

She curtsied with icy politeness. "There are many persons who seek the ear of the Governor at a time such as this. I have enjoyed your attention overly long. If your excellency will excuse me I will rejoin my friends."

He bowed, his eyebrows drawn in puzzlement, and when he raised his head she was gone. He watched her walk rapidly toward Caballero and the Bacas, her head held high, and his throat was suddenly dry. He lifted his finger to a servant and drained the glass at a single draught.

When Soledad reached the others she said: "The little devil." She tapped her foot furiously.

"Which little devil?" Caballero asked.

"The Corvera girl. Madre de Dios! The one who threw the eggshell."

"It is the custom," he said evenly. "Have you forgotten so quickly? Do they not follow the old traditions in the City of Mexico?"

"They do not drench the President of Mexico with stinking cologne. La puta!"

"You are wrong, Soledad. The girl is no whore."

"And Don Manuel is not the President of Mexico," Baca said.

"He is the chief of New Mexico, and it is fitting to treat him as such. And did you see the way she shook her behind? Why did she not ask him openly to crawl into bed with her?"

"There was no need," Baca said, watching the bubbles rise in his glass. "She knows he will ask her, in time."

6

MAGOFFIN MOVED from place to place ministering to the comforts of his guests with the practiced ease of an experienced host, his keen, blue eyes observing everything that was going on. He encountered the Governor as Don Manuel was rising from a monte table. The dealer knew his business. Don Manuel was jingling a handful of coins.

The Governor was in a pleasant mood. He took Magoffin by the arm and walked away with him. Looking across the room to where Doña María Trinidad was seated with her coterie of admirers, "She is a happy woman, Don Santiago," he said.

"It is my hope that all my guests are happy."

Armijo squeezed his arm. "There is no need for the renowned Magoffin tact at this moment, my old friend." He gestured with his chin. "The ugly chick is happy among roosters."

"Yes, excelencia."

"One could not tell from the outside what fires lie within," Armijo said musingly.

Magoffin shifted uncomfortably. It was the kind of confidence he preferred to avoid.

"We are good friends, Don Santiago," Armijo said.

"Many thanks, excelencia."

"Eh? You and I? Of course," Armijo said warmly. "But I was not referring to us. It was of Doña María Trinidad and myself that I spoke." He gazed at his wife. "There are many reasons why I am thankful I am Governor of New Mexico. One of the most important is that it has brought happiness to the lonely woman who is my wife and my dearest friend." He smiled curiously. "Do you think it is strange for me to speak in this manner, Don Santiago?"

"You are in your own house, excelencia," Magoffin said.

"Tell me, Don Santiago, do you know the meanings of the word 'cabrón'?"

"I believe so, excelencia."

"It means, firstly, cuckold," Armijo said. "But it has other meanings. It means more truly a man who consents to the adultery of his wife. Among my other titles I am also the chief cabrón in New Mexico."

Magoffin was silent.

Armijo looked at him steadily. "I do not live by the rules, Don Santiago. For me and mine there are rules that belong to us alone."

"Yes, excelencia."

"It would please me greatly, señor, for you to understand that I find happiness in the happiness of my wife." Don Manuel again looked across the room, and for a moment his eye caught the eye of his wife and an expression of felicity spread over his face. "Perhaps there are many kinds of love a man may have for a woman," Don Manuel said. He tightened his fingers on Magoffin's arm. "Come and see me tomorrow, Don Santiago, and we will make a special arrangement for you on the taxes."

Magoffin looked at him in astonishment. Armijo smiled again. "Keep your silence about it, Don Santiago. The favor will be for you alone." He added very quietly: "What I will lose on you I will more than balance in the duties to be imposed on the gringo Carson."

"Carson?"

"This is not a large country, Don Santiago. I hear everything that is said in it. Look, the satire is about to begin. Come, let us listen to it together."

It was several moments before Magoffin could recall Carson to his mind, and then he remembered. He lit a cigar slowly. It was all right to forget about Carson, he thought, but he would take care in the future not to forget Damasio Salazar.

The master of ceremonies who had been supervising the complicated group dancing now waved his cane of office and the maestro on the raised platform where the musicians were seated strummed his guitar loudly. The room quieted instantly.

"Where does your excellency desire to sit?" Magoffin asked.

"In the front, where everyone can see me, of course." Don Manuel grinned. "The people must be able to watch me squirm and so laugh at my discomfort. That is the whole point of the satire."

"I was surprised to hear that your excellency had restored the old custom."

"Were you, Don Santiago? You should not have been. For hundreds of years the Spanish governors permitted their subjects to laugh at them occasionally. I allowed it when I was Governor a decade ago. Santiago Abreu abolished the custom of the satire, and those who followed him did not bring it back. They said it was undignified. They were fools. The people like to feel they are in on a joke, even when the joke is on them."

The two men took seats near the musicians' dais. As Magoffin watched with admiration, Don Manuel entered his part of buffoon immediately. The Governor pretended fear. He pretended embarrassment. He sat gingerly on the edge of his chair as though prepared to make a run for it if the satire got too sharp. The gestures were traditional and Don Manuel did them well; before the first words were sung the guests were chuckling.

The guitarist strummed his instrument and began the old familiar melody, simple and rhythmic as a nursery jingle. A young man named Gilberto Digneo, who was known in Santa Fe for his skill in composing doggerel, stepped forth.

> *"Viva! Viva to our good New Mexican folk,*
> *Who love to do many things, to dance, to sing,*
> *To eat, to drink, to listen to church bells ring,*
> *But most of all to laugh at a joke!"*

He paused and the guitarist played the melody again. The guests chanted the last line. Armijo winced exaggeratedly and the audience roared.

The singer resumed:

> *"Consider the happiness of the poor paisanos,*
> *They have no worry about the weight of gold,*
> *Nor about sheep that are not in the fold,*
> *Nor about houses to keep out the cold,*
> *Nor about wealth, by many others extolled,*
> *For if the truth about this can be told,*
> *It is all taken east by the kind americanos."*

Don Manuel pointed ostentatiously at Magoffin. Many of the guests shouted: "Hola, hola, El Don!" Magoffin grinned.

> *"To the excellent Juan Bautista Vigil give hail,*
> *His interest in his countrymen is without compare,*

157

It fills his heart like the morning air,
Their troubles and worries he strives to share,
Their heartaches and joys are his daily fare,
To prove his love is true and rare,
He carefully reads all of their mail!"

The room swept with laughter. Armijo, shaking with merriment, craned his neck to see Vigil. The postmaster, seated in a corner, laughed ruefully. He shook his fist with pretended anger at the singer, and the guests laughed more loudly.

Magoffin glanced at Don Manuel. The verse had mentioned Vigil but the barb was intended for the Governor. Everyone knew that when Vigil opened the mail he was obeying Don Manuel. The Governor's face was artless.

"The Indians say we love them 'a big heap,'
We love them as brothers,
We love them as mothers,
We love them beyond all others,
To prove it we give them our sheep!"

Magoffin knew that the Indian raids on Mexican herds were growing constantly as the buffalo herds were slowly being decimated. The Indians referred to New Mexicans as their "shepherds." The peasants in the remote villages were bitter about the lack of protection given to them by the government. This, Magoffin reflected, was satire on the grand scale with no holds barred. His respect for Don Manuel was increasing with each stanza.

The singer continued with verse after verse, each a set of lines jabbing at some cause of public discontent. Armijo, Magoffin thought, was superb. He was the supreme mummer. He dodged as though things were being thrown at him. He frowned, he grimaced. His reactions pointed up the satire and he was as much entertainment as the singer.

Watching at his side, Magoffin saw something else. He saw that Don Manuel's eyes never lost their alertness no matter how much he jested, that under the clowning the Governor was listening carefully to what was in truth the public voice of criticism of his administration. Magoffin knew that according to the old custom the singer was given free rein with a guarantee of no reprisal.

He knew too that for weeks before the baile Digneo had been assisted by people everywhere. He silently saluted Don Manuel. Armijo, he thought, did not have Pérez's polished manner of a grandee, but he was attuned to the people he ruled.

"To our Governor, Don Manuel, give hail . . ."

Armijo's face was without expression. Magoffin could see some of the guests moving worriedly in their seats.

> *"His courtesy to his enemies is everywhere known,*
> *This kindness he has always shown,*
> *Throughout the years it has steadily grown,*
> *And in this clemency he is almost alone,*
> *Ask those in the palace jail!"*

This time the verse was followed by no hilarity. The room held a dead silence. Men and women looked aghast at the temerity of the singer. Magoffin alone saw the white line that cut across the Governor's lips. Don Manuel allowed the silence to continue almost to the breaking-point and then in an expansive gesture he raised both arms and laughed, a loud, clear laugh intended to carry to every part of the sala. The laugh flashed across the room like a bolt of lightning, and the tension snapped instantly. The guests echoed the laugh, nervously at first, and under their high-pitched sounds were the booming roars of Don Manuel and finally the nervousness was gone and the laughter everywhere was free.

Don Manuel took a handful of coins from his pocket and tossed them on the dais. This signaled a similar rain from others. The flinging of the money was in itself a subtle thing, Magoffin realized. By it Don Manuel indicated he understood the satire was ended, and by recognizing that, he showed that he accepted the gibe at him as the crowning point and that nothing that could be said thereafter could surpass it. The people understood instantly that he was showing them he took the most pointed sarcasm for himself, and as he limped away, the laughter began again, and this time it was laughter of affection.

7

Don Guadalupe Miranda entered Armijo's office with an armful of papers. Don Manuel raised his eyes in mock despair. "More?"

"More and more," the secretary said.

"And it makes you happy to see me labor."

Miranda nodded contentedly. "It does, excelencia."

"I know. You still like to see your pupil practicing his lessons. I remember, maestro, how you used to say: 'Work, work, always work, read more, study more, write more.' Well, secretario, are you satisfied with your student?"

"Most satisfied, excelencia. Especially with the signature." Miranda rolled his eyes. "It is the most beautiful in New Mexico."

"Well, then, what have we here? Papers and more papers. I drown in papers!" He took them from his secretary and let them cascade on the desk. "Papers from all over. From the North District, from the South District, from the City of Mexico, from Chihuahua, from Durango. I suppose I must begin to look through them and see what they are about before any others come along."

Don Manuel thumbed through the papers. "Indian trouble with the Lagunas. A man from Bado is accused of theft. An Apache woman at Las Vegas says she was raped." He looked at the mass of papers in sudden disgust. "Where else in the world is the governor of a country bothered with such trivialities?"

"It was your excellency's own idea to dissolve the subprefectures and the lower courts," Miranda said carefully.

"Of course! How else could I get absolute control? Besides subprefects and judges cost money." He looked up at Miranda and grinned like a small boy caught in a pantry. "I know what is going through your mind, Don Guadalupe. If I want to hold a tight rein I have no business complaining about details. You are right. I consider myself properly rebuked by my old teacher."

Miranda removed his steel-rimmed glasses and wiped them. "Do not use the word 'rebuke,' excelencia," he protested, blinking slowly.

"No, you are quite right, maestro. The work is necessary and

I shall read through each paper before the day is out. But I will not pretend it interests me."

When he was alone he jumped up and began to pace nervously in the room, stopping now and then to look out on the plaza. He wondered when she would call. She had been in his mind from the moment of his waking. Each time Miranda had come in to announce a visitor he had grown tense, thinking it might be she. This was not a day when he could concentrate on the problem of an Apache woman getting raped.

It was not that she truly resembled Doña Rafaela. There was a little something, in the manner she held her chin, in the sudden widening of her eyes, but it was very little. The thing was more in him than in her. The pressures were so strong even that little was enough. After all the years he was still unable to forget Doña Rafaela. Perhaps it was only that for years he had been seeking a frame into which he could fit the picture he carried in his mind.

Juan Bautista Vigil bustled in with his summation of the latest batch of mail going out of Santa Fe. The postmaster was particularly concerned about a letter sent by an American who lived permanently in Santa Fe, a merchant named Pickett, to a friend in San Antonio de Bexar, Texas. Vigil was offended at the Governor's lack of response to that hated word Texas. Although the Texans had failed to respond to Gonzales's appeal for help, fear of that country was never far removed from the minds of New Mexicans. "Señor Pickett says the American merchants are unhappy about the new impost levies," Vigil said grumpily.

"That does not surprise me," Don Manuel said indifferently. He thought of how it would be to take her to his bed.

"He says the discontent is not limited to Americans, but that the New Mexican people are discontented."

"He lies." There would be pride there.

"He says the army is restless."

"He lies again." There would be resistance.

"He says this discontent exists not only among the peasants; that there are many influential persons—citizens, army officers, ricos—who would not be unhappy to see Texas make good its claim that the boundaries of Texas include to the Río del Norte."

Armijo sat erect. "What do you say?"

Vigil laughed mirthlessly. "So you begin to listen."

"What was the last thing you said?" Vigil repeated it. "More lies," Armijo said angrily. "My officers are loyal. What the ricos and the rest think is of no interest to me."

"Shall I destroy this letter?"

"Reseal it and send it on its journey."

"But this is dangerous sedition, Don Manuel."

"Since we know its contents and the name of the man who wrote it, it no longer is dangerous. It is more dangerous unsent."

Shaking his head dolefully, the postmaster left. There were other callers. It was not until just before four o'clock in the afternoon that Soledad came. He felt a tightness in his groin. The resemblance was stronger than he had thought. She was dressed in a riding habit, English style, and she carried a crop and he knew that she was defying him. She was strong as he was strong. The room was suddenly warm. He heard the buzzing of flies. "Come in, señorita, you bring sunshine into my office."

She curtsied. Her cheeks were pink from the riding. "Do I disturb, excelencia?" She looked at the desk piled high with papers. "You are busy, I think."

"I am not busy. You have been riding." While the day dragged out, minute after minute.

"I wanted again to see the Sangre de Cristos. I used to ride there often with my father. It was little use, excelencia. Even the mountains appear different now."

"It was the wrong time of day. The sun was too high. The Sangre de Cristos do not stain until the sun is setting."

"It was not the hour, excelencia." She sat down in a chair near the desk. "Forgive me for taking you from your affairs of state, excelencia. But I could not speak at the baile last night nor could I leave Santa Fe without giving you my thanks."

"Your thanks? For what, señorita?"

"My name is Abreu, excelencia."

"I know your name," he said slowly.

She gripped the crop. "When I heard the manner of the death of my father I thought I would never again feel anything. I waited for the men of New Mexico to rise and oust this mestizo and avenge the names of Abreu and Pérez and Alaria and Sena and the others. But the men of my country were silent. It appears they were willing to bow their necks to this man who not only was murderer and revolutionary but half-breed as well." Her voice became scornful. "I tried to inspire the officials in the City of Mexico to send an army north for vengeance. But their bodies were too filled with sheep milk. And then it became known to me that after all there was a man left in New Mexico. You, excelencia! When I learned how you avenged the outrage I knew that feelings were still alive in me. I cried with joy!" She raised her head. Her eyes were brilliantly alive. "I was proud that day to be a New Mexican!" She struck her boot with the crop. "Only one thing was lacking, excelencia, and that was that I was not at your side."

He sat spellbound. "And you would not have been useless!"

"Por Dios, and I would not have, Don Manuel! I could do more than this scum that calls itself manhood in New Mexico. I said prayers for your success and I vowed to the Holy Virgin of Guadalupe that one day I would face you and express to you my gratitude. I do so now!"

"I have received no other such reward," he said fervently. "I did only what had to be done."

"Do not depreciate yourself, excelencia. There was no other to do it." The warmth in the room heightened the flush on her cheeks.

"And now, having fulfilled your vow, you make ready to leave Santa Fe," he said.

"Yes, excelencia."

"Why must you leave?"

"I explained to your excellency that I came up here to see if the insurrectos left anything. Now I must return to Mexico."

"Your presence is not needed there. What must be done may be done by writing."

She shook her head. "I must watch the lawyers personally and see that they do not swallow what is left like vultures."

"But you need not remain away after the affairs are settled."

"It will take time, excelencia. My father's business extended as far away as Spain. It is a labyrinth that has to be searched."

"But even that will not take forever," he persisted. "One day there will be no reason for you to remain away from Santa Fe."

She made a cigarette and he held out a light. "There is little reason for me to return to Santa Fe, excelencia."

He got up and walked toward a window. "There are many

reasons for you to return," he said, not facing her. "This is your home. This is where you were born."

"I have no home, excelencia. Gonzales made certain of that. I have nothing but memories, and they do not summon me."

He turned to her. "I will provide you with a dwelling."

Her chin raised. "Thousand thanks, excelencia, but no."

He walked back to her eagerly. "Why not?"

"I own more indebtedness to you now than I can ever pay, excelencia. I can incur no more."

"You owe nothing to me. And the gift will not be from me. It will be a just restitution from the government of New Mexico. Your father served his country well, and for many years. He lost his life and all he owned here in an insurrection that was directed not against him but against the government he represented. The government has a duty to make reparation."

"You sweeten the pill most graciously, excelencia," she said with unconscious coldness. "But I cannot accept what you offer."

He sat down heavily. Because she was an Abreu, he thought. "Do not close your mind to the offer, señorita," he said. "Remember that I do not make the offer in the name of Manuel Armijo. It is as the head of the legally constituted government that I seek to make amends to the daughter of the Judge Abreu."

She looked at him appraisingly and he was unable to meet her eyes. "I think, excelencia, when my father's affairs are settled, there will be funds enough for me to purchase my own house in Santa Fe if I should desire to return here." She stood up. "I will not clutter your day longer. I thank you again from my heart for what you did in my father's behalf. I shall always be beholden to you."

He rose, resting his hands on the desk. "Do not mention it, señorita," he said, his voice as polite as her own, his face sullen.

She was surprised at her dislike for him at that moment and she felt she had to make amends. "Before I go, excelencia, I remember you said last night there were some things you desired to ask of me. Have you forgotten them or have you decided not to ask them after all?" Her mouth hardened. "Or was it only that you wanted to offer me a house in Santa Fe?"

He thought: they are all alike, the dogs and the bitches, in their pride and their rigidness. They opened until one thought they were ordinary beings and then came the arrogance, like a slap.

"There was nothing, señorita. And the offer of a dwelling came to me only after your arrival here."

"I have offended you, excelencia," she said penitently. "Believe me, on the memory of my father, it is the last thing I would do. Let me atone, for favor. I would not go on this note of unpleasantness."

He knew he should let her go. "I did want to question you, señorita, on what they say about me in the City of Mexico."

"I can give you joy there, excelencia." Her voice was remotely mocking. She wondered at this compulsion to hurt him. "In the City of Mexico I have heard from the highest persons in the government only that your excellency is one of the great leaders of the country and that but for your courage and alertness the Gonzales insurrection might have spread beyond the borders of New Mexico."

"They say that?"

"And more. With my own ears I have heard General Santa Anna remark that if there had been a Manuel Armijo in Texas, that territory would never have been able to secede."

Don Manuel beamed. "The general said that? Himself?"

"Himself." He looked, she thought, like a child given a sweet. "I have returned the happiness to your face, excelencia. With your permission, I now will take my leave."

He walked around the desk. "It is I, señorita, who now am debtor." He kissed her hand. "God, and we will see each other again."

"Do you believe so?"

"It was not an expression of certainty," he said. "Consider it a prayer."

She withdrew her hand and curtsied and, filled with confusion, hurried from the room.

8

THERE WERE GUESTS for dinner in the palace that evening. Don Manuel needed all his will to show interest in his friends. He noticed Doña María Trinidad's suppressed excitement. He suspected what lay behind the animation. When the guests were gone at last, she came to him, her eyes sparkling. He tried to respond. "Who is it tonight, Mariquita? What little pigeon have you caged for me?"

"You have spoiled my surprise," she said in disappointment.

"I read it on your face all evening."

She pouted, as though she were comely. "It is Carlota Lucero."

His interest quickened. The Lucero girl was impudent and saucy. "You are an angel." He kissed her on the forehead. She clung to him tightly.

"Hurry, you are late," she said.

He raised her chin with his fingers. "And you are late too, querida?"

She giggled.

"Let us both hurry, then. We must keep neither of them waiting."

He hurried to his room. It might be something with the Lucero. She was the daughter of Ernesto Lucero, an ambitious but unsuccessful merchant who had been trying to persuade Don Manuel to allow him to have a small interest in the Chihuahua trade of the firm of Armijo & Speyer.

The girl was seated, sipping wine. She rose instantly, putting the goblet on a table. She was tall and her complexion was dark, but her features were regular and finely made. Her eyes, which he had remembered for their piquancy, were subdued. He bowed. "I am sorry to have kept you waiting, bonita. My guests were long in leaving." He waited for the pertness. It was now she should say something bold and fresh and then he would begin to feel the excitement. "How old are you, Lolita?"

"Fifteen, excelencia."

He poured himself some brandy. "Drink your wine, chiquita."

"I have had enough, excelencia." She moved her head from side to side like a rabbit seeking escape.

"Come here," he said. He felt his interest wane. "Let me look more closely at you."

She came to his side instantly. "I hope your excellency finds me pleasing."

"Do you, niña? And why?" There was a small quickening.

166

"My father will be angry if I do not satisfy your excellency."

He saw she was trembling. "Are you certain you do not desire more wine?"

"If it would please your excellency."

"Would it please you?" He began to feel irritation.

"My only desire is to make your excellency content with me."

"Then you may stop calling me 'excellency.'"

"If that will please your excellency."

"Call me Don Manuel," he ordered.

She swallowed hard. "Yes, Don Manuel."

"Now you must have more wine. This wine has come all the way from Spain, across the great ocean."

"Has it?" She gripped the cup.

He poured more brandy. "Now, salud, muchacha."

"Salud, excelencia—your pardon, Don Manuel."

He drained the goblet, watching her. Under his gaze she lifted the wine cup to her lips and tried to sip from it. She could not make her throat work. He put his goblet down. He cursed Lucero. He could have repeated word for word what her father must have said to her before sending her to the palace. Without her impudence she was nothing.

He sat on a sofa and called her to his side. He slipped his hand into her loose cotton chemise. "Who has been here before me, niña?"

"Before you? Oh, no one, Don Manuel."

"I am the first?" He closed his eyes and waited for the excitement.

"Yes, excelencia, truly."

"Lola."

"Don Manuel." She tried to smile. "Do my little breasts please you?"

"That is better. So I am the first. That is something, is it not? Do you like this, corazón?"

"It is most pleasant, excelencia. Oh, forgive me!"

He opened the blouse. Her arms crossed instinctively over her breasts, and her eyes became more frightened than ever. He laughed shortly and pulled her toward him. He kissed her breasts and he thought: "Now the feeling will come." There was nothing but the pounding of her heart. "Stand up, Lolita. Now uncross

167

your hands. There is nothing that you should hide. I want to look at you. Now, niña, untie your skirt and drop it, and quickly. You are well made, dulce. Your body was intended to give pleasure to a man."

"I am happy, Don Manuel."

"Have you ever seen a man unclothed?"

"No, Don Manuel."

"Have you longed to see a man disrobed?"

She shivered. "Yes, Don Manuel."

"You have wanted to know for yourself what it is that a man can be to a woman, have you not, Lolita?"

"Yes."

"Now keep your eyes on me. Watch me as I undress."

"I will watch, Don Manuel."

"And now do you see this, niña, this scar on my thigh?"

"I see."

"That is where I was shot in a fight with Indians. It is what makes me limp. Does my lameness offend you?"

"No, Don Manuel."

He picked her up and çarried her to the bed. He kissed her body. "Make sounds, niña," he commanded roughly. "I would know that this does not displease you."

"What kind of sounds, Don Manuel?"

"Nombre de Dios!"

She pulled away in terror. He kissed her more violently. Her body was like ice. Then he felt the tension begin to leave her.

"That is good, Don Manuel. Oh, that is very good."

He pushed her away from him and got out of the bed. He poured more brandy and swallowed the fiery liquid. "Dress, Carlota, and return home."

"Dress?" She sat up slowly. Her long, coarse black hair fell over her face. "Is that the finish?"

"Get dressed."

"Why do you speak to me so harshly?"

"Por amor de Cristo! Put on your clothing and go home."

She began to cry. "I have displeased your excellency."

"You have not displeased. Dress and leave."

She held out her hand. "Do not send me away, excelencia."

"Go, quickly."

"The thing was not finished. It was wrong of me to think only of myself. I did none of the things I should have done for your excellency. Return to the bed, excelencia, and I will think only of you."

He put on his robe. "The time has passed. Dress, Carlota, and go."

She swung her feet from the bed. "My father will be greatly angered."

"Tell him he will receive that which he has asked. He will not be angered."

She pressed her hands under her breasts. Her face was pinched. "Look upon me again, excelencia. You said before that my body was made well. Return to the bed with me and I will work to please you. I will make all the sounds you desire to hear. It was wrong of me not to make the sounds."

The brandy glass shattered in his hand.

"What have you done, excelencia? Your hand is bleeding. Ah, Dios, it is my fault!"

"Go."

She began slowly to dress. "What shall I say to my father?"

"Tell him you were a success."

"I cannot lie to my father. It would be sinful."

"Then tell him nothing." His voice was almost inaudible. "It was nothing of your doing, señorita. Say nothing to him. He will get good tidings from me and there is no need to tell him anything."

She finished dressing, holding her chemise together with a thin hand. "I ask forgiveness for my incompetence, excelencia. I am without experience. It pleased me so much and it was so new I forgot it was your excellency who was to have been pleased. I would try again one night and that time think only of you."

Later he poured brandy over the tiny cuts in his hand and went to bed.

9

THE EARLY MORNING was cool. The buildings in the new sun were the color of pink pearls. The smell of burning piñon filtered into the plaza. Soledad stood at the side of the carriage she would share with James Magoffin. Her face was tight. "I cannot believe he will permit me to leave without saying farewell. And yet he has avoided me since the night of the baile."

"It was not avoiding," Ramón Baca said quickly. "He is an officer. He has duties." He lowered his eyes before hers.

"Are you certain you have everything you will need?" Lupe asked. "The salts with the strong smell if you fell faint?"

"I have everything." She stared at the palace.

"It is useless to look for him," Baca said. "His company is not due to return until tomorrow evening."

"What is it that eats into him, Ramón?"

"You ask that again. I have told you it is your imagination."

"I imagine nothing. He has changed so that of all of him only the outside is the same. Something burns in him all the time. What has done this to him?"

"He needs a woman," Lupe said.

"Poof!" Baca grunted.

"This little one with the homely face was the same way," Lupe said, talking rapidly. "At the beginning when he called at the home of my parents he was a perfect caballero. Dios mío! So kind, so gentle. But then he changed. He became moody and filled with unpleasantness." Lupe nodded knowingly. "It was the last struggle of the selfish male. Immediately afterward he asked for my hand. And look at him now. He is still ugly, but he is the happiest man in Santa Fe. And they all are alike."

"Santa Madre de Dios!" Baca exploded. He caught his wife's eye. "She is right, Soledad."

"The truth, Ramón," Soledad said. "Was it his turn to take a patrol against the Indians at this precise time?"

"These things work on a list that rotates," Baca said vehemently. "Each of us has to take his proper turn."

"And his name came up? The day after the baile?"

"Exactly."

"There was no way he could have made exchange with another officer?"

"Ah, no, Soledad. That is not permitted. Capitán Caballero is very strict about that. Each takes his turn at the proper time and there is no way one may avoid it. It was a most unfortunate coincidence."

She made a cigarette. "It is better that I do not ask you to repeat that on oath, uncle. You are too much of your name to lie."

"Your hamper with food and wine is in the carriage," Lupe said.

"It is his own affair. If he does not want to see me it is no concern of mine." She looked around impatiently. "When does the caravan depart? They have been ready for hours, it seems to me." She puffed rapidly on the cigarette. "Ramón, Ramón, what is it that is troubling him? I can feel it. All our lives he and I have been frank with each other. Neither of us knows the meaning of lies and evasions with the other. Now it is as though his heart is held in a trap. He listens to himself before he speaks, and when he speaks, it is only from a corner of his tongue."

Lupe took her hand. "Don Esquipulas no longer is the same," she admitted. "Even this blockhead has noticed it and has remarked on it to me. But we know no more than you do."

"But you are his friend, Ramón," Soledad said. "It is your duty to find out."

He shrugged. "I have no powers of magic, nor am I priest to whom he may come to confess. No man is closer to my heart, but he has drawn a curtain in front of me as well."

She looked again at the palace. "And that one begged me to remain here and offered me a house."

"For which he would carry the key," Baca said.

Her eyes flashed. "And why not? It was an honest offer, so much for so much."

"Soledad!" Lupe said.

"In many countries it is considered an honor to be mistress to the king," Soledad continued rapidly. "Here this one is no less than king. As the whore to the Governor I might even have a little something to say about this list that makes such opportune coincidences." Her hand trembled as she lifted the cigarette to her mouth.

Lupe's eyes filled with tears. She kissed Soledad tenderly. "He is a bad rooster, this Esquipulas, and he has injured you greatly."

"*He* did not offer me even that," Soledad said.

"He knows that one named Abreu is no whore," Baca said in fury.

Soledad ground the cigarette under her shoe. "We will allow it to remain at that. Here comes Don Santiago. I believe that we now leave. I thank you both for all your kindness to me."

Lupe held her tightly. "Soledad, chiquita mía, do not think too hard on this thing with Caballero. Whatever it is, it will pass. Everything passes. Remember only that Santa Fe is your home and you must return here."

Magoffin came up to them, smiling. "Are you ready, señorita?"

"Yes, Don Santiago."

"You have forgotten nothing?"

"Nothing, thanks, Don Santiago."

"Then if you will do me the honor to get into my carriage we will begin our journey, con el favor de Dios."

She looked around slowly, to the Sandia Mountains to the south, to the rippling Jemez range in the west, brightening in the rising light; to the Sangre de Cristos in the east, now dark and without blood. She kissed Lupe and then Baca and entered the carriage.

"Is there a message for Don Esquipulas?" Lupe asked, hesitantly.

"Not a word."

Magoffin gave the signal to the driver, and the carriage pulled away. From a window in the palace Don Manuel watched the dust rise and then settle again.

1

SOLEDAD ABREU returned to Santa Fe in the early fall of
1840. When she left the city, she promised herself she was breathing the dust of the plaza for the last time, but even then she knew
she would come back.

From Chihuahua she journeyed to the City of Mexico, and
while the lawyers wrangled over her father's estate she threw herself into the gay life of the national capital. Her beauty and her
name gave her success, as it had before, and for a little while she
believed again she could remain away from Santa Fe. When her
father's affairs at last were adjudicated she was frightened at the
speed with which she packed to leave the City of Mexico, and she
knew that in all the recent months she had not conquered herself.

She assured her friends she was going back to Chihuahua only
to report to her mother and sister on the settlement of the estate
and that she would then return to the City of Mexico. On the
dusty miles north she told herself she would go no farther than
Chihuahua, and to show herself her indifference she broke her
journey for a visit with friends in Durango.

She arrived in Chihuahua at last, and after her duties there
were accomplished she hung on, making plans from week to week
to return south, but instead in conscious surrender she accepted
an invitation to visit with friends in El Paso del Norte. Three days
after she reached the border city she walked alone to the bank of
the Bravo, its water swollen with the summer rains of New Mexico.
She felt the wind from the north on her face, and tears filled her
eyes in rage at her weakness.

From El Paso del Norte she went to visit with relatives of her
mother in Albuquerque. There was no joy in stepping again on the
soil of New Mexico; it was only that she did not possess the will
to stay away.

In Albuquerque she was shocked by the prices in the stores. When she commented to a shopkeeper one day that things cost two and sometimes three times what the same articles cost in El Paso del Norte or Chihuahua or even in the City of Mexico, the shopkeeper froze into silence. This departure from the usual garrulity and good manners of her countrymen was so unusual that she remarked about it to the cousin with whom she was visiting.

"It is not so strange," the cousin said. "They thought perhaps you might be an agent of the Governor."

"I do not understand," Soledad said.

Her cousin shrugged. "The prices are high because all the taxes are collected that way."

The cousin's husband interjected: "Don Manuel is too clever to tax the people directly. He still pretends to be their champion but only the very innocent are still fooled. At first it was only the yanqui store-owners who were taxed, but that did not last long. Now the levies—and they are monstrous—are made on all. They are all worked into the prices people must pay."

"Money is needed to maintain a government," Soledad said.

"And to maintain Don Manuel. Half of the taxes and the proceeds from the collections from the peasants fall into the depthless pockets of the Governor on the way to the treasury. His house here has become the true Palace of the Governor."

"Gossip!"

"More than gossip. With my own eyes have I seen figures. Not all who call Don Manuel 'excelencia' are blindly loyal."

"At the beginning there were complaints. Not openly; no one would dare," the cousin said. She looked around nervously. "It was then the storekeepers became convinced Don Manuel had spies everywhere. Hoodlums broke into places whose owners had whispered protests, so that no one knew who was friend and who was informer. Goods were stolen and fires were set." She added quickly, glancing at her husband: "Of course it may be those were just coincidences."

The haciendas of the ricos were more peopled than ever before. Since Don Manuel had restricted the sale of arms and ammunition, many of the peasants were no longer able to protect themselves on isolated farms and had abandoned their holdings and moved for safety to the walled estates. For these peasants, who dealt not in money but in services, the inflated prices meant they had to work longer to keep alive, and since hours could not be added to the day, many had begun to pledge unborn children to peonage.

As for the ricos, their loathing for Don Manuel remained unchanged. At the great feasts, at the bailes, in the fabulously lavish course of their days and nights, they pursued their hatred for him. It seemed to Soledad that abomination of Manuel Armijo had become to the ricos another kind of religion. But, she noted, it never went beyond poisonous words.

She was aware for the first time of a paralyzing weakness in the class she called her own, seeing with new clarity how the vigor that belonged to the syllables of the names they bore was trapped in ancient suits of armor gleaming silently in darkened corners, in crossed swords untouched on walls, in great black Bibles in which the names were listed, going back through generations to those who had worn the armor and wielded the swords.

At a fiesta given in her honor by Don Antonio Sandoval, who still held the title of prefect of the south, the talk as always fastened itself on the Governor, and in the group that surrounded Soledad it dwelt with particularity on Don Manuel's notorious lusts. As ladies tittered delicately behind fans, it was said that Don Manuel was putting on airs and now denied untamed peasant girls his presence and admitted to his bed only the daughters of the best families.

A youth languishing in a suit of wine-colored velvet, his face soft and beardless, his eyes gentle as a doe's said with a simper: "But now it is the wife of the Governor who holds the key to success. The sow is the important one. All the young Rurale officers travel to her bedroom as though it were a military duty. Each performs his exercise and then emerges from the dark cave with a promotion in his hand!"

The gentlemen roared and the ladies laughed appreciatively, their fans wiggling rapidly, and, emboldened by the success of his wit, the youth leaned closer to Soledad and, giggling mischievously, attempted to snatch a kiss. With the swiftness of cat she pushed the epicene face away. The youth tumbled backward awkwardly and fell on the floor. In the stupefied silence that followed she said: "Señor Sandoval, all these words ill befit your house, you who are personal deputy to Governor Armijo." The prefect's face turned the color of old cheese. Soledad moved her eyes slowly around the room. "If you all hate this Armijo so, why do you not stop gossiping endlessly like toothless women and do something about it?" she asked with frigid scorn. "The weapons for your deliverance are on your walls and in your armories. You go by the names of men. Arm yourselves, hombres! Draw your swords! Destroy this one you call monster!"

As she spoke they moved away from her, their faces warping with the great fear. Women crossed themselves and men held up their hands to ward off a curse. She looked down at the youth still sprawled on the floor, his mouth agape. "Save your kisses, señorito," she said. "I own no dark cave that contains your prosperity." She laughed contemptuously. "But what there is, maricón, you would get lost in."

She placed her wineglass on a table with care and walked unhurriedly from the room. The next morning she set out for Santa Fe.

2

SHE STEPPED DOWN from the carriage with the feeling that she had been for long arrested in time, that this moment was the moment following that other moment when she had waved farewell to Ramón and Lupe from almost this same place in the plaza. It was as though for her the only hours that could be reckoned were the hours of Santa Fe. She filled her lungs and looked at the plaza. There was no change. She knew then how she had feared secretly there would be change that might have escaped her. It was like cutting up intricately patterned material for a dress; the design had to meet perfectly at the seams. Only then could one believe in the illusion that the pattern had not been broken and put together again.

It was the early afternoon of a brilliant day. The air was clear with the purity that natives believed was reserved for New Mexico. The mountains were outlined with such cleanliness against the turquoise sky that she thought almost she could see over and behind them. In the plaza men and women were idly wandering among the usual stalls. Against the walls of buildings, under the shade of the portales, men slumbered in peace. Among the sleepers squatted beggars, themselves half asleep, their bony and ragged buttocks resting on calloused heels, their arms extended, their lips moving in endless chant for alms. Shoppers drifted slowly in and out of stores, greeting one another as though they were singing songs, walking to their houses and their siesta. A priest stepped from the door of La Castrense and surveyed the scene. Somewhere in the distance someone was plucking laggardly on a guitar.

This, she thought, was the true face of the city, with none of the agitation brought in with the gringos. She drank it in and knew how parched earth must feel under a gentle rain.

A huge, brightly gilded carriage turned a corner and swept into the plaza, churning the soft dust. Instantly several guards lounging before the main entrance to the palace sprang to attention. The horses were pulled up violently. Two soldiers jumped down from the tailpiece of the carriage, crying: "Make way! His Excellency Governor Armijo!" A groom opened the carriage door, and Don Manuel stepped down.

"Make way for his excellency!" the soldiers shouted. They shouldered their way into the crowd on the plaza, swinging their muskets. Don Manuel, waiting for the path to be cleared, stood as though he were alone in the world. The people scattered. A beggar, cross-legged near the palace door, did not move. One of the soldiers kicked him. The beggar screamed.

Don Manuel remained motionless. The entrance was cleared, the soldiers presented arms, and the palace door was opened. As Don Manuel, limping heavily, walked into the building, the soldiers turned sharply and followed him. The door was closed, the carriage taken away. While the dust settled, moments passed before the people closed in again where the Governor had passed.

Soledad rushed to the entrance. Several persons were looking down with sympathy at the beggar, whose cheek was bleeding. His head rolled from side to side. Soledad looked more closely at him. "This man is blind," she said.

One of the men standing there said: "And deaf. It is why the other léperos permit him always to have the best place by the door to the palace."

"Blind and deaf," Soledad said.

"Thus he could not hear the order to clear away."

"That brute who kicked him must have known that."

The man nodded and then noticed she was well-dressed, a rica. He moved away from her and again she saw the fear. "This filthy beggar should not block the path his excellency uses," he said in a loud voice, looking at the two guards.

His words and manner alerted the others. They nodded, their lips turned down, pity no longer in their faces. "It is true," a woman shrieked.

An old man with a drooping mustache and a stubble on his chin said viciously: "This one makes a stink in the air his excellency must breathe."

A short, swarthy man with broken teeth spat at the moaning beggar. "His excellency is too lenient with this filth!" he bellowed. He too looked at the guards at the palace door.

The beggar in his world without light or sound was still shaking his head. The short, dark man kicked him in the shoulder, and the beggar screamed again.

"Stop, hombre," Soledad said to the short man. The beggar whimpered. She touched his cheek. He recoiled and then he moved his head forward tentatively, and when he felt the hand did not strike him, he kept his cheek against it.

"We were not sympathizing with this scum," the first man explained to Soledad, his eyes scurrying to the door.

"Filth!" a woman screamed.

"It is too late, señora," Soledad said. "This one cannot hear you. Only God may speak to him."

She put some coins into the beggar's hand, closing his fingers over them. She touched his mouth to still his thanks, straightened, and walked away. The plaza no longer belonged to her.

3

SOLEDAD WENT DIRECTLY to the Casa Baca. Her heart was beating rapidly as she left the plaza. It was not that she had great sympathy for common people, who were, after all, not far above the animals. But beggars were different, and beggars who were afflicted were more different. They were blessed; they suffered for the fortunate. One was kind to them always if only to show one's gratitude that one was spared the evils of poverty or disability. She would like to have that brave soldier under a whip. But he was not the worst of it; the worst was the other people's turning away. What had entered into their hearts to make them forget lessons they had learned all their lives from the padres?

The Bacas welcomed her joyfully. Lupe, rosy-cheeked and bulging with new child, presented the first-born, a solemn little girl named Filomena María de los Remedios. The child curtsied gravely.

When they were sipping the hot chocolate that Lupe produced immediately, Soledad asked: "Where is my caballero?" She paused in the act of lifting the steaming cup to her lips. "He is on patrol, I think."

Baca nodded. "Did you inquire at the palace?"

"No."

"He is on patrol. How did you know?"

Soledad could not explain to them that the pattern required he be on patrol, that he had been on patrol when she left Santa Fe two years before and that there had been no time in between. She drank the chocolate. "How is he?" Baca shrugged. Lupe lifted her eyes heavenward and lowered them. "How is he?" Soledad asked again.

Lupe took a breath so deep Soledad was fearful she would burst from her blouse. "Unhappy."

"Why unhappy, Lupe?"

Lupe sighed again. "It is how it is said in the old proverb: 'Donde hay amor, hay dolor.'"

Baca snorted. "'Where there is love there is sorrow,'" he

mimicked. "Madre de Dios! With this one everything is connected with love!"

"Why does he grieve?" Soledad asked.

Baca put down his cup with a loud noise. "Who knows?"

"What is it that you do not wish to tell me?" Soledad asked.

"It is nothing that we hide, niece," Baca said. "We know nothing. My friend no longer confides in me. I know only what I see."

"And what is it that you see?"

"You saw it yourself before you left here. Only it has become worse. He now is almost a stranger to everyone."

"Tell her what you have said to me," Lupe said.

"I was mistaken, without doubt," Baca said.

"Tell her," Lupe commanded.

"What is it?" Soledad asked.

Baca's face crossed with pain. "God forgive me for saying this, but I have come to think he no longer cares whether he lives or dies."

"Mi madre!" Soledad clasped her hands. "What is it that you say!"

"I have tried not to believe it," Baca said quietly. "The thought is sinful. But it has seemed that way."

"What has he done?"

He shrugged. "Nothing, perhaps, when you come to talk of it. Except that he asks for more expeditions against the Indians than are his due. And on these missions he is reckless. He has always been brave as a hidalgo, and his soldiers respect him; he has never avoided risk, but it goes beyond this. He seems to expose himself where there is no need to expose himself."

"Tell her how you saved his life," Lupe said.

"One is always helping another. But it is true. One day both our companies were on joint patrol. His horse was shot from beneath him. That could have happened to anyone. But he made no effort to get under cover. He remained standing there in the open, loading and firing his pistol, not even protecting himself behind the carcass of the horse. I called to him, but he paid no attention to me."

"And then Ramón risked his own life," Lupe said proudly. "He was the hero of the day, my little husband! He galloped to where this idiot was standing and lifted him to his horse and rode off with him." She crossed herself. "Virgen santísima! It is not enough that my husband performs his own duties, but he also must touch fingers with death because his friend has gone crazy!"

"There was an expression on his face," Baca said in a low voice. He held his hands together as though in prayer. "It was the expression of a man who has walked a long path and sees salvation at last. At that moment, God forgive me, he was awaiting death."

"But why?" Soledad's lips were white. "Why, Ramón, why?"

Baca rubbed his face tiredly. "One could believe almost it was a family taint. Capitán Caballero tries to find his own death these days, in a bottle."

"Don José always has drunk too much," Soledad said.

"But not as he does now. He drinks not for pleasure and not even to ease pain. He looks into the bottle to find a place to lose himself." He stood up. "I must leave. I go on duty. What are your plans, Soledad? This time, by means of God, you remain with us. This is no short visit."

"I plan to stay in Santa Fe."

"Thanks to God! Our house is your house."

"You are kind, uncle. But you know it is said that one roof, no matter how large, is too small for more than one family. It is my intention to rent a house."

"Santa Fe has many empty houses."

"Ea, pues, that at least is good news."

"Their owners are away, on long vacations. They are guests of Don Manuel." He snapped his fingers. "Por Dios, I know of exactly the place. It is only two or three houses away from here, the house of Don Facundo Cubero."

"Don Facundo? Has he removed from Santa Fe?"

"He is in the City of Mexico awaiting trial on a charge of treason. His wife and children have moved to the country."

"Don Facundo a traitor?" Soledad asked with astonishment. "But he was a friend to my father. He came often to our house in the old days. How can that be true?"

"You must understand the new definition of words, Soledad," Baca said. "Among other things, Don Manuel is engaged in altering the language. A traitor no longer means what it has meant since the Spanish language was invented. I will tell you what happened. One evening at a small dinner party Don Facundo drank a little more than he should. There was a lively conversation going around the table, a conversation about love and marriage—although for my part I do not see how the two are related—and Don Facundo made the observation that some persons believed marriages were made in heaven, while others believed as strongly they were made in hell, but no one would deny that the marriage between Don Manuel and Doña María Trinidad was made in a pigsty. It was less than a week later that Don Facundo was arrested and sent in chains to the City of Mexico."

4

SOLEDAD STARED at the stiff white card, feeling that Don Manuel had reached out and touched her. It was an invitation to a formal reception at the Palace and attached to it was a note in Don Manuel's hand expressing the hope that she would find it convenient to accept. She had made no secret of her return to Santa Fe and she had known the Governor would hear of it sooner or later, yet she found herself startled that he had discovered it so quickly. She tossed the card into the fireplace. It fell short of the smoldering logs and she retrieved it. Trembling for what reason she knew not, she fingered the card and then placed it and the note in her silver tray and tried to forget it.

She busied herself in her work redecorating the sala of the Casa Cubero. Since she had engaged the house she had occupied herself so she would not have too much leisure to think of what Ramón had said to her about Esquipulas Caballero. As she moved about the room she could not keep her eyes from turning to the gleaming white card on the tray.

It was on the evening of the reception that Don Esquipulas called on her, and when she saw him, there was no happiness, just the ending of the pain.

He kissed her hand with formality. When he raised his head

she saw how much older he appeared. His face seemed narrower and longer and more Spanish. There was gray at his temples. "You have returned to Santa Fe," he said. "You are going to stay."

She took her hand from his. "The prospect appears to give you no pleasure, señor."

"Pardon. I did not mean it that way. Only it is strange to see you as mistress of the house, particularly the house of Don Facundo Cubero."

"It is a very attractive house."

"It is very nice," he agreed politely.

"May I offer you some of the vino de Jerez?"

"For favor."

She poured the amber wine into two glasses. "*Salud, mi caballero.*"

"*Salud,* Soledad." Then he said, almost angrily: "Why have you come back?"

She set down the glass slowly. "Is there any need for a reason for my returning to the place of my birth?"

He shook his head, his jaw muscles knotting. "No, no, for certain! What do I say?" He finished the wine. "I have been in the saddle for many days, muchachita, and I returned only this afternoon. I am wearier than I think." He smiled. "The proper question is why you have remained away so long. We all have missed you."

She looked at him silently, noticing he still bore the rank of ensign, and she took away his empty glass. "I think you need more wine, señor. My memory of Don Esquipulas Caballero was that of the gallant." Her eyes filled with hurt. "Of a man with charm greater than that of any other caballero in Santa Fe. Of a man whose face took on a certain tenderness when he looked on me." She leaned closer to him, holding the empty wineglass against her breast as though it were a chalice. "What has happened to you, mi corazón? Are you now without any love for me?"

He lifted his hand slowly and touched her cheek as a blind man might seek identification. And then there appeared upon his face an expression of such naked agony that she turned her head quickly so his pride could suffer this weakness alone.

"You spoke of more wine, señorita," he said, releasing her.

"Yes."

183

"It is necessary that I attend the Governor's reception. It is a duty required of all presidial officers when they are not away from Santa Fe. Would you do me the honor to accompany me?"

"It is kind of you to ask me," she said courteously. "I accept, with much pleasure."

5

THE MASTER OF CEREMONIES, in blue satin jacket, white satin vest, white satin knee-breeches, long white stockings, and pumps with square, silver buckles, rapped his cane of office sharply and the guests in the drawing-room hushed as he announced in a piercing voice: "His Excellency Brevet Brigadier General of the Mexican Army, Governor and General Commandant Inspector of the Department of New Mexico, Don Manuel Armijo, and Her Excellency Señora the Governess, Doña María Trinidad."

With the precision of a company of trained ballet dancers every man in uniform came to vibrant attention, every civilian bowed deeply, and every woman curtsied almost to the floor. Don Manuel looked at the bowed heads. He lifted a finger. The master of ceremonies bawled: "You may rise!"

The hum of conversation resumed. Doña María Trinidad was surrounded immediately by half a dozen or more young men who escorted her away with the dexterity of male dancers carrying off a prima ballerina. Men paid their respects to the Governor. Don Manuel replied to them without interest, his eyes roaming the room. He wondered if Soledad had come. His face became sour as he saw a small pursy-looking man detach himself from the Americans who were huddled as an undigested lump in one corner of the room.

"Excelencia," the man said, pronouncing it "exthaylenthia."

"Señor Alvarez," Don Manuel said coldly.

Manuel Alvarez, the new American consul, in black evening dress, with a stock so tight it almost strangled him, waved a forefinger. "I have been seeking an audience with your excellency for a fortnight. I have a number of important matters to discuss with your excellency."

The Governor regarded him with undiguised distaste. When Alvarez first arrived in Santa Fe some months before, Armijo had been flattered that the government of the United States had seen fit to establish diplomatic relations with him. He had been astounded to discover that the new consul was not a native American but a naturalized Spaniard. His satisfaction changed to anger at what he decided at last was a studied insult on the part of the American State Department in sending to represent the gringos a native of Spain, the single country in the world which New Mexican officials detested more than the United States.

Armijo said silkily: "Señor Alvarez, I do not know in what school you were tutored in the arts of diplomacy, but surely you must have learned that a social function is no place to discuss matters of state."

Alvarez, breathing heavily, replied: "But, excelencia, it would appear that I can reach your person only at a time such as this, and it is most necessary that we discuss the new tax structure."

"I will not discuss business here, señor."

"It is only of business that I would speak to your excellency. The American business men here wish me to make protest on their behalf on your new ruling which doubles the license fees of Americans owning business establishments."

Armijo nodded almost imperceptibly to two officers who had trailed him into the drawing-room. The officers placed themselves between the consul and the Governor. Armijo turned and walked away. Alvarez tried to follow him, but the officers blocked his way. The consul, reddening, moved quickly in several directions. Each time the officers intercepted him. Alvarez cried out: "Don Manuel!" The officers took him by the arms and led him out of the room.

Soledad, watching the scene with Esquipulas Caballero, tightened her fingers on his arm. "Who is that little man and why are they being so rude to him?"

"It is the American consul."

"How dare they treat him in such manner?"

"Governor Armijo lacks love for him."

"But he is a foreign diplomat."

"This would shock your friends in the City of Mexico, would it not?" he asked sarcastically.

"For certain! Beyond the rudeness to a guest there is the special privilege enjoyed by envoys."

"They enjoy none here."

"And who were those two men dressed as officers?"

"They were officers, señorita," he said distinctly. "The young one is Don Tomás Martínez, a nephew to Governor Armijo. The other is Teniente Damasio Salazar."

In an ante-room a large group surrounded a roulette table and watched the play. Soledad and Caballero looked over the shoulders of the seated players. The croupier called out: "Number twenty-eight," and reached out to rake in the money. A knife blade flashed and the point was driven through the sleeve of the croupier's jacket, pinning his outstretched arm to the green board. Don Tomás Martínez shouted: "Thief! You interfered with the spin of the wheel!"

The croupier, held across the board by his trapped arm, turned white. "The ball stopped on number twenty-eight, Don Tomás. Your stake was on number eleven."

Don Tomás's eyes were glazed with drink. "Thief! I did not see it stop on twenty-eight. What kind of game do you try to run at the palace?"

The croupier, making no attempt to remove the knife, looked pleadingly at the other players. "There are others who saw," he said with agitation. "Others saw where the little ball stopped."

It was as though he had said nothing. The other players remained silent, their faces vacant. They did not look at the croupier or at the officer.

Don Tomás laughed harshly. "Eh? Son of whore! Who speaks for you? They all know you for a thief. I order you to return my money and the money belonging to everybody else at this table."

The croupier looked around helplessly and then his face became transfixed with horror as he saw Don Manuel walking toward the table. He jerked his arm free, ripping his sleeve, and began to count out money.

"A little moment," Soledad said. "I saw the wheel stop. There was no interference and the ball stopped on number twenty-eight."

The croupier waved his arm frantically. "Perhaps you were mistaken. Perhaps the wheel had not properly stopped."

"But that is ridiculous," Soledad said.

Don Tomás twisted his head. "Do you call me liar?"

"I call you nothing, teniente," she said evenly. "I was not speaking to you."

"For favor, señorita, it is better to make the refund and bring about no trouble," the croupier said. He held a palmful of silver dollars toward the lieutenant. His hand trembled so cruelly that several of the coins fell to the board.

"What is the trouble here?" Don Manuel asked.

The croupier shook his head and tried to smile. "Nothing, nothing, excelencia, nothing, nothing at all."

Don Tomás grinned at his uncle. "Just a small matter of cheating, mi general. The dog played tricks with the wheel."

"That is a lie," Soledad said.

"I am making restitution, excelencia," the croupier said.

Armijo looked down at the other players. They were still silent, their heads bowed. Then Caballero said: "Don Tomás is in error, excelencia. There was nothing improper about the play."

For a moment Armijo closed his eyes and his face was bleak. "Think you, Don Esquipulas."

"I will make restitution," the croupier chanted.

"There is no need, señor," Armijo said.

"The filth cheated!" Don Tomás screamed. "Word of honor!"

"Leave the table, teniente," Armijo said.

"Why must I leave the table? Whose word do you take?"

"Leave the table."

"My money is as good as any other's!"

"Summon Coronel Chaves, for favor, Don Esquipulas," Armijo said. To the croupier he said: "Have the generosity to forgive my nephew, señor. I fear he has emptied his glass too often."

"I am not drunk!" Don Tomás shouted.

Armijo, ignoring him, waved his hand gracefully over the table. "Resume your play, señores y señoras. My nephew has made a small mistake. The croupier, Don Felipe Valdez, is known to all of us for his honesty."

The croupier, still pale and shaken, made a small bow. "Thank you, excelencia."

"You take sides against your own blood!" Don Tomás fumed.

187

"Silence, Don Tomás," Armijo said. "Stand at attention. You are in the presence of your commanding general."

Don Mariano Chaves, now commander of all the Rurales, came to the table. "You called for me, excelencia."

"One of your officers has had too much to drink, mi coronel," Armijo said. "Have him escorted from the palace and taken to a place where he may rest until he regains control over himself."

"Don Tomás, excelencia?" Chaves asked in astonishment.

"Yes."

Chaves saluted the Governor. "Follow me, teniente."

Don Tomás stiffened as though he might refuse to obey. Then he threw back his handsome head and laughed. He clicked his heels and saluted the Governor. Before following Chaves away, he glanced at Caballero.

Don Manuel said tightly: "I ask again that the play be resumed. I make apologies to all for the manners of my nephew. And I thank Señorita Soledad Abreu and Don Esquipulas Caballero for preventing a wrong from being committed against Don Felipe." He turned to Soledad. "This incident has brought on a small headache, señorita. Perhaps you would do me the honor to share a little breath of air with me in the placita." He extended his arm. "With your permission, Don Esquipulas."

After a moment's hesitation she accepted the proffered arm, murmuring: "I will find you later, Don Esquipulas."

Caballero listened for a while to the clicking of the ball in the wheel and the monotonous announcements of the croupier. One of the players rose and left and Don Esquipulas took the seat and joined the play.

6

THE NIGHT AIR was fresh after the heat and smoke inside. It was the time called el veranillo de San Martín, the season known to the Americans as Indian summer.

Don Manuel spoke as though he were not opening but resuming a conversation. "I know what they are thinking now, por Dios, all of them who eat from my table and drink from my cup."

There was such bitterness in his tones she looked quickly at him. In profile the heaviness of his face did not show. He looked young and curiously exposed. She felt uncomfortable, perturbed at the need to alter her view of him again. She had prepared herself for many things, but not for sadness.

"They will say now that Don Tomás has behaved like a lout. Many men may be coarse. Many men may get drunk. There are fights always around gaming tables. But this time it will be different. Because Tomás Martínez is nephew to Manuel Armijo."

She did not want to look on the sensitivity of his lips. "Don Manuel," she said.

"He is no better than others, nor is he worse. He is young and he is arrogant and he drinks too much. There are many who do the same and of them it is said only that such action is natural to high-spirited youth. But for the nephew to the Governor there are other words."

"Don Manuel."

"The words are boor and brute. He is called vulgar. They attach these words to the name of Don Tomás because they are afraid to apply them to Manuel Armijo!"

"Don Manuel, please."

"They come as close as the son of my sister and they feel brave."

"You must stop!" She shook her head. He was drawing her to him in terrible intimacy.

He looked at her in distress. "Why must I stop, señorita?"

"Your excellency has just been disturbed and embarrassed," knowing what he implied could not even be acknowledged. "You speak in reaction. Tomorrow you will regret this weakness."

He said nothing as they walked several steps. The music came to them faintly. "You are quite right," he said gravely. "I presumed. I ask your pardon."

"Excelencia," she said in a choked voice.

"You are saying to me: 'We are not that close,' are you not?" he asked with immense gentleness. "I have been speaking as a friend and we are not friends of that kind?"

"You are the Governor of New Mexico."

"And you are an Abreu? Is that what you are saying?"

She shook her head again. "It is not of me that I speak nor of my feelings nor of who I am. Madre de Dios, I am nothing, excelencia! It is only that you are shaken from yourself."

"And I expose my feelings in a manner you consider strengthless and unmanly."

"My considerations are of no importance, excelencia. I do not want you to despise yourself tomorow for what you say tonight."

He nodded soberly. "That is the kind of world we live in. At all cost the code must be followed. One may not speak. One must never yield spontaneously to the mood of the moment. One must always think of the next day. One must always remember how one's words will sound if they were to be repeated, particularly the words of Manuel Armijo."

"There is no question of repeating, excelencia!"

He made a comical face. "Por Dios, señorita, and what can I say to you that will not come out wrong? I would do anything not to offend you." He abruptly stopped his walking, turned to her, and, laughing, held out his hands. "Let us begin over again. Let us begin at the proper place as the code prescribes. In my forgetfulness I omitted even to make decent greeting. I spoke to you tonight as though I had spoken to you yesterday and not two years ago. I will not try to explain this stupid error, for that would only lead us again to the path you are avoiding. I will say only how happy I am to see you again."

"Thank you, excelencia." Was there another who could shift so bewilderingly, she wondered.

"You look extremely well, señorita," he said, burlesquing the tones of polite speech.

"You are kind."

"And how does it feel to be back in Santa Fe?"

"In some ways, good."

"In some ways only?"

"In some ways only, excelencia."

"That of the beggar?" he asked with a smile.

"You know of the beggar?"

"I know of everything."

"Yes, that of the beggar! Upon arriving in Santa Fe I saw a blind man kicked in the face by a soldier who wore your uniform. I saw people look on and approve."

"They need that. The people need that."

190

"Tonight I saw a foreign envoy dragged across your drawing-room by two of your officers, and no one thought it strange. Do they need that too, excelencia?"

"Yes," he said patiently. "Perhaps even more than the other. He represents the United States."

"Not a person was shocked."

"Except you," he said gravely.

"I am happy to be of amusement to your excellency."

"You should be, señorita. Very little amuses me these days."

She drew herself up. "I think it grows chilly, excelencia. And your guests must deplore your absence."

He touched her arm. "Here is a bench. Let us sit down for a little while."

"So that I may provide more entertainment for your excellency?" she asked icily.

"Say relaxation more than entertainment. No one speaks to me in your manner any more. No one raises a voice of anger against Manuel Armijo." He grinned. "At least not so that my ears can hear it."

"From what I have seen since my return to New Mexico it does not surprise me, excelencia. Nor would you want anyone to do so."

"No, I would not," he said frankly. "It is a luxury I cannot permit either to myself or to my subjects. But I have not lost the memory of it, as an honest sound, and when it comes from one so lovely as you it is filled with tanginess. It is like the spicy taste of good chile after a diet of sweet chocolate." He held his hand toward the bench. "For a little moment, señorita," he pleaded. "The evening is short enough."

She sat down, taking out the makings of a cigarette, and rolled one swiftly.

"Gracias, señorita. We will smoke and talk as friends. May I tell you a little about the people you speak of?"

"If it would please your excellency."

"They are like children. They respect only strength, and for them strength cannot be an inner quality but must be held before them like a blazing torch." He held a light for her cigarette and then lighted a cigar.

"Is kicking an old man this blazing torch?"

"It is."

"I do not believe it."

"It is true."

"And you consider such an act beneficial?"

"Either to myself or to New Mexico."

"In the order named?"

He laughed happily. "Madre de Dios, how you delight me!"

She lifted the tongs to her mouth. "It is a better word than amuse, excelencia."

"I am overjoyed that the days of your travel are ended. I have missed you very much."

"I think we must now return to the baile, excelencia," she said.

"When do we meet again?"

"This is not a large city, excelencia. We shall from time to time be at the same places at the same times."

"I did not mean that, Soledad," he said, saying her name for the first time. "When shall we meet again privately?"

"I cannot say, excelencia. I am an unmarried woman."

"And an Abreu!"

"That is the name to which I was born, excelencia."

"You must not refuse to see me alone."

Her head reared. "*Must* not, excelencia?" she asked coldly. "Because of the power of which you spoke?"

"Ah, Dios, no. I have been able to speak to you tonight with honesty. It has been a rare experience for me. You were filled with compassion when a beggar was injured. Tonight you burned with sympathy for à stranger, a Spaniard. Have you not the smallest amount of charity for me?" He seized her fingers and kissed them.

She tightened with aversion. "What do you suggest, excelencia? That I sneak through the back door of the palace to your chamber?" She stood up and drew her mantilla over her shoulders. "Or will you come in the night to my house? Or perhaps we could make a compromise and meet each other halfway—in the center of the plaza."

As she walked back into the palace he could think only how he had almost called her Rafaela.

7

ON THE WAY to her house after the reception Caballero was silent. When she opened the door, he bowed and turned away. "Do not go," she said. "Come inside for a little moment." As he stood there, still turned away, she said: "For favor, mi caro. We will share a cup of chocolate."

The dueña, Doña Dorotea Engracia, a cousin of Soledad's mother, who had come back with her from Mexico, was in the sala, still awake. She retired to her own room when they entered.

Soledad held her hands before the embers glowing on the hearth. "The summer of the good San Martín has been a little one," she said. "Put more wood on the fire, for favor, while I prepare the chocolate."

He set some mesquite logs on the coals, and presently the pungent smell filled the room. He stared into the blaze. She returned with a tray bearing a pitcher and cups and set the tray on a table near the fire. "Pull over two chairs, querido. The warmth is so good."

He carried two leather-backed chairs to the fire. She handed him a steaming cup of chocolate, sat down, her legs curled under her, and held the other cup in her two hands. She held her face toward the burning logs. She sniffed the smell of the mesquite and closed her eyes in pleasure.

"You were a success at the baile tonight," he said.

"That is not unpleasant to hear."

"Many persons asked me who you were."

She opened her eyes and sipped the chocolate. "Make me a cigarette, hombre. I am so content at this moment I do not want to move."

"You were a success with Don Manuel as well."

She continued to look at the flames, sucked cracklingly up the chimney by the wind that had risen. "You desire to know, of course, of what we spoke."

"It is no business of mine."

"It is not. And yet you were black with anger when I returned from the placita."

"I was angry? You should have seen your own face. Every-one else saw it."

"And what conclusion did all of you draw?"

"Where Don Manuel is concerned, there can be only one conclusion."

"I see." She raised the cup to her lips again. "You begin to sound like Ramón. Ah, Dios, how I love the taste of chocolate! I will tell you what Don Manuel said to me."

"I have no curiosity," he said sullenly.

"He spoke of many things, but it is only what he requested at the end that will be of interest to you."

"It is no affair of mine."

"It is not," she agreed again. "He asked me if he could visit me alone." She saw the muscles tighten in his jaw. She finished the chocolate and, setting down the cup, stretched her open hands toward the fire. "Of course your pride will not suffer you to ask of me what reply I made to this request. I will tell you. I said to Don Manuel that I was unmarried and that I could not grant him the private meetings he desired."

"Half the people who were at the palace undoubtedly think you are in bed with him at this moment!"

"Instead of sitting innocently in front of my own fire with a very old friend?" She crinkled her nose. "I do not believe so. To-night is the night for Inés Domínguez and everybody knows that."

"Inés Domínguez?"

"The little girl who is so thin but who has the enormous breasts."

"Por amor de Dios!"

"She winked at him. "It is a return engagement, you know."

"What the devil are you talking about?"

She looked around with exaggerated carefulness. "As the story was revealed to me, and it was revealed by one to whom it was told by a good friend of Inés herself, there was an earlier engage-ment, and on that occasion Don Manuel for one reason or another was unable to bring the play to a successful conclusion. Inés per-formed the role of an innocent, which I am informed is an im-portant feature in these sessions with Don Manuel, and in this particular case the display of innocence must have required art-istry, since the same informant told me little Inés has had a lover for more than a year. Nevertheless, it was a flat failure." She looked owlish.

"Dios, Soledad, and what are you saying!"

She shrugged and jutted her lower lip comically. "Ea, pues, it appeared then that the little father of Inés was highly incensed. Señor Domínguez owes the government a sizable sum of money in back taxes and he was in high hopes that Inés might inspire Don Manuel to leniency. The fury of Señor Domínguez was said to be so great that he threatened to drive the girl out of his house. In his generosity, however, Don Manuel granted the girl a second audience, and this return engagement was scheduled for this very night after the reception, as, apparently, almost all of Santa Fe except you well knows. Therefore, hombre, despite your fears, no one thinks that it is I who is supplying his excellency with rapture at this time."

"Body of God," he breathed, "in what manner have you spent your time in the City of Mexico?"

Her laughter rippled. She uncurled her legs and stood up. "Let me pour you more chocolate, señor," she said gravely, taking his cup. She looked at him for a moment, her eyes twinkling, and then made a moue. "You appear shocked, Don Esquipulas," she said. "Do you know not of these things that happen between men and women?" As she handed him the cup she said: "Or is it that you know all about little Inés? Perhaps you yourself have served her better than did his excellency." She sat down and stirred her cup reflectively. "After all, your reputation as lover is unsurpassed by any."

"I have had nothing to do with Inés Domínguez."

"Why not, mi caballero? Is she not to your taste?" she asked banteringly. Then she twisted in the chair and all the laughter went from her voice. "It is not comical between us any more, is it?"

He did not reply.

"We cannot sit and laugh together as we used to, can we?" she asked. "You find no pleasure in my words, do you? And yet the words are all the same and here we are alone as we used so often to be and it is all different. Is it gone from us, corazón? Are we to be strangers always?" She saw the tiredness on his face, and her eyes filled with tears. "What has removed you so far from me that I reach to you and cannot touch you?" she asked in a fright-

195

ened voice. "What curse has been laid upon us? What is this dark wall that separates us so that our eyes can never meet?"

"Wall?" he said hoarsely. His face grew old.

"You did not ask me why I spoke as I did to Don Manuel," she said. "Do you believe truly that it was because I am unmarried? He did not believe it was that. But neither did he know the reason. Do you?"

"No."

"You do. It is because I love you."

He stood up slowly. "No," he said. "No, Soledad."

"Do you find that offensive as well?" she whispered. "It is necessary for me to tell you so there can be no mistake in your mind about it, even if you hear it with no pleasure."

"No."

"If we are still to remain strangers, it must not be because you are unsure of me." She spoke slowly and evenly, her face imprisoned in quiescent ecstasy, so that her speech and her manner became a kind of personal liturgy. "You I love, hombre. You I have always loved."

He remained hunched over the fireplace and there was no sound but the wind and the seething of the flames, and then his eyes closed briefly and he straightened himself and raised his head. She watched him from her place of bondage and saw in his rigid composure, his arms lifted stiffly from the elbows, his mouth indrawn with a stringent reconciliation, the imperative dedication of the killer of bulls at the ordained time of climax in his bitter ritual of immolation. He was composed as the true matador is composed, everything in him held to the fullest, retained to the final culmination of the austere thrust in which there was no joy, only the abatement of the compulsory and irrefutable need.

He turned to her until he faced her fully and he held out his hand. She rose from the chair and went to him, knowing she had entered his world as though she had crossed a line, and she remained still and silent as he removed her clothing with consummate care. He lowered her gently and composed her before the fire. His movements were angular and fixed. He paused for a moment as though in final resistance, his face sunken with an exhausted asceticism, and then he delivered himself of the purgative making of the wound. It was an act of exorcism and the manner of purification was only accidental; he fought violently and alone with his mysteries, and when he removed himself from her and lay back drained, she knew that as yet he had not touched her.

Presently she asked: "You know? You were able to tell?"

"Who was it?"

"It does not matter."

"Where was it?"

"It was not here."

"Who was he?"

"Nothing of it matters."

"When was it?"

"After I left here. The second time. In the City of Mexico." Then she asked: "Why should I not have? There was no reason not to."

"Did you love him?"

"You allowed me to go."

"Did you love him?"

"I returned to you after the first time and you allowed me to go."

"Did you love him?"

"Yes. I believed so then."

"Why did you not remain with him? Why did you return here?"

"There was no question of that. He had a wife, a very lovely wife." She raised herself on her elbow. "You should know it all. I was presented with a reckoning. I carried his child and I lost it and there can be no other child in me."

"Is there more to say?"

"Yes, there was one other, in El Paso del Norte, not like the first, which was a thing of many months, but a single time, done with no emotion. I did not want to cross the river. I would have done more than that for strength not to cross the river. But it was useless, and while it was happening I knew it was useless, and after that I did not try any longer to remain away."

He thought he now had his absolution. It was not defeat but victory. There now was in both of them a pollution, and now his ghost could rest. There was restored balance, not by a lifting of one side, but by the lowering of the other. He turned to her in malign triumph and sealed his relief.

197

1

Don Ramón Baca held up his hands and the shouting died down. "Soldiers, attention! You are not acting as loyal members of the presidial troop. You behave more like the savages you have just fought so bravely. It is the policy of his excellency to make payment of your salaries in wheat. Nothing can be done about this. I ask you to take your bags of wheat and go to your houses in peace."

One of the soldiers gathered before the barracks shouted: "We have just returned from the market. Now the dogs do not even pay a dollar a fanega. It has dropped below even that!"

Another soldier shouted: "The louse-ridden merchants say they do us a favor to take the wheat from us at any price!"

"They say the market is choked with wheat!"

One soldier waved his fist. "My woman says she will leave me if I appear again with this grass. Why cannot we at least have corn?"

Baca held up his hands again. "It is useless, soldiers. We must all obey orders."

A huge soldier stepped forth. "We mean no disrespect to his excellency," he said in a rumbling voice. "We are loyal to Don Manuel. Look at this leg, señor. The wound of an Apache arrow has not yet healed. At any time I stand ready to die as a soldier of his excellency. But until I am dead I must live, and my family must live. Speak to his excellency, señor. Tell him that the men who serve him cannot live from month to month on a handful of wheat. Tell him that while we protect New Mexico from the savages our wives and our children hunger."

"Tell Don Manuel! Tell Don Manuel!" other men shouted.

"I will speak to him," Baca said.

2

Don Manuel glowered across his desk at the detested face of the American consul. The Governor was in the worst of tempers. He had arrived at his office that morning outraged at his inability to persuade Soledad Abreu to visit him privately. For more than three weeks, since the night of the reception, he had tried again and again without success to arrange a meeting with her.

When he reached his office he found a number of disturbing reports awaiting him. There was a communication from his deputy in the City of Mexico, Padre Juan Felipe Ortiz, in connection with the trial of Don Facundo Cubero. Don Facundo, the prelate wrote, had proclaimed that Manuel Armijo was conducting a reign of terror in New Mexico. So violent had been his charges that the central government was considering sending a commission to New Mexico to investigate.

There was a report from Don Diego Archuleta, Armijo's northern prefect, telling of new riots in Taos due to rising prices and increasing depredations by wild Indians. As though that were not enough bad news from the Rio Arriba, there also was a furious letter from Padre Martínez relating to a grant of land north of Taos that Don Manuel was making to his secretary, Guadalupe Miranda, and the French Canadian trapper Carlos Beaubien. Although the granting of the land was within Don Manuel's rights, rights carried down from the days of the royal Spanish governors, the priest protested that the turning of the enormous tract of almost two million acres into a private grant would bring about the eviction of hundreds of peasants. In his anger Padre Martínez was tactless enough to point out that while the law provided that Don Manuel benefit to the value of twenty per cent of the returns, it was obvious that by naming his secretary as joint owner his profits would be considerably more.

There was another report that an American engineer working at one of the placer mines had been slain by New Mexicans and that the local authorities had neglected to arrest the slayers, who escaped. Other Americans sent a petition to their Minister in

Mexico. And to add to all these things, by a devilish coincidence, Don Manuel had previously given the American consul an audience for that morning.

Señor Alvarez had arrived at the exact minute of the audience and had looked with barely concealed disgust at the strings of dried Indian ears which were draped around the Governor's office. His lips crimped, Alvarez had spread out a sheaf of notes of alarming proportions and had launched immediately into the matter of the slain engineer.

"I have said, Señor Alvarez, that I will order an investigation," Don Manuel said for the third time, biting savagely on his cigar.

"There must be more than the usual investigation, excelencia," Alvarez lisped vehemently. "There were many witnesses to the murder, and their depositions were taken. Each says the attack on my countryman was unprovoked. The criminals must be brought to justice before they disappear forever into the mountains."

"I said I will look into it. What else is there?"

The consul listed half a dozen crimes committed against Americans in various parts of New Mexico. In all instances the guilty ones had not been apprehended. When he looked up from his notes at last, Don Manuel was staring at him through half-closed eyes, his cigar dead between his lips. The festooned ears seemed to have moved closer to listen in. Alvarez ran his hand around his collar. "The United States and the Republic of Mexico have a treaty between them which guarantees the rights of citizens of each country when in the other country, excelencia. The attitude to nationals of my country which I find here in New Mexico is not the attitude of a civilized government. Your nationals are given protection in the United States, excelencia, and my government considers that our nationals are entitled to the same protection by you."

"Do you then presume to call us barbarians, Señor Alvarez?" Don Manuel's voice was dangerously quiet.

"I do not, excelencia," the consul replied. "I say only that American citizens do not receive the protection normally accorded foreigners in civilized countries."

"Do you call us uncivilized?"

"Your excellency chooses not to defend his officials."

Armijo gave the desk a violent blow with his fist. "Por Dios, and I am the one who decides what questions will be answered and in what manner! What protection is it that you speak of, señor? For example that given to Mexicans in Texas?"

"I do not represent the Republic of Texas, excelencia." Alvarez pulled out his kerchief and mopped his brow. "I am consul for the United States."

"It is all the same."

"It is not all the same. Your country has always enjoyed the friendliest relations with the United States. Your own Constitution was based on that of the United States."

"Gringos are the same, whether they call themselves Americans or Texans," Don Manuel roared. "The leaders of your country are no friends of mine and they are no friends of my country. I know what they think of this country. I know how they connive with the traitors in Texas, that place which you call the Republic of Texas, but which is still legally and morally and in every other way a part of Mexico. And this mendacity is not restricted to Washington, señor. Here in Santa Fe the Americans whose cause you plead are up to their necks in intrigue with the same traitors in Texas."

"Your excellency is mistaken, I assure you."

"Why did the trader Gregg route his caravan this year so that it almost passed through the northern part of Texas?"

Alvarez looked puzzled. "It is true, excelencia, that Señor Gregg explored a new route across the prairies, but I do not see how that constitutes intriguing against your excellency."

Armijo gripped the desk. "Yes, he explored a new route, far to the south of the old route, which has proved satisfactory enough for twenty years; so far south, in fact, that the Texans could smell the money that was passing under their noses! You know as well as I do that the Texans have been trying for a long time to have the caravans pass through Texas so that some of the money of the Santa Fe trade would stick to their fingers. And now this Gregg deliberately brings his wagons almost to their border to show them how easily it could be done. How long do you believe the Texan dogs will be able to resist such temptation? If I were to do my duty as a patriotic Mexican governor I would throw every American in New Mexico out of the country!"

Alvarez threw up his hands. "You cannot be serious."

Armijo sat back, breathing hard. "No, señor, I cannot be serious because my poor country is the tail to the American dog."

Alvarez wiped his perspiring face. "Don Manuel, forgive me for contradicting you, but you are mistaken. In all of New Mexico there are no more loyal supporters of your excellency than the American merchants. There may be a few exceptions, but they are without influence. The Americans want only peace and security so they may continue to conduct their business affairs with profit. They would be foolish to want changes. If Texans were admitted to New Mexico, they would become competitors of my countrymen. Surely your excellency can see that."

Armijo contemplated him somberly. "Continue your complaints, señor. The day is running its course."

Alvarez hesitated and then said boldly: "I wish to talk about the customs taxes." The consul knew this was a touchy subject with the Governor. The year before, Don Manuel had changed his system of taxes on imports from an ad valorem assessment on the goods to a flat tax of five hundred dollars per wagon, regardless of the value of the merchandise. The traders had protested against the inequities of such a method of taxation, but Don Manuel was adamant. This year the canny Yankee traders had struck back. The night before they reached Santa Fe they repacked their wagons, consolidating the loads of two or three wagons into one. The main caravan passed through the customs in this manner before Don Manuel discovered what had been done.

Alvarez cleared his throat and picked up a memorandum. "In July of this year, excelencia, there arrived in Santa Fe a small auxiliary caravan belonging principally to New Mexicans, though a few of the wagons were owned by Americans. For the few articles belonging to the citizens of the United States your customs officials exacted almost double the amount of tax required from the Mexicans. Last month another small caravan arrived with goods owned by my countrymen, and these merchants were compelled to pay duty even higher than that imposed on the Americans who arrived in July." He looked up. "Does your excellency have any comment to make on that?"

"Custom imposts are the law of the land," Armijo said levelly. "That is the only comment I make."

Alvarez nodded, expecting nothing else. "I have used every means open to me to win justice for the citizens of the country I represent, excelencia. I have had no success. Therefore I have prepared a document in which all the injustices I have described to you, together with many others of a similar nature, are listed in full. I propose to send this paper to the Secretary of State of the United States. I conclude the petition with the following observation, which I take the liberty of reading to your excellency." He adjusted his glasses. " 'This convinces me that Governor Armijo is determined by such means to keep from the market the competition of the industrious and enterprising citizens of the United States. He is the positive ruler and regulator of the duties and of the customhouse affairs, as he is in everything else in this department.' "

Armijo was on his feet before Alvarez finished. "That is an infamous statement, señor! Of course I tax the gringos more than I do my own people. This is New Mexico! It is not a province of the hungry colossus. The customs regulations are our own internal affairs and none of your business. The gringos take thousands of dollars out of this country every year. Everybody has his hand in New Mexican pockets, from the gringos in the United States who manufacture the goods to the gringos who bring them here. Por Dios, I make them pay for that privilege of doing business here! And I make them pay more than my own poor countrymen have to pay! There is no injustice there, señor. There is only love for men of my own blood. Your petition is a lie and you are a liar and provocator to prepare it!"

"I seek to provoke nothing, excelencia. As you have outlined your reasons for the unjust taxes they take on an air of validity. I would accept your policies as unpleasant to the country I represent but nevertheless as justifiable save for one thing. It so happens that not all your 'poor' countrymen draw benefit from your love for them."

"What do you mean, señor?"

Alvarez adjusted his glasses and looked again at his notes. "This year Don José Antonio Chaves, who holds the title of customs inspector, entered eleven wagons in his own name and was taxed twelve hundred dollars. That is a little more than one hundred dollars a wagon. Similar concessions were made to Don Juan

Estevan Pino, Don Alberto Speyer, Don Juan Bautista Vigil, and others who are intimate friends of your excellency."

"They are all natives of Mexico!"

"Including Speyer? Let us say they are. However, at the same time several other native-born Mexicans—for example, Donato Heredia, Pedro Jesús Arrillaga, and many more who do not enjoy your excellency's favor—paid the five-hundred-dollar fee."

"How do you know all these details?" Armijo asked.

"I have examined the books in the customhouse."

"How did you arrange to see my books?"

"That is my own business, excelencia. Do you deny the truth of what I have said?"

"Spy! Who showed you the books?"

"I am no spy, excelencia. And I cannot reveal the name of my informant."

Don Manuel laced his fingers together. He leaned across the desk. "Who opened the books to you, señor?" he asked cajolingly. "Tell me. It will not go badly with you."

"I gave my pledge, excelencia."

With a violent curse, Armijo sprang up and ran around the desk. He seized Alvarez by the lapels and lifted him and shook him violently. "Who opened the books to you!" he shouted.

Alvarez tugged feebly at the iron hands that held him. "Release me, Don Manuel," he gasped.

"What traitor showed you the books?"

"Release me," Alvarez said faintly. "I am an American citizen, Don Manuel."

With another oath, Armijo flung him back into the chair. "I will have you flogged! I will have the skin torn from your bones! Who opened the books?"

Alvarez pulled himself to his feet. He lurched away from the Governor, staggered to a window, and bathed his face in the fresh air. When he turned to Armijo he was pale but composed. "You have failed in every way to understand me, Don Manuel. I am not a rich man, but I do not desire to be bribed. I am not a brave man, but I do not fear flogging. You are correct when you say I am not an American by birth. I was born in Spain. But perhaps that has helped make of me a somewhat better American than some who were born in the United States. Perhaps it is the mem-

204

ory of corruption that I left behind in Spain that makes me more sensitive to it when I see it duplicated here. Perhaps it was because I was born in a country where there is no personal freedom that I have come to have a love for a country that now honors me with its citizenship and its trust."

He walked calmly to the desk and gathered his papers. "With your permission I will take my leave, excelencia. Before I go I wish to tell you of one thing more. I have assembled many incidents for inclusion in this document I shall send to Washington. But there is one incident I have not included. Late this fall an American citizen named Joseph Persifer was slain and robbed near the eastern border of New Mexico while on his way to this country from the trading establishments on the Platte and Arkansas Rivers. Another American, James Bonny, subsequently investigated the murder with the alcalde of Las Vegas. They found some of the property stolen from Mr. Persifer in the possession of a New Mexican named Juan Angel Apodaca. Apodaca signed a confession in which he admitted he and two others attacked Persifer. He swears that one of his two confederates, a man named Ascensión Montoya, was content to rob Mr. Persifer, but that the third confederate insisted that the American be killed. Apodada and Montoya argued with their partner, but in the end he prevailed upon them and Mr. Persifer was shot in cold blood." He slipped his notes into his attaché case and, holding the case under his arm, faced Armijo. "The name of this third man, excelencia, is Juan Cristóbal Armijo. He is your nephew." He bowed. "Good day, excelencia."

3

FOR SEVERAL MINUTES after Alvarez departed, Armijo did not relax from his taut position. Then slowly and painfully he eased himself around the desk and fell into his chair. His leg ached and he rubbed it abstractedly. He did not know how much time had passed when Guadalupe Miranda announced that Don Ramón Baca desired a few moments of his time.

"Send him in," he said. He looked up as Baca entered. Stiff and correct. The old manner. The stiff-necked Bacas.

"Excelencia, I come as spokesman for soldiers," Baca said.

"Which soldiers, Don Ramón? There are many soldiers."

"Those in my own company."

"Ah."

"They protest against again being paid in wheat, and especially do they protest against the rate at which the wheat is valued."

"So?"

"They are loyal soldiers, excelencia. But they must eat and their wives and children must eat. They say they cannot feed their families on wages that are paid in wheat set at four dollars a fanega."

"You are quick to emphasize their loyalty, Don Ramón."

"It is but the plain truth, excelencia."

"Loyal soldiers do not rebel."

"They do not rebel. They do but protest, in humility. They think perhaps that your excellency does not realize how they are being paid for their bravery."

"Is their bravery something that must be bought?"

"In order to be brave a soldier must first be alive, excelencia. And after being alive he must know in the heat of battle, when the next arrow or musket ball may be the one designed for him, that at least those at home whom he loves have enough to eat."

"And you agree with them that the rate computed for the wheat is exorbitant?"

"Wheat is a glut on the market, excelencia. Today the men were informed by the merchants whose houses and stores they risk their lives to protect that the price has dropped to less than one dollar a fanega. On the pay sheets it is charged to the men at four times that much. Some of the merchants refused to accept the wheat at any price, saying it was moldy. I appeal to you, excelencia, to reconsider. These men are the backbone of your army. They are the firm support of your government. They love your excellency, but they can no longer go to their houses and look upon the hungry faces of those who depend upon them for support."

"And now they will no longer love or support me?"

"I did not say that, excelencia."

"But you imply it. You threaten?"

Baca shook his head. "I neither think it nor threaten your excellency. I ask only that justice be done to loyal soldiers."

"Justice! Justice! I begin to want to vomit at the sound of that word! Why is it always your company? Why no other company?"

"I do not know, excelencia. It was my company that returned today from a fortnight in the field to find the wheat awaiting them."

"And they refuse to accept it?"

"You insist upon harsh words, excelencia. They plead."

"This approaches open rebellion, señor."

Baca looked at him steadily. "We live in a republic, excelencia, which men died to create. It is not improper for men to protest against the slow starvation of their wives and children."

Don Manuel felt a throbbing in his head. This was not the City of Mexico, where Facundo Cubero was spreading lies against him, nor was it Taos nor was it something lost in the slimy secrecy of his own customhouse. This was here, within his grasp. "Do not remind me of the form of my government, señor. I know my government. I created it. I am the only government and the only law! And I say that what your soldiers do is treason! Treason!" His hair fell over his forehead. He lifted his arm and pointed toward the door. "Go back to your men. Tell them that I command them to close their mouths and accept their pay in the manner I have decreed all my soldiers shall be paid. That is a direct order, señor, from your commanding general. Do you understand that?"

Baca saluted. "I obey, mi general."

"Then go! Pronto! Pronto! And tell the soldiers I know who they are. Tell them I shall not forget their names." He stood up. "Nor yours, señor! Nor yours!"

Baca returned to the waiting men. "The order stands. His excellency commands that you take your wheat and go home."

The swarthy giant who had spoken before shouted: "I will not take this filthy stuff!" He picked up his sack and threw it against the wall. The bag split and the grain spilled out.

The action served as a signal. Cursing, yelling, each man

threw his sack against the wall, and when the sacks were burst they waded in the mound of grain, kicking it wildly in all directions.

A whistle blew. The men stopped. A platoon of soldiers marched up, led by Lieutenant José Silva, second in command of the presidial companies. "General Armijo orders that every man in the Baca company consider himself in barrack arrest," he said. "No one will leave quarters."

The newly arrived soldiers herded the now docile rioters out of the courtyard into the barracks. Then Silva said: "The order applies to you as well, Don Ramón. You will deliver yourself to the jailer and will remain prisoner until released."

Baca unbuckled his sword and handed it to Silva. His face white, he walked firmly to the military prison.

From a window in another part of the palace Don Manuel observed the execution of his orders. He returned to his office and drank several brandies but he could not lessen the pounding in his head or shut out the ringing in his ears.

4

CAPTAIN JOSÉ CABALLERO replaced the quill in its stand. He sprinkled sand over the paper, and when the ink was dry he funneled the sand back into its container. Tugging at his lower lip, he slowly read over his formal resignation as commander of the presidial troop.

For the last six months, as he had gradually relinquished his responsibilities to Lieutenant Silva, he had written and rewritten his resignation. It was not a long statement, but the words had to be exactly right, for this would be his last public pronouncement. The version he now studied was perhaps the hundredth draft he had prepared. At this time there were not a dozen of the original words left. They stood battered but erect, veterans of a lengthy campaign.

Captain Caballero sighed at length and laid the paper in the center of his desk. He was finished at last. There was not a single word he could change. The words were all correctly spelled. There were no ink blots. There was nothing left now but for him to sign his name.

And now that he had at last composed his valediction, he felt the full weight of his sadness. When this paper was accepted by General Armijo he would then be separated forever from the career to which he had devoted his life.

He reached out automatically to the decanter of brandy that was always near to his hand and he removed the glass stopper. He replaced the stopper and pushed the decanter away resolutely. From now on, there would be nothing left but the brandy and on this day he owed it to himself to remain sober. He closed his eyes and the small, neat face sagged. He wondered what had gone wrong.

It had been conceived in devotion to his country, and the execution had fulfilled the conception, but somewhere it had gone wrong. It was not to him to whom the wrong had been done. Although he was an old man he had been given back his command exactly as Don Manuel had promised. The wrong had been done to his son, Don Esquipulas, who was not an old man, who had drawn his sword for Don Manuel in the beginning, and who had not prospered when victory had been won. Although he had courage and skill, Don Esquipulas was still in the lowest rank of officers after three years. Again and again Don Manuel had passed over his promotion until now men who were not even officers in 1837 were superior to him.

Captain Caballero's hand stretched out again to the brandy and again he withstood temptation. He had found forgetfulness in the brandy. It was a reliable friend when his thoughts became too painful. Don Esquipulas had no such escape. When Captain Caballero emerged from his own world he saw the same corrosion was in the soul of his son. He knew that his son wanted to speak to him and he fled back to the bottle each time with a kind of terror, knowing he would have no answers.

He had imagined it would be different—he restored to the command of his troops, his son working and learning at his side, so that when the time came for him to step down, as now, his son would be ready to take his place. Instead he and Don Esquipulas had become almost wholly separated from each other.

He had become separated from his troop as well. When Don Manuel had arrested Ramón Baca and his company, he had omitted going through proper channels. Don Manuel should have communicated his wishes to Captain Caballero and he would have issued the order. He was the one responsible for the discipline of his troops.

It was a harsh order, but Don Manuel had gone further. After keeping the men in quarters for a week, he had sent them out on another patrol, though it was not their turn, making a campaign against the Indians into a punishment. If Don Manuel had only asked him he could have explained to him that one did not punish soldiers by permitting them to perform their duty. It would have been a greater punishment if the men had been denied the privilege of going out on patrol the next time their turn came up.

He stopped his thinking abruptly. In criticizing Don Manuel he was guilty of even greater transgression, that of disloyalty to his commander-in-chief.

He picked up the quill and wrote: "Submitted with the most profound respect, Capitán José María Caballero." He hoped until the finish of the final twirl of the rubric that he might make a blot and be forced to recopy the page again. He was denied the reprieve.

5

CAPTAIN CABALLERO was annoyed to find Lieutenant Damasio Salazar in the Governor's office. Salazar was sprawled in a chair, trimming his fingernails with his knife. Captain Caballero flushed slightly as the lieutenant glanced up at him and then resumed paring his nails. The captain held himself stiffly as he marched to Don Manuel's desk. He tried to keep his eyes from straying to the dried ears. The ears always made him a little sick at his stomach. "Capitán Caballero," he said, "reporting to His Excellency General Armijo."

Don Manuel said: "How does it go, my old friend?"

The presence of Salazar discomfited Captain Caballero. He had planned for a long time precisely what he would say, and the words were not intended to be spoken before a third person. "Excelencia, I am an old man and for a long time I have not been well." He could sense Salazar's sneer.

"Your ill health has long been a concern of mine, Don José," Don Manuel said.

"I have felt increasingly that my health does not permit me to continue in my duties as captain of the presidial companies."

"I have hoped with all my heart you would recover."

"I no longer believe it is possible, excelencia." He heard Salazar shift in his chair. "I have prepared my resignation. I have the honor to present this resignation to your excellency at this time." Caballero laid the paper, rolled into a cylinder and held together with a white ribbon, before the Governor.

With deep gravity Don Manuel picked up the cylinder and read it soberly. "I accept this resignation with the greatest reluctance, my dear captain. In all of New Mexico there has been no one more loyal that you. Your departure from public service will leave a void that will not for a long time be filled."

"Thank you, excelencia, thank you," Caballero said.

"It is painful to see an old compañero go, Don José," Armijo said in a quiet voice.

Captain Caballero felt tears rising to his eyes and he was embarrassed that Salazar should see them. "We have done things together, excelencia."

"You have been a right arm, Don José! It could not have been done without you. Together you and I have changed the history of New Mexico."

Caballero could not speak.

"And now, Don José, you feel the weariness of your years and you find it necessary to remove yourself from me," Don Manuel said. "The cornerstone of my government will be taken away. And yet, while you enjoy your deserved rest, you will be happy in the knowledge that your strength was given in service to your country." Don Manuel smiled. "Who knows, Don José, in a little while perhaps you will surprise yourself by regaining your vigor. In that happy event, remember there always will be a place for you in my government."

Caballero blinked his eyes. "I shall always be at the disposal of your excellency."

Now Don Manuel stood up. "You have said your farewell to me, Don José. But much as I love you, there are those who love you more. I speak of your troops. You must not retire without bidding them farewell. I will order a formal retreat. You must not deny them this honor." Don Manuel smiled cordially. "And you must remember, Don José, that I shall always be in your debt."

Caballero thought of his son. "I have a favor to ask, excelencia."

"Ask it."

Again Salazar moved in his chair. Caballero lowered his eyes. He could not speak of his son before Salazar. "It is a small thing, excelencia. It will be strange for me to shed this uniform. I ask for the privilege of wearing my uniform on important occasions."

"At all times," Armijo said heartily.

"Not at all times, excelencia, just the important ones." Then Captain Caballero thought of a way in which he might bring up the name of his son. Perhaps just to mention Don Esquipulas might do good at this time. "I hope there will be such an occasion in the near future, excelencia. It is possible there will be a marriage in my family."

"A marriage? Are you considering honoring some fortunate woman with your proud name, Don José? I approve! The life of a widower is a lonely one." He winked at Caballero. "Am I at last hearing the true reason for your resignation?"

Caballero colored. "Not I, excelencia. It is of my son, Don Esquipulas, that I speak."

Armijo laughed loudly. "That rooster? Is he going to settle down to one woman at last? That is difficult for me to swallow, Don José. If true, it is bad news for the muchachas of Santa Fe."

"It is by no means arranged, excelencia," Caballero said hastily. "It is just that I have thought it may come about."

"And who is the girl?" Armijo asked, grinning broadly.

"She is an old family friend, excelencia. Her name is Señorita Soledad Abreu. I believe your excellency knows her."

Don Manuel heard a thud. He looked up. He had forgotten Salazar was in the room. The lieutenant was still slumped in the chair, but he no longer was working on his fingernails. He was looking at the door that had just closed behind Captain Caballero.

Armijo followed his gaze. The knife was in the door, buried half-way to the hilt.

"A little too high for the captain, excelencia," Salazar said. "Just right for the son." He lifted himself indolently to his feet and retrieved the blade. "There could be no marriage without a groom."

"What the devil are you talking about?" Armijo said.

Salazar walked slowly back to the chair, balancing the point of the knife on his forefinger. "It should not surprise you, excelencia," he said calmly. "That kind seeks itself out like animals of a special breed. It is a commodity they have for each other. It is all so convenient." Salazar resumed his seat. "In the great empty house of Facundo Cubero." He sheathed his knife violently. "They always win, excelencia. They are always beaten and they always win."

"You are skillful with the steel, Don Damasio."

"I have also practiced a great deal with the pistol, excelencia."

"That is useful for a military man. You have heard, of course, that Don Esquipulas is one of the finest swordsmen in New Mexico?"

"The sword? An antique weapon, excelencia. I have heard an interesting expression recently. Do you know what the gringos call the pistol?"

"No."

"They call it an 'equalizer.' It is a very appropriate word. It equalizes many things; for example, the relative positions between two men, one of whom had time in his youth to study the obsolescent art of fencing and the other of whom had time only to learn how to throw a knife or point a muzzle in the right direction."

"Why do you bear such hatred for Don Esquipulas?"

Salazar removed the blade from the sheath again. He pushed the point into the soft part of his finger. A bubble of blood rose. He touched it with his tongue. "It is a simple thing, excelencia. He was born to this world with everything. I, with nothing."

"You are superior to him in rank."

"Through your kindness, excelencia. It is not the puppy Caballero alone, though it seems to concentrate in him. It is all of them who despise the people. It is their manner, their speech, the way they walk. It is everything. One smells it when one enters their houses." He raised his eyes. "It is something you would not understand perhaps, excelencia. I do not know why I reveal these feelings to you. I do not love to reveal them to myself. But they have the quality, the ricos, to make me feel an impostor in this uniform. I seem always to hear the private laughter they reserve for themselves. This Caballero hides it, but I think it is stronger in him than in the others."

"You exaggerate, Don Damasio. New Mexico is part of a republic. Men win their own places in life."

"That may be, excelencia. But the ricos are leftovers from a great feast. They belong to another time."

"They are citizens of the Republic of Mexico."

"Are they, excelencia? They are more Spanish than Mexican." Then he said: "Your pardon, excelencia. I do not mean to say anything that would be offensive to you."

"You do not offend me."

"Were it not for your excellency they would try to remake New Mexico into an imitation of a royal province."

"Perhaps you are right, Don Damasio."

"Of all Mexico only New Mexico took no part in the great Revolution. I think for the ricos it is as though there has never been the Revolution."

Don Manuel warmed to Salazar's words. He felt an impulse to reply in kind, but he checked himself. To exchange confidences was to deliver a small part of oneself.

Salazar leaned toward the desk, clutching the knife tightly. His eyes glowed with a dull hatred. The line of his mouth was almost invisible. "I should like nothing better than to show it is only in the accident of birth that this coxcomb is better than I," he said. "The favor would be for me. There is no need even for your excellency to grant me permission. It would be enough if your excellency does not command me not to do so."

Don Manuel dangling the temptation before him like a bright jewel. It could be easily done. The deserted dark street and the silent passage of the knife through the air. But then he remembered a day when Caballero had come to him wounded and another when he had ridden up a hill. Their time was not yet worked out. He knew the threads were intertwined and now it was only that they were intertwined in this as well, the three strands of a plait. He sat erect. "You talk nonsense, Don Damasio. My officers are not assassins."

Don Manuel enjoyed the pleasant contemplation of his mercifulness. He had forborne. To move a finger one way meant death; the other way, life. If Esquipulas Caballero had once almost lost his life in his service, he had not repaid the debt.

He smiled as he remembered the disappointment on Salazar's face as he left and he recalled the lieutenant's parting remark: "Perhaps you have not lost her after all, excelencia. Perhaps it is that you have just won her."

He moved his finger one way and then the other. Jesucristo could not determine life and death more easily.

1

FROM HIS OFFICE Don Manuel watched the people gather in the plaza on the clear January day to witness the ceremony for Captain Caballero. The people were in a holiday mood. He saw some of the local American shopkeepers mingling with the natives, something the yanquis had not done for some time. As the soldiers from the presidial companies and the nearby Rurale units took their positions, he could see the cheer was on them as well.

The good humor of the capital reflected his own affability. He had been in an agreeable frame of mind for weeks and had gone out of his way to iron out various unpleasantnesses. He had called together the American business men who had permanent establishments in Santa Fe and other communities and had overwhelmed them with graciousness. He had suggested that perhaps the stubborn and implacable Manuel Alvarez was their own worst enemy. He had reminded them that before the consul had appeared on the scene, the Americans and New Mexicans had always managed to get along. How could he, he had asked them, show the friendliness he felt in his heart toward Americans when Alvarez was sending insulting papers to the Secretary of State in Washington? And, in any case, who was Alvarez? Was he an American? Or was he not a Spaniard, farther removed from both Americans and New Mexicans than they were from each other.

Many of the merchants had seen the point and had disavowed Alvarez's protests. Some of them sent letters to Washington, denying the charges the consul had made. Armijo made a small concession immediately: he ordered a slight decrease in licensing fees. The merchants turned in a body on their consul.

Then Don Manuel had turned his attention to the soldiers. He had appeared among the men as he had been in the habit of doing in the early days, a rough man among men. He had made a minor adjustment in their salaries. He had slapped backs and had sworn round oaths.

He had sent a message to Carlos Beaubien instructing him to be more lenient in his policy of dispossessing the peasants who had for generations lived on the land he had just granted. To remove a source of irritation to the impoverished peasants in the north, he had also ordered Beaubien to route the pack trains with the peltries representing Armijo's percentage of the rapidly developing trapping industry so they would not pass through Taos or other Rio Arriba communities on their way to Santa Fe.

He had sent a courier to the leaders of the Mimbres Apaches tribe and had concluded an arrangement to exchange barrels of American whisky for skins. He had promised a bonus if the Apaches devoted themselves to trapping and decreased their raids on the flocks of sheep.

His cheerfulness was such that he was not at all perturbed to hear from Padre Ortiz that Don Facundo Cubero had prevailed upon the central authorities to appoint the commission to investigate conditions in New Mexico. It would take weeks to select members for such a commission, more weeks for the appointed men to make preparations, and then many more weeks for the arduous journey. Anything might happen to the group before it reached Santa Fe. If they arrived safely, Don Manuel was confident he could make the men see things his way. If by some chance he failed, then the investigators still had to go back to the City of Mexico and there were many wild and dangerous miles over which they would have to travel even to reach El Paso del Norte. A word to Mangas Coloradas, chief of the Mimbres Apaches, would be enough.

2

THE PRESIDIAL BAND marched out from behind the palace playing a stirring march. The sun shone on their polished instruments. The people cheered as the bandsmen took their stations in the center of the plaza without missing a beat.

The officers and soldiers came to attention. At a signal from the bandleader, the bugler sounded the piercing "Call to the Comandante." When he finished, the palace adjutant moved forward. "His Excellency General Manuel Armijo!"

The officers flashed their sabers. The soldiers brought up their muskets in salute. Don Manuel rode onto the plaza.

He charged down the line of presidial soldiers, reining in when he reached the edge of the plaza with such violence that his horse snorted and reared and the spectators shrieked with delighted alarm. With great strength he brought the powerful animal under control and then he raced across the plaza and down the line of Rurales, formed at the opposite side, and again he reared his horse in a tower of dust and again people cried out and women swooned rapturously. Now Don Manuel trotted the horse to the center of the plaza in front of the band and there he stopped him with such gentleness that the horse froze into immobility. Don Manuel sat erect in the saddle, his back arched, his chest expanded, forming, with the motionless horse, a heroic statue.

Don Manuel gestured and the adjutant stepped forth again. "Capitán José Caballero! Capitán José Silva! Present yourselves to his excellency!"

The two officers appeared from opposite sides of the plaza. They walked their horses at a stately pace until they met, and then each executed a sharp turn and resumed the slow walk until they reached the Governor. They halted and drew their swords.

When the cheering of the people quieted, Don Manuel said: "In our language the word 'caballero' means cavalier. It means knight. It means nobleman. It would seem that the founders of our language must have had in mind the type of man we honor today!"

The deep voice carried the words to all corners of the plaza. When Don Manuel paused, the people cried: "Olé!"

"In the terrible hours when insurrection swept over the land, when savage murderers led by a madman threatened to destroy us all, no one responded more nobly than did this man who has given so much of himself in the service of his country that he has exhausted himself before his time. And throughout the years of loyalty his character has remained wholly unblemished, so that today as he steps down from his duties he remains forever after an inspiration to others who must still continue.

"Loyalty, devotion, courage, are virtues that should make a man ageless. Unfortunately, remorseless time does not permit such miracles. The years go by and add their weight to all, the loyal and the disloyal, the brave and the cowardly. And so today I am forced to perform the saddest duty in the life of a commander-in-chief. I am forced to accept the resignation of my most trusted deputy. I do so only because the powers at my command do not include that by which I can turn back the passage of time."

He accepted from the adjutant a small velvet box. "There is one last honor I may bestow upon you, Capitán Caballero. It is a small expression of thanks from your commander and your country. It is with pride and humility that I salute you and present to you this medal of the Order of the Cavaliers of Guadalupe."

He opened the box and took out a ribbon from which hung a large, enameled medal. He hung the ribbon around Captain Caballero's neck.

"There are two fortunate circumstances that to a degree mitigate the sadness of this moment," Armijo resumed. "One is that although one Caballero departs, another remains and the glorious old name is not entirely removed from the presidial troops. The second circumstance is that your place, dear Don José, is being filled by another officer in your own tradition, Capitán José Silva. Capitán Caballero, your commanding general extends his regrets and his wishes for many more years of good life! Capitán Silva, your commanding general congratulates you and wishes you well!"

The people broke into the loudest cheers of the day, and now they were joined by the soldiers in the plaza. Captain Caballero bowed his head. When there was quiet, he attempted to speak. He opened his mouth, but no words came. He opened and closed his mouth again, but he could say nothing. He wiped his eyes and coughed and saluted Don Manuel. He turned to Captain Silva and saluted him.

The lonely notes of retreat sounded in the square. A drummer started a slow dirge. Captain Caballero faced his troops for the last time. He rode slowly past them, and when he came abreast of

219

his son, he paused and the two men gazed silently at each other, and then Captain Caballero moved on. When he passed the final platoon of men he continued until he was gone from the plaza.

3

THE PARTY given by Don Manuel to honor Captain Silva was attended by Soledad Abreu in the company of Ramón Baca. Lupe had almost reached her time and Esquipulas Caballero was on duty with the palace guard and would not be relieved until midnight. When she saw the governor approaching her, her face colored slightly and her fingers went to the choker of pearls on her neck.

After greetings were exchanged, Don Manuel asked if Baca had drunk a toast to Captain Silva.

"We have but just arrived, excelencia."

"In that case may I suggest you find Capitán Silva and give to him your salutations?"

Don Manuel thought that he was not wrong about Soledad and Caballero. There was new luster to her skin. The eyes had new life. He felt his chest tighten. "You are very beautiful tonight, Soledad."

"My thanks, excelencia."

Did she hold her head with new assurance, or was it only a new hair style, the hair built up off the neck and high on the head? Was it the pearl collar that gave her a look of chasteness, so that all he could think of was lack of chasteness? He knew everything and he knew nothing.

"You stare at me oddly, excelencia. Is there something wrong with my appearance?"

"No."

"Is it the dress?"

"It is not the dress. You have changed, señorita."

"Changed, excellency? In what manner?"

He was in control of himself now. "I am not a schoolboy, Soledad."

"Your excellency chooses to speak in mysteries."

"Something happens," he said banteringly, his cigar held at a jaunty angle between his lips. "Is it the new look in the eyes? Perhaps it is that. Is there less shyness, a new knowledge that makes a woman closer to all men?" He removed the cigar and pursed his lips. "Perhaps it is that."

"This, then, is a night for riddles, excelencia. Is this a new game to which I am being introduced?"

"It is not a new game," he said gravely. "It is a very old game, the oldest of all."

"Excelencia, we are being observed by a thousand eyes."

"We are but in polite conversation."

"It was a beautiful ceremony in the plaza," she said, waving her fan rapidly.

"A polite conversation between two civilized persons."

"Capitán Caballero should have been most proud."

"You do not appear to be tranquil. Perhaps a glass of wine would refresh you." He beckoned to a servant and took two glasses from a tray. "Your face seems flushed, señorita. Is the room overly hot? The wine is cold."

He lifted his own glass to his lips without removing his eyes from her. As she brought the wine to her mouth, her eyes met his and he was less sure of himself. It was a duel, a constant duel, a playing for position, and he knew that his own balance was so insecure that the moment she recovered her calm it would be he who would be without tranquillity. "How is Don Esquipulas?" he asked quickly.

"He is in excellent health. But you should know this better than I."

"I am confident I see much less of him than you do, señorita."

"Your excellency returns to his little game."

"There is no need to blush. It becomes you, but it is unnecessary with me. I believe that I told you once before that there is little that occurs in Santa Fe that does not reach my ears."

She held back her head. The pearls gleamed softly. "Perhaps it would be better if we ended this saraband, Don Manuel. If your excellency is implying there is something between Don Esquipulas and me, then your excellency is entirely correct."

His fingers dug into the palm of his hand. "Do not say it so

221

challengingly. You must know this information can bring nothing but pleasure to me."

"Pleasure?" she repeated. "You are a curious man, Don Manuel."

"In what way?"

"I should like to believe that your excellency is serious."

"I am wholly serious. And why not?"

"Your excellency well knows why not."

He held out his hand. "Because he wins where I lost?" He smiled. "It is true, mi cara, that I gave my heart to you. I say it in all frankness. I dreamed dreams. My imagination became a wild horse that galloped in all directions. For a little while many lost things seemed again possible. I was again a young man with the hopes a young man might have." He shrugged and his smile became rueful. "But circumstances said no. I am Manuel Armijo and I cannot act to a woman as another man might. And I am married. Our belief does not permit the sacrilege of divorce even when the marriage has nothing left. I forgot all those things for a little moment. I was like a child lost in a forest. Nothing of what I felt was familiar to me. But the quest was lost before it truly began." He hunched his shoulders boyishly. "And so, little girl of the eyes, I accept my fortune, as always. One must do this as one must accept the next card turned by the monte dealer. And if what is so important to me is to be denied me, then the next best thing is that it be given to one who is himself bound to my life and who has his own place in my heart."

Her fan was motionless.

"Has he asked you to marry him?" he asked.

"No, excelencia."

"He will. He is a young rooster and the idea is alien to him and will take a little time to find root. But he will."

"Do you believe so, excelencia?"

He felt the tightening again at the anxiety in her voice. "With my heart," he said. "And when the time comes, as it will, I will consider it an honor to sponsor the wedding myself."

"I have no words for your excellency," she whispered.

"Think of how much worse it would have been for me if you had found no love here so that you would have removed yourself from us forever. No, señorita, I lose well. It is a talent I developed long ago when there were more defeats than victories. And this time it is not too difficult to lose well. Will you not still be part of my official family?" He took her hand and raised it to his lips. "May a merciful God watch over you both and protect you. That is the wish of your Governor."

4

THE ORCHESTRA was playing a slow waltz as Don Esquipulas Caballero entered the sala. He looked down the line of dancers until he saw her. She was advancing toward her partner, curtsying, rising, extending her hands. As the partner clasped her fingers and she arched her back, Caballero saw the line of her throat and then the partner released her and she retreated from him, waving her kerchief to the slow strains of the music.

While waiting for the waltz to end he sought out Captain Silva. He saw the captain, his head cocked, listening to a story Damasio Salazar was telling him. Caballero picked up a glass of wine and joined them. "*Salud, mi capitán*," he said. "Accept my felicitations."

Silva lifted his head and laughed loudly. "Many thanks, Don Esquipulas." He continued to laugh, wiping his eyes.

Caballero bowed to Salazar. "Señor teniente."

Salazar ignored him. He put his arm around Silva's shoulder, turning the captain away from Caballero. He put his mouth close to Silva's ear and began to tell him another story. Caballero walked away.

Back at the refreshment table, he saw Soledad coming toward him, her walk still half a dance. Before she reached him she pirouetted, her arms upraised. He could see the sparkle in her eyes.

"Here is my caballero," she said.

"How does it go, little drunk?"

"Filled with the burning hatred."

"And with wine to put out the fires of the hatred."

"With much wine, but the fires of the hatred still consume. I am filled with so much of this hatred, hombre. I feel it is a sign that I wear."

"I dislike you too."

"Dislike? Santo Dios, is that all? I loathe and detest you."

"You have had assistance, many glasses of assistance."

"The hatred has nothing to do with the assistance. I hated you before then."

He held his glass to her lips. "You missed me, then, little friend of my heart?"

"I gave you not so much as a thought all evening." She crinkled her nose. "Except in pity."

"Why in pity?"

"I gave a single thought to the poor little one who had to perform his dull military duties while others danced and drank, and I wanted to go to your office with a glass of wine but Ramón forbade me to do so. He was stern and very proper. He said there was a regulation that stated specifically that one is forbidden to bring even one small glass of champagne to one's lover while he is on duty."

"There must be such a regulation. He knows them all by heart. But I thank you for the thought, little lady."

"Look, I have finished your wine, mi caro."

"There is more." He gave her a filled glass and took one for himself.

She held up the glass. "With aversion."

"With much aversion." Then he asked: "By the way, where is Ramón?"

"I have not seen him for some time. He was angry with me."

"Why was the good uncle angry?"

"Don Manuel spoke to me at some length. The uncle did not approve."

"Oh?" He sipped his wine. "And what did his excellency have to say to you that took such time? Did he again beseech you to visit his bedchamber?" He tried to get it off lightly. "I wonder what there is in that room that he is so anxious for you to see."

"I begin to grow curious myself," she said solemnly.

He examined the bubbles in his glass. "You should go."

"Do you believe so?"

"Just once. You should go just once to allow his excellency to verify that your body is no different from any other."

224

"Is it no different, hombre?" she asked blandly.

"Outwardly?" He shrugged. "The same."

"So?"

"The usual things, all in the correct number and in proper locations."

Her foot began to tap.

"It is below the surface the difference evidences itself. But only in the imagination."

She shook her head slowly. "How I hate you, truly, truly!" She set down the glass and made a cigarette. "Are you not interested in what Don Manuel actually had to say?"

"If you are inclined to reveal state secrets."

"It is no secret, idiot. The Governor knows about us."

"What does he know?"

"He knows that we love each other."

"Now, how could he have found that out?"

She cleared her throat and puffed her cheeks. "There is little that occurs in Santa Fe that does not sooner or later reach my ears," she boomed.

"And he is right," he laughed. "He includes all the ears in his office."

She tilted her head. "It does not surprise me that he knows."

"And does it not, little light of my life?"

"I have always thought when it is happening with us that bells must surely be ringing all over Santa Fe."

He touched her cheek. "You are the side of my heart."

She closed her eyes and shivered. "It is too big for the one room, hombre. At that moment all the people in the world must raise their heads and know of it."

"Jesús mil veces! We might as well make love in the plaza!"

"And it is all the times between times as well. Do I not wear this affliction as a sign?" She asked slowly: "How could he not know?"

"Do not make me leave so much wine untasted. We must stay a certain time here for politeness."

"I have passed that time."

"But I have just arrived. Tell me, how has his excellency digested this knowledge? I think there is another little regulation providing that taking away the woman of the Governor is a court-martial offense. I must check with Ramón."

"I never was the woman of the Governor, friend."

"That is a technicality."

"If you would know, the Governor approves of us."

"No!"

"He does, truly. He told me it made him very happy. It made me quite angry. He has given up too easily. He should have challenged you to a duel at the very least."

"I do not understand. What did he say?"

"I will not tell you what else he said, hombre."

"You have secrets with Don Manuel." His voice edged.

"We have this secret, but I hope only temporarily. At the proper time and the proper place I will reveal this to you also."

He glanced over the room. "Where is his excellency? I have not seen him since I came."

"He left earlier in the evening with the horrible Salazar."

"Salazar?"

"I saw him go up to Don Manuel in great excitement and they left together. Salazar returned later, but Don Manuel did not."

"Salazar must have brought him a new woman. A real woman."

"A real woman." She snapped open her fan.

"Don Manuel must have been expecting her. Why else should he have been so generous in abandoning you?" He stepped back and surveyed her critically. "You know, Don Manuel is older and wiser than I am. Perhaps I should profit from his judgment."

She made an angry sound in her throat. "It is what enrages me. I do not enjoy being tossed aside by his excellency before he has even conquered me."

He thought he could not listen to this even as a joke. It was only when he was lucky that he could get it off himself. He held up his glass. "With your permission."

"Not too much wine, hombre."

"Just enough to catch up to you."

"Not too much." Her eyes danced. "A small drunk is good. A big drunk—no good."

"Do not worry," he said. "The bells will ring tonight."

. . .

Later there was the slow ingathering, a summoning from far places, and the senses began to trickle in streams, slim at their origin, spilling into each other until he thought he could not endure it, reaching the single place so that there it was all together, everything that was within him that had life, and then it was too much and no longer could be contained, and in the peace he knew that nothing had happened before to either of them and that, having this, he could not again be without it. He asked the words quickly, almost with defiance, lifting a cross to banish the devil.

"Yes," she said. "Yes, I will be your wife."

He knew that for him the devil was gone, but whether it was because of his question or her answer he did not know.

5

DON MANUEL had been annoyed when Salazar came to him at the party and asked if he could speak to a man who had just arrived in Santa Fe. "Who is he? And can he not wait until tomorrow?" he asked testily.

"I would not have dared to suggest the interview for this time if it were not of the greatest importance, excelencia," Salazar said earnestly.

Don Manuel nodded abruptly. "Bring him to my office."

The man who followed Salazar into the Governor's office was a burly Mexican peasant wrapped in a torn blanket. His face was almost as dark as that of a Negro. On his left cheek was a long scar, extending from his ear to his mouth. He was covered with dust, and his lips were blue with the cold.

"Excelencia," Salazar said, "permit me to introduce a cousin, Carlos Gutiérrez."

Don Manuel made the slightest inclination of his head. Gutiérrez held his sombrero against his chest and bowed deeply.

"My cousin came originally from Taos, excelencia. He is a hunter and a restless man. He has chased animals all over New Mexico and he has made his home in many places. Some time ago, excelencia, perhaps eighteen months ago, Carlos came to me when I was stationed at San Miguel and asked to borrow money from me. It was his wish to go to Texas."

Don Manuel sat up straighter and looked at Gutiérrez with more interest.

"I gave him the money, excelencia, and I drew from him the promise that he would keep his eyes and ears open and if he learned anything that would be of benefit to your excellency he would return."

Again Don Manuel looked at Gutiérrez. The man's eyes were closed and he appeared to be asleep on his feet.

"My cousin went to Texas and obtained employment as a mail-carrier between Austin and San Antonio de Bexar. He won the respect of the Texans quickly because he is a man with courage. He worked faithfully and he had several close escapes from Indian attack. He became regarded as one of the most trustworthy of mail-bearers. All the time he was familiarizing himself with the language of the Texans. He kept this knowledge to himself because besides being brave he also is prudent. He happened to be present at a number of meetings among high Texan officials. He was alert. He learned something at last that he believed should be brought to your excellency's ears. He informed his superiors he had received word of sickness in his family and then hastened to Santa Fe. He arrived only tonight and sent word to me immediately at the palace."

"What is the information?" Don Manuel asked.

"Speak, Carlos," Salazar said. "His excellency listens."

Gutiérrez opened his eyes. He rolled a cigarette with slow peasant calm. "The Texans are making preparations to send an armed expedition to Santa Fe."

Don Manuel's thigh ached suddenly. "I must show no fear before these men," he thought. He gripped his leg. "What kind of expedition?" he asked. "Of what size?"

"Three hundred men," Gutiérrez said.

His fingers loosened. "Three hundred men! Do they believe they can conquer New Mexico with a corporal's guard?"

"Three hundred men and fifty merchants with wagons of goods, excelencia," Gutiérrez said.

"Merchants? Wagons? Goods? What kind of invasion is this?"

"It is not exactly an invasion, excelencia. The Texans say they have no intention to make war."

Don Manuel exhaled slowly. "Let us take this carefully, Don Carlos," he said. "There must be no misunderstanding."

Gutiérrez raised his head at the title of courtesy the Governor placed on his name. "There is no misunderstanding, excelencia. The Texans say the expedition is chiefly for business. The Texans need money and they hope to open trade with New Mexico. They are not looking to fight, but the soldiers are not without purpose."

"What of the soldiers?"

"They come not to war but to liberate."

"Liberate whom?"

"The New Mexicans, excelencia."

"Liberate from whom?"

"From you, excelencia."

Salazar said hastily: "My cousin reports only that which he has heard in Texas, excelencia."

"The Texans say that New Mexico east of the Bravo belongs to them and they have heard that the people of New Mexico are not happy under the rule of your excellency," Gutiérrez said. "The President of Texas believes that all that is necessary is for him to send a small force here, no more than these three hundred men, and that the appearance alone of these soldiers will cause New Mexicans to flock to them as liberators."

"You said the intentions were peaceful, for trade."

"There is to be no war, excelencia. If the people do not choose to become Texans, there is still to be no fighting. The merchants are to sell their goods and make arrangements for future business and then all are to go back to Texas."

"Tell his excellency of the circulars," Salazar said.

"Papers have been printed to distribute to the people of New Mexico," Gutiérrez said. "They are written in Spanish. I have read them."

"My cousin was taught the art of reading by Padre Martínez before he left Taos, excelencia," Salazar said proudly.

"The papers promise all freedom to the people of New Mexico if they turn against your excellency and annex themselves to Texas."

"They try to conquer a country with pieces of paper?"

Gutiérrez shrugged. "The Texans believe that all persons would prefer being Texans to anything else, particularly New Mexicans."

"And this is called a peaceful expedition!" Don Manuel exploded. He jumped to his feet. "Santa Madre de Dios, and what kind of slimy snakes are these Texans! To come into this country disguised as friendly business men and while I would honor them as such to try to steal my country from me behind my back! How clever they must believe they are! They risk nothing. If the country does not fall into their hands like ripe fruit they keep the smiles on their faces and go away to return another time and try again. When do they plan to start, señor?"

"In the late spring."

"By what route?"

"They do not know that themselves. There are no maps for the land between the borders of New Mexico and Texas. They talk of finding the Red River and then of following that."

"They must truly be mad!"

"I have listened carefully, excellency, because that unknown land is not unknown to me. I have hunted there often. They enter into a world no gringo has ever explored."

"Can they be such fools? Even Texans?" Don Manuel marveled. "Dios mío, what arrogance! Do they think the earth itself will contrive to do their bidding? Do they have papers printed to send ahead to water holes and grazing lands as well."

"Such is the plan, excelencia."

Don Manuel's eyes were bright. "Amigos, partake of more brandy. I must think on this for a little moment." He walked to a window and opened it. He filled his lungs with the cold night air. "Santa Virgen de Guadalupe," he said silently, "thank you for revealing to me that the heretics come to challenge me not with guns but with trickery." He held his hands clasped in devotion. His teeth gleamed. "Sweetest Mother of Mexico, of all weapons it was the last they should have chosen."

His thoughts came together swiftly and full-formed. He went back to the men. "Don Carlos," he said briskly, "you will return

immediately to Texas. The illness in your family now is cured.
You resume your work as faithful carrier of mail and government
dispatches."

"Serve the Texans again, excelencia?" Carlos asked, puzzled.

"You become more faithful than ever, so there is no one who
does not trust you. And when the expedition is formed, you will
volunteer to join it. As guide, if that is possible."

Gutiérrez looked at his cousin and then at Don Manuel in
slow bewilderment. "Do I understand that your excellency desires
that I lead Texans into New Mexico?"

Don Manuel slammed his hand on the desk. "For certain,
friend!" His face creased without mirth. "But by a route of your
own choosing. A long route that goes in circles through the wildest country. A route that turns up water holes only days apart, just
often enough to keep the heretic dogs alive." His eyes glittered.
"And then at a certain time you disappear and come to me."

Salazar clapped his hands. "Santa Madre! I understand! What
brilliance, excelencia! Carlos leads the Texans to nowhere and
then abandons them so they will die of hunger and thirst, so their
carcasses feed wolves and their bones remain to bleach on the
desert as eternal reminders for all others who would come to us in
enmity. Excelencia, God has given to New Mexico a man of
genius!"

"But they are *not* to die," Don Manuel said.

"Not to die?"

"I want them only *half* dead. You are to lose them, Don
Carlos, but in such a place that sooner or later they will find their
way to Santa Fe. You will lose them so far along they will be
unable to do anything but continue on."

"Now *I* do not understand, excelencia," Salazar said.

Don Manuel smiled. "If you did, Don Damasio, you would
be clever enough to be Governor of New Mexico and then we
would not be friends."

"Excelencia—"

"It is my wish that the Texans arrive here, finally, as shadows
of men," Don Manuel said. "They will tell me they are business
men. I will not accept them as such. I will proclaim them an army
of invasion. Only by then the real battle will be ended. The forces
of nature will have done the fighting for me. I will capture this

231

army. It will be a historic victory. And only we will know the Texans were defeated before they faced us. To the world it will be simply that the Republic of Texas sent up an army to claim land it calls its own, and that this army was defeated by Manuel Armijo."

"Dios santo," Salazar whispered with awe.

"Now do you understand, Don Damasio?"

"I called your excellency a man of genius before. I do not know now what word to apply to your excellency."

"Governor is enough," Don Manuel said dryly. "It is good that you understand. It is more important that *you* understand, Don Carlos."

"It is entirely clear to me, excelencia," Gutiérrez said.

"I am pleased to hear that, señor. Now there are one or two things more. You will find a courier and the day the expedition starts out send him to me with the password 'God and Liberty.' Make certain this man knows how to reach here."

"I will do so, excelencia."

"You have said the plans call for three hundred soldiers and fifty merchants. If there is any change in strength, give the courier the details."

"Yes, excelencia."

"It is possible that in some manner you will be discovered."

"I will not talk, excelencia."

"Every man can be made to talk, Don Carlos. But there is no need for you to endure pain. If they find you out, talk, but do not tell much. Enough only to satisfy them. Now, this is the important thing: they may be clever enough to conceive the idea of sending a message to me under your name to deceive me. In that event you will admit, after a little pressure, that the password between us is 'solitude.' "

Salazar grinned.

"I will know that any message purporting to come from you with the word 'solitude' is not to be believed. That word will tell me you have been unmasked and I must make new plans. Do you understand all that, Don Carlos?"

"Yes, excelencia."

"Repeat your instructions," Don Manuel ordered. When Gutiérrez finished, Armijo said: "Magnificent! You are a man of intelligence, Don Carlos. You may believe that when this venture is over, you will not be forgotten."

"I am a loyal New Mexican, excelencia."

Armijo opened a small silver box on a side table. He took out a leather pouch. "This contains gold, Don Carlos. It belongs to you for the service you have already rendered your country. I will not give it to you now. If it were found in your possession in Texas you would have difficulty explaining how a poor carrier of mail had such a sum. But it is here for you, and when you return to me I will give it to you and another exactly like it."

Carlos's hands opened and closed. His lips twitched. "My life is at the disposal of your excellency."

Don Manuel dropped the pouch back into the box and snapped the cover. He walked slowly to Carlos and embraced him. "Do not dispose of that life. Preserve it to serve your Governor and your country. Now, Don Carlos, you must depart immediately. Let no one here see you. Half of the gringos here are in league with the Texans and in some way you might be recognized. Adiós, dear friend, my gratitude journeys with you." He turned to Salazar. "I do not forget your part in this either, *Capitán* Salazar."

When he was alone he knelt before the crucifix on the wall. "Nuestro Señor Jesucristo," he whispered, "everything is answered. Everything, the troubles in the north, the discontent, everything, even the commission from the City of Mexico. Señor Padre, thank You."

1

PADRE MARTÍNEZ said the words of absolution and made
the sign of the cross. The dying man jerked his head violently as
though he were trying to tear himself from that which was holding
him, and then he fell back exhausted and died.

The priest stood up wearily. "Do you have friends who will
dig the grave?" he asked the dead man's wife.

"There is no money for holy burial, padre," the woman said.

"Have the grave dug," Martínez said. "I will give him Catholic burial."

Martínez left the house. Fifteen or twenty men and women
were awaiting him. They set up a clamor.

"I am next, padre," a woman cried, tugging at his cassock. "It
is Antonito. He is your student, padre."

"I was here before this one," another woman cried. "My husband, Gilberto, he who assisted with the repairs on the south wall
of the church. On his belly is already the sign of the rose."

A man shouted: "I was here before the dawn, padre."

"And I came right after him," another woman screamed.

Martínez raised his hands. He leaned against the door. "Peace,
peace, I will make time for all." He shook himself to keep awake.
He had not been in bed for three days.

Taos was filled with refugees from the Beaubien land grant.
They had come in endlessly for weeks, on foot, on burros, dragging
small carts, and they filled the streets and the fields so that Taos
now had the appearance of a camp rather than of a community.

It was spring and the food they had was what was left from the
previous fall. The food of the citizens of Taos was also that stored
from the last harvest. The snows had not yet begun to melt in the
mountains, and the supply of water was low.

The dispossessed sat silently beside their belongings, waiting
for they knew not what, and after the first weeks the epidemic
started. The homeless were huddled together; they defecated in

the streets and the meadows, the flies swarmed on the warm days, and when the sickness started, it went from one family to another, always the same. First the fever and then the aching in all the bones and then the nosebleeds; then there appeared the red rash on the abdomen, the sign of the rose. Each victim hoped all along it was a mistake until the rose appeared. From then on, nothing could be done. There was no doctor in Taos. The sick remained strewn on the ground or on pallets in houses, and the flesh fell away until it seemed impossible the bones would not push their way through the skin. Some of them died and some of them recovered, and no one could say why the black angel touched one and passed another by.

Padre Martínez looked down at the supplicants. If a man could only divide himself so that he could do more than one man! What right had he to decide who should die without grace? He pointed to the mother of his student Antonito. "I will go with you," he said.

"Thanks to God, padre," the woman said.

The other people did not protest. They stepped back to make way as the priest hurried off with the woman, and they followed them to take up the vigil at the house of Antonito.

In the house the flies buzzed. The boy, who was eight, lay on a mattress made of cornhusks. There seemed to the priest to be nothing in his face but eyes. He touched the child's forehead and pulled off the sack with which the child was covered.

The mother screamed: "The mark of the rose! Santa Madre, it was not there before, padre!"

Antonito recognized the priest. "Good day to him of God, Padre Martínez," he said.

"That God may give you many good days, little son," the priest replied.

"Am I going to die, padre?"

"Die? How foolish! Only very old people die."

"Is Pepe well?"

"Pepe?"

"It is his kid," the mother said.

"He is very well," Martínez said.

Antonito smiled. "He is very young. He must have food many times a day."

Martínez took his hand. "I will take Pepe to my own house and I will feed him myself. When you get well he will be so fat you will not recognize him."

Antonito nodded tiredly. "Thank you, padre."

"And now you must sleep. When you sleep, little son, then the sickness becomes frightened, and if you sleep often enough, then the sickness says finally: 'Well, I cannot stay with this muchachito any longer. I believe I will go away.' And, presto! You wake up and you are better."

"I will sleep, padre," the child said.

Martínez stood up. The woman was biting the knuckle of her forefinger. Her eyes asked the question. The priest prayed and crossed himself. "God makes His own decision, my daughter." He left the house and chose another supplicant from among those waiting.

The epidemic went in waves. For days the incidence of contraction fell off. Then, as though it had been resting to gather its strength, the disease would strike again and people who had felt encouragement on one day toppled over on the next.

On a warm, sunny morning Padre Martínez was holding a pan of milk under the long chin of Pepe. He was watching the slender tongue slop up the milk when he received word that Antonito had died during the night. The priest's chin fell upon his chest. He held the pan until Pepe finished the last of the milk. He stroked the animal's soft neck and then he put down the pan and started for the office of Colonel Diego Archuleta, prefect of the north.

2

"In what capacity do you call upon me, padre?" Archuleta asked. He was a tall man with a heavy, tight-lipped face. "As deputy to the departmental Junta or as priest?"

Martínez fingered his crucifix. "You know as well as I do that the rank of deputy is a meaningless one, Don Diego. I come to you as a Christian, as a human being, as a New Mexican."

"Then I say to all the three men that I exist here but to obey the commands of the Governor of New Mexico."

"Something must be done about these people."

"I have no authority to do anything without orders from Don Manuel."

The priest's face was glassy with sweat. "Then communicate with his excellency and tell him of the conditions that exist here. The refugees must be allowed to return north."

"Don Manuel is aware of everything that happens here. If he desired to do anything he would give me his order. Are you ill, padre?"

"No, señor, I am not ill, not in the way you mean," the priest said bitterly. "My illness is only because of the callousness that permits people to die as though they were animals without souls. Where is your conscience, Don Diego? How can you sit here as though made of stone while your countrymen fall dead on all sides of you?" The sweat streamed on his face.

"Is this an official protest? Have the people appointed you to speak for them?"

"They do not complain, Don Diego. They accept their sufferings as though the disease were an act of God."

"They are wiser than you, I think," Archuleta said. "We all must die when our time comes. Go back to the people and serve them as priest and leave the affairs of government to those whose business it is."

"It is no act of God! It is the act of Armijo!"

"In either case there is no recourse, padre," Archuleta said impassively.

The priest pushed himself to his feet. He left the office. The sun smote him like a hot blade. He staggered and recovered and then fell over into the street.

He lay between life and death for three weeks. When he emerged from the delirium, he tried to sit up.

"Do not try to move, padre," a woman said. "You are still in the shadow."

He blinked his eyes and looked at the woman. "Morena, what do I do here?"

"There were many in your house, padre. The little children. It was thought safer to keep you separated from them."

"And you offered me your house, Morena?"

"It was an honor, padre. You must not speak more."

A week later, over the protests of the woman, he climbed on his burro. "I will not try to thank you, my daughter," he said. "God bless you."

"My house is already blessed, padre."

He started south for Santa Fe.

3

DON MANUEL helped Martínez to a chair. "In the name of God, padre, what has happened to you?"

"I have been ill, excelencia."

"The epidemic?"

"Yes."

"Why was I not informed? You might have died."

"Many have died. Others die at this moment."

Don Manuel sighed as he sat down. "It is a terrible thing indeed, Don Antonio. And to come at such a time."

"Is death less welcome now than it might be at another time?"

"Death is never welcome, padre, it is true," Don Manuel said gravely. "But to strike like this at our time of national danger!"

"It does constitute national danger, excelencia. But I did not understand you regarded it as such."

"The whole country is in uproar," Don Manuel said, surprised. "And am I not the leader of my country?"

Martínez smiled with relief. "I cannot express to you my happiness at finding you in this sympathetic mood, excelencia. I gathered from Coronel Archuleta that you were not concerned in the least. He himself is indifferent."

"Not indifferent, padre! He has but the calm attitude of the trained officer."

"Then you have definite plans to assist the refugees? You will allow them to return to their homes?"

"If there are any they will be permitted to return to their homes."

"If there are any? Taos is filled with refugees, excelencia, and with the refugees, the sickness."

"I was not speaking of those persons who were required to leave the land granted to Carlos Beaubien, padre," Don Manuel said. He waved his hand expansively. "Oh, they give me concern, of course. And, believe me, they would concern me more if it were not for the war."

"War?"

The two men gazed at each other. Then Don Manuel asked quietly: "Where have you been the last month, padre?"

"I have been ill with the fever."

"Did you notice nothing on your way down from the north? Has the capital not surprised you with its military activity? No one may leave or enter the city without permission. Santa Fe is under martial law."

"It has been for some time, excelencia," the priest said. "I was stopped and questioned once or twice by soldiers, but my way was not barred."

"You were recognized."

"What war, excelencia?"

Don Manuel shook his head in amazement. "Can it be possible you do not know that an army of Texans is on the march? Madre de Dios, what have we been talking about?"

"I believed we were talking about the dispossessed and the dying in Taos."

"At this moment the heretics are on their way to invade New Mexico and you talk of sick people in Taos!"

"What trick is this?" Martínez rasped.

"Trick?" Armijo shouted. "We are at war!"

"You are not as disturbed as you should be," the priest said. "I have followed the workings of your mind before. What kind of scheme is this?"

For a moment Don Manuel's face was dangerous and then he smiled. "You have been sick, padre," he said in a controlled voice. "It was just ten days ago I received word by Comanche courier that an army left Austin on the 21st day of June to make war on the Department of New Mexico."

The priest was stunned. Presently he looked at Don Manuel with his sunken eyes and said: "I wonder for what special fate you are being saved."

"My destiny will take care of itself, padre," Armijo said

evenly. "At the moment I can think only of the defense of my country."

"Naturally."

Armijo's eyes narrowed. "It is not a war of conquest alone. It is a religious war as well. The Texans have no love for Catholics, padre."

Martínez sighed heavily. "How convenient for you that this happens to be true!" he said.

As he undressed to rest in the chamber provided in the palace by Don Manuel, Martínez thought how the sick and the dying in Taos were now to be deprived of relief in the name of patriotism and religion. He thought how, in order to defend the Church, it was necessary for him to stand again at the side of Manuel Armijo.

4

IN THE LAST WEEK of August, Carlos Gutiérrez returned to Santa Fe and reported to Governor Armijo that he had abandoned the Texans about one hundred and fifty miles from San Miguel.

Don Manuel, who had been getting reports on the progress of the Texans from Indians in his hire, heard this news with the keenest excitement. By now the people of New Mexico were in panic. For weeks the priests, led by Padre Martínez and Padre Juan Felipe Ortiz, who had returned from Mexico, had thundered from the pulpits that the Texans would burn churches and slay priests, would commit arson and pillage and rapine as they had done five years earlier when they rebelled against the motherland.

The campaign of fear and hatred was not directed against the Texans alone. During the summer, bands of youths roamed the country armed with clubs and staves and assaulted Americans and destroyed their property "in the name of Armijo, the name of the true Church, and the name of Mexico." Scores of Americans, many of whom had lived in New Mexico for years, were killed, injured, or arrested. The victims were on all levels, from a deaf-mute in Taos who was clubbed to death because his ailment prevented him from responding immediately to a summons from the alcalde, to Charles Bent, one of the brothers who owned Bent's Fort on the Platte and Arkansas Rivers. Bent, who was married to a New Mexican woman in Taos, was arrested and sent in chains to Santa Fe and was kept in prison for a week before Don Manuel released him.

The demonstrations in Santa Fe were quieted, almost by magic, during the time of the arrival of the annual caravan, which was a good one that year, the traders bringing in more than one hundred and fifty thousand dollars' worth of merchandise in sixty wagons. Don Manuel used the natural concern of these traders over what the next few weeks might bring to persuade them to dispose of their merchandise at lower prices than normal. When the merchants departed, the rioting resumed.

In all, Don Manuel was content with the way he had managed things. He welcomed Gutiérrez cordially and asked him immediately about the condition of the Texans.

"There have been many deaths, excelencia," Gutiérrez said. "Those remaining can be said to be not dead and that is all."

"In no condition to fight?"

"They fight only to remain alive."

Don Manuel rubbed his hands together contentedly. "Begin at the beginning, Don Carlos." He sat on the edge of his desk and pushed the brandy decanter toward the peasant.

When he had refreshed himself Gutiérrez made himself comfortable and told the Governor he had signed on as a wagon-driver for the Texans. "At the start I did nothing else, excelencia. There was no need for me to help the Texans go wrong. From the very first everything that was to be done was improperly done. If your excellency had been there yourself you could not have aided yourself more than did the leaders of this expedition. The men were without discipline. They obeyed no one. It was as though they were going out for sport. The start of the expedition was delayed for five weeks, and I knew then they would be in the driest country in the hottest part of the summer.

"They were not on the trail a week before the water trouble started. Between the 1st day of July and the 4th day of July men died from eating wild berries they thought would satisfy their thirst. By the middle of July they were mired down in the quicksands of the Brazos, and when they crossed the stream they were beset by a prairie fire.

"By the third week of July they reached the Cross Timbers, and there they had to fight every foot of the way. They had to cut down trees to make passage; the land was filled with ravines and they traveled twenty miles to move five miles ahead. When they reached a stream at last, they decided they had to strip themselves of excess baggage, and it was then they discovered that much of the dried beef they had brought from Austin had spoiled. When they discarded it, the air filled with vultures like black rain and for the first time the Texans began to believe they might soon be without food as well as without water.

"Despite the lightening of the load the expedition bogged down again in the Cross Timbers. That is terrible country, excelencia. The train was strung out over a long distance. No wagon could pass another. The men were choked with thirst, and the oxen refused to draw. The men now were like maniacs, galloping in all directions, looking for water. Nobody could find water and no one could eat because their throats were too parched to swallow food. In the nights many of the mules broke free and then more wagons had to be abandoned. When we passed through the forest at last, we found a stream and made camp. The water tasted good, excelencia."

Don Manuel nodded and touched the decanter. Gutiérrez poured himself another drink. He made a cigarette and the Governor held a candle toward him.

"The camp was a pleasant place, excelencia. The men seemed to recover quickly. They began to laugh and to sing songs. They are brave men and they are strong. They set up a blacksmith forge and made repairs on wagons. They felt so cheerful some of them began to say they were certain the Red River was only a short distance away. These men boast a great deal and pretend to have knowledge of things they have no knowledge of, and they talked so much about the Red River they convinced themselves they would see it the next day or the day after that.

"We did not see it the next day or in the next several days, as I knew we would not, and the men became as discouraged as they had previously been confident. It was then that it appeared to me to be a good time to speak up. One of the officers spoke a very good Spanish, and he translated for me. I told the general in command that I was from Taos and that I had hunted and trapped in the country of the Red River, which is true, and that I believed we were near the stream, which was not true. The general asked his officers if any of them knew me, and several of the officers and merchants said they recognized me and that I was a man who could be trusted."

Don Manuel smiled demoniacally. "Good, good, compañero."

"Then the general asked me if I would serve as guide. I did not have to offer, excelencia."

"Madre de Dios!"

Carlos Gutiérrez's face became somber. "It made me understand that God is truly on our side, excelencia." He was at that moment all Spanish, involved in the relationship between Spaniard and the God who is Spaniard. "I said also that I expected to be paid more money as guide than wagon-driver."

Don Manuel clapped his hands softly. "Dios mío, Don Carlos, but you have imagination."

"It was the demand for more money that convinced the general more than anything else that I could be relied upon. The next day we encountered a large party of Indians. I knew again that God had His hand upon my shoulder, excelencia, because no one could speak the language of the Indians but I. They were forced to use me as interpreter. The Indians were of great size and were mounted on beautiful ponies, and they had rifles that looked like gringo rifles. I told them the Texans were on a peaceful trading mission and they said they knew that and told me how many soldiers and how many wagons we had."

"They were Indians of the Waco tribe, Don Carlos," Armijo said with satisfaction. "They were employed by me."

"Later we found the village of these Indians, but it was abandoned. The Texans were astounded at the appearance of the village with its little houses and the storehouses and the fields of pumpkins and melon and corn. The Texans believe all Indians are savage. I was proud then of my Indian blood and I knew that while I could respect the Texans as brave men, I could never love them. In the night one of the Waco men came secretly to the camp and found me and gave me the password, and I told him about the condition of the Texans."

"He came faithfully to me, Don Carlos," Armijo said.

"The next day I explored the country, and when I returned I told the general I was confident that the stream on which the village was located was the Red River." He made another cigarette and leaned toward the candle to light it. The scar was a white slash on his cheek.

"It was not the Red River," Don Manuel said.

"It was not. It was the Wichita. The general looked at some sketches he had and said the bend in the river where the village was must be a place called Coffee's Upper Station. Only if that were true, he said, then the stream should be going southwest and not northwest. I told him the Red River twists like a snake. I said that though the journey would be longer by following its course, the country was easier. The general pondered for a little while and then decided to take my advice.

"We followed the stream for three days, and the land was easy land as I had promised and everyone was in good spirits. We were going in a southwesterly direction, which everyone knew was not the way to reach New Mexico, but I assured them the river soon would shift its direction. Then one day the stream joined another larger stream and I said that this new stream was my old friend the River Utah. I said I had often trapped there and that this was the exact place where the buffalo-hunters crossed with their carts. I showed them the ruts of the cartwheels and everyone was happy, and now they had complete faith in me. I said that the narrows of the Red River were perhaps sixty miles distant and that another sixty miles beyond that we would come to the first ranchos of San Miguel.

"The beef had been growing worse daily, because of the poor feed and the long marches and the lack of water. The sugar was gone and the coffee almost gone. Three pounds of beef were still being given out for each man each day, but because its quality was poor it did not nourish properly. At least it did not nourish Texans. I found it ample.

"I waited until all were asleep that night and then I went to the corral and struck the oxen across their soft noses with my quirt. I returned to where I slept and in a few moments heard cries of 'Stampede!' Much equipment was ruined. In the morning it was as though a tornado had struck the camp."

"And no one suspected you?" Don Manuel marveled.

"No one. From then on, the country grew rougher than before, as I knew it would. There were mountain ranges with no passages through them, and the men again became discouraged. The earth was very hard and the oxen suffered in their feet. Many oxen had to be unyoked, and that made it worse for the others. Three days later we came to a high mesa where the ground was heavily covered with grass. I said that this was the place where my countrymen brought their sheep. That night I told them that San Miguel was but eighty miles away.

"I was asked whether it would be possible for a rider with a light pack to make the distance in three days, and I said it could be done easily. Then a gringo named Samuel Howland, who said he had been a merchant in Santa Fe, offered to ride ahead."

"I know that man," Don Manuel said.

"He said he spoke Spanish well and that he would find your excellency and tell him about the expedition and make things ready for its reception. He departed with two other men. They did not go in the direction of San Miguel and I knew they would not reach there in three days or three times three days.

"The course now led away from the river. There was no water at all. The men sucked bullets and pieces of rawhide. The animals became almost unmanageable. Then in the middle of one afternoon we came to what seemed to the men to be the end of the world. We reached a precipice that dropped more than three hundred feet. I do not know what would have happened then if some of the men did not spy a small river in the valley below.

"About fifty of them went down to see about the water. I knew it had turned salty many years before and was not fit to drink, but I did not say anything. I knew when the men found that out, it would be too much; there would be trouble and I would be the first to suffer. It was time to go, excelencia, but there was one thing more that could be done. I waited until twilight and then I started a small fire in the tall grass where we were camped. The dry grass caught like gunpowder. A wind came up from the west and drove the fire in the direction of the men and the animals and the wagons.

"Then, I tell you, there was panic. The men recovered and tried to keep the flames from reaching the wagons, but they were not successful. The first wagon to catch fire was one that contained a great deal of ammunition. This wagon exploded, and then other wagons caught fire. Soon more than ten wagons were blazing. The animals went wholly crazy and ran in all directions. Some of them tumbled down the cliff.

"For a while I helped with the fire-fighting. When I could, I found a horse and rode away. Hours later I looked back. The prairie was still blazing and the fire had spread so greatly it seemed as though the sky had caught fire too. And that is what happened, excelencia."

Throughout the recital Don Manuel had not moved from his position on the edge of the desk. As he listened to the peasant he thought how Carlos Gutiérrez was not different from the things he had described. He was as hard as the earth, as hard as the rocks, as hard as the mountains. He had spoken of the thirst and the hunger and the exhaustion as though he too had not hungered and thirsted, as though he had been a spectator who had had food and water and had not wearied as the other men wearied. It was because to him none of these things were new, Don Manuel thought as he listened to the words fall with no emotion from Gutiérrez's lips. To the peasant of my country to be hungry and tired and despairing is the manner of life.

For a long while after Gutiérrez finished, Don Manuel said nothing, leaning forward from the desk top, his eyes fixed on the harsh, scarred face, and then he sighed deeply. "It was enough, Don Carlos. It was more than enough."

He stood up stiffly and limped to the strongbox and took out two pouches. He hefted them and then handed them to the peasant.

5

CAPTAIN CABALLERO, dwarfed by the large chair in which he was seated, looked down the long dinner table and beamed at his son and Don Ramón Baca. "This is your time, young men. This is what you have been trained for all your lives. War means glory and promotion. Dios mío, if only I could be at your side!"

He smiled to Soledad and Lupe Baca. "You will be proud of your two men!"

"You went to see Don Manuel, did you not, Don José?" Soledad asked softly.

The pleasure left Captain Caballero's face. He nodded heavily. "I told his excellency I did not expect to take command again, but that I would serve in any capacity. He thanked me, oh, most graciously, but nothing was done." He twisted his wineglass in his fingers. "To miss out on this, a war with Texans!"

"I do not think you miss much, Don José," Esquipulas said quietly. "It would seem Don Manuel does not intend that the presidial companies will do the fighting. Only the Rurales were given training and equipment and they have already been dispatched to the field under the command of Archuleta and Salazar. The presidial troops are not to stir from the capital."

"The presidial troops belong to the capital," Captain Caballero said proudly. "It is their historic duty. Don Manuel holds them here so they may defend Santa Fe in the event the Rurales are unable to stop the Texans, which is quite possible with the militia."

Ramón Baca asked: "What makes everyone so certain there is going to be a war?"

"The Texan barbarians will be satisfied with nothing else," Captain Caballero said with vehemence.

"How do we know Texans are marching upon us?"

Captain Caballero frowned. "I do not understand, Don Ramón."

Baca's lips curled. "We have only the word of Armijo."

"Don Ramón!" Captain Caballero said sternly.

"Your pardon, señor." Baca emptied his glass.

Lupe threw up her hands in disgust. "You drink too much and you talk too much," she said to her husband. "War! War! Let us forget about this war and talk instead of the marriage. To me that is more exciting than war."

Soledad crinkled her nose. "To me as well, Lupe. I am not distressed that the presidial companies are being held in Santa Fe." She reached across the table and touched Esquipulas on the hand.

Lupe glared at Baca. "Always are you sneering at Don Manuel, and yet in the midst of all his great responsibilities now, he still has found time to arrange the marriage and stand as its sponsor. This Don Manuel is a big man, husband, and I am not alone in that belief. People talk of it more than they do of the war. They find it difficult to understand and yet there it is."

"I find it difficult to understand too," Baca said.

"You should not," Soledad said.

Baca refilled his glass and drained half of it. "Why should Don Manuel be happy about this marriage?"

"It was what he wanted long ago," Soledad said quietly.

"What do you mean by that?" Baca demanded.

"He told me so himself. It was on the night of the party to honor Capitán Silva. You will remember, Ramón, that you were angry because Don Manuel spoke to me at such length. And you will remember, Esquipulas, my dear one, that I told you the Governor and I shared a secret. The secret was only that Don Manuel assured me you would ask me to be your wife and he told me then how much it filled his heart with gladness and how he wanted to sponsor the ceremony when it would take place since I had no father alive to do it." She looked steadily at Baca. "Don Manuel's words gave me peace, Ramón, because at that time I wondered whether Esquipulas would offer me the honor of his name, and it was on that same night after the party that Esquipulas made the Governor's words true."

"What have you to say to that?" Lupe asked triumphantly.

Baca finished the rest of his wine. His upper lip was beaded with sweat. "I say only that there is nothing that this Armijo says that I do not believe he means just the opposite. I think he is a poltroon and I know nothing of whether Texans come or do not come. This I know, that Armijo is no man of courage. If he appears to be resolute, it is only that for some reason he knows there is nothing to fear." He looked at each of the other faces. "I also do not believe in his good will toward the marriage. Don Manuel has not changed overnight. He has found no nobility. I do not know what he plans, but he plans something. I love you, Esquipulas, as my friend, and I love you, Soledad, as my niece and as one who is to become wife to my friend, and I tell you both to be on guard." He stared at his empty glass. He muttered: "*Guarda!* *Guarda!*"

6

ESQUIPULAS CABALLERO and Soledad Abreu were married on a morning early in September in La Castrense, favorite church of Governor Armijo. The ceremony was performed by Vicario Juan Felipe Ortiz, who wore for the first time a chasuble embroidered in purple and gold which he had had made in the City of Mexico. In his plain, white dalmatic Padre Martínez, who served as deacon at the nuptial Mass, was almost lost from sight.

The sponsorship of the Governor gave to the ceremony an official air, and the plaza in front of the military chapel was thronged as the guests arrived. The fortunate women who had been invited wore gowns over which seamstresses had labored feverishly for weeks, from the day the new material was brought in by the summer caravan. The wealthier ladies had had three gowns made, one for the church, one for the reception later in the palace, and a third for the baile scheduled for that evening. The men were in uniform or native dress. No Americans were invited.

There was a stir and quickening of breath in the beautiful church when the bride appeared wearing a gown made of white satin and Valenciennes lace. The guests agreed too that Don Esquipulas, in his uniform, was a handsome man, in the old Spanish way. But it was plain that Don Manuel was the first man in the land, a picture of serene nobility as he gave the bride to the groom.

The Latin words were pronounced by Padre Ortiz, and in the name of the Father, the Son, and the Holy Ghost Soledad Abreu became Doña Soledad Caballero de Abreu.

The presidial companies and the palace band were formed in the plaza as the couple emerged from the church just before noon. The officers drew their swords, the soldiers cheered, and the band struck up a lively march. The people under the portales joined their voices.

By order of Don Manuel the band remained in the plaza, and when the area was cleared of the military and the wedding party, the musicians began to play again and the people flooded in and sang and danced and there was the spirit of the fiesta.

7

AT THE WEDDING RECEPTION Don Manuel presented to the bride a silver and turquoise necklace made by the renowned local silversmith Don Francisco Patania. As he fastened the necklace around the neck of Doña Soledad, and as Captain Caballero wept without shame, Don Manuel clasped Doña Soledad in one arm and Don Esquipulas in the other and hugged them tightly. "Here," he said, "is the future of our country."

It was more than an hour later that some of the guests noticed that the music in the plaza had stopped abruptly on a long, broken note, as though sound were ripped, and that there was silence outside and then the sounds of hoofs. One of the guests looked from a window and said: "Excelencia!"

Don Manuel walked to the window. The part of the plaza directly in front of the palace was cleared except for a semicircle of mounted soldiers. Leading the cavalrymen was the nephew of the Governor, Lieutenant Tomás Martínez. Don Tomás held a thick piece of rope. At the other end of the rope were three barefooted, emaciated men, tied together neck to neck like draft animals.

When the Governor appeared at the window, one of the three prisoners pulled forward. "Don Manuel!" he cried. "Succor! Succor!"

Don Tomás whipped the man across the back. "Down on your knees, dogs!" he commanded. He jerked the rope and the three men fell to their knees. "Excelencia," Don Tomás said loudly, "I bring you the first of the Texan prisoners!"

1

Lieutenant Tomás Martínez herded the prisoners into the Governor's office and again ordered them to kneel. Now not only were the men bound to each other but their hands were tied behind their backs. One of the men fell on his face. Don Tomás booted him. The man pulled himself to his knees.

Seated in tribunal line with the Governor were Captain Silva, Padre Martínez, Juan Estevan Pino, Juan Bautista Vigil, and one or two other men summoned from the reception. The appearance of the prisoners had caused fearful excitement among the guests, but after asking these men to accompany him Don Manuel had requested that the reception continue as planned.

Before he left the window the Governor had listened for a few moments to the people in the plaza shouting "Death to the Texans" and then he had announced: "Your Governor is going to interrogate them, amigos. There is no danger. Your Governor has put eyes and ears everywhere on the border."

He had ordered the band to play again, but the fiesta mood was ended.

At a command from the Governor the prisoners got to their feet clumsily. The prisoner who had pleaded for succor stepped forward again. He was a tall, sandy-haired man with light, blue eyes. A week's stubble of beard did not hide his fine features. His clothing was in tatters, as was that of the other two men. "Don Manuel, how happy I am to see you at last!" he said in fluent Spanish.

"Señor Samuel Howland," Don Manuel said, "so it is you."

Howland seemed relieved that Don Manuel had recognized him. "And you, Don Juan Bautista, and you, Don Juan Estevan Pino. And Padre Martínez. It is good to see all of you again. Excelencia, I have told my friends there has been a mistake and that as soon as we reached your excellency it would be straightened out."

251

"Who are your friends?" Don Manuel asked.

"This is Señor Rosenberg, excelencia, and this one is Señor Baker."

"Are you all Texans, Don Samuel?"

"We are, excelencia."

"Do you call yourself Texan as well?"

"Yes, excelencia."

"When you lived in Santa Fe you were known as American."

"I was born in the United States, excelencia."

"But you now term yourself not American but Texan. What you say, señor, is that there is no difference between an American and a Texan, is that not so?"

"Most Texans come originally from the United States, excelencia. I do not understand what your excellency tries to prove."

"I prove only that a Texan and an American are one and the same thing," Don Manuel said in sudden fury. He nodded, with a grim smile, to his friends. Padre Martínez's face arrested him. It was a concentration of hatred. At that moment, Don Manuel knew, the priest was closer to him than he had been at any time since Taos. "It is what I have said all along, Don Samuel. I have known from the beginning that the Americans conspire with the Texans, and you are proof of that conspiracy!"

Howland's eyes clouded and he shook his head. "There has been no conspiracy," he said in a tired voice.

"You were welcomed into this city as a friend," Armijo said relentlessly. "You lived among us for many years. You spoke our language, and our people bought goods from you, and you made a living from us. We trusted you innocently, like children. And then without word, without reason, you left. And now you return not as an American and friend, but as a Texan, leading a party of war against us. And you say there is no conspiracy!"

"I am not the leader of the expedition, Don Manuel, and it is not a party of war," Howland said. The two other prisoners, who understood no Spanish, looked at him worriedly.

"You helped to guide the expedition," Armijo said.

"Only because I knew something of the country, and even then not for long. I come as a business man, excelencia, with other business men, only to renew old friendships and re-establish my business affairs."

"And I say you return with the treachery of a snake, leading an army to destroy people who gave you their trust!"

"Your excellency is mistaken. There is no thought of war."

"There is little use to lie to me," Don Manuel shouted. "I know the President of your country calls New Mexico part of Texas."

"That may be true, excelencia, but the men who crossed the country between Texas and New Mexico have come in peace."

"With three hundred soldiers armed to the teeth!"

"The soldiers were for protection against Indians."

Don Manuel smiled craftily at his friends. "Your intentions were wholly peaceful, then?"

"I swear it, excelencia."

"With no thoughts of war, of siege?"

"No, excelencia." Howland's eyes filled with hope. "I swear it on my word of honor."

"The word of a heretic!" Padre Martínez said harshly.

"I am not of your faith, padre, but I am a man of honor," Howland said.

Don Manuel asked softly: "And what of the proclamations, Don Samuel?" He stood up and leaned over the desk. "Yes, Don Samuel, the proclamations, printed in Spanish for my people to understand. Telling them they are citizens of Texas, asking them to welcome the Texans as liberators and to turn against me. What of these, señor?"

Howland lowered his head. "I think they were a mistake, excelencia."

"What kind of fool do you think I am!" Don Manuel roared. "What kind of fool does your President think I am! To send an expedition in the name of peace with a loaded gun in the hand of each man and a wagon filled with papers urging my people to overthrow me! Do you still talk of peace and friendly trade?"

"The President did wrong, excelencia."

"Of course you say that now," Don Manuel sneered. "You are my prisoner. What else can you say?"

"I have said nothing I did not believe to be true."

"With whom do you think you deal, señor? Do you believe we are savages without power of reasoning? We are a nation older and more legal than your own! Do not tell me lies about peace. I call this expedition an act of war!"

"Then there is nothing more to be said, excelencia," Howland said quietly. He squared his shoulders. "You are in command, excelencia. You will do as you choose. I can only repeat for the last time that my friends have come in peace. If President Mirabeau Lamar was presumptuous, it is not their fault. They come as business men and not as conquerors. As God is my judge, I swear this to you."

2

A KEY TURNED in the lock and the door creaked open. Howland raised his head. A guard asked: "Who is the one who speaks Spanish?"

"I," Howland said.

The guard looked down the dark corridor. "The way is clear. There are three horses outside and muskets. Follow the road to San Miguel. Do you know the road to San Miguel?"

"What is this?" Howland jumped up.

"There is food in the saddlebags. There is not much time. Go!"

"What is he saying?" Baker asked.

"He says we can escape. He says there are three horses outside with guns and food."

"Then what in the name of God are we waiting for? Let's go."

Howland hesitated. "I smell a rat."

"We could get word to the others, Sam," Rosenberg said. "We could warn them about Armijo."

"There's something fake about this," Howland said.

Rosenberg clutched his arm. "Listen, Sam, you've been saying Armijo is planning something dirty for us. If we stay here, he shoots us or hangs us. If we get out, maybe we can fight. And we might get through and bring word to the others. They're all walking into a trap and we're the only ones who know about it."

"He's right," Baker said.

"Why are you letting us free?" Howland asked the guard.

The guard shrugged. "We do not all love Don Manuel, señor. You talk too much. I risk my life. Go before it is too late."

Howland translated. "I don't believe any of it. We've done nothing wrong. Why should we run like criminals?"

"Because we haven't got a chance here," Baker said.

"And the others," Rosenberg said. "My God, what will happen to them if they're not warned?"

"I'm getting," Baker said.

"And I," Rosenberg said.

The two men ran out of the cell and down the corridor. After a moment's hesitation Howland followed them. Outside were the three horses. There were muskets in the saddle scabbards. There was food in the bags. The three men galloped off. It was just past midnight.

They rode through the night. They passed through the narrow mouth of Apache Canyon and then headed southeast. They slept during the day and traveled at night. Howland planned to lead them around San Miguel and try to intercept the Texans on their way to the village. Just before they reached San Miguel, in a pocket in the hills, they were attacked in the night by half a hundred New Mexican soldiers.

The three Texans formed a small circle. The New Mexicans opened fire. Rosenberg was killed at the first volley. The New Mexicans closed in. A soldier swung his saber with both hands in a great arc. The blade cut off Howland's right ear and part of his cheek and almost severed his right arm at the shoulder. Baker dropped the soldier with a musket ball in his heart. The two men fought until they were overwhelmed and knocked unconscious.

They were tied to their horses and Lieutenant Tomás Martínez gave the order to return to Santa Fe. Rosenberg's body was left for the wolves.

Don Tomás reported on the fight to Governor Armijo as soon as he reached the capital.

"Were there Mexican deaths?" Don Manuel demanded.

"Four, excelencia. Seven others were wounded, two so badly they may not live."

Don Manuel nodded with satisfaction. "They will be buried in a large public ceremony with all military honors. I will make a speech."

"The two Texans who live are back in their cell," Don Tomás said.

"Neither they nor any of the other Texans now will be able to proclaim they came in peace," Don Manuel said. He smiled affectionately at his nephew. "You arranged everything well."

3

IN THE CLEAR AUTUMN AFTERNOON from his headquarters in the grounds of an abandoned mission, as Don Manuel waited for the arrival of five more Texans captured by Captain Damasio Salazar, he watched his soldiers marching on the road to San Miguel. From time to time he swallowed a mouthful of brandy against the increasing chill. The winter was coming on early.

The sun was setting over the western mountains when a soldier galloped up to Don Manuel. The Governor signaled. The bugler sounded the command and the honor guard formed its ranks. Don Manuel was assisted onto his lavishly caparisoned horse. He adjusted the rich blue, embroidered serape he wore over his uniform. Drummers began a rhythmic beat. Pennants were raised.

A small platoon of cavalry rounded a bend in the road from the direction of San Miguel. Strung out between their lines were five prisoners, on foot. The leader of the platoon, a fat moonfaced man with sweeping mustaches, saluted flamboyantly. "Excelencia! Teniente Jesús Alpuente, reporting with the Texan prisoners!"

Don Manuel returned the salute languidly, riding past the quivering officer until he reached the prisoners. He gazed silently at the five fettered men. Their clothing hung in rags. Their faces were haggard with hunger and exhaustion; their arms and legs were torn with scratches, and the lips of two of them were broken with sores. Boots had burst and the right ankle of one of the men was swollen. Don Manuel sighed. "Unbind the prisoners," he said in a mellow voice. When the men were freed he leaned over and shook each man's hand. "Friends, I have heard of your capture.

Have the goodness to identify yourselves. As for me, I am Don Manuel Armijo, Governor and General Commandant of New Mexico." He sat back gracefully in the saddle, a sad and friendly smile on his face.

One of the prisoners, a rangy, blond man, said instantly in perfect Spanish: "We are merchants from the United States, excelencia."

Another of the prisoners pushed him aside. "That is not true, excelencia. Four of us are Texans. Only one of us is a citizen of the United States."

Don Manuel's smile vanished. He seized the blond man by his tunic, jerked him from the ground, and shook him roughly, pointing to the buttons on his tunic. "What does this mean?" he shouted. "I can read. 'Texas!' No merchant from the United States ever travels with a Texan military jacket!"

"I made a mistake, excelencia," the man said. "I offer a thousand apologies to your excellency."

Don Manuel flung him to the ground.

"Forgive me, excelencia," the man sobbed. He crawled to his knees. "It is only that I am so worn from our terrible experiences. I did not realize what I was saying to your excellency." The four other prisoners stared at him.

Don Manuel turned to the man who had contradicted the blond man. "Perhaps you can speak the truth, señor."

The storm left the Governor's face as quickly as it had come. In a polite manner he questioned the man, who said his name was Peter Van Ness. The prisoner told him that the Texans had split into two groups, and that one group under the command of the leader of the expedition, General Hugh McLeod, had remained at Palo Duro, some one hundred miles from San Miguel, and the other had continued on until it reached the Gallinas River. The five men, he said, had ridden on ahead of the Gallinas River group.

Van Ness answered the Governor's questions straightforwardly and Don Manuel listened courteously. From time to time the Governor glanced appraisingly at the blond man, who had got back on his feet and was now keeping himself apart from the other men.

"We are a mercantile expedition pure and simple, excelencia," Van Ness said. "Our intent is peaceful. We are accompanied by

257

commissioners authorized by President Lamar to establish trade arrangements with your excellency." Van Ness pointed to the prisoner with the swollen ankle, a quick-eyed man with dark, wavy hair. "This gentleman, excelencia, is an American journalist, Señor George Wilkins Kendall. He is no part of the expedition. He traveled with us only for protection against the Indians. He has a passport from the Mexican consul in his native city of New Orleans, in the United States. He speaks Spanish well and he was sent out by his newspaper to write articles about Mexico. After he visits Santa Fe he wishes to continue down into Mexico."

Lieutenant Alpuente offered Kendall's papers to the Governor. Don Manuel examined them and returned them to the officer. "The passport is a good one," Don Manuel said. He looked slowly at each prisoner. "However, Señor Kendall, since you are found in the company of the *enemies* of New Mexico it will be necessary for me to detain you until I can investigate you further."

At the word "enemies" the blond man groaned. Don Manuel regarded him with mounting interest. "There is nothing to fear if all is as you say it is, señores," Don Manuel said briskly. "I am a man of honor, and New Mexico is a civilized country. We are not assassins nor savages and you will be given every opportunity to defend yourselves legally." He gripped the handle of his sword and stiffened arrogantly. "I have the reputation of being a warrior leader of a warrior people! We do not war upon the innocent or upon those who come to us without enmity." His face became pleasant again. "I need an interpreter. Who among you speaks my language best?"

The blond man rushed forward so quickly he stumbled. "I speak Spanish almost like a native, excelencia. I have lived for many years in Chihuahua and in other parts of your great country. Your excellency would find no one better suited than I to serve as your interpreter."

Don Manuel nodded with a small smile. "Your name, señor?"

"William Lewis, excelencia."

Don Manuel ordered a mule. "Mount, Don Guillermo."

Lewis climbed eagerly on the mule and moved away so that he was among the Mexicans. He averted his face from the other prisoners.

"Were there papers carried by these Texans?" Don Manuel asked Alpuente.

"Yes, excelencia, Capitán Salazar collected them all." Alpuente unstrapped his saddlebag and handed the papers to Don Manuel. The Governor thumbed through them rapidly until he came to one of Lamar's incendiary proclamations. He read the circular through and returned all the other papers to Alpuente. The circular he folded and slipped into his pocket. "Take the prisoners back to San Miguel, teniente," he said. "I will question them again tomorrow."

Alpuente, tired from a long day in the saddle, said plaintively: "The prisoners have already walked more than twenty miles today, excelencia. One is wounded and the American has an injured ankle. They are hardly able to walk back tonight."

"They are able to walk twenty miles more," Don Manuel said. "The gringos are an energetic and tireless people." His voice did not change. "If one of them pretends to be sick or tired on the road, shoot him down and bring me his ears."

4

DON MANUEL put his arm in friendly fashion on Lewis's shoulder and led him to the front window of the house of the alcalde of San Miguel. "Look on the plaza, Don Guillermo. You will see something of interest."

A corporal and six soldiers were leading a man with bandaged eyes across the plaza.

"Do you know that man?" Don Manuel asked.

Lewis started violently. "It is Baker."

"There were three originally," Don Manuel said placidly. "They were arrested and they attempted to escape from the prison in my palace. They were recaptured and one was killed on the spot."

The blindfolded man was brought to the center of the plaza. He was pushed to his knees. The corporal shouted an order. The six soldiers stepped back three paces. The corporal gave another command. The soldiers fired their muskets at Baker's back. Baker fell on his side. His legs kicked convulsively. The corporal drew a pistol and pushed the writhing man flat on his back. He pressed the muzzle against Baker's heart and pulled the trigger. Baker kicked out again and lay still. The blast from the pistol started a small fire on his shirt, which burned until the fire was blotted out by the dead man's blood.

Don Manuel studied Lewis's face. "I am going to order your four friends brought before this window, Don Guillermo. I wish to find out more about them."

The prisoners were lined up outside the window. Don Manuel questioned Lewis exhaustively about each man. He asked the questions loudly, so that the four men could hear each word. Lewis whispered his answers in Don Manuel's ear. When he was finished, Don Manuel ordered Lewis to follow him and went out of the alcalde's house. He walked up to the men with dignity, his face again without animosity. "Friends, you told me the truth yesterday. Don Samuel has corroborated your statements, as has your good friend Don Guillermo. I save your lives. I have ordered Don Samuel to be shot. He ran away from Santa Fe and was retaken. His fate will be yours if you attempt to escape."

Then Lewis gasped: "God in heaven!"

The other men followed his horror-stricken eyes. They saw Samuel Howland being led across the plaza by the corporal and six soldiers.

"What happened to him?" Lewis whispered.

"He was struck by a saber," Don Manuel said. He shrugged. "In a moment or two his wounds will be of little concern to him."

The men could see Howland's teeth through the hole in his cheek. Because of the mutilation his face seemed in a ghastly grin. As Howland passed them he raised his eyes. The four men moved forward instinctively to speak to him but they were held back by their guards. "Good-by, boys," Howland said. "I've got to suffer. You must . . ." He passed from hearing.

Howland was led to where Baker's body still lay, covered now with flies. A piece of cloth was tied around Howland's eyes and he was forced down to his knees. As the soldiers raised their muskets, Don Manuel again placed his hand on Lewis's shoulder. When the soldiers fired, Don Manuel tightened his fingers.

5

THE GOVERNOR was subdued as he and Lewis returned to the house of the alcalde. Don Manuel poured brandy into two glasses and gave one to Lewis. "My heart is filled with pain for those two men," he said somberly, "but my people would not be denied. If only they had remained quietly in prison until this whole affair could be investigated, nothing would have happened to them. I put them in a cell for their own protection, but their American friends in Santa Fe helped them escape, and when they were retaken they killed five New Mexicans." He sighed. "I knew Don Samuel for many years, but my people demanded vengeance and even now they are unsatisfied because there were only three Texans to execute."

Lewis's hand, holding the brandy glass, trembled. He bit his lip.

"By the way, Don Guillermo, Don Samuel told me something about you when I questioned him this morning."

"About me, excelencia?" Some of the brandy spilled from the glass.

"He referred to you as *Capitán* Lewis." Don Manuel smiled gently. "You did not tell me you were a military officer."

"I did not think it would be of interest to your excellency."

"Did you not? As one officer to another? Where did you hold your rank, Don Guillermo? Was it in the Texan insurrection against Mexico?"

Several moments passed before Lewis could reply. Don Manuel gazed at him attentively. "Yes, excelencia," Lewis said. "But—"

The governor held up his hand. "There is no need to justify yourself, capitán. We all of us fight for that in which we believe."

"Thank you, excelencia!"

"Only do not allow this to reach the ears of my people."

"No, excelencia."

"We are a frontier people," Don Manuel said musingly. "We have lived with war and death in one way or another for hundreds of years. Our methods of justice often are violent, but we in New

Mexico have never had security long enough to learn moderation."

Lewis lifted the glass convulsively and emptied it. He set it on a table and looked out of the window. The bodies were not yet removed. He rubbed his hands together, cracking his knuckles.

Don Manuel poured more brandy into his glass. "Tell me, dear friend, how were you regarded by the leaders of the expedition?"

Lewis whirled. "I believe they thought highly of me, excelencia. They considered I had had more experience in Mexico than almost any of them."

"They listened to your counsels?"

"Always, excelencia!"

"Then they would be inclined to listen to your advice now, would they not?"

"I believe so, excelencia," Lewis said more slowly.

"You allow your brandy to stand overlong, Don Guillermo." Armijo stood up and walked back and forth. His countenance was grave. "Capitán Lewis, I know the affection you must have for these men who shared so many difficulties with you. When men face death together, they achieve brotherhood. Yesterday and today you witnessed the stream of soldiers marching to the front. You must be filled with concern about the outcome of a battle between your poor, half-starved countrymen and the soldiers of my powerful armies. Thousands of Mexican fighting men wait only for my word to fall upon your little band of friends. Believe me, Don Guillermo, nothing would make me unhappier than to have to give that word."

He stopped abruptly and faced Lewis. "In addition to all the soldiers I have here at my command, five thousand of the finest troops are being sent to me from Chihuahua. I do not need these soldiers, but they are on their way."

He resumed his seat, rubbing his thigh, and he stretched his legs. "At the present moment, Don Guillermo, I am able to offer certain concessions to your friends. Once these soldiers arrive from Chihuahua—" He shrugged. "Then, I do not know. Since you have lived in Chihuahua you know the military department there has jurisdiction over New Mexico. The commander of the Chihuahua troops may have specific battle orders that I would have no authority to countermand. Despite my desire to be lenient to your misguided companions, I might then be powerless to prevent a war of extermination. Time is working against the Texans in all ways. Each day they grow weaker. Victory over men in such condition would be victory without satisfaction."

"I understand, excelencia," Lewis heard himself say.

"And some of my countrymen would inevitably be slain as well. It would all be such waste."

Lewis listened to the singing of soldiers as they marched through the plaza. He finished the brandy. "Exactly what do you want me to do, excelencia?"

6

THE GUARD dipped his knee and looked worried. "His excellency gave orders that no one was to be admitted, padre."

"I must see the Governor," Padre Martínez said.

"There were to be no exceptions, padre."

The priest pushed the guard to one side. He entered the house Don Manuel had commandeered in the little village of Anton Chico on the Pecos River. He found the Governor sprawled in a chair in the sala, a half-empty brandy bottle dangling from his hand. The room was dark except for the fire on the hearth.

Don Manuel's face was flushed and sullen. His eyes glinted dangerously. "Do you want me to execute my guard for disobeying my orders?"

"Why not?" the priest asked bitterly. "And why stop with him? Why not have one man kill another until in all of New Mexico none is left alive but Manuel Armijo?"

Don Manuel lifted the bottle to his lips. He wiped his mouth. "This is a time I would have preferred to be alone, presbítero. I believed I had arranged it so. But my orders appear to make no impression on you. You are here. What do you want? Say it quickly and then go!"

The priest strode up to the Governor and faced him. The lines were deep in his face. "There is no need for me to ask if it is true that you have ordered the execution of the hundred Texans who surrendered on the bank of the Pecos."

"There is no need. It is true."

"Even though they surrendered honorably and were guaranteed their safety?"

"Even so."

"On the pledge of Mexican honor?"

"I feel bound in no way to respect the surrender agreement!" Don Manuel said violently. "I have read the manifestoes the dogs brought with them. They came under a mantle of peace—with a secret plan to bring about revolution in my country. They came without honor and they deserve no honor!"

"That is all true, Don Manuel," the priest said. "But they remain men. You cannot order them butchered like so many sheep."

"I order what I please! I am the Governor!" He tilted the bottle to his lips. His throat jerked spasmodically.

"They came in dishonor," the priest said. "But you pledged your honor."

Don Manuel spat. "Treachery beckons to treachery." His lips pulled down jeeringly. "What would you have me do? Turn them loose among my people so they may foment the insurrection for which they traveled a thousand miles?"

The priest clasped his hands. "Send them to the City of Mexico, Don Manuel. Your triumph will be no less. Your victory will be made plain to everyone who dwells between here and there. Let them be tried and judged in Mexico."

"I need no higher authority than myself!"

"There is none to gainsay that. But for whatever reason these men came here, you pledged your word and they accepted it."

Don Manuel squinted curiously at the priest. "This plea for lenity comes oddly from your mouth, padre. These men are heretics. Their plan was to wrest New Mexico from the Holy Church and give it to the infidels. For weeks you have raged up and down the land calling for death to heretics. And now you ask for mercy. Why, padre, why?"

"They were the enemy before. Now they are prisoners and helpless," Martínez said quietly.

"What difference does that make? The same blood flows in the same bodies. The same thoughts fill the same heads. I have removed the fangs, but the snakes must still be destroyed."

The priest closed his eyes. "It is because they are heretics and we are not that our honor must be greater than theirs. I beg you to reconsider, Don Manuel. The shame would never leave you."

Don Manuel finished the brandy in the bottle and threw it against the hearth. "You priests are all alike," he grated. "You condemn heresy and inveigh against heretics—in the abstract, when they are far away, a cloud on the horizon, a distant idea like the devil whom no one sees. Your mouths are filled with brimstone and your words clap like thunder. But when the same heretics become captured men, where goes your fury? You slobber like old women and beg for tenderness!"

He lurched to a sideboard, opened another bottle of brandy, and took a deep draught. "Name of God! What kind of people are we? Am I the only man among us? Here are our natural enemies. Here are men who would drive us from our houses and destroy us. Here are men who desecrate our churches and defame our religion. And you come sniveling to me and wring your hands and ask that I refrain from killing them as I would kill wolves who do no more than attack sheep!"

"They are not wolves. They are men."

"It is the same everywhere! I have tried to give this country a backbone. Instead of fighting to rip out the eyes of the enemy my people share tears with them."

"Your people are Christians who have not forgotten the teachings of the Saviour." The priest drew himself up to his full height. His mouth tightened. "You do not order the prisoners shot for their heresies, Don Manuel."

Brandy trickled from the corner of the Governor's mouth and dripped on his shirt. "I do not?" he asked hoarsely.

"I can tell you the true reason, Don Manuel."

"Speak then, presbítero. Reveal myself to me!"

The priest folded his arms and walked slowly toward him. "These Texans surrendered themselves and laid down their arms without resistance."

"Every child knows that by now."

"*But not to you.*"

Don Manuel recoiled. "What has that to do with it!"

"Everything. The Texans gave themselves up not to you but to Salazar. They were prisoners in a sheep-pen here in Anton Chico when you arrived from San Miguel." Martínez pressed close on him, his eyes burning. "Your mind has few secret places from me, Don Manuel. It is old, familiar terrain. You prevailed upon the gringo Lewis to betray his comrades in some way, but you had not the heart to go with him to accomplish it, for fear something might go wrong and there might after all be battle. So you sent Salazar to take the risk in your place and then you arrived here in your glory to discover the Texans had laid down their arms without fight and there had been no risk. And at the beginning you exulted. But then Salazar told you how he had accomplished this miracle and you came to realize that while the plan was yours, the triumph belonged to Salazar."

"Enough, Don Antonio!" Armijo backed away.

"You found out how easily it had been done and how there had been no danger," the priest continued pitilessly. "You knew you had played it too safely once again, and that you were denied, as you were denied when you trembled with fright once before and sent Capitán Caballero into Santa Fe only to learn that José Gonzales had already fled."

"It is enough!" Don Manuel looked from side to side, a cornered animal.

The priest folded his arms. "And so you ordered every Texan to be executed, not for heresy, not for the secret treachery, but because they gave themselves up without resistance to Salazar, so that their surrender became the greatest act of treachery of all."

"Silence!"

"Salazar could capture them," the priest said, "but only Manuel Armijo could order their death. So you gave the order."

"Do you love these dogs so greatly you would die in the line with them!"

"It is the answer you have found for everything, is it not, Don Manuel?" the priest asked softly. "When confused, kill." He put his hand on the Governor's arm. "Do not talk of killing me. That in each of us that can die was slain long ago."

Armijo pulled away. He wiped his wet face. "Your calling gives you unfair advantage, Don Antonio." His voice broke. "You own a key to open doors to hearts."

"I do not need to read your heart," Martínez said. "I need only to look into my own."

266

Don Manuel thrust his head forward like a beleaguered bull. His face again was ugly. "You may open doors that would be better left closed, padre, but you have no command. The men die!"

"Why must they die?"

"They are enemies."

"Then let them die as enemies. Free them. Return to them their weapons. Set them back on the east bank of the Pecos and fight them honorably. I will ride at your side and share your bullets!"

"You are crazy!"

"Your own officers consider your order unjust."

"My officers think only what I think."

The priest contemplated him silently. "Are you quite certain of that, Don Manuel?"

"Yes! Yes!"

"Then you would permit them to vote on the matter and you would abide by their decision?"

"For certain!" Don Manuel waved his finger under the priest's nose. "And will you in your turn agree to yield to the vote?"

Martínez nodded slowly. "I will, excelencia, if you do not command them how to cast their ballots."

"Agreed." Don Manuel straightened. He pushed back his hair, pulled down his tunic, and began to button it. "A gamble between you and me, padre. And a hundred lives for the stake."

Don Manuel told the officers gathered in the sala what was to be done. Each man was given a slip of paper. "A cross will be the sign for the execution," Don Manuel said. "A circle will charge that they live. Señores, mark your ballots."

Martínez collected the folded papers. He put them on a table and opened them, one by one, looking at the marks and putting slips to the right and to the left. The piles mounted evenly. When the last slip was exposed he counted the piles. "The verdict is by a single vote, excelencia. The prisoners are to be spared."

7

DON MANUEL drank brandy and stared at the slips of paper and brooded over the weakness of his countrymen. When the Texans were on the east bank of the Pecos, armed and ready to fight, the natives of Anton Chico had huddled in their houses and prayed that the heretics be destroyed. When the Texans had surrendered to Salazar, the people had gone hysterical with joy, had hailed Salazar as hero and deliverer. But when the Texans had been herded into the sheep-pen something had happened to the people of Anton Chico. Now the Texans were not heretics and enemies but were pobrecitos, poor little ones, and the people had come with food and drink to the sheep-pen in droves and had struggled with the guards to get to the prisoners to comfort them. "How does one understand such a people?" he demanded savagely of the empty room. "How does one deal with such a people?"

He drank the brandy from the bottle until the slips of paper blurred before his eyes, thinking how the weakness was in his officers too and remembering how the officers of the presidial troop had once refused to obey his order to execute the four Gonzales men, and he felt a sudden cold fear at the disobedience of his officers. He swept the slips of paper from the table, picked up his cane, and ran out of the house.

He tore through the village, his eyes glaring wildly, his hair hanging over his forehead, swinging his cane at people in his way. He pushed past the guards and rushed into the sheep-pen. "These dogs are untied!" he shouted. "Guard! Guard!" He struck the first guard who ran up. "Do you leave prisoners untied? You are under arrest!" He caned the other guards and ordered them to bind the prisoners hand and foot.

He was not satisfied when the men were fettered. He ordered the guards to unbind the prisoners and tie them up again more tightly. With his cane he flailed right and left at prisoners, at soldiers who moved too slowly to suit him. He disliked how a Texan happened to look at him and, spewing curses, he beat the prisoner unconscious. He took a buffalo robe from a prisoner whose expression did not appeal to him. He struck a prisoner who turned away his face when he approached.

The prisoners had been kept to one side of the pen away from the piles of sheep dung. When the men were bound tightly enough to satisfy him he ordered them tied together, in bundles of six, like staves, and then dragged to the other side of the pen and dumped on the mounds of manure.

He returned to the house, muttering to himself. He threw the cane across the room, put the brandy bottle to his lips, and drank until he started to choke. He coughed until tears flowed from his eyes, his face was scarlet, and the brandy was vomited over his tunic.

Suddenly the rage departed. His face was fixed for a moment and his eyes glittered. Then he began to laugh. He threw back his head and roared. He fell into a chair, his body shaking with mirth. One hundred Texans had surrendered to Salazar and that was done, but there were others waiting to be taken. And Salazar's prisoners had been commanded by a colonel, but the commander of the remaining Texans was the general. "The general will hand me his sword!" he shouted. "A general! A general!"

8

THE NEXT MORNING he woke still in the chair. He got to his feet stiffly. His tunic was stained with dried vomit.

He started out immediately for San Miguel for a change of uniform properly to receive the surrender of General McLeod. The news of the surrender of the first batch of Texans had preceded him to San Miguel, he found. The people had celebrated all through the night. Guns had been fired and church bells rung and the people had gathered in the church and joined in a Te Deum of gratitude for the great victory. The priest had carried the figure of San Miguel around the plaza, followed by delirious men and women. Entertainers with mandolins and guitars had played and sung until daylight and the people of San Miguel had sung with them. When Don Manuel rode into the village the cheers echoed back from the mountains.

He listened happily to the acclamation. Perhaps there was some hope for his people after all. He waved his hands and allowed women to kiss the tips of his fingers. In triumph he rode to his quarters in the house of the alcalde, where he bathed and shaved and changed to a clean uniform. He could not contain his joy. He had to give a little to others. He ordered the three Texan prisoners and the American journalist to be brought to him and greeted the men cordially.

"Caballeros, you have heard the news without doubt," he said, offering them brandy and cigars. "A third of the Texan army has surrendered to me at Anton Chico. Now I go to meet General McLeod. I hope that he lays down his arms as quietly. If he does not I shall be forced to kill him and every one of his men. I have brought you here to bid you farewell. I have left orders with the alcalde to treat you well. You shall be fed properly and you shall want for nothing."

"What is to happen to us in the end, excelencia?" Van Ness asked.

Don Manuel shrugged. "I have no choice, señor. I must send all of you to the City of Mexico, where you may plead your case to the highest authorities."

"But that must be two thousand miles, excelencia."

"You may consider yourselves lucky," Don Manuel said. "Would you believe it, but some of my officers wanted to have all of you executed. There was an argument about it down in Anton Chico. The officers decided to put it to a vote, believing that since Mexico is a republic, important matters should be settled by the ballot. It was a curious thing, my friends. The vote was split exactly even. Half of the officers voted to shoot all prisoners and the other half voted to send them to Mexico."

"My God," Van Ness whispered in English.

Don Manuel shrugged again. "Fortunately for all of you, it was just at that moment that I myself arrived in Anton Chico. Of course I ordered that all lives be spared." He smiled at the four men. "But I tell you, señores, it was a very close thing."

Van Ness asked: "What about Señor Kendall, excelencia.

You will remember I explained to you that he is not a Texan and he has a passport to visit Mexico."

Don Manuel's teeth flashed in a broad smile. "When the last of the Texans are in my hands I will release Señor Kendall." He beamed on the American. "I beg you to do me the honor to be my guest in Santa Fe, Don Jorge." Don Manuel extended his hand. "I must leave now," he said. "Let me shake the hand of each of you." He took their hands in a firm grasp. "Return now to your quarters," he said. "Of course you must not try to escape. You would be executed immediately."

A few minutes later the plaza was shattered by a trumpet blast. Don Manuel galloped out of San Miguel. The fiesta continued.

Three days later as he was riding toward Palo Duro with his bodyguard, composing in his mind the words of the ultimatum he would deliver to General McLeod, he was intercepted on the road by courier with the news that General Hugh McLeod had surrendered his entire force to Colonel Diego Archuleta without firing a shot. Don Manuel turned back to San Miguel.

9

GOVERNOR ARMIJO gazed moodily from the house of the alcalde at the jubilant people in the plaza of San Miguel. The capitulation of McLeod, ending the Texan threat to New Mexico, had made the natives insane with joy and relief. They roistered for days, and again and again the priests brought from the church the effigies of the patron saint and the Virgin of Guadalupe and paraded with them around the plaza while the villagers chanted their prayers of thanksgiving. From time to time the revelers gathered in front of the alcalde's house and cheered their Governor, and Don Manuel appeared before them and smiled and waved his hand and listened to their vivas, trying to force himself to believe that he deserved them all.

Then the prisoners themselves began to straggle into the village, and though they were enemies and the people had been told they had come to destroy them, when the men and the women of San Miguel saw them their happiness vanished.

The prisoners were as close to death as men could be and still hold the breath of life. They staggered into the village, gaunt, starved, feeble skeletons of men, almost all naked, almost all barefoot, their feet bleeding and lame. Their faces were bearded, their hair was matted, and their skin was burned raw from wind and sun. Half of them were unable to stand upright without the help of others. They coughed and spat and the eyes of some were haunted wildly; others were drugged with the dull listlessness of animals in stupor. They filled the plaza, aimless as dust, and some of them keeled over as soon as their feet stopped moving and others immediately fell asleep erect.

Now the people stilled their elation and were suffused with almost unendurable compassion. They looked pleadingly to their priests, and their faces became weighted with sorrow, their hands were extended in the ancient gesture of pity, and their prayers of gratitude to the good San Miguel and the ineffably merciful Virgen de Guadalupe for their deliverance from the gringo monsters turned into supplications for mercy for the wretched creatures who stood and lay helpless and mute in the sun.

Don Manuel saw the change in his subjects, and his heart tightened and blackened with bitterness as he looked at the miserable derelicts from Texas. He suffered the exquisite torment of knowing almost with awe how well his plan with Carlos Gutiérrez had succeeded and how he had failed to take full advantage of it. It was always the same, first with Gonzales against Pérez, and then with Captain Caballero against Gonzales, and now with Salazar and Archuleta against men whose names alone were a scourge in his country. He could think and he could plot, but he could not make courage.

Then the wagons that had lasted through the journey from Texas arrived in San Miguel, and Don Manuel bestirred himself and with the generosity of a pirate chief distributed the spoils to his officers and men, working with frenzy to becloud their minds over the precise details of the historic victory. Frequently Captain Lewis pointed to something or other, and he separated it from the rest and set it aside for the renegade.

On the evening of the 14th of October, Don Manuel ordered a bonfire built in the center of the plaza. He made a feverish speech to the people and then he ordered that the proclamations which the President of Texas had sent with the expedition be consigned to the flames. The soldiers shouted boisterously as they threw in load after load and the flames lighted the square murkily and flickered on the faces of the Texan prisoners, who stared from buildings in which they had been quartered.

When the last of the manifestoes was tossed into the blaze the soldiers and officers, led by Don Manuel, began a dance of triumph around the great fire. Presently some of the villagers joined hands in the dance. Before long, Don Manuel wandered off, his arm around the waist of a young girl. Many of the military heroes found women and drifted away with them.

The following night, on the eve of his departure for Santa Fe, Don Manuel gave a banquet for his officers. Although he pretended to drink as much as the others, he kept his wits about him. He was keenly interested in seeing how their triumphs affected Diego Archuleta and Damasio Salazar.

Colonel Archuleta appeared unimpressed with himself. He remained taciturn, as always. He drank freely, but his tongue did not loosen. When he was congratulated on winning the surrender of the Texan general he nodded his head stiffly, and his stony Indian features indicated he preferred the matter to be dropped. Don Manuel observed him with satisfaction. Archuleta, he thought, was the perfect subordinate officer, skillful and with no ambition beyond winning military victory. Then he overheard Salazar talking loudly.

"They put down their arms like cowardly dogs," Salazar was saying. "I gave the command and the weapons were scooped up as though they were playthings for children. Damasio Salazar gave the command, and they were helpless!"

Don Manuel watched Salazar stagger from group to group, emptying glass after glass, retelling the story of his victory.

Before leaving for the capital, Don Manuel sent for Salazar. The captain appeared with a greenish face and bloodshot eyes. His hand trembled as he saluted.

"Well, dear Don Damasio, the entire Texan affair has been

brought off with the greatest success," Don Manuel said with immense good nature. "And you have had a most important part in it, beginning with the night you brought your cousin to me."

Salazar, who had worried over having talked too much the night before, said fervently: "Thousand thanks, excelencia. My life is always wholly at your disposal."

"It is too bad, of course, that poor Carlos was set upon by thieves. How is your cousin, by the way, Don Damasio?"

"His arm is broken, excelencia. The other injuries were of no importance."

"And all the gold was taken from him?"

"All, excelencia."

"I have made every effort in Santa Fe to track down the hoodlums. I am afraid it is hopeless. He was drunk. He did not see their faces." Don Manuel sighed. "Well, there will be other chances for him to benefit from me."

"He believes that, excelencia. He is devoted to your excellency."

"Ea, pues, now to business, Don Damasio. As you know, I have already sent the Texan leaders and some of the prisoners on their way to Mexico. You will take the remaining prisoners to El Paso del Norte."

Salazar's face fell. He had looked forward to a lengthy celebration, financed by the sale of the goods Armijo had given him. He recovered instantly. "I live only to obey your excellency," he said, realizing he *had* spoken too much at the banquet.

"You will have a strong company of your own Rurales, Don Damasio, with Teniente Jesús Alpuente as your chief assistant. I have also ordered down some officers of the presidial companies to go along with you under your command."

"May I ask your excellency who they are?"

Don Manuel waved his hand indifferently. "Don Esquipulas Caballero is one. His friend, Ramón Baca, is another. One or two more. Now, Don Damasio, you will take the prisoners by the shortest route to El Paso del Norte, and there your responsibility will cease. General Elias will supply the escort for the journey through Chihuahua. I have allocated eighteen head of cattle to feed soldiers and prisoners. I have also set aside one of the Texan wagons, filled with odds and ends. From time to time, as you pass through the villages on the way, you will exchange these bits of goods for fresh bread and other foods to enlarge your supplies."

"I understand, excelencia."

Don Manuel's face became stern. "The prisoners are honorable men, Don Damasio. I want you to treat them with severity, but also with justice. There is to be no undue harshness in dealing with them. Is that understood?"

"Perfectly, excelencia."

"You will start out two days hence, on the 17th."

"I will obey your excellency to the smallest detail."

"Included among the prisoners will be the American, Kendall." Don Manuel patted Salazar on the back. "That is all, Don Damasio. Good luck to you." He walked him to the door.

He would have freed Kendall as he had promised, Don Manuel thought, but Captain Lewis had pointed out that Kendall might take the story of his part in the affair back to the United States before he could dispose of the merchandise with which Don Manuel had rewarded him. Don Manuel had reminded him that Kendall planned to visit Santa Fe and other parts of Mexico before returning to the States, but Lewis had argued that the journalist might well change his plans after his experience, and that even if he did go to Santa Fe he would have the opportunity to tell other Americans of Lewis's betrayal. Since Don Manuel had given Lewis a much larger share of the loot than he was entitled to, with the understanding that Lewis would dispose of the goods in Chihuahua and turn back some of the money, the argument of the Texan captain prevailed.

Don Manuel, however, considered that he had been charitable in yielding to the urging of Padre Martínez that the prisoners be supplied with sufficient food for the march to El Paso del Norte, and he did not give his dishonesty with Kendall another thought.

Now all the strings were neatly tied. He left in his carriage for Santa Fe to receive the welcome of a conquering hero. On the road north he passed the cadre of officers riding to San Miguel to supplement Salazar's command. Don Manuel peered from the window. The officers saluted. Don Manuel waved his hand.

1

THE PRISONERS lined up in the plaza in the morning glare. Their clothing still was in tatters, many were still without boots, and the mark of their terrible journey from Texas was still on them, but they were rested and stronger and there was flesh on their ribs. The people of San Miguel had adopted them as their own particular poor, and though Don Manuel's guards had tried to discourage them, the women had insisted on sharing their meager supply of food with the men who were quartered in their houses.

Esquipulas Caballero leaned indolently on his saddle horn and looked at Ramón Baca quizzically. "Do you still have doubts, monkey-face? There are Texans. They are real."

"I can see them." Baca shook his head. "I still do not understand."

"There were more. Many have already left for Chihuahua."

"Look at those faces, chico," Baca said wonderingly. "These are men. These are hard men and they all have the look of knowing how to handle guns."

"How then do you explain it?"

"I cannot explain it. But I refuse to believe that at the command of Manuel Armijo these men meekly laid down their arms. This is a breed that fights to the death rather than surrender. You may have heard of the place in San Antonio de Bexar called the Alamo."

"Except that these men *did* surrender," Caballero said sarcastically. "Madre de Dios! No one has ever accomplished what Don Manuel has done. This is victory greater than any ever won by Mexican generals. It is something that will go down in history. Stop trying to spoil it!"

Baca made a face. "If it will make you happy, little husband, I will feel proud with you." He grinned. "Tell me, friend, were you happy when you were ordered to come here to serve as nursemaid for Texans?"

"I would have preferred to have some part in the campaign before it was over, but this is better than nothing."

"I do not mean as a warrior. Were you happy as a husband?"

"What do you mean?"

"Santa Madre! Were you not relieved to be removed for a little while from the female?"

Caballero's lips twitched. "I was not."

"Novice!" Baca snorted. "It is too soon. You have not yet reached the time when campaigns in the field will be welcomed and considered less hazardous than the fighting that occurs every day in one's house. And the bride? Did she weep?"

"She wept, monito."

"Did she wring her hands?"

"She did."

"Did she beg you to be careful and not get your feet wet? Did she say unpleasant things about other females you may encounter?"

"Was your ear at the door?"

"The words were not invented by my niece."

"Did Lupe tell you these same things?"

"Lupe? Nombre de Dios!" Baca laughed. "She kicked me out of the house and ordered me to prolong my absence. No, friend, that part of my marriage is lost in the past. That is why, in a mood of nostalgia, I attempted to reconstruct the last, sad moments when you separated yourself from your bride." He sighed. "How tender!" He wiped an eye.

"The devil!" Caballero made as though to move off.

Baca detained him. "Before we leave the delicate subject— you will be away from Santa Fe for some time. Do you think perhaps you will find a different woman when you return?"

"How different, fool?"

Baca held his hands in front of his belly. "Bigger—here."

"I do not know," Caballero said tightly.

"You can tell me. I am almost your uncle."

"I do not know!" Then Caballero said: "There is Salazar."

Don Damasio rode into the plaza. A drummer brought silence with a fanfare. Salazar surveyed the prisoners. "Texans, today your holiday comes to an end. We start out for El Paso del Norte. You will be happy to hear I shall be in command. My first order is that every prisoner is to be counted. I have been commanded to deliver to the commandant in El Paso del Norte every man who leaves San Miguel, and if I cannot produce the man I must at least produce his ears to show he has not escaped."

As the tallying started, Caballero and Baca noticed one of the prisoners limp out of the line. A soldier rushed up to him and pushed him back. Salazar was given the results of the count.

"There are exactly one hundred and eighty-seven of you," he said. "That is the number for which I am accountable. The rest of your friends have already started out on the march, which will not end until all of you reach the City of Mexico, where you will be punished for your crimes!"

The lame man stepped out of line again. "Capitán Salazar!"

Salazar walked his horse to him. "Did you call to me, Señor Kendall?"

"I am an American citizen, capitán. Why am I being included among the prisoners?"

Salazar separated his lips. "Perhaps it is because you are one of the prisoners."

"Governor Armijo told me I was to be freed."

Salazar scratched his chin. "Did he, señor? Perhaps. But for some reason I was not told the same thing." He shrugged. "So you are a prisoner."

"I am an American citizen!" Kendall repeated loudly.

"Get back in line, gringo," Salazar said, "or you will be freed forever."

Baca leaned toward Caballero. "What do you make of that?"

"Who knows?"

Salazar rode to the head of the line. A bugler sounded the order to march. The prisoners moved slowly out of the plaza. As they passed, women wept and covered their heads with their shawls.

2

THE NARROW STREET echoed with cheers. Doña Dorotea
Engracia, who had grown fat in her lazy life as dueña, waddled to
a window. She threw up her hands. "It is the Governor's carriage!"

Soledad glanced up from her needlework pattern. "Have you
never seen Don Manuel's equipage before?"

"The people cry out and wave their hands and call his name!"
Doña Dorotea Engracia said with great excitement. "He leans
from the window and waves back to them." Her hand flew to her
throat. "Virgen santísima! The carriage stops before this house!"

"It is true then, as they say, that Don Manuel never sets foot
on ground any more," Soledad said. "This house is but around the
corner from the palace."

"Such as he may not walk!"

"Why not?"

"He is the Governor."

"It would do him good." Soledad giggled. "His excellency
grows fat."

"How can you say that?" Doña Dorotea Engracia asked in a
shocked voice. "He is a large man. *Muy hombre!*"

"It is too bad you are not younger, aunt. And not so fat yourself." She chuckled again. "Though it would be something to see,
you and Don Manuel."

Doña Dorotea Engracia turned scarlet. "Close your bill,
shameless!" Her voice changed. "He steps from the carriage. He
smiles at the people. Dios mío, why does he come here?"

"To see Capitán Caballero, undoubtedly. Now stop your
gawking and come from the window."

"What a manner! What an air!" The dueña clasped her
hands rapturously. "What a hero! In all of Mexico no one is so
great."

"He has greatness," Soledad said.

"The greatest of greatness. Not even Santa Anna ever won
such victory over Texans." She closed her eyes happily. "The
fiestas! The bailes! Santa Fe was never before so joyous. And the
long faces of the gringos! It has been a tonic just to see them."

Soledad smiled. "The Americans have not been happy."

"God was on our side," the dueña said with fervor. "It was as Vicario Ortiz said so beautifully at the time of the Te Deum. 'When the moment of decision arrived, Nuestro Señor Jesucristo took His stand irrevocably against the heretics.'" Doña Dorotea Engracia wiped her eyes. "What a beautiful phrase!"

There was a knock on the door. Sighing, the dueña crossed the room and opened the door. A servant whispered something to her. She closed the door quickly and hurried back to the chaise-longue on which Soledad reclined. Her eyes, almost lost in the plump cheeks, dilated with excitement. "He has come to see you, Soledad! Rise quickly and dress!"

"I had no appointment with his excellency."

"It is Don Manuel! Does Don Manuel need to make an appointment? Hurry and dress. You must not keep his excellency waiting!"

"It is not fitting. I am a married woman, and my husband is from the city."

The dueña threw up her hands. "Santo Niño de Atoche! This is no lover calling! This is Don Manuel Armijo!"

"It still is not fitting." Soledad bent over her pattern. "Send word that I am not at home."

"Madre de Dios! Who is not at home when Don Manuel calls?"

"Then send word that I am indisposed."

"Rise and dress, Soledad," Doña Dorotea Engracia said firmly. "In Santa Fe one does not refuse audience to Don Manuel."

The Governor was limping impatiently in the sala when Soledad entered the room. She curtsied. He bowed and kissed her hand. When he raised his head she could smell the brandy on his breath.

"This is a great honor, excelencia."

"I am the one who is honored, Doña Soledad."

"But not entirely unexpected."

"You knew I would call."

"Yes, excelencia," she said coolly, "I knew you would call."

He stepped back and looked at her. "Marriage has been good to you, Doña Soledad."

"It has not displeased me, excelencia." She walked past him to the table with the drinks and biscuits. She noticed Doña Dorotea Engracia was not in the room. It was the classic scene, she thought, smiling, and she must remember all the details to tell her husband. "May I offer your excellency some of the vino de Jerez? Or perhaps you would prefer some brandy?" She smelled the brandy fumes over her shoulder.

"The brandy, señora, for favor."

"Since you have already started with it," she said, her back still toward him.

"It is true. I have had a number of brandies."

"It is something I should not have suspected."

"I needed courage to present myself to you," he said into her ear.

She poured brandy into a glass, then turned and faced him. "You need no courage to visit this house, excelencia," she said calmly. "In it dwell only your most loyal and devoted subjects." She gave him the glass and poured some sherry in another. "Salud, to the conqueror of the Texans!"

His face became stern. He squared his shoulders, pulled in his belly, and emptied the glass. "Thousand thanks, Doña Soledad. Were you proud of your Governor when you heard the glorious news?"

She eyed him candidly. "I was very proud, excelencia, as was my husband, Don Esquipulas. How could one of Mexican blood not be proud?"

"It was a great victory." He strutted in front of her.

He is like the rooster parading lustfully before the hen, she thought. Esquipulas, mi corazón, even the sash is the right color for the comb. He is comical, querido, and you will laugh when I tell you of this, and she wondered why she did not laugh even to herself.

"Three hundred of them!" he said. "Many of them veterans of the rebellion against Mexico, and they surrendered to me like frightened children!"

Muy hombre, very man, Doña Dorotea Engracia had called him.

He waved his fist. "I could have ordered every one of them executed. My officers begged me to do so. But I preferred to show

mercy! I sent them on foot to the City of Mexico so the entire
nation could see Texans for what they are!"

He was un macho, Lupe had said, a he-animal, a bull.

He ended his swaggering. "You are most beautiful today,
Doña Soledad," he said.

She inclined her head. "You are kind to say so, excelencia."
It was a simple compliment and yet she felt her face begin to
flush as though he had said something improper to her. She saw
his head lower slightly and his shoulders hunch and she thought
he now looked like neither the bull nor the cock but a boar, ready
to charge. Madre mía, Esquipulas, my soul, this one is all the
creatures of the menagerie in one! He is truly comical, querido.
She gestured to a chair. "Will your excellency sit down?" she
asked, feeling the trembling in her throat. "This is a comfortable
chair. It is the favorite of my husband, Don Esquipulas."

He reared at this second mention of Caballero and glared
at her truculently; his mouth went ugly.

I must remember to tell you, my husband, of the thought
of the menagerie and of the exact manner of this look, she
thought. I must forget none of these details.

He took the chair she offered and held out his glass. She saw
the wetness of his lips. She refilled the glass. "Have you received
word of Don Esquipulas, excelencia?"

"He is performing his duties."

"In a manner that satisfies your excellency, I hope?"

"He does well enough."

She sat down, not too close. "You honor this house, excelencia, to come to it when all of Santa Fe clamors for your presence
to give you congratulations. But perhaps it was your intention to
call upon Don José."

"The old man is in the barracks with the soldiers. He relives
the victory through those who were there."

"You knew he would not be here," she said.

"I left orders that he be entertained with anecdotes and
brandy."

"I thank you for honesty, Don Manuel. Did you also send
away your carriage so people would not gather in front of this
house?"

"Yes, señora."

"You omitted nothing." She swallowed some wine and smiled brightly. "One hears of nothing but your triumph."

"You should hear of it from no one but me," he said, suddenly angry.

"From you, excelencia? With the many things you must do?"

"I would bring my triumph to you as I would a jewel." His eyes glowed somberly. "It is what I lack."

"You lack not for worshippers, excelencia."

"Hundreds of worshippers, thousands of worshippers, crawling so low they lose faces and become as ants. There is no end of worshippers." He rubbed the moisture from his lips. "I return to Santa Fe, the greatest victory in the history of my country in my hands, and my happiness is turned to ashes."

"Your people welcomed you as hero!"

"To hell with the people! There is no one to whom I can speak as a man should speak to a woman. I glory less than the commonest of my soldiers who finds waiting for him the woman he loves, who receives from her that which the victorious warrior has for due."

"You have a wife, Don Manuel."

"It is true," he said slowly. "And I love this wife. I love her as my friend. I do not love her as wife. I have never." He shook his head, and his face filled with pain, and with the hurt on it the years of it fell away. "It is you, Soledad, God help me. It is you."

"Excelencia, please."

"I shall speak. The growth is in me. It is a robust plant. The nurturing has been lean. It has survived winter cold and drought and it has grown thorny and hard like the cactus on the desert. But it does not die."

Her eyes softened. "Pobrecito."

"I sit alone on a peak. I breathe air no one else breathes. I am without companion." He stood up. "I need you."

She closed her eyes. "It is not decent to speak to me so."

"To the devil with decency! Do not speak to me of decency. Cuerpo de Cristo, decency is for other people! You and I are above decency. I rule New Mexico. The law for myself is what I make it."

"That may be true, excelencia. But the superiority is yours alone."

"I include you in it!" He loomed over her. "Do you still refuse to understand me? I love you. Listen to me, Soledad. The
last time I said those words I was kneeling before a dead woman.
I thought that part of me was dead in her dead body. But I know
now it was less than this."

"You honor me overly much, Don Manuel," she whispered.

"Honor!" he groaned. "Jesucristo!"

"No, excelencia." She held out her hand as though to keep
him away. "Listen to *me*. You have made yourself the greatest
man in New Mexico, in all of Mexico. I grieve for your loneliness.
But to be alone is a demand of greatness, for you have raised your
head above others. Call upon me for a duty. I will follow, I will
obey. I give thanks to our Holy Virgin that at this time we have
one such as you to guide the destiny of our land. But that is not
the same thing you ask. I feel many things for you, excelencia. I
lower my head before you. But I share my bed with a single man,
and you are not he."

"I love you, Soledad."

"And I have love for you, excelencia."

"My nights are agony."

"If you were to give me a musket and command me to march
against an enemy I would obey you gladly. But that is not the
same thing, excelencia."

"I am not good enough," he said savagely.

"I did not say that, excelencia."

"I am not born well enough to sleep with an Abreu."

"I did not say that, excelencia," she repeated very gently.
"The thought was not in my mind. How can one such as you talk
of birth or lack of birth? In all this land none is higher than you."
She looked at him clearly. "It is nothing of that, and I swear
it to you. It is only that one man alone may take me to his
bed."

His lips set hard. "I hold the life of that man in my hand."

"That is true, excelencia."

"I can lift him or throw him to the ground."

"That is true."

"He lives or he dies on a word from me."

"That is true, that is true."

He crouched before her eagerly. "He need never know. What

I ask takes nothing from him. I accept the leavings from his table, and gladly, humbly."

She rose and turned away from him. He is no macho, no gallo, Esquipulas. He begs.

He followed her. "It is you who hold this life. You determine whether he lives or dies. You can raise him, step after step. His future would be without limit."

"If I but sleep with you," she said coldly.

"It is more than that, but that."

"Until you tire of me."

"There will be no tiring."

"One time, twice, three or four times a week, and then less, and then still less, and I am cast off."

"That will not be true."

"It is true of all your other queridas, excelencia. The city is filled with women you have used."

"It is true of the others, but not of you. Soledad, I stand before you without guile. I open myself. Do not remove your eyes. I hide nothing. Heed me, cara, heed me." He held out his hand pleadingly. "I will promote Caballero," he said so quickly the words became a single word. "He will never know the reason."

She looked at him silently, with slow comprehension. "You planned this from the beginning, did you not, excelencia?"

"I will not deny it."

"Everything you said, the sponsorship of the marriage, all of it, was preparation for this."

"Yes!"

Then she said quietly: "You are without pride, are you not, Don Manuel?"

His head snapped as though he had been whipped. "You are saying pride is something reserved for your own kind?"

"I am saying that you act in a manner unworthy of the Governor of New Mexico."

"You remind me that the world is filled with two different kinds of people, and that you were born an Abreu and that you are married to a Caballero, and that perhaps I have not the right even to the name Armijo!"

"You put words between my lips, excelencia. I remind you of none of these things. I say only that it has happened to me

that I am wed to the one man I can love as you ask for love."
Tears rose to her eyes. "Do not twist my words. Ask anything of
me to prove my devotion to you as a loyal subject. You compliment me unduly, I think, when you say you need me as listener
to your victories. But if I can soothe your difficult way by understanding and affection, I am here. I shall always be here. My
house is your house, excelencia."

"All of it except your bedroom."

"Except the bedroom, excelencia."

He dropped the glass to the floor and took her hand between
his and began to kiss it. "We would be discreet. It would be the
same between the two of you as before. It would be better. I will
make his career into an unparalleled success. He will be happier,
far happier."

"Enough, enough, excelencia!"

"You told me you were beholden to me for having avenged
the death of your father, Don Santiago. I now claim the gratitude!"

She removed her hand from his and covered her face. "You
strike hard, excelencia, and low and deep. I *am* beholden to you."

"Prove it, Soledad!"

"But my mind is an ordinary one. It is not broad enough to
permit me to leave your body and then turn to that of my husband."

"We will keep the secret."

"There would be no secret. Your seed would burn in me like
acid. I am not capable of looking at his face after you have raised
your body from mine."

"It could be done, it could be done!"

"My ears cannot absorb two declarations of love. When my
husband sighs his relief on me, it is all the sound I can bear. Sometimes even his cries are too strong and I think I shall die with
them. My husband uses all that part of me, excelencia, and leaves
none unused."

He shouted her name and closed his arms around her, and
she thought of the pasture. "You are my duchess!" He kissed her
mouth, her face, her neck. He tore at her as a dog would tear at a
bone. "You are mi duquesa! You are mi duquesa!" He pushed her
body against him.

She felt the pressure of his groin and twisted to get away, and then with remote and shapeless horror she felt the oncoming of languor. Her breath slipped away and her legs would not support her and she slumped against him.

He kissed her again and again and in an explosive motion ripped open her dress and cupped her breasts in his hands. "I have eaten here before, mi duquesa," he said. "In the nights all the bodies have been your body." She pushed at him and he fell to his knees and pressed her thighs against his cheek. "Have pity, duquesa, have pity. I kiss the ground on which you walk." He groveled at her feet, kissing her calves and her ankles.

She held one hand over her exposed breasts and looked down at the thick black hair, and the weakness no longer was in her. She stepped back. He looked up at her, and what he saw in her face forced him to rise.

"You have seen what no one should see, señora," he said. He stopped at the door. "You should not have caused me to act so."

3

DAMASIO SALAZAR climbed upon a broken wall of the old mission where Don Manuel had encountered the first five Texan prisoners. "Friends! Today is another day. We have a long road ahead of us. To march, one needs food. I give you food!"

Lieutenant Alpuente held up a sack. Salazar took out a handful of stale corncakes. "Catch!" Don Damasio shouted. He threw the cakes out as though he were scattering grain to chickens.

The prisoners could not control themselves. They fought with each other for the cakes. Men were knocked down and trampled on.

Salazar roared. "Like dogs! Like dogs!" He tossed another handful of cakes into the air. Again the starved prisoners scrambled and Salazar shook with laughter.

Ramón Baca shook the coffee grounds out of his tin cup. He made a cigarette. "Well, chico, do you like what you see?"

"They are Texans," Caballero said.

"And in your eyes that makes it proper for them to be treated as animals?"

Caballero stretched. The morning sun had not yet warmed the air. He worked his arms. "I have heard it said that in their own country Texans do not treat Mexicans with kindness."

"Perhaps not. But these men are not just Texans. They are prisoners of war. There is a tradition on the treatment of such."

Caballero took Baca's cigarette to light his own. He sighed luxuriously. He looked forward to the day in the saddle. "I am wholly without love for Salazar, monito. But I also find it difficult to work up sympathy for Texans. They came to betray us. They were unsuccessful. Now they suffer."

"They appear to have suffered enough before they reached here. And what of the American among them?"

Caballero shrugged. "All gringos are alike to me."

"Not for the present purpose. Don Manuel said we were at war with Texas and not with the United States. The Americans still are doing business in Santa Fe. The caravan came as usual this year." He gazed across the camp toward the prisoners' compound. "I believe I will talk to this American when a chance presents itself."

Caballero waved a finger. "Do not offend Salazar."

Baca spat. "I defecate on Salazar."

"And I. When you would speak to the gringo, inform me. I will join you."

A sergeant of the Rurales strolled toward them indolently, his hands on his hips. "Capitán Salazar orders that both of you join him in a conference of officers," he said. He turned on his heel and started back.

"Sargento," Caballero said. The sergeant paused and looked over his shoulder. "Return here," Caballero said. The sergeant shambled back. "Remove the hands from the hips," Caballero said. "Now approach us in military fashion and salute and address us properly." The sergeant made a move as though to walk away. Caballero's hand went to his pistol holster. "*Pronto, sargento, pronto,*" he said.

The sergeant's face filled with malevolence. He dropped his

hands from his hips, walked up to the two officers and saluted, and repeated the message.

"Thank you, sargento," Caballero said. The man strode off.

Baca mashed out his cigarette. "Have you noticed, little friend, how all of Salazar's men come to resemble Salazar? I tell you he is a contagious disease!"

"I have the feeling we are not going to be among the popular officers on this journey," Caballero said as they walked toward where the other officers were gathered.

"Would you not be insulted if we were?" Baca asked.

Captain Salazar was in the process of assigning officers to various duties. Presently he looked at Caballero and Baca and smiled. "I have been puzzled about you two gentlemen," he said. "I do not anticipate a battle with an enemy between here and El Paso del Norte, so there is no need for you to guard the standard. And at the same time I hesitate to humiliate you by ordering you to command Rurales." The other officers snickered. "But I have found tasks for you to perform, señores. Don Ramón, undoubtedly you have noticed that with us there is a wagon filled with valuable merchandise confiscated from the Texans. Your assignment will be to guard this wagon with your life. As for you, Don Esquipulas, we have with us on this journey almost a score of precious cattle. I entrust to you the responsibility of guarding them. Unfortunately it is not something you can do alone and so you will have to accept half a dozen of my Rurale soldiers."

Caballero moved a step forward. Baca put his hand on his arm. "We obey your orders, mi capitán," Baca said.

The march that day was thirty miles down the Chihuahua Trail. The terrain was grassy, but the bandaged feet of many of the men opened up again and the trampled grass got dark and greasy with blood.

Salazar called a halt at sunset in front of a large corral. He and Lieutenant Alpuente straddled the corral fence and counted off the men as they stumbled into the clearing. The air stank of sheep dung. When the last prisoner was tallied, Salazar gave some sacks of meal to Alpuente, and the lieutenant distributed a small amount to each prisoner.

Salazar ordered Caballero to bring up the cattle. He counted the stock with elaborate care. "You have lost none, Don Esquipulas. My compliments."

Baca, standing next to Caballero, began to whistle softly.

Later Salazar called the prisoners to one side of the corral. "You should know, prisoners, that Governor Armijo ordered me to tie you together each night, but I have too much humanity for such cruelty. But you must not cause me to regret my Christian mercifulness, so I tell you that if a single man is missing any morning, all of you, every single one of you, will be instantly shot."

4

CAMP THE NEXT NIGHT was made alongside a stream. Salazar issued a stale barley cake, hard as stone, to each man. It was the first food they had been given since the evening before. They soaked the cakes in the stream to soften them. They washed themselves and bathed their bleeding feet, and in the morning they formed their column briskly and some of them began to joke with one another.

"Listen to them," Baca said in wonderment.

"They are fools," Caballero said. "Salazar will believe only that he has been too lenient with them."

"I can admire such fools," Baca said. "Look at those men, Esquipulas, and then repeat to me that you still believe they are men who would quietly hand over their guns to Manuel Armijo without pulling the triggers at least once."

"I know only that they did."

"But not why," Baca said.

They reached the pueblo village of Santo Domingo at noon. Indian women came from the apartments with tortillas, baked pumpkins, and dry ears of corn. The Indian women did not weep as the Mexican women had. They looked at the emaciated, ragged prisoners and then they looked at the Mexicans guarding them and their eyes became remote and their faces filled with the bleak hatred of Spaniards.

Salazar became enraged as the women pressed the food upon the prisoners. He ordered his soldiers to drive the women off. The soldiers galloped up and down the line of prisoners, swinging their muskets at the women. The women would not be denied. They managed to get the food to the prisoners though many of the women were left with bruises when the column was gone.

In San Felipe the scene was repeated and again Salazar flew into fury. He shouted orders and his soldiers filed out and attempted to bar the women from the prisoners. Two women pulled one of the soldiers from his horse. They threw him to the ground and a score of women closed in. Other soldiers beat their way through the women and pulled the soldier to his feet. His uniform was torn and his face was covered with scratches. He climbed back on his horse and galloped out of the village, followed by the jeers of the women.

Then suddenly a woman cried out: "Down with Manuel Armijo!"

The cry cut through the air with the sharpness of a razor. For a moment there was a silence of horror. Caballero looked quickly at Baca. Baca's homely face was puckered with a fiendish grin.

The cry was taken up. The imprecations grew in violence and soon included all those who served Manuel Armijo. Salazar, his face grim, ordered the prisoners hurried through the village. Soldiers struck the prisoners to make them quicken their pace. Soon the prisoners were lurching along at a trot. Even at the faster speed it took time for all of them to get through the village, and all during their passing they listened to the shouting of the women.

Squatting a few feet from the campfire, chewing his food, Salazar looked up with annoyance as two soldiers led Peter Van Ness before him. "What do you want?" he asked from his full mouth.

"The men are freezing," Van Ness said. "They have asked me to appeal to you for some shelter for the night."

"Freezing? Is it cold?"

"It is very cold, Don Damasio. We were cold last night and the night before, but now it is freezing. The feet of many of the men already are frostbitten."

Salazar looked at his officers. "Can this possibly be true? How do you know their feet are frostbitten, señor?"

"Nails are falling from toes," Van Ness said. "Feet are sore and there is no feeling in them. If this continues, gangrene will set in and the feet will have to be amputated or the men will die."

Salazar raised his hands and his eyes piously. "Nombre de Dios, but this must not happen! I shall see about this shelter, as soon as I finish my meal, señor."

"Thank you, capitán," Van Ness said quietly.

"Go back to the men, señor, tell them I shall not forget."

Later Salazar went to the shivering prisoners. "Line up, hombres, I have found good shelter for you this cold night." He led the men to a small, two-room adobe house. "Here is a roof for your heads. Enter and I will count you to make certain all are here."

"This building will not hold fifty men, Don Damasio," Van Ness protested. "There are almost two hundred of us."

Salazar nodded gravely. "You will be crowded, it is true; but that will make for warmth. Enter!"

The men went into the building. They soon filled both rooms and more than half of them were still outside. Soldiers pushed more and more of them through the door. The men were pressed so tightly no one could move and there were still prisoners outside. These were forced in. The soldiers wielded their muskets as staves and pounded the prisoners. Toward the last the soldiers turned their backs and linked arms and in that way got the last of the Texans into the building. The door was swung shut and a heavy wooden beam was dropped across it into iron braces.

Salazar peered through a narrow window next to the door, the only window in the building. "Rest well, friends. I think you will not be cold tonight."

Ramón Baca gestured to Caballero to remain at the building, which was just outside the village of Algodones, when Salazar and the other officers strolled away. Baca put his face to the opening and then he stepped back and Caballero looked inside.

No man could move a limb. Those whose arms happened to be caught at their sides could not raise them. Those who happened to have their arms upraised could not lower them. There was hardly enough room for men to expand their chests to breathe.

Then the men in the rear room screamed: "There's no air! There's no air!"

"They are like grain in a sack," Caballero said.

The men in the back shouted: "We're smothering! Try to break down the door!"

Caballero turned away. "They will die like animals."

The two men heard a thud as the prisoners tried to break through the door and then they heard groans and cries of pain and then another thud and more groaning. Baca looked into the opening again, turned abruptly, and hurried to the officers' fire.

He found Salazar warming himself at the fire, puffing contentedly on a cigar. "The prisoners suffocate, capitán. Some of them must be allowed to come out of the building."

Salazar removed the cigar. "You have pity for heretics, Don Ramón?" The firelight played evil tricks with his face.

"Governor Armijo ordered the Texans brought to El Paso del Norte. He said nothing of leaving half of them dead on the way."

Salazar smoked and considered. "You are right," he said at last. "I allow some of them to come out. Just fifty, not a man more."

Baca gave Salazar's order to the guard. The beam was lifted. The door flew open. Men, soaking in sweat, bleeding from the nose and ears, reeled out of the building into the icy night, and, paralyzed by the cold, some of them fell over like logs. When fifty men were counted off, the door was forced shut and the beam was replaced.

A huge, red-haired prisoner, half-blinded by the sweat in his eyes, shouted: "Where's Salazar? I'll kill him!" He staggered in a circle, swinging his arms. "Where is the greasy bastard? I'll kill him!"

Baca saw the lame American try to quiet him. The red-haired man shook him off. He waved his fists. "Where are you, Salazar? In the sweet name of Christ, where are you?" A Rurale hit him on the head with the stock of his musket. The prisoner tottered and fell to his knees and then stood up again. "Where are you, Salazar?" The soldier hit him harder and the prisoner went down unconscious. The soldier lifted his musket.

"Stop that!" Baca ordered.

293

"Tu chingada madre!" The soldier drove the butt down on the prisoner's shoulder.

"Stop!" Baca commanded again. He drew his pistol. The soldier lifted his musket again. Baca shot him in the shoulder.

"Bring Ensign Baca to me," Salazar said to Lieutenant Alpuente. "And call the other officers. This should be amusing." He seated himself on a pile of folded blankets and crossed his arms. When Baca faced him he cleared his throat and said with severity: "It has been reported to me that you shot one of my soldiers, señor."

"That is correct, capitán."

"That is serious business, the shooting of a soldier."

"It is more serious than you believe," Baca said shortly.

Salazar was disconcerted for a moment by Baca's attitude. He knew the other officers were waiting. He cleared his throat again. "Yes, it is serious," he said.

"When we return to Santa Fe I shall prefer charges against the man at a court martial," Baca said.

Salazar's mouth dropped open. "*You* will prefer charges?"

"It is military law that a soldier obeys the commands of an officer. It is my understanding that this is true even in the Rurales."

"There is as much discipline in the Rurales as in the presidial companies!" Salazar shouted, his judicial manner deserting him entirely.

Baca smiled coldly. "With your permission, señor capitán, I must disagree. If I believed that to be true I would not have shot the man in the arm."

"That sounds better, Don Ramón," Salazar said.

"I would have put the bullet into his heart."

Salazar bounced to his feet. "What!"

Baca regarded him calmly. "I have no way of knowing whether or not you have ever read the manual of military regulations, Don Damasio, but in it there is an entire section dealing with the action to be taken when a soldier refuses to obey the commands of an officer in the line of duty. The section is explicit. I could have shot the man dead. If he had been one of the presidial soldiers I would have shot him dead and he would have expected no less, except that among true soldiers such things do not occur."

Salazar struck his fist against his chest. "I give all the orders here!"

"Did you order the soldier to beat an unconscious man to death?" Baca asked politely.

"Of course not," Salazar spluttered.

"I did not believe so. Then, señor capitán, so long as I hold rank as officer, I expect to be obeyed by your soldiers. If that is unacceptable to you, you may place me under arrest." He saluted and turned on his heel.

During the evening meal Salazar held to a moody silence. The other officers talked loudly among themselves. Salazar chewed his mustache. He said suddenly: "I wonder how it is going up there in Santa Fe with Don Manuel returning as a great hero. Everybody will worship him, I think."

"It is true," Alpuente said. "Who among our people does not worship Don Manuel?"

"And now more than ever," Salazar said. "Now he is a hero."

"The greatest hero," the fat lieutenant agreed.

"It is astonishing how women idolize a hero. There is nothing a woman will not do for such a man. You know, Don Jesús, I am happy I did not have to leave a wife unattended in Santa Fe."

The Rurale officers began to understand Salazar's talking was not aimless. They stopped their own conversation and listened intently.

"Women are strange people, Don Jesús," Salazar continued reflectively. "You never know what a woman will do. You believe she is faithful and then suddenly she is not. No, if I had a wife in Santa Fe, particularly a wife who attracted Don Manuel, I would be a worried man now."

The officers looked at Caballero.

"How are all your little cows?" Baca asked him cheerfully.

"They are all tucked in for the night," Caballero said.

"I would have pictures in my head," Salazar said. "I would see this wife and Don Manuel doing things together."

Baca dug his fingers into Caballero's thigh. "Give me some tobacco, hombre," he said.

"I would think of myself lying on the ground under a military blanket and I would think of my wife in a warm bed with Don Manuel." Salazar chuckled. "He is a bull, it is said."

Baca's fingers were iron. Caballero relaxed. He took out his tobacco sack. Baca made a cigarette and lit it with a brand from the fire. "I am officer of the guard tonight, friend," he said to Caballero. "I must inspect the prisoners. Come, stretch your legs with me." As they walked away they heard the officers laugh. Caballero stiffened. "You will have a better reason," Baca said. "The longer you wait, the more pleasure it will be. Killing that filth will be one of the great things of your life. Do not do it in haste."

The wind had risen. They walked to the building where the Texans were imprisoned. The guards were huddled in their blankets. Baca held his lantern to the window. He heard sounds of pain.

"What were your thoughts today when you listened to the people in the streets of San Felipe?" he asked, lowering the lantern.

"I did not know what to think," Caballero said.

"One thought was in my head. It was that New Mexico still had a conscience and that at that moment we listened to it."

They walked to the pigpen where the fifty men had been taken. The stink, even in the bitter cold, made them gasp. Baca held the lantern aloft. He moved among the prisoners until he found the red-haired man. He held the light closer. A blood-soaked bandage was tied around the man's head. Baca looked around and saw the American. "How is this man?"

"He will live," Kendall said, "because of what you did. I thank you for him, señor."

Baca took a flask from his pocket. "I have some brandy. Do you believe you can rouse him?"

"Yes," Kendall said eagerly. He threw back his blanket and lifted the injured man to a half-sitting position. "Fitz, here is some brandy," he said.

"Tell them to keep their brandy," the man said.

"Fitz, this is the officer who saved your life. Drink some of the brandy."

The man opened his mouth. Several of his upper teeth were missing and the gums were still bleeding. Baca held the flask to his lips. The man choked. Kendall slapped him on the back. "Try to swallow, Fitz," he said.

The man managed to get some of the brandy down. He blinked his eyes and tapped Baca on the arm. Then he passed out again. Kendall laid him down gently and drew his blanket to his chin.

Baca handed the American the flask. "Keep this, señor. Give it to him when he needs it. When the flask is empty, return it to me and I will refill it. And do not let Salazar know about it."

"God bless you," Kendall said.

Baca straightened. "How are you called, señor?"

"George Kendall."

"And he?"

"Cornelius Fitzgerald."

"Make him understand he must not provoke Salazar, Don Jorge, else he will not live to reach El Paso del Norte."

5

CABALLERO watched the prisoners stumble out of the building. His hand tightened on the hilt of his sword. "Look at them, Ramón, they are stuck together, as though with glue."

Five men emerged in a clump. When they separated, the man in the center fell over unconscious. His friends dragged him out of the path of the others. The men sucked air into their lungs. From the pigpen came the hacking coughs of the men who had been released the night before.

Salazar lined up the prisoners. "We do not travel quickly enough," he said. "After all, the winter is coming on us and we do not want you to freeze to death. So you may know the exact rate I wish you to travel, I will provide one to set the pace." He rode up to where Fitzgerald was standing. He uncoiled his lazo. "Lift your hands high in the air, señor," he said. When Fitzgerald did not move, Salazar said pleasantly: "Quickly, señor, raise your arms or I take them off you from the shoulders." Fitzgerald held up his hands. Salazar cast the loop over his wrists. He allowed Fitzgerald about six feet of the rope and tied it to the pommel. "Now we start," he said. "This man who has so much energy he does not know what to do with it will keep up with me. And the rest of you will travel as quickly."

They started toward Sandia. Salazar kept his horse at a walk at first and then gradually let it out. Fitzgerald had to trot to keep up. The jogging started the blood flowing from his injured skull. At Sandia, Salazar announced there would be a short rest to keep the horses from becoming winded.

That night Baca and Caballero walked over to the corral near Alameda where the prisoners were herded. They found Fitzgerald, surrounded by a dozen men, telling of some of his experiences as a soldier of fortune in different parts of the world. When the officers appeared, he jumped to his feet and gripped Baca's hand. His wrist was swollen and chafed raw.

"I respect your strength, señor," Baca said.

Fitzgerald struck himself on the chest. "I was born an Irishman and I became a Texan."

Baca glanced around the corral. The prisoners, who had just finished their meal of the day, an ear of raw corn for each man, were in good spirits. "I do not know how they do it," Baca said.

"They are hardy boys," Fitzgerald said. "The weak ones died on the way up from Texas. Anybody who was able to survive that trip has iron in his bones."

"Was it a difficult journey?" Caballero asked.

Fitzgerald laughed. "I do not speak your language well enough to tell it to you, señor."

"Perhaps Don Jorge can find the words," Baca said.

"Tell them, George," Fitzgerald said. "Words are your business."

Baca took a bottle of brandy from under his poncho. "This may help you along."

The men sat down in a circle and wrapped their blankets around them, and George Kendall told of the journey up from Texas and of how Carlos had abandoned them. "The strange thing is that the man could not have been lost," Kendall said. "I saw him in San Miguel the day we began this march. His arm was in a sling."

"Santa Madre!" Baca said. "Was this a large man with a scar on one cheek?"

"He had a scar," Kendall said. "Do you know him?"

Baca nodded. "This Carlos who served as your guide, Don Jorge, is a cousin to Salazar."

The prisoners were stupefied. Kendall said slowly: "Then we were betrayed from the beginning. Nothing was accidental—the mistaking of the rivers, the wandering—it all was done deliberately."

"He must have been sent by Don Manuel," Baca said. "You noticed his arm was in a sling. He was beaten up in Santa Fe and it was said a large amount of gold was taken from him."

"The payment to the Judas," Fitzgerald said.

"I can understand now why Don Manuel appeared so unworried about Texans," Baca said. "What I do not understand is why all of you surrendered with no resistance." He looked at Caballero.

"We broke up into two groups," Kendall said. "One group went on ahead of the other, and then five of us left the first group. We were taken first. We had very little choice, Don Ramón. We suddenly were surrounded by a small army commanded by our friend Salazar. He promised us fair treatment and a friendly reception from the Governor if we surrendered our weapons."

"And you believed him?" Baca asked in amazement.

"We had never encountered your captain before."

"That explains what happened to you," Baca said. "But what of the others? There were hundreds of you. For years we have heard of the valor of the Texans. I understand how you suffered on your journey from Texas, but you still could have fought."

"I told you that the men divided in half," Kendall said. "The first group reached as far as the Pecos River at Anton Chico. They were under the command of a man named Cooke. He was visited by Salazar. The captain was cordial. He sent freshly butchered sheep to men who were almost starved to death. He sent wine and brandy and cigars to Cooke and other officers. Then he told Cooke the law of New Mexico required that they give up their guns before they went on to Santa Fe. He said this custom was accepted by the men who crossed the Santa Fe Trail year after year. He said Governor Armijo and the people of New Mexico had nothing but the friendliest feelings for them and wanted to do business with them, and that if they gave up their weapons they could go on to the capital. When they started back for Texas the weapons would be returned to them.

"Cooke did not wholly believe Salazar, and some of his officers believed Salazar less. They were for holding onto their guns and fighting if necessary. But there was something else. You will remember I told you five of us from Cooke's party were taken first. One of the five, a man named Lewis, sold out to the Governor and agreed to betray his comrades. This Lewis had been an officer in the Texas war and was greatly respected. As the other officers were urging Cooke to resist, Lewis came forth. He said that everything was as Salazar had represented. Still there were men who did not want to lay down their arms. It happened that both Cooke and Lewis are Masons. Lewis swore to Cooke on his Masonic oath that Salazar was telling the truth and that it was the custom for all foreigners to give up their guns before they entered Santa Fe. Cooke could not doubt his word, given in that manner. He ordered his men to put down their guns, and five minutes later they were prisoners."

"So that is how the great victory came about," Baca breathed.

"As for the others who remained with General McLeod, they were without food," Kendall went on. "They were eating lizards and snake meat and desert tortoises and one day they killed a polecat and ate the flesh raw. They were attacked by Kiowa Indians and their horses were stampeded. When they continued on foot, men fell dead, one after another, and it was then that they encountered a large force under the command of a man named Archuleta. This Archuleta too demanded that they lay down their arms, and he told them the same story Salazar had told Cooke. The officers with McLeod wanted to fight, as had the officers with Cooke, and McLeod gave orders to get ready to fight. It was then he discovered that on the march men had thrown away their guns and ammunition when they became too weak to carry them, and though he counted more than one hundred and fifty men, there were less than three dozen rifles among them. He surrendered."

Caballero lowered his head. Baca could not look at his friend's face.

6

SALAZAR sent soldiers into Albuquerque in advance of the prisoners and he ordered the prisoners to go through the town in double time. The soldiers lined up on both sides of the main street and prevented the people from giving food and drink to the Texans, but they could not keep the people silent. The shouts against Governor Armijo were louder than at the pueblo.

Someone threw garbage at Salazar. The refuse missed the captain but splattered on his horse. Salazar drew his sword, but did not attempt to charge the crowd.

Because of the demonstration, Salazar refused to issue food to the prisoners that night. "I have observed how you eat the corn the women give you," he said. "You eat it raw in what must be the manner of your country." He pointed to where the animals were feeding. "Go there with the other animals! The grazing is excellent!"

It was not until they reached the village of Valencia the following evening that Salazar relented and gave a small measure of wheat flour to each man. The flour required fire for baking, and some of the men found wood and built small fires and made cakes. Although they had not eaten for two days, many of the prisoners were too exhausted to prepare the flour and they lay down and slept.

The camp was wakened in the morning by the screams of one of the prisoners. The man pointed to the body of another prisoner. "We slept together last night," he babbled. "We wrapped our arms around each other to keep warm. When I woke this morning, I was sleeping with a corpse!" He gagged, but there was nothing to come up.

The dead man was stiff from the cold. Salazar removed his ears and strung them on a rawhide thong he kept in his saddlebag. He waved the thong in the air. "The trophies increase more and more. Whose ears will be next?" He looked down at a prisoner hobbling up to him. "What do you want?"

The prisoner, a man named John McAllister, was permanently lame in his left leg from a fall from a horse many years before. He told Salazar he had twisted his right ankle and could not walk. "Would you like to ride with me?" Salazar asked sardonically. "There is a small cart used to carry camp equipment, capitán," McAllister replied. "I have a silver dollar to pay for a ride on it." Salazar took the dollar. An hour later the cart broke down. Salazar distributed the equipment to other carts, and McAllister crawled to one of the other wagons.

"Now you continue on foot," Salazar said.

"You agreed that I might ride," McAllister said.

"I agreed that you might ride in that cart."

"But that has come apart."

"Therefore you walk."

"I cannot walk, capitán."

Salazar swung his sword. "Move on!"

"I beg you to allow me to ride on one of the wagons until my ankle gets a little better," McAllister said.

"Move, swine!"

McAllister attempted to take a step and fell on his face. Two of his friends lifted him and supported him. Salazar whipped them away with his sword. "The heretic pig walks alone!" he shouted.

"I am a Catholic, capitán," McAllister said.

"Move, I said!"

McAllister fell down again.

"Get up and walk!" Salazar screamed. "Forward, or I shoot you on the spot!"

McAllister slowly stood erect. He cast down his blanket. He crossed himself, murmuring: "Jesus, forgive me my sins." Then he said quietly: "Go ahead and shoot, you Mexican dog. The sooner the better."

Salazar fired a bullet into his heart. A soldier removed the ears and gave them to the captain. Salazar permitted the soldier to keep the blanket. Another soldier pulled off McAllister's trousers. Another ripped a religious medal from his neck. The body was pushed to one side.

7

Now the march was through the great valley of the river that was called the Río Bravo and the Río del Norte and the Rio Grande. The wind swept through the country, which was open and bare, and the land had true loneliness. It was the big country that had made the first men from Spain remember the Castilian plateau that surrounded Madrid.

There were no villages and few houses. The men marched in apathy and cold. They tore buttons from their jackets and bought brief rides behind soldiers. When the soldiers kicked them off, they held their jackets closed and leaned against the wind as they marched. Now and again men lay down and died as though death were a thing of the will.

The food for the soldiers began to run out and Salazar ordered Caballero to butcher one of the beeves, the first since they had left San Miguel, confirming what Baca had suspected, that Salazar was trying to salvage as many of the cattle as he could to sell in El Paso del Norte. The raw lungs, brain, and entrails were left for the prisoners to fight over.

Caballero woke at Fray Cristóbal to find that snow had fallen during the night. The camp was desolate. A slowly rising vapor gave him a feeling of unearthiness. All around, men were sprawled, looking like felled trees. The morning silence was broken only by the coughing of prisoners who had taken fever after the night in the building.

Soldiers stirred and prodded prisoners awake with muskets and lances. Salazar called the Texans together. "We reach the difficult part of the journey, hombres," he said. "Before us lies the Jornada del Muerto."

The prisoners repeated the name, "the Day's Journey of the Dead Man," among themselves.

"It is a crossing of ninety miles," Salazar said. "I will not describe it to you. I will say only that the name is not inappropriate. There is no drinking water anywhere. The crossing must be made without break. We rest here this morning and start out this afternoon." His mouth twisted. "On the other side is El Paso del Norte. Those of you who get across will perhaps live after all."

He ordered Caballero to butcher a second beef and again allowed the prisoners to scramble for the refuse. The lucky prisoners feasted on the raw leavings. The men huddled together during the day, drawing what warmth they could from the bleak sun, and talked about the Jornada. A raw wind came up in the afternoon and it turned still colder. Salazar gave the order for the column to move. Kendall clutched a two-quart gourd he had filled with water. His puffed-up ankle turned on a stone. The gourd slipped from his fingers and shattered on the frozen earth and the water began to turn to ice.

It got steadily colder. Now the soldiers dismounted and walked to keep from freezing. Later that night they passed a column of Mexican dragoons who had been ordered to Santa Fe to reinforce Governor Armijo in his war with Texas. The dragoons were on foot for warmth as well. Where they found a patch of grass or a few pieces of wood they built fires. The tiny blazes were stretched out for miles on the plain.

Salazar made no attempt now to hold the prisoners in formation. Some of them sneaked over to the fires. The dragoons and the women followers with them moved aside for the prisoners and some of them gave them brandy.

"This is a journey of enlightenment, is it not?" Baca asked Caballero. "Life is confining in Santa Fe, chico. I think perhaps this Texan President was not wrong. Do you recall what Señor Kendall said the other night? 'Your country is called a republic,' he said. 'In a republic men govern only with the consent of those governed. When the consent is withdrawn, the governor must go.' That is an interesting thought, is it not?"

The prisoners drifted on through the night. The fires and the friendly dragoons were soon behind them. The cold grew still worse. The veterans among the Texans sent word up and down the line: "Keep awake, keep awake, don't fall asleep. If you fall asleep you will freeze to death."

The men who were well tried to watch over the sick. Despite the repeated admonition, which became a kind of marching chant, men fell over and were asleep before they hit the ground. Their friends slapped their faces and shook them. They begged to be left alone.

At dawn the prisoners were staggering like drunken men. Some were asleep on their feet, dragged along by friends. There was no pause. Salazar rode up and down the column and kept the men moving. By noon they reached the Laguna del Muerto, "the Lagoon of the Dead Man," and Caballero told Kendall to pass the word to the men that they had come halfway and that forty-five miles were behind them.

In the afternoon an American named Richard Golpin, a merchant who had joined the Texans in Austin, fell to his knees. His bleeding feet would no longer bear him. He had already bargained away all his buttons and had left only his shirt and trousers. He offered the shirt to a soldier for a ride. The soldier accepted. Golpin began to pull the shirt over his head.

Salazar rode up. "Kill that man!" he ordered. The soldier looked at him in astonishment. "Kill that man!" Salazar repeated. "You, the one who was going to take the shirt!"

The soldier hesitated and Salazar struck him with his sword. The soldier pulled out his pistol and shot Golpin while he still had the shirt over his head. The soldier was unable to aim properly and only wounded Golpin.

"Kill him!" Salazar fumed. "Or I kill you!"

The soldier felt for Golpin's head under the shirt and fired a second bullet into his brain.

At sundown Salazar called a brief halt. He left orders for the march to start again before midnight and then he and Alpuente climbed into one of the supply wagons and covered themselves with blankets and finished a bottle of brandy. When the prisoners started again, they passed the wagon and heard the snores of the two men.

Toward the early morning the cold increased to a point beyond anything the men had experienced. The soles of the prisoners' feet stuck to the ground and pieces of flesh tore off. Water froze in gourds held by men against their chests. The prisoners had had no food in thirty-six hours. A man lay down and said he could go no farther. A soldier said in a mild voice: "Move on, hombre, else I have to follow the order of Capitán Salazar and kill you." The man tried to pull himself along on the ground. He collapsed, crying. "I will have to kill you," the soldier explained in the same unangry voice. The man clasped his hands in prayer and shook his head. The soldier brained him.

It was four or five hours after sunrise and the men had been walking for more than forty hours when a shout rose from the head of the column: "It's the Rio Grande!"

Swaggering, half drunk in the camp that night, Salazar stumbled over a sleeping man. Salazar cursed and beat the man with his saber. The man spoke no Spanish. He had learned only two words, which he had found occasion to use to people who had given him food. The words had always brought a smiling response. He now sat up and said: "Muchas gracias."

Salazar struck him again. The man said: "Muchas gracias."

Salazar went insane with rage and beat the man with the saber blade again and again, and each time the man murmured his thanks. It was Kendall who shouted: "For God's sake, stop thanking him or he'll beat you to death!"

The man understood for the first time why he was enraging Salazar and he closed his mouth. Like a spring that needed time to unwind Salazar continued to strike him, the blows becoming slower and slower, until he stopped and walked away.

On the 5th day of November the survivors of the march entered the plaza of El Paso del Norte.

8

CABALLERO'S MOUTH fell open. "Madre de Dios! Don Jorge, can this truly be you?"

Kendall grinned and looked over the fine hidalgo suit he was wearing. He twirled his mustache. "Compliments of General Elias. He makes caballeros of all of us."

Caballero looked at Van Ness and then at Fitzgerald. "Ramón," he said, "do you know any of these men?"

"We hardly know ourselves," Van Ness laughed.

"That bath," Fitzgerald said. He kissed his fingers. "That first bath!"

"And the bed," Kendall said.

"The cigars," Fitzgerald said.

"And the wine. Don't forget the wine," Van Ness said.

The three men laughed. Caballero and Baca were staring at them speechlessly when General Elias entered the room. The officers came to attention. The ruddy-faced, gray-haired military commandant of Chihuahua looked at the three prisoners with satisfaction.

"You are a little different from the three men I brought into my house yesterday, señores," he said.

"It was all worth it, general, all of it, for the bath," Kendall said. "I think I would do it all again for how I felt when I stepped into that hot water."

The general turned to Caballero and Baca. "These gentlemen told me of your kindness to them, señores. I have asked you to dine with us this evening in gratitude for them. I have also arranged for something that may interest you later."

They sat down to dinner. Kendall looked at the linen and silver. He picked up a fork and shook his head. "This is the first meal we have eaten at a table since we left Austin."

After dinner, in the rich atmosphere of cigars and fine brandy and strong coffee, the prisoners told of their experiences on the march from San Miguel. The general listened in stony silence; from time to time his jaw muscles bunched. He said, at the end: "There are many things I should like to say at this time, señores, and many things I may not say. I am the military commandant of Chihuahua and technically you are my prisoners of war."

Kendall said: "You have already said it all, señor general. None of us shall forget your kindness to us."

A servant came to the table and whispered something to the general. Elias nodded, the servant left, and a moment later Salazar entered the room. He saluted cockily and then his eyes went around the table.

"Señor general," he said, he eyes bulging, "Capitán Salazar has the honor to report to the general the conclusion of the duties imposed upon him by General Manuel Armijo, Governor and Military Commandant of the Department of New Mexico."

"I know the name of your Governor and the title he affixes to his name," Elias said.

Salazar again looked around the table. The other men contemplated him quietly. "Don Manuel entrusted to my care a number of the Texan heretics," he said. "They were captured through the skill and bravery of Don Manuel as they were making a treacherous attack upon New Mexico. It was my assignment to bring a number of these prisoners to your excellency. I have discharged my duties as ordered. I have brought all the prisoners except those who died on the way." Now Salazar raised his head with something of his normal manner. "They died, excelencia, but they did not escape. I bring you proof!" He pulled from his pocket the rawhide with the ears.

"I have heard," Elias said, "of Don Manuel's predilection for those portions of the human anatomy."

"Each man is present or accounted for, excelencia," Salazar said proudly.

"Excepting those who were lost or who perished in the night," Elias said quietly.

Salazar frowned. Then his yellow teeth seemed to spring from his lips. He held out his hands. "There may be some missing, excelencia."

"You are attention, señor capitán," Elias said.

Salazar's hands dropped to his sides. He glanced at his former charges, now lounging negligently, cigars dangling from their lips.

"Capitán Salazar," Elias said in the same polite tones, "you are a coward, a scoundrel, and a disgrace to your country and to the uniform you dishonor."

Salazar's sallow face flushed. He pounded his chest. "I am a brave man and a true officer, excelencia. When I am on guard, my chief, Don Manuel, sleeps peacefully."

"I have no interest whatsoever in the feelings Don Manuel has for you," Elias said. His voice now was like chilled steel. "I talk only of the men you caused needlessly to die. Because of you our country has become a stink in the nostrils of these men, and the smell will spread when they return to their homes and the whole world will think Mexico is made of Salazars!"

"You must not speak so to me," Salazar choked.

"I wish only I had authority to deal with you as you deserve,"

308

Elias said. "I would not order you arrested. I would simply turn you over to the men you brought down here."

"Holy Mother of God!" Fitzgerald half rose from his chair.

"I do not have that authority, however," Elias said. "There are those in Mexico who live by the law. So you may return to your chief and report to him you have accomplished your mission. I will tell you only, señor, that I am a Christian and that I believe with all my heart that you will not go unpunished for this."

Salazar trembled. "Is that all, General Elias?"

"It is not all. There are, on the other side of the Bravo, fifteen head of cattle which were given to you by Don Manuel, who does not share your love for senseless cruelty, to feed your prisoners. There are also horses and mules that were stolen from citizens of El Paso del Norte and then acquired by your Governor in traffic with the savages. You will order soldiers to where all these animals are waiting and have them brought here immediately, together with a wagon of merchandise which also was given to you as a means of obtaining food for your prisoners. Until everything is in my hands you will consider yourself under arrest and you will not leave the limits of this city. If you do, I will send a squad after you with orders to kill you on sight. I would willingly lose the stolen animals for that pleasure."

9

PEDRO MUÑOZ, the colonel in command of the dragoons from Mexico, presented himself to Governor Armijo in the palace at Santa Fe. Don Manuel laughed. "Take your soldiers back to Chihuahua, mi coronel. Tell them I do not need soldiers. Tell them that my weapon is here." He tapped his forehead. "I think, señor coronel! I reason! Take your soldiers back to Mexico, where they are needed. Here all that is needed is Armijo."

1

Soon after Esquipulas Caballero and his wife arrived for the spring rodeo at the rancho of Juan Estevan Pino, Caballero said he wanted to look at the bulls that were to be used in the tailing.

Soledad waited for him to ask her to go with him. When he did not, she said: "Have a look at the horse you will ride too."

"I shall do so." He bowed formally. "You will excuse me, Doña Soledad."

"Of course." She looked at his somber eyes. "Esquipulas."

"Yes, señora," he said politely.

"Shall I see you again before the contest?"

"It is possible, but I do not believe so."

She touched his wrist. "May God favor you, husband." She watched him walk stiffly away and she wondered again as she had wondered since he had returned from El Paso del Norte what had happened on the journey with the Texans that had changed him.

During the weeks Caballero had been gone she had thought of her experience with Don Manuel. She had planned how she would tell her husband of all of it, making it into something comical that they would laugh over together, and she had the words put together in her mind, a story of a fat man strutting like a lecherous rooster; and then she had remembered how for a little while Don Manuel had not been comical and she knew that she would not be able to tell her husband about it so he would think it was comical either. She could hear the words as they came from her mouth and could see what would happen to her husband's face as he listened to them, and she knew that before she was finished he would be on his way to kill the Governor.

She had thought then of telling him only part of the story— all but the end of it—making the secret into a half secret, but where would she stop with the truth and begin the invention, and would he not know exactly when the lie began? And what ending would she give to it? And finally she knew she could tell her husband nothing. Then he had returned from Chihuahua and she knew that her torment had been unnecessary because he was a different man, and in his present state communication was impossible. From then on, through the winter, into the spring, they had acted toward each other with careful courtesy and she wondered how much of it was due to him and how much to her for what she had not told him.

She chatted pleasantly with friends in the sunny patio of Don Juan Estevan's rancho, which he had picked up for next to nothing during the winter from a disgraced rico, and she was joined by James Magoffin, who had just come up from the south on his way to the United States to get together his annual wagon train. Magoffin was one of the few Americans present. The previous October, flushed with his victory, Don Manuel had lifted the interdiction against travel and there had been an immediate exodus of Americans, including many business men who had liquidated their holdings at a loss. The American consul, Manuel Alvarez, had departed as well, and the Governor considered it good riddance, and for a little while matters were almost amicable between Armijo and the Americans who still remained. Then Armijo had learned that Alvarez had gone to Washington to make a personal, formal complaint against him to the United States Secretary of State, Daniel Webster, and the Americans were in greater disgrace than before. The rioting against them had stopped and they were unmolested, but apart from Magoffin and one or two others, they were socially ignored.

She felt a curious, unexpected security with Magoffin. "I had heard you were back in Santa Fe, Don Santiago. I was hoping I would have the pleasure of seeing you here. How is your wife, Doña María Gertrudis?"

Magoffin's blue eyes clouded. "She is not well, Doña Soledad."

"What is the matter with her?"

"I do not know. Whatever it is, it has baffled every doctor in Chihuahua. If she has not improved when I return there, I am going to take her to Independence to see whether anybody there can help her."

The air was rent by a sudden blast of trumpets. They both

311

looked up. A dozen horsemen galloped into the clearing in front of the house. Behind them was the Governor's carriage. The trumpets were blown again. Don Manuel and his lady descended from the carriage.

Juan Estevan Pino rushed up to the couple. He held his sombrero against his chest and bowed, as a peasant would before his patrón. "This is a great honor, excelencia. My poor house and everything in it is at your disposition and that of your lady."

Don Manuel raised his hand with lordly graciousness. "We were pleased to come, Don Juan Estevan," he boomed.

Soledad took Magoffin's arm impulsively. "Look how quickly the mood of the guests has changed, Don Santiago."

He gazed at her curiously. "It is easy for your people to accept Don Manuel's greatness," he said. "It is less easy for them to carry the weight of the greatness he imposes on them."

She pulled her hand away with the same swift gesture. "Do you deny this greatness, then, Don Santiago?" she flared.

"You know better than that," he said quietly. "It is only that greatness becomes a burden after a very little while. Don Manuel tells his people they live in a historic time and that is a thrilling thing, I think, but a man can keep his shoulders squared and his chin thrust out and his eyes stern only for so long. Then he wants to relax. And I mean that for Americans as well as Mexicans." His eyes twinkled. "I believe I can say I know your people, Doña Soledad. They have a special maturity of their own and I think they get bored at being reminded they are heroes." He took her arm. "I believe the entertainments are going to begin now. Show me that I have not offended you by doing me the honor of sitting with me."

The guests were moving toward where seats had been set up on one side of an immense corral. For a moment Soledad held back, and then she smiled and squeezed Magoffin's arm. They strolled to the seats together.

The first exhibition in the corral was a demonstration of the art of the lazo. Mounted men charged after racing animals and cast the ropes deftly on the horns, necks, and hind legs of oxen, horses, and calves.

"Watch Fernando!" Soledad cried. "He is the best of all."

"Fernando?"

"The large man there, on the black. He is servant to Don Esquipulas. Even as a child there was no one to match him with the lazo." Her eyes sparkled. "With him the rope becomes an instrument of art."

"Would you like to look through the glasses?"

She shook her head. "I excite too much, Don Santiago, and what happens always happens outside the little circle."

He watched Fernando Rael. Lounging carelessly in his saddle, Fernando did everything everybody else did. "He makes it appear so simple," Magoffin murmured.

"It is the style," she said. "He has the true style."

The other lazo-throwers left the field. A steer was released from a chute. Fernando tossed the noose under the galloping animal, tightening it on its off foreleg.

"Olé! Olé!" Soledad cried out. "Santa Madre, but that was a thing of beauty!"

Twice more, steers were released and twice more Fernando caught them in the same manner. The guests in the seats stood up and shouted their approval. Don Manuel presented a purse of silver to Fernando. He accepted the gift and then rode up to Vicario Juan Felipe Ortiz and gave the purse to him to be distributed among mendicants. Don Manuel frowned and then joined others who were applauding Fernando for his generosity.

The next event was the correr el gallo, the running of the cock. A live rooster, his head greased, was buried up to his neck. Horsemen raced past at top speed and, leaning down from their saddles, attempted to grab the cock by the neck and pull it out of the ground. Many missed the target altogether. Others who managed to get their fingers around the slippery neck could not hold onto it. One man succeeded at last and then the others tried to wrest his squawking trophy from him. He dodged back and forth, and in the struggle the cock was ripped to pieces, but the successful rider eluded his pursuers finally and galloped to where his sweetheart was seated and he presented to her what he still retained of the mangled fowl. The girl tore a feather from the wing and stuck it in her hair, to wear later at the baile, and the spectators shouted their olés.

Servants brought refreshments and the guests settled down to that for which they were most eagerly waiting, el coleo, the tailing of the bull. The details of the sport, as Magoffin knew, were deceptively simple. A bull was released. Men rode him down and jockeyed to seize the bull's short tail. He who succeeded lifted his leg, still in the stirrup, over his wrist so that the wrist was held under the inner part of the knee, and then he turned his horse violently away from the bull and, by pulling the bull half around itself and twisting his wrist at the same time, tried to flip the bull over. In the perfect execution, as the trader had seen it done before, the bull was turned over so that he rolled on his back and got up on the other side and the rider, as soon as he turned the bull, continued on without breaking his stride, without glancing again at the bull, to where his lady was seated, his hat off his head and held across his chest. There he swung the hat in a wide circle and bowed before her.

It was, Magoffin thought, as with all things Spanish, not what was done but the style in which it was done. The disdain that started with the moment of danger was sustained in the rider's not looking back at the fallen bull, in the rider's assuming it was turned properly, for if the bull were not and got to his feet without the complete roll over, the rider would not know it until the spectators he faced jeered at him.

There were preliminary contests at first, boys working with smaller, less dangerous bulls. Magoffin was aware again of the preoccupation with death which was the birthright of the people. Death was not the inevitable. Death was not something to be awaited, but must be courted during life. For them, he knew, there was no sight to compare with that of a man entering on the area of death, remaining there however briefly, then departing. Each observer traveled with him and felt the cold breath on his own face.

He watched the expressions that passed over Soledad's face. In the bright, strong sunlight she flushed and she paled, her eyes dilated and then grew tired, her lips moistened and tightened and separated. Her hands opened and closed, and as a rider came abreast of a bull and leaned from his saddle and groped for the small handle of the tail, at that moment, which was that of the greatest danger, when the bull might turn or the rider might fall under the bull, she became rigid and her teeth closed on her upper lip.

One of the novices seized the tail. He was leaning far out and he raised his right leg to make the grip. He lost his seat and the bull swept from under him. The youth held the tail of the bull and was dragged half across the corral before he released it. The bull whirled and before any of the other riders could drive him away he scooped the fallen boy with his sharpened horns and tossed him into the air. When the boy fell, the bull gored him in the chest.

The dead boy was carried away. Magoffin looked at the people around him and thought: "This boy is not mourned, he has died for everyone here."

The final coursing included the most skilled horsemen, such persons as Ramón Baca, Damasio Salazar, Esquipulas Caballero, Tomás Martínez, and José Silva. For this event Don Juan Estevan had reserved his heaviest and most dangerous bull.

"This will be the most exciting," Soledad said, breathing rapidly.

"And even more so because Don Esquipulas is in it."

The corners of her mouth turned down. "I know Americans believe it is uncivilized with us—this and the bullfighting.

"I did not mean that."

"We have no fear of death, Don Santiago. He is an old friend."

"And yet there might be other uses to which an unconcern toward death might be more usefully put."

"But there must be no use to it!" she said, stamping her foot. "That is the whole thing, the uselessness of it. To face death for a purpose is noble, but it is another thing." She stiffened. "Here! Here comes el toro! Madre de Dios, it begins!"

The bull, saliva dripping from his mouth, pawed at the earth and then trotted down the length of the corral, and then the earth shook as a dozen horsemen thundered after him. Magoffin raised his glasses. Caballero's face was without expression. He had, Magoffin thought, the true indifference.

"Are you looking closely at Don Esquipulas?" Soledad asked.

"Yes."

"Is his face disinterested?"

"Yes."

"That is the meaninglessness, señor," she said proudly. "I can tell you, no other will have it as truly."

She was right, he thought. There was much of it on the face of Baca, but there also was excitement there. That was healthier, but it did not make the tenseness. Salazar rode with his face set in a sneer, his substitute for disdain. Silva was careful and he made no excitement. Martínez, the nephew to the Governor, made some of it.

The bull stopped abruptly and veered, running off at a sharp angle with clumsy grace. The riders reined and turned and spurred and charged after him. Again the bull doubled and caused the riders to overshoot. Magoffin then saw an expression of appraisal appear on Caballero's face. Magoffin felt excitement rise in him. He understood Caballero was judging the sharp, sudden turns made by the bull and was calculating how to turn that to his advantage.

"Madre de Dios!" Soledad said. "Watch, watch, watch that one now!"

As the riders descended upon the bull for the third time, Caballero cut away to the right, taking the short leg of the triangle the direction of the bull would complete if he had estimated correctly and the bull veered again.

"He has done it!" Soledad cried.

The bull stopped short and turned right, and Caballero now had a clear field ahead of him several hundred yards in front of the other riders.

Soledad clutched her throat. "Dios mío! That Caballero has outguessed el toro! Go, caro mío, go, go, go, mi alma, go! Virgen santísima, go!"

Magoffin glanced at her. Her face was enraptured. Her lips were bloodless. Her eyes were enormous. He looked past her to where Don Manuel was seated. The Governor too was staring at Soledad.

The spectators were now on their feet. Magoffin looked back on the field. Caballero was riding down hard on his quarry, coming at the bull from an angle, and Magoffin saw him slow his horse slightly, so as not to reach the point of intersection too soon, and then brace himself in the saddle and incline his body outward for the lunge for the tail. As he decreased the speed of his horse the other riders began to close the gap. The bull was on the near side, between Caballero and the spectators, and as Caballero brought himself into position and extended his arm, the bull put on a sudden burst of speed and there was daylight between them again.

Again Caballero closed in, and now the other riders were almost caught up with him. Magoffin's fingers tightened around the binoculars. He saw Caballero lean out again so that now he was altogether free of the saddle and was resting his weight entirely on his right boot in the covered stirrup. His left leg was half bent over the top of the saddle. Then Magoffin saw Caballero's fingers come to within six inches of the tail, then three inches, then an inch.

He heard Soledad talking, through the screams of the spectators: "María, Madre de Dios, for favor, just a little more, just a little more! Santa Virgen, just a little more! Hombre, hombre, push a little harder and you have it!"

Then he saw Caballero's hand close around the tail and Caballero started to shift his balance back to the saddle, and then Magoffin saw something else. He saw Salazar pull up on the other side, boxing Caballero with the bull, and then Salazar moved slightly ahead and kicked backward with his spurred right boot and Caballero's horse screamed and reared. The bull's tail tore loose from Caballero's hand.

Magoffin felt Soledad's nails dig into his wrist like dagger points and he heard her cry: "Hombre! Guard! Guard!" Then he saw Caballero's horse plunge to its knees and then rise and then rear again. Caballero was still more than half out of the saddle. He levered himself powerfully with his right leg, twisted his body, and caught the pommel with his left hand and threw himself upward and over the saddle. The horse reared again, but the danger was past.

Magoffin lowered his glasses and looked around. Apparently no one had seen what he had seen and now even he was not entirely certain of it. It was impossible to know what had happened, in the dust and confusion, and with Salazar on the far side. The other spectators had dismissed Caballero as soon as he had relinquished his grip on the tail and they continued to watch the others. José Silva took the lead and then was forced to one side

317

by Tomás Martínez, and it was Martínez who finally took the tail and tossed the bull, doing it well. He galloped to the Governor and saluted him and then he held out his hand toward a young woman. Don Manuel beamed and the girl blushed with pleasure.

Magoffin looked again at Soledad. She was breathing heavily. Her bosom rose and fell rapidly and her upper lip was wet with perspiration. "Did you see that, Don Santiago?" she was asking him. "Could any man but that Caballero have stayed on the horse then? Santa Madre, but that one can ride!"

She too appeared to have noticed nothing unusual, and Magoffin wondered whether he had seen what he thought he saw. "It was brilliant," he said.

"It was bad that pig of a horse had to pick that moment to smell the sky. My husband had the bull. Everybody saw it. But he has nothing for which to feel shame. Nombre de Dios, but it was beautiful!"

The riders now lined up before the Governor and saluted him. Caballero threw Soledad a kiss. Armijo gave the winner's purse to his nephew. "I know," he said, "that Don Tomás will not disagree when I say that the excitement was not alone in his success but in what was done by Don Esquipulas Caballero as well."

Caballero inclined his head. "Thousand thanks, excelencia."

Soledad cried out: "Caballero, you are muy hombre!"

"Who should better know?" a man yelled.

2

THE BAILE lasted long into the night. Caballero drank heavily. For the time being, he seemed to have forgotten what was bothering him and it was good between him and Soledad. "Santa María, mujercita," he said, "you are sweet to look at."

She crinkled her nose and curtsied. "My thanks, hombre."

"Do you know something? I think I hate you."

She tried to keep it light, but she could not. "Do you?"

"I think I hate you very much."

She thought: this was not a time to weep. "You have returned to me."

He looked around with a broad gesture. "Have I been away?"

"You have been away, mi caro."

"I do not want to be back. Back is here, at the rancho of Don Juan Estevan Pino. Let us go to our house."

"So soon?" She grinned. "The baile is just well started."

"You know something else?"

"Tell me something else, corazón."

"When I came into this room tonight, there was a jolt."

"Was there?"

"Boom. Like that." He slapped himself on the back of the head. "Right there!" He leaned closer to her. "You know something? I thought I was being assaulted. It gives me an idea. Let us go to our house. I desire to make an assault."

"On the back of my head?"

"Everywhere. I will make the general assault."

"Madre María, but I hate your person!"

"I hate you too. Let us go to our house. We talk too much of hatred and do nothing about it."

"And leave all this lovely champagne?"

"Now, at once. It is a command."

She looked at him demurely. "You forget, señor. You no longer are the lover. You are the old husband now. What you desire is at your disposition at any time. There is no call for haste."

"The time is now. Place it as my disposition."

"The other guests might be embarrassed."

"Let us go to our house." He lifted her chin. "Hey, woman, I feel a fire."

She felt the weakness in her thighs. "We will go."

"This minute."

"This minute, hombre, I can wait no longer than you can."

"Then why do we wait?"

"Let us find Don Juan Estevan and Señora Pino and express our gratitude."

"A waste of time."

She slipped her arm under his. "The delay will sweeten it, my soul."

They walked among the guests seeking their host and hostess, and then Soledad stiffened and tightened her grasp on her husband's arm as Don Manuel walked up to them.

319

Don Manuel bowed. "You have not as yet honored your Governor with a dance, Doña Soledad."

"We are just leaving, excelencia."

"So early? You will offend your hosts."

"Don Esquipulas strained his leg today," she said swiftly.

"It is too bad. But surely there is time for one small dance with your Governor. They are just now starting a slow waltz and is the dance I may enjoy." He said to Caballero: "You will not deny me, señor?"

Caballero bowed. "We are honored, excelencia."

He watched them depart, and when he turned to go to the refreshment board he found himself before Doña María Trinidad. He kissed her hand. She held out an empty glass. "Fetch me some wine, Don Esquipulas, and have a glass filled for yourself."

"With pleasure, señora la gobernadora."

When he brought the filled glasses she took his arm. "Let us walk a little in the placita, señor."

"You honor me, señora."

The night was warm and the air smelled sweetly of the newly flowering lilacs. She led him to a bench. There she made a cigarette and pulled the smoke deep into her lungs. "That was magnificent riding today, Don Esquipulas."

"Thank you, señora."

She sighed. "It is lovely here in the dark. I was not made for light."

"It always is a pleasure to look upon la gobernadora."

"Save your compliments." Then she said: "You are foolish."

"Pardon, Doña María Trinidad?"

"You might easily have been killed today."

"It is a risk one takes when one tries to tail the bull."

She pulled on the cigarette and breathed the smoke through her broad nostrils. "Your risk was perhaps greater than others'."

Caballero wrinkled his brow. "A horse may rear at any time."

"You are right. A horse is an unpredictable animal. A horse may rear at any time, and if he happens to choose that time when the man on his back is stretched out to turn a wild bull—" She shrugged. "Who knows? In nine times out of ten the rider is thrown and perhaps trampled or gored as that young boy was earlier." She blinked at him calmly. "So much youth, so much handsomeness, to be destroyed by the horns and the feet of a bull."

Her words seemed to filter through to him from a distance and he strained to listen to her. He shook his head to rid it of the wine fumes. There were words behind the words and he did not understand what they were, and yet he felt the back of his neck grow clammy and looked around as though there were snakes in the darkness.

He wet his lips, took out the makings for a cigarette, and tried to put one together. His fingers were clumsy and he spilled the tobacco. She took the husk and the tobacco pouch and rolled the cigarette deftly and put it between his lips. Then she brushed the crumbs gently from his lap, and her fingers lingered where his thighs strained against the tight cloth of his trousers.

"You are young, Don Esquipulas," she said. "You have the intelligence to become an important officer under his excellency. You have a name second to none in New Mexico. You should have the rank to accompany it."

He dragged on the cigarette and stared at where the fat, jeweled fingers were stroking him. "I have hoped for a good future, señora," he said.

"And yet you do nothing to ensure it."

"I do my best, señora."

"Do not be such a fool!" Her eyes glowed like those of a cat. "Don Manuel is powerful. He is more powerful than many kings. When he smiles on one, his fortune is made."

"I serve him loyally."

"That may be true. But it is not enough."

She sat back and brought the glass to her lips, and he thought: "The nest of snakes was on my lap and it has been taken away."

"How does your marriage go, Don Esquipulas?" she asked.

"My marriage? It is a happy one."

"It becomes monotonous, does it not?"

"Less than others, señora."

"But still the first excitement is gone. It is the tragedy. Marriage can never remain on the plane on which it starts."

He wiped his forehead. Her face seemed to distort as though he were seeing it in unstill water. "What is it that you intend for me to understand, señora?"

The mole on her lips seemed to enlarge monstrously. "You are married to a woman with beauty, Don Esquipulas. Men have been willing to permit their fortunes to be made with the help of their wives."

"I have read history, señora."

"Don Manuel is a man of history. That is a truth I myself had to accept many years ago when I knew less than I do now and when Don Manuel was less than he is now."

The drunkenness was gone in the night, and there were, he knew, snakes in the darkness. He asked harshly: "Is this not a matter Don Manuel might better discuss with my wife?"

"He has tried. She has refused."

"That was before we were married. He might have more success now."

"It was since." She peered closely at him, her eyes shrewd. "Did she not tell you? It was when you were away with the Texans."

And now the change that had come over him gradually on his way to El Paso del Norte, in which the validity of the great lie that lay between him and Soledad was denied in the denial of the honor of Manuel Armijo, reached full size.

"She did not tell you?" Doña María Trinidad asked again. "I said no marriage can retain itself. In her secretiveness she has herself taken the first step."

"That is not true!"

"Why else does she remain silent? Is it her habit to keep secrets from you?"

He thought how of all the things of her he remembered from the earliest days, that which had belonged to her most was the candor in her eyes.

"Was this not something a wife with clear conscience should tell to her husband?" she asked. "Or perhaps her conscience was not clear." She took his hand and rubbed it gently. "How could she have taken you to herself with this secret locked away?"

"Señora."

"Was she different from before? Had you any suspicion at all that she was being devious?"

"Señora, for favor—"

"A truth cannot be made to vanish by ignoring it," she purred. "If she kept this secret from you, what else may she be concealing? She has learned to curtain her thoughts from you. You must learn to do the same." She pressed the palm of his hand against her bosom. "There would be no mark left upon your wife, Don Esquipulas, and no man will adjudge you cuckold."

"And if not, señora?"

She dropped his hand and made another cigarette before replying. "You almost stepped into the black abyss today, my friend. How many more times can you hope to be as lucky?"

3

Don Esquipulas found Ramón Baca gazing wistfully at the dice table. "I want to talk to you, Ramón."

"What passes?"

He led him out of the hearing of the gamesters. "At the tailing this afternoon, Ramón, you rode behind me."

"And was I proud! Never have I witnessed a more magnificent recovery."

"Why did the horse rear?"

Baca shrugged. "Who knows? Why do horses rear? There are many reasons. They see something on the ground. They get excited. They know there are other horses around and they believe it is a good time to show off."

"They get spurred."

Ramón looked around swiftly. "Por amor de Dios, fool! Not so loud!"

"It is true then."

"I do not know."

"As you are my friend and my brother."

"It may have been accidental. You are alive and unhurt. Give your thanks to the Virgin and let it remain at that."

"Who was on the other side of me?"

"I do not know."

"I heard a horse near to me on the other side. I could not see who it was."

"Nor I. There was dust. We were all mixed together."

Caballero shook him by the shoulders. "Cuerpo de Cristo! Do you no longer call yourself my friend?"

"It was Salazar," Baca said slowly.

"Salazar!"

The homely face became grim. "And I do not think it was an accident."

"Come with me to the stable."

"There is no need. En el nombre de Dios, leave it a suspicion. It is better not to be sure."

"Do you come or do I go alone?"

Baca breathed heavily. "Let us go, but quietly."

In the stable Caballero looked from stall to stall until he found the horse he had ridden. He held a lantern to the horse's left side. Then he said: "Here, Ramón, look! There is a deep gash in the stifle. I have never dug spur into a horse so deeply and I have never cut him in the stifle."

Baca looked closely at the long cut in the upper part of the left leg. "Now you know and your knowledge can be your sentence of death." He took Caballero in his arms. "As you love your wife, teach yourself that you know nothing!"

Caballero pushed him away roughly. His eyes blazed. "Muerte!" He pulled out his knife and started out of the stable.

Baca seized his wrist and forced him against the wall. "Whose death? Your own! Your own!" Baca said fiercely. "You cannot fight Salazar. Armijo would order a bullet in your neck before you could wet your steel."

Caballero tried to wrench his wrist free. The small fingers held it with the grip of a vise.

"Armijo would say you tried to kill for no reason," Baca said. "You could prove nothing. What is a spur slash on a horse? How could you prove it was not done by yourself? In God's name, control yourself!"

Caballero suddenly quieted. Baca released his wrist. He took the knife from lifeless fingers and returned it to its sheath. "You have learned a new thing," Baca said. "Keep this knowledge tucked away with the other things we have learned lately. One day we will find a use for all of them. Until then you are a wise man if you do nothing and say nothing, to Soledad or to anyone else."

"Why not to Soledad?" Caballero said angrily. "Why do you specify not to Soledad?"

"Because she is an innocent woman and should not be burdened with this poisonous information. It must be kept from Lupe as well. We both are enemies to Salazar. Today it was you. Tomorrow may be my turn." Then he frowned. "What is the matter with you?"

Caballero slumped against the wall. "Nothing."

"You did not think it was you alone, did you? The honor of being hated by Salazar is too much for one man. I too made friends with the prisoners."

"The prisoners?"

"Kendall and the Texans. Salazar will never forgive either of us."

"The prisoners," Caballero repeated. He started to laugh.

"What the devil is the matter with you!" Baca looked around. "Do you want to wake the dead?"

Caballero laughed until the tears came to his eyes. "I will tell you a funny thing, monito. I had forgotten all about the prisoners."

4

THE CARRIAGE LAMPS seemed to give no more light than two fireflies. Soledad snuggled against him and softly hummed the tune of the waltz she had danced with Don Manuel. "How do you feel, hombre?"

"I feel very well," he said.

"You are not tired?"

"No."

"Do not get tired. Side of the side of my heart, I am so happy."

"Are you?"

She looked up at him. In the light from the lamps his face was set. "What is the matter, caro?"

325

"What did Don Manuel have to say to you while you danced?"

She giggled tipsily. "You are jealous."

"What did he say?"

"You are jealous, you are jealous," she chanted. She pulled his face to her and kissed him. "My husband is jealous." She held out her arms and began to hum the song again.

"What did he say? Or is it secret?"

She pouted. "Perhaps."

"Jesucristo!"

She stopped the humming and looked at him more closely. "I am sorry, querido, but I do love to tease you," she said in a small voice. "You become so angry and little white lines come out on either side of your nose."

"What did Don Manuel say to you? Or are you taking this time to invent a story?"

She sat upright. She pressed her fingers to the sides of her forehead. The little lamps jiggled back and forth. "We talked about you."

"What about me?"

"He told me how happy he was you escaped injury today."

"Dios!"

She closed her eyes and tried to remember. "He said to tell you to be careful with yourself and not allow anything like that to happen again." She filled her cheeks and imitated the voice of Don Manuel. " 'Be certain you do not neglect to tell him that, Doña Soledad. Promise me you will warn him to take better care of himself.' " She snuggled up to him again. "And he was right, my soul. You must be more careful." Her voice was sleepy. "By the way, hombre, what were you doing in the patio with the witch?"

"We were talking," he said. "About you."

But she was asleep by then and she did not hear him, and later it was no good and she knew that what had come back to them for a little while was again gone.

5

CABALLERO took his saber from Fernando and buckled it on. "You will watch, Fernando, as usual."

"You have no cause to worry about Doña Soledad," Fernando said quietly.

"I do not ask your opinion, Fernando. I give an order."

"Your order will be obeyed, Don Esquipulas."

"You do not like the part of spy?"

"I do not, Don Esquipulas."

"I do not like the part of husband who needs to spy on his wife."

"There is no cause, Don Esquipulas."

"He came here the last time, did he not? You told me so yourself."

"They did not leave the sala, Don Esquipulas."

Caballero picked up his cap. "The next time they may reach the bedroom," he said viciously, and turned to go.

"Don Esquipulas," Fernando said, "may I speak?"

"Have I ever forbidden you to speak?"

"You are wrong about this. He is the Governor. She may not bar her door to him."

Caballero nodded slowly. "It is true, Fernando. No door is barred to Don Manuel." His face tightened with pain. "But why does she not tell me? Why, en el nombre de Dios, does she not tell me? Why does she believe I will think it is my father the Governor comes to visit?"

"A woman does not always reason as does a man," Fernando said. "But you are wrong to suspect her." His voice altered. "Don Esquipulas, she is Soledad. She is the same child with whom we shared our childhood. You cannot think evil of her."

"Men and women are not children." Caballero's lips drew in. "Would Soledad believe that the companion of her childhood aided in the slaying of her father?"

"You were a man and a soldier, obeying orders."

"And she is a woman and also no longer a child. I hold a secret from her, Fernando. Why should she be better than I?"

Fernando lowered his head. "There is enough evil in the time, Don Esquipulas, but it has not penetrated to this house. She would die before she would dishonor you."

Caballero put his arm on Fernando's. "I can understand everything, Fernando," he said in a low voice. "Most of all can I understand why Don Manuel follows her with his tongue hanging like that of a thirsty dog. But why does she keep her counsel from me? If there is no intrigue, why does she not speak out?"

On the way from his room to the sala Caballero felt remorse, but when he saw her he hardened again.

"How long will you be gone this time?" she asked in the flat voice they now used with each other.

He shrugged. "Who knows? The orders are always the same: make contact with the Indians and bring back as many ears as possible."

"But it is so soon since your company was sent out the last time."

"Is it, señora?"

"Is your company not being sent on patrol more often than others?"

"That is what we are being paid for, señora."

"But is there not supposed to be a rotation?"

"I do not question posted orders, nor does Ramón."

"Ramón?"

"We go out together this time." He bowed. "*Hasta luego*, Doña Soledad."

She ran to him suddenly and buried her face against his chest. "What is happening to us, husband?"

He felt the remorse again and then he thought it was to this room Don Manuel came to make love to her. "I must go."

"It is because I cannot give you a child," she said. She held his body tightly. "If my belly could fill as it should, it would not be this way."

"Perhaps not," he said. "But we cannot undo the past." And, he thought, it makes it safer. He separated himself from her and kissed her hand. "Adiós, señora."

She lowered her head and clasped her hands. "Adiós, señor."

When he was gone she lit three candles before the crucifix on the wall and knelt before it, crossed herself, and kissed the tips of her fingers. "Santa Virgen de Guadalupe," she whispered, "sweetest Mother of Mexico, bring him safely back to me. Let nothing happen to him while there is still this untruth between us. We need time, dulce Virgen, we need so much time."

6

CABALLERO AND BACA finished their evening meal and stretched out on the riverbank. They listened to the protests of the crickets and the assurances of the frogs. Baca said: "It is pleasant here, is it not, chico?" He pulled on his cigarette. "It is a funny thing, but I feel safer here than I do in Santa Fe."

"I agree, monito," Caballero said.

"That is something, is it not? To feel more secure in the country of the Apaches than in the capital of New Mexico?"

"The world is upside down."

"Not the world, chico. Our world."

Caballero shrugged. "Our world is the world."

"It is not the world." Baca stared at the stars. "It is only that Armijo would have us think it is the world. New Mexico is a tiny place."

"It is all the place we have."

"You know something, chico? I cannot forget what Kendall and the others told us during those nights."

"I have thought often of it as well," Caballero said.

"We all are men before God. How is it possible for some to live as they do in their countries and for others to live as we do?"

"When I was a child I was taught Mexico fought a war so Mexicans could live as free people."

"It is almost amusing, is it not? To think that men died fighting against Spanish oppression only to make way for Manuel Armijo." Baca lifted himself on his elbow. "You know what I have been thinking? New Mexico never fought in the war against Spain. The Revolution was ended before the people of New Mexico even knew it had begun. The Spanish Governor in Santa Fe received word from the City of Mexico that there had been a revolt and that Mexico no longer was part of Spain but a republic, and he pulled down the Spanish flag and sewed together a new flag and he continued as Mexican Governor; and that was all anyone in New Mexico had to do with the Revolution. There is no memory here of that fight for independence. Perhaps that is why we put up with Armijo."

"He is here, monito, for whatever reason."

"For how long?"

Caballero flipped his cigarette into the river. "Forever."

Baca said: "I believe he can be overthrown."

Caballero sat up. "What are you saying?"

"You listened to the people when we were traveling with the Texans. Do you believe the people of New Mexico love Armijo?"

"People do not make revolutions. For that you need soldiers."

"Soldiers are people like other people," Baca said calmly. "They have wives and children and relatives, and when they go to their houses they talk. Why should peasants who wear uniforms be different from peasants who work in fields?"

"They eat better."

"Only on duty. It is why soldiers do not dislike being sent out to look for Indians even though they may be killed. And though the field rations are not generous, there are soldiers in my company who put aside food to take back home."

"Soldiers obey orders."

"That is true too, chico. It comes down to the officers."

"And Don Manuel has been careful in selecting and promoting his officers," Caballero said. He added dryly: "Particularly in promoting them. Do you believe that Capitán Salazar would assist in an insurrection against Don Manuel?"

"I believe Salazar would insurrect against his own mother if he thought he would profit. But there are officers who are truly wearied of Manuel Armijo."

"There must be," Caballero agreed. "But who would lead them?"

Baca said: "I would."

"Ramón!"

Baca got up and squatted on his heels. "The name of Baca is not unknown. It is a name men can rally around."

"How long have you been thinking of this?"

"All my life, it seems."

"Have you talked to others?"

"I have. That is how I know. Men have sworn they would join me in ridding New Mexico of Armijo."

"Cuerpo de Cristo, and how can you be certain one of them is not a spy for Don Manuel?"

Baca shrugged. "That is a necessary risk."

"Why have you not told me of this before?"

Baca looked at him candidly. "I was not sure of you before."

"Why do you tell me now?"

"I am sure of you now."

Caballero twisted his head. "Did you hear that?"

"I hear nothing but the snores of soldiers. No, chico—"

Caballero leaped to his feet. "Listen! Now!" He pulled out his pistol. "There! Madre de Dios!"

An Apache Indian walked toward them, his hands held out in the sign of peace. "Hold," the Indian said in Spanish. "Hold."

"Come closer," Caballero ordered. "Here."

"I am alone," the Indian said. "I come in peace." He walked closer, lightly as a cat, his hands still extended, palms outward. "I am Nolgee. I am a Mimbres Apache. I want to talk."

"Santa Madre," Baca breathed. "He came in like a ghost. Where were the guards!"

"Guards?" Nolgee sneered. "Mexican guards? When did a Mexican guard know when an Apache was in the forest?"

"What do you want?" Caballero asked, looking closely at the Apache. He saw a man below middle height with the barrel chest of an Apache warrior, his naked body painted for war.

Nolgee pointed across the Mora River. "Over there, a day's journey away, there are many Mimbres Apaches, four of them for each one of you. They wait for you. You walk into a trap. You will be killed."

"Why do you tell us this?" Caballero asked. "Do you not live to kill Mexicans?"

Nolgee's black eyes flickered balefully. "My people are filled with drink sold to them by your chief. Drunken men do not fight carefully and they have whisky enough to remain drunk for many days. They will kill all of you, but you will kill many of them too because they will be careless. There are not enough of us to lose this way. I come to tell you to go back."

"Drink that our chief sold to you?" Caballero asked.

"Two days back a mule train came to us. There were two drivers, a little man named Pedro and a fat one called Mario."

"I know those men," Baca said. "They work for Armijo."

"They brought many barrels of drink. They were exchanged for horses and mules we captured in Chihuahua. I argued that animals should not be exchanged for drink. I said we should trade them only for guns. But I am not chief. Now the men are wild and crazy and the drinking has only started. Go back, Mexicans! We will fight you another time."

Caballero asked Baca: "Do you believe him?"

The Indian looked at him coldly. "I am Nolgee. I do not speak with the forked tongue."

"I believe him," Baca said softly.

"I tell you one thing more and then I go," Nolgee said. "Your chief does not love you."

"What do you mean by that?" Caballero asked.

Nolgee smiled contemptuously. "The tame Apache who led the mule-drivers to us told us where to look for you."

"Apaches will betray us, even those we have befriended."

The smile hardened. "It was not the tame Apache who betrayed you. He told us your chief wanted us to know where you were. He told us your numbers and the direction of your march. Your orders will take you tomorrow to a small canyon to the east, there, over the river. The walls of the canyon are filled with Apaches. If you come there, you will all die."

"And we will take many of you with us!" Caballero spat.

The Indian nodded. "You will. Too many. Go back. We will find another time to fight."

Baca said quietly: "Many thanks, Nolgee, we will think on what you have said."

"Do not thank me, Mexican," Nolgee said savagely. "I do not come here because of love for you."

"Still, thanks," Baca said.

Nolgee looked at him curiously. "What kind of people are you that your own chief betrays you to the enemy?"

"That is a question I cannot answer," Baca replied. "Perhaps it is not the people but only the chief."

"Then you are foolish not to kill your chief." He turned and instantly was gone.

The camp was quiet. In the night men stirred in their sleep, and somewhere a man muttered.

"To condemn eighty men to death," Baca said. "Eighty men, Catholics, his own soldiers who trust him and would die for him. He has gone mad, chico. Power is poison. A mind must be made of iron to contain it. And why? Because he believes we know the secret of his victory over the Texans?"

"It is not that, monito," Caballero said. "I have something to tell you. I have wanted to tell it to you for a long time."

When Caballero was finished, Baca said nothing for several minutes. Then he asked: "You have never told Soledad?"

"No." Caballero's face, in the light of the small fire, was like a death mask."

"I can understand. She loved her father even more than most."

"I could not bring myself to tell her," Caballero said in a dull voice. "Not at the beginning, nor since."

"It explains many things. Tell me, chico, at the time did you truly believe in Don Manuel?"

"Yes."

"You believed and your father believed. You had no choice." He placed his hand on the shoulder of his friend. "You have made your expiation."

7

THEY DISMISSED THE TROOPS at the barracks and made their report to the officer of the day. They walked up the side street to the front of the palace and turned under the portal. They saw Salazar lounging against the palace in conversation with Tomás Martínez and other officers. Baca and Caballero saluted and passed on.

"Hola, friends!" Salazar called after them. "A little moment. Did you find Indians?"

"No," Baca said.

Salazar wagged a finger. "Don Manuel will not like that. There are many Indians. He believes soldiers should find them."

Caballero saw then that Salazar wore the insignia of a major. He looked at Martínez. The Governor's nephew was a captain. He glanced rapidly at the other officers. Almost all had been raised in rank. Two men who had been sergeants were now ensigns.

Salazar, watching him, laughed. "You missed some excitement, friends. While you were gone, there was a big ceremony in the plaza. Don Manuel made a speech to the people and told how much he loved his brave officers and how happy he was to have the power to reward them with promotions and medals. There was a big baile."

"I do not believe either of them would have been happy at the baile," Martínez said.

Salazar nodded gravely. "I think they would both have been embarrassed. Perhaps that is why Don Manuel made certain they would be away during that time. You would not believe how many persons wondered why Ensign Caballero and Ensign Baca were not promoted, and if you were there you would have had to explain."

At the corner of the Calle de la Muralla, Caballero asked Baca cruelly: "How many of those officers were included among the men you talked to?" He walked on to his house without waiting for a reply.

He went directly to his bedroom. As Fernando helped him out of his uniform, he asked: "Where is Doña Soledad?"

"She is visiting with Señora Baca," Fernando replied.

"Lay out my dress uniform, Fernando." Caballero bathed and shaved. When he was dressed he snapped on his short dress sword.

"Where do you go?" Fernando asked.

"Is my father awake?"

"I believe so, Don Esquipulas."

Caballero paused with his hand on the door. "Do you not have something to report to me, Fernando?"

"Señor!"

"I asked a question."

334

"He was here, Don Esquipulas. They remained as usual in the sala. Where do you go now?"

"Are you certain, Fernando, that my wife is visiting with Señora Baca?" Caballero asked.

He walked down the corridor to his father's room. The elder Caballero had been confined to bed for several months. Don Esquipulas knocked on the door and heard his father call out weakly for him to enter. He opened the door and closed it gently behind him. The room was almost in darkness. He knelt at the side of the bed.

"Who is it?" Captain Caballero asked.

"It is I, father." He kissed his father's hand.

"Did you have a fight?"

"No, Don José, there was no fight."

His father chuckled. "We always had a fight."

"We found no Indians."

"Not like the old days, son of my soul."

"No, señor."

Capitain Caballero struggled for a moment. "Esquipulas, help me to sit up. Then open the blind." In the light the old man's small face revealed its devastation. It was shrunk and wrinkled like an old apple. He peered at his son from his rheumy eyes. "What have you done that is improper?"

"I do not know," Esquipulas lied.

"What has gone wrong? In what way have you displeased Don Manuel?"

"I do not know."

"Have you been brave?"

"Yes, señor." He looked at his father's sword on the wall.

"Have you obeyed all orders?"

Esquipulas closed his eyes. "Yes."

The old man shook his head. "I do not understand it." The watery eyes brightened. "Perhaps you should speak to Don Manuel."

"I go to him now. Give me your blessing, Don José."

Captain Caballero touched his head. "*Dios te bendiga, hijo mío.*"

Esquipulas kissed his father's hand again.

8

A GUARD barred the door to the Governor's office. "It is necessary to search you, Don Esquipulas."

"It is a new order," Guadalupe Miranda said quickly. "No one may enter Don Manuel's office bearing weapons."

"An excellent order," Caballero said. He unbuckled his sword and handed it to the guard. "I have no other weapons."

"My orders are to search," the guard said. He ran his hands over Caballero. "Pass, señor."

Don Guadalupe announced him, and Caballero entered the Governor's office, walked briskly to the desk, and saluted.

"So you and Baca have returned," Don Manuel said. "And with empty hands."

Caballero looked at the truculent face of the Governor and thought of the change that would come over it when he told him of Nolgee. As he started to speak he realized suddenly that he could say nothing at all about the Indian or of what he had learned about Don Manuel's traffic with the Apaches and his betrayal of the soldiers, because he would also expose Ramón Baca's knowledge of it. His mouth closed on the words.

"What do you want, señor?" Don Manuel asked irritably.

It was without dignity, Caballero thought, but there was nothing else. "I desire to make formal protest to your excellency in connection with the new list of promotions," he said, the words tasting like ashes in his mouth, forcing himself to say them.

"Protest? Do you protest to me?"

"I desire to remind your excellency I am the ranking ensign in point of service in all the presidial companies and have been for some time. I desire to remind your excellency I have done my duty to the best of my ability at all times. In passing over me again and again your excellency has subjected my name to ridicule. If I have failed in the execution of my duties I am prepared to resign my commission. If I have not failed I believe I am entitled either to promotion or to explanation."

"Your service?"

"I have performed all duties asked of me by your excellency,"

Caballero said with icy respect. "All military duties. And I desire to remind your excellency that from the beginning I have undertaken duties that were not required of me."

"A hundred men would have been eager to serve me! A thousand men! At any time!"

"Undoubtedly, excelencia. But there was only one who did."

"It might have been any other."

"No other with the name Caballero."

"And that name was an important thing?" Don Manuel asked with a terrible smile.

"For no inconsiderable time, Don Manuel, the name of my father ringing in the ears of men was the sole bridge between your excellency's success or failure. There were many who pleaded with that gentleman to place himself at the head of his country."

"José Caballero to take command of New Mexico? That spineless brandy-soaked weakling!" Don Manuel lifted his head and roared.

Caballero went for the handle of the sword that was not at his side. "You forget, excelencia, that Capitán José Caballero had spine enough to lead soldiers into Santa Fe when your excellency did not dare to enter the city for fear that Gonzales might be waiting for him."

Don Manuel arrested his laughter and his face became still. The room was silent, so that when he opened the drawer of his desk to take out his heavy pistol the sound of the scraping of the drawer was a large sound. Caballero looked at the weapon and a faint, frosty smile appeared on his lips, and now all that had been said between them had form.

The Governor held the weapon with composure. He stood up slowly and limped around the desk until he was less than a yard from Caballero. "You know, señor, I had thought you would come to see me."

"But not this way, excelencia."

"No, not this way, I will admit it."

"You believed it would be because I at last saw the light as other men of my class have seen the light."

"And you come with blackmail."

"No blackmail, excelencia. With the report of a junior officer to his commanding general."

337

"Is there more to this report?" Don Manuel asked evenly.

"Only to repeat the advice given by Doña María Trinidad that all the service I have performed in your excellency's behalf was as nothing unless I permitted my wife to serve too, as your excellency's personal whore."

"Is that all, señor?"

"With the advice, of course, was the suggestion that I perform the same service for señora la gobernadora."

Don Manuel sighed. He lifted the pistol slowly and pointed it at Caballero's heart.

Caballero smiled and touched the muzzle delicately. "I doubt me that you can do it, excelencia. That requires strength. Your excellency is capable only of ordering other men to kill." It was not much, he thought, but if he was to die it was something.

The muzzle wavered. Don Manuel called for rage. His finger on the trigger was without feeling. He felt empty inside. "Give me it," he commanded himself, but there was no response. Now when he needed rage there was none to be summoned and he was again denied.

"How did your excellency plan it?" Caballero asked, still smiling, knowing he had won. "Were we all to use the same bed at the same time?"

Don Manuel whipped the pistol across his face.

Caballero staggered, but he did not fall. "Do you find this easier, excelencia?"

Don Manuel smashed the barrel on his face again, and this time Caballero's eyes closed and the mocking smile was a ghastly thing as he collapsed on the floor. Don Manuel gazed down at him somberly, knowing their lives still were bound. He dropped the pistol lifelessly and lifted the unconscious figure and carried it to the door. He called out: "Guard!"

The guard rushed in and then stopped abruptly. Don Manuel held out Caballero as though he were an injured child. "Put this man in a cell," he said tonelessly. Then he said to his secretary: "Don Guadalupe, make out the charge. High treason against the state in time of war. The penalty is death."

Miranda rose painfully to his feet. "How shall the charge be worded, excelencia? This one is a Caballero."

"While accompanying the Texan prisoners to El Paso del

Norte the traitor Caballero visited with the prisoners and held conspiratorial conversations with them in direct violation of the regulation that no intercourse be held privately with prisoners of war," Don Manuel said.

1

"IT IS LESS than it might have been," Soledad said. "He is alive."

Lupe Baca sobbed without restraint. "Why did he have to go to see Don Manuel? Why was it important what rank he held?"

"He found it necessary to go," Soledad said.

"Why? Why?"

"Silence, woman," Baca growled. "It is something you cannot understand."

"He *is* alive," Soledad said. "You do not just tell me that?"

"He is alive," Baca said. "He no longer is handsome, but he is alive. The prison guard told me Don Manuel presented him with a new nose, one that is spread across his face almost from one ear to the other, but he is alive."

"Then we must make plans," Soledad said calmly.

"When is the execution scheduled?" Fernando asked Baca.

"Don Manuel has not yet set the day."

"We will have time," Soledad said with a strange smile. "Don Manuel will not hasten."

"How do you know that?" Lupe cried. "It may be tomorrow, or even today. At this moment Don Esquipulas may be facing the squad!" She burst into fresh sobs.

"It will not be so soon," Soledad said. "When Caballero dies, Don Manuel loses his lever. He will wait like a spider, hoping that each day will bring me to the palace to plead for the life of my husband."

"You will never go," Baca said.

"Have no fear, Ramón."

"There are men in Santa Fe who could be persuaded to strike a blow against Armijo," Fernando said slowly. "They would need guns and a leader."

340

Baca raised his hand. "All can be provided. But before anything we must bring the news to Don José."

"He is very sick," Fernando said.

"Don Ramón is right," Soledad said. "He must be told, and now. He cannot die without knowing."

The men went to Captain Caballero's room and Baca told him bluntly what had happened. The information had a galvanic effect on the old man. His squandered face burned with two bright spots of color and his eyes gleamed feverishly. He threw back the cover and for the first time in half a year he rose from the bed unaided. "Fernando," he said, "bring my uniform."

When Fernando hesitated, Baca said in a soft voice: "Obey."

The uniform hung loosely on the wasted body. Captain Caballero's head was almost small enough to fit into the high embroidered collar. On his left breast was the medal Don Manuel had presented to him. "My sword," he said.

Fernando took the sword from its place on the wall and handed it to him with reverence. Captain Caballero buckled it on and straightened himself. He walked from the room into the sala.

Soledad knelt and kissed his hand. "It will serve no purpose, Don José."

Captain Caballero placed his hand on the hilt of his sword. "My son bears the name Caballero. Men of that name were loyal servants to their rulers before there was one called Armijo. If my son is traitor, then so is his father, because what my son knows he knows from me."

"You are right," she said humbly. "And when you speak to this Armijo tell him your son's wife is Abreu."

"I will not forget," Caballero said. As suddenly as it had come to him, his strength deserted and his knees buckled. Fernando sprang to his side and caught him. "Take me to Don Manuel," Captain Caballero said.

"You are unable to stand, Don José."

"At the necessary time I will stand. Put me in a chair and have me carried to the palace."

As she watched him being carried from the house, Soledad remembered a Spanish book she had once read about a man in medieval Spain who tilted at windmills.

. . .

341

In the street in front of the Casa Caballero were people who had heard of the arrest. When Captain Caballero appeared, men removed their hats. Caballero kept his eyes fixed ahead of him, and as the chair moved through the street the people followed as far as the plaza, and then, suddenly fearful, they hurried away.

The chair was set down in the office of Guadalupe Miranda. "Lift me to my feet, Fernando," Captain Caballero said.

Fernando set him on the floor. His bones were as light as dried sticks.

"Release me, Fernando," Captain Caballero said. "Don Guadalupe, have the kindness to inform his excellency that Capitán José Caballero asks for the honor of an audience."

Miranda entered the Governor's office silently. He came out a few moments later. "His excellency apologizes, Don José, but he is too busy to see you."

"Return to him and ask again," Captain Caballero said.

"He will not see you."

Captain Caballero held back his head with supreme pride. "Return to his excellency and say that it is Capitán José Caballero of Bernalillo who desires an audience."

Miranda shook his head sadly. "It is useless, Don José." He wrung his hands. "Return home, old friend, and rest yourself. Perhaps in the end something can be arranged."

Captain Caballero unfastened the medal from his uniform and threw it on the floor in front of the Governor's door. He turned in the military manner and walked to the chair, and then his back arched and he walked past the chair. It was not until he was outside the office that he started to sag, and Fernando, watching him like a hawk, rushed forward and caught him in his arms. He carried him from the palace to his house and laid him on the bed.

Captain Caballero opened his eyes. "Thank you, Fernando," he said. "When you again see Don Esquipulas, tell my son the truth came to me too late."

He turned to the wall and died.

2

ESQUIPULAS CABALLERO heard the key turn in the lock and the creaking of the door and then he heard Ramón Baca's voice call out: "Hola, chico, where are you?"

"Ramón!"

Baca entered the cell, holding a lamp. Behind him was a soldier. "Thousand thanks, Clemente," he said. "I will not forget this."

The soldier looked nervously down the corridor. "Only that you do not remain too long, Don Ramón."

"I will be brief, Clemente. Go to the end of the block and stand watch." The door shut behind him. "Now, chico, let me look at you."

"What are you doing here?" Caballero demanded.

"I am no prisoner. Let me see you. Madre de Dios!"

"Don Manuel—"

"I defecate on Don Manuel! Dios mío! What has he done to you?"

"I do not look so good?"

"You have looked better." Baca held the lantern closer. Caballero blinked in the unaccustomed light. His broken nose was still swollen; his lips were puffed and cracked. "The girls will no longer swoon, chico," Baca said. "How do you feel?"

"It is difficult to breathe, that is all."

"Be happy that you breathe at all."

"For a long time there was a sweet ringing in my head, but now the song has gone away. How long have I been here?"

"Almost five weeks."

"Madre mía! Why does he not execute me?"

Baca set down the lantern. "He still is in hopes Doña Soledad will throw herself at his feet."

Caballero clutched his arm. "She must not, Ramón!"

"She will not."

"Do you understand, she must not!" Caballero said hoarsely. "If she frees me in that manner, I will find her heart with a knife."

"There is no need to worry. She is no peasant woman."

343

"Of course not, of course not," Caballero muttered. "Is she well?"

"The happiest woman in Santa Fe."

"What are you doing here?" Caballero asked suddenly. "You may have been seen."

"I have come with news."

"You must get out of here." Caballero shook violently. "One of us is enough, Ramón."

Baca gripped him tightly. "Easy, chico, easy. Santa Madre, what have they done to you! There is little danger. The name Caballero still means a little something in the presidial troop. No one will betray me."

"Have you something to smoke? I have died a thousand times for a cigarette?"

Baca made a cigarette and handed it to him. He held up the lantern. Caballero pulled on the cigarette. "Ah, Dios, but I have needed this."

"Chico, you are an ugly man now. Maybe I will have a chance at last with the muchachas."

"What is your news? Tell it, and quickly, and leave."

"Something only a friend should bring to you. Your father is dead."

Caballero turned away his head.

Baca told him how Captain Caballero had tried to see Don Manuel and how he had failed. "Fernando carried your father home and he died, quietly, peacefully. And he died knowing the bucket of defecation was too frightened to see him. He knew that Armijo could not look into his eyes, knowing how many debts he owes to the name Caballero and how you are the last man in New Mexico to be labeled traitor to Armijo. He died well, chico. He was going rapidly and he might not have died so well or so usefully."

The end of the cigarette brightened as Caballero pulled on it.

"Your face, your face, I cannot tell what expression there is on it, or if there is any at all," Baca groaned. "It is as though a mule kicked it. Do you hear what I am saying?"

"I hear, monito, and do not worry about the expression upon my face," Caballero said.

"Then listen more. Your father did many good things for

344

this country. He was wrong about Armijo. But perhaps in the end he did the best of all. He would have died without purpose, but in her mercy the sweet Virgin gave to him one other chance. On his way to see Armijo, people followed him in the street, and at the burial were many hundreds even though they knew their names would be in Armijo's hands within the hour. Americans were there even though they knew that because of it they might be stoned. There was no priest because none here would risk Armijo's fury, but Santiago Magoffin, who is a good Catholic, said the words of a prayer. It was all something to see, chico, and the old man did it."

Clemente appeared at the door. "It becomes dangerous, Don Ramón."

"A little moment, amigo. Esquipulas, remember this: Armijo is frightened. The tub of tallow is filled with unholy fears. He is learning how much he is unloved. I have heard he has quarreled with Don Juan Bautista Vigil and that the old postmaster avoids him. He has threatened Miranda, who taught him to write his name, and he has publicly insulted his partner, Alberto Speyer, and almost struck him. This is all from fear, chico, and a small, dead man brought it to him. Courage, amigo, and keep hope in your heart!"

"When I left my house I asked my father to give me his blessing," Caballero said. "I thought it was I who would die."

"You might well have been killed," Baca said. "This is no time for such luxury." Clemente again came to the door. "When it gets bad here, remember that Armijo is afraid," Baca whispered as he left, "and that one day his fears will destroy him."

Caballero lay back on his pallet and tried to remember how his father had looked the day he bade him farewell, but he could not. The only picture that came to him was of how Captain Caballero must have appeared when he led the presidial troops into Santa Fe, and that was something he had not seen. There were no pictures after that. He lay motionlessly on the pallet and his eyes were dry. He had no way of telling time in the cell and did not know how long it was before he wept.

345

3

FERNANDO RAEL entered Santa Fe from the Taos Road at an early hour of the morning and went directly to the house of Ramón Baca. Baca was awake, awaiting him. "The men are at Pojoaque," Fernando said.

"How many in all?" Baca asked.

"Twenty-eight. It is no great number."

"They are all armed?"

"Twelve of them with the muskets you provided. The others managed for themselves in one way or another. We have no army."

Baca shook his head impatiently. "It was impossible to take any more guns from the armory. And twenty-eight determined men can do many things. Besides, I do not believe I shall have to call on them at all."

"You are still confident about this palace revolution?"

"The men are ready. They were ready before, but the arrest of Don Esquipulas was the final thing they needed."

Fernando asked slowly: "When you say men, Don Ramón, you mean officers, do you not?"

"Who else?"

"Have you spoken to any of the soldiers?"

"Unnecessary. Soldiers obey their officers."

"How can you feel so certain of these officers?"

Baca laughed. "Tell me, Fernando, have you heard so much as a word anywhere about this?"

"I have not."

"Then there is your answer," Baca said proudly. "For more than four months I have been talking to officers I decided I could trust, and not a word of it has reached Don Manuel or anyone else. The men have kept my confidence."

"How do you know that Don Manuel has not been informed and that he does not wait for you to make your move?"

"Don Manuel is a coward, Fernando. The officers who have sworn to follow my lead command more than two thirds of the presidial troops. If Armijo had any inkling of what was going on he would never permit these officers to retain their commands."

Fernando breathed out hard. "You may be right, Don Ramón, and yet I do not like it. It would be better, I believe, to secure more guns from the armory, one or two at a time, and build up a force of size."

"While Caballero rots in a cell?"

"He is not dead. There still has been no day set for the execution."

Baca's lips tightened. "If he stays there much longer, Fernando, an execution may not be necessary. I have visited him twice now. That one was not made for solitary confinement. He goes a little crazier each day. I have given him my word of honor that Doña Soledad will not buy his freedom the way Armijo offers to sell it, but a man has a bad time of it alone. He lies in that hole and imagines terrible things." He shook his head slowly. "We do not have as much time as you think we have."

"Have you told him of your plan?"

"No."

"Would that not make it possible for him to wait with more ease?"

"It might. But there is always the chance that Armijo may decide to put him to the question. In that event the knowledge would be a dangerous thing for him to possess. It was difficult not to tell him, Fernando, but I felt he was safer not knowing. I have not even told Doña Soledad or my own wife."

"And tomorrow is the day?"

"The officers have been alerted. They are set." He looked up with the eagerness of a young boy about to play a prank. "You would not believe it, Fernando, but even I did not realize how much Armijo is hated."

"And is hatred enough, Don Ramón?" Fernando asked quietly.

"It is enough for the start. I have added the rest—the plans, the leadership, the organization."

"And what exactly do you do tomorrow?"

"I have sent word to the officers to join me on the plaza at eleven o'clock. I will pronounce against Armijo and then we will march upon the palace and order him to surrender his office."

"And if he refuses?"

"He will not refuse. He is a coward."

347

"Supposing he refuses."

"His power rests solely on the support of the army. That support now belongs to me. He may shout and he may rave, but he will be unable to give commands."

Fernando raised his eyebrows. "And if you succeed? What will you do with Don Manuel?"

"We will not harm him. We are gentlemen, not savages. This will be an orderly protest by orderly men. We will place him under arrest and send him to the City of Mexico with an account of his treachery, tyranny, and thievery. And there is plenty! The indictment will stretch from Santa Fe to El Paso del Norte." He laughed and slapped Fernando on the back. "Are you answered now, doubter?"

"Your plan rests on the good faith of officers who have received many favors from Don Manuel and who have feared him for many years and have no learning in revolt, Don Ramón," Fernando said stubbornly.

"Armijo has remained in power only because no one has had the courage to challenge him. That challenge now will be made, and made by one who is called Baca!"

"And what are your orders for me, Don Ramón?"

"To return to Pojoaque and there await my word."

"I will leave immediately." He picked up his hat. His strong, hard face remained unconvinced. "I wish you all luck, Don Ramón."

"I will have it," Baca said heartily. "By this time tomorrow Manuel Armijo will be prisoner in the same cell now occupied by Esquipulas Caballero, and for the first time in many years the people of New Mexico will breathe air that is free."

Fernando touched his forehead and walked to the door.

"Revolutions start from the bottom, Don Ramón," he said quietly, "not from the top."

"Do they?" Baca exclaimed. "Then we will make a revolutionary revolution!"

4

RAMÓN BACA walked his horse onto the plaza. It was exactly eleven o'clock. He looked around. In different parts of the square he saw the officers were waiting and he saw that with them, in little groups, were noncommissioned officers and some soldiers. He drew his sword. The blade flashed in the sunlight. "To me, hombres!" he said in a strong voice.

Slowly, in pairs, in groups, the officers and the men collected under the portal on the side of the plaza opposite the palace. Curious citizens paused and watched. Baca waited, his blood tingling in his veins, until all the military men were assembled and then he pointed the tip of his sword at the palace and shouted: "In the name of the people of New Mexico I pronounce against Manuel Armijo! In there is the tyrant!"

He moved slowly across the broad width of the plaza toward the main entrance to the palace, his sword still extended. He glanced confidently over his shoulder. The men had not moved. He drew back on the rein and waited. The men remained motionless. He turned and rode back to them.

"Compañeros! The time is now!" he shouted. He waved his sword. "We are gathered together at last in the name of liberty! Follow me!"

No one moved. He scanned their faces. He saw the emotions drift across them in inexorable procession: resolution, consideration, hesitancy, and then, finally, fear.

The plaza was silent. Slowly Baca sheathed his sword. He looked again from face to face. "Hombres, you have made your decision," he said in a low voice that carried to all parts of the square. "Our country writhes under the heel of a despot. Today we would have destroyed his power forever. We would have brought freedom to this country we love. It would have been a better land for you and your women and your children. But you have decided to remain as you are, prisoners to the dictator, cowards, defeated men. I can no longer remain among you. Adiós, amigos, and may God guard you!"

From the silence he heard Lupe's voice raised in a terrified, animal cry. He waved his hand in the direction of the cry and he spurred his horse and galloped across the plaza onto the Taos Road to the north.

5

Don Manuel, in his office, going over his accounts with his partner, Albert Speyer, heard nothing of what went on in the plaza. The Governor was in a comfortable frame of mind. The Santa Fe Trail business had reached a total of one hundred and sixty thousand dollars, and of the seventy-odd wagons that brought in the merchandise, a sizable number was owned by the prospering firm of Armijo & Speyer. The two men were poring over figures when Guadalupe Miranda burst into the room. Don Manuel looked up with an irritated frown. "I left orders not to be disturbed until we concluded our business."

Miranda told him rapidly what had happened in the plaza, and Speyer was on his feet before he finished. "We sit here adding and subtracting while fifty feet away somebody is making a revolution? What kind of a country is this!"

Don Manuel said nothing as Miranda burbled the news. He walked to a window. The plaza was no different from any other time. Vendors hawked their wares. Children played. Dogs slept. Beggars sprawled in the warm sun.

"What are you going to do?" Speyer demanded.

"I have already done," Don Manuel said.

"What the devil do you mean?"

Don Manuel turned to the men. "In the end they were afraid. There was no need even for confrontment. The treason was organized, but at the moment of decision the thought of Armijo stopped them." He laughed gratingly. "Where is the firebrand? Where is the maker of insurrections? Where is Baca?"

"He fled to the north, excelencia," Miranda said.

"Let him go," Don Manuel said with contempt. "He has done me a service."

"A service?" Speyer cried.

"A great service. He exposed to the officers their own timidity.

They will harbor no more thoughts of revolution. Let him go and give Indians somewhere a bloodletting. The vultures await him."

He dismissed Miranda and sat down again at his desk. "Back to work, Don Alberto," he said calmly. He lit a cigar and bent over the books, and then he began to tremble. He said: "Leave me for a little while, Don Alberto. Return this afternoon, for favor."

Alone, he puffed rapidly on his cigar. He rubbed his sweating hands and felt the painful trobbing in his leg. His stomach knotted. His eyes fell upon the wall where there still was a faint scar from the gash made by the lance of José Gonzales. The officers had refused to follow Baca; but supposing they had not refused. It had been that close. They were afraid to go through with their insurrection. But they had schemed. This thing was not the product of a day or a week. The planning must have gone on for some time for Baca to believe he would succeed. How long? Por Dios, how long! And no one had been loyal enough to inform him. Not one of his officers had come to him to warn him that a plot was being made against him. Against his life. They would have shot him, he did not doubt that. What else could they have done? Pérez and then Gonzales and now, Madre de Dios, now Manuel Armijo!

The walls quivered and the structure of his government seemed to split open before him. He had nothing if he did not have the army. The ricos hated him, and the peasants who he had believed belonged to him were erratic children, ready to acclaim him one moment and turn away from him the next. When he had heard how the people shouted against him as the Texans passed through their towns and villages, he had at first been stunned and then he had consoled himself with the explanation that children always were fickle and that many who had hailed him as deliverer from the madness of Gonzales now undoubtedly resented him as the executive who demanded their livestock and their grain. He had told himself that he no longer needed the people, other than as sources for taxes, that he had the army, that the architecture was based on the army, on his faithful officers, whose careers he had enriched. And now he saw the façade in its weakness, its instability, an adobe wall that could be washed down by sudden rain.

The room rotated and he felt naked and exposed and abandoned. He shouted hoarsely: "Miranda! Miranda!" And when the secretary put his face into the doorway he ordered him to get Salazar. He chewed on his parched lips as he waited. He could be certain of Salazar. Of all the men in New Mexico, Salazar was the last one with whom Ramón Baca would conspire.

He shook as though with the ague as Salazar strode into the office. "You know of what occurred in the plaza, Don Damasio?"

"It was monstrous, excelencia." Salazar smote his sword.

"Take men and the fastest horses. Go after Baca. Bring him back to me, but alive."

Salazar saluted. "I obey, excelencia."

"Alive! Do you hear? Alive!"

Don Manuel canceled all appointments for the day. He waited alone in his office. Shortly after dark he heard the clatter of horses in the plaza.

A few moments later Salazar rushed into the room, his face triumphant. "Your commands have been obeyed to the letter, excelencia!"

Don Manuel gripped his desk. "He is unhurt?"

"As you commanded, excelencia."

Don Manuel exhaled slowly. "He is your prisoner, Don Damasio," he said. *"Put him to the question. I desire to know the names of all who were involved with him."

Salazar's lips crept back from his teeth. He stretched his fingers. "I will do so with much pleasure, excelencia."

"Be skillful," Don Manuel warned, his finger outthrust; "I do not want him to die before he speaks."

"I shall be most skillful, excelencia," Salazar replied.

"Send Miranda in," Don Manuel said. When his secretary stood before him he said: "I have thought on this matter, Don Guadalupe. The danger is greater than I at first realized. An example must be made of the traitor Baca and of his good friend Caballero. Major Salazar has a few questions to ask of Baca and that may take a few days. I order that the date of the execution of both men be set at two weeks from today at the garita. Publish the order and circulate it throughout the country so that all may know the fate that awaits those who plot against the government."

Miranda shuffled his feet. "Excelencia, the two officers have friends. Two weeks is a long time to give these friends a chance to organize another attempt at revolt."

"What do you suggest, secretario?" Don Manuel asked sarcastically. "Shall I free them and escort them to the border?"

"I do not dare to suggest that to your excellency," Miranda said in a low voice. "I say only that if your excellency is resolved to execute them, do so, but quietly. Announce the execution only when it is over."

Don Manuel pinched his lower lip. "Perhaps you are right, Don Guadalupe. Do not publish the order. But it remains the order. The date remains the same." He looked at the calendar on his desk. "On the 17th of December the two traitors will be put to death secretly by firing squad at dawn at the garita."

"I obey, excelencia." He turned to go.

Then Don Manuel said: "A little moment, Don Guadalupe." His eyes narrowed. "Not entirely secretly. I desire that the order be communicated to the prisoner Caballero, and to the wife of the prisoner." He rubbed his fingers together gently. "Also give word to the Señora Caballero that I permit her to pay a last visit to her husband."

Miranda looked at the floor. "On the night before the execution, excelencia? That is the customary time."

"At any time from now on," Don Manuel said.

6

THE PRISON GUARD, Clemente, held his lantern ahead of him as he shuffled down the narrow, dark cell block. He hung the lantern on a hook outside the cell door. "You will speak through the grill, Señora Caballero," he said. "The order was explicit: no more than five minutes, and the door must remain locked." He left her.

Soledad pressed her face against the barred opening. "Esquipulas," she whispered. There was no answer. She felt the cold slip under her cloak and grip her legs. "Esquipulas, amante, can you not hear me?" She heard a stirring in the cell. "Hombre, hombre."

"Who is it?"

"It is I, Soledad. Come to the door, my soul, there is very little time."

There was sudden movement in the cell. "Soledad, you are not a prisoner!"

She took the lantern from the hook and held it in front of the grill. On the other side was a bearded alien face with a flattened nose. The eyes were closed almost to slits against the weak light. The skin was yellow. On each cheek was a grimy cleft, like an eroded gully in the desert.

"The light blinds me," he said. "I cannot see you. Stand back and hold the lantern against your face." Then he said: "It is you, it truly is you." His voice became frightened again. "You are not a prisoner?"

"No, my heart."

"You do not lie?" His fingers, black with dirt, gripped the bars. "Swear to me that you are not prisoner too."

"I swear it."

"Then what do you do here?"

"Don Manuel gave me permission to visit you."

"Why? Why?"

"I do not know," she lied.

"It is a trick." He gripped the bars more tightly. He lost his voice and it came out in a whisper: "It is a trick."

She slipped her fingers between the bars and felt his lips. Then she felt something at her feet and looked down. In the yellow light from the lantern she saw the two small eyes of a rat. She kicked out and the rat scurried away. The cold swept up under her clothing. Her fingers caressed the leathery lips.

"Why should he let you come here?" Caballero asked again. He wondered if she knew the date of his execution had been set. When he had been told, he had prayed she would not learn of it until it was over.

"We do not have much time, querido," she whispered. "Let us not waste what we have in talking about him." She did not know whether he knew of Don Manuel's decree and she could not tell him.

354

"There must be a reason," he persisted. "He does nothing generously."

"He gave no reason."

"You have not gone to see him?"

"No, husband."

"Has he come to see you?"

"Not since you were imprisoned. He came before." She closed her eyes, and two tears trickled down her cheeks. "He came often before."

"Then that is the reason!" he croaked. "He believes that after you have seen me here, you will go to him."

"That is what I too believed."

"You will not go!"

"No, caro."

"You will not free me that way!"

"No."

"I would kill you! I would kill you with my own hands!" His voice rose hysterically and then left him. She could see his lips moving behind the bars, but there was no sound. He rubbed his throat savagely and wet his lips. ". . . the first thing," he said. ". . . kill you myself."

"I will not go to him."

"Swear it by that which you hold most holy," he whispered.

"On the memory of my father." She felt the nibbling again and kicked her foot. She pressed against the bars. "The minutes fly, querido. Let us use what are left to speak only of ourselves. Side of the side of my heart, you I love."

"You I love, wife."

"The nights are without sleep for me. Our bed is too large, hombre, and I am lost in it alone."

"Put your fingers through the bars again, linda. Let me taste the tips of them again."

"Here, here, here they are. How close the bars are!"

"And thick."

"Can our lips touch, even lightly?"

"No, querida."

"Try, try, my heart, try."

She pushed her lips against the bars. Her tongue tasted the filth on the grill. The rat was gnawing again on her shoe, but now

355

her feet were numbed with the cold and she did not feel it. "I cannot reach," she sobbed. "I cannot reach."

"You have reached. All of you has reached. You are here inside with me and I embrace you."

"Hold tightly to me. Touch me with your fingers."

"They touch all the places, the cheek, the breasts, the belly, the hollow in the thighs."

"If at this moment I could die!"

"Yes," he said. "It would be a good time."

Clemente appeared. "You must leave now, señora."

"A little more time," she begged. "En el nombre de la Santa Virgen."

"The time has gone around twice already, señora."

She nodded dumbly. "I must go," she said to the bars. "*Dios te bendiga*, Esquipulas."

"Adiós, Soledad." His fingers tightened on the bars.

She kissed them. "Walk with God, husband."

"With you."

7

IN A CELL in another part of the prison three men bent over Ramón Baca. "He has fainted again, Don Damasio," one of the men said disgustedly.

"Waken him, Mateo," Salazar said. "He finds comfort in unconsciousness."

Mateo dumped a pail of water on Baca. Baca gasped. He moved his head slightly and opened his eyes. He was in a heavy chair, bound with iron bands across the chest, thighs, and shins. His forearms were held down with smaller bands to the broad chair arms. The bands flattened his hands, palms down, on the chair arms so he could not move his fingers.

"Who were some of the other men?" Salazar asked again.

Baca said nothing.

"Try another finger," Salazar said.

Mateo took a sharpened wooden splinter from his jacket

pocket and inserted the point under the nail of the little finger of Baca's right hand. He pushed. Baca jerked his head and screamed. Sweat flooded his cheeks.

"Who were some of the other men, amigo?" Salazar asked. When Baca remained silent, he said: "Light the wood."

The other man struck flint and held the flame to the splinter. It burned slowly to the finger. When it reached the finger Baca screamed again and his head fell on his chest. The little room was filled with the smell of burned flesh.

"Waken him," Salazar said. Then he asked: "Who were some of the other men?" He waited. "It grows a little monotonous, Mateo. Try another finger."

"There are none left on this hand, Don Damasio," Mateo said.

"There are five fingers on the other hand."

"I think that of the teeth is better."

"Por Dios, but you are a stubborn man," Salazar said.

"They do not faint so easily with the teeth," Mateo insisted. "Besides, this smell sickens my stomach."

"Finish with the other hand, Mateo. After that you may try your specialty with the teeth."

8

DON MANUEL was sprawled gloomily in a chair in his apartment in the palace. His collar was open. His left hand cupped his right hand over his chest. A bottle of brandy stood on a small table at his side. He glanced at Salazar indifferently. "I can see that you have not succeeded," he said without tone. "And in a few hours it is the time. Help yourself to a drink. You appear to need one."

Salazar was tired and dejected. He gulped down the drink. "I cannot understand that fool!"

The Governor seemed in a reverie. "You lack skill, I believe," he said disinterestedly.

"There was no lack of skill, excelencia!" Salazar retorted. "It was done with great skill. The splinters were thrust under the nails of each finger of each hand. They were lighted. My assistants almost vomited. Baca shook the prison with his screams."

"But he would not talk." There was a ghost of a smile on Don Manuel's lips.

"Then one of my men did something else, something for which he has developed great talent. He applied a small chisel to each of Baca's front teeth and tapped with a hammer. The blow was delivered with great delicacy so that each tooth was broken off neatly just below the gums. I thought Baca would lose his mind with the pain."

"But he still would not speak," Don Manuel mused.

Salazar looked embarrassed. "I argued with him. I said: 'Don Ramón, how can you be such a fool? You are protecting men who failed you. What makes their names so precious to you?' " He held out his hands. "I cannot understand it, excelencia."

"Of course you cannot, Don Damasio."

"In the end we pulled out the fingernails one by one, but by then he was past speaking." Salazar leaned forward eagerly. "Postpone the execution, excelencia. Give me a little more time. There are other things that may be done. Sooner or later he will speak."

"He will not speak." Nor, he thought, would she come to him. He had counted each hour from the time she had visited her husband in the cell and he had told himself she could not stand by and allow Caballero to go to his death, and yet a part of him knew from the beginning she would not come to him.

"Just give me a few days more, excelencia," Salazar pleaded.

Armijo had not moved from his slouched position. Now he pulled himself erect. He poured some brandy into his goblet and stared at the rich amber liquid. A few more days for Salazar would mean a few more days for him, and perhaps in the end she too would break down and speak. And it was more than just the woman. There was the old thing between Caballero and himself, the intertwining of the strings. There was himself and there was the priest, Martínez, and there was Caballero, and the threads wove in and out. When Caballero died, the pattern would be broken.

He remembered the first journey to Taos and the bringing of the muskets to the priest, and he remembered how Caballero had come to him twice in Albuquerque, once with his side opened by

Indian arrow, and he remembered how he had known then that the threads were twisted together. He listened to the sound of the wind rising in the cold night, and his eyes lost themselves in the dark distance of the room, and he thought how under other pressures it might have been different. "Except," he said to himself, "nothing can be changed. It is written down and the text must be followed, word after word." It never was men alone, but always men in relation to the circumstances, and even without the woman it would have been the same.

The plea to extend the time was tempting, but the pact had been made and it was necessary that he live up to his part of it. Caballero deserved to die in dignity. He knew the mind and he knew that the two of them had contained themselves during the allotted time and he could ask no more of them.

He drank the brandy. "The execution takes place as scheduled."

Salazar bowed. "Your excellency commands. I live but to obey."

"Select your men immediately."

"I can do it myself, excelencia, and gladly."

Armijo's face hardened. "This is a lawful punishment, Major Salazar, and not the settlement of a personal quarrel."

"Six men will suffice, excelencia," Salazar said humbly.

"Select them, then, and name them a legal squad of execution in conformity with the law. They are servants of the government, not assassins."

"Yes, excelencia."

"Walk the prisoners to the garita, and as silently as possible. Use no horses. I desire above all that there be no disturbance in the city." He rubbed his face tiredly. "Have the men put to death at first light. And report to me when it is done."

At the door Salazar paused. "What kind of man is this Baca, to die for men who betrayed him?"

Don Manuel again was staring into the distance. "Do not try to understand Don Ramón, nor the other, nor the wife of the other. Be content there are so few of them."

9

CABALLERO was led into the palace courtyard shortly after two o'clock in the morning. Snow had begun to fall before midnight, and now a strong wind swirled the flakes in wild gusts. Six militiamen, one of whom held a lantern, huddled together in the yard. A few moments later Salazar emerged from the prison, pushing a stooped figure ahead of him.

Caballero was dumfounded when he recognized Baca. "When were you arrested?" Baca tried to reply and Caballero looked at him more closely. "Madre de Dios!" he gasped.

Baca's face was that of an old man. His lips were drawn against toothless gums. His eyes were lifeless. He swayed slightly in the wind, and Caballero thrust out his fettered hands and caught him. Baca groaned. Caballero raised his wrists and looked at the fingers.

Caballero dropped the hands and rushed toward Salazar, his hands lifted like a cudgel. Salazar waited for him calmly and kneed him in the groin. Caballero went down, his mouth and nostrils filling with snow. He got on his knees and then tried to stand up.

"Stop," Baca said. "It is useless."

"Let him alone," Salazar laughed. "This pleasures me."

It was the sound of Baca's broken and quavering voice and not what he said that quieted Caballero. He pressed the heels of his hands into the pain in his groin and then he got awkwardly to his feet and limped to his friend. His eyes were scalded with tears. "Ramón, Ramón, what has he done to you?"

"Enough," Baca said through his missing teeth. "But less than he desired."

"But why? En el nombre de Dios, why?"

"Because he attempted to insurrect," Salazar said. "It was an insurrection that reduced itself to a single man: Ramón Baca. At the last minute his associates refused to follow him and now the fool dies to protect them." He lifted Baca's chin. "Do you want to tell me the names of the others? There still is a chance to save what is left of yourself."

Baca spat in his face.

Salazar knocked him down, his eyes filled with murder. He wiped away the spittle. "Your life already is dedicated," he said. "It is an unfortunate thing. I should like a little more time with you. There are other games we could play together."

The prisoners were pushed forward into the face of the wind. The six soldiers selected by Salazar followed, their serapes wrapped around them, the barrels of their long muskets sticking up behind their necks. Salazar trudged in the rear, his blanket covering everything but his eyes, his head lowered against the icy blasts. He cursed the wind and the cold and the snow and the fact that he had to make the long walk to the old Spanish sentry box on the hill on foot instead of on a saddle over a warm horse.

The city was in darkness. The snow piled in drifts. Caballero and Baca were dressed only in shirts and trousers.

"So it failed," Caballero said. The wind drove the words back into his mouth.

"What?" Baca asked loudly.

Caballero put his mouth against Baca's ear. "The officers deserted you at the last minute," he chattered.

Baca said into his ear: "Fernando was right."

"Fernando? What do you mean?"

"He said my revolution would fail. He said it must start from the bottom. If I could do it again, I would know better. It is not the officers, chico, it is the people."

"The people make no decisions."

"Perhaps not. But no decisions can be made without them."

Their talking, in the wind, made them breathless and filled their lungs with cold, and they closed their mouths and lowered their heads and walked for a little while in silence. Then Baca said: "I do not mind dying. Only it is annoying to die knowing it could have been successful. I would give my life for another chance." He grinned toothlessly. "I made a joke, chico."

"Death will come as it might have a dozen times before," Caballero said indifferently. "My regret is for a few who remain alive."

"Ah, that is true. For the first time in my life I would willingly have Manuel Armijo for companion to share everything that is about to happen to me."

"And Salazar, do not forget Salazar, monito."

· "I do not forget Salazar. Only I do not think of him as one to shoot. I think of stepping on that one and then grinding with my heel." He grinned. "Hey, chico, I have a thought. Let us agree to haunt those two."

"Ramón," Caballero said, "you are a crazy man."

They reached the foot of the hill. The wind swept down. The stinging snow blinded them. The soldier carrying the lantern shifted it from one hand to the other and then held it lower so he could keep his blanket wrapped more tightly around him.

"Where we are going it will be warmer," Baca shouted.

Caballero bent his head. "Ramón," he said, "you are a crazy little bastard."

They started up the slope, buffeted by the wind, and then the night was filled with horsemen. There was no signal of their coming, no warning of sight or sound in the maddened night, so that it was as though they had materialized from the snow and the wind itself, and they galloped against the soldiers in whitened and terrible silence and bowled them over like tenpins. The soldiers rolled over, large, clumsy bundles in their blankets, and when they recovered from the shock of the ghostly assault, they struggled with numbed fingers to extricate themselves from their weighted and stiffened blankets and get at the muskets slung across their backs.

His head ringing from the force of his fall, Salazar sprang to his feet almost instantly. His nerveless fingers fought for his pistol. "The prisoners!" he shouted. "Guard the prisoners!"

Baca picked up the lantern knocked from the soldier's hand. "Hold fire!" he commanded. "Hombres, do not shoot at each other! No one of you is enemy to another! You are brothers! Join hands against the tyranny of Armijo!"

Now Salazar had his pistol free and he fired it across the ten feet at Baca, the single light in the darkness. Baca dropped to his knees with a gasp that became part of the wind and then he fell over slowly and in the lantern light the snow on the earth colored red. Caballero rushed at Salazar, and Salazar fired again and Caballero felt a burning blow in his side and stumbled. Then he felt himself being lifted and flung over a horse and he heard a shot from a musket. As he struggled to get down he heard two more shots, and then he heard nothing.

10

CABALLERO opened his eyes, to the rhythm of the horse's trotting. He lifted his head. "Ramón."

He heard Fernando say: "We have Don Ramón."

He tried to say something else, but the sleepiness was on him again and he could not make his lips move. He pressed his cheek against the warm neck of the horse.

He awakened again as he was being lowered. His side burned. "Ramón," he said hoarsely.

Fernando said: "He caught a bad one, Don Esquipulas."

"Where is he? Where is Ramón?"

Fernando carried him into a small adobe building. A candle guttered on a table. He saw Baca being laid on a pallet. He pulled away from Fernando and seized the candle and knelt at the pallet. As he held the candle close to Baca's face, he saw Baca's lips drawn back and the death already on his face.

"Ramón."

Baca opened his eyes. "Hola, chico." The corners of his mouth bubbled with blood. "Am I going to die?"

"Yes, monito," Caballero whispered.

"It is not a good time. I am just beginning to learn. Were you wounded too?"

"Yes."

"Are you going to die?"

"I do not know."

"Do not. There are things for you to do."

"Yes, Ramón."

"Now there is only you, chico. Use yourself well." His eyes rolled back. "Jesucristo, forgive me my sins." Then he said: "Lupe." The bubbling at the corners of his mouth stopped.

Caballero closed the eyes. He shut the mouth to cover the empty places where the teeth had been. He folded the hands. He touched the charred fingertips. He whispered: "Señor Padre, have mercy on his soul." He kissed the lips and he tasted the blood.

1

PADRE MARTÍNEZ looked at the snow falling in the night as he shut the door behind Fernando. "I suspected you would come here."

"Do you know about us already?" Fernando asked.

"Already? It is a week. Everybody knows about you. Archuleta has been notified by Don Manuel. His men are making search everywhere."

"We kept to the hills, padre."

"Both men are wounded, are they not?"

"Don Ramón is dead."

The priest crossed himself. "God have mercy on his soul. And your master, what of him?"

"He lives. The musket ball is still in him."

"Where is the wound?"

"In the right side, above the hip."

"It must be gangrenous by now. The lead must be removed and the wound cleaned."

"Don Esquipulas said you had skill as a surgeon."

"I have a little skill in everything, Fernando. Where is he now?"

"We are all encamped in a small canyon to the south. Don Esquipulas is unconscious."

"He must be brought to Taos under cover, immediately."

"Here, padre? To your house?"

"No, not here. There are women and children here. It would be unsafe." He thought for a moment. "There is a house not far from here. A woman lives there, one named Morena. She knew Don Esquipulas before. He will be safe there."

"What of her husband, her family?"

"She has neither. Her man died last year in the plague. She is alone."

"Can she be trusted?"

"She will keep silence."

Fernando looked at him intently. "And what of you, padre? Can *you* be trusted?"

Martínez's eyes glowed. "I am a priest."

"In this country today that does not mean everything, padre."

The priest smiled painfully. "Even in New Mexico a priest is still a servant of God. Wait here. I will make ready." He returned a few minutes later. In his hand was a slim knife and a pair of surgical forceps. "*Vamanos*, my son, there is no time to lose."

Fernando lifted the cross on the chain around Martínez's neck. "Swear that you will not betray him, padre."

Martínez nodded. "It is fitting," he said quietly. He took the silver cross from Fernando's hand. "I swear on the cross I will betray none of you."

Fernando lowered his eyes. "Forgive me, padre."

"Your devotion requires no remission, mi hijo. Now, *vamanos!*"

As they left the house, dogs barked. "They make enough noise to rouse the dead," Fernando said angrily.

"Be tranquil. A path has been worn to my door by those who call upon me at all hours of the night. No one will think anything is unusual and no one will be about in this storm." He climbed on his burro. "We will stop first at the house of Morena and prepare her."

A little more than two hours later, as the first touches of the gray dawn lighted the sky, the two men brought Caballero to the house he had visited five years before. The room was warm from a new fire laid in the corner hearth. A pot of water boiled over the flames. They placed the unconscious man on the pallet and the priest undressed him. Morena stared at the bearded face and the broken nose. "You would not recognize him, would you?" the priest asked grimly. "The mark of Armijo is heavy."

"He was so handsome," Morena said.

"Now he is wise. He has profited in the exchange. Fetch the water now, mi hija."

She set the pot of water on the floor next to the pallet and gave the priest a clean rag, and he wiped around the wound. The edges were as hard as leather and the skin was black. Martínez put the point of the knife into the wound and spread it open. Caballero groaned and opened his eyes.

"Give him brandy," the priest said to Fernando. "Make him drink it."

Morena fell on her knees and took Caballero's face between her hands. She kissed him on the lips. "Pobrecito, pobrecito, it soon will be over." She took the flask from Fernando and held it to Caballero's mouth. His throat swallowed convulsively once or twice and then the brandy filled his mouth and spilled over. "Swallow more, pobrecito," she said. "It soon will be over."

The priest held down one side of the wound with the flat of the knife and inserted the forceps into the opening. Caballero arched his back and screamed. Morena covered his mouth with hers, and Fernando pushed down his chest and held it under his knee, and the priest moved the forceps and then grunted and pulled out hard. "It is done," he said.

Morena took the pincers from the priest. She looked at the slug. "Such a little thing to cause so much trouble."

"It is large enough," Fernando said. "It is as big as the world."

Martínez cut away the rotted flesh around the wound and then he kneaded it and the blood began to flow. The blood was black before it became red. "Now the poker, Morena," Martínez said.

She took an iron bar from the bed of the fire and hit it against the stone to free it of ash. The end of the bar glowed a dull red. She handed it to the priest.

"Now, both of you, hold him down," Martínez ordered. He pressed the sides of the wound together and laid the end of the poker on it, and the air thickened with the smell of cooked flesh. Caballero screamed again and arched his back with such force he almost threw Fernando off his chest, and then he became limp and his head rolled to one side.

The priest handed the iron back to Morena. He remained on his knees, and his lips moved silently. He crossed himself and stood up.

"Will he live?" Fernando asked.

"Con el favor de Dios, I believe so. It will take a little time, but I believe he will not die." He swallowed from the brandy flask, then gave the flask to Fernando.

Fernando lifted the flask to his lips and then he paused and held it out to Morena. "Here, woman," he said gruffly. "You need this before I do."

Her eyes widened. She swallowed a little of the brandy. "Many thanks, señor," she said softly.

"Now, Fernando, what of your men?" Martínez asked. "They cannot remain in that canyon."

"It is true, padre. What do you suggest?"

The priest held his hands in front of the fire and pondered for a moment. "Tell them to enter Taos singly. The Rio Arriba is filled with refugees from the north. They come every day from the land grants. The new faces will not be noticed. Little by little I will find places for them to stay. Only hide your weapons somewhere. They will make questions." He saw a look of suspicion cross Fernando's face. "You do not wholly trust me yet."

"I trust no one wholly, padre, but him and myself," Fernando said impassively.

The priest's face was somber. "You have read and understood the book of the times." He gestured toward the knife and the forceps. "Has that not proved me to you?"

"Men have been saved from death before to be kept alive for their executioners."

The priest held up his cross. "And this? The oath on this?"

"I will say that I do not distrust you, padre," Fernando said. The muscles knotted in his cheeks.

"Well, in any case, that is a beginning," Martínez said with sarcasm.

"I also will say that I would kill any man who betrays him."

Martínez fingered the cross. "Even a priest."

"Even a priest, padre."

"No!" Morena cried. "That is blasphemy!"

Martínez regarded Fernando gravely and then his dark eyes filled with pain. "Do you believe I would betray you to a man who has planted such seeds in the hearts of Catholics?" he asked harshly. He threw his serape over his shoulder and left the house.

Morena crossed herself. "You should not have spoken to him so. He is a good man."

Fernando sat down heavily. His head fell on his chest. "I was wrong, it may be. I am very tired. And it seems that almost everyone in New Mexico says one thing and means something else."

She ladled out a bowl of atole and gave it to him. She put freshly made tortillas before him and poured a cup of chocolate. He devoured everything. When he finished he stretched and then he made a cigarette and with the third puff he yawned and his eyes closed. "I need to return to the men and give them instructions," he said sleepily.

"Take a little sleep, hombre," she said. "There is time." He looked quickly at her and his face turned suspicious again. She pointed to the crucifix on the wall. "Do you want me to swear too?"

He lay down on the earth floor near the hearth and was instantly asleep. She took the cigarette from his fingers and put it in her mouth, moved Caballero's matted hair from his burning forehead, and bathed his face. Then she sat down between the two men and smoked the cigarette and listened to their breathing, Caballero's discordant and broken, Fernando's deep and rhythmic, and her face was serene.

2

THE FEVER held for six days. Each morning and each evening Morena washed Caballero's body with cold water, and she remembered when the enfeebled frame had belonged to a young exquisito from Santa Fe who had shared her pallet. On the seventh day the fever broke and on the afternoon of that day Caballero opened his eyes and there was sanity in them for the first time. His eyes moved slowly around the room. He frowned when he saw Morena. He tried to raise himself on his elbows.

She pushed him back gently. "Do not make an effort, Don Esquipulas."

He wet his parched lips. "Whose house is this?"

"It is mine."

"Where is it?"

"In Taos, señor."

"Fernando? The men?"

"They are well and safe, señor."

He closed his eyes. His breathing rasped in the small room. His face broke out with sweat. She touched the wet cloth to his cheeks and wiped his brow. "*Agua*," he said. She lifted his head and held a cup of water to his lips. As he drank, his eyes opened. "Who are you?" he asked. "How am I here in your house?"

She looked away to hide the hurt. "You have been in this house before, Don Esquipulas."

There was silence and then she felt his hand touch her wrist. "Morena! It is you. And this is your little house. Pardon, chula! Do not turn your face from me."

"I should not have believed you would remember."

"It is only that my eyes are not yet fully opened. Morenacita, I could not forget you. Look at me and smile a little. Have I been here long?"

"A week, Don Esquipulas."

His hand went to his side. He grimaced.

"Padre Martínez removed the ball," she said.

"And you have been my nurse?"

"It has pleasured me."

"Morena, let me look at you. You have altered little. The face has still the loveliness of a flower."

"You have changed, Don Esquipulas."

He laughed weakly. "So I have been told," he said. He rubbed his beard. "I have not yet had the pleasure of looking upon the new arrangement made by Don Manuel." He wet his lips again. "I am hungry, woman."

She smiled happily. "It is a good sign. I have broth waiting." When she sat down next to him again with the broth, his eyes were closed and she thought he had fallen asleep again, but he opened them and she fed him the thick mutton soup. She made a cigarette and put it into his mouth.

He sighed contentedly. "I am a happy man, bonita. Was I a bad patient?"

"You said many things with the fever."

369

"Did I? Of what did I speak?"

"Doña Soledad. Padre Martínez told me she is your wife and that she is a great lady and that she is beautiful."

"You are no less beautiful."

"Do you love her?"

"Yes, Morenacita, I love her very much."

"You spoke also of Ramón and of a monito," Morena said quickly. "I asked Padre Martínez about these and he said that Don Ramón was your friend and that he had been killed, and that a little monkey is an animal that lives in the trees in jungles in foreign lands. He did not know about the monito, but he said he has heard that sometimes great ladies have little monkeys for pets. Does Doña Soledad have such a pet?"

"The word was what I called Don Ramón in affection."

Her eyes filled with tears. She shook her head and said briskly: "You have spoken enough for a sick man. Now you will sleep again."

When he woke, it was night and he heard Fernando's voice in a low whisper. He turned his head. He saw Fernando and Morena seated at the small table, their faces close. In the light from the tallow he could see the shining in her eyes as she looked at the big man. He saw on Fernando's face an expression he had never seen there before. "Hola, Fernando," he said. "What passes, friend?"

Fernando was at his side instantly. "Morena told me you spoke with sense today," he said, his voice filled with gladness. "So you will live."

"I will live. The wrong man was killed, Fernando."

"It is important only that you live."

Caballero shook his head. "The wrong man was killed," he repeated bitterly. "My quarrel with Armijo is a personal thing and extends to no one beyond Don Manuel and me. Don Ramón's fight was for all of you."

"To fight is to fight. You know what he knew."

"I know only the beginning of what he knew."

"You will learn more, señor. We all will teach you, and the dead eyes will help you to see."

"It is possible," Caballero said. "Morena, I die of hunger."

"Be thankful it is only hunger," Fernando said soberly.

"It would have been a great loss," Caballero grunted. "Only I have forbidden myself to die by Salazar."

"He is here."

"Here! In Taos?" Caballero tried to sit up.

"He arrived with one hundred men the day before yesterday."

"Does he know anything?"

"I do not believe so, Don Esquipulas. I learned he gathered some of the people in Las Truchas and put them to the question and one of them finally revealed that men fitting our description had passed near the village headed north. I think he just followed that lead, with nothing more certain to go on. Since his arrival here he has conferred with Archuleta, and his soldiers have searched, but without confidence."

"They will not remain long in ignorance. You must all leave here," Caballero said.

"Salazar may go somewhere else."

"He has the nose of a ferret. He will not go away."

"You cannot be moved yet."

"Then you must all go without me."

"We will not leave you," Fernando said quietly.

"The loyalty of the men was given to Don Ramón, not to me. They owe me nothing."

"They call you leader. They will not leave you."

Again Caballero tried to sit up. "Then as leader I command that you all go and save yourselves."

"Until you are recovered I am leader," Fernando said. "We will not go."

Morena squatted next to them. She held a steaming bowl. "Go back to the table, Fernando. Let this man eat."

Fernando rose without dispute and returned to the table. Morena fed Caballero savory mutton stew. He felt his strength increase with each mouthful. When he was finished he lay back. "Fernando."

"May I speak with him now?" Fernando asked Morena.

"For a little moment only. He must sleep again."

"Nombre de Dios!" Caballero said petulantly. "Who gives this woman such authority?"

371

"This is my house," Morena said. "In it I am leader." She smiled. "I welcome the sound of anger in the voice of Don Esquipulas. The man returns to earth."

Caballero snorted. "When may I be moved, Fernando?" he asked.

Fernando shrugged. "Who knows? It depends on the distance of the journey and the difficulty."

"How many days?"

"A week. Two weeks. When Padre Martínez gives the word."

"Where is the priest?"

"He has gone to the pueblo."

"Leave word at his house for him to come here when he can."

"It is not necessary. He comes every day."

"That is enough now, I think," Morena said.

"Do you believe he will come here today?" Caballero asked.

Fernando sat down at the table and closed his mouth.

"Fernando!"

"The talking is ended," Morena said.

"Por Dios, I have not finished!" Caballero shouted.

"You have finished, señor," she said. "No one will speak to you."

"Fernando!"

"There is no use in arguing," Fernando said placidly. "She has the nature of a sergeant."

3

Padre Martínez visited the house the next day. He readily admitted the danger of Salazar, but he said flatly Caballero could not undertake a lengthy journey on horseback. "Where would you go?" he asked Caballero.

"We would cross the border and go to Bent's Fort."

"Winter has closed the pass."

"We would get through."

"The wound is healing, Don Esquipulas. The cauterization has stopped the infection." The priest shook his head. "But a day in the saddle would split you open again, and when the infection comes to the same place a second time, it always is worse than before. You cannot leave yet."

"Do I stay in bed like an old woman and wait for Salazar to come here and get me?" Caballero demanded.

"He has no knowledge of your presence in Taos."

"How can you be sure of that?"

The priest smiled. "There are men who keep me informed of what goes on in the office of Prefecto Archuleta."

"Salazar is a ferret. He will find out."

"Possibly. But he knows nothing yet. He stamps about Archuleta's office and has angered the colonel so that if he did not bear orders directly from Don Manuel, Archuleta would order him out of the North District. He has demanded that Archuleta turn Taos inside out. The colonel has told him with truth that it would take months to search every house and interrogate every person in the Rio Arriba. The matter stands at that place. It is not comforting to have Salazar here, but for the moment the danger is not immediate. You must remain here and heal yourself. It would be a greater danger to try to escape." The lined face softened. "I think of you, Don Esquipulas, and of your wife, and of the least uncertain way to keep you alive."

"I believe you, padre. I will do as you say."

"Does Doña Soledad know that you are not dead?"

"One of the men went to Santa Fe and informed her. She wanted to return with him to me. It was only when the man convinced her that Armijo must be watching her that she would consent to let him go without her."

"Now let me see my handiwork," the priest said. He examined the wound. It now resembled a severe burn. The flesh around the burn was firm and healthy. The priest applied ointment to the scab. "A little more rest, just a little, and you will be better than new." He stood up. "I must leave now. A man is dying of the disease that devours the stomach. He has shrunk to the size of child. He needs comfort." He looked around the room, at the fire on the hearth, at Fernando and Morena seated at either side of the pungent blaze. "This house is blessed," he said.

Caballero recovered his strength steadily during the next few days. He began to take tentative steps in the room. The first time he got up from the pallet his legs collapsed under him and he realized how foolish he had been to think he could have stayed in a saddle. Once he was back on his feet the threat of Salazar seemed somehow less. He began to hope that perhaps Salazar would leave Taos without learning anything more than he knew then.

Outside, Taos was locked in the bitter winter weather. Snow fell frequently. At night the wind rose and the howling of the timber wolves was close. Inside was warmth and there was food and drink and it was the whole world.

On afternoon Morena said laughingly: "I have pretended, to please the others, that I believe you are truly Don Esquipulas. But under that jungle there could be the face of any man. Fernando, get your shears and razor and prove to me this man is who he says he is."

Fernando obeyed immediately, with the marvelous docility with which he responded to all of Morena's requests. Caballero seated himself in a chair and Fernando prepared to remove his beard. Suddenly Caballero stopped him. He stroked the beard, and his eyes were thoughtful. "Salazar has seen me but once this way," he said, "his soldiers never. This hair is a useful thing."

"It is true," Morena said instantly. Her face blanched. "Madre mía, but I would have imperiled you with this childish request!"

"No, it will serve a good purpose," Caballero said. "Do not put away your instruments, Fernando. Without doubt a description of my present appearance has been given to Salazar's men. They look for me as I was before or as I am now. We will fool them and give them a third face. Trim the beard, Fernando. Bring it to a state halfway between what it is now and the complete removal."

Fernando set to work. He was almost finished when Padre Martínez entered the house. "Sit down," Caballero said cheerfully. "You are next." Then he read the expression on the priest's face and he pushed away the shears. "What is the matter, padre?"

"Salazar has arrested one of your men."

"Santa Madre!"

"Salazar has been more clever than we anticipated," the priest said grimly. He warmed his hands at the fire. His face was red with the cold. "On the surface he has been doing little beyond antagonizing Archuleta, but he had a plan all along. He has had men

374

in civilian clothes scattered in taverns, acting as provokers. They
made insulting remarks about Don Manuel. The natives thought
they were refugees from the land grants, but they did not respond
to the remarks because they have learned to shut their ears and
their mouths when the name of Armijo is raised. Last night in a
small fonda one of Salazar's agents mumbled something about
overthrowing Don Manuel. It was then one of your men shouted
his agreement. He was taken immediately."

"Has he given away anything yet?"

"He was too drunk to be questioned."

"Why have the men been permitted to get drunk in public
taverns?" Caballero demanded angrily of Fernando.

Fernando hunched his shoulders. "They are men who have
volunteered, Don Esquipulas. They may not be disciplined as
soldiers."

"When he is sober he will be put to the question," the priest
said. "Meanwhile Salazar has alerted all his men, particularly the
guards he has placed at all exits from Taos. Everyone who leaves
is scrutinized."

"He has had guards there from the beginning," Fernando said.

"Who is the man?"

"One called Joaquín Mainez," the priest said.

"He is a good man," Fernando said. "He is foolish when he is
drunk, but he is strong."

"He will not be strong when Salazar is finished," Caballero
said.

"Salazar will make him talk," the priest said. "And he should
not have to suffer so. You must get out now, you and all of the
men. How do you feel, Don Esquipulas?"

"I am ready."

"The other men are no problem. Neither Salazar nor his men
know any of them by sight or they would have arrested them before
now. Does he know you, Fernando?"

"I do not believe so, padre, not to recognize."

"Then it is only you, Don Esquipulas. The others can get by
the blockade. With you it will be more difficult."

"Order the men to move, Fernando," Caballero said. "We
will arrange about me afterward."

"To the north?"

"It is the only way. Anywhere else and they are deeper in the trap. They must cross the border. They will find safety only among the Americans at Bent's Fort."

"What do we know about that place?" Fernando asked.

"Charles Bent is married to a Mexican lady, and his house is in Taos," Martínez said. "He is a good man." He nodded approvingly. "It will not appear in the least out of the ordinary if the men go singly or in pairs. Since the Beaubien land grant was made, a small settlement called Cimarron has developed between Taos and Raton Pass. There is much traffic between Cimarron and Taos, especially now with hunters and trappers."

"We will make this Cimarron the meeting-place," Caballero said.

"But what of you, Don Esquipulas?" Fernando asked. "This arrangement does for the others, but you may not be able to pass Salazar's guards."

"Get the men moving," Caballero ordered. "I will begin to think of something for myself."

"Think of something first," Fernando said.

Now the priest spoke. "Since I learned of the arrest of this man Mainez I have been trying to concentrate. I have thought of something that might work successfully, with the help of God."

"What is it, padre?" Fernando asked eagerly.

"The man I spoke of the other day, he who was dying. He is dead. The funeral is tomorrow. The cemetery is outside of Taos on the north road. I have thought Don Esquipulas could attend the Mass and join with the mourners following the coffin from the church to the place of burial. The guards at the barrier will perhaps be less alert on such an occasion and may not look upon the faces of the mourners as carefully as they do others."

Caballero twisted his beard. "It will work. They will not recognize me."

Fernando looked worried. "It is a great risk. And if you are discovered, the men will not be there to help you."

"There can be no better plan," Caballero said decisively. "Fernando, go instantly and give the word to the men."

Fernando scratched his head. "There is still something about this that bothers me."

"You worry too much," Caballero said. "Move quickly."

Then Fernando snapped his fingers. "How will you get from the cemetery to Cimarron. You still are unable to ride alone."

"You can wait at the cemetery for him," Martínez said.

Fernando and the priest left the house, and Morena ordered Caballero to lie down and gain as much strength as possible. He obeyed her meekly and was gratified to see her expression of content. Presently he slept. He wakened a few hours later and ate a substantial meal. "I am much pleasured by what has happened with you and Fernando," he said.

"It is good, señor."

"You love each other, do you not?"

"Yes, señor."

"There is no better man."

She placed wood on the fire, sat next to him, and folded her hands in her lap. "I have not forgotten that which occurred long ago with us, Don Esquipulas," she said.

"There is no need to remember that, bonita. I have never said anything to him."

"I have told him."

"Why?" he asked with surprise.

"I could not start with him with a bad secret," she said. "It was simpler to tell him at the beginning, of you and of others. Now there is no lie between us."

He thought of his wife and asked: "What did he say?"

"He was not angered. He understood that it was nothing that affects that which is between him and me. Forgive me, Don Esquipulas, but with you it was a rico relieving himself with the body of a mestiza. It touched none of the things that Fernando and I touch together." She smiled gently. "Nor does it affect the love he has for you, señor."

He lifted her hand to his lips. "I am less than either of you."

"Do not believe that, Don Esquipulas," she said peacefully. "I served you and it did not leave me unmoved. It is only that this is a different thing. Fernando and I are the same."

4

HE SLEPT AGAIN, fully clothed, and when he woke early in the morning he saw Fernando had returned and was lying on a blanket with Morena in his arms. He spoke out quickly and Fernando told him that the men had started moving out of Taos before sunset and had passed the inspection of the guards and that all of them should be on the road to Cimarron before dawn. "I shall take you to the Church of San Fernando de Taos just before the sun rises and then I will go ahead and wait at the cemetery."

Caballero sat up and began to pull on his boots. "Take me there now, Fernando, and then return here to Morena."

"There still are several hours, Don Esquipulas. It is very cold and the church is without heat."

"You will take me there now." He stood up. He took Morena's hands. "I will not try to thank you," he said. He wrapped a blanket around him. "Don Fernando de Taos," he said, "*vamanos*."

His eyes watered and he began to shake as soon as he got outside. He held himself tight to show no weakness before Fernando. He knew that if Fernando believed he would not be able to make it to the cemetery, he would not leave him.

Fernando grunted at the cold. "Do you know something strange? This man who died was a poor man."

"Why is that strange?"

"To be buried from a church with a ceremony by a priest. Do you know that Padre Martínez makes no charge?"

"I did not know, but it does not surprise me." His heart was pounding. He wondered if he could take a short rest without making Fernando too suspicious.

"I thought he surely must have been a rico," Fernando said. "There is to be a Mass for the Dead and all that goes with it including a cross-bearer and acolytes carrying candles. I found he was a carpenter. The funeral would cost one hundred and fifty dollars in Santa Fe." He shook his head wonderingly. "When I have to die, I hope I can arrange for it to take place in Taos."

"It would be fitting with your name," Caballero said. "But

I make a promise. Wherever you die I will see that you have a proper funeral, even if it costs one hundred and fifty dollars."

The effort was too much. He leaned against the wall of a building and tried to cover his gasping. Fernando looked anxiously at him and he managed a smile. They pushed on again. The streets were deserted. The night was clear and very cold. Caballero felt himself getting weak. He wondered how much farther it was to the church. His feet got heavy; they dragged and his boots scraped on the ground. Then he stumbled and Fernando caught him. "It is nothing," he said. "I caught my foot on something." He started to walk again. His side began to twinge with each step, and then it felt as though there were a knife sticking him there. His eyes blurred and he tasted the mutton he had eaten. The ground whirled and he passed out.

He opened his eyes in darkness. "Fernando."

"Easy, Don Esquipulas. We are inside the church."

He tried to control his breathing and speak easily. "Good. Padre Martínez will find me here. You return to Morena." When Fernando did not move, he gave him a push. "Go, Don Fernando de Taos! Do not waste on me minutes you have to spend with your woman."

He listened to Fernando's departing footsteps and gave thanks that he had been able to convince him he was all right. He hoped he would be all right, but he no longer thought so. But if anything happened on the way, they would all be beyond the barrier. The church was damp as well as cold. He clamped his teeth together and made his blanket into a tight cocoon and fell asleep.

"How far did you say it was from the church to the cemetery?" he heard Fernando ask.

"At least thrice the distance from Morena's house to here," he heard the priest say.

"He will never be able to make it. He collapsed before he came halfway from the house. I had to carry him here."

When Caballero was able to bring his eyes into focus, he saw the two men leaning over him, the priest holding a lantern. "Of course I shall be able to make it," he said. "It is too late to make new plans."

"I will not let him start out," Fernando said.

The priest pinched his lower lip. "Instead of going ahead, Fernando, perhaps you could walk at his side, to be there in the event he could not go on."

"If he broke down, a crowd would collect," Fernando said. "He would be caught like a beaver in a trap. I do not argue with you, padre. He does not leave Taos on his own feet." As Caballero opened his mouth to protest, he said: "Save your breath, Don Esquipulas."

Martínez set the lantern on the floor and clasped his hands behind his back. He strode back and forth. "And yet he must be moved." His shadow danced crazily on the wall. He clapped his hands behind him savagely and then stopped in the treading and the bitter smiting and turned his head slowly and looked at the other men, his eyes alive with a new thought. "We will place him in the coffin," he said.

"What will you do with the body, padre?" Fernando asked.

"Nothing. They will go together."

"Los dulces Nombres!" Fernando crossed himself. He looked down at Caballero.

Caballero asked: "Would there be room, padre?"

"Room enough. The box was made for a man of full size. When this one died he was bones without flesh. In his shroud he is lost in the box." He knelt before Caballero and took his hand. "The corpse will make no objection," he said. "Could you do it?"

"Yes," Caballero said. "How would you arrange it?"

Martínez thought for a moment. "You and Fernando could wait in the apse during the Mass. I will send the acolytes and the mourners from the church ahead of the coffin. It will then take but a moment for me to raise the lid and for Fernando to set you inside."

"Is the coffin not sealed?"

"The cover is held down only by hasps and pegs. There are no nails in Taos to waste on coffins."

"How would he breathe?" Fernando asked.

"The grooves in the hasps are long enough," the priest said. "We will insert small wedges of wood in the corners. They will keep the cover open enough to admit air."

"What then of Fernando?" Caballero asked.

"The procession to the cemetery will be a slow one," the priest said. "He will have time enough to hasten from the church and ride past the barrier before us. Then he can wait at the place of burial as we planned originally." He pressed Caballero's hand. "It will not be pleasant for you, mi hijo, but we are almost at the end of our time and I can think of no other way."

Caballero looked steadily at the priest. "This is a big thing that you offer to do for me, Don Antonio."

The priest's face was caught by the wan gleam of the lantern in dull lights and shadows so that it might have been a map in relief of his own country with all the bony hills and the empty valleys and the eyes two midnight lakes in dead craters. "I am not a conventional servant of God," he said. "I can think now only that it is necessary for you to escape from the hands of Manuel Armijo. Your men are a beginning, but they are aimless unled. You must survive to lead them and the other men who will join you." His eyes glowed with a raw flame. "I have had my call and for half of my life I have tried to obey it as I have seen best, and I have succeeded in some small things and I have failed in many large things, and now you have your call and our call is the same. There is sickness and starvation and ignorance and tyranny in the land, and the summons of the people is no less than that of God. Do not be grateful to me, mi hijo. You perhaps are my second chance, and that implies forgiveness for my errors. It is I who give thanks to you."

5

IN THE RECESS Caballero heard the shuffle of feet as people entered the church and he thought how it had been given to him, despite himself, by Fernando at the beginning, by Ramón, by his father, by his wife, by Morena, and now by the priest and how all the pieces fitted together relentlessly so that, having accepted the parts he now possessed the whole. Then he heard the voice of the priest, harsh and compelling: "*Ego sum resurrectio et vita,*" and he thought if he had belief it was belief taken from the belief of others. He had walked in a narrow and limited corridor and now he had come to the end and had stepped out to look upon a world. He heard the voice, which had in it the force of the winds that assaulted mountains, muted now in *"Resquiescant in pace."* The journey of the dead was ended. He stirred himself and flexed his legs as the absolution of the body was made and he smelled the sweet odor of incense. He stood up. His own journey was to begin.

He heard the priest request that the mourners leave the church before the coffin was carried out and he sensed the surprise at this alteration of ritual. For a moment his breathing stopped. He heard the tread of many feet and then there was silence, and then the priest was beckoning to him.

He had hoped the coffin would be a simple oblong, so he could lie reversed, head to feet, but instead the box was built with its greatest width for the shoulders, narrowing at the feet. The dead man lay immaculate in a white cotton shroud. Fernando lifted Caballero and laid him prone on the corpse so that his face was above the shriveled face. Then he lowered the lid and placed the wedges in the corners. Caballero felt himself being pushed down on the brittle bones and heard the dull clasping of the hasps and the low squeak of pegs being inserted, and he was alone in the darkness and the smell of freshly hewn pine, with lips against his cheek.

The smell of the sap smarted in his eyes. He blinked as he felt the box being lifted. He felt himself being carried slowly, and then a sliver of light broke through the raised slit and cold, fresh air filtered in. The box was set down and he heard the creaking of wheels. He twisted his neck and strained his head to get his face as close as he could to the crack. He could see men and women lined up on the side of the street, the men with hats removed, all of them crossing themselves as the cross-bearer passed before them.

His arms, pressed rigidly against his sides, tingled. His right hand, gripped around the butt of his pistol, slowly lost feeling. He felt sudden panic at the thought of being paralyzed in the box, so that if he were discovered he would be helpless to defend himself. He moved his body as far as he could to the left and flexed his hand and shifted his arm as much as he could. His left arm went dead altogether, but he felt the return of the blood to the other arm. He gripped the pistol.

He had to keep control over that hand, he thought, his head

swimming with the smell. If the carriage were stopped and the lid lifted and one of Salazar's soldiers appeared above him, he must not be wholly defenseless. But the carriage would not be stopped. Who would demand that a coffin be opened? Salazar might, he thought. Not even Salazar. Salazar might, he thought.

The cart jolted on the rutted road. He grew increasingly dizzy with the accumulating noxiousness of the sharp odor, and his stomach turned and he felt sickness in his throat. He compressed his lips and fought back the queasiness. He must not vomit on the corpse. "Then man is dead and shriven and stainless and the dignity of his death must not be violated," he said inside him. "Santa Virgen de Guadalupe, help me to contain my stomach," he prayed. "Dulce Madre de Méjico, assist me to not defile this silent man who has accepted my companionship without protest."

He kept his face as close as he could to the crack and then he saw the crack lessen and looked quickly at the corner of the box. He saw that the jouncing of the wagon had loosened the wedge there, and as he watched, the wedge shook free and dropped away and the lid closed at that end so that he again was in darkness.

He twisted his head and tried to see over his shoulder. At the other end he could make out a faint slit of light. The wedge there still held intact. He pushed himself up and lifted the lid with his shoulders. The light crept in again and with it the clean air. His head fell against the face of the man and the lid closed. He gathered his strength to lift it again and then he realized he could not do that, that the lid must not be seen rising and falling.

"It is necessary to breathe slowly," he told himself, a little drunk on the smell, "to hold the air in the lungs, to exhale slowly, to wait, to inhale slowly. I must not lose the control. I must do nothing without the control. There is not much farther to go. I must retain everything. Dios santo, let me keep myself for the little while longer that is necessary."

The wheels sighed in relief as the wagon came to a halt and he knew they had arrived at last at the barrier. He heard voices, among them the voice of Padre Martínez, and he gripped the pistol butt more tightly. His head seemed to have a wide circular motion of its own, wandering crazily in capricious orbit. He listened to the voices and struggled against a lunatic, unhinged impulse to cry out, to join his voice with the other voices, to become part of the living again, to loose himself from the dead. He felt the unyielding body under him, urging itself against him, and he thought of Soledad and seized upon that thought and clung to it and bought time and reason with it.

And then he knew the wagon was moving again and it was simple and easy. It was in back of him. Everything was in back of him. He felt friendship for the partner of his darkness and he closed his eyes and thought he would sleep a little to seal their intimacy.

The opening of the coffin restored him to partial consciousness and he felt himself being lifted out, and then he felt a saddle between his legs and an arm around his chest. He murmured thanks to the priest, but he did not know whether that was then or a long time afterward. When he opened his eyes again, he was being helped down from the horse. It was late afternoon. The air was cold and fresh and he filled his lungs gratefully. He looked around. Fernando and Morena, their hands clasped, stood before him. He saw the uncertainty in Fernando's face and the fear in the eyes of the woman. "I am glad that you came with us, Morena," he said. "We would be incomplete without you."

She fell to her knees and took his hand. "You are without anger, Don Esquipulas?"

"You belong nowhere but with us."

"I can ride as well as a man," she said. "And you still have need of me. I will be of use to you."

"Do not talk of use," he said. He stroked her cheek. "We are three friends."

"Gracias, Don Esquipulas."

"Morena—Fernando. The title belongs to other people and to another time. Honor me by speaking to me as you do to each other." He held both of them in his arms. "We are friends," he said, "*somos amigos.*"

They crossed the snow-laden Sangre de Cristos and made camp that night on the Cieneguilla. The following day they traversed the length of the Moreno Valley through forests of naked aspen. From time to time Caballero moved over to Morena's horse. They reached Cimarron the following afternoon. In the bustling village they found the men waiting for them and for the first time

384

Caballero greeted each of the men who had pledged himself to him.

He paused before a large, swarthy man. "Friend, your face is not unfamiliar to me."

"He is called Carlos Gutiérrez," Fernando said.

"The name is familiar as well," Caballero said, frowning.

Gutiérrez shifted his musket from one hand to the other. He looked embarrassed.

"He has important family connections," Fernando said. "He is cousin to Damasio Salazar."

Caballero snapped his fingers. "Nombre de Dios! You are the man who misguided the Texans! Why have you left the service of Don Manuel?"

Gutiérrez told him how he had been assaulted and robbed. "I thought at first I was an unfortunate man, señor, destined always to be penniless," he said. "But then I learned that Don Manuel's nephew, Tomás Martínez, had boasted that it was he who had broken my arm." He wiped his mouth slowly. "You need have no doubt of my loyalty, señor."

"I believe him," Fernando said.

"Then that is enough," Caballero said. He looked around. "There are more men here than I expected."

"Men of Taos joined us," Fernando said. "We now number almost twoscore."

Caballero looked soberly at the faces. "You would be better led if it were Don Ramón who stood here in my place, señores. I will do my best to fail neither him nor you."

Their path led along the slim bench cutting off the Rayado and Cimarron Valleys from the Sangre de Cristos to the west. They journeyed slowly in the snow and the ice. The course followed roughly the original mountain branch of the Santa Fe Trail, but the marks of the road were obliterated.

Soon after the beginning of the first day's journey the pain started again in Caballero's side. He rode slumped over, his elbow in the side, and he bit his lips until blood came to keep himself from crying out when his horse stumbled or fell. Fernando remained close. He ordered Fernando to say nothing about his condition to the others nor to allow their speed to be retarded beyond the impositions of terrain and weather. He felt a new and curious responsibility to these men.

Huddled in their whitened serapes, their faces burned with the cold, their eyes streaming tears from the wind, they crossed a vast, sage-strewn plateau. Here the winter wind swept with such force they had to turn their heads away to breathe. The horses labored. They crossed the Canadian River and began the slow ascent to Raton Pass, and on that afternoon one of the spies in the rear rode up to Caballero and pointed backward. Caballero lifted his glass to his eye, and below him in the distance, crawling like ants on the glaring snow, he saw horsemen.

He handed the glass to Fernando. "How many of them do you make them to be?"

"At least a hundred. It must be Salazar. There would be none other in such numbers so far north at this time of year."

The following day the pursuers appeared to have gained on them. They crossed the Raton Mountains, descended from the pass, and reached Trinidad in the foothills of the Culebra Range. They camped on the bank of El Río de las Animas Perdidas en Purgatorio, where there still could be seen the bones of the men who were massacred by Comanche Indians. That night Caballero found his shirt was sticky with blood.

In the morning he scanned the country behind them. "There is no sign of them, Fernando."

"Perhaps we were mistaken. Perhaps it was not Salazar."

They continued in a northeasterly direction and late the following day they crossed the river, the name of which had been translated and shortened by French trappers to Purgatoire, and they entered upon another sprawling plain, covered with scattered mesquite and sage and innumerable villages of prairie dogs. They replenished their supplies with as many of the rodents as they could kill and they moved on. There still was no more sign of their pursuers. They came to a country of stunted cedar and cane cactus. Caballero was paralyzed on one side from his shoulder to his knee.

They reached the Arkansas River and across the bleak landscape they saw the massive walls and the two watch towers of Bent's Fort.

1

Damasio Salazar leaned across Don Manuel's desk. The manacles cut into his wrists. His voice trembled with fear and bewilderment. "It was not my fault, excelencia! I made the man talk at last and I started after Caballero immediately. I saw them on this side of El Paso del Raton. We halted that night only long enough to rest the horses, and the next day we gained on them. I gave the order to go faster and then I was suddenly arrested by my own subordinates and brought back here as prisoner. They said it was by your orders." His voice rose. "By your orders! By your orders!"

Don Manuel started to laugh. Salazar drew back in alarm. The laughter spun around the room. Don Manuel slapped the desk with his hands. His eyes teared. And then as quickly as it had begun, the laughter ceased. Don Manuel pulled himself erect. He wiped his face with a kerchief, blew his nose, and surveyed Salazar from head to foot. "Por Dios," he said at last, "but you are an ugly man!"

"Excelencia," Salazar said weakly.

"Remove the manacles," Don Manuel said. He signaled to the guards to leave the room. "Sit down, Don Damasio, you have had a difficult time."

Salazar sat on the edge of the chair and rubbed his chafed wrists. He straightened his disheveled uniform. "Was there a mistake, excelencia?"

Don Manuel began to chuckle again. "Yes, there was a mistake. There was a great mistake."

"Is it comical, excelencia?"

"It is very comical."

"Would your excellency explain it to me?"

Don Manuel shook his head. "No, I do not believe it is a type

387

of humor you would understand. It is a private joke between Don Esquipulas Caballero and me."

"He is out of New Mexico now. He has escaped us."

"That is part of the joke," Don Manuel said.

Salazar pushed back his long hair. "Whatever this joke is, excelencia, it has served to disgrace me."

"That is true," Don Manuel said wryly. "And that is another corner of the joke. But do not worry; I will announce that this mistake was made and but for that you would have been successful."

"And I would have, excelencia," Salazar said vehemently.

"This follower of Caballero that you put your hands on in Taos—what else did he tell you? Did he say who sheltered Don Esquipulas? Who attended his wound?"

"Once I learned that the bird had flown with the woman, excelencia, and the direction of the flight, I took up pursuit. I did not stay to question the man more."

"That was right. Where is he now? We may still learn things from him." He rubbed his hands together.

"The man has died, excelencia," Salazar said miserably.

A terrible light appeared in the Governor's eyes and then vanished. "You have many qualities, Don Damasio," he said very quietly. "Unfortunately, restraint is not one of them."

"He was a stubborn man, excelencia. Extreme measures were necessary."

"They are always stubborn," Don Manuel said, "but never so much as when they are dead."

He dismissed Salazar, ordered his carriage, and told the driver to take him to the Caballero house. The afternoon was gray and cold.

2

"Suffering becomes you, Doña Soledad," he said.

"Does it, excelencia?"

"Before, your face had beauty and pride, and now to that something else has been given."

"You may take satisfaction in that, excelencia, since it was you who gave it."

He stood by the fire. "It was kind of you to receive me."

"It has become a folk custom not to deny the door to Don Manuel Armijo."

"I thought to bring you news of Don Esquipulas and to tell you a joke." He waited for her face to change expression. They were inhuman in their pride, he thought. "You do not ask whether your husband is alive or dead, señora."

"He is not dead."

"How do you know that?"

"You would be unable to hide your triumph, excelencia."

He stared into the fire. "He has escaped to Bent's Fort."

"And that is a place that does not respond to your excellency's commands." Her voice rose. "He has defeated you."

"I have defeated myself, Doña Soledad. That is the joke." He faced her with a curious smile. "Your husband is free because of my orders."

"I am certain of that, excelencia."

"It is true. But for me he would be back in his cell, or perhaps dead. It is very funny."

"Tell me your joke, excelencia. It is long since I have laughed."

"When Don Esquipulas and Baca were abducted from Major Salazar, I threatened him with serious punishment. Then I gave to him a second chance and sent him out to recapture the prisoners. It occurred to me that he might try to escape from the country and I gave a secret order to his next in command to arrest him if it appeared he had that in mind. It was almost on the north border that he finally got within sight of your husband and he would have caught up with him the next day."

"Only he was arrested!"

"He was made prisoner and returned to me. It struck me as very comical, señora. Do you believe you can laugh?"

"I am laughing, excelencia. It is a pity that the widow Baca cannot share the laughter with us."

"How did you know Baca was dead?" he asked quickly.

"I knew that Don Ramón was killed and that my husband lived."

"How did you find that out? Who came and told you?"

She looked at him mockingly. "Does your excellency intend to put me to the question? No? Then your excellency will never know, at least not from me." She looked at her hands. "How long do you believe I would hold out, excelencia? To the third finger, perhaps, or only to the second?"

He started, and turned away his face.

"I believe I could keep silent for at least three fingers," she said decisively.

"Stop," he said in a dull voice.

"Incidentally, how long do you believe you yourself could hold out? Certainly you could never equal the record set by Don Ramón. That was a singular achievement, was it not? All the fingers of both hands, and the interesting game with the teeth. How many teeth were involved, excelencia?"

"I did not inquire."

She raised her brows. "Did you not? I should have thought you would have needed to know, to the last tooth. Of course you cannot hang teeth the way you hang ears." She smiled bitterly. "But no matter, it was quite a demonstration."

"Baca was a fool!" He clenched his fists.

"You might call it that. Others might use a different word."

"He was a traitor and a fool."

"And he defeated you as well. Do not forget that. It must give you something to think about, to be defeated twice in such rapid succession, and by two men who belong to a class your excellency has persuaded himself capable of defeating nothing."

"Two men," he said with contempt. "Believe me, señora, they mean very little."

"What is the saying? 'Muchos pocos hacen un mucho.'"

"These littles will never make a much. The one is dead and the other occupies himself with a mestiza whore."

"I beg your pardon, excelencia."

He grinned savagely. "You were not informed of that, were you?"

"I do not know what your excellency is talking about."

"Then I will tell you, and gladly. Your husband was wounded when he was snatched from the squad of execution."

"Yes, he was shot by this incomparable Salazar, the same who killed Don Ramón. And both men fettered."

Don Manuel's eyes sparkled malevolently. "But what you did not hear, Doña Soledad, was that your husband was brought to Taos and that he was taken in by this whore whom he had known before and that when he went north he took her with him."

She looked at him pityingly. "You become obvious, excelencia."

"It is true!"

"It proves nothing. If he did so, he had good reason."

"There can be but a single reason."

"I will wait to hear from his own lips what that reason is." She walked to the sideboard. "What may I pour for you?"

When he spoke again, his voice was as unruffled as hers. "You have faith in the integrity of your husband."

"Yes, excelencia. Your preference, for favor."

"Some brandy."

She handed him the goblet. "It is the drink for heroes."

"On what do you base this sublime trust in your husband?" he asked, walking back to the fire.

She sat down and held her own glass in both hands. It was some time before she replied. "I was instructed by my father from the very beginning in the recognition of honor," she said.

He nodded meditatively. "Honor."

"A human attribute that once was widespread, excelencia."

The room now was quite dark. The parts of Don Manuel's face that did not reflect the fire merged into the murkiness. The light made formless hollows of his eyes.

"And you consider Don Esquipulas possesses this rare quality?" he asked.

"As my father possessed it, excelencia."

He poured himself another drink and drank it down; then he splashed more brandy into the goblet. She had delivered herself to him and he knew that soon he would say what he had to say.

"Do you believe that I love you?" he asked.

"Yes, excelencia."

"It has no meaning for you?"

"Not as you comprehend meaning, excelencia. I am in love with my husband."

"The man of truth and honor."

"Yes, excelencia, and of pride and dignity."

"All of the virtues."

"Enough of them, at least, for me."

"Are there other reasons?"

"None other are necessary, but there are some."

"And what are they?"

"You bear the smell of death on you."

His lips thinned. "It surprises me that you are affected unpleasantly by that odor, Doña Soledad. The true Spanish blood has an affection for the dark angel."

She raised her face slowly. "There are different kinds of death, excelencia, and each gives out its own scent," she explained with withering patience. "There are deaths that walk with the probities and whose perfume can set fires in men's hearts. But there also are deaths that are kin to cowardice and dishonor and they stink to the highest heaven and surround one who has involved himself with them so that he smells like a dog who has rolled in the flesh of a skunk." She stood up and walked toward him, frozen with remorseless regality. He seemed to retreat as she approached and yet he did not move. "Death! Death! It is everywhere about you. It is the odor of Armijo."

"It is the burden of my office!"

"Will you explain that to the widow of Don Ramón? I doubt that she would hear, excelencia. Words do not penetrate to her easily now. She is in a merciful world of her own. But perhaps you could command her to listen to you and understand."

"Baca was a traitor. He deserved his death."

"Will you go to the grave of Don José Caballero and tell the ghost of that gentle old man whose unique sin was that he believed you to be a man of honor that he too was a traitor and deserved his death?"

"The old fool was a sot, consumed by alcohol."

"And where does my husband fit, excelencia? Is he a traitor or is he only a drunk or is he something else altogether, a category invented by you for him alone?"

It is the time, he thought. "Yes, Doña Soledad, it is all death and there is more death than you know."

"My husband is dead, then, and all this has been but your manner of revealing it to me?" she asked quietly.

And believing it could be that, he thought, she was able to hold it to no more than that, the still voice and the bleakness in the eyes. "I regret I cannot say it is so. It was not to Don Esquipulas I referred. I was speaking of the death of your father and of his two brothers."

"They are long dead."

"With the help of your husband."

They regarded each other in silence in the dark room and he thought briefly and with terror that she would be able to refuse the words and then he saw the dying begin.

"What are you saying, excelencia?"

"Only that your husband had his hands in those deaths."

"My father and uncles were killed by Indians."

"After an insurrection that was made successful only because the Indians were armed with the newest muskets. And the muskets were brought to the Indians by Don Esquipulas, and when Pérez and your father and the others tried to defend themselves on the mesa at San Ildefonso, the Indians were directed in their firing by this same man of truth and honor. If your father was not killed on the spot it was not because Don Esquipulas did not try to do it."

"You lie."

"You know I do not. I myself supplied the muskets that Don Esquipulas brought to the mestizo Gonzales."

"You lie, excelencia."

"Don Esquipulas delivered the muskets to Padre Martínez in Taos under instructions from his father, the saintly Don José, the gentle old man of whom you spoke," he continued without relenting. "Those muskets were given by the priest to Gonzales and the other insurrectos, and Don Esquipulas remained with the Indian and showed him how to lay the ambush that routed Albino Pérez and permitted the Indian to march unchecked to Santa Fe and do what was thereafter done."

The dying was more than half over. His voice took on a kind of desolation. "Did he tell you none of this?" he asked, knowing that the code would not have permitted it. "When you returned from the City of Mexico, bewildered at what had occurred, did he not explain the reason to you? Or was marrying you with your

393

father's blood on his hands explanation enough? And what of the smell then, señora? Did you detect it mixed with the sweat of your bodies. Which of the smells of death was in the air as you lay side by side in the dark hours? Your lips have known all of him. What of the smell?"

Now she raised her dead eyes. "Are you done, excelencia?"

"Do you believe what I have told you?"

"Yes."

"All of it? Your husband and his father and his servant?"

"Even Fernando," she whispered.

"All of them, all of them, in conspiracy hidden from you for years by these men of probity."

"I believe," she said, her voice barely supporting her words. "But in believing I also must believe that you yourself were chiefly responsible for the slaying of my father. If Don Esquipulas was involved, it was because of you."

"I was responsible, señora."

"And how should that endear you to me, excelencia?"

"I was gambling for a country. It was unfortunate your father was set in my path. I do not apologize for my part in his death."

"And why have you waited until now, until just now, to tell me all this?"

"It is the time, Doña Soledad. There is a time for all things and it was the time for this. I had an exit arranged for Don Esquipulas. It failed through error. But there was another way to remove him from you."

"You did not fail the second time, excelencia. You should be content. You have reached into space and you have plunged your dagger."

His hand reached out to her. She shrank back. And then as though this act of flinching touched something within her which had not yet been touched, she stopped it and drew herself erect. "Once before, excelencia, I told you I was beholden to you. Again I say it. A thousand thanks for this information you have brought to me. It was long coming. Your diligence must not go unrewarded. You may come with me." She walked past him, her head elevated, her eyes fixed straight before her. She led him to her bedroom and turned and faced him. "Does it pleasure you to watch your women undress, excelencia, or does it pleasure you more to do it for them?" she asked. "Or would you prefer again to tear off my chemise?"

He stared at her speechlessly.

"What is your pleasure, excelencia?" she asked docilely. "What is your custom at these times? If it is the tearing off of the chemise that pleasures you most, you may tear mine."

She waited patiently. He continued in stupefied silence, making no move to come nearer to her. She shrugged, removed her clothing, and dropped it at her feet. "I await your orders, excelencia." She regarded him placidly. "That which you have sought for so long now is available. Why then do you hesitate?"

He uttered a low, choked animal sound and seized her and kissed her wildly. She remained passive, her arms dangling limply at her sides. "You will weary yourself unnecessarily standing up, excelencia," she admonished sympathetically. "Would you not prefer to enjoy me in comfort in bed?" He pressed his burning cheek to her breast. She said: "Give me your commands, excelencia."

"You are the one to give commands," he said hoarsely.

"Not I, excelencia," she protested mildly. "With your permission, I am here only to serve your excellency."

"To you I would submit."

"Because I am your duchess?" she inquired.

"Command me!"

She looked shocked. "I have no such authority, excelencia."

"Tell me what you want me to do," he beseeched.

"But that is impossible, excelencia," she explained. "I am one of your subjects, no different from other women who exist but to attend to the pleasures of your excellency."

"Soledad!"

"Please tell me what gives you the most intense satisfaction. I will do my utmost to effect it. With permission."

He fell to his knees and kissed her bare foot. "I am your slave, mi duquesa."

"With permission, you are in error, excelencia. You are no slave. You are the Governor."

"Not to you." He kissed the sole of her foot.

"You are extravagant, excelencia."

"Make your demands upon me."

"I have no demands."

"I kiss the ground on which you walk."

"You have told me that before," she reminded him. "And there is no need for such impassioned entreaty. I do not require wooing, excelencia. With your permission, I am won." She stepped away from him and walked to the bed. She lay down. "I am wholly at the disposition of your excellency." She smiled amiably. "Before you begin, excelencia, tell me only this: now that you see me, am I different in any way from the others?"

"Soledad, por el amor de Dios!"

"Pardon, excelencia," she said humbly. "I shall be silent until you are done with me." He fell upon her and presently she asked: "What is the matter with your excellency? Have there been too many others and too recently?"

He looked down upon her and knew now she had always understood with terrible clarity that which he had sought in her, that which had disjoined her for him and had isolated her, and with this new, sickening vision he realized that from the start she had deftly and surely withheld it from him so that now, offering everything, she offered nothing.

"Would your excellency like to rest a little? Or perhaps return another time?" she asked. "I will consider it a debt to be paid."

He saw the quiet amusement in her eyes and he was possessed of hysterical frenzy to defeat her purpose. He labored again, but the new perception had further reduced him and he moved away and stood up. He picked up his dagger and looked morbidly at her.

She raised herself on her elbow, and the amusement spread to her whole face. "You make a heroic picture, excelencia. On what would you use the steel? On myself or the evidence of your impotence?"

He sat down slowly on the edge of the bed, moving as though drugged, and raised the point of the knife over her heart.

She laughed. "You no longer are amusing, excelencia. Nor do you fill me with fear." She pushed aside the knife. "You begin to bore me. Go, excelencia, the evening is still new. You have the time to find yourself some whore who may be able to persuade you that you are yet a man."

He continued to sit and stare at her with glazed eyes from which all will was gone. Her words penetrating finally, he sheathed the blade as though he were under compulsion to obey and he stood up as dutiful as a child and limped to the door.

He heard her say with deadly stillness: "Capon!"

3

"Is it useless to try to dissuade you from returning to Santa Fe?" Fernando asked.

"It is useless," Caballero said. "Say no more. I go."

"We both know what Doña Soledad must have found out at last," Fernando said. "What need is there to go?"

"I must hear it from her."

"Then let me go with you."

"That would but double the risk. I go alone."

Fernando looked at him piercingly. "Go if you must. But I ask one thing of you, Esquipulas. Whatever you learn from Doña Soledad you must attempt no reprisal against Armijo."

"I make no promise," Caballero said coldly.

Fernando seized his wrist. His broad face darkened with anger. "You will promise! He is surrounded at all times by an army of guards. You would not kill him and you would yourself be slain."

"Remove your hand, Fernando."

"Do not use that tone with me. There no longer is master and servant between us."

"I did not mean that. Release me."

Fernando took him by the arms and shook him violently. "You will promise first."

"Nombre de Dios, I make no promise!" Caballero blazed. He pushed Fernando away. Morena crouched in a corner of the little room in the residential quarter of the fort.

"You will not waste yourself," Fernando said with deep passion. "Your life no longer belongs to you alone. Too many men have risked their own lives to save it, and three men have died. They who still live have given up everything—their families, their houses, even their country—to keep blood flowing in your body.

Your life belongs to them as much as it does to you, and you will not squander it." He raised his great fist. "And if you kill Armijo it is even worse than if you fail and get yourself killed."

"What the devil do you mean by that?"

"He must not be murdered for private revenge. Not even by you. His life is too precious for that. You will not make a martyr of him." His hands dropped to his sides. His face twisted with pleading. "You must understand what I am trying to say to you. This filth must not be presented with nobility. It is not Armijo, it is the idea of Armijo that must be destroyed. He must be discredited while he is alive and vulnerable. Men must rise and stand against him, and it must be done against a man. It never can be done against a memory. The instant he is dead by your bullet, Manuel Armijo becomes a saint. You will promise me not to give him that or I will break your bones myself!"

Caballero pulled Fernando's head toward him and pressed it against his breast. "You have my promise."

4

THE MULE TRAIN loaded with peltries from Charles Bent arrived in Santa Fe late in the afternoon and was brought to the government warehouse, where the value of the consignment would be assessed and it would be determined how many of the skins would be paid to the government of New Mexico in legal impost, how many others would be given as presents to the customs officials for their helpfulness, and how many would be set aside for Don Manuel for his kindness in permitting the trappers employed by Bent to operate in New Mexican territory. Weary from their tedious journey and smelling strongly of their recent charges, both living and dead, the muleteers, free until the next morning, when the return trip would start, took off immediately for the pleasures that awaited them.

Caballero, who wore the long drooping mustache of a muleteer and the rest of whose face was covered with two weeks' growth of beard, pulled the wide brim of his sombrero low on his forehead and left the warehouse with the other men. He found a small, low-class tavern and ate frijoles and tortillas and washed down the food with cheap wine, and then he dawdled over other glasses until it was well into the evening. He refused the blandishments of a whore and bought her a glass of wine. After ten o'clock he left the place and strolled idly through the city, making a wide, unhurried circuit so that he approached his house from the rear. He slipped into a narrow alley, remembering how when he was a child he had used this means of getting into the house unobserved when he had stayed out later than his father permitted, and climbed over the patio wall.

The house was in darkness. He crossed the patio and entered the sala. There he paused, but he heard nothing and walked slowly down the corridor to his wife's room. He crossed the threshold and went to the bed. In the pale light coming through the windows he could see her lying asleep, her face turned away from him. He struck flint and looked around until he saw a tallow, which he lit. She stirred and her lips parted and he gazed silently at her for a few moments and then whispered: "Soledad."

An expression of fear crossed her sleeping face. He repeated her name and she stirred again and opened her eyes, and he lifted the lamp so she could see his face. She sat up and opened her eyes wide, and the pupils dilated and the expression of fear disappeared and was replaced by something else.

"How did you get here?" she asked.

He set the lamp on a small table next to the bed. "I came with a train of mules." He searched her face. It was awake now and in her possession. Nothing in it had changed, and it was the face of a stranger. "Señor Bent gave me the message you gave to his agent," he said. "I wanted to hear the same words from you."

She drew the cover up to her neck. There was still winter in the night, and the room was without heat. The act was not unnatural, yet he understood its truer meaning.

Her eyes were flat and lifeless. "If Señor Bent told you I considered my husband as dead, then he repeated my words with accuracy, señor, and you have endangered yourself needlessly."

"I did not doubt he relayed your words without mistake."

"If you did not, then you must also have understood the reason for them."

He nodded. "I believe I did, Doña Soledad."

Her face contorted. "Don Manuel has revealed your secret!"

"And what has Don Manuel told you?"

"About my father and how he was killed."

"It is in the open at last," he said quietly.

"It is true, is it not?"

"It is true, señora."

"All of it? You delivering the muskets and then serving the stinking Indian at San Ildefonso?"

"All of it."

She held the cover against her chin. "And you had neither manhood nor truth to tell me, nor belief in me to believe I could be made to understand?"

"None."

"Instead you married me with the disease in your heart."

"Would you have understood?" he asked.

She was silent for a moment and then her lips pulled down and her voice trembled with disgust. "No, you are right, the original crime would have sufficed. But the second was boon companion. They march together, hand in hand, and I do not have to judge which was worse!"

"I am happy that you know." He gripped the brim of his hat. "It is a strange thing, but I feel for the first time since the death of your father that there is true peace between us. The disease has been destroyed. It is a pity that all else has been destroyed with it. There was this concealed thing with us from the beginning, and if one believes in the justice of God, then all that has happened to us since then grew from that, from the first doing of wrong and from the silence that compounded it. I will tell you only this: when I served Don Manuel I believed I was doing right. When I carried out his orders, there was no plan to kill your father or his brothers or even Pérez. My own father would not have subscribed to that. Now it seems foolish beyond all reason not to have realized it could have worked out no other way." He held out his hands. "Tonight you have wiped these clean."

Her head moved slowly from side to side. "Your words are late and without meaning for me and useless," she said bitterly. "Go, coward, I hate your person." Her eyes filled with horror.

"Do you?" he asked.

He disappeared in the darkness.

1

CABALLERO pushed away his plate and sat back from the table.

Morena looked at the dish unhappily. "But you have only tasted it!" She held out her hands. Fernando shrugged.

"I have had enough, thanks," Caballero said.

She leaned toward him, her hands on her hips. "What do you exist on these days? You do not eat enough to fill the belly of a small bird! You waste to a stick!"

Caballero smiled. "Only compared with yourself, little mother."

She looked at her swelling belly and blushed and moved closer to Fernando, who put his arm around her. Fernando touched the belly with his finger. "Has he been beating the drum lately?"

The blush deepened, and she pulled away. "Virgen santísima! You are no better than he! And what makes you believe so surely it will be a son?"

"It is the way it should be," Fernando said. "First the son, then the daughter. But it matters little. Either will be acceptable and there is time for more."

She tossed her head. "*Toma! Vaya!* Listen to the man boast." She removed Caballero's plate from the table. "It is this meat from the cow that is given out in this gringo place. How can one make stew that may be eaten from beef flesh? Beef is for Americans. Here there are two brave men in my household. If only one of them would bring me some decent meat from sheep, I could make a stew that even this sorrowing one would eat."

"The stew is delicious, chula," Caballero said. "It is not that."

"You think too much. A small amount is useful, but too much interferes with the digestion." She would have said more, but the suffering on Caballero's face stopped her.

She cleared the table. Fernando watched her devotedly. Soon

401

after their arrival at Bent's Fort they had been married by a French priest. Morena was still only partly convinced they were man and wife. She would not believe it wholly until the ceremony was performed again by a priest she could understand.

Caballero stood up. He said he would stretch his legs outside.

"I think you had better make up your mind about the Texans, hombre," Fernando said. "Soon there will be no mind in you to make up."

Caballero left the little room that had been assigned to Fernando and Morena by Charles Bent. He breathed deeply of the cool, spring night air. He walked slowly across the broad clearing in the center of the fort, which could contain a hundred wagons and which now was empty. He could hear murmurings of talk, laughter, a song being sung, from the rooms that lined the inside of the fort walls.

The noise from the bar was somewhat louder, but even that was lost in the black emptiness. He tried not to think of her. The fort was a place for loneliness, and when it got too bad there was nothing to take it away.

When he had come back from Santa Fe he had told himself that now the lie was dead between them, the wall was razed, that he would never again lie awake in the night and listen to her breathing and wonder how it would be if she found out and despise himself for not having the strength to tell her. He had thought that one day they might begin again, in honesty. He still thought it could be that way and it gave him a portion of peace until he remembered that he was an exile and she many miles away and that there was no communion between them and that nothing was being begun.

He walked to one corner of the fort and climbed up the ladder to the parapet. There he identified himself to the sentry. He walked down the parapet, leaned against a musket vent, and looked out. Below him were the tents of the Indians camped outside the fort. Small cook fires twinkled in the area and he saw the Indians and their women moving about. The night was silent and clear and the fort was the end of the world.

It now was almost five months since he had come wounded to Bent's Fort and with his companions had been taken in without question, and he still marveled at the size and complexity of the isolated bastion and at the force and imagination and driving will that made it possible. It was more than a fort, he thought; it was a walled city, a microcosm of alien civilization. It was the frontier of the United States, dragged piece by piece over half a thousand miles of plain and mountain.

Once the Spaniards could do that. They carried Spain and the cross with them where they went, and where they halted became a piece of Spain in defiance of all who tried to stop them, and when they moved they left Spain forever behind them. The Spaniards no longer could do that. Their time had passed and somewhere in the passing those who had followed them had lost it.

But was that true? Had his people no more of the old indomitable spirit than the sheep they tended on the hillsides? It was true in New Mexico, but did that mean it had gone from the people? Had the blood of the conquerors diluted so much in its course through the centuries that it now was content to meander placidly in the present vessels? Or perhaps was it more accurate to believe that it was the climate that no longer was there?

He felt excitement rising in him. It was a new idea and he wanted it clear. He remembered listening after dinner one evening to the legendary American scout Kit Carson, who was married to the sister of Charles Bent's Mexican wife and who had been employed as hunter for the fort. "It does not surprise me that a man like Manuel Armijo can be the unchallenged dictator of New Mexico," Carson had said in his soft voice. "The world is growing up around you, but New Mexico does not change. It does not even reflect Spain. It reflects a medieval Spain that even the Spaniards have rejected. The New Mexicans have been cut off from time. Their ideas are the same ideas that were brought over centuries ago by the conquistadores and the priests who came with them." He had smiled disarmingly. "Do not be offended, Señor Caballero. I speak because of the love I have for your people and an unhappiness to see them so misused."

As Caballero had slowly recovered from his wound he discovered that the men who had come with him from New Mexico had found places for themselves in the intricate operation of the fur trade at the fort. Fernando, with his proficiency with the lazo, had been engaged as a vaquero for the cattle kept in the corral outside the west wall. Carlos Gutiérrez worked as a trapper. Other men had joined the guards. One or two who could speak Indian dialects were serving as traders. A man who had joined them in Taos labored in the blacksmith shop. Morena helped in the kitchen. Each person was accepted and respected in direct proportion to his demonstrated capabilities. Fernando rapidly achieved a kind of celebrity for his marvelous dexterity with the rope.

Of them all, Caballero realized, he alone had not proved himself. Men who in his own country were of a class lower than himself were held in higher esteem than he was. No one was unfriendly to him. It was only that as yet no one had a basis on which to judge him. His name and his family meant nothing. As soon as his health permitted he asked Bent to assign him to military duties with the guards who were kept on duty around the clock. Bent, who knew of his experience, appointed him a lieutenant, and he satisfied the sentries that he was a trained officer who knew his business and thereafter he was respected at least as much as the majority of his men. He was not held in as much admiration as was Fernando and he could never reach the status of Carlos because the trappers were in a class by themselves. Caballero was surprised to discover that this did not annoy him.

As the weeks passed he observed a gradual change in his men. It was so subtle and it took a direction so outside his experience that for a long time he could not analyze it, and then he came to realize that his companions simply were ceasing to have those qualities which he had always believed were inherent in his people and irremovable from them, and were becoming more and more like the men around them. At first their language limitation segregated them, but by degrees, in the intoxicating freedom around them, they picked up words and phrases in English, and from the Canadian and French trappers they learned a little French, and soon their broken English mingled with all the other accents and dialects, French, Irish, Scotch, and the different and confusing American intonations that caused an American from New England to sound as though he were speaking a different language from an American from Georgia or Virginia.

But it was more than their speech alone. Their natures were undergoing profound change. The men were shedding the characteristics and habits of a lifetime as they might peel off layers of skin. They developed new assurances, a new respect for themselves as men. They discovered new traits in themselves, new skills, new humors. It was as though they had stepped forth from cocoons and were drying and developing their limbs in the exhilarating air. They still considered Caballero their leader, but he sensed that his leadership itself had sustained a change as deep as the change in the men themselves: he was their leader only because they had chosen him as such.

They achieved, and this amazed Caballero perhaps more than anything else, a new kind of dignity that protected them from the attitudes they had been led into before by the unyielding dignity he had believed to be the last thing any man of Mexican blood would surrender. He had a vivid example of it one night when he and Fernando were seated at a table in the saloon and one of the New Mexicans was standing at the bar drinking with a bearded hunter. The two men at the bar were talking about something when Caballero suddenly heard the hunter shout: "You're crazy, you dago greaseball!"

Caballero moved immediately to prevent what he believed would be an inevitable knife fight. Fernando pulled him down. The Mexican at the bar, instead of reaching for his blade, punched the hunter in the chest and yelled back: "Who you calling 'greaseball,' you Irish bastard!"

Caballero listened and watched with stupefaction. Fernando laughed. "Those two men fought off a dozen Indians for five hours a week ago. Do not worry about them."

"But they insulted each other," Caballero said.

"As friends insult each other. With friends, insults are a sign of friendship. It is something they have learned from the gringos."

"There is a great deal to learn from these gringos," Caballero said slowly, watching the two men at the bar toast each other with refilled glasses of whisky. "In Santa Fe there would be a dead man on the floor now."

"It is another thing they have learned," Fernando said. "When a man knows he is brave he does not have to kill to prove it."

Standing now on the parapet in the brilliant night he knew there could be no such emancipation for New Mexicans under Manuel Armijo. The existence of the dictator was predicated on the denial of personal liberty. And yet there were three more years

405

to Armijo's term, and when this term was ended, it would be followed without question by another and another. Armijo would go on forever. He was stronger and more entrenched than the central government from which he theoretically derived his power. In the two decades since the Revolution only one President of Mexico had lasted out his full term of office. Only one President of Mexico had reached office without an insurrection against his predecessor and the killing of men. Presidents came and went in the City of Mexico with each shift in the wind. Compared with the central government, the government of New Mexico was a mountain of stability.

In time Armijo might be driven out. But would that be enough? Would there not always be someone put into his place who would be Armijo with another name? The struggle between liberal Federalism and dictatorial Centralism was a bloody and endless thing in the capital of the nation, but no matter how much the opposing forces there disagreed on everything else, they concurred on one thing: because of its geographical position it was necessary that New Mexico be ruled by a strong man.

He felt a sudden chill. His thoughts had led him to the edge of a precipice and he was dizzied as he looked down into the dark depth. For logic now required that he ask himself the most terrifying question of all: could New Mexico ever hope for lasting and true freedom as part of Mexico?

He covered his eyes to shut off this staggering vision. He wanted to retreat from the precipice and return to safer ground. A revolution against Armijo was a big thought, but how small it was next to the thought of revolution against Mexico itself! He looked around in fright, certain that everything must have changed in the explosion of the thought. But nothing was different. The night was cold and still and bright, and the guards paced slowly on the parapet, and below him the Indians crouched over their fires. Nothing was different and yet he knew he had crossed a line and never would be able to cross it back.

He had never forgotten words spoken quietly on dark nights by men from Texas who seemed, while defeated and prisoners, to be more than men, and now by another route, his own, he had been led to friends of these men now gathered again on the border of his country. He had gone beyond Ramón Baca. He understood what the people of Texas had understood and what the Indian, José Gonzales, had grasped in the fevers of his mystic illumination. And he understood for the first time why Manuel Armijo had been unable to rest until Gonzales was put to death before his eyes. Gonzales had more than soldiers: he had an idea.

2

CABALLERO called together the twenty-nine of his followers who were at the fort. He looked at them with pride. "Hombres, this gringo place has been good for you," he said. "You all look good. You all are better men than you were six months ago. The gringos do not think of you as Mexicans. They think of you as hunters and trappers and soldiers and Indian-fighters and clerks and traders, the way they think of everybody else up here. Nobody is French or Mexican or American or anything else except what he does. It is a good way to live.

"You are content. You work hard. You eat well. There is enough liquor. Some of you have found Indian women. The life up here has become your life and it is hard to remember how it was before. It is hard to realize that back in New Mexico people work only to make Armijo fatter and richer. Up here you can tell any man to go to hell, and if you fight, it is just between the two of you and who is stronger wins and that is the end of it. That is how men should live. There is nobody up here with wooden splinters to stick into your fingernails, and when someone comes to your door at night it is probably just a friend who has drunk too much and not soldiers to drag you to prison. You have learned here how you can work together with men from different countries, with different religions, one man as good as the next and one religion as good as the next, and it is hard to remember that in our country men only obey Armijo and are taught that all who are not Catholics are heretics and all who are not Mexicans are enemies.

"Now, all this may be good enough for you. If you believe that, I do not blame you. You have found your way out of the woods. You have risked your lives for Ramón Baca and for me.

Three of you are dead. You do not have to do anything else. But it is not enough for me. I cannot forget that while we enjoy this sweet freedom, those in New Mexico have no freedom. I want to do something about it. I am going back to New Mexico."

He looked at their faces. If there was surprise at his announcement, he could not see it. The men listened in silence.

"The Texans are in arms against Armijo, looking to avenge their countrymen," he continued. "They cry for the blood of Armijo and Salazar. The Texans have different reasons for fighting the battle, but it is the same battle. I would join my hand with the hands of the enemies of my enemies." He paused again. He said in a low voice: "I know this has the sound of treason. It *is* treason, hombres. The motherland has failed us. It has failed us in forcing Armijo upon us. It has failed us in giving no protection against wild Indians. It has failed us in the hunger and the sickness of our people. I shall be called traitor. But I am charged with treason now, so the label is an old one. It is different with you. You can stay here as long as you like and even return home and no one will know what you have done. You must think of that.

"Señores, liberty must come from the outside. Don Ramón Baca did not know that and he paid for his lack of knowledge. I believe our hopes are with the Texans who proved that freedom could be won. I go to join them."

He looked again at each face as though to seal it within him.

"That is all I have to say. I have thanked you before for my life and I thank you again. I will bear no resentment against those who choose to remain here. Perhaps that is the wiser thing. If any of you return with me you may have to fight your brothers. I will take as many as desire to come. I leave at sunrise on the day following tomorrow."

When he rode up to the main gate of the fort he counted twenty-two of the men waiting for him with Fernando at their head. His throat filled. A bugle call cut through the still air. The gate was swung open. He raised himself in his stirrups. "Hombres, let us go to our country," he said.

3

They crossed Raton Pass, where the winter snows were yielding to the new spring, and they cut away from the old trail and headed south toward Las Vegas, following the course of the Canadian River on the Cimarron Branch of the Santa Fe Trail east of the Cimarron Mountains.

It was a time for action. The country was ridding itself of winter. The air had the smell of spring, and the mountains were just beyond the reach of a man's arm. The Canadian rode high with its cold draughts of melted snow. A twig that fell into the churning stream might be carried a thousand miles down New Mexico, across Texas, across Indian Territory, into the Arkansas River. It might drift down the Arkansas into the Mississippi and float finally into the great gulf.

The months they had been away were as years. They looked at the yucca from which spears were beginning to emerge and at the aspen with the new leaves already quivering in the smallest air and at the lupine and the columbine. The mountains, which sprawled like sleeping animals, and the long valleys with the early shadows, and the sky with no stain filled their eyes, and when they spoke there was excitement in their voices. This was the land they had named for memories and for saints and for how it looked. No matter how much they had taken on the ways of the gringos, Caballero thought, they had not lost this. This was theirs, and everywhere else they were visitors.

At the confluence of the Canadian and the Ocate they met some buffalo-hunters, and the ciboleros told them they had seen a band of Texans traveling west along the Mora River, which ran roughly in the same direction as the Ocate and about a day's ride to the south. Caballero reckoned the Texans probably were going to the frontier settlement of Mora, which would be one of the good bases for an envelopment of Santa Fe.

They saw smoke as they entered Mora, and above the sound of their horses' hoofs they heard the wailing of women. They drew up in the little plaza. The square was deserted. Buildings were smoldering. Dead men lay on the ground. The crying women were not to be seen and their lamentations seemed to come from the earth. Caballero shouted: "Hola! Hola! Where are the people of Mora?" His shout was followed by silence except for the snapping of flames. He looked wonderingly at Fernando. "Hola!" he shouted again. "Hola!"

Fernando raised his deep voice. "We are New Mexicans!"

From doorways and from behind the walls of burning buildings men began to appear. They looked warily into the plaza. Their faces were blackened with sweat and smoke. Many were wounded. They carried staves and spears and bows and arrows, and one or two of them had old-fashioned muskets. They walked slowly to the plaza. Caballero dismounted. "What has happened here?"

A short, thin man whose head was covered with a bloodied rag asked: "Who are you?"

"We are your countrymen."

The man looked at the unfamiliar clothing worn by Caballero and the men and at the new Colt repeating percussion rifles they carried. "You do not look like New Mexicans."

"We are all countrymen," Caballero said. "What has happened here?"

The man tottered. Caballero caught him and held his canteen to his lips. The man drank thirstily. He wiped his mouth with the back of his hand. "It is as you see, señor," he said. "We were attacked."

"Indians?"

The man shook his head. "Texans."

"Texans!"

"They came without warning. They galloped through the plaza like insane men and they shot at men who were sitting and doing nothing and who were unarmed. There they lie where they fell. We tried to fight back, but it was useless. There are four muskets in Mora. The Texans threw burning brands into houses and then they opened the corral and took all the horses. They left Mora as you see it."

"How do you know they were Texans?" Caballero asked, a knot in his stomach.

"They were Anglos and they were commanded by a large man with a big mustache the color of gold, and before they left they shouted this was only a taste of what the people of this country would suffer for what was done to the prisoners taken by Governor Armijo."

Caballero turned away. The sickness filled him. Now the women and children of Mora were coming out of hiding. A small girl watched flies light on blood coming from her leg. Women recognized their dead and set up new howling. They covered their heads with their shawls and squatted at the sides of the dead and rocked back and forth. A priest appeared. Wounded men looked somberly at their wounds, and some of them lay down in pain.

Caballero remembered then that the village had been named for the river which the French always called L'Eau des Morts after trappers had found whitened bones of a massacred party. "How many Texans were there?" he asked.

"It was hard to tell, señor," the man said, "they raised such dust. I would guess no more than two dozen."

"And which direction did they take when they left?" he asked, though he knew. The man pointed east. Caballero climbed heavily into the saddle. He said: "We go after them."

4

FERNANDO pointed to the ground. "They make no attempt to cover their tracks."

"Why should they?" Caballero said bitterly. "They were confident no one could follow them."

Caballero rode on in silence, his face tight. The men were silent behind him. Late in the afternoon they saw droppings, and Fernando estimated the Texans had passed there six hours earlier. They rode into the evening and into the night. The trail led them north of the junction of the Mora and Sapello Rivers. At the first dawn Fernando lifted his head and sniffed. Caballero smelled it too, the smell of wood fires. He held up his hand and the men slowed up. They went up a slight rise, and on the far side of the rise they saw the camp of the Texans.

The men were still asleep around the campfires. A sentry, rifle cradled in his arm, moved from fire to fire and tossed a few pieces of wood into each. Then he walked to the west edge of the camp and, leaning on his gun, peered into the slowly dissolving darkness in front of him.

Caballero whispered a few words to Fernando. Fernando dismounted and handed the reins to Caballero. He uncoiled his lazo and shook it loose. Crouched low, he slowly worked his way down the hill toward the sentry. Caballero gave another order and the men unslung the new rifles that had been given to them by Charles Bent. Caballero leaned forward and followed Fernando with his eyes. The sentry was outlined clearly against the brightening eastern sky and Caballero knew he and his men were not visible in the darkness still around them. He saw Fernando rise and twirl the noose and cast it, and the loop fall on the neck of the sentry. At the same moment Fernando jerked the rope so powerfully the sentry's cry was choked off. The sentry dropped his rifle. It went off. The camp was instantly awake.

The chance of a surprise attack lost, Caballero gave the order to open fire immediately. Three of the Texans fell at the first shattering volley. Caballero waved his arm to the right and to the left and his men spread out and fired again. The Texans, unable to see anything but the flash of the guns, returned the fire, and then one of them tied a shirt to his rifle barrel and waved it in the air. Caballero ordered his men to hold fire. "Put down your guns, Texans!" he shouted in English.

The Texans dropped their rifles. Caballero led his men into the draw. He gave an order and three of his men jumped from their horses, disarmed the Texans, and gathered up the rifles.

Caballero dismounted. He walked to a red-faced, thick-necked man with a flowing yellow mustache. "Are you the leader?" he asked in English.

The man blinked bloodshot eyes. He jutted his lower lip and said: "I am Colonel Charles A. Warfield, of the Army of the Republic of Texas."

"*Colonel* Warfield," Caballero repeated. He looked at the Texans. "And do Texas regiments amount to only twenty men?"

"The rest of my soldiers are not far from here," Warfield said blusteringly. "The sound of the gunfire probably will bring them here in the next few minutes!"

Caballero considered him impassively. "Why do you not wear

uniforms?" He saw a look of fear appear in Warfield's eyes. Moving slowly among the men, he recognized among them a few of the prisoners from the march to El Paso del Norte and he had the sickness in him again. "There are no uniforms," he said. "You are not a colonel and these men are not soldiers. You are—you are—" He fumbled for the word in English.

"Bandits," Fernando said.

"Yes, bandits! Bandits!" He strode back to Warfield. "You are bandits and murderers. Why did you attack a peaceful village and kill innocent persons who have never harmed you?"

"Our countries are at war," Warfield said, trying to get the bluster back into his voice.

"That may be. Wars are fought between armies. Are there no enemy soldiers for you to shoot at in your war or are you afraid to attack men who can shoot back? Are you at war with farmers and their women and their children?"

"We are at war with New Mexico," Warfield said. "We have come to avenge Texans who were tortured and killed."

"They were tortured and they were killed, but not by the people of Mora. Not by any of the people. The people of Mora have never seen Texans. Your countrymen suffered, but from Armijo. From Manuel Armijo!"

"They are all the same. They are all Mexicans."

"You fool!" Caballero shook his head helplessly. "I cannot say it all in your language. Listen, fool. It was all done by order of Armijo. Can you understand that? And these people hate Armijo as much as you do. If you had come to them and told them you were going to war on Armijo, they would have welcomed you and given you shelter, and if you gave them weapons they would have followed you. Instead you ride on them like Apaches and kill five men and wound many others, even small children, and you steal horses and burn houses and you end by driving these people into the arms of Armijo. From now on, the people of Mora and everybody else who hears what you have done will hate Texans and will try to kill them when they see them." He lifted his fist. "Greatest of fools! I should kill you for nothing else than for the new friends you have made for Manuel Armijo!"

Warfield's mouth dropped. "I do not understand. Are you not all New Mexicans?"

"Yes, yes, we are New Mexicans! Madre María! If only I had the words in American to explain!" Caballero's face ran with sweat. "All of these men are New Mexicans. But we too are at war with Armijo. Do you know why we are here? We heard at Bent's Fort that a new army of Texans had come to fight Armijo and we came down to join you."

"There has been talk enough," Fernando said in Spanish. "Let us hang them from trees and be off. He may be speaking truth when he say there are others."

Several of the Texans started. One of them repeated the words in English to Warfield. "You have no right to hang us!" he cried.

Fernando shrugged. "Maybe you are right," he said in English. "Maybe we just shoot you the way you shot people in Mora."

"No," Caballero said, "we will neither hang nor shoot them."

"What are you saying?" Warfield demanded. "For the love of Christ speak English so I can understand you."

"I said we would not kill you," Caballero said.

"Why not?" Fernando asked.

"They surrendered and we accepted their surrender," Caballero answered. "We are not murderers."

"They deserve no consideration," said one of the New Mexicans.

"He is right," Fernando said.

"We will not kill them," Caballero said, "for the reason I have given and for another reason. If we put these men to death, the word will get back to other Texans and it will not be known why we killed them, only that we killed them. What they did in Mora will never reach their countrymen. All they will know is that more Texans were killed, and that will mean more vengeance. There are not enough of us to guard all the border. More innocent people would die and we would make more friends for Armijo and more enemies of those who should be our friends."

"What in Christ's name is he saying?" Warfield shouted.

"I am going to turn you all free," Caballero said to him. "You killed five of our people in Mora and you will leave eight of your own dead here. The score is even." He walked past Warfield and pointed to one and another of the Texans. "I know these faces. They were on the march to Mexico. I forgive them for the hatred they have for our people. For what they suffered they may have

414

hatred, even hatred so blind it makes them shoot children." He rubbed his face. "Dios santo! I can speak no more English. I am run out of words. Who among you understands my language?" One of the Texans stepped forward and Caballero hurried to him, put his hand on his shoulder, and looked at him with burning eyes. "Go back to your people, amigo. Tell them to come to us with an army to drive out Armijo. From one end of New Mexico to another you will find friends. Do you understand?"

"Yes, señor."

"Good, gracias á Dios! Tell your countrymen that people of New Mexico have grieved for that which was done to the Texan prisoners. Make it clear it was done not by the people but by Armijo, only Armijo! And when they understand that, tell them to come and deliver this country from the tyrant." He stepped back and held out his hand.

The Texan gripped it. "I will repeat your words, señor."

"Your face is not unknown to me. You were on the march?"

"I was, señor."

"Is it possible you would know of one called Fitzgerald?"

The man laughed. "Fitz? The red-haired Irishman? Of course I know him."

"My name is Caballero, señor. If you see Don Cornelio again, give him my friendship and tell him my eyes ache to look upon him again."

"I will do so, Señor Caballero, and gladly."

Caballero returned to Warfield. "You are free to go."

"Without guns? Through Indian country?"

Caballero said to Fernando: "Return half the rifles. Give three rounds for each gun." He turned back to Warfield. "You will go on foot. I do not trust you. Without horses you will not be able to attack any more villages, and during the long walk you will have time to think on what I have said to you. I will give your horses and the rest of your guns to the people of Mora."

"On foot!" Warfield sputtered. "Back to Texas!"

"You can go to Bent's Fort. Others have done it on foot."

"You're like all the rest of your damned breed!"

Caballero made a cigarette slowly. His fingers shook as he rolled the husk. When he spoke, it was almost in a whisper. "Señor, I have given good reasons why I will not kill you, but almost

415

do you make me reconsider to make one exception in your case. You stand next to death. Leave quickly before he takes you into his arms."

When they were gone, Fernando asked: "And now what do we do?"

Caballero sat down wearily on a stump. "I do not know."

1

Don Manuel held his hands against his ears, but he could not shut out the shouting from the plaza. "Why does some-one not stop them? Why do my soldiers not drive them away?"

Colonel Diego Archuleta removed his cigarette. "The plaza is a public place, excelencia."

Don Manuel took his hands from his ears and looked at Archuleta from red-rimmed eyes. "What do you say?"

"People have always gathered in the plaza, excelencia."

Don Manuel pounded the desk. "Honest people going about their business, yes! Not rioters! Listen to them. They are danger-ous!"

"They are frightened."

"They have no right to howl like madmen in front of the palace," Don Manuel shouted. His hands shook. "They shold be driven away."

"Soldiers would have to shoot half the people in Santa Fe to clear the plaza, excelencia."

"Let them! Let them! Kill them! Nombre de Dios, kill them! They are not honest citizens; they are insurrectos. Kill those who will not go, and drive the others away."

Archuleta mashed out the cigarette. "Is that an order, excelencia?"

"Yes! Yes! Order out the troops and clear the plaza!"

Archuleta gripped his sword, made a stiff military about-face, and marched toward the door.

Don Manuel bellowed: "No, no, come back! I revoke the order! They are my children! They are all my children! I cannot kill them!" He buried his face in his hands. "Madre de Dios, and what do they want of their poor Governor?"

Archuleta returned to his seat. He rolled another cigarette. "They are panic-stricken, excelencia. They have heard what happened in Mora. They hear that the enemy is marching on the country. They want you to take command of the troops and disperse the Texans."

Armijo raised his head. "They want! They want! Who are they to want? Who are they to give orders to Armijo?" He ran to a window and glared at the shouting mob being held back from the portal by a line of guards with joined muskets. "Do you hear me?" he roared against the bedlam. "Armijo gives the orders! The Governor commands!" The words were absorbed in the noise like drops of water in a sea. He leaned against the wall and covered his ears again. "Enough, enough," he said. "Silence yourself, my children. Go to your houses. Stop, por amor de Dios, and give your sick Governor rest." The rash on his back began to itch again and he attacked it with the fury of a dog scrabbling for fleas. "It is an easy thing for them to make demands. They are safe. They have nothing to fear. The Texans do not want to cut their hearts out. The Texans cry only for Armijo." He rushed back to the desk and slammed his fists on it. "They curse Armijo. The Texans do not scream for vengeance on Archuleta!"

Archuleta flicked the ash from his cigarette. "No, excelencia."

"Do you know that I was hanged in effigy in every town in Texas? Were you ever hanged in Texas, Don Diego?"

"I believe not, excelencia."

"The Texans do not even know of the name of Archuleta!"

Don Diego looked at the end of his cigarette. "If your excellency will give the order I will gladly take out the army and give battle to the Texans."

Armijo nodded violently. "Do so, Don Diego, do so! I give you complete command of the troops!" He dug his fingers into his back. Dios en cielo! The rash would drive him insane, and the old witch had sworn to Doña María Trinidad that the new ointment would put out the fire.

"Would your excellency be good enough to put that in writing?" Archuleta asked.

"Immediately, Don Diego, immediately. In writing. In the proper form." He sat down and scribbled the order and signed his name and rubric. He thrust the paper into Archuleta's hand.

The colonel read it carefully. "I will give the necessary orders, excelencia," he said tonelessly, "and leave within twenty-four hours."

Don Manuel jumped up and hugged him. "Splendid, coronel mío." He stepped back and rubbed his hands. "You will be the hero of the people. I will give you a medal. *Vaya con Dios*, Don Diego, and return to your Governor victorious!"

He watched the tall, square-shouldered colonel leave the office. Why had he concerned himself so needlessly? It was so simple. Then the smile froze on his face and he ran to the door. "Wait!" he shouted. "Come back, come back."

Archuleta returned to the office. "Does your excellency have further orders for me?"

Armijo stared knowingly at the colonel's face. It was like a slab of rock, he thought. It was like the side of a mountain. It was without human expression, without joy and without disappointment, without satisfaction and without anger. Jesús mil veces! An ordinary man could never read such a face. An ordinary man would never have understood what went on behind the eyes like pieces of charcoal and the tight mouth and the voice that never changed. Give him the order and he would gladly take out the troops. *Gladly!* First it was the Texan general McLeod and now it would be with this Texan commander. *Put it in writing.* That was clever. But it was too clever. Complete command of the troops. And he would be the hero of the people. What could he not do with that piece of paper!

"I should like to reread that authority I gave to you, Don Diego," he said. What if Archuleta would not give it back? The colonel frowned and unhestitatingly took the paper from his pocket and returned it to the Governor. Armijo grabbed it. His eyes sparkled. He had fooled him! How could this blockhead believe he could match his brains with Armijo? He unfolded the paper to make certain it was the same and then he tore it into little pieces. Archuleta was regarding him calmly. He had raised this man to be colonel and he could break him as easily. "As easily," he said aloud.

"Pardon, excelencia?" Archuleta asked.

"Nothing, nothing. I have changed my mind. I will take out the troops myself," Don Manuel said quickly.

Archuleta shrugged. "It is not at all necessary, excelencia, but if your excellency thinks best—"

"I think it best! Did I not just say I think it best?" He had outwitted him. The fool had not realized what he had in his pocket. "You may go now, Don Diego."

"Does your excellency desire me to accompany him on the campaign?"

"No, there is no need."

"Does your excellency desire me to remain in Santa Fe while you are gone?"

Another trick, Don Manuel thought. "Return to Taos. You have a company of militia there."

"Yes, excelencia."

"Get them in readiness. I will attach them to my army as we pass through Taos on the way north." Don Manuel smiled to himself. Did Archuleta think he was stupid enough to leave him in command of soldiers while he was away? Archuleta had stolen the surrender of one Texan general from him, but he would steal nothing else.

The colonel hesitated. "Does your excellency intend to use the northern militia in combat with Texans?"

"I said I would add them to my army. Does that not explain itself?"

"May I remind your excellency that the militia in the north is composed almost entirely of Indians from the Taos pueblo," Archuleta said. "The captain in command is himself a pueblo Indian."

"What the devil difference does that make?"

"The pueblo Indians do not consider Texans their enemies."

"What!"

"May I remind your excellency that Gonzales sought the support of Texans, and the Taos Indians have always looked upon gringos as allies. Your excellency may have some difficulty in making the northern militia go to war against Texans."

Don Manuel's face began to turn purple. "Are you telling me soldiers wearing my uniform will refuse to obey my orders?"

"I am not saying that, excelencia," Archuleta said quietly. "I say only that if I were in your excellency's shoes I would not feel I could depend upon Taos Indians in battle against Texans."

"But you are not in my shoes!" Don Manuel roared. "And the northern militia is under your direct command, and if the Taos Indians are disloyal, that is your responsibility."

Archuleta's fingers tightened on his sword. "The militia will be ready when your excellency arrives."

Don Manuel pushed past the colonel and ran to the door. "Don Guadalupe," he called to his secretary, "prepare a bulletin immediately. General Manuel Armijo will lead his troops personally in a campaign against the Texan army." He looked back gloatingly at Archuleta, as though daring him to contradict.

2

ON THE 1ST DAY OF MAY, General Armijo left Santa Fe with four hundred and fifty troops to protect his country against the newest Texas threat from the north. He had no idea of the size of the new enemy force reported gathering in the general vicinity of Bent's Fort, but he knew that the band that attacked Mora had numbered no more than twenty and he did not believe this second band would be much larger. He assured himself he had nothing to fear. The Texans had surrendered before and they would do so again. It was better, he thought with satisfaction, to be considered brave than to be brave.

His departure was accompanied with the usual acclaim of his subjects. It was the feature of warfare he relished as second best. The greatest pleasure was the victorious return. But he would have that too. He rode along happily, filling his lungs with the dry air. The mood did not last long. When he arrived in Taos his back and sides were so chafed he had to be helped from the saddle and he went to bed immediately in Archuleta's house.

He remained in retirement for three days, suffering greatly. He swore to himself that his first act upon returning to Santa Fe would be to import a personal physician. The old Spanish governors had had their private doctors; there was no reason why he should not. It was ridiculous for the Governor of New Mexico to have to depend on peasant women because there was not a single physician in the capital.

He brought the irritation under some control at last, aided by an ointment obtained by the military surgeon from some pueblo medicine man, and then he consented to receive the leading men of the Rio Arriba, including Padre Martínez. From his bed he proclaimed his determination to protect his people against their enemies, at no matter what cost to his health. His listeners were moved.

As the men were leaving he requested the priest to remain behind, knowing Martínez had no inconsiderable skill as a doctor. He asked Martínez to examine the inflammation, which had started several weeks before on his back and was spreading around both sides of his body. "It is not the mal francés?" he asked anxiously.

"I believe not, excelencia," the priest said gravely. "I have never known the French disease to start on the back."

"Then what is it, padre? Nombre de Dios, rid me of this affliction and then ask anything of me in return!"

"I do not believe it is within my power to cure you, excelencia."

"Why not? What is this cursed thing?"

The priest looked at him quizzically. "Once before I saw something that resembled this, excelencia. And yet I cannot believe it is the same thing."

"What was it? Tell me about it."

"I gave comfort once to a man who was condemned to die. He too had this outbreak on the flesh, and at the time I attributed it to only one thing."

"And that was?"

"Fear."

Don Manuel fell back. "Fear!"

The priest nodded soberly. "I questioned the man and from his answers I concluded the condition was one of nerves, brought on by the fear of his impending execution. I spent much time with him and persuaded him that what we call death is nothing more than the start of a new existence, a happier one by far than this one. The inflammation abated, excelencia, and when the man finally made his peace with God, it was gone entirely."

Don Manuel pulled the covers over him. "Of what would I feel fear?" he growled.

The priest bowed. "Your excellency must know better than I."

When he was alone Don Manuel tried to sleep. What the devil was the priest trying to tell him? There was nothing the matter with his nerves. And he had no fears, of anything or of anyone. He closed his eyes and sought for sleep, telling himself he was without fears.

3

DON MANUEL was in no great hurry to engage the Texans and he took advantage of the suggestion made by Archuleta that he remain in Taos until the colonel's spies returned from the north with information about the enemy. He found it surprisingly pleasant to tarry. Taos had adapted itself to the demands of the mountain men who made rendezvous there. There were gambling halls in profusion and women, and the Governor found himself lucky with both. He was pleased to discover he could even drink the potent Taos Lightning without irritating his skin condition too much.

Where he went he was greeted with deep respect. Archuleta had told him the people resented the fact he was taking away the militia, leaving the area unprotected against Navajos, who had been active all spring, but the subdued and deferential attitude of the natives confirmed what Don Manuel had suspected from the start: that Archuleta had been exaggerating grossly for some purpose of his own. Don Manuel did not know that within the first week of his arrival Archuleta's agents had arrested seventeen men for making treasonable statements and that afterward the natives kept their thoughts to themselves.

In the middle of May, Damasio Salazar arrived in Taos to report to Don Manuel that he had trailed Caballero to Mora and had lost him again. With the best of humor, Don Manuel asked him if he had put any of the natives of Mora to the question. When Salazar said he had not, Don Manuel asked pleasantly: "Why not, Don Damasio? Have you lost your taste for such things?"

"Mora is an armed camp, excelencia. It would have caused bloodshed to impose my orders there."

"I do not understand, Don Damasio."

"I told your excellency how Caballero caught up with the Texans who attacked Mora."

"Yes, it is very considerate for Don Esquipulas to kill my enemies for me."

"Before he left he gave to the men of Mora weapons he had captured from the Texans. They are armed to the teeth with the latest gringo revolvers and rifles."

"That is contrary to my law," Don Manuel said angrily, "and they know it. Why did you not order them to turn the weapons over to you?"

Salazar hesitated. "Caballero left more than guns."

"What do you mean by that?"

"I do not myself know. The men in Mora had a new attitude. They were not without respect and yet it was plain they would not be roughly handled. They had the guns, but it was more than guns."

"You talk in riddles!"

"Only because it is in fact a riddle. I do not know what lies Caballero told the villagers, excelencia, because they were in a mood to tell me only what they chose to tell, but I could see they had an independence and that that independence was supported by some of the most modern weapons I have ever looked upon."

"It is fortunate this Caballero is unable to supply each community with an arsenal to implement this new thinking," Armijo said dryly.

"I amuse your excellency," Salazar said, abashed. "Perhaps I have exaggerated. I admit frankly I was shaken more than a little by this defiance I read in the faces in Mora."

Don Manuel laughed. With his army under his eyes and reverent natives all around him he could not get worked up at the moment over the activities of a couple of dozen outlaws, particularly when he had the smell of Salazar's fear to bring out his own courage. "All the more reason for you to capture this dreadful man as quickly as possible, dear Don Damasio," he said mockingly. "Unless you have grown so fearful of Caballero you prefer to join me in my campaign against the Texans." He tapped Salazar playfully on the chest. "I am told that you are a great favorite among the Texans and that next to me there is in all of New Mexico no one they would like better to meet again."

In the last week of May, Archuleta's spies arrived with their information. Archuleta told the Governor the spies reported the enemy numbered about two hundred men. Don Manuel tried not to reveal to the colonel that the number was higher than he had expected.

"The commander is a man named Jacob Snively," Don Diego said. "He is said to have the habit of turning his men loose with knives among the prisoners when the fighting is over. His men do not kill all the prisoners. They content themselves with merely castrating some."

Don Manuel sucked hard on his cigar. "The answer to that is not to allow this man to take prisoners," he said evenly.

There was no more reason to delay in Taos. Don Manuel left just before the end of the month and proceeded as far as Agua Fria, a little more than twenty miles to the northeast, and set up his field headquarters there. The tiny settlement, with its altitude of nearly ten thousand feet, was cool and invigorating.

He sent his troops on a series of patrols to make contact with the enemy. When it came to the turn of the northern militia, he found Archuleta had not exaggerated after all. Fully a third of the Indians refused to obey. They were joined by a small contingent from the pueblo of Santo Domingo. Almost apoplectic with rage, Don Manuel ordered that the rebellious Indians be tied to their horses and kept tied until they were well out on the plains. He sent two New Mexicans with the Indians to make certain his commands were not disobeyed.

When the pueblo Indians reached the territory of hostile Indians, their commander, Captain Ventura Lobato, a stocky, bandy-legged Taos Indian whose name was the Spanish translation of his Indian name, Lucky Young Wolf, unfettered the thirty Indians who had been bound hand and foot to their saddles, and, speaking in Taos dialect, told his men of the plan he had conceived. "We will seek out the Texans exactly as Don Manuel ordered, only if we find them we will not return to Agua Fria to bring the news to him, but we will give ourselves up to the

Texans," Lobato said. "We will offer to lead them back to where Don Manuel is encamped and to fight at their side against him."

The Indians shouted their approval, and one of the New Mexican observers asked Lobato what he had said to make the sullen men so happy. "I told them that after we defeated the Texans there would be much loot to divide," Lobato said.

The Indians scoured the country. They crossed Raton Pass and on the 19th day of June, just off the Santa Fe route in the sand hills south of the Arkansas River, they sighted the Texans under the command of Colonel Jacob Snively. They shouted with jubilation and galloped toward the Texans, their muskets still slung around their shoulders. The Texans waited until they got within range and then opened fire. Eighteen of the Indians fell dead. Twenty more slid wounded from their saddles. The two New Mexican observers turned tail and raced back to the pass. A few of the Indians returned the fire, and then all of them surrendered.

4

Don Manuel was unable to sleep. He squatted at the side of the stream that gave Agua Fria its name and smoked one cigar after another, listening to the sounds of the night. It was not a time he liked. There was no activity in the camp now, no rough soldierly speech and laughter and song to interpose themselves between him and the endlessness around him. Now it was just himself alone and the night and the mountains and the cries of the coyotes.

He rubbed his itching back, wondering whether there could be any truth in what Martínez had said. He cursed the priest for introducing such a thought into his mind. And yet despite the plain living the camp made necessary, the rash was not abating.

Could it be nerves? The only things to which he could not issue orders were those which went on inside of him. His word was supreme law, but he could give no commands to his thoughts or to his imagination or to his memories. His mind went round and he thought of things he did not want to think of and he remembered things he desired to forget. He stared at the moonlight on the rippling water, and his head was a pail filled with the smells of rotting garbage.

It had been easy to laugh at a frightened Salazar in the brightness of day in Taos. Neither Snively with his two hundred soldiers nor Caballero with his pitiful handful of men had amounted to much against the cheery clicking of ivory balls in roulette wheels and the clinking of bottles against glasses. The defiance of the men in Mora was lost in the passion of the women of Taos. The Texan cries of vengeance were drowned in their cries.

But there was none of that now. The night in the austere mountains was an amphitheater of stillness, and his life uncoiled before him, a twisting path through a graveyard filled with the bones of men he had destroyed. He heard the noise of the people in the plaza and the voice of the priest telling him he was afraid and the voice of Salazar telling him men were growing strong and the voices of pueblo Indians who had stood up against him knowing he could order them shot.

The night was an enemy throwing invisibility around other enemies. Somewhere in the night men were looking for him. It was not war between two countries; it was war against Armijo. Men had journeyed for hundreds of miles nourished by a single burning desire: to kill Armijo. And they could be anywhere. They could be just across the stream. Each tree protected them. The night and his own earth conspired to betray him.

He threw an unfinished cigar into the water and jumped to his feet, knowing he was the hunted. He was the mountain lion with the yelping dogs at his heels. He was the buffalo with the ciboleros on his trail. He was Pérez and the Abreus and the half-breed Gonzales. A hundred rifles might be pointing at him. "Guard!" he screamed. "Guard!"

A man appeared instantly. "Yes, excelencia."

"Did you hear anything?"

"No, excelencia."

Don Manuel wiped his face.

"Does your excellency desire anything?"

"Nothing, hombre, nothing, but a thousand thanks."

The man touched his sombrero and vanished. The shout had wakened other men and now Don Manuel heard voices everywhere around him. "I am not alone," he said to himself. "I am in the

427

center of devotion and alertness." He felt his trembling lessen. He bathed his face in the cold water. Nombre de Dios, could the priest be right? Could fear reveal itself in scales on the skin? He listened to the low voices. "Speak," he said, "speak, speak, and let me know that you are here." The water refreshed him. It was ridiculous. But could Martínez be right? He lit a fresh cigar. He was not alone. He was in an armed camp. There were loyal men everywhere. He had but to raise his voice. The priest was mad. He knelt again at the stream and drank of the water. And then, his head close to the earth, he heard hoofbeats.

For a moment he was paralyzed. And then he shouted again: "Guard! Guard! Rouse the men! Horses from the north!"

The alarm was sounded. Men grabbed muskets. Officers bellowed commands. And into the camp, their horses foaming, galloped the two men Don Manuel had sent north with the pueblo Indians.

"Where is the general?" one of the riders shouted. "Where is Don Manuel?"

"Here!" Don Manuel bawled. "Here!"

The rider gasped: "Excelencia, the militia was attacked by the Texans. Half of Captain Lobato's men were killed or wounded in the first barrage. The rest were taken prisoner. We fled through a hail of bullets to bring you the word."

"Where?"

"On the other side of the pass, excelencia. The Texans were on their way south on the Santa Fe road when we encountered them."

The other rider said: "They may be behind us, excelencia!"

The officers waited and then one of them cleared his throat and asked: "What are your orders, excelencia?"

The paralysis was on him again.

"There may not be much time, excelencia," the officer said.

"Break camp!" Don Manuel screamed. "Bring my horse."

His horse was saddled and led up to him. He could not move. He was lifted into the saddle.

"What are the orders, excelencia?" the officer asked again.

"Bring the army back to Taos. Place yourself under the command of Colonel Archuleta."

He whipped his horse and rode off alone to the south.

5

He flung himself from the saddle and staggered into his apartment in the palace. He shouted for his wife. A servant reminded him that la gobernadora was out of the city, visiting relatives. He fell into a chair and ordered the servant to pull off his boots. He stood up in his stocking feet. His shirt was bloody.

"Was your excellency wounded by the Texans?" the servant asked.

"Take off the shirt. With care!"

Pieces of his flesh were matted to the shirt. Don Manuel screamed. He picked up his cane and beat the servant. The man fled from the room. Don Manuel stumbled after him and fell. He lay on the floor in a paroxysm of pain, his eyes filled with tears. He beat his fists on the floor. "Virgen santísima," he sobbed, "Virgen santísima, give me relief. Santa Madre, take the flames from my skin." He stared at the fresh bleeding and whimpered: "Madre de Dios, what have I done to deserve this?"

He got to his feet and removed the rest of his clothing. He ordered a tub to be filled with cold water and got into it. The water felt like the fingers of angels. He rested his face on his knees, feeling the pain go away, and he thought how he needed someone. Doña María Trinidad was gone, now when he needed her more than he had ever needed her before. He had no one. He was alone, an abandonado. "Rafaela, why were you taken from me?" His tears fell into the water.

He looked up. Was there not someone? Not as he had seen her last, but as she had come to him so long ago, her eyes shining with love and devotion. "I am beholden to you," she had said. "I said prayers for you. I wished only to be at your side," she had said. She would not refuse him. She was of the pure blood, one who held an obligation a sacred trust. She would give him compassion.

He dried himself. He was ailing and she would respond generously. He put on a silk dressing-gown. He would not go to her house—her house was filled with bitter relics. He sent a servant to summon her.

He sat down and clasped his hands to compose himself. He saw her face and thought of the things he would say to her. There would be no passion, but a man in torment asking for comfort.

The servant reappeared. He looked up eagerly. "Is she with you?"

"She is away from the city, excelencia. There is only a caretaker in the house. He said Señora Caballero left more than a week ago for Albuquerque and left no definite time for her return."

Don Manuel fell back into the chair. "You too, mi duquesa, you too."

"Is there anything else, excelencia?"

"Nothing." He thought: "You too, Soledad."

There were many things he had to do. He had to order Rurales up from the south in the event Archuleta could not hold off the Texans. He had to make arrangements to defend the capital. He stared at the great empty room.

THE TIME OF THE GRINGO   PART XIX

1

Hᴉs ᴊᴀᴡs clamped on a slender stogie, Colonel Jacob
Snively listened to the flat, unaccented voice of Captain Ventura
Lobato, and when the Indian finished, Snively translated what
he had said to Colonel Warfield. "What do you think?" he asked.

Warfield spat. "I don't believe any of it, Jake. I think it's a
typical dago trick."

"It may be," Snively agreed.

"Why should these guys suddenly want to sell out their country? These bastards must have all eaten out of the same feedbox.
The gang that jumped me near Mora handed me the same stuff,
but it didn't stop them from killing eight of my boys. You listen
to this guy and you'll find Armijo all ready and waiting."

Snively tugged at the whiskers on his chin. He was a tall,
gangly, blue-eyed man, originally from Pennsylvania. He had
worked as a surveyor for the Mexican government in Texas, and
when the Texans rebelled he had joined them and had fought
through the war, rising from private to full colonel. When the
Texan prisoners returned from Mexico with the account of their
experiences, he had asked permission from President Houston to
raise a force of eight hundred volunteers to raid Mexican caravans.
He had been able to attract only a quarter of that number, but
he had gone ahead with his plans. He had made a wide swing to
the north of New Mexico, and while waiting on the Arkansas he
had been joined by Colonel Warfield, who had made it to Bent's
Fort and had there been deserted by his followers.

Despite Warfield, Snively was impressed with Lobato's offer.
To go down and surprise Armijo and then take the capital! It was
a heady prospect.

Having spoken, the Indian waited. Lobato realized his error
in galloping toward the Texans as though he were attacking and

431

he did not condemn them for opening fire. He still wanted to attach what was left of his company to Snively's army and then guide the Texan colonel to Agua Fria. The commander of the Santo Domingo Indians, Lieutenant Hernandez Angel, concurred. Lobato had emphasized that a quick decision was necessary, for the two New Mexicans who had turned back would undoubtedly warn Governor Armijo.

"You do not believe Armijo's men will fight?" Snively asked.

"I do not say that, señor coronel," Lobato said. "They are soldiers. Some will fight, but I believe you would win. The people of Taos would welcome you as liberator and there would be nothing between Taos and Santa Fe."

When Snively repeated this to Warfield, he snorted. "It just ain't reasonable, Jake. Even Mexicans got a feeling for their country."

"These are not Mexicans," Snively said. "They are Indians."

"They're Mexican Indians. That makes them double double-crossers in my book."

Snively scratched his beard. "He sounds like he might be on the level."

"The greasers who double-crossed McLeod and Cooke sounded on the level too," Warfield said.

For more than a week, during which time five of the wounded Indians died, Snively tried to make up his mind. On the 28th day of June his decision was made for him. A spy came into camp with the news that the big summer Santa Fe caravan was approaching from the east, escorted by three companies of United States dragoons under the command of Captain Philip St. George Cooke. Snively sent for Lobato and gave orders to break camp. "I have decided not to accept your offer, señor capitán."

"The caravan," Lobato said.

"Yes, the caravan. But I believe you spoke honestly to me and I am going to turn you all loose. You are free to return to Taos." He looked at the Indian's expressionless face. "What is the matter? Do you not understand what I have said? You are all free. Get your men together and go home."

"We must pass through the country of the wild Indians," Lobato said. "They are our enemies. You have taken our weapons."

"What the hell is he beefing about now?" Warfield demanded.

"He wants his guns back."

"So they can follow us and jump us some night?"

"I'm sorry, capitán," Snively said. "No guns."

The Indian's eyes were blank. "Many thanks, coronel." He saluted and turned on his heel. Half an hour later the Indians were saddled up and on their way south. The Texans started east.

2

COLONEL SNIVELY intercepted the caravan at a point on the Arkansas River just below the Caches, more than two hundred miles east of Bent's Fort. Warfield pointed out with satisfaction that the river at that place marked the boundary of the United States and that Cooke and his dragoons could proceed no farther. From there on, the wagons would travel over territory claimed by both Texas and Mexico, and in Washington it was Sam Houston's claim that was acknowledged.

"Looks like the U.S. cavalry mothered our little chicks nice and safe for us," Warfield chuckled. "And now the soldier boys are going to deliver the package right into our hands."

Snively made camp on the disputed side of the river and then, as former Americans, he and Warfield forded the stream and paid a social call on Captain Cooke. The American officer, a tall, bearded, hawk-nosed man, greeted them thoughtfully and opened a bottle of whisky. Warfield, glass in hand, leaned against the open fly of the tent and gazed at the long line of wagons strung along the river. "Nice packet of freight you been escorting, captain," he said.

"I suppose you gentlemen intend to pick up the escort at this point," Cooke said.

"Well, captain, they're entering Texas territory now, you know. Seems fitting their chaperons should change to Texas boys. We're Southerners, captain. Couldn't hardly expect us to be less hospitable than you Yankees."

"Just what do you plan to do, Colonel Snively?" Cooke asked.

Snively and Warfield exchanged grins. "Well, captain, I don't aim to be impolite or anything like that but I reckon what takes place in the Republic of Texas is Texas business," Snively said.

"You plan to attack the caravan as soon as they leave us, of course," Cooke said quietly.

"Didn't say that, captain," Snively said.

"Didn't say no, neither," Warfield said.

"You've done your job, captain," Snively said. "Your orders were to escort the caravan to the boundary of the United States. You've done fine. They're all safe and sound with nary a scratch on anybody. What happens to them from here on out doesn't concern you at all."

Cooke refilled his glass and pushed the bottle toward Snively. "Colonel Snively, what you say is absolutely true. Officially my obligation ends at this point—"

"Then let it end!" Warfield interrupted.

". . . I know why you feel as you do toward the New Mexicans," Cooke continued earnestly, as though Warfield had not spoken. "I don't blame you. My own cousin, Bill Cooke, was involved in that business. If I were a Texan I think I would feel exactly as you do."

"Glad to hear you say that, captain," Snively said. He poured the whisky and drank it down. "Damn fine drink."

"But only a part of this caravan is composed of Mexicans," Cooke said. "More than half of the wagons belong to Americans. More than half the riders and drivers are Americans. How do you propose to weed out the Mexicans when you make your raid?"

"I think that will just have to work itself out at the proper time, captain," Snively said.

"You don't think Americans are going to put up a fight to defend dagos, do you?" Warfield asked.

"I mean just that, gentlemen," Cooke said quietly. "These traders, Mexicans and Americans both, have known each other for years. Some of them are close friends. Some of the Americans have Mexican wives and families. When you start shooting they are not going to stand by. If you attack the caravan you attack the entire caravan."

434

Snively fingered his glass. "Maybe so, captain, but it's still no concern of yours. If there's trouble it will be settled between your government and my government. Your job is over."

"You mean you would kill Americans to rob Mexicans?"

"That's a hard word, 'rob,' captain," Snively said. "I mean I have authority from the President of Texas to try to get back some of the goods stolen by Mexicans."

Warfield turned away from the opening. "In Texas territory only Texas law applies, and up here we're Texas law!"

Snively nodded. "We don't aim to quarrel with you, captain, but we got the law on our side, and you know it."

Cooke walked to the open flap. "There are women there."

"That's too bad, captain," Warfield said.

Cooke looked at the wagons, at the people around the cook fires, at the unyoked draft animals and the unsaddled horses. "I'm not going to let you do it, gentlemen," he said.

"How you going to stop us?" Warfield asked.

"I'm going to disarm all of your men."

Snively jumped up. "Just a minute, captain—"

Cooke's face was grave. "I'm sorry, colonel, but I have not brought these men and women across the plains for you to kill them. I order that your men surrender their arms to me immediately."

Warfield threw back his head and roared. "How do you figure you're going to make that order stick, captain? Supposing the boys say no."

"I have two hundred soldiers," Cooke said.

"So have we," Warfield said.

"I will also call upon every man in the caravan. I don't think you will doubt they will assist me." He faced the two men. "There is nothing in the world I would less rather do than shoot at men from Texas, but if you force my hand I will give the order."

Warfield began to say something abusive, but Snively stopped him with a glance. "You know that you are exceeding your orders by a long shot, don't you, captain?"

"I do, colonel."

"And you know you may be brought before a court-martial for this."

"I stand to lose either way, colonel," Cooke said. "I am ex-

435

ceeding my authority and I may be called to account for it. On the other hand, if I permit American citizens to proceed to certain destruction without making an attempt to prevent it, I am just as liable. And if I am going to be punished I prefer that it be for saving lives rather than for not saving them. Only I am not making this decision on a basis of liability, either way. These are peaceful merchants, engaged in peaceful trade between my country and New Mexico. I will not knowingly deliver them into the hands of men pledged to destroy them. The order stands, gentlemen. We will disarm you without a fight, or, if you insist, with one."

Again Warfield opened his mouth and again Snively stopped him. "How do you propose to carry out this order, captain? My men now are in Texas. I won't order them to cross the river to surrender their arms."

"I will take a company of dragoons across the river and accept the surrender there," Cooke said.

"In Texas?" Warfield asked.

"I take full responsibility," Cooke said. "When you return to Austin you may prefer whatever charges against me you please."

Snively fingered his beard. "Are we to consider ourselves your prisoners, captain?"

Cooke smiled with great charm. He gestured toward the bottle of whisky. "You are my guests."

An hour later, as the sun was setting, the three men crossed the Arkansas River followed by seventy-five dragoons. As soon as they reached dry land on the south bank, Snively turned stiffly to Cooke and said: "Captain Cooke, you now are in the Republic of Texas. A state of war exists between my country and the Republic of Mexico. You have attempted without authority to interfere with a Texan army in pursuit of duties imposed upon it by the President of Texas. As commanding officer of this army I order you to surrender your arms and to consider yourself my prisoner."

The Texans, gathering around, listened to Snively with astonishment. Cooke smiled gravely and bowed. "I expected nothing less, Colonel Snively. You are a resourceful officer. Nevertheless I a· 1 constrained to reject your demand and repeat my own."

"Captain Cooke, I'm in my own country now and I outrank you!" Snively said, losing his temper for the first time.

"Order your men to produce their weapons, colonel."

Warfield pushed his way forward. "God damn it, we outnumber these soldier boys three to one. Why the hell do we stand here and listen to him?"

Cooke drew his heavy cavalry pistol and pointed it upward. "I expected something like this too, Colonel Warfield," he said in his low, courteous voice with its Virginia accent. "If I pull the trigger the rest of my troops, together with the men from the caravan, will cross the river before the sound of the shot dies away. Colonel Snively, will you please be good enough to give the order to your men."

Snively's eyes seemed to charge with blood. He opened his mouth. Cooke cocked the pistol and in the dead silence the click was heard clearly. Snively waved his fist. "Cooke, you'll regret this! So help me God, I'll bring charges against you to Sam Houston himself!" Then, through his teeth, he ordered his men to give up their weapons. "Each man turn in a gun," he said meaningfully. "One gun for each man."

Cooke knew nothing of the acquisition of the weapons from the pueblo Indians, and the stipulation had no significance for him. Its purport was understood by many of the Texans. They surrendered weapons, as ordered, only the firing pieces they turned in were not their Colt repeating rifles but the old muskets they had taken from the Indians.

The following day Cooke permitted the caravan to continue on its way, and that evening he called the Texans together and explained to them why he had done what he had done. His words had a profound effect on the majority of Snively's men. More than a hundred of them renounced all further raiding on the plains because it would inevitably bring them into conflict with the Americans, and half of this number asked Cooke if they might return to Independence with him. Included was the redheaded Irishman, Cornelius Fitzgerald. Cooke gave his assent heartily.

For protection against the Indians, the American officer returned ten muskets to the remainder of the Texans, believing them to be unarmed, and three days later he started east.

3

WITH TROUBLED EYES Fernando watched the rider leave the camp. He said to Caballero: "That is the fifth man, hombre. Soon there will be no one left but you and me. How much longer does the brooding continue?"

Caballero walked away without answering him. The men were camped in the Rincon Mountains behind Mora, where Caballero had taken them to escape Salazar. After Salazar had left Mora he remained there, dispirited and morose, wondering what he should do next and where he should go. His hold over his men declined with his irresolution and they had begun to drift away.

Fernando caught up with him. "You must make a plan, and soon, Esquipulas. These men have no talent for doing nothing."

"I will try to think of something," he said.

Three more days passed. Another man left. On the afternoon of the fourth day two men from Mora came to the hide-out and told him that a Texan army was reported gathering on the plains below the Arkansas, and for the first time in weeks Caballero showed interest. He questioned the men, but they could tell him little beyond the facts that the force was said to be sizable and was commanded by a Texas colonel.

When the villagers left, Caballero pondered over the information. He called his men together. He had been in error, he told them, in judging all Texans by the gang commanded by Warfield. "In the north is a real Texas army," he continued, becoming increasingly enthusiastic. "It is commanded by an army officer. They are in force and that can mean only one thing: they are here to war on Armijo."

They broke camp and started north, and with each mile his spirits rose. How foolish he had been to be discouraged because of one band of scoundrels! It was just after ten o'clock one morning when they were to the south and east of Raton Pass that they heard the thunder of hoofs and the sound of scattered gunfire.

"It may be the Texans!" Caballero shouted to the men.

"It sounds as though there are enough of them," Fernando said. "But why the shooting?"

"Maybe they have found themselves some of Armijo's soldiers," Caballero said excitedly.

"In that case, why do we loaf?" Fernando asked.

They galloped toward the sounds and reached the rim of the closed end of a rocky, precipitous canyon. In the distance was a column of dust. Caballero raised his glass to his eyes. "They are not soldiers from Texas," he said. "They are men fleeing from Navajos." He stared longer and then said: "Por Dios, it is the militia from Taos! I recognize the figure of the captain, Lobato."

"Let the Navajos get them," Fernando grunted.

Caballero strained at the glass. "I do not understand. Lobato and his men are without weapons. They do not even carry sidearms."

"All the better."

"They will be trapped in the canyon."

"That means there will be one company less to which Armijo will be able to give orders," Fernando said. "Let us rest our horses and watch. We are at a good place to see the pleasant sight."

Caballero lowered the glass, frowning. "Why should they be unarmed?"

Fernando shrugged. "It would be interesting to know. Unfortunately, the Navajos probably will not give them the opportunity to explain it to us."

"We must help them," Caballero said.

"Who? The Navajos? I believe they can do the job themselves."

"They have no chance. Every one of them will be slain." He raised the glass again. "There are men riding double-saddle. They must have wounded."

Fernando's eyes widened in disbelief. "Do you mean help the Taos militia? Jesucristo! I have been thinking all along that we *wanted* Armijo's soldiers to be destroyed."

"Lobato and his men are pueblo Indians."

"They wear Armijo's uniforms."

Now they could hear the screaming of the Navajos.

"The Taos Indians bear no love for Armijo. These men were formed, not to fight his battles, but to protect the north country from these same wild Indians," Caballero said.

439

"They still wear Armijo's uniforms and draw his pay," Fernando said coldly. "I see no reason to lift a finger."

"You are wrong, Fernando. And these men are unarmed. I will not watch them slaughtered like sheep. I know Lobato and he is a man of decency."

"How can we help them? There are but fifteen of us. There must be more than fifty Navajos in that pack. We do not assist the militia by getting ourselves killed with them."

"Our rifles give each of us the fire power of six men. We are more than their equal."

"Then let us fight," Fernando said indifferently.

Caballero grinned. "Now listen. You take half the men and cross to the other side of the canyon. Protect yourselves behind boulders. Watch me. When I wave my hat, open fire. Not before. Do you understand?"

"Of course I understand."

"Then go. And on foot."

"On foot!"

"Run around and keep out of sight and stir up as little dust as possible. *Pronto! Pronto!*"

Fernando selected half a dozen men and they dismounted and scurried around the rim of the canyon. Caballero and the remaining men took their positions. The militia now was almost at the dead end of the canyon. The Navajos were some two hundred yards behind them. The pueblo Indians jumped from their horses and tried to climb the steep walls. The Navajos picked off two or three of them, and then the rest stopped climbing and stood with their backs to the wall and waited for their enemies to capture them.

Caballero, on his belly, waited until the Navajos came within range. Then he lifted his hat, and rifles cracked from both sides of the canyon. Half a dozen Navajos fell from their horses. Caballero worked his rifle lovingly. To be able to draw and fire, again and again, por Dios, the gringos were magicians with their guns! The fifteen men aimed and fired relentlessly, and, as Caballero had said, they might have been fifty. The Navajos jerked back on their horses and looked up the canyon walls and then they raced away, screaming their rage at having to abandon the prize that had been so close and so certain.

The pueblo Indians, who had resigned themselves to the torture and death they knew to be expected at the hands of their old enemies, now stepped away from the canyon wall and looked up. Caballero got to his feet. "Hola, Capitán Lobato! What happened to your friends?"

Lobato, shading his eyes from the sun, squinted up. "Don Esquipulas!"

"Is it safe for us to come down?" Caballero shouted. "You know we are outlaws."

Lobato held out his arms. "Come down, mi hermano."

When Caballero and his men reached the bottom of the canyon, Lobato looked around. "Where are the rest of you?"

"This is all we are, señor capitán."

"You mean that all that shooting was done by just you?"

Caballero held out his rifle. "The new gringo guns. They turn each man into a half dozen."

Lobato shook his head incredulously. "Santa Madre! With such rifles a company could defeat a regiment."

"Speaking of guns, Don Ventura, how does it happen that the Taos militia roams in Navajo country without its own muskets?" Caballero asked. "Has Don Manuel forbidden you to carry guns these days?"

"That is a good question," Lobato said, "and I have a good answer for it. Sit down and make yourselves comfortable, hombres, and I will tell you a little story." He looked keenly at Caballero from his dark eyes. "I know what has happened between you and Don Manuel and what you have been doing, so I can tell you all of this and leave nothing out. Since we now return to Taos, you will understand when I am finished why the story must be forgotten immediately." Thereupon he related everything that had happened to the militia from the time Don Manuel ordered it out of Taos to make war on the Texan army, and as he spoke, Caballero's animation dried up and his face became gray. "I told the Texas colonel we had to cross the country of our enemies," Lobato concluded. "It made no difference. They turned us loose without so much as a pistol, and then this morning the Navajos picked up our trail and the chase started, and you know how it ended."

Caballero began to laugh. Fernando whirled. Caballero's face

441

was lifted to the sky and his throat pulsed with his laughter. Lobato looked at him in astonishment. "Was my story amusing?" Lobato asked.

"It is very amusing," Caballero said. "Fernando, tell him how amusing it is."

Fernando said in a low voice: "We were on our way to join forces with Snively. We believed he came here to make war on Armijo."

Lobato lowered his eyes and looked at the cigarette between his fingers. "It was that kind of laughter," he said. "I would laugh with you, Don Esquipulas. You were deceived as we were deceived. I have heard of the attack on Mora and I have met Warfield. By this time he and Snively may have massacred the caravan. That is what the Texans come here for, whether they number twenty or two hundred, to raid and to steal and to kill! They do not come to fight Armijo." He looked away. "This Don Manuel is a lucky man. A puff of wind would blow him away and yet everything that happens to him happens in his favor."

As the Indians made ready to continue on to Taos, Caballero gave Lobato five of the rifles. He explained the working of the weapons and showed the Indian how to use the ingenious loader, which filled all six chambers with powder and ball simultaneously.

Lobato watched him with silent wonder. Then he said quietly: "With two or three hundred of these we could change Don Manuel's luck." He embraced Caballero. "You have made friends, Don Esquipulas. There will always be sanctuary in the Taos pueblo."

Lieutenant Hernandez Angel, a tall, muscular youth, said: "And in the pueblo at Santo Domingo as well!"

The Indians rode off and presently the canyon was empty save for Caballero's followers. Fernando sighed heavily and asked: "And where do we go now?"

"That is a good question," Caballero said bitterly. "I think maybe the answer is nowhere."

"It has not worked out as you planned, so now you are ready to quit," Fernando said roughly.

"Can you suggest something better?" Caballero asked. "It seems none of my ideas are good and I am run out of even bad ones."

442

Fernando's face twisted with scorn. "You believed you would lead us to the Texans and we would join hands and overthrow Armijo and everybody would live happily ever after as in a fairy tale." He spat. "I piss on fairy tales, señor! But there is enough of the rico left in you to believe it would work out just as you had planned it. And because it has not you sulk like a spoiled child."

Caballero made a cigarette and contemplated him quietly.

Fernando clenched his fists. "There is much you could learn from the people, *Don* Esquipulas. They are your strength, and not gringos from Texas. The people could teach you that nothing works out the way it is planned. It is always different and it is always worse. The people were born knowing that, and that is why they are never disappointed and why they survive. The ricos have not been able to destroy them in hundreds of years because they know that. They cannot be hurt because they know in the beginning that the worst is going to happen to them. It is something a peasant child could explain to you. The people of Mora know it. Lobato and his people know it. Your own men here know it and have always known it. Only you do not know it."

He searched Caballero's face for some response, and when he saw none he continued, his voice heavy with contempt: "Did you believe freedom was easy? Did you believe it was a whore you could take to bed by just raising your finger? It is not easy; it is hard. It has to be worked for. It is more than hard; it is impossible. And yet the impossible can be made to come true! You have not lost, fool, you have gained. You have found out who are not friends, and that is much of a thing. But because you are a rico and not yet a man, you do not seize upon this knowledge as a weapon more powerful even than the new gringo rifle. You have won a victory, but you prefer to look on it as defeat and you sit there and pout over your lost cause. Nombre de Dios! It is easy to see why Armijo has been able to defecate on the ricos for so long without anyone lifting his head to murmur in protest!"

Caballero raised his eyes. He squinted over the cigarette smoke. "You have a dirty mouth, Fernando," he said mildly.

"Then get up and pull out your knife and have go at me!" Fernando roared. "Draw blood! Only do not sit there like an old woman."

Caballero rose slowly to his feet. Fernando assumed a de-

443

fensive stance. The other men watched them tensely. "I dare not," Caballero said at length, in the same diffident voice. "Morena would never forgive me."

For a moment Fernando was speechless and then he shouted a laugh that echoed throughout the canyon. "Santo Niño de Atoche! The man is still alive!" He shook Caballero's hand violently. "Now give us orders, hombres! And make them good!"

"We will go back to Bent's Fort and re-equip ourselves."

"And then?"

"And then we will return to New Mexico and you will introduce me personally to the people." He looked at Fernando from large, solemn eyes. "I want most of all to meet this peasant child who can teach me so much."

4

At Bent's Fort they discovered Morena had been delivered of a son. Fernando stared for a long time at the tiny creature while Morena and Caballero awaited anxiously his first statement as a father. Finally Fernando scratched his chin and mumbled: "It is a good thing, woman, that you obeyed orders and produced a man child!"

While Fernando remained to gaze at his son, Caballero went to see Charles Bent. The American, a large, open-faced, quiet-spoken man, told him the final chapter of the Snively story. "Do you mean gringo soldiers took guns away from other gringos so they could not attack the Mexicans in the caravan, Don Carlos?" Caballero asked.

"There were Americans in the caravan too," Bent said.

"But Snively was out to attack only my people, and this captain prevented him." He peered at Bent as though he were seeing him for the first time. "How is such a thing possible, Don Carlos, gringo against gringo, in behalf of Mexicans?"

The hard-bitten trader was embarrassed by the intensity of Caballero's question. "Right is right and wrong is wrong," he managed to say at last.

Caballero leaned back in his chair. "You are strange people, Don Carlos," he said slowly. "To believe in right and to believe in wrong."

Bent shuffled some papers on his desk. "Are your men getting everything they need up here?" he asked gruffly.

"Do not change the subject for a little moment," Caballero said. "What did you say was the name of this captain?"

"Cooke. Philip St. George Cooke."

"San Jorge," Caballero repeated. "It is the name of the patron saint of England, he who killed the dragon."

"I suppose so."

"Was there not one of the name Cooke who was leader among the Texans who were captured by Don Manuel?"

"William Cooke."

"Are these men of the same blood?"

"They are cousins, I believe."

"Are they enemies?"

"Not that I know of."

"And with a cousin who was one of Armijo's prisoners this captain risks his career to protect Mexicans?"

Bent nodded uncomfortably.

"Because of belief in right and wrong?" Caballero persisted.

Bent took a black cigar from a box on his desk and pushed the box toward Caballero. Caballero selected a cigar with care. He bit the end and dipped it in the brandy glass in front of him and then he leaned forward to take a light from the American trader. He looked into Bent's gray eyes. "We are getting everything we need here, Don Carlos."

5

Don Juan Bautista Vigil shuffled into the Governor's office, open mail in his hand. The Governor was bent over the day's dispatches. The office was chilly and the postmaster shivered slightly. "There is no need for me to read the reports, Don Manuel," Vigil said. "It is all on your face. More of the same?"

"The same," the Governor said in a weary voice.

445

"And what is it this time?"

"The corn at Socorro."

"How much of it was saved?"

"None."

Vigil clapped the side of his head. "Madre María! That corn meal was tax for half a district. You said you would order that a company of Rurales escort the wagons to Santa Fe."

Don Manuel rubbed his eyes. "The Rurales were assigned."

Vigil sat down slowly. "Do you mean to tell me this wild man now attacks Rurales in company strength?"

"He attacks them and he defeats them and disarms them and robs them."

"And what are the brave soldiers doing the while?" Vigil asked with heavy sarcasm.

"They are fighting bravely," Don Manuel said. "Eight were killed and twice the number wounded."

"How is this possible?" Vigil asked in disbelief.

"Caballero is clever, and he has gringo guns."

"It is unfortunate you did not recognize this cleverness before he obtained gringo guns," Vigil said.

The Governor's dull eyes flickered over their dark pouches. "They say they will search for him."

"Search for him!" Vigil said angrily. "But they will not find him. And they will search for the grain, and though every bag of it will be returned to the farmers, they will not find that either. And they will search most of all for the muskets that were taken from them, but of all things that will be the last they will find!" The old man jumped up, dancing with rage. "Nombre de Dios! What kind of soldiers are these? And what kind of men officer them?"

"They do the best they can."

"It is not good enough! There is one man who would run the outlaw into the ground."

Don Manuel jerked his head. "Do not talk to me again of Archuleta. I need him where he is, in the City of Mexico."

"He is no politician! He is a soldier!"

"He now is my deputy."

"Then recall him!" Vigil shouted. "There are a dozen other men who can listen to politicians argue in Mexico."

446

Don Manuel sat back in his chair. He picked up his cane. "And there is but one Archuleta."

"Who else is there?" Vigil asked defiantly.

Don Manuel fingered the cane and shook his head. "Don Juan Bautista, you are a bigger fool than even you look."

The postmaster leaned across the desk, white lines bracketing his mouth. "*I* am a fool! And *you* are the wise man! And it is wisdom to provoke the people to riot in the north because Archuleta is not there to keep the wild Indians off their necks. And it is wisdom to permit Caballero to run hog-wild. The wheat in Taos—the sheep at Mora—the cattle at Belen—and now this in Socorro. All stolen from your agents and all given back to the peasants so that now they take off their hats when they speak the name Caballero. And the man who could stop all that sits on his ass and listens to speeches in the City of Mexico!"

"Archuleta remains where he is."

"And the taxes remain where they are! On the farms instead of in the treasury!" Vigil wagged a finger under the Governor's nose. "You are a lucky man, Don Manuel, that the caravan was so big this year."

Don Manuel smashed the cane on the desk. "I am lucky? *I!*" he roared. "When things go well it is all of us, but when the trouble comes it is Armijo alone!"

The old man cowered. "I did not mean that, excelencia."

"What have you got there?"

"A few letters. One or two of interest, excelencia."

"Leave them here and go."

Vigil put the mail on the desk. "I did not mean it that way, excelencia," he said again.

Don Manuel pushed the mail to one side. "I will send it back to you when I have finished."

"We should not speak to each other in this manner, Don Manuel."

The Governor rubbed his back against the chair. His eyes closed, his mouth twitched. "It is forgotten."

Vigil blew his nose and wiped it slowly. "Are you ill?"

"Nothing but this damned rash. I cannot sleep." He squirmed in the chair and grimaced when he touched a tender place.

"You do not look well. The gringos are gone and things are

447

quiet. Why do you not go to El Paso del Norte and see a doctor and then go to your estate for a little while and rest yourself?"

"I do not need a doctor. I need sleep."

"You need a vacation from Santa Fe. It has been six years."

"I will think about it," Don Manuel mumbled. His shoulders slumped.

Vigil looked at the loosely fleshed face. The Governor looked worse every time he saw him. His skin hung away from his face like that of an old woman. He looked at the cane, which Don Manuel no longer used as a prop to emphasize his limp. The cane was needed now, was seldom out of his hand, either on the ground or raised to strike at people in the street who did not bow low enough to suit Don Manuel as he passed them. Vigil shook his head and left the office.

Don Manuel tried to ease his itching back against the chair. His eyes became vacant. His mouth hung loose. If he could go away for a rest—but who would do the thinking? He pressed his fingers against his eyes. Then he sat upright. His face got ugly with suspicion. To recall Archuleta and leave the capital, to go to Chihuahua—it fitted together.

He tugged at his lip, remembering how Archuleta had looked at him when he arrived breathless in Taos and told him the army was following him and that the Texans were advancing and for Archuleta to take command and defend the country. And he remembered how Archuleta had looked when he brought the troops back to Santa Fe behind the caravan with the story of how the gringo officer had stripped the Texans of their weapons. At first he had considered it a monumental joke that one of his enemies had eliminated the other enemy for him, and then he realized what a fool he had made of himself and how ridiculous had been his flight. It was Archuleta again, as it had been Archuleta before when the Texans had come the first time.

He had wondered how many others would think the same thing and he knew he had to get rid of Archuleta. He had not rested until he had sent him to the national Congress as deputy to occupy the post that had been vacant since the return of the priest Juan Felipe Ortiz. It could not be helped that the natives of the Rio Arriba, who had been in ferment since their militia had returned, depleted and mauled from its collision with the

Texans, were thrown into an uproar when Archuleta was taken away. It was more important for the time being to remove that man from his position of military command. And Don Manuel had no fears that Archuleta would do anything to injure him politically in the City of Mexico. He knew the colonel did not have that kind of mind.

And now Vigil was pleading with him to bring Archuleta back, and was urging him to leave the capital, even to leave New Mexico. He had called Vigil a fool, but was it foolishness? Was it just the blabbing of an old man or was there something else behind it? It could be nothing else. Not Vigil. Of all people, not Vigil. Everything Vigil was he owed to him. But could it have been introduced into the old man's mind by someone cleverer than he, someone who believed Don Manuel would not be suspicious of his old crony? No, it probably was nothing. There was no one. And yet he must watch it. He must watch everything. Vigil was either intriguer or fool, and either was bad. He must remain alert at all times. They all were lined up against him, the enemies without and the enemies within. It was the world against Armijo.

He swallowed a mouthful of brandy, and color returned to his cheeks. His eyes began to glitter craftily. He was tired and he was sick, but he was not that tired or sick.

He was filled with sudden zeal. He scratched his back furiously. The rash would go away and all would be well again. It was just sleep. He picked up the opened letters and began to read through them, tossing them aside rapidly, one after another, until he came to a letter written by Antonio Sandoval in Albuquerque to a relative in the capital. Don Antonio wrote letters as gossipy as those of a woman, and Armijo lit a cigar and settled back to enjoy it. Halfway through the letter he put down the cigar.

"You know Doña Soledad Caballero de Abreu, the wife of the outlaw," the prefect from the south had written. "It will interest you to hear that she is attempting to stir up an insurrection against the Governor! She is holding secret meetings in some of the haciendas here and is making most inflammatory speeches against Don Manuel. She reminds us of our 'birthright' and urges us to rise and throw his excellency out!

"She has as yet conjured up no army, but the gatherings are well attended and the woman is cheered lustily when she orates

449

about Don Manuel's 'crimes against the country.' These meetings are the most popular events in the Rio Abajo this fall. We all come to the meetings masked and at all other times we pretend not to know those of us who attend them. It is deliciously exciting. Doña Soledad is an extremely beautiful woman, you know, and it is difficult to say whether she attracts for the passion in her words or the passion in her face. . . ."

Don Antonio named some of the people who attended the seditious gatherings and concluded with the warning that "all of this is, of course, told to you in the greatest secrecy. I knew how amused you would be, but I must ask you to burn this letter as soon as you read it."

The Governor read through that portion of the missive twice before he could bring himself to believe his eyes, and then he indulged in the first genuine laughter he had enjoyed in a long time. "*Qué diablita! Qué mujer!* Soledad, Soledad, mi corazón!" He could see her, ablaze with passion, trying to stir up ricos in fancy masks. Madre de Dios! What he would give for some magical power to make himself invisible so he could listen to her. And how foolish she was! Trying to make blood of tepid water. Virgen de Guadalupe! What he could have accomplished with such a woman at his side! "Soledad, it is useless. That is all gone from your ricos, and even if it were not, no Spaniard will listen seriously to a woman speak of anything but love!"

1

IN THE THIRD WEEK of October Don Manuel received a communication from the City of Mexico which caused him to forget the troubles in Taos and the activities of the two Caballeros. He was stupefied to read that the government of Mexico had formally accused the United States of being primarily responsible for the presence of raiders on the prairies and in retaliation the northern ports of New Mexico were ordered closed immediately and all trade between New Mexico and the United States forbidden henceforth. The communication was signed personally by General Antonio López de Santa Anna, who sent with it his warmest felicitations to his "pillar of strength in the north."

The order left Don Manuel stunned. His first reaction was outrage that the economy of New Mexico should be used so callously as a pawn by the distant central government. "In retaliation," the decree stated. In retaliation against whom? A few gringos would be annoyed, true, and would be inconvenienced until they made arrangements to trade elsewhere, but in the end the only sufferers would be the innocent Mexicans who supposedly were being avenged. The northern ports were the nostrils through which New Mexico breathed. With them sealed, the country would strangle.

He reread the paper, hardly able to credit his eyes. Then his sense of transgression evaporated and he wondered how the situation could be put to his use.

He summoned his secretary and pushed the missive toward him. Miranda's face turned white as he read it through. "Surely General Santa Anna cannot mean this seriously, excelencia," he blurted.

Don Manuel arched his hands. "I believe he means every word of it."

"But this will destroy the country, excelencia! There will be

451

no money for anything. It would be no worse if wild Indians razed New Mexico from Raton Pass to El Paso del Norte."

"You are right, Don Guadalupe," Armijo said somberly. "You have used the precise word. The order will destroy the country."

"But you will not obey it!"

Don Manuel tapped the paper. "The command is here."

"Disobey it! Ignore it!" Miranda waved his small fist.

Don Manuel widened his eyes. "Disobey a command from General Santa Anna?"

"You have thrown away orders from the City of Mexico before. You are stronger than Santa Anna, excelencia. Tear it up! He would not dare do anything about it."

"You give dangerous advice for a schoolteacher, Don Guadalupe," Armijo said mildly.

"Your responsibility is to your people and not to Santa Anna. If you enforce this decree, you pronounce the sentence of death on them."

"Not I. The central government."

"Santa Anna knows nothing of conditions here. He could not or he would not issue such an order."

"But he has issued it, and here it is." Don Manuel squared his shoulders. "I have no choice but to obey my superiors."

"New Mexico will be ruined, excelencia. I appeal to you—"

Don Manuel held up his hand. A small smile appeared on his lips. "How long do you believe Santa Anna will allow this decree to remain in effect, secretario?"

"It says permanently, excelencia."

"It *says* permanently. How long is permanently?"

"I do not understand, excelencia."

Don Manuel began to limp back and forth, poking his cane at the floor. "Santa Anna is an impetuous man. He thinks only to teach the 'Colossus to the East' a lesson. He forgets one little thing. I am the first Governor of New Mexico who has never asked the central government for a single centavo. Where did this money come from? From the Santa Fe trade! The trade that started as a little baby at fifteen thousand dollars a year and which this year reached almost half a million and the end not in sight. And now the commerce is ordered ended. Just like that! And what happens? Chaos. Chaos, Don Guadalupe, chaos!"

He leaned heavily on the cane. "Chaos within, secretario, with the government running down and the army deserting and the Indians inspired, and on three sides our little country besieged by enemies. And then what?" His lips curled away from his teeth. "Then the General Santa Anna has to make the big decision if he does not want to see New Mexico go back to Indians or to Texans or even possibly to Americans. He can do one of two things: he can send gold up here or he can remove the embargo. And when the general must make a choice between his pride and his pocketbook, what do you think he will do?"

Miranda blinked his weak eyes and smiled tentatively. Don Manuel's words lifted a load from his mind and yet there was something about the Governor's attitude which prevented him from feeling relief. "In that case, excelencia, why should you permit it to happen at all?" he asked timidly.

The animation left Don Manuel's face, and his jaw set under the flabby cheeks. "Perhaps it is the will of God that the people suffer a little." Laughter suddenly splattered like hail from his lips. "Perhaps they need to be taught a small lesson."

Miranda shuddered as he listened to the wild laughter and saw the feverish gleam that appeared in the Governor's eyes.

"They conspire with the Texans," Armijo said. "They weep in the streets when the heretics pass and they fight with my soldiers to give them to eat and drink. They shout insults at Armijo for driving the priest-slayers from the land. They defy my orders and protect outlaws who are enemies of the state. The ricos listen to revolutionary talk and spit at my name. Everywhere there is discontent. Perhaps suffering will do good. Perhaps it will purge them of their dissatisfaction. When the Navajos set up hogans in the plaza, then perhaps the people will know the value of Armijo." His eyes stared off broodingly. "Children are precious things, Don Guadalupe, but they require discipline now and then to teach them their places." He sat down and placed his cane carefully upon the desk and his eyes were still away.

Miranda removed his glasses, wiped them, and gathered all the force that was within him. "I can be no part of this, excelencia." He drew back in fright.

Armijo only nodded and smiled sadly. "You desire to leave me, Don Guadalupe," he said, not as a question. "You deserve a rest. You have been a faithful secretary for six years and it is time that you rested. We both are in need of rest. I am worn out, amigo, and you must be almost the same."

"What are you planning to do, excelencia?" Miranda asked bewilderedly.

Don Manuel clasped his hands. "Have you noticed that when life becomes too turbulent in the City of Mexico, General Santa Anna retires to his estates? And how, when he removes his hand from the helm, the vessel begins to founder? His people come to him on their knees and beg him to return and set the ship back on course. He is more effective against his enemies with his absence than with his army. I will take a page from the book of the President of Mexico and retire to my peaceful orchards." He smiled gently. "Did you know I have orchards, Don Guadalupe?"

Miranda nodded mutely.

"Yes, amigo, I have many beautiful orchards, as many as any rico in the Rio Abajo. In fact, I am a rico though I have always protected my people against that class. In the spring the blossoms fill the air with perfume. I will go there and allow my body to rediscover its health and the whole country will see the emptiness that is made when Armijo is removed." He regarded Miranda tenderly. "And you too must take a rest, Don Guadalupe. Is it not true that it is a custom in the great universities for the teachers to take what is called a sabbatical leave?"

"Yes, excelencia."

"You have labored without cessation for six years and you are entitled to your sabbatical leave. You are a big landowner, Don Guadalupe. There is a vast tract in the north which has been granted in your name. It develops amazingly under the supervision of Don Carlos Beaubien, but still you should go there yourself and see how your affairs progress. I will retire to the south and you will retire to the north and we will leave our poor Santa Fe to endure the fate decreed for it by the President of our country."

Don Guadalupe stood up, his head whirling. "Should I make public the order, excelencia?"

"Not yet, not yet." Don Manuel held up his hand. "There are things to do first. You will send word to my warehouse that all merchandise belonging to my firm be taken from the market instantly. Then you will send agents around to my competitors'

454

warehouses to purchase everything that is for sale. Make certain that the other merchants do not know it is for me. But everything, everything, do you understand?"

"I will follow your excellency's instructions, but I do not understand."

"Because you are a scholar and not a business man," Don Manuel said affectionately. "But I will tell you. When the word gets out that the ports are closed and that the merchandise in the warehouses is the last that will be brought into the country, overnight the goods will be worth double."

2

At the beginning the people refused to believe the curt announcement of Santa Anna's decree when it was posted on bulletin boards in the plazas of all the villages. The trade with the Americans was like a drug that had been administered to them for twenty years, starting in small quantities and increased year after year in strength, and now it was suddenly to be denied to them. But it was true, there on the paper, with the name of the President of Mexico on the bottom to make it beyond all appeal. And when they realized at length that it was no joke without humor, no error, that it was the plain truth as the cold, terse words stated, that henceforth there would be no wagons arriving in the country laden with all the wonderful things the fabulous Americans manufactured in their distant country; that the wool which had been sheared and carded so painstakingly and the pelts that had been taken with so much risk and effort and the pennies put together one at a time from hours in the salt lakes and the mines were all without value since soon there would be nothing for which to exchange them, and even now the prices of everything had already vaulted into the sky, they wandered about in a stupor; and when the numbness wore off, there was left a dull hatred for this man whom they had never seen and who had never seen them but who had the power to stretch out his arm from the City of Mexico and choke them to death.

455

They called Santa Anna cojo, for his missing leg, and said it was his soul that was crippled more than his body, and they hurled maledictions on his head. By this single directive Santa Anna, who had been until then only a remote and bodiless name, became the most hated man in New Mexico, and peasants who had not before asked questions now asked themselves what kind of country they lived in when such havoc could be brought about by the whim of a single alien man. For it was borne upon them that Santa Anna was an alien and that Mexico was an alien country and that below the border were not brothers and fellow countrymen but foreigners with no concern in their welfare.

For twenty years they had been seeing Americans in increasing numbers and they had done business with them and had taken on some of their ways along with their wares. Everywhere the people repeated the folk tale of how American soldiers had disarmed the Texans so they could not attack Mexicans, and they talked about what it now seemed they must have known all along, that they were closer in their experiences with the Americans than they were with the Mexicans below the Bravo.

In their unhappiness they found compassion for Don Manuel, who accepted the blow with them, with dignity, with sympathy, and with helplessness. They spoke of the health he had lost in their behalf and of how he would suffer more than most because of the terrible edict. He was no gringo who could take his trade elsewhere. His business, which he had developed with as much acumen as he had developed the business of the country, would go bankrupt. Don Manuel was a New Mexican, and he was hurt with every other New Mexican.

3

As HE WOUND UP his business affairs, unloading his merchandise, including that bought up from his competitors, at a tremendous profit, and keeping his plan to retire still secret, Don Manuel had only one concern: whom would he name to command the army during his absence? He had privately decided to appoint his old friend Don Mariano Chaves to serve as provisional governor, but the military chieftainship was another matter. He was safe from Archuleta, but any officer to whom he gave control of the army, even temporarily, would become instantly powerful and inevitably dangerous. He considered and rejected one officer after another and he had reached no solution to the problem when there arrived in Santa Fe in December a general from the City of Mexico named Mariano Martínez y Lejanza and Don Manuel knew that his fortune was still with him.

The appearance of General Martínez was the direct result of conversations in the national capital between the military authorities there and Colonel Archuleta. Don Diego had been questioned about the state of the New Mexican army, and while he had no wish to be disloyal to his superior, General Armijo, and kept his mouth shut about many things, he could not disguise his opinion that military conditions in the northern department were less than perfect and that despite all efforts the troops were making no headway in bringing the wild Indians under control. General Martínez was dispatched to Santa Fe to try to bring about an improvement. His orders stated explicitly that he was not being sent to supersede General Armijo but to serve under his command, and he was cautioned against offending the notoriously thin-skinned New Mexican Governor.

General Martínez was a flinty professional soldier, a harsh, unpleasant man, with a long, cadaverous face. He was coldly respectful to Don Manuel, but he was unable to hide the fact that along with many other Mexicans from the national capital he considered New Mexicans as inferior people and that he felt he was slumming when in their midst. Don Manuel welcomed him with open arms. General Martínez was first of all an alien, which was enough to prevent him from entrenching himself, and beyond that he obviously was the last man in the world to build a political party around him.

To the general's astonishment, Don Manuel tore up his limited orders, telling Martínez his health was so bad he had to relieve himself of some of the pressure. He wrote new orders naming Don Mariano military chief of New Mexico. He then asked Mariano Chaves, who held the rank of senior deputy in the moribund Junta, to serve as temporary governor. Chaves, who was not in the best of health himself, was reluctant to burden himself with the task, but when Don Manuel promised him it would be but for a brief period, he yielded. On the 15th day of January 1844, Don Manuel sent a letter to the Minister of Exterior Relations in the City of Mexico, informing him that he was sick and had to leave Santa Fe and apprising him of the appointments he had made.

Two weeks later, on the last day of the month, Don Manuel vacated the office of governor. He paused in the anteroom at the desk of Guadalupe Miranda. The secretary was clearing out his desk. The two men gazed at each other and were silent. Then Don Manuel said: "It has been a long time, maestro, and a long way."

Miranda nodded and lowered his head so Don Manuel could not see the tears that came to his eyes.

"Adiós, patrón," Don Manuel said, giving Miranda the title that belonged to him as landowner.

"Adiós, excelencia," Miranda said. "I pray that your excellency recovers his full health."

"Thanks, Don Guadalupe." Don Manuel walked with a heavy limp toward the corridor.

"Don Manuel!" Miranda cried out. Armijo paused and turned his head. Miranda was on his feet and made no effort now to hide the tears. "Vaya con Dios, Don Manuel!"

Don Manuel lifted his hand and moved it slowly. "And may God watch over you as well, little teacher."

He left the Palace of the Governors and climbed into his waiting carriage, his fingers lifted to the people gathered in the plaza. He took Doña María Trinidad's fingers and held them tightly as the carriage rolled out of Santa Fe.

4

" . . . The government has fallen apart like a bundle of staves from which the rope has been removed," Don Juan Bautista Vigil wrote in alarm two weeks later. "Chaves labors to bring order from the confusion, and the Junta meets daily in its effort to help him. But Chaves is without experience, and the Junta has forgotten how to make decisions. . . ."

How could they have not forgotten? Don Manuel chuckled. I was always there to make the decisions for them.

In the same mail was an appeal from Chaves for him to return to Santa Fe and resume office. He wrote back that he was too ill. A week later another entreaty came from the capital, signed not only by Chaves but by the members of the Junta and General Martínez as well.

"Nothing would give me greater satisfaction than to be able to serve my country at this difficult time," Don Manuel replied. "But in my present condition a return to Santa Fe and the toil of government would be nothing less than suicide."

There were more letters and more pleas to come back to the capital, including a personal visit from Chaves, and then, in April, Don Manuel received a lengthy personal communication from the President of Mexico.

"Our concept of government is identical," Santa Anna wrote, "so I know it will give you much pleasure to learn that a new Constitution has been adopted for our country which greatly strengthens the principle of Centralism. Among many other changes, with which I will not tire you at this time, the terms of departmental governors are reduced from eight to six years. This means, of course, that a new appointment must be made for New Mexico at this time.

"Despite your ill health, which has given me much worry, I would normally insist that you take on the office of political chief and the additional responsibilities of military leader for at least another six years, since there is none else in New Mexico of your quality and you have been a bastion of strength in the north.

"It so happens, however, dear Don Manuel, that at the present time I have in the town of Sabinas, near the Texas border, a commission engaged in discussions with a commission from Texas to the end that a treaty of peace be drawn up ending the conflict between our two countries under the terms of which we will recognize Texan independence on the condition that Texas will not annex itself to the United States.

"We have none of us forgiven the United States for its lightning-quick recognition of the Republic of Texas in 1836, but we are faced with the inevitable. Political realities require us to accept the accomplished fact of Texan independence, but we can

459

ensure that that also means independence from the United States.

"The commissioners from Texas have stated that their President, Don Samuel Houston, has agreed to this condition, and I am desirous of surrounding the conferences with the greatest atmosphere of harmony. Unfortunately, mi compañero, your name is not a popular one with the Texans and there are among the Texan negotiators at Sabinas men who were members of the Texan Santa Fe Expedition. Obviously it will facilitate affairs if you do not hold the rank of Governor of New Mexico at the present time.

"The situation is but temporary and, gracias á Dios, you are still a young man with many years of service to your country ahead of you. I do not desire to nourish any permanent opposition to you among your fellow New Mexicans, because before long I will again call upon you to accept power. Therefore I have decided to name General Mariano Martínez y Lejanza, whom you appointed military chief, to the position of governor. This will all be entirely understandable to you, I am certain, my old friend.

"One thing more. There is in the United States among the political leaders in the North a strong feeling of opposition toward the annexation of Texas to the United States because of the issue of slavery. It is my wish to win as many friends as possible among these leaders in order doubly to ensure against the absorption of Texas at a future time. Most of the Santa Fe Trail merchants come from these Northern states and so at this time I am rescinding the embargo on the trade and authorizing General Martínez to reopen the northern ports.

"I close with the most cordial expressions of friendship and the fervent prayers to Our Lady of Guadalupe that you may soon be restored to your former good health and so make it possible for us again to walk, hand in hand, toward the future of our beloved country."

General Martínez's formal appointment as governor was brought up from the City of Mexico by the same courier who carried Santa Anna's letter to Don Manuel, and ten days later Don Manuel received a heated communication from Vigil.

". . . What an idiot this man is! He knows nothing about nothing and he is grabbing at everything with both hands. You will not believe this, but his first official act as Governor of New

Mexico was to dismiss Don José Antonio Chaves from his post as head of the customs and take over the post himself. In one stroke this fool has made himself an enemy to the whole Chaves family. . . ."

Don Manuel was content to recuperate in peace.

5

IN JULY, Don Manuel interrupted his bucolic existence for a trip to Santa Fe to meet Albert Speyer and the wagons. It was his first visit to the capital since his abdication. As his carriage entered the plaza he was vaguely aware of a change. It took him a moment or two to realize that rows of cottonwood trees had been planted around the borders of the square. The sight of the trees angered him. By what right had the foreigner made permanent changes in Santa Fe behind his back! The trees had been planted with military precision, each exactly the same distance from its neighbor, giving to the plaza an air of primness. The plaza no longer looked like Santa Fe.

The carriage stopped in front of a mercantile establishment where Don Manuel had engaged rooms for his stay in the capital. He was recognized as he descended. A dozen men removed their hats and bowed and there were cries of "It is Don Manuel! It is Don Manuel!" The irritation left his face and was replaced instantly with an expression of benignity. He raised his hand in the familiar gesture and as he entered the building his ears were gladdened with the shouts of "Viva Don Manuel!"

His temporary quarters became a salon to which all his cronies flocked. Their excitement at the manifest signs of his returning vigor was pitiful. His authority filled the small rooms so that his friends felt almost they were visiting him as of old, in the office of the governor.

Vigil now was serving the Junta as its secretary. "The deputies squabble all the time, Don Manuel," he said querulously. "They are always arguing and no one is friend to another. It is not like the old days."

461

Don Manuel considered it sensible not to point out that in the old days the Junta rarely convened, and when it did, it was for the purpose of confirming his commands and that no one had been permitted to argue with anyone.

"The palace now has the air of the headquarters of a general who hopes he will not be reduced to colonel," Vigil grumbled. It hardly matters whether one wears a uniform or not—everyone is considered as a soldier. Any day now I expect to hear of a new order requiring everybody to salute him, including small children." The peninsula of chin closed on the promontory of nose. "Everything is set on schedule. Everything must be done precisely on time. It is not that we live in a garrison, but in a garrison in the middle of a war. The smallest request comes in the form of an order, as though Santa Fe were under enemy attack."

"At least the troops must enjoy the military atmosphere," Don Manuel said.

"The troops hate it! He drills them all the time."

Among Don Manuel's visitors were Don José Antonio Chaves, the discharged head of the customs; his cousin, Don Mariano Chaves, and his uncle, Don José Chaves y Castillo, who now was senior deputy of the Junta. Don José told him Governor Martínez had asked the central government for funds.

"That will endear him to Santa Anna," Armijo chuckled. "But why does he do this? The caravan soon will be here."

"He is like a child with a new plaything. It amazes him that when he dips his hands into the treasury they come out with money sticking to them," the senior deputy said with contempt.

"We plan to inform on him to the central authorities," Don José Antonio said.

Don Manuel bade them be patient. "What is a little dishonesty among government officials? It is expected. How else can they live? Do not fire your guns prematurely. Keep a record among yourselves of all the peculations you can discover, in exact detail. One day the right moment will arrive."

"How will we know, excelencia?" Don José Antonio asked, unable to rid himself of the habit of giving Don Manuel the title.

Don Manuel patted him on the arm. "I will tell you."

1

AN OLD MAN with a fierce white mustache rode slowly up the trail on the bare back of a burro. As they approached the summit the burro halted. The old man kicked him without anger. The burro turned his head and gazed at him and then with a grunt got over the last rise.

Dark had settled in the valley below, but here there was a little light. A guard appeared from behind a rock, his rifle at the ready. The old man regarded him with boredom.

"Who goes?" the guard demanded.

"Friend. Put down the machine that explodes, hombrecito. A rifle is for a grown man. You may do yourself some small hurt."

The guard looked at him more closely. "It is you."

"It is not my father. He is long dead."

"Go, old man. You talk too much."

"Where is your leader, Señor Caballero?" the old man asked politely. "If I do not trouble too much."

"There, by the fire."

The old man bowed. "Thousand thanks, guarda, and may your castanets dance with frequency."

"On the belly of your daughter, old man."

"For certain! As soon as she loses her sense of smell." He kicked the burro mildly again and the animal ambled toward the fire. "Hola, Don Esquipulas!" the old man called out.

Caballero looked up. "Hola, Don Elías. How go you?"

The old man twisted his mustache. "Strong enough to join your flea-bitten band."

Caballero nodded gravely. "You are a valiant old man and I respect you, but we are peaceful citizens. You are thirsty for blood and would kill and steal from soldiers and get us in trouble with the authorities."

"It is true."

"But where are your young ones?" Caballero asked. "They are not so ferocious as you and perhaps we could make use of them."

The old man spat. "I defecate on the young ones."

"I believe I grow not to love them too much either," Caballero said. "What brings you here?"

Don Elías took a folded piece of paper from his pocket. "This notice the alcalde received with orders to post it on the bulletin board in the plaza. Since it was intended for your eyes, he asked me to bring it to you."

Caballero took the paper. "Some brandy for the courier?"

Don Elías shook his head. "I should like nothing better, Don Esquipulas. Aguardiente, brave men, the night, a fire!" He sighed. "But the animal is old and his eyes are faulty. I will take him to his house before it grows too dark."

"Many thanks, Don Elías. Until presently."

Caballero held the paper open before the fire. It was an official document from the Palace of the Governors in Santa Fe. Fernando leaned over his shoulder and read it with him.

The decree of outlawry was pronounced against the Sr. Esquipulas Caballero and his followers by Sr. Governor Don Manuel Armijo.

Don Manuel Armijo no longer is Governor of New Mexico.

The present executive invites the Sr. Caballero to come to the Palace of the Governors at his convenience for discussions to the end that he and his loyal followers be restored as lawful and useful citizens.

The Sr. Caballero is guaranteed safe-conduct to Santa Fe, and in the event the discussions fail in their purpose, he and those who accompany him are similarly guaranteed safe-conduct hence.

The Sr. Caballero, wherever he may be when he hears of this, is invited to notify the alcalde of the nearest village of his reply to this request.

MARIANO MARTÍNEZ Y LEJANZA
Governor and General Commandant
Department of New Mexico

464

"It is a trap," Fernando said instantly.

Caballero read through the document a second time. He rubbed his mouth slowly. "Is it?"

"I get the distinct smell of Salazar."

"Salazar has not been in our hair for many weeks."

"It is some trick, Esquipulas."

"How are you so certain it is a trick? He guarantees safety."

"I piss on his guarantee."

"He is an officer in the army, Fernando, and a general. He would not dishonor his word."

"Santa Madre! And are you so foolish as to believe still in the honor of politicians?"

"He is an officer," Caballero repeated stubbornly.

"Armijo is an officer. Salazar is an officer. How far would you trust the guarantee of either of them?"

"This one is different. He is an officer in the Mexican Army."

"God help you for being such a fool!" Fernando looked into his eyes. "And what if it is not a trick and he persuades you to stop what you are doing? What of the people who have come to depend on you. This man may be a general in the Mexican army, but he takes from the people no less than Armijo did."

Caballero raised his head. "They do depend on us."

"We have done good things for them."

Caballero looked at him earnestly. "Have we, Fernando?"

"We have stood between them and the Rurales like a wall."

"In doing that, have we truly done them good?" He looked back into the fire. "We have fought for them and we have retrieved that which was seized from them and we have returned it to them as one might toss a bone to a dog. We have been good for their bellies. But have we been good for them? All their lives they have depended on strength in some form or other, and now we are another kind of strength and they depend upon us. In what way does this make for strength in them?"

"Salazar found them strong," Fernando said harshly. "Did one of them ever betray us to him? He has put the question to a hundred of them and every mouth remained sealed."

Caballero nodded reflectively. "They have that kind of strength, Fernando. They can suffer. They can resist. They are like the rocks. But they are afraid."

"Afraid! Can you use that word to men who have set with closed lips while their fingernails were pulled off because they would not reveal where you were hiding?"

"They are able to endure," Caballero said. "But they have no talent to revolt. They would die rather than run the risk of dying." He looked painfully at his friend. "Can you understand?"

"I understand only that you no longer believe in them."

"I believe in them, but for what they are and not for what you imagine them to be. Nothing can defeat them, but they cannot act. When I speak to them a little light glows in their eyes, and when I stop, the light goes out."

"In time it will remain."

"No, Fernando, they have been too long in the yoke. They are like oxen who would allow themselves to be beaten to death by a man whom they could trample underfoot. The people have never known freedom and they will never lift a finger to fight for that which is unknown. Their liberty must be handed to them. They will then accept it as the unfamiliar dish it is and take little bites until they accustom themselves to the strange taste. In the end they will find it palatable and it will give them sustenance. *But it must be given to them!* They will never go into the dark forest to take it for themselves. And that was what we set out to do. All we have accomplished is to make them weaker."

He held out his hands to the fire. Fernando dropped to his knees. "You are not being just, Esquipulas. You have not given them time."

Caballero laughed shortly. "It has been almost a year, and in that time has a single peasant offered to join us? Por Dios, has one man come to us to say: 'You are fighting our fight and I would be at your side?'" He snapped his fingers. "Pardon! I forgot. There has been one. The ancient who brought up this piece of paper. He who has grandsons old enough to bear arms has offered himself. But who else, Fernando? We have left four of our men dead from government muskets and who has stepped forth to replace them?"

"There has been no one," Fernando said in a low voice.

"And why should there be?" Caballero asked scornfully. "Why should men tear themselves from the sides of their women when we have made all of them our wards? When was it that you last slept next to your wife, Fernando? Your son must be starting to walk upright like a human being, but when did your eyes see him last?"

Fernando looked at the drawn face on which the skin clung tightly as though there were not enough of it for the bones underneath. "We have all denied ourselves many things, and you perhaps more than others. No one knows this better than I. The earth makes a hard wife. But what do we know of this man to make ourselves trust him?"

"Nothing."

"And you would still deliver yourself to him?"

"It is a danger. We have long embraced danger."

"For a reason. Is there reason now?"

"I believe so."

"And what is that reason?"

"At the start we believed liberty must be brought to the people and we thought the Texans would do it, but they failed us. Then we talked of the day when the Americans would open the door and let in fresh air, but the Americans seem content to send in business men instead of soldiers. Then we tried to make it come from the people themselves, and that was the biggest failure of all." He turned to Fernando. "Perhaps we were wrong in all these things. Perhaps that which we have sought can come from one of our own."

"From this man who was given power by Manuel Armijo?"

"We do not know that is true."

"We know that the Rurales infest the country exactly as they did under Armijo."

"Perhaps this man just needs a little time," Caballero said. "We know a few things about him. We know that he is not Armijo, and that is a big thing. And we know he reduced Salazar to the rank of captain and assigned him to garrison duty in San Miguel. And we heard that when he did this he said some very unpleasant things to Don Damasio. There are one or two things else. This Governor has made the plaza a thing of beauty. He has built a little park in front of the Rosario." He rolled a cigarette and picked up a brand from the fire. "I wonder how Santa Fe looks," he said.

467

Fernando said: "Then you are resolved to go?" knowing it was not Santa Fe.

"I am resolved only for myself," Caballero said quietly. "I know that at the end of the road may lie a trap. I would order no one to come with me. Here is the paper. Take it to the men and let them consider it and decide for themselves."

Fernando went over to talk to the men, whose numbers had been increased at the last visit to Bent's Fort by those, including Carlos Gutiérrez, who had declined to leave the fort originally when the plan was to join the Texans. Caballero stared into the fire thinking how the name alone, Santa Fe, became her name, became Soledad, became his wife, so that seeing it on the paper he saw her face and the palace just the building that was near the house where she lived. He thought of the days and the weeks and the months that had gone, lost irretrievably, each day widening the emptiness between them, each day adding to the strangeness they would have for each other, and the hollowness that was never far away sucked at his belly and he could not endure it.

Fernando looked down silently at the thin, racked face and then he said: "They have voted to accompany you."

"All of them?"

"All of them."

Caballero raised his eyes. "And you?"

"I cast the first vote."

2

FROM A CRAG high in the Rincons, on which the new winter snow had already fallen, Damasio Salazar watched the slow progress of the riders on the narrow trail far below. His eyes, tearing from the icy wind, gleamed with satisfaction. He pointed to a small hand-drawn map spread on the rock in front of him. "Here they are, Don Tomás," he said. "They follow the trail here and then they enter the Canyon of the Little Fox. We will swing around and enter the canyon from the west and be inside before they get there." He showed his yellow teeth. "We will provide welcome."

Tomás Martínez, his face blue with the cold, asked: "Why

must we go the long way to the west entrance?" He put a gloved finger on the map. "We could cut down the trail here and slip into the east entrance ahead of Caballero and save making the big circuit."

Salazar picked up a handful of snow. "Because of this. The entrance from the east must show no tracks."

"The canyon is far below," Armijo's nephew retorted. "The snow will not have reached there as yet. It is only in the high places."

"That may be, friend, but if there is no snow there will be earth, and earth can tell a story as easily as snow. We take no chances, we go in from the west."

Martínez tightened his serape around his neck. "I do not know why we had to come to this freezing wilderness in the first place. Caballero could have been taken on the plaza in Santa Fe as easily as out here."

"Without doubt," Salazar said. "But his excellency wanted no disturbance in the capital. I have told you this."

"And he is right, I think," Martínez sneered. "He will not go down in history as Don Mariano the Well-Beloved. Por Dios, if Caballero were to enter Santa Fe with more than a dozen armed men, he might find himself acclaimed Governor of New Mexico before he crossed the plaza!"

"The Governor is less than adored," Salazar said, "but for the time being he is the Governor. It was difficult for me to persuade him to give me this chance. And I had grown to like the rank of major. I should like again to face forward on my career instead of backward." He slapped his cold hands together. "Give the orders to the men to mount and get started. We must be there to act as hosts when the outlaws come into the abode of el zorrito."

Caballero and his men picked their way carefully down the treacherous, snow-laden trail. They descended below the snow line; the hoofs of their horses rang on the frozen earth. They passed below the frost to where the winter had not yet stretched its cold fingers. The vapor vanished from their lips and from the nostrils of the horses. The men pushed back their sombreros and wiped off the sweat that was suddenly there. The earth was loose and the horses churned up dust. The men slipped out of their serapes, rolled them into bundles, and tied them to their saddles. They crossed a dry riverbed. The sun was close to the rim of the mountains, and the floor of the valley was filling slowly with a blue haze.

Fernando craned his neck. The sun was tan on the bare sides of the eastern hills and then became a garland of rosy flowers higher up in the snows. "When do you want to make camp, Esquipulas?"

"There is a canyon half an hour's ride ahead. The walls will make protection against the night wind. We will ride that far."

The men were slouched casually in their saddles, but their eyes were alert. Their rifles were cradled in their arms. Caballero had sent word to the alcalde of Mora that he was accepting the Governor's invitation and he had waited long enough to give the alcalde time to notify the Governor. He did not believe Governor Martínez would violate his pledged word, but he was taking no chances. He had scouts riding in the front and rear and he had ordered his men to be prepared for attack at any time.

The sun was resting delicately on the mountain line when they came to where the valley narrowed to the mouth of the canyon. Caballero called a halt and sent the advance scouts into the canyon to reconnoiter. They reported the interior was apparently empty and there were no tracks of horses anywhere. Caballero waved his men toward the defile, and the band entered. They passed through the narrow opening that debouched onto the floor of the canyon and continued on for about fifty yards and then the walls on either side of them exploded with musket fire.

"Ambush!" Caballero shouted. "Follow me!" He kicked his spurs into his horse and the animal leaped forward with a wild whinny. He tore down the length of the canyon, his men thundering behind him, and then he turned abruptly to the left and galloped up the boulder-strewn south wall. Behind them Salazar and his Rurales were streaming down from their positions. "Make your horses gallop if it kills them, hombres!" Caballero commanded. "Raise all the dust you can!" A third of the way up the side of the canyon he pulled his horse to a rearing stop and flung himself on the ground. "Take positions behind rocks and open fire! *Pronto! Pronto!* Do not wait for the dust to settle!"

The men leaped from their horses and knelt behind the boulders and began to shoot blindly through the dust. They heard cries of surprise and then of pain, and when the air cleared at last, they saw that Salazar and his soldiers had taken shelter behind trees and stones in the bed of the canyon.

Salazar commanded: "Fire at will!"

"At what?" Martínez asked.

"At the rocks! At anything! Keep them pinned down while I make a plan."

A rifle ball channeled the earth next to Martínez and he rolled hastily to one side. "Nombre de Dios! How many men does he have?"

Salazar sighted and squeezed the trigger. "I forget, Don Tomás, that this is your first experience with the gringo repeating rifles."

The gunfire poured down. "Santa Madre de Dios," Martínez whispered with awe.

Salazar grinned balefully. "I seem to remember in San Miguel you wondered often and out loud why I had not been able to capture Caballero and his scanty following. Now you know. But do not dirty your trousers, friend. This time we have enough men, even with those rifles."

"It is incredible!"

"You will believe soon enough. Meanwhile go down to the extreme end of my left flank and see to it that the men there are not so astounded that they forget to shoot back."

Fernando threw himself down at Caballero's side. "Do you see who is down there?"

"Salazar. I recognized him before. I have taken three shots at him, but he keeps himself well covered." He twisted around. "Say it, Fernando. Say it, and say it all."

"I will save my compliments for later."

"If I should be killed here, Fernando, do not bother to mark my grave with my name. Label it only 'The biggest fool in New Mexico.'"

"I will do so. Meanwhile what is your plan?"

"Salazar has more than two hundred men down there. For the

time being, we can keep them down there. In the end there is only one thing he can do. He will charge. And he must charge before the night falls or else we can slip away in the dark."

"What is he waiting for? It will be dark in less than an hour."

"I have tried to put myself in Salazar's shoes," Caballero said.

"That must have been pleasant."

"It will get dark down there before it does up here. He must be planning to make his attack when his men will be barely visible and we will still be in the light."

"And do we just lie around up here and wait for him to overrun us?"

Caballero smiled faintly. "I have proclaimed myself a fool, but even you will have to admit my foolishness occasionally does not extend to battle."

"Then you have a scheme?"

"Spread the word among the men to get themselves behind boulders that can be moved. When Salazar begins his charge they will wait until the Rurales reach the base of the rise and then they will fire a final volley and push down the boulders."

"Jesucristo!"

"The rocks will start a landslide and will cause confusion and will also raise dust."

"Then we jump onto our horses and take off."

"Yes, but not on up the canyon wall. I think Salazar will expect us to continue as we started, away from him. Instead the men will ride along the wall at the level we are now, back toward the canyon mouth we just passed through, and then about two hundred yards from here they will ride down into the canyon."

"Down to the canyon floor?"

"The darkness will protect us there too, Fernando."

Fernando nodded with respect and slithered away. He crawled from one man to another and gave Caballero's instructions. When he reached Carlos Gutiérrez, the huge man grabbed his arm. "Have you seen who is down there, Fernando?"

"Salazar, your admirable cousin? I have seen him."

"The nephew of Armijo is there."

"Por Dios, I had forgotten your little experience with him."

"I have not forgotten," Carlos said. His eyes burned like coals.

"Fernando, I have a favor to ask of you."

472

Fernando cocked his head. "In connection with Don Tomás?"

"Yes! How much time does our leader believe we have before the charge is made?"

"Less than half an hour now."

"It will be time enough. Fernando, listen to me."

"To save time I better get the lazo first."

Carlos's teeth gleamed. "He is there, waiting for you, the last man on the end."

His lariat in his hand, Fernando made his way carefully down the side of the canyon. Moving silently as a cat, slipping from rock to rock and then, as he came to the floor of the canyon, from tree to tree, he brought himself finally to a point less than fifteen feet from where Martínez was directing the fire of the soldiers, who, concentrating on their work, did not notice the solitary figure creeping through the dusk.

Fernando uncoiled his rope with great care, and then he cast it and it snaked out and the noose dropped over Martínez's shoulder. Don Tomás was catapulted into the air as though something had exploded under him, and then he was dragged on the ground as rapidly as Fernando's powerful arms could haul him in. His scream of surprise was drowned in the shooting, and when the soldiers who had been nearest to him realized what had happened he was in Fernando's arms.

Fernando lifted him as though he were a child and, using his body as shield, he scampered back up the hill. He deposited Martínez on the ground. "Here is an old friend who is anxious to see you, Carlos," he grunted. "He could not wait for the charge."

"Tomasito," Carlos said, with suppressed ecstasy. "Tomasito, what passes, little friend of my heart?" His fingers worked convulsively as though he were almost afraid to touch him. "Fernando, he does not speak," Carlos whispered. "Perhaps it is that the lazo squeezed the breath out of him." With consummate delicacy he loosened the noose. Martínez stared at him with horror. "Look, Fernando," Carlos said. "He still holds to his musket. He must believe he is not among friends." He took the gun from Martínez's limp fingers. "You do not need this here, Tomasito," he said gently. He tossed the musket away. "Now perhaps he will say something. He is still without voice, Fernando, and usually he has so many words he does not know what to do with them."

473

He snapped his fingers. "Perhaps he does not remember me! Hey, compañero, I am Carlos! Por Dios, do you not recognize your old friend Carlos?"

Martínez opened his dry lips. "What are you going to do with me?"

"He speaks!" Carlos chortled. He slapped his thigh.

"Time grows short," Fernando said without interest.

"Take me to your leader," Martínez said, trying to get authority into his voice.

Carlos scratched his head. "It presents a difficulty, mi bonito. He is engaged at the moment. There are bad people down there firing at him." He grinned. "Besides, he would only order that you be shot. He is a cruel man, that caballero."

Martínez pressed himself against the rock, his eyes rolling wildly. Carlos took him tenderly by the wrist, his dark, scarred face placid. Then Carlos's forehead wrinkled. "No, it was the other one," he reminded himself. He closed his massive fingers around Martínez's right wrist. His other hand wrapped itself lovingly around Martínez's arm, just below the elbow. Then he raised his knee and with an easy gesture that seemed to have in it no force he broke the arm as he would break a piece of kindling.

Martínez screamed. Fernando spat. "All right, you are even, Carlos. Now kill him."

"No," Carlos said.

"Why not?"

"I desire that he have a broken arm."

"He has a broken arm."

"To have a broken arm a man must be alive," Carlos said. "What would a corpse know of a broken arm? This one must live now. When his arm is in one piece, then I will kill him."

Fernando shrugged. "At least put a little ball in each knee. Or even one knee. For a bonus."

"No!" Carlos roared. "Not a thing but an arm that is broken." He lifted Martínez above his head and strode out from behind the rock. "Dogs! Catch this filth!" He hurled Martínez down the side of the canyon. He stood there ignoring the musket balls that spattered around him and waited until Martínez rolled to a stop and crawled to his own line. Then he stepped behind the rock.

A little later Caballero cried out: "They are beginning to

move!" He peered down the long barrel of his rifle. The bottom of the canyon now was almost dark. He could see figures moving about and now and then a piece of metal caught a stray gleam from the fading light. He heard the dull, deep beat of horses' hoofs. "Get ready," he ordered. The hoof-beats quickened and got louder and a moment later the line of soldiers appeared below them. He cried out: "Now, fire!" The rifles cracked out with almost a single sound and he shouted: "Heave!"

The boulders began their slow roll down the side of the canyon. They gathered momentum, tearing up other stones and bushes and small trees and clumps of earth, and the rumble became a roar and a wall of dust and Caballero clambered into his saddle and shouted: "Hombres, to horse!" He slapped the animal's rump and guided it toward the east. He could hear the terrified shouts of the Rurales and the whinnying of their horses, and then the cries were mixed with yells of pain from the soldiers and trumpeted screams from the horses and he knew that some of them had not been able to dodge the avalanche.

He reined sharply to the left, his men strung behind him, and his horse picked its way down the canyon. Presently he felt the ground level off under him and he spurred the horse toward the east again and then they passed through the mouth of the canyon.

3

SOLEDAD stirred the sweet, thick chocolate and wondered why Padre Martínez had called. Her eyes remained on the priest, who leaned against the hearth in the house on the Calle de la Muralla, motionless as a santo, and she tried to put from her mind the memory that this one was among those who had conspired in the death of her father.

"How many more of the meetings were held after Don Manuel arrived in the Rio Abajo?" Martínez asked.

"None, padre," she said, cold and disquieted.

"None? Not one?" He turned his head.

"Not one, padre." Dulce Virgen, she asked, why had he

chosen now to come when she was just beginning to find a peace and a manner of life? From the moment he had appeared in the room, his harsh face set in anger, she had trembled, and it was only by remembering what she knew of him and his part in the conspiracy that she controlled herself; and she knew that she should not think of that, for with it all he remained a priest.

"The little ricos ran back to their holes," he said contemptuously.

"Yes, padre. They gave the excuse that since Don Manuel no longer was Governor, there no longer was reason for the meetings."

"But when he first went to Albuquerque he still legally was Governor. Don Mariano was not named until months later."

She nodded wearily, biting her lip. It was true and with all his perceptiveness he would never know what the realization of that truth had meant to her. "It was just an excuse, padre. They were frightened. They were frightened to death. His presence was enough. On one day they were deep in brave plans, and on the next they were scattered and silent as mice." Her lips thinned. "He has said all along the ricos no longer are men, and he was right. Virgen santísima protect me! In this he was right!"

He shrugged. "Even Armijo can be right about truths."

She set down the cup and made a cigarette. "I saw the fear creep into their faces when they heard he was there. Their eyes fluttered like those of girls. Their mouths were agape. Santa Madre, but it was disgusting!"

He turned his head back to the fire so she would not see the smile on his lips and the twinkle in his eyes. "Did you see him?"

"I did not."

"And what did you then, my daughter?"

"The air could no longer be breathed. It stank of men's fear and of Armijo. I went to Chihuahua and visited with my sister and mother."

"And then you learned that Don Manuel had been removed as Governor and that there was a new Governor in the palace?"

"Yes, padre."

"And you returned to Santa Fe."

"As you see, padre."

He turned violently. "Why did you return?"

She looked puzzled. "This is my house, padre. Why should I not return to it?"

"But you waited until Don Manuel was gone!" He walked swiftly toward her, his cassock flaring, and he leaned over her. "Because you believed, now that Armijo was gone, it would be different here."

The puzzlement left her eyes. She smiled faintly. She held the cigarette to her lips with the gold tongs. "It is true, padre, that I thought things would be changed, but not in the way you mean. The new Governor was a Mexican officer and a gentleman, as Don Albino Pérez had been. I could remember how it had been then and I thought that perhaps that was how it might be now."

"And that the interdiction might be lifted from the name of your husband?" he rasped.

"I have no husband, padre."

His hand flew out, the fingers curled like the talons of a great bird. "Do not speak blasphemy!"

The cigarette shook. "I have no husband."

"You accepted the holy sacrament of matrimony before God!" he said. "As long as you both live you remain husband and wife."

"I understand, padre. But God will have to content Himself that the marriage lives in His eyes. For me it exists no longer."

"You have no right to alter it in the smallest way."

"I make no attempt to alter that which was sealed in His name," she said quietly. "I seek no other husband."

He knelt before her and stroked her hand. His eyes were luminous. "Doña Soledad, pobrecita, can you truly condemn yourself to this life of loneliness?"

The harsh voice was tender and the calloused hands seemed softer than her own. She wanted to weep and she hated herself for the weakness. She pulled away her hand and thrust it behind her back, and she turned her head so she would not look upon his eyes, which carried a pity she could not bear. "The condemnation was made before the sacrament was taken, padre. I do but accept that which was made inevitable."

"Only death and the Judgment are inevitable. All lesser things are not so predestined."

She uttered a low cry and stood up and walked away from him. The trembling was on her again. She threw the cigarette into

477

the fireplace, and she gripped her kerchief and prayed: "Dulce Virgen, give me strength," and she thought how the holiness was on his side and her head fell helplessly. "What is done is done and cannot be undone," she cried.

"It was done in another time."

"It is the same time. The dead are still dead."

"He who did what was done is no longer the same."

"He is the same, the same."

The priest rose slowly to his feet as though his body were filled with aching bones. "There are many who no longer are the same."

"My concern is not with others—only with him who married me with my father's death in his heart."

His fingers traced a cross with great weariness. "May God pity you for the hatred that has shriveled you."

"I need no pity!"

"Then you are more alone than you know."

"I have found this hatred a nourishing diet." The trembling was gone now. She walked toward him, her head erect, her eyes flashing. "It is not sweet and it does not cloy."

"Then you have no interest in Don Esquipulas, where he is, whether he lives or is dead?"

"Your words have informed me that he lives, padre," she said coldly. "I would not have asked."

"Then I will tell you this not because of any concern you might have in your husband's welfare, for you have assured me you have none, but to acquaint you with the character of the man who now is Governor." He looked at her from under the heavy brows. "Governor Martínez posted an invitation in every plaza of New Mexico asking your husband to come to Santa Fe to see if their differences could not be resolved. He guaranteed Don Esquipulas his personal safety, even to leaving Santa Fe unharmed if they could not reconcile themselves. Don Esquipulas, who apparently also believed in the qualities of a gentleman and an officer, accepted." He paused and looked blankly at her tenseness. "Would you like to know what happened?"

She recovered. "If it pleases you, padre."

"As soon as Governor Martínez received word through the alcalde of Mora that your husband would come to Santa Fe, he sent out Damasio Salazar with two hundred soldiers to lay ambush."

"He could not have dishonored his pledge!"

"That is what your husband must have thought," Martínez said dryly. "I believe he must have concluded otherwise when the musket balls began to fly."

She walked to a table and began to make a cigarette. "But Don Esquipulas escaped the ambush?"

"With great skill he fought his way to safety."

"Then he will know better than to trust Governor Martínez in the future," she said with studied indifference.

"The Governor was understandably enraged at the failure of his plan—so enraged that he himself is now going to take to the field against your husband."

"He will not catch him." There was unconscious pride in her voice.

"I am not so certain, Doña Soledad. Governor Martínez is determined, once and for all, to put an end to your husband's acts against the government. He entrusts this assignment to no small group of Rurales. He leaves Santa Fe at the head of five hundred presidial troops."

The color drained from her cheeks. "Five hundred men to make war on a few outlaws? You joke, padre."

"No less!"

"The man will make himself the laughing-stock of Mexico, even if he captures Don Esquipulas."

The priest sighed. "He has thought of that, my daughter. He does not announce publicly that he leads an army against a handful of men. It will be said that he is going to make war on the Utes, which is a respectable venture. He may even go on and shoot a few Indians when he is finished with your husband."

She was silent for a moment and then she struck the flint with a steady hand and held the flame to the cigarette. "Why do you reveal to me these secrets of state, padre?" she asked in a conversational tone of voice. "Even if I were so minded I could not go to the Governor and ask him to change his mind. This is a different Governor, padre, and Don Esquipulas has committed crimes against the government."

"Crimes!" The word rolled like a peal of thunder. "That is a strange word to pass your lips, señora! His 'crimes' are no greater than those you urged upon the ricos in the Rio Abajo. You are guiltier than he. You called for open revolution. He merely returns to the people what belongs to them."

"My efforts were a joke, padre," she said.

"You meant them as no joke. Your intent was as fully serious as that of your husband." He came close to her, his hands joined. "You were the other side of the coin. And you knew it, you knew it! In your heart you knew you were working with him, hand in hand, and that was what gave purpose to your actions and timbre to your voice and eloquence to your speech!"

Her face was white. "It is not true."

His eyes burned on her. "It is true! You cried hatred and drove him from you when he risked his life to look again upon your face, and you even tricked your mind into believing this hatred to be true, and yet you were compelled to stretch your hand across New Mexico to touch your fingers to his."

What was it the voice had said through the blackness of the cell? *Put your fingers through the bars, linda, let me taste the tips of them again.* It was not fair, los dulces Nombres, it was not fair! "You put motives into my design that did not exist, padre!"

He shrugged. "So be it," he said, suddenly calm.

"I still do not know why you have told me of this."

"It does not matter now."

"You have started, padre. Finish!"

He fingered his cross. "I have been ordered to go with the troops as chaplain. There is every chance that your husband and his followers may be massacred. He is a clever leader but cleverness cannot balance the disproportion of the forces and I do not believe he will permit himself to be taken alive. If he is wounded mortally I will attempt to reach him to give him final sacrament."

"That is your function."

"It also is my function to give a dying man temporal as well as spiritual consolation," he said. "If Don Esquipulas spends his last minutes in my arms is there any word from his wife that I may repeat to him?"

"Nothing."

"Nothing?"

"*Nada! Nada!*"

"We leave at sunrise tomorrow, Doña Soledad."

"*Nada, nada.*" She held out her hands. "I have put out the flames, little by little, and my hands are charred, padre. I am just coming to know a peace. En el nombre de Dios, do not try to start the fire again." She fell to her knees and pressed the cross to her lips and she no longer tried to withhold the tears. "Let me own my peace, padre. There is nothing, nothing." The syllables beat on her head like the drums in the pueblos. "*Nada, padre, nada, nada.*"

4

Don Manuel pulled his sombrero farther down on his face against the afternoon sun. He stretched his legs. He clasped his hands over his belly. The sheltered patio was warm. On a table, still unopened, was the latest letter from Don Juan Bautista Vigil. It was not until four o'clock, when a servant appeared with refreshments, that Don Manuel bothered to break the seal.

". . . There has been the greatest excitement here, Don Manuel. As you know, the Governor led the troops to the eastern plains, ostensibly to engage with Utes but in reality to take Caballero, your old friend. Since Caballero's acceptance of the Governor's original invitation had been received through the alcalde of Mora, he went there first, as Salazar had done, but this time the bird had flown. The question was put to a number of the villagers, but no one would speak—this Caballero has the people under a spell!—save some old man, and his speech was so insulting the Governor ordered him executed and ordered further that the body remain in the plaza for three days as an example to the others.

"The Governor could not return to the capital with nothing to show for his campaign, so he moved about the plains until he encountered a small party of Utes. There was an engagement near the Ocate. He defeated the Indians and took some prisoners, and from them he learned that a band of New Mexicans, apparently the outlaws, had been seen heading north toward Raton Pass, and he was satisfied they had fled the country, doubtless to their winter nest at Bent's Fort. He released two of the Ute prisoners with a request to their chief, Panasiyave, to come to Santa Fe to make a treaty of peace, and then he returned here.

"The Indian chief agreed to discuss peace. He arrived here with six subchiefs and an escort of twenty-five warriors. It was a sight to see, Don Manuel! The leaders went into the palace and the warriors remained in the plaza, and before long the entire city was crowded there gaping at them.

"I was not in the Governor's office during the conference, so I am unable to tell you exactly what happened there. I do know the Governor had some sheets stretched across part of the office and that he secreted about fifty soldiers behind the curtain. He argued at considerable length with Panasiyave and the other Ute leaders and was apparently unable to come to terms with them. Panasiyave got up to leave, and the Governor, apparently, interpreted this as a threatening move. He picked up his chair and brained the old man and at the same time shouted an order to the soldiers hidden behind the curtain. The soldiers came out immediately and started to shoot.

"The Indians, who had all been disarmed before they were admitted to the Governor's presence, fled from the office. The soldiers chased them into the plaza, shooting the while. The chiefs and the warriors waiting outside jumped on their horses and galloped out of the plaza, and in the end there were eight dead and more than thirty wounded, mainly among the men and women standing in the plaza. The commotion was greater than anything since Gonzales.

"I have been able to learn that an investigation has been ordered by the commandant in Chihuahua and that a general of higher rank than the Governor is coming here from El Paso del Norte to look into the affair. . . ."

Don Manuel went into his house and bathed and perfumed himself. He stood naked before a mirror. The rash was gone. His body was brown from the sun and without blemish save the scar of his old wound on his thigh. His belly was flat and hard from the days in the saddle and his long walks on his broad land.

He dressed and summoned a courier and dispatched to his former head of customs, Don José Antonio Chaves, a message that consisted of a single line: "It is the right moment."

5

IN THE CITY OF MEXICO in the month of December 1844, in another of the interminable insurrections, General Santa Anna was overthrown, imprisoned and finally exiled by a faction led by José Joaquín Herrera, leader of the liberal Federalists. Although the violent change in government was accomplished as usual with the assistance of the garrison of the city, it appeared this time to be a genuine move in a new direction and not another clash between opposing military cliques.

Herrera was opposed to military dictatorship. He believed the Republic of the United States was the highest political statement mankind had made and he desired that the Republic of Mexico follow the same path. He believed in the dignity of his people. He believed his government should represent these people—all of the people, including peasants. He believed in open discussion and in the blending of many minds for the general welfare.

He believed too that Mexico and Texas and the United States could exist side by side in peace and even in friendship. He was considered by his enemies to be an idealistic fool, but he had for the moment the support of the country, and the generals and the colonels elected to lay low, confident that in the end he would ruin himself.

The greatest problem that confronted him was the still unsettled question of Texas. The commissioners at Sabinas had drawn up the treaty Texas had asked for, under the terms of which Mexico recognized Texan independence and the Lone-Star Republic agreed not to join the United States. The treaty was not as yet ratified by either the Texan or Mexican governments, and Herrera undertook as the primary task of his administration the difficult job of persuading the embittered Mexican Congress to approve this agreement which would forever separate Texas from the mother country.

Neither Herrera nor anyone else in Mexico knew that while the Texan commissioners were signing the treaty in Sabinas, other Texan negotiators were at the same time concluding a secret agreement with President Tyler in Washington opening the way for admission of Texas to the Union. And because of the delays in communication he did not know either that in the same month of December the Congress of the United States, having been informed at last by Tyler of the secret agreement with the Texans, voted its approval of annexation.

In January 1845 a courier arrived in the City of Mexico from Santa Fe bearing an impeachment against Governor Martínez drawn up by the Junta of New Mexico, charging Martínez with embezzlement. The same courier brought a separate indictment prepared by the former head of customs in Santa Fe, detailing a long list of peculations and frauds. At the same time Governor Martínez's private secretary arrived in the national capital with a request from the Governor for another ten thousand dollars to keep the government wheels turning in New Mexico, supplementing the fifteen thousand dollars Martínez had asked for and had received earlier. Before the month was out, Herrera was presented with the findings of the general who had investigated the shooting in Santa Fe, for which the blame was laid entirely on the Governor. President Herrera removed Martínez. Unable to swallow Armijo, whom he considered another Santa Anna, Herrera appointed José Chaves y Castillo, senior deputy of the Junta, as provisional governor.

From Washington on the 3rd day of March 1845, a day before he was to turn over his office to the newly elected President Polk, Tyler, empowered by the vote of the Congress, sent his representative to Austin to make formal offer of annexation, a move that Mexican leaders and the Mexican press had declared would bring about war between the United States and Mexico. As one of his first official acts President Polk sent a strong naval force and an army under General Zachary Taylor to New Orleans to be ready for any emergency.

When it learned of Tyler's action, the proud Mexican Congress was thrown into uproar. On March 21 Mexico broke off diplomatic relations with the United States. Herrera felt peace might still be salvaged. He reminded his countrymen that Texas had asked for the treaty originally and he argued that if Mexico ratified the document, Texas would be bound by its honor to turn its back on the United States. On May 17, making no attempts

484

to hide its misgivings, the Mexican Congress gave in to the eloquence of its President and endorsed the treaty.

When the Texas lawmakers convened on June 12, their country was in the enviable position of a beautiful woman whose favors were being sought by two suitors. On one hand was the envoy from the United States, offering admission; on the other, the representative from Mexico with the validated Treaty of Sabinas. It did not take the Texan officials long to choose; they rejected the treaty and accepted annexation, a decision later approved by the almost unanimous vote of the citizens of Texas.

Although the decision was a shocking personal blow to Herrera, he still attempted to stand against the tide of opinion in his country. He was accused of disgracing Mexican honor. The militarists proclaimed him a weakling who tried to make his way with words in a world where only the mailed fist was respected. They cried out that only blood would remove the stain from the national blazon.

In his dogged pleas for moderation, Herrera was not aided by the sudden appearance in the City of Mexico of a plenipotentiary from President Polk, who offered to settle the differences between the two countries by buying California and also paying the Mexicans something for their "imaginary interest" in Texas. The proposal was taken by the hypersensitive Mexicans as adding insult to injury and served only to rub salt into lacerated hearts.

Herrera continued to dream that by some miracle conflict might yet be averted, but he was not wholly devoid of a sense of practicality. He was aware that New Mexico was the least protected part of his country, a thumb stuck out into alien territory. And he knew too that Texas had claimed as its own all the territory east of the Rio Grande and that this claim had been recognized by the United States. Now that Texas was part of the United States, the country he had idolized would undoubtedly consider New Mexico a part of the annexation.

With a heavy heart he turned to the strong man of the north and in the spring of 1845 reappointed Manuel Armijo political and military chief of New Mexico. It was the third time Don Manuel had been called upon to serve his country as Governor and the first time in New Mexican history a man had been so honored.

In July, General Taylor was ordered to sail from New Orleans to Corpus Christi, and he established a position on the west bank of the Nueces River. Between the Nueces and the Rio Grande to the west lay one hundred and fifty miles of land claimed by both Texas and Mexico. Taylor and his army remained encamped for six months. In December the militarists in Mexico had their way and Herrera's government was overthrown and his hard-won constitutional reforms were torn up. Mexico reverted to naked military dictatorship. An appeal was sent to Santa Anna, begging him to return from his exile and once again take over the rule of Mexico.

Upon the fall of Herrera's regime General Taylor was ordered to march across the disputed territory and take a position on the east bank of the Rio Grande. Mexican officials and citizens protested, but Taylor was ordered to hold his ground. General Mariano Arista crossed the Rio Grande with his army and the long-awaited conflict began, between two generals each of whom within a few years would be elected President of his country.

On May 11, 1846 President Polk announced to the Congress of the United States: "War exists, and not withstanding all our efforts to avoid it, exists by the act of Mexico itself."

6

THE NEWS of the dismissal of Governor Martínez reached Santa Fe at a time when his popularity, always less than great, hit bottom. Martínez had just imposed a direct tax upon his subjects, a step that cost Albino Pérez his life and that might have cost Martínez his, since among the private citizens so taxed was Manuel Armijo, assessed five hundred dollars.

Don Mariano was more fortunate than Don Albino: he was able to leave the country with his whole skin. The money he had just collected stuck to him. When Don José Chaves y Castillo took over, the treasury was bankrupt. The Junta found itself with insufficient funds to purchase the stationery and ink necessary for its business. In order to raise a few dollars for this purpose, the deputies moved out of their meeting-hall to a room in the palace and rented out the Assembly Hall for bailes.

Funds always were low at this time of year, however, just before arrival of the annual caravan, and the fiscal year of the New Mexican government was timed for this event. Although conditions had never before been quite so bad, the deputies were encouraged by the prospect of the advent of the wagons. The provisional Governor reappointed his nephew, Don José Antonio Chaves, to his old post as head of the customs, and the deputies sat back and waited for the merchants to come.

That year the wagons did not arrive. They were lined up by the score in the meadows outside of Independence, their owners afraid to give the word that would start them on the long journey across the prairies. The traders looked at the war clouds collecting in the sky and refused to risk sending their goods into a country with whom the United States soon might be at war.

Most of the New Mexican merchants were equally cautious. They feared that if war started, Santa Fe might be attacked and possibly destroyed and everything stored in warehouses there lost. They were reasonably certain no Mexican army would attack Missouri.

A few of the New Mexican traders took their chances. They banded together and drove through to Santa Fe. They were greeted by Don José Antonio Chaves, who asked them where the others were. They told him there were no others.

Within a month the government of New Mexico was paralyzed.

When the official courier arrived from the City of Mexico with the appointment of Manuel Armijo, the citizens in Santa Fe flocked to their churches and gave prayers of thanks, and a delegation was sent to Albuquerque to escort him to the city. As the well-remembered carriage entered the plaza the hearts of many persons were so filled they could not even raise their voices to cheer, and as the old familiar figure with its resolute, confident face stepped down and limped into the palace, there were few who did not weep.

Don Manuel was back. Now all would be well.

The deputies looked upon him as a savior.

1

IN THE LATE SPRING of 1846 Esquipulas Caballero and Carlos Gutiérrez returned to Bent's Fort after a winter of trapping on the remote reaches of the Snake River. The breakup of the cold that year had been followed by heavy rains. For more than a week they had ridden in a downpour that at times turned so blinding the pack animals trudging behind them loaded with the winter catch became heads without bodies.

The men huddled in their ponchos, enjoying the exquisite misery known only to Mexicans who have not for days looked upon a blue sky. The rain beat against their faces, the fur hats without brims which had served them so well in the winter now offering small protection against the driving water. Carlos made a cigarette and tried to light it. He sank his face into the recess of the poncho. The rain spilled in. When the flame finally was going, the cigarette had dissolved. He threw away the shreds, cursing. "I have discovered the secret at last," he said. "It is the beavers."

"What is the beavers?" Caballero inquired.

"This rain."

Caballero considered. "Are you saying that the rain is the beavers?" he asked at length.

"No, por Cristo, I am saying that the rain is because of the beavers."

"That is an interesting observation, Carlos. Would you do the favor of explaining what it means?"

Carlos waved his arm. "It is because of all the dead beavers, the ones we have trapped and the ones that have been trapped by all the others."

"Have I missed a sentence somewhere?" Caballero asked politely.

"What is the function of a beaver?"

Caballero scratched his soaking beard. "He assists in the making of small beavers?"

"He makes dams."

"That is true."

"What is the function of a dam?"

"The catechism gets easier. It holds back water."

"Exactly!" Carlos shouted. "And since beavers are being killed, they are prevented from doing what they were intended to do."

Caballero nodded gravely. "You have struck upon a great truth, Carlos. We must not fail to warn Señor Bent that if he does not desist he will cover the earth with a flood."

"We shall all drown," Carlos said lugubriously.

"Perhaps we shall learn to build dams."

"I do not believe so. We are not so clever as the beavers."

They rode in silence. Presently the rain abated. Here and there the clouds parted and revealed a touch of blue. Carlos wrung the water from his hat. "I defecate on a hat of beaver," he said with disgust. "I like fur on one place of a body, and it is not on the head of a man. Ah, Dios, a clear sky and a bright sun and a broad brim to keep the face in the shade and a little sweat in the small of the back! I am a tolerant man and I do not in the least object to rain when it is modest and brief. But, por la Virgen, this is too much!"

Caballero grinned. "We shall have the sun before long, and as much as even you can want."

"It will be good to return. Up here the country is not very different and yet it is in no way the same. When do you believe we will start back?"

"As soon as we settle our accounts with Señor Bent and re-equip ourselves."

"We must all get the new revolving pistols Señor Colt is making."

"Señor Bent has agreed to put some aside for us."

"Why is it that we are unable to invent such things as revolving pistols and repeating rifles?" Carlos asked.

"Perhaps it is because we are too busy inventing Don Manuels."

Carlos's teeth showed white against his weathered face. "It will be like the old days with Don Manuel in Santa Fe." He shook his head. "Somehow it did not have the right taste with the other."

"I agree, Carlos."

"Fernando says it makes no difference. Perhaps it does not to him. He has a big mind. But I have a small mind. I find it difficult to hate an idea. I can understand an enemy only as a man. When I look through the front sight of my rifle I see no idea but only the face of Don Manuel or that of Tomás Martínez."

Now the rain had stopped and the air was clean and smelled of the spring. There were large pieces of blue in the sky, and in the distance across the plains they could see where the sun was shining. They took off their ponchos and stretched in their deerskin clothing, from which most of the fringes had long since been removed to repair the rents made during the winter work.

Caballero filled his short trapper's pipe and lit it. It had been a good season. The haul was heavy. The Indians had bothered them, but not too much. The months of isolation had drawn from them all that was in them of fortitude and strength. What it was he had seen in the mountain men when he first had come to Bent's Fort was in them now: the reliance of a man on himself. And now it was ended and soon they would be back at the fort and would exchange the hours of their work for new weapons and ammunition and new horses. Then they would return to their country.

The mountains there were good friends who waited patiently for their return, and the air would be dry and their own, and the old enemy, the true enemy, would be in Santa Fe. Carlos was right, he thought. There had to be a face on the far side of the rifle sight. The other things were important and no man was removed from his thoughts, but the core was Armijo, and now Armijo was back.

He knew the struggle was not against the man, but the man gave it form and substance. The palace was a mold, and those who entered the governor's office and held power were shaped in the end in one way. Don Manuel had given to the palace his own features. He had come to be bigger than himself and was now enacting a role, and no matter how often the actor changed, the role would remain the same. But in Caballero's life the role had been created by Armijo, and to war against anyone else was to war against an understudy.

It was futile. It always would be futile. It was a conceit to believe it was war. It was no more than the biting of gnats. There could be no resolution. And yet, he knew now, he could never discontinue it.

The Indians were encamped as always on the great clearing in front of the main gate of the fort. As he and Carlos rode slowly between the rows of conical skin jacales, smelling the acrid smoke of the cook fires, he reflected, as he had done often before, on the miracle of the administration of the Bents. Here gathered in front of their wigwams were warriors of the most savage tribes: Apaches, Navajos, Cheyennes, Utes, Comanches—Indians whose hatreds were so unquenchable that they killed among themselves as readily as they fought with white men. They sat quietly now, eating, smoking, talking, listening to the low chanting of their medicine men. None of them paid any attention as the two New Mexicans passed by.

In any other place in the world except there in the shadow of the fort those same Indians were their enemies. The braves who did not lift an eye as their horses picked their way through the camp would kill them as automatically and as instinctively as they would kill rattlesnakes if they encountered them an hour's ride from there. And it was not one-sided. But here it was as though they all had another vision, as though they saw and yet did not see. Even the horses, who would whinny at the faint smell of a single Indian in the wilderness, seemed to understand that here it was different, that this was a place of truce.

Perhaps Charles Bent was right, Caballero thought, impossible as it always sounded, when he expatiated on a favorite theme that one day this peaceful intermingling would be everywhere.

The two men approached the gate and prepared to enter the fort. The guards glanced at them. They were no different in appearance from other returning trappers. Their faces were weather-beaten and Caballero's cheeks, where the gray-streaked beard did not cover them, were as dark as those of Carlos. There were claw-marks around their eyes from the endless squinting against the snows and blinding waters. Their unkempt hair hung in coarse tangles below their shoulders.

One of the guards asked with a straight face: "Been somewhere?" He waved his arm to wave them in when suddenly another guard stepped up to him and whispered something in his ear. The first guard frowned and looked puzzled. "I'm sorry, boys, you'll have to wait a minute," he said. He placed himself directly in their path. The other guard trotted over to a corporal and spoke to him, and the corporal hurried away.

"What is the matter?" Caballero asked in English.

"It'll be straightened out in a minute," the guard said. "The corporal's gone to fetch Mr. Bent."

"For what reason?"

"We'll have to wait for Mr. Bent," the guard said firmly.

Caballero leaned on the pommel, conscious of the now curious stares of the Indians around the gate. He and his men had passed through the gate for years and had never been stopped.

The corporal returned. "It's all right, boys, come on in."

The guards moved aside with evident relief.

"What is all this?" Caballero asked.

"Mr. Bent asked for you to come to his office," the corporal said.

Caballero shrugged and they rode into the fort. He quickly sensed an atmosphere of excitement. He gave his horse to Carlos and walked over to Bent's office.

When he entered, Bent got up immediately and walked around the desk. "It is good to see you, Don Esquipulas. I am sorry you were held up at the gate. The order did not apply to you."

"What order? What goes on here, Don Carlos?"

"Have a drink first and sit down." He poured whisky into a glass and filled a glass for himself. "Welcome back."

Caballero emptied the glass and set it on the desk, sat down and stretched his legs wearily. He took a cheroot from the box Bent extended to him. "And now, Don Carlos, what is the great mystery?"

Bent sat down behind the desk. He looked at Caballero keenly. "First of all, Don Esquipulas, you must forgive the guards. I have issued an order that no Mexican may enter my fort without my permission. The guards knew who you both were and were perhaps overzealous. I did not intend to cause you embarrassment."

"There was none," Caballero said politely. "But why this order?"

Bent leaned back in his chair. "Don Esquipulas, for a long time now, a year or more, things have not been going well between your country and mine. And what happens in Washington and the City of Mexico comes here as a backwash. We both are subject to actions taken by men thousands of miles away."

Caballero stiffened. "There is going to be war."

"It may have already started," Bent said quietly.

"I grieve for you, Don Carlos," Caballero said instantly. "And for your wife and your children."

"Thank you. It is kind of you to think of them."

"But I still do not understand why you take such precautions up here, Don Carlos. The Texans have been fighting a war with Mexico for many years and it has never reached up here. We only hear of distant battles. We get no chance to take part in them."

"It will be different this time," Bent said.

Caballero removed the cigar from his mouth and rose slowly to his feet. On his bearded, worn face only the eyes were alive. "Are you saying that an American army is coming to New Mexico, Don Carlos?"

"Yes."

He saw her face before him. He clenched his hands. "For what purpose?" he asked in a still voice.

"What is the usual purpose of an enemy army?"

"The Texans sent men to attack innocent peasants." Now in the quiet room it seemed to him that she too was listening.

"This army will come here to rid the government of New Mexico of Manuel Armijo and to make New Mexico a part of the United States."

"A part of the United States? With what status, Don Carlos?"

"Equal to that of any other territory."

"And the people?" It was the people, he told himself rigidly, the people and the idea and the removal of Armijo, only the face now was not as he had seen it over the drawn cover, but as he remembered it from how many other places?

"Those who desire may go to Mexico with all their possessions."

"And the others?" In those times they could not be near

493

each other without touching, and now how long had it been?

"Will remain and become citizens of the United States."

"Inferior to Americans?" It was the people, he told himself.

Bent stood up and put his hand on his shoulder. "Sit down, Don Esquipulas," he said. He was silent for a moment. "Your countrymen will be Americans," he said quietly. "They who swear allegiance will be citizens, no different from citizens in any other part of the Union."

Caballero dug his fingers into his knees to stop the trembling in his hands. He was silent for several moments. "Where is this army now, Don Carlos?"

"It is being formed in Fort Leavenworth, on the Missouri."

"That is not far from Independence."

"It is not far."

"The army will travel west on the Santa Fe Trail."

"More or less."

"Do you know the commander, Don Carlos?"

"Yes. He is Colonel Stephen Watts Kearny."

Caballero regarded him intently. "Is this Kearny a good man, Don Carlos?"

"He is a very good man."

Caballero stood up. He put his half-smoked cheroot in a tray. "I go to Fort Leavenworth."

There was a knock on the door and Bent called out: "Come in."

Fernando entered the office. Caballero embraced him and then asked Bent: "He knows, does he not?"

"He knows about Kearny. Not that you go to him."

"Where else could he go?" Fernando asked. He said to Caballero: "Carlos told me you returned. I have fresh clothes laid out for you and two horses saddled and ready to go."

"Two horses," Caballero said.

"Do you mean you go with him?" Bent asked.

Fernando shrugged. "It is too late to change the habits of a lifetime."

2

THE SERGEANT ON DUTY at the main gate of Fort Leavenworth folded his arms across his chest. "He'd have my head! I've been telling you that for more than three weeks. Why don't you boys just go and enlist?"

"We may do that," Caballero said patiently, "but we desire to see Colonel Kearny first."

"Why? Why must you see the old man?"

Caballero studied the large chevrons on the thick arms of the sergeant before he replied. "I want to look into his eyes and speak to him."

"Are you crazy?" The sergeant looked helplessly at the other guards. "Listen, we have almost two thousand men here! Supposing each one of them had to see the color of the old man's eyes before he swore himself in." He wiped the sweat from his face. "Why don't you two go off somewhere and make up your minds whether you want in or not. But for the love of God stop pestering me to take you in to see the colonel. It just isn't possible."

Caballero bowed courteously. "Many thanks, señor sargento. Come, Fernando."

"And don't come back when someone else is on duty," the sergeant yelled after them. "You'll get the same answer." He turned back into the fort. "He wants to look into his eyes. My God, are all Mexicans loco?"

Caballero and Fernando walked down the dirt road toward the settlement that had grown up near the fort. The sun beat down. "What do we do now?" Fernando asked.

"We go to the cantina and get a drink."

"And when we are finished with the drink?"

"I will think."

"You have been thinking for almost a month."

Caballero hunched his shoulders. "Sooner or later the right thought will come to me."

"The war will be ended by then. What is the matter with this gringo coronel?"

Caballero mimicked the sergeant. " 'He is a busy man.' "

Fernando spat. "Do you know what I think of this sergeant with the red face? *No vale cagada!*"

They heard the sounds of hoofbeats and carriage wheels and they moved to one side of the road, holding their hands in front of their noses because of the dust. Caballero glanced at the carriage as it passed. They resumed their walk toward the settlement and then Caballero stiffened and seized Fernando by the arm. "Santa Madre! In the carroza!"

"What in the carriage?"

"Señor Magoffin! Por Dios, it was he inside!" He turned and ran after the carriage, hampered by his loosely hung spurs, shouting: "Don Santiago! Don Santiago!" He saw the carriage pause for a moment at the gate and then disappear inside the fort. He stopped, breathing hard.

Fernando caught up with him. "Are you certain of this?"

"Of course. Do you believe I do not know that face?"

Fernando spread his hands, palms up. "Well, we have lost him. We are no better off than before."

"Only for the moment, Fernando, only for the moment." He slapped Fernando on the back, a gesture he had noticed was popular among the Americans. "If he has gone in he will come out again, and he will not get away the second time."

The sergeant at the gate said: "Oh, no, not you two again."

"Do you know who was in that carriage that just entered, señor sargento?" Caballero asked courteously.

"I sure do. It was Colonel James Magoffin."

Caballero saucered his eyes and thrust out his lower lip. "*Colonel* Magoffin. With your permission, señor sargento, we will wait here for him to come out again."

The sergeant jerked his thumb. "Outside the fort is free territory. Make yourselves at home."

Caballero and Fernando sat down and leaned against the wall and pulled their sombreros over their eyes. They made cigarettes and waited.

The sergeant leaned into Magoffin's carriage. "Your pardon, sir, but have you ever seen those two men before?" He gestured over his shoulder.

Magoffin looked at the two men squatting against the wall,

their heads lowered, their arms clasped around their knees. He noted the white cotton clothing and the high, conical broad-brimmed hats. He smiled reminiscently. "Many, many times, sergeant. All over Mexico. And you'll see them yourself before very long."

The sergeant stepped back and saluted and Magoffin gave the order to his coachman to drive on. At that moment one of the men pushed back his hat and sprang to his feet. "Hola! Don Santiago!" he called out. "A little moment, friend, for favor."

"Hold it, driver," Magoffin said. He looked curiously at the man walking rapidly toward him. He was a Mexican obviously from his dress, but he did not walk like a Mexican. There was less of the indolent swagger and more of a light, purposeful tread, the walk of a mountain cat. And around his waist Magoffin saw a gun belt and a holster containing a very un-Mexican revolver, one of Colt's. The lean face was bearded.

Caballero reached the carriage. He put his hands on his hips and lifted his head, and his teeth flashed white in the strong light. "*El Don, viejo amigo, qué paso?*"

"*Muy bien,*" Magoffin said automatically. He stared at him puzzled and then at the big man who joined him.

Caballero laughed again. "Regard this hombre, Fernando. He does not recognize us. I think he is not polite. I said always that when El Don was back among the gringos he would forget everyone he knew in New Mexico."

The sergeant spoke up. "Should I have these men taken away, colonel?"

Caballero looked at the sergeant. "Get back to your post. This is not your business." The smile did not leave his lips, and the command, in English, was accented, and yet it had authority and the sergeant stepped back a pace and wrinkled his brow.

Magoffin snapped his fingers. "Don Esquipulas, it is you! God in heaven, what are you doing here?" He flung open the door of the carriage and jumped out and gripped his arms.

"Gracias á Dios," Caballero said, "his eyes have opened."

"I was getting tired," Fernando said.

"You know my friend, Don Fernando Rael," Caballero said.

Magoffin's eyes flickered for a moment. He remembered Fernando as Caballero's servant. He extended his hand instantly.

497

"Of course, Don Fernando." He surveyed both men wonderingly. "What *are* you both doing here?"

"We came from Bent's Fort to see the American coronel who is going to bring the army into New Mexico."

"You came all the way from Bent's Fort to see Kearny?"

"Yes, Don Santiago."

"Is it permissible for me to ask why?"

"I wish to talk to him if he will listen."

"He will listen," Magoffin said.

"Can you arrange it with this ox of a sergeant so that we may be taken to him?"

"I can do better than that. I am now on my way to my house in Independence. Coronel Kearny is dining with me there tomorrow evening. Come back to Independence with me and you can see him then."

Caballero heaved a sigh of relief. He held out his hands to Fernando. "Por Dios, I have always said there is nothing El Don cannot arrange."

"That is not what you always said a few minutes ago," Magoffin said dryly. He stepped back and allowed Caballero and Fernando to enter the carriage and he climbed in after them. Caballero waved his hand pleasantly to the sergeant. Magoffin gave the order and the horses trotted off.

Caballero leaned back luxuriously in the comfortable leather seat. "The sergeant called you Coronel Magoffin," he said.

"I have a mission with the army," Magoffin said. "I was given that rank."

Caballero winked at Fernando. "I believed it was only in the New Mexican army that a man was promoted from nothing to coronel."

"It is only honorary, I assure you."

"I was told you resigned your post as consul in Chihuahua and moved with your family to Independence."

"Yes, almost two years ago."

"It will be a great pleasure to go to your house. My wife—" his eyes darkened—"Doña Soledad spoke often of Doña María Gertrudis. I look forward to the honor of meeting her."

Magoffin was silent for a moment. "I am afraid that will not be possible just now, Don Esquipulas. My wife died last year."

498

Caballero raised his eyes swiftly and then lowered them. The yellow dust filled the air with golden motes.

3

COLONEL KEARNY pushed his chair away from the table and sighed contentedly. "The reports of your hospitality were in no way exaggerated, colonel. I cannot remember when I have so much enjoyed a dinner. My compliments to your judgment in wines and to the skill of your cook."

"It is my pleasure, sir," Magoffin said. "Shall we go into the parlor? Brandy and coffee will be served there and I have some cigars I believe equal to the wines." He looked across the table at Caballero and Fernando. "It amuses my old friends to hear you call me colonel. Don't worry, amigos, the rank was given to me only to impress Armijo."

"You should have been made a general, then," Caballero said. "Don Manuel will consider himself your superior officer."

Kearny's eyes widened slightly, but he said nothing.

"I intend to remain in civilian clothes," Magoffin said. "There is only one colonel in the Army of the West."

"I don't know," Kearny said. "If anything happens to me you may find it necessary to take command of the troops."

Magoffin lifted his eyes piously. "Let us hope that never happens! The parlor, gentlemen?"

The men seated themselves in the parlor and Caballero thought of what Magoffin had told him about Kearny. He saw a man slightly above middle height, with an erect and muscular frame. He thought him to be about fifty. The clean-shaven face was grave. The black hair over a high forehead was sprinkled liberally with gray. The gray eyes were thoughtful.

When the brandy, coffee, and cigars had been served, Kearny looked keenly at Caballero. "Colonel Magoffin has informed me that you have some matters to discuss with me, sir. I shall be most pleased to listen to anything you have to tell me which will enlighten me on your country and your countrymen."

"Before you begin your conversation," Magoffin said, "perhaps it would be useful for me to tell you something about this man and about his activities during the last few years."

"Of course, sir," Kearny said. "I am at attention."

As Magoffin related rapidly the essential details of Caballero's career, his break with Armijo, and his subsequent guerrilla warfare in behalf of the peasants, Kearny's eyes remained full and unwavering on the New Mexican and there emerged gradually upon his sober face an expression of deep respect.

"In all the years that Manuel Armijo has been in absolute power," Magoffin said, "the guerrilla force of Señor Caballero has constituted the only organized opposition to tyranny in New Mexico. The number of his followers has remained few, pitifully few, but he has been a sharp thorn in Armijo's side and by his example he has reminded his people constantly that opposition was possible. But he has become more than a tenacious guerrillero. He has won the faith and the trust of the people whom he has aided. They believe in him, sir. He has proved himself to them by risking his life again and again."

When Magoffin was finished, Kearny said with simplicity: "I am very proud to know you, sir, and I am honored that you have sought me out." He was oddly gratified to see a brief light appear in Caballero's somber eyes. "Would you be good enough, señor, to tell me exactly what is in your mind?"

"I thank the colonel," Caballero said. "It is I who am honored. May I ask exactly what is in his mind with regard to my people?"

Magoffin looked quickly at Kearny. He saw the gray eyes flicker for a moment and then become cold and flat and he opened his mouth to intercede. Then he saw the chill depart and a ghost of a smile appear on Kearny's lips, and he heard Kearny say very quietly: "That is an honest question, sir, and I will try to answer it as honestly."

Kearny put his cigar carefully in a tray, he rose to his feet, and clasped his hands behind his back. "It is an honest and forthright question," he repeated, "and it was asked by a brave man. The gentleman has the right to ask it of me. He has come to the United States to seek me out and he must know what are the intentions of the soldiers who soon will tread the soil of his country." He paused and then continued slowly: "The government of the United States desires to take New Mexico into the United States

500

on terms of absolute equality. No one who does not resist will be harmed. No property will be confiscated. No one will be persecuted for religious beliefs. It is the hope and the wish of the United States to extend its own freedom and prosperity and education to the people of New Mexico. No attempt will be made now or at any time in the future to make your people forget the language of your fathers. Spanish and English will stand side by side as the two tongues of New Mexico for as long as your people desire it, and all official documents will be printed in both languages so that all may understand them."

"As citizens of Texas?" Fernando asked.

"As citizens of the United States. New Mexico will not be made part of Texas, but will become a separate territory of the United States, in which your people for the first time will have a true voice in their own government. It is the intention of the United States to establish public schools, build hospitals, encourage the publication of newspapers and periodicals, giving to all opinions the greatest latitude of expression. Freedom of speech and assembly will be extended to all persons, and the American concept of justice, by which a man is considered innocent until he is proved guilty in fair trial, will be introduced into New Mexico. There will be no cruelties, your women will not be injured, nothing will be stolen by my soldiers. I do not go to New Mexico to punish New Mexicans. I go with no enmity. I go with good wishes." He paused again. The room was silent. "Your people, your women, your religion, your priests, your houses, your farms, all will be treated with honor and justice. I pledge this upon my word of honor as an officer in the United States Army."

Before he was finished Caballero was on his feet. His right hand went instinctively to his side, where his sword once had hung. "We will guide your army into New Mexico," he said.

4

CABALLERO AND FERNANDO returned to Fort Leavenworth with Kearny two days later and they were enlisted in his headquarters as scouts on his staff. Caballero wandered over to a wall on which hung a large map. After studying it with interest for several minutes he asked: "What is this, mi coronel?"

"It is a map of New Mexico," Kearny said.

Caballero looked at the map again. "It is a work of art," he said. "But it is not New Mexico."

Kearny smiled. "I did not think it was very accurate. And yet it is the latest map of the area."

"Look, Fernando," Caballero said. "This shows the Ocate going through Cimarron. There is a small stream that passes through Cimarron, señor coronel, but it is not the Ocate. And this map does not show the Mora River at all."

Fernando traced the markings of a mountain range with a thick forefinger. "The Sangre de Cristos do not live here."

Kearny peered at the map. "It has been made up from various reports and it apparently is even less accurate than we believed," he said. "Would you as your first assignment restore the natural features of your country to their proper places? And then I will have my draftsman make a new map. One of my officers, Captain Cooke, who knows more about that country than any of the others, has been stationed at Fort Crawford in the Wisconsin Territory. He is on his way here and I had planned for him to look over this chart, but it now appears he will not get here before we depart for the West. He will join us at Bent's Fort, however."

Caballero turned his eyes from the map. "Captain Cooke? Is he the same officer who took guns away from the Texans so they could not attack New Mexican traders?"

"Yes, I remember that incident," Kearny chuckled. "The Texas government was out for his scalp for that Snively business, but he managed to survive."

"I have wanted to meet Captain Cooke."

"I promise you that pleasure before long. Now I will leave you gentlemen to your work."

The two men began to make the changes. To Caballero it was as though he were looking at the face of a friend on which the features had been distorted. There was no part of the north section of his country with which he was not intimate and which did not hold a memory. The mountains had provided retreats and the streams had supplied water and the canyons had been places for ambushing savage Indians and later Rurales. The land was as familiar to him as the lines on the palms of his hands, and as he made alterations he could hear the voice of Ramón Baca in the camp on the bank of the Mora. "I believe he can be overthrown," Ramón had said, and now Caballero thought how it would be if he were alive. "You should be here now, monito, with me in this greatest of all adventures, you at my side and the women awaiting us." The three of them together, Ramón, Fernando, and himself! How they would have been!

When the changes were completed Kearny called a meeting of his senior officers, who included Colonel Alexander William Doniphan, in command of the First Regiment of Missouri Cavalry; Major Meriwether Lewis Clark, in command of two batteries of artillery, equipped with six-pounders; Major Edwin Vose Sumner, in command of three squadrons of the First Dragoons; and Captain William Z. Angney, in command of two companies of infantry. Together their forces totaled 1,657 men.

Kearny did not miss the surprised reaction of the officers when he introduced the two New Mexicans. "I realize it strikes you gentlemen as strange that two Mexican nationals have elected to come over to our camp," he said. "I do not propose at this time to go into the details for that change of allegiance. I will state only that Señor Caballero and Señor Rael were first vouched for by Colonel James Magoffin, who was sent to me by the President, and that after listening to them I personally am also wholly convinced of their sincerity. That will be taken for granted from now on." He looked into the face of each officer before he continued. "Now, these gentlemen have discovered some serious inaccuracies on the chart of New Mexico. They have made changes, based on their long familiarity with the terrain. Señor Caballero, if you will be good enough to take that pointer and step up to the map, we shall listen attentively."

Caballero walked to the map. "I will try to speak only English, señores," he said. He studied the chart for a moment and his bearing underwent a subtle change. His posture became military and his face took on authority. "There is only one way to come down, señores," he said. "That is through Raton Pass as you see here. When you come down from the pass you have to make a choice. There are mountains to the east of Santa Fe. You must decide whether to continue along the west side of the mountains or the east side. I will try to explain to you the good things and the bad things of both routes.

"The west route takes you across the Sangre de Cristos here, just below Agua Fria, through the Taos Valley and Taos, and to Santa Fe along the valley of the Rio Grande. That route is what is known as the Mountain Branch of the Santa Fe Trail, and it has been used for many years by the traders and by persons traveling between Bent's Fort and Santa Fe. It is a good way. The trail is marked well. It is known to the scouts who have escorted the wagons on that branch and you will find many men at Bent's Fort who know every step. But it is very mountainous. The worst place is here, through the Sangre de Cristos. There is nothing bad enough at this time of the year to stop you altogether, but it will take a great deal of strength out of the soldiers on foot and it will tire them greatly.

"The east route is a little shorter, maybe. It also is easier to march over. It is not so well known to the Americans. This route takes you here—" he moved the pointer—" across the Ocate River and the Mora, through Las Vegas, around the south end of the Rincons, and then northeast through Pecos and Apache Canyon. The land all along is almost level and would be much easier for the infantry. It also is a less settled part of New Mexico and there would be better chance to find game, though at this time of the year most of the wild animals go up into the cooler places in the mountains. This route has one very bad thing about it. It goes through Apache Canyon. Apache Canyon is the best place in all New Mexico for Armijo to make a defense. If you come that way and Armijo decides to resist, he will make his stand there. It is a terrible place to try to force. There is a very narrow opening, no more than the width of eight or ten wagons. There are high mountain walls on either side. About one hundred men could do a good job of holding off an army indefinitely, and Don Manuel can call upon many more than a hundred. Your artillery would be useless. If you charged with cavalry you would be cut down by fire from both sides. I think so long as Don Manuel chose to defend it he might keep out your army. In addition to everything else, you would run out of food, and there is no supply for an army of your size in that country."

The officers now were leaning forward intently. Colonel

Doniphan, a large, florid-faced man, asked: "Is it possible to turn that position by a flanking move, Señor Caballero?"

Caballero hesitated while he translated the unfamiliar military terms into Spanish in his mind. Then he understood. "It is possible, coronel, by continuing on down here, to Galisteo. But that would take many more days and make your food problem serious, very serious. I think if you take the east route you must find some way to get through the pass. If you went as far down as Galisteo and ran out of food, the same thing might happen to you that happened to the Texans who came up in 1841. They were almost dead from starvation."

Kearny cleared his throat. "Well, gentlemen, there we have the difficulties we must face. On the one hand there is this mountainous terrain which will drain the strength of the men, and on the other a stone wall of mountains and a narrow pass."

Caballero laid down the pointer and made a cigarette. "As you say, señor coronel, that is the story of the land. There is another story, the story of the people, and that story too is different on each of these routes. I will tell you about Taos. The people of Taos always have been great fighters and revolutionaries. They are mostly pueblo Indians and part Indian up there. They were friendly to the Anglos. In their religion there was a belief that one day a great army of Anglos would come from the east and deliver them from the Spaniards."

"I'll be damned," Doniphan said.

"Three years ago the Texans sent an army to New Mexico to make revenge for the prisoners Armijo took in 1841. Armijo went to meet them. He took with him the Taos militia. The men did not want to fight the Texans for Armijo. They found the Texans and went to surrender to them and join them to fight against Armijo, but the Texans killed many of them and sent the rest, with no guns, back to Taos through the country of wild Indians."

"My God!" Sumner said.

"When they returned to Taos and told the people what the Texans had done, the people rioted and they did not understand any differences between Texans and Americans. They drove out all the Americans living there and burned their property, and from then on they have a great hatred of all gringos."

505

"Couldn't someone explain the difference between Americans and Texans to them?" Sumner asked.

Caballero shrugged. "What is the difference now, señor? Texans are Americans now, are they not? In time you could teach the people so they would understand you are not the men who sent the militia unarmed to the plains, but the men who took the guns away from the Texans; but that would take too long, and while you were doing it, Armijo's agents would be telling them other things and your army could not wait for them to make up their minds who was telling the truth. I believe you would have great trouble if you passed that way, and Armijo would find many men to stand with him. And there is something else. There is a priest in Taos, Padre Martínez."

He looked at Fernando and smiled. "What shall I say about Padre Martínez? He saved my life and he is a good man. But he also is an ambitious man and for many years he has had the dream that one day Taos would be separated from the rest of New Mexico and that he would be the ruler. He has not opposed Armijo openly all these years because by some trick or other Don Manuel has made him think that one day he might give him the north country. The priest has a good mind and he believes in many of the things the Americans believe in; but he knows too that when New Mexico becomes part of the United States his dream is dead and that he will lose even some of the powers he has under Armijo."

"The priests will remain undisturbed," Kearny said quickly. "I have already told you that."

"They will remain undisturbed in their priestly functions," Caballero said. "You have told me that and I believe it. But many of the priests also are politicians, and Padre Martínez is the biggest politician of all. He has been deputy to the Junta since before even Armijo came to power. Do the Americans allow Catholic priests to hold political office, Coronel Kearny?"

"We believe religious leaders should restrict their activities to their churches," Kearny said quietly.

"Do not believe that Padre Martínez does not know this! And he is not one content to be a simple parish priest. In the Spanish tradition the Church has always mixed in political affairs and has

506

encouraged its priests to be politicians as well, and Padre Martínez has been brought up in that tradition. But even as a priest his powers will be lessened in a country where there are many who are not Catholics. Now he has great power in the north and ambition for more, and his religious hold over his people is supreme. Afterward he will have no political power and he will see priests of other faiths come into the land to compete with him." He shook his head. "No, it cannot be said what Padre Martínez will do. Once he risked his own neck to save my life so that I might one day oppose Armijo. But I am a Catholic. I do not know what he will do now. I suggest only that he may do much. If you try to pass through Taos and he calls for his people to rise up and give support to Armijo, you will pass only over the dead bodies of the entire Rio Arriba."

Colonel Doniphan raised his finger. "Señor Caballero, there is one thing that puzzles me more than anything else. You have said 'if' Manuel Armijo resists. Is there any question that he will oppose us? The United States and Mexico are at war. Can this Governor do anything other than defend his land?"

"Don Manuel can do anything, señor coronel," Caballero said evenly. "And he has done so many times. I have said 'if' because I do not know what he will decide to do."

"But that's fantastic!"

The end of Caballero's cigarette glowed. "He is a fantastic man, señor." The smoke filtered slowly through his nostrils. "He is many men, this Armijo," he said in a low voice. "I believe that all the things of our blood are in him and they battle at all times with each other. When the time comes, señor, Don Manuel may be hero or he may be coward. He has been both. He may lead his troops with valor or he may run away like a frightened sheep. He has done both of those too. I believe in his own way he has a love for his people. It is twisted, but it is a kind of love. He may decide it would be useless to let them be killed for a cause that was lost. Or the moment when he must decide may be a moment when he sees himself as a man in history and he may believe he must fight so people later can say he was a patriot and a brave man."

"My God, it is like trying to find your way through a fog!"

"A fog? What is that, señor?" When the word was explained

to him he nodded somberly. "That is true. There is but one thing that can be done with safety, and that is to be ready for the worst. If you are surprised, it will be a pleasant surprise."

"What about this other route?" Kearny asked presently. "What is the feeling of the people there?"

"It is different there. They have priests there, but no one so big as Padre Martínez. Also the area is greater and the people are scattered and not in one group as in Taos."

"And these are the people you have helped all these years."

"Yes, mi coronel, we have been with them for many years. It could be said we have helped prepare them for this day. What the people of Taos will do is a question, but if I go among the people on the east frontier ahead of your army and speak to them and explain who you are and what you will do, you will find few enemies apart from those who work for Armijo. I do not like to make big promises, Coronel Kearny, but I believe I can lead you on this route so you will come to Apache Canyon without fighting a battle." He took a deep breath. "What would happen at Apache Canyon, no man can say."

5

ALTHOUGH the American merchants had declined to risk sending their wagons across the Santa Fe Trail the year before, when there was only threat of war, now that the war had started they changed their minds. There was sound business reasoning behind the reversal.

The seaports of Mexico were blockaded by the United States Navy. The merchants knew that goods would be scarce in Mexico and would consequently command higher prices, and they had the previous year's loss to recoup. But there was another and a vastly more important motive behind their decision. The canny traders understood perfectly that the war with Mexico would bring an end to the commerce of the prairies as they had known it for almost a quarter of a century. They had little doubt of the outcome of the war, and they realized that when New Mexico became part of the

United States and was occupied by their countrymen, the unique monopoly they had held since the Mexican Revolution would be a thing of the historical past. There was one more jackpot to be collected, and they proposed to get it.

In the early part of May, Albert Speyer set out secretly from Independence with a large train carrying more than seventy thousand dollars' worth of arms and ammunition ordered two years before by the Governor of Chihuahua. Shortly thereafter the American traders left Missouri with the largest caravan of all time. The time of departure was earlier in the season than usual because the traders had to get to Santa Fe before Kearny in order to take advantage of the war conditions in disposing of part of their goods there, and also to obtain from Governor Armijo, while he still was in power, the guía, or customhouse permit, which would enable them to proceed to Chihuahua and other parts of Mexico to sell the remainder of their merchandise.

They traveled under forced draft, presenting the curious spectacle of American business men hastening to reach an enemy city to do business there before that city was attacked by an American army, and then to arrange for commercial concessions from the Governor of New Mexico at a time when that official was making preparations to defend his country from the American assault. They were not unaware that they were running a considerable risk, but they were men used to danger and they gambled on their knowledge of the character of Manuel Armijo and on the approach of Kearny's forces to protect them.

During that same month of May and into June, Kearny was sending his own supply trains across the prairies to stockpile equipment at Bent's Fort. On the evening of the 4th of June he received an express from an officer escorting some of the supply wagons, informing him of the race of the traders toward Santa Fe and of the merchandise Speyer was carrying. The following day Kearny sent a dispatch to Captain Benjamin Moore ordering him to overtake the traders and stop them. "It is the object of the greatest importance that we get possession of Governor Armijo's goods (ammunition, arms, etc.) and I rely upon you and your command to do it," Kearny wrote. "Tell the Mexicans that we do not intend to deprive them of their property but to stop its progress for the present."

Captain Moore led two companies of the First Dragoons from the Kansas River on June 7 and made forced marches for eleven and a half days, arriving at the crossing of the Arkansas on June 19. Although he had averaged a stunning thirty-five miles a day, the wagons of Speyer and the other traders were more than two hundred miles ahead of him and now beyond all interception. He returned to Pawnee Fork and stopped all later traders.

6

THE ARMY OF THE WEST began its march on Santa Fe officially on the 26th day of June with the departure from Fort Leavenworth of four companies of Missouri Mounted Volunteers, their guidons waving in the brilliant sunshine. The units were followed in rapid succession on the days following by other cavalry companies of the Missouri regiment, the infantry companies, the artillery battalion, and, at the very end, the squadrons of First Dragoons, which constituted the only regular army units in Kearny's command, all others comprising Missouri civilians who had enlisted at the outbreak of the war.

Riding slowly alongside the long lines of infantrymen stretched across the baked prairie, Esquipulas Caballero looked with wry admiration at the men who had been transformed in a few weeks from boisterous civilians—farmers, ranchers, clerks and shopkeepers from St. Louis, adventurous sons of rich and poor families, even river-boat men from the Mississippi—into disciplined soldiers who were, he knew, man for man, more than a match for the best regulars Armijo could put up against them. They all seemed to have been born with guns in their hands, he thought. Even the office workers, whose clerical pallor had been replaced by healthy tan, carried their rifles as though they had never been without them.

Rubbing his newly shaved and somewhat tender face, he listened to the laughter and the joking and the raillery that went back and forth and he marveled at the inexhaustible good humor with which these men tramped toward unknown dangers. It was another approach to the dark angel, he thought, as authentic for the gringos as was the cold indifference that men of Spanish blood selected for an attitude as they walked toward the same lady. He did not know which was the better way, but he admitted to himself it was not unpleasant to listen to men march to war as though they were going off on a holiday.

He was ruminating placidly on these differences between peoples who presently would find it necessary to reconcile these and other differences when he heard a voice that struck deeply into his memory. He stiffened in his saddle and cocked his head and he felt a chill go through him on the broiling summer day.

"I don't know why the rest of you laddies joined up in this lousy army, but this Irishman has a reason and a damned good one," the voice said. "I have an appointment in New Mexico that's five years old."

A man laughed. "Do you think she'll still remember you?"

"She probably has six kids, and only one speaks with a brogue," another man called out.

"It's not a she, it's a he," the first voice said. "A greasy little bastard name of Salazar. There are a lot of dead men waiting for me to catch up with him. I don't mean to disappoint them."

"Friend of yours?"

"When I find him I'm going to carry him off to some quiet place and take him apart. When I'm through with him, there won't be enough left to shovel away."

"We're supposed not to be mad at those people, Fitz."

"You know, boys, for five years I've had the same nightmare. I dream that somebody else got to him first and that he's dead. I wake up in the middle of the night all broken out with cold sweat."

Caballero leaned down from his horse. "You may rest easy, Don Cornelio," he said. "Salazar still lives."

By the 31st day of July the entire Army of the West was camped on the banks of the Arkansas at a point nine miles downriver from Bent's Fort. The five hundred and sixty-four miles from Fort Leavenworth had been covered without a single mishap, and to the hilarious joy of the infantrymen the foot soldiers had reached the rendezvous ahead of the cavalry. Although this feat

511

was accomplished at the expense of many blistered feet, the infantry proved, as Cornelius Fitzgerald remarked, that "a man is as good as a horse any day."

The army had made the prairie crossing with the orderliness and stamina of seasoned veterans, averaging more than eighteen miles a day. Each unit reached the predetermined point on the exact day fixed by Colonel Kearny, and many of the battalions arrived at the end of the march at the precise hour the commander had specified in the orders he had drawn up at Fort Leavenworth.

7

COLONEL KEARNY, who had been brought down by fever and who had spent most of the crossing in an ambulance wagon, arrived at the encampment on July 26. He immediately called a series of staff conferences, which were attended by his senior officers as they arrived and by James Magoffin, Charles Bent, and his brother, William; by Caballero and, upon his arrival with his company, Captain Cooke.

Mountain men, recently returned from New Mexico, reported the country was up in arms, especially in the Taos area, that the wildest propaganda against the Americans was being spread everywhere, particularly by the priests, and that Governor Armijo was calling for volunteers and was making energetic preparations to resist the American advance.

Kearny, showing the ravaging evidence of his illness, listened grimly to this information. "I am under instructions from President Polk to occupy New Mexico peaceably, if possible," he said. "As far back as June 20 I sent an express to Governor Armijo, requesting him to tell his people if they laid down their arms and would take the oath of allegiance to the United States they would receive the same protection and enjoy all the liberties of American citizens. Apparently he has chosen to withhold this message from his subjects and has decided to receive us as enemies."

"You can't hold the people to blame, sir," Charles Bent said grimly. "They don't know what to think. They are being pulled in all directions. I think if they were left to their own inclinations they might very likely welcome your troops. But the priests have great influence, and Armijo is an orator."

"That is exactly what Señor Caballero has been saying," Kearny said. He turned his sunken face to the New Mexican. "What suggestion would you make?"

"The propaganda against the Americans is successful because my people have heard nothing from you to contradict it," Caballero said. "New Mexicans have faith in the word of the Americans. Your people have treated them fairly, for many years. And the New Mexicans know, Don Manuel has lied to them. If you send word that you have not come to hurt them, it may do much to quiet them."

"I agree, sir," Magoffin said.

"It would help a great deal, I think," Bent said. "The New Mexicans would want to believe you."

"There is a difficulty," Caballero said. "Most of my people cannot read. When proclamations are sent out to the villages by Don Manuel, they are posted outside the offices of the alcaldes and the people gather in the plazas and the words are read to them by alcaldes or priests. I do not believe these men would read what you had to say."

"How could we get around that?" Kearny asked.

"Your word must be taken to the people by men who would read it to them," Caballero said. "If you prepare a statement, señor coronel, I will take a dozen of my men and ride down to Taos Valley and read it to the people. There may be those who will believe it."

Kearny made a note on his writing tablet. "I will issue such a proclamation, Don Esquipulas, and make as many copies as you think necessary." He then spread open the map, and the Bents and the mountain men confirmed the revisions Caballero and Fernando had made. "How far down into New Mexico can I go before I must decide whether to proceed to Santa Fe by way of Taos or by way of Las Vegas and Apache Canyon?"

"I believe you would have to make your decision at the Ocate, mi coronel," Caballero said. "Beyond that point you would have to return to the river to go in the other direction."

William Bent, who had explored the eastern frontier exten-
sively, concurred. "That's about it, sir. Beyond the river you'd
either have to retrace or try for a mountain crossing, which I
wouldn't recommend."

Kearny rolled up the map. "Thank you, gentlemen," he said.
"Señor Caballero, as soon as the proclamation is ready you will
start out. The army will move out August 2. You will rejoin me on
the Ocate. Before you leave, gentlemen, there is an announcement
I wish to make. President Polk desires that the New Mexicans
shall not be treated as a conquered people. It will take some time
to set up machinery for a territorial government, but I do not want
even the interim government to be a military one. It becomes
necessary for me to appoint a temporary civilian governor who will
administer affairs in New Mexico under the Constitution of the
United States. I have decided to appoint Mr. Charles Bent to be
the first American Governor of New Mexico."

Bent was taken completely by surprise. The other men congratulated him. "I will do the best I can, colonel," Bent said. "It
is an honor."

Kearny's face was gray with weariness. "It is a responsibility,
Mr. Bent."

The following day James Magoffin and Esquipulas Caballero
brought to Kearny twelve copies of the translation they had made
of the proclamation he had written:

"The undersigned enters New Mexico with a great military
force with the object of seeking union and ameliorating the condition of its inhabitants, doing all this under the instructions of his
Government, by which he will be effectively sustained in ac-
complishing its views. He therefore recommends to the inhabitants
of New Mexico that they remain tranquil in their houses and continue in their peaceful vocations with the assurance that while
they continue their daily occupations and labors they will not be
molested by the American Army but on the contrary will be respected and protected in all their rights, both civil and religious.
All those who shall take arms or incite and approve resistance to
the Government of the United States will be looked upon as
enemies and treated accordingly."

Kearny signed all of the copies: "Camp at Bent's Fort, July

31, 1846—S. W. Kearny, Colonel of the 1st Dragoons," and then he asked: "Señor Caballero, are you prepared to depart?"

"Yes, mi coronel. I have chosen ten of my men. They are saddled up and ready to go. The others will remain with you to serve as scouts."

Kearny turned to Magoffin. "I am going to send Captain Cooke and twelve dragoons with you when you go to see Governor Armijo," he said.

Caballero's eyes widened. "See Don Manuel?"

"Colonel Magoffin has been instructed by the Secretary of War to have a private conversation with Governor Armijo," Kearny said somewhat dryly. He smiled at Caballero's astonishment.

"I thought I would go alone, colonel," Magoffin said. "Don Manuel may resent the appearance of armed troopers."

"I have considered that," Kearny said. "But I believe it would be unwise for you to go without protection. I know you are familiar to these people and it is not likely that they would harm you. It is possible, however, that if you were alone you might be detained somewhere, and that would defeat your mission as surely as if you were assassinated. I do not believe Governor Armijo will consider a captain and twelve dragoons a military invasion. They will escort you under white flag."

"Very well, sir," Magoffin said.

"I have another reason, Colonel Magoffin," Kearny said. "Captain Cooke will carry a personal message from me to Governor Armijo. I do not want to neglect any opportunity to address myself personally to the Governor."

There were sounds of commotion outside the tent and an orderly stepped in. "I beg your pardon, sir," he said to Kearny, "but patrol has just captured three Mexican spies across the river."

"Bring them here," Kearny said.

A few moments later three Mexicans in white cottons were pushed into the tent.

Caballero said: "That one is Tomás Martínez. He is nephew to Governor Armijo."

Martínez started when he saw Caballero and then he drew himself erect. Kearny looked at Don Tomás meditatively. "These men are not in uniform. Señor Caballero, ask them if they realize that under the rules of war they may be executed."

Caballero translated the words. Martínez squared his shoulders and a sneer appeared on his handsome face. The two other men clasped their hands in a gesture of prayer.

Martínez said coolly to Caballero: "Renegado, tell the American coronel to call his firing squad and I will show him how a Mexican officer can die." He turned away his head indifferently.

Caballero repeated the words, including the epithet "renegade," and Kearny murmured: "He is a brave man. Ask them if they are willing to give us information if we spare their lives."

"Only that the people of New Mexico have risen as one man under the standard of General Armijo," Martínez replied when this was translated to him. "The gringo soldiers will be slain to the last man, and the traitors who help them will be hanged from the portales in the plaza and people will spit on their bodies." He spat at Caballero's feet.

Kearny nodded gravely. "Take them away." When the prisoners had gone he said: "I cannot deny that arrogance appealed to me."

"He was not pretending," Caballero said quietly. "He would die well."

"I will not order them executed," Kearny said. "I'll ask the Bents to hold them here until our business is finished."

"May I make a suggestion, mi coronel?" Caballero asked.

"Certainly, Don Esquipulas."

"You are merciful not to have these men put to death. It is more than Don Manuel would do if he captured American spies. But as prisoners in Bent's Fort they will serve you no purpose. These men can be put to use."

"In what way?"

"You have wanted to get word to Armijo. His nephew is close to him, and Don Manuel will listen to him. Instead of putting these three men away in the fort let them look instead upon your army, at its size, at its equipment. There is nothing that is secret. Soon many New Mexicans will see your army and report on it to Don Manuel. Let these men see it now. Martínez is an officer and he will understand the power in the rifles and the cannon and he will not fail to understand the quality of your soldiers. It will prove to him that you consider yourself so strong you do not bother to hide anything from spies. Then, when they have seen everything, give them a good meal and send them back to Santa Fe. Martínez will go to Don Manuel immediately and tell him what he has seen, and the other men will spread the word among their friends."

Late that same afternoon, Tomás Martínez and the other two spies were brought before Kearny again. The Governor's nephew was more subdued than he had been in the morning.

With Kearny was his official interpreter, Antoine Robideaux, a trapper from St. Joseph, Missouri, who had been associated for many years with the Bents.

"You can go home tomorrow and tell your countrymen all that you have seen," Kearny said quietly. "To Governor Armijo you may say that I shall cross the river day after tomorrow and advance with my army on the great trail to Santa Fe. Tell him that we are not coming at night, secretly, or through the mountain passes like an enemy, but in broad daylight, that, like people who are not ashamed of their intentions, we are ready to regard the citizens of New Mexico as American citizens and treat them as our equals."

He looked closely at Martínez from his gray eyes. "Tell General Armijo that we shall take and occupy Santa Fe and all other cities in New Mexico, and that if anyone places an obstacle in our way, we shall remove it immediately. We shall respect all the rights of citizens and protect their property as well as their persons. If your countrymen have food for men and animals which they might be inclined to sell us, tell them they might bring them to us, and we shall give gold and silver for them.

"Furthermore, be assured that if any one of our soldiers does an injury to the lowliest among you, I shall punish that soldier severely. At the same time, however, be assured that I shall also treat you in a similar manner if you injure one of us."

As Robideaux translated the words, Martínez came slowly to a position of attention, and when Kearny concluded he saluted the colonel. He turned on his heel in a soldierly manner and strode from the tent. The other two men, unable to believe they were being let off with their lives, hastened after him.

The following night Kearny sent his last communication before embarking on his campaign to Brigadier General Roger Jones, the Adjutant General of the United States Army: "It is impossible for me to tell what opposition will be made to our entering New Mexico, but I, at this time, feel confident that our force is sufficient to overcome any that may be offered. I have done all in my power to obtain possession of the Country quietly & peaceably, and I hope to succeed."

He sealed the paper and then walked to the opening of the tent and looked at the campfires glowing in the black night.

At dawn the Army of the West crossed the Arkansas River into New Mexico.

1

DON MANUEL woke in excellent spirits after an unusual night with a Haitian dancer who was part of a traveling company of entertainers spending a week or two in Santa Fe. He stretched his hand, hoping that by some chance she might still be there. The other half of the bed was unoccupied, as he had been afraid it would be.

Doña María Trinidad was steadfast on that one point. She would supply all the queridas he wanted, but they must not be there when he woke in the morning. A woman during the night was one thing, but that same woman in bed in the morning was something else. She no longer was a female body, but changed by some subtle process into a human being who enjoyed a social relation with her husband, and that Doña María Trinidad would not permit.

He sighed and picked up a calendar from the bedside table. It was the 6th day of June and the theatrical company was scheduled to leave Santa Fe for El Paso del Norte on the 11th, he remembered. He would arrange for the dancer to visit him again on the 9th. That would not make him appear too anxious in the eyes of Doña María Trinidad and it would give him time to renew his strength. He shivered pleasantly. With that one he needed all his powers.

When he entered his office shortly before eleven o'clock, it was to find Don Juan Bautista Vigil impatiently pacing there. He lifted his voice in friendly salutation.

Vigil glared at him sourly. "So you have finally come to life."

"I have finally come to life. I should like also to say I feel very good."

Vigil's face was engulfed with sudden anger. "You feel good! The world goes up in flames and you feel good!"

"Pardon, Don Juan Bautista?" Don Manuel asked politely.

Vigil picked up a dispatch lying on the desk and flung it before the Governor. "Read this, Don Manuel. It arrived this morning while you were wallowing in bed with your whore."

Armijo regarded Vigil with distaste, feeling his well-being draining before the old man's testiness. "I suppose you have read it," he said. "What is the news? Another revolution in Mexico?"

"War!" Vigil shrieked. "War is about to start between the United States and Mexico. I went to your apartment three times this morning to bring this news, but you could not be disturbed. Well, be disturbed now!"

Don Manuel sat down and lit a cigar. "It appears to me you are lacking in respect this morning, Don Juan Bautista."

The old man wilted at the mild voice. "Pardon, excelencia," he mumbled, wringing his hands. "I meant no disrespect." He sat down. "It is a terrible thing, war. People die."

Don Manuel read the dispatch carefully. "It has not yet begun."

"The dispatch is more than a month old. It has begun."

"Then it has begun."

"Is that all you can say?" Vigil's voice rose again.

"What would you like me to say? That it is too bad? Would you consider that appropriate?" He tapped the paper with his finger. "We have expected this for a long time. Now it is here. Let us consider how it will affect us and how we may benefit from it."

Vigil was aghast. "Benefit from it!"

Don Manuel drew in a rich mouthful of smoke and exhaled a blue cloud. "There are few situations from which benefit may not be realized with the application of some small intelligence," he said with the air of a schoolteacher. His finger traced a line in the dispatch. "It says here the gringo navy is blockading the ports, including that of Santa Cruz. What does that suggest to you?"

"War!" Vigil held up his hands. "War, excelencia!"

"Curious," Don Manuel murmured. "To me it suggests that merchandise soon will grow scarce in Mexico. Prices will rise."

"Santa Madre de Dios!" Vigil gasped. "Do you talk of merchandise and profits?"

Don Manuel sat back. "What else should I talk of?"

"Perhaps about defending your country!" Vigil rose half out

of his seat. "At this moment while we sit here and you talk of business an American army may be marching on us."

Don Manuel removed the cigar. "From where, friend?"

Vigil leaped up and ran to a wall map and began to pound it with his fist. "From here, from Missouri, from where the traders come from."

"Ah, now consider what you are saying. With the best draft animals and with the best of luck the crossing of the prairies takes at least two months. It can be done only at a certain time of the year when there is feed and water. Now tell me, Don Juan Bautista, how is an army that cannot march as rapidly as a mule going to cross this prairie? What army can walk from Missouri to New Mexico with everything it needs to make war?"

Vigil walked back slowly from the map. "It is a strange thing, Don Manuel, but all these years you have said that one day the gringos would take your country from you. And now that we are at war with them, suddenly you are confident they cannot do it."

"When I have said it, it has been for a purpose," the Governor said. He touched the paper again. "Just as I will put this to a purpose. It does not mean I have believed it. At least not in this way." His eyes darkened. "I have not imagined New Mexico as conquered by a gringo army. The gringos have too much money invested here to destroy our country. What I have foreseen is an economic conquest. That is why I have urged New Mexicans to enter more and more into this commerce of the prairies, even those men who thought it was without dignity for descendants of hidalgos to engage in trade. I have wanted to postpone that day and, in postponing it, perhaps eliminate it."

Vigil sighed heavily. "I pray that you are right about this, Don Manuel."

"I may be right or wrong. But even if I am wrong what can be done about it? The army may be sent out from Missouri or it may not. If not, there is nothing to worry about. If so, it may reach here in condition to fight or it may come to grief as the Texans did. I can change none of these things."

"If a gringo army comes, it may be that some of the people will not oppose it," the postmaster said cautiously.

"The people will do what I tell them to do."

"God grant that you are right!"

"The people will speak to the gringos with my mouth and they will see them through my eyes and they will listen to them with my ears." He looked challengingly at Vigil. "Do you doubt that?"

"No, no, for certain," Vigil said quickly.

"Another thing, did we not receive an express from Independence less than two weeks ago stating the traders had started?"

"Yes, excelencia."

"Did they come last year? Does it look as though they expect New Mexico will be made into a battleground?"

"No, excelencia. But these gringos now will be enemies."

Don Manuel broke the ash from his cigar. "Business men are never enemies. They are only competitors. The gringos understand that. The proof is that they are coming here." He picked up the dispatch and glanced at it again. "I will do something with this."

That afternoon Don Manuel prepared a circular in which he informed his subjects of the contents of the dispatch.

". . . My friends, in the name of the supreme government, I am writing that you may be prepared for conflict," he concluded. "It is not courage and discipline alone that I would obtain by my entreaties to you, but also constancy and endurance, that you may prepare yourselves for trials yet harder than those in the past from the wretchedness of our Treasury. I hope that you will suffer it all with the resignation and discipline whereby you shall make yourselves distinguished in future epochs solely for saving the Fatherland, and that in the moments of danger, whenever it may arrive, you, filled with enthusiasm and courage upon seeing for a second time the enemy that surrendered his pride at your mere presence, shall find at the head of your lines in every exigency your comrade and best friend, Manuel Armijo."

In the days that ensued Don Manuel beguiled himself with the charms of the dancer who called herself Anne-Marie Leclerc. The troupe elected to remain in Santa Fe longer than it originally planned in order to take advantage of the patronage of the on-coming and notoriously free-spending merchants, and Don Manuel generously extended its amusement license without extra charge.

During this period the Junta was holding regular meetings.

The deputies had got into the habit again of convening during the administrations of Chaves and Martínez and had been permitted to continue in this democratic process by Don Manuel, who regarded the practice as harmless now that everyone understood he was indispensable. His confidence was such that he permitted former political enemies who had supported Governor Pérez, and who had returned to government during his retirement —such as Donanciano Vigil—to remain in office.

During these meetings the Junta made plans for the arrival of the Americans—not the soldiers, but the merchants. In the daily record of the sessions for June 18, a few days before Kearny left Fort Leavenworth, there was entered the following notation: "As the arrival of the United States caravan was about due—the time for the payment of the salaries on the list of civil officers— Donanciano Vigil moved that a committee be named to secure from the treasurer's office a statement of the advances that have been made to the Assembly for their secretary and other employees for the year past to date, in order that an estimate might thereby be made of the cerdit due each one, as also of the expenses of office and any other extraordinary expenses."

The caravan was awaited eagerly by the Junta for another reason. That spring it had placed an order with James Magoffin for a "new press with all accessories at a moderate price," and the members expected the press would be brought in with Magoffin's wagons. The press would make simpler the publication of government circulars, and the deputies could hardly wait to see it.

2

THE FIRST WORD OF KEARNY was brought to Don Manuel by his partner, Albert Speyer, who had ruined half his mules in driving them across the prairies in forty-five days.

"We all heard in Independence that Kearny was going to try to hold up the caravan so he could get into Santa Fe first," Speyer said. "I started out immediately. The others cannot be much behind."

"How big is the gringo army?"

"I do not know for certain. Somewhere around two thousand men, perhaps more."

"Delay the caravan so he could get here first!" the Governor exclaimed. "This man appears confident he will enter Santa Fe." He began to feel the fear. He rubbed his chin hesitantly.

"Volunteers arrived in Independence by the hundreds for weeks and set off immediately for Fort Leavenworth. They boasted they would be in Santa Fe before the summer was out!" Speyer retorted with a vehemence unusual to his Prussian stolidity.

"How do they expect to cross the prairies?" Don Manuel demanded. "Did not the Texans teach them it could not be done?"

Speyer toyed with the gold chain that hung across his vest. "The story is a little different this time, Don Manuel," he said. "This campaign is being planned by professionals. For almost two months they have blackened the plains hauling supplies to Bent's Fort. The men will travel under light pack, and when they arrive at the fort they will find everything they need."

Don Manuel smote the desk with his fists. "They will get lost on the way, as the Texans did!"

"Do not depend upon it. There is little country between Missouri and Bent's Fort that is unknown," Speyer said, regarding him steadily. "These men will follow the Santa Fe Trail. And Kearny is no novice in the West. He has just led an army in a journey through country more savage than the plains."

"He is a colonel," Don Manuel said disdainfully.

"It is a grade that is considered respectable enough in the American army," Speyer said dryly. "The rank is symbolized by an eagle, and in this instance the wings are broad enough to spread over two thousand men."

"Then they will reach here and we will defeat them."

Speyer's eyes were flat. "You have enough men to do that perhaps, Don Manuel, but not all your troops have modern guns."

"The sons of New Mexico will stop the enemies with their bodies!" Don Manuel said ringingly.

"Bodies stop only one thing, lead balls. After that their stopping days are ended."

"The country will rise to a man and destroy the gringos!"

"Save that for who need it, Don Manuel. Exactly how do you plan to defeat Kearny?"

524

"With my army, por Dios!"

"Your army is inadequately armed."

"I cannot help that."

"You can."

"How? I cannot make guns out of air."

"There are the latest repeating rifles and ammunition in our wagons."

Don Manuel looked at him in astonishment. "They do not belong to us. They were ordered by the Governor of Chihuahua."

"We are in possession of them," Speyer said.

Don Manuel was a long time in replying. "Those guns are worth seventy thousand dollars, Don Alberto," he said. "There is not the tenth part of that money in my treasury."

Speyer's pale blue eyes took on a faint animation. "The people of New Mexico have been good to us. We have made much more than seventy thousand dollars out of this country, and if we defeat Kearny we will make still more in the future."

"What the devil are you getting at?"

"Donate the guns to your country."

Don Manuel's mouth fell open. "Are you insane?"

The harsh lines in Speyer's face deepened. "No, Don Manuel."

"Are you suggesting seriously that we throw away not only the profit but even the original cost of seventy thousand dollars' worth of merchandise?"

"I am more than willing to sacrifice my half," Speyer said levelly.

"Well I am not!" Don Manuel shouted. "I am not in business for my health."

"Nor am I, normally. This is war."

"We are not yet at war. I have received no official word."

"You are at war, Don Manuel."

"Damn the Americans!" Don Manuel screamed, pounding the desk.

"It is more important to turn them back."

Don Manuel's eyes glittered balefully, like those of an enraged bear. "Since when do you hate gringos so much?"

"I do not hate them," Speyer said in the same quiet voice. "I have even thought that perhaps they might bring benefits to

New Mexico. That is not the point. The point is that they come as enemies. I believe your people should have the opportunity to defend themselves." He rubbed the gold chain between his fingers. "I should like to help give them that opportunity."

"To hell with your rectitude!"

"It is not a question of rectitude," Speyer said. "I pretend to no such virtue. It is not even a question of patriotism. My patriotism lies at the door of one country, my own, and that country is in no way involved in this conflict." A flush appeared on his severe features. "The New Mexicans have been my friends. I desire only to stand by them."

For several minutes there was silence and both men could hear the noises in the plaza. Then Don Manuel said coldly: "I will not contribute the guns."

Speyer's wintry eyes fixed themselves on the Governor. "I appeal to you to reconsider, excelencia."

"We made a contract with the Governor of Chihuahua. The firm has always honored its contracts. It will honor this one."

"The guns are needed here more than they are in Chihuahua. They are the newest American percussion rifles. Turn them over to your men."

"I refuse to do so," Armijo said with finality.

Speyer rose slowly to his feet. He contemplated his watch chain for a long while. "Then I will make a contribution of my half of the weapons, excelencia," he said. "As soon as they clear the customs we will divide the load and I will present the part that belongs to me to your army."

Don Manuel knocked over his chair as he stood up and leaned across the desk, his face blackening. "I am the Governor of New Mexico! I am commander of the army! I make the decisions!" He struck his chest. "I! I! I!"

"You are both of those persons," Speyer said unemotionally. "But in neither capacity do you control property belonging to me."

"I am also head of the firm! I make decisions for the firm!"

Speyer nodded. "Then let us sever our partnership, Don Manuel. Separate what is yours from what is mine and we will then do with our own property as we see fit."

Don Manuel quivered with rage. "The partnership is dissolved! But its contracts will be honored to the letter! Every last gun will be delivered to Chihuahua!"

Speyer looked at him calmly. "It is not within my power to oppose you," he said. "I think you are making a mistake." He turned and started to leave the office.

"Guard! Guard!" Don Manuel shouted. "Guard!"

The door flew open. The officer on duty, Captain Tomás Ortiz, brother to the vicar, rushed into the room drawing his sword. "Excelencia!"

Armijo thrust out his arm. "Arrest that man!"

Speyer stopped in his tracks. He stood quietly, his high shoulders squared, his long arms hanging at his side.

Captain Ortiz looked at Don Manuel in amazement. "Arrest Señor Speyer, excelencia?"

"Throw him into a cell!" Don Manuel frothed.

"Your partner, excelencia?"

"Do you defy me as well, capitán? Do you want me to order you arrested?"

Ortiz said to Speyer bewilderedly: "You are under arrest, señor."

Speyer walked slowly toward the open door. Ortiz, shaking his head, fell in behind him, sword in hand.

"Wait! Wait!" Don Manuel cried.

Ortiz turned. The Governor was seated, his hands gripped tightly in front of his eyes, his head drooped.

"I countermand the order," Don Manuel said. "Señor Speyer no longer is under arrest."

Speyer, his back still turned to Don Manuel, walked from the room without a word. Ortiz sheathed his sword and followed.

"Damn the Americans," Don Manuel muttered in a broken voice. "Damn the Mexicans."

Captain Ortiz closed the door quietly.

Don Manuel remained alone in his office. He forgot about the quarrel with Speyer almost instantly. He could think of only one thing, Kearny. To hold up the caravan until he could occupy Santa Fe! How could Kearny be so positive it would be so easy? He felt the fear again.

He sent for Speyer two hours later and in a dull voice informed him he wanted to sell his share of the business. The Prussian, who had thought the dissolution of the partnership would be the other way around, that Don Manuel would want to buy him out, made an opening offer, prepared for the usual bargaining he assumed must follow. Don Manuel agreed to the figure without argument.

The necessary papers were drawn up and then Don Manuel, changing abruptly from business man to Governor, ordered Speyer to leave immediately for Chihuahua. Speyer needed no urging. He departed the next morning before his former partner recovered his sense of business and changed his mind.

3

IN THE BRIEF TIME that Speyer's drivers were in Santa Fe they spread the word about Kearny and within forty-eight hours many of the ricos closed their houses and fled to the south. Outside the city, peasants drove their livestock into the mountains. In the north the priests and alcaldes urged men who had guns hidden away from the days of Gonzales to bring them forth and prepare to defend their country against the invader. Ultimately the agitation affected Don Manuel himself. He became suspicious that Speyer had withheld information from him and that the threat was even more immediate than the Prussian had let on. He sent spies to the frontier and dispatched his nephew to Bent's Fort.

In the midst of the rumors the caravan arrived and the people in the capital reversed their emotions. Here were old faces and old friends. Here were Americans, but not soldiers. The traders confirmed the prospect of an invasion by Kearny, but their presence was incompatible with thoughts of war, and from fear the people catapulted to rejoicing. The fiesta spirit was never more pronounced than it was that July, and the bailes never were more splendid.

Don Manuel now believed that Speyer had exaggerated the gravity of the situation in order to swindle him. He saw now what a bad deal he had made and he cursed his former partner for his trickery. To make up in part for the money he lost, he raised the customs duties and charged exorbitant fees for the guías he granted to the merchants. Their willingness to pay anything he demanded strengthened his belief that the American menace was far less than Speyer had said.

In the early part of July he received his first official word from the central authorities that his country and the United States were at war. He had not doubted that the two countries would eventually be drawn into conflict, but the formal document attesting to its reality came as a shock. With the communication from Santa Anna in his hand he looked from his window at New Mexicans and Americans milling around happily in the plaza and he felt his mind reel at the lunatic paradox. He was going mad, he thought, or the people were going mad. On the 10th day of July he received the express from Kearny asking him to lay down his arms and receive the Americans in peace. The courier told him Kearny had no less than four thousand soldiers. Don Manuel listened to the boisterous tumult in the plaza and he was certain he was living in a world that had gone insane.

He needed help. He needed counsel. He turned at last to the men he had considered little more than nonentities for almost ten years. He ordered the Junta to consider what must be done. Somewhere among the deputies, he thought, there must be men who would have something to contribute.

The greater number of deputies had returned to their own towns and estates when rumors of Kearny's approach had first begun to circulate, and they were unwilling to come back to Santa Fe. Don Mariano Chaves rose from a sickbed in response to Don Manuel's summons and fell dead of a heart attack. Don José Chaves y Castillo, as senior deputy, issued summons upon summons for other deputies, but he was almost wholly ignored. Upon orders from Don Manuel, Chaves notified the deputies that if they did not return to the capital immediately they would forfeit all pay. Even this drastic threat failed to persuade more than a handful.

The few who attended the emergency session called themselves to order and did nothing else. The years over which Don Manuel had sterilized their minds of all thought now claimed their toll. The men who had been prevented from thinking for a decade were now unable to think. For the first time since he had assumed power in 1837 Don Manuel would have listened to advice, but his deputies had none to give him and he again knew how much he was alone.

Toward the end of July the Santa Fe traders left the capital and went south, and with them went the theatrical company, including the delectable Anne-Marie, who had transferred her affections to a snub-nosed curly-haired American named Jones, who had promised to take her back to his home in Baltimore in the United States. Don Manuel had pleaded with her to remain in Santa Fe, and the dancer, fearing he might keep her there by force, had pretended to yield and then had slipped away with Jones, disguised as a man.

After the merchants left, the city quieted and many persons began again to doubt the existence of an American army. All doubts were resolved when Captain Tomás Martínez returned to Santa Fe from Bent's Fort. There was an army and it had somehow crossed the plains and now was without question already marching on New Mexican soil.

Don Manuel listened with increasing apprehensiveness to his nephew's account of the American strength, but it was not until Don Tomás told him of the presence of Esquipulas Caballero in Kearny's council that the fear ceased to be solely a physical thing.

"I do not know his status, excelencia," Don Tomás said as the fear spread stickily through the Governor's mind. "He wears no uniform, but he has great influence with this Kearny. It was Caballero who interceded in our behalf and it was at his suggestion that I was shown through the camp and permitted to examine the equipment."

Don Manuel bade his nephew report to the Junta on what he had seen, and when Don Tomás was gone he sat numbed and did not move until his sweat and the heat of his fright stifled him and he jerked off his tunic and opened the collar of his shirt and fell back again, panting. He brought himself to pour a glass of brandy and he thought how in the vast office of the Governor of New Mexico he was alone. His head rocked with old scenes and old sounds and he saw the pattern again, and now the Americans were part of it. The Americans no longer were a strange officer and

530

hordes of faceless men but were part of the design that had begun long before on the road to Taos. The American army now had the face of Caballero.

He drank another brandy and then abruptly put on his tunic and left the palace for the house on the Calle de la Muralla.

4

SOLEDAD was dressed in the American fashion, her sleeves puffed at the shoulders, her waist slender as a reed, and he remembered a time when she had curtsied before him and had asked him if her costume had offended him.

"I did not know about Don Esquipulas, excelencia," she said. "It does not surprise me."

"You knew nothing of this?"

"I have not been in communication with Don Esquipulas for some time."

He looked at her earnestly. "What are your plans in the event the Americans enter Santa Fe?"

"I have made no plans, excelencia."

"Your husband would arrive with them."

"I will decide what to do when the time comes."

He could not take his eyes from her. "It may be necessary to abandon the capital, señora," he said.

"After you have defended it to the utmost, excelencia."

"After or before."

"Before, excelencia?" she asked with surprise. "How before?"

"Resistance may be useless. If it becomes necessary for me to leave Santa Fe, would you consider coming with me?"

"No, excelencia."

He nodded slowly. "It is too late, is it not? It is too late for everything."

"It is not too late, excelencia, because it could never have been," she said. "I will not go with you, but so long as you remain here and defend your country I will support you in every way that lies within my power."

He smiled crookedly. "Even though you plotted against me?"

"So you knew of that too."

"From the beginning."

"And you permitted it?"

"Yes."

"Why, excelencia?"

He shrugged. "Who knows? It gave you amusement."

She sighed. "You are a strange man, excelencia." Then she lifted her head proudly. "I do not deny it. I tried to persuade men to drive you out and restore New Mexico to those whose ancestors took it from Indians. I failed miserably. But the Americans are not the descendants of the conquistadores. The Americans are aliens on the land. I forgive nothing you have done and I forget nothing. But in this war I am on your side of the barricades."

He went to her and lifted her hand to his lips. "How different it might have been, señora!"

She rose from her chair and walked away from him. "It could have been no different," she said. "We do what we must, you and I and Don Esquipulas. Even the gringos, I suppose. What Don Esquipulas does at this time you have driven him to do. I am under no such compulsion. You have injured our country greatly, but you are of the blood of New Mexico." She turned and faced him, her chin high. "Raise your standard, excelencia, and men will follow you. Do not even think of not resisting."

"There may not be many, señora."

"There may not," she agreed. "You are not greatly loved by your people, and properly so. But you are the leader. You are the only leader. There is no other. Summon your people. Not all will fail you. But if you were forsaken by all men and you had to stand alone in the path of the Americans with but your own sword in hand, you would still have to resist!"

"If I order resistance Santa Fe may be razed to the ground."

Her eyes flashed and he felt his blood quicken. "The Santa Fe that is made of mud and water may well be razed, excelencia. There is more mud and there is more water. *That* Santa Fe can be rebuilt and will rise prouder for its demolishment. What can never be re-created if it is destroyed is the honor of the people of New Mexico. You hold that honor in a shining vessel in your grasp. It is a sacred trust. You may not betray your people before history."

He looked at her quizzically. "You speak only of national honor," he said; "you say nothing of my own. Has it no value for you?"

"Your honor is your personal concern, excelencia," she said evenly. "Your own conscience must dictate to you how you treat with it. The honor of New Mexico was brought into this land by men who died gladly for it. That honor belongs to all of us."

He bowed. "I will try to remember that."

THE TIME OF THE GRINGO PART XXIV

1

AFTER the Army of the West crossed the Arkansas River it entered upon a barren and angry land. The earth itself seemed to look upon the Americans as an enemy and set out to defend with the force of nature the country that lay ahead. A scorching southwest wind blasted sand and dust into the faces of men and animals, blinding and almost suffocating them. The soldiers who had marched with such high spirits and notable success from Fort Leavenworth broke out with sore eyes and bleeding noses and heat rashes and they got sick of the desert fever. Many of them crawled into the wagons of the later Santa Fe traders who had joined the army at Bent's Fort and there collapsed.

Water was in short supply from the start and enough was issued only to keep men alive. Feed for the animals was almost nonexistent, and in the ninety miles of desert that lay between the Arkansas and the Purgatoire, Kearny was forced to divide his troops into bands and to scatter them over separate trails to take advantage of every blade of sere grass and every drop of brackish water which the caravan that had passed through weeks earlier had not consumed. Horses and oxen fell dead from heat and thirst and the struggle of dragging their way through the deep, sucking sand, and the army soon was being followed by another army, of wolves and coyotes and vultures, which pounced avidly on the carcasses of horses that were abandoned. Although he had stockpiled supplies, Kearny had planned to augment his food with game, which did not appear. For safety he placed the army on half rations.

Upon crossing the Purgatoire on August 5, the army found a greater supply of water and grass, but the men were maintained on reduced rations and the weather continued hot. The desert fell

534

behind and the country became mountainous. To the right of the march were the great Spanish Peaks and in the distance to the east were the endless plains. Ahead reared the naked mountains with the bony and precipitous cliffs.

Mules and horses perished on the rough roads and bristling hills leading up to Raton Pass. From time to time it was necessary to haul the artillery carriages with ropes up abrupt mountain spurs and to lower them in the same manner on the other side. The vista that lay before the men as they reached the summit of the pass was breath-taking, but there were few not too tired and too sick and too hungry to enjoy it.

On August 10 Kearny reached the Cimarron. During the night a Mexican on his way to Taos arrived at the camp. Kearny gave him copies of the proclamation he had prepared as well as letters to the alcalde of Taos and to Padre Martínez and permitted him to continue on his journey. Later that night two different groups of spies from Armijo were captured. Kearny showed them his army and his weapons.

"I come as a friend of your people," he said. "I desire to protect their property and religion, to defend the weak against the strong, and the poor against the rich." The faces of the spies brightened, and Kearny turned to an officer and said quietly: "If I have to fire a round of grape into such men, I shall think of it with remorse all my life."

He sent the men away unharmed, with additional copies of his proclamation, urging them to distribute them among the people.

The next day the army came to the Ocate, and there Kearny found Caballero waiting for him. Caballero's report was discouraging. Taos Valley, he told Kearny, was an armed camp and the hardy natives of the Rio Arriba were determined to put up resistance. He had with him a number of prisoners and one of the captives had a proclamation issued by the prefect of the Rio Arriba calling upon New Mexicans to destroy the "Americans who are coming to invade your soil and destroy your property and liberties." The captives told Kearny that the wild Indian tribes—Utes, Comanches, Navajos, and Apaches—were flocking to Armijo to join in the fight against the Americans.

535

Kearny, who was suffering again from the desert fever and who had lost more weight since his departure from Bent's Fort, called Caballero and Fernando into his tent.

"There is no doubt that Don Manuel has issued this proclamation and others like it," Caballero said soberly. "He is master of that kind of thing. He is telling them that your soldiers are here to plunder and destroy, and the priests are saying that you have given orders to brand the initials 'U.S.' on the cheeks of women after your soldiers have raped them so that all other American soldiers will know them for whores."

"My God, what kind of men are these priests?" Kearny asked angrily.

"Some of them may even believe it," Fernando said.

Kearny mopped the sweat from his haggard face. "If I march down by way of Taos, where is Armijo likely to make his stand?"

Caballero shrugged. "There are several places. Pojoaque, the mesa of San Ildefonso, others."

"None as strong as Apache Canyon."

"I know of no place in New Mexico as strong as Apache Canyon, mi coronel," Caballero said quietly.

"But I would have to kill civilians to get to him."

"Through Taos, yes, señor."

"Thank you both for the risk you have taken. If you will be good enough to leave me now, I will consider the choice before me and make my decision."

In the torrid, airless tent the ailing colonel faced the terrible loneliness of a commander at the time of decision. The intelligence was in. He could ask no more and learn no more.

From a military viewpoint there was no problem. To march through Taos would mean fighting, but he had no doubt of the outcome and after that he could fight Armijo in the open. His army was more than a weapon however, he knew. The men were carrying intangibles into New Mexico, and the intangibles would remain long after the soldiers departed. What the army did in the next few days would set the tone of relations between Americans and New Mexicans for a long time to come. Generations not yet born would be presented with an attitude based on what his soldiers did. He could win his war for today and at the same time lose it for the future.

A half-hour later he issued orders for the Army of the West to march down the plains to Apache Canyon.

Caballero went to the tent. "God bless you, sir," he said in English. He walked quickly away.

2

LATER THAT DAY two natives from the village of Mora entered the camp. When they were brought before Kearny they said they had come to him without fear because they had faith in Americans. Kearny gripped their hands warmly, feeling that somehow they had underwritten his decision. When the two Morans saw Caballero they wept with joy, and though Apache Canyon still lay far ahead and the military issue had not even been joined, Kearny had the strange feeling that his true victory had already been won. "These men appear to be good friends of yours," he said to Caballero.

"Good friends and old friends, mi coronel," Caballero said. "When we hid out from the Rurales our camp was not far from the village of Mora. These people were our eyes and our ears, and many times they were our food supply as well."

Kearny cocked his head. "You bring up an interesting subject, Señor Caballero. Since I have entered New Mexico my army has been on short rations. I have given orders that nothing shall be stolen. I have attempted to buy cattle and sheep, but I have not had much success. Do you think these men would sell to us?"

Caballero spoke to the two men and when he finished they began to talk rapidly, both at the same time. Caballero's face reddened.

"What is their reply?" Kearny asked.

Caballero looked embarrassed. The two men began to talk again and they nodded vehemently and gestured with their thumbs at Kearny.

"What are they saying?" Kearny asked again.

Caballero rubbed his lips with his fingertip. One of the men took his arm and shook it. Caballero said in a strained voice:

"They say that if they have cattle and sheep in their fields it is because of me." His voice became hardly audible. "They say the village of Mora would be honored if the American commandant would accept as a gift the animals they have."

Kearny stared at the two men. They grinned and nodded again. He said: "Tell your countrymen I will accept every animal they can spare, but that I will pay for them."

When Caballero repeated what he had said, the two men fell upon him with a new barrage of words and stamped their feet on the ground. "They will take no money from you, señor coronel," Caballero said. "They say you must take the animals as a gift from Mora." He hesitated. "Accept their offer. They will have it no other way."

"Then I accept with all my heart," Kearny said.

The two men broke into joyous smiles. One of them said something rapidly to Caballero. "He says they will start back for Mora immediately and round up the animals and they will bring them to you before you reach Las Vegas. He apologizes for the condition of the animals. He says the grazing has been bad because of lack of rain and they will not be fat."

Kearny took a deep breath. He wanted to say more, but the men were mounted and already riding out of the camp.

3

Don Manuel heard the clatter of the horse and he flew to the window. He saw the rider whip his foaming horse across the plaza and then jerk it to a stop. He saw the man slip down from the saddle and stagger to the portal. "The Governor!" the man gasped to the guards. "I must see Don Manuel!"

"Here!" Don Manuel shouted. "I am here!"

The man tottered to the window. His face was ashen with fatigue. "Excelencia, more than five thousand American soldiers are marching down the eastern plains. They were six days' journey south of Bent's Fort when I left them and dashed across the mountains. Excelencia, they are boasting in a loud voice that they are coming to take possession of New Mexico at any cost!" He fell over unconscious.

"Give this man help," Don Manuel ordered. He stepped back from the window, walked to the desk, and sat down. He lit a cigar, but it was tasteless and he put it down and let it go out. The office seemed extraordinarily large. Governor Martínez had thrown out the collection of Indian ears. The room seemed to grow bigger with each day that passed. The fear crept in him.

He could not bear to be alone. The Junta, which was meeting that day, was useless. He made out a list of the principal citizens of Santa Fe and sent word for these men to come to his office immediately. He ordered Colonel Diego Archuleta to attend the conference. Archuleta, who had been sent back from the City of Mexico at the outbreak of hostilities and who had been appointed by Don Manuel as second in command, was engaged in supervising the fortification of Apache Canyon.

Don Manuel buckled on his sword, and buttoned his tunic, and stood stiffly and with forced calm as the men gathered in the office, and as they formed nervous little groups, their eyes avoiding his, he could see their fear and his own left him. He read the faces and made out the men who had already privately surrendered to the Americans and the men who were planning how to make a good thing of the Americans and the men who were too frightened to have any thoughts at all.

The large majority of the citizens urged him not to try to oppose Kearny. A small group, led by Archuleta, contended the Americans must be fought, and the colonel, in his cold, impressive voice, reported that the fortification of Apache Canyon was progressing rapidly and that the narrow mouth of the canyon would prove impassable to the enemy.

"Cannon have been placed where they can sweep the opening and an abatis has been constructed across the east entrance," Archuleta said. "And now we know definitely that Kearny is marching down the eastern plains and will have to attack at the canyon."

"Why can they not climb the sides and attack from above?" demanded one of the men who had counseled surrender.

"It is possible, theoretically, for infantrymen to crawl up the sides of the mountain," the colonel replied with the icy disinterest of a military man explaining military problems to a civilian. "They would need both hands and both feet to reach the summit. The outer walls of the canyon are almost straight up and down. The summit will be ringed with defenders, who would easily pick off enemy soldiers attempting the climb. The enemy could not stop to fire back without risking falling to the bottom again. I do not believe Coronel Kearny would give such a suicidal order, and as a matter of fact it would please me much if he did."

"What if they force their way into the entrance?" the same man asked.

"I do not believe they can. If they should, the length of the pass is lined with timber and rocks offering natural breastworks. More are being constructed. We would sweep the Americans with fire from both sides." He turned to Don Manuel. "Excelencia, the pass can be successfully defended."

"Many thanks, Don Diego," Don Manuel said. He felt unexpectedly brave. He thought of Soledad and his chest puffed out.

The men who had urged surrender now turned hysterically on the colonel. They accused him of wanting to sacrifice Mexican lives to further his military ambitions. Archuleta remained silent, his face impassive.

"Quiet!" Don Manuel said at last. He looked again at the faces and he relished the fears. "I have listened to you. There will be no more talk of surrender. We will fight! We will fight and win!"

The small minority who had supported Archuleta broke into cheers. Most of the other men accepted the decision in silence. A half dozen continued to protest, and when Don Manuel, standing now at the side of Colonel Archuleta, his hand on the colonel's shoulder, did not deign to reply, they gave way to complete panic and turned their abuse upon him.

Don Manuel's frigidity now matched that of the colonel. He called for the guard and ordered the offenders imprisoned. As the others filed out, all of them now pledging their support in the defense of their country, he gripped his sword proudly and he thought: "Soledad, I have not forgotten." She would hear of this meeting, he knew.

Later in the day the skeletonized and benumbed Junta came to life at last and acted decisively. The deputies voted Don Manuel full dictatorial powers, authorizing him "to dictate all those measures which may be necessary for the conservation of the national honor, which, for the moment, is threatened by the Republic of the United States, our neighbor." The deputies vested him with "extraordinary powers to maintain the military forces at his command" and granted him the right to make whatever levies he deemed necessary to pursue the war. After thus reaffirming the unlimited authority they had presented to him years before, the departmental Assembly made preparations to adjourn.

She had spoken the simple truth, Don Manuel thought when he read the minutes of the meeting. He was the leader. He was the father, and when disaster threatened they turned to him and cried out: "Don Manuel, save us." He raised his eyes and looked into space. "Have no fear, niños," he whispered. "I will protect you. I will think for all of you and I will protect you."

He did not neglect to decree a stiff war emergency tax and he sent agents out immediately to collect it.

On the 10th day of August a courier arrived from Don Juan Dios de Maes, the alcalde of Las Vegas, with word that James Magoffin and an escort of dragoons had arrived in Las Vegas on their way to the capital to discuss terms with the Governor. The dispatch dovetailed with Don Manuel's momentary mood of confidence.

He called a public meeting in the plaza and rode out to the people on his charger. "My fellow countrymen," he boomed. "I have just received information that the gringo leader wants to confer with me. You know what that must mean! They came here believing our country would fall before them like an old house in the wind, but they have learned instead that our brave fighting men have risen with irresistible fury to the call of your Governor. Now the gringos quake and they want not to fight but to talk! I answer them: you have come as invaders with false promises. We do not treat with you. We stand ready to die to the last man to preserve the independence of our country!"

His sword flashed. The cheers became wine in his veins.

4

SHORTLY AFTER the rise of the sun on the 12th day of August, Magoffin's party was escorted by a company of New Mexican cavalry through Apache Canyon.

Cooke's keen military eye quickly took in the defensive construction that was being completed. The abatis of stones and trees had been erected just inside the east mouth of the forty-foot pass. Redoubts and ravelins had been built on the sharply sloping inner walls. Soldiers were dragging pieces of artillery to the strong points and were setting them in place. The field of fire was concentrated on the opening. Cooke estimated rapidly that at least one thousand soldiers were at work. As the Americans rode by, the Mexicans paused in their labors and gazed at them silently.

The cavalry left them when the trail debouched on the broad plain to the west. "What do you think of it, captain?" Magoffin asked Cooke.

Cooke's face was grim. "Nature has provided a powerful place of defense, Colonel Magoffin, and it is being fortified with great skill."

"Unless they have sent up a trained officer from Mexico I know of only one man who would have that skill: Don Diego Archuleta," Magoffin said.

"Whoever it is, he intends to do more than just keep us outside the canyon. He plans to kill as many Americans as he can. Did you notice how the abatis was built not against the mouth to block it entirely, but far enough inside so that a few men at a time could filter by it. They would then be subjected to murderous defilade. The man knows his business."

"Do you consider it possible to breach the pass?"

"It is always possible to breach any defense. I hate to think of the number of lives it would take," Cooke said.

The party was met on the outskirts of the capital just before noon by a company of finely armed and mounted cavalry led by an officer who filled his saddle with superb grace. The officer saluted Cooke. "I am Capitán Tomás Ortiz," he said. "I have been sent to escort you to the palace. Your lives would not be safe without the protection of my soldiers." Although Ortiz knew Magoffin, he ignored him. "I will not ask you to surrender your weapons, capitán, if you pledge your word of honor that under no circumstances will your men use them."

As they rode into the city, it became evident that Ortiz had not exaggerated the attitude of the people. Women screamed in terror at the appearance of the Americans and scooped up their children and ran off, sheltering them. Men cursed and jeered and shouted: "Death to the Americans!"

The city was overflowing. There were over three thousand volunteers there and more were coming in steadily from all directions. Captain Ortiz, his face reflecting his pride in the belligerent mood of his people, gave the order to his men to draw their swords to guard the Americans from attack.

Upon reaching the plaza, Magoffin, in accordance with an arrangement he had made previously with Cooke, slipped away to the office he used in Santa Fe. It had been agreed that the official conference would be between the Governor and Cooke. Magoffin's session with Don Manuel would be a private one.

After having encountered everything in the New Mexican people from shy friendliness to hostility, Cooke wondered at the reception he would receive from Don Manuel. Aware of the Mexican predilection for ceremony, he suspected there might be a great deal of pomp. He was surprised, upon being admitted to Don Manuel's office, to find the Governor alone. He stood at attention as Ortiz said with profound respect: "Excelencia, I have brought to you the American officer, Señor Capitán Felipe San Jorge Cooke, as you ordered."

Cooke saluted the Governor. Don Manuel regarded him gravely and the American sensed immediately an undeniable dignity. "Excelencia, I come as a representative of my commanding officer, Coronel Kearny. I bear from him a communication for your excellency." Cooke discovered his voice instinctively echoing the deferential tones of Ortiz.

Don Manuel extended his hand. Again surprised, Cooke accepted it and found his own gripped hard. "I welcome you to Santa Fe, señor capitán," Don Manuel said in his rich voice. "I regret only that in our first meeting we must assume the roles of enemies."

Cooke snapped open his dispatch case and reached into it. Don Manuel raised his hand elegantly. "There is time enough for unpleasant business, Don Felipe. You must be wearied from your journey. First you must refresh yourself. Capitán Ortiz will show you to the quarters that have been set aside for you. You will be informed when the official reception will take place and you may present the communication from Coronel Kearny at that time." He rose and his imposing manner became even more evident. "Good day, Don Felipe."

Cooke, who had thought Armijo would not be able to wait to see what Kearny had written him, saluted again with some confusion. Armijo dismissed him with another graceful gesture and the American followed Ortiz out of the office. He was taken to a comfortable room in the officers' section of the barracks. There he found clean linen laid out for him and a variety of toilet articles set on a table. A bottle of wine, a bottle of brandy, and a box of fine Cuban cigars were on the table as well.

Ortiz ran his eyes over the room. "I believe you will find here everything necessary to recover from the fatigue of the road, mi capitán. If by any chance anything has been omitted, you need only ask for it of the orderly who will remain on duty outside this room. He has been instructed to obey your commands. When you are ready he will show you where you may bathe." He bowed and departed.

Cooke stood quietly for several minutes, stroking his beard. Then he walked over to a mirror on the wall. He had not realized how grimy he was. He picked up a cigar and sniffed it. He poured some brandy, tasted it, and drained the glass. He poured more and, shaking his head, sat down slowly in a deep chair.

When he returned from his bath he found that all signs of travel had been removed from his uniform. His boots were polished. He poured another glass of brandy and lit a cigar. It was three o'clock in the afternoon when an orderly tapped on the door and announced the reception was scheduled for an hour hence.

At four o'clock exactly Captain Ortiz returned and led him to the sala in the Governor's apartment. This time Don Manuel was not alone. In the room were almost a score of men, some in uniform. All were dressed richly. The air was aromatic with the smell of fine cigars. Governor Armijo walked over to Cooke instantly and put his hand on his shoulder. He took him from person to person and introduced him. Some of the names were familiar to him from his conversations with Magoffin. He shook hands with Don Juan Bautista Vigil, Don Juan Estevan Pino, an Otero, a Sena, Don José Chaves y Castillo. A tall, lordly priest in a magnificent cassock held out his hand for Cooke to kiss. The American officer, trying to hide his astonishment at the priest's flaming red hair and blue eyes, took the hand and inclined his head. The last man to whom Cooke was presented arrested his attention.

"Señor Coronel Diego Archuleta," Don Manuel said.

Archuleta nodded coldly and, unlike the others, did not offer his hand.

"This morning I had the opportunity to see the fortifications at Apache Canyon," Cooke said. "I was told the work probably was directed by Coronel Archuleta."

"You were informed correctly," Don Manuel said.

Cooke bowed. "May I express my compliments to the coronel? The work is that of a master."

Even this praise did not lessen the iciness of Archuleta's face. "We are not without knowledge of military art, capitán," he said. He turned and walked away.

"Before we proceed to business, Don Felipe, there are refreshments," Don Manuel said, an amused smile on his lips. "Would you do me the honor to drink a glass of wine with me?"

"With pleasure, excelencia," Cooke said. He looked across the room at Archuleta.

Don Manuel followed the glance. "You must not mind Don Diego," he whispered. "He is a hothead."

A servant brought the wine and Don Manuel raised his glass. "Health and money and time to spend it!" he said cheerily.

As Cooke sipped the excellent wine, another man entered the room. Don Manuel smiled broadly. "Don Enrique," he said heartily.

"I am sorry I am late, excelencia," the newcomer said. "I came as quickly as I could."

"You are in time, my old friend," Don Manuel said. "Here is your countryman Señor Capitán Cooke. Don Felipe, here is another American, Señor Connelly."

Henry Connelly, a wiry man of middle height with an up-turned Irish nose and a pair of twinkling blue eyes, greeted Cooke warmly. "It's a pleasure to meet you at last, captain," he said in a voice that danced with faint brogue. "We've heard a lot about you in these parts."

Cooke, startled at finding an American in the conclave of the enemy, asked weakly: "You have heard my name, sir?"

"Who hasn't, captain, who hasn't? You're the officer who disarmed the Texans under Snively, aren't you?"

"Yes."

"You're a pretty famous man here, captain," Connelly said. "A lot of Mexicans look on you as a kind of hero."

Don Manuel had listened affably to the exchange in English. He now sighed and said: "It would be most pleasant to continue this discussion, señores, but I fear there is business at hand and we must get to it. Don Felipe, Señor Connelly has lived long among us. I have asked him to act as interpreter."

The men took seats and the room hushed as Connelly un-folded the paper Cooke handed to him and, after reading it through, translated it in a clear voice:

" 'Headquarters of the Army of the West, in camp upon the Arkansas, at Fort Bent, August 1, 1846. Sir: By the annexation of Texas to the United States, the Rio Grande, from its delta to its source, forms now the boundary line between the United States and Mexico and I am coming by order of my Government to take possession of the country over a part of which you are presiding as governor. . . .' "

Several of the men raised their voices. Don Manuel lifted two fingers and they were silent. Cooke looked again at Archuleta. The colonel's mouth was a tight line.

Connelly continued: " 'I come as a friend with the disposition and intention to consider all the Mexicans and other inhabitants as my friends if they should remain quietly and peaceably in their houses attending to their own affairs. All such persons shall not be molested by any of those who are coming under my orders in their persons nor in their property nor in their religion. I pledge myself to the fulfillment of these promises.'" Connelly raised his eyes for a moment and cleared his throat. "'I come to this part of the United States . . .'"

Archuleta was on his feet immediately. "This is not the United States!" he said in a deadly voice.

Don Manuel smiled at him gently and shook his head. Archuleta resumed his seat, his hand gripping his sword hilt.

"'I come to this part of the United States,'" Connelly repeated, "'with a strong military force, and a still stronger one is following us as a reinforcement. I have more troops than I need to overcome any opposition which you may be able to make against us, and for that reason and for the sake of humanity I advise you to submit to fate, and to consider me with the same sentiments of peace and friendship which I have and protest for you and those under your government.

"'Should Your Excellency do this it would be eminently favorable to your interest and that of all your countrymen, and you will receive their blessings and prayers. If, on the contrary, you should decide otherwise, if you should make up your mind to make resistance and oppose us, with such troops as you may be able to raise against us, in that event, I notify you that the blood that may be shed, the sufferings and misery that may follow, shall fall upon your head, and instead of the blessings of your countrymen you will receive their curses, as I shall consider all Your Excellency may present against us armed, as enemies and they shall be treated accordingly.

"'I am sending you this communication with Captain Cooke of my regiment, and I recommend him as well as the small party of twelve dragoons, to your kindness and attention.

"'With much respect, I am Your Obedient Servant, S. W. Kearny, Colonel, First Dragoons.

"'To His Excellency, Governor and Commanding General, Don Manuel Armijo, Santa Fe.'"

The Governor stood up immediately. "There will be no discussion," he said, looking directly at Archuleta. "Señores, you have all heard the words of the American coronel. I will consider them and I will give my answer to Capitán Cooke before the day is out. And now, amigos, let us join in refreshments."

Cooke sat alone in his room and tried to collect his thoughts. The conference, called to determine the question of war or peace, had in the end been turned by Governor Armijo into a pleasant social event. Archuleta left immediately, and after that there was no note of anger anywhere. Don Manuel did not again refer to Kearny's message. He remained at Cooke's elbow constantly, the attentive host, pressing champagne on him, suggesting he try this or that bit of sweetmeat, proffering a cigar when he noticed Cooke was without one.

The other men chatted like so many birds; they drank wine and nibbled biscuits as though they had not a care in the world. They clustered around Cooke and he discovered Connelly had not been merely flattering him when he said he was held in esteem by the New Mexicans. Connelly himself seemed to be more native than American. More and more Cooke felt he had entered into some fairy-tale world. After a while even he found it difficult to realize that only a short distance away an army was marching on Santa Fe and that there was a very good chance that not too many hours hence he would be directing grapeshot at these men who now expressed their affection for him with such genuine sincerity.

At seven o'clock the gathering broke up and an officer returned Cooke to his quarters. And there he attempted to rationalize the strangest afternoon of his life.

It was ten o'clock and he was on his third cigar and wondering where Magoffin was and what his part would be in the bewilderment when a soldier came to the room and told him that Governor Armijo requested his presence in his office.

Don Manuel was alone again, except for Archuleta. The colonel turned his back on Cooke as he presented himself to the Governor. Don Manuel appeared to be in as amiable a mood as ever. He asked Cooke if his accommodations were to his liking and if there was anything he desired that had not been provided. Upon being assured by Cooke that he wanted for nothing, Don Manuel picked up Kearny's letter and glanced at it. His face saddened. "I have studied this ultimatum delivered by Coronel

Kearny," he said. "I regret to tell you that there is but a single course open to me. I am a soldier, señor capitán, and I have personally experienced the unpleasantness of war. My body still bears the scar of a wound. War is not new to me! But my honor and the honor of Mexico and the responsibility I owe to my people and to my government require that I reject the demand made by your commander. I do not love war, Don Felipe, but I have no choice. I must lead my troops against the Americans and pray that God and the Blessed Virgin give victory to our side."

Cooke was deeply moved by Don Manuel's words. "I am unhappy to hear of your decision, excelencia."

"I would be recreant if I did less, Don Felipe."

Cooke leaned forward. "Have you considered all things, excelencia? You refer to the message of Coronel Kearny as an ultimatum. It is not that, I assure you. It is an expression of friendship, a plea that lives, Mexican and American, be spared."

From a corner of the room Archuleta snorted. Don Manuel smiled. "It may be called an expression of friendship," he said. "Your commandant says to me that he will be my friend—if I surrender. You must forgive me if I fail to detect in his words the true notes of friendship. I believe the Apaches would be my friends too if I handed my country to them."

"It is not the same thing, excelencia," Cooke said earnestly, "if you permit me to disagree. If you accede to the request of Coronel Kearny your people will immediately have all the rights of other Americans."

"I have heard it said that the Americans are very proud of their government and so it must appear to you that you are being generous in offering to share it with us and that I am being foolish to refuse it," Don Manuel replied quietly. "You have forgotten only one thing. It is a small thing and you may be forgiven for having overlooked it. It so happens, my dear capitán, that we are not Americans, but are Mexicans. That cannot be changed by a stroke of the pen. I will not argue that your government is not a good government. It may be the best government. But it is not our government."

"We do not come to conquer you, excelencia."

"Nevertheless, Don Felipe, you will *have* to conquer us," Don Manuel said with noble sadness.

Cooke straightened. "I will convey your excellency's reply to Coronel Kearny."

"You will leave in the morning, señor," Don Manuel said. "I have asked Señor Enrique Connelly to accompany you. He also will bear word from me to your commander. You may tell Coronel Kearny I will have no less than six thousand men, fully armed and equipped, and that I shall myself lead this force against him. You also may tell him that at this moment additional soldiers are on their way up from Chihuahua. Don Enrique will support you in all this and perhaps there may still be hope that your commander will be dissuaded from taking the step that will prove fatal to your side."

"I shall do as you request, excelencia," Cooke said. "May I express my deep regret that I have failed in my mission."

Don Manuel rose briskly. "Now we will visit El Don," he said.

5

Don Manuel seated himself in the most comfortable chair in Magoffin's office. He set his sword upright between his legs, crossing his hands over the hilt. "You are here to offer me a bribe, Don Santiago," he said bluntly.

"I have some facts to present to your excellency," Magoffin said. "It is my hope that when they are understood by you, you will feel impelled to come to a certain conclusion."

For Cooke, the unreality of the afternoon, which had disappeared before Don Manuel's simple and impressive declaration of his determination to resist, now returned. His eyes crossed those of Archuleta. Don Diego's were fathomless.

"What are these facts, Don Santiago?" Don Manuel asked politely.

Magoffin offered the men whisky and cigars before he replied. Archuleta refused both. Magoffin took a chair opposite the Governor. "Let us consider the situation, excelencia," he said. "Except for a brief period you have been Governor since 1837. You know better than anyone else how tenuous are the ties that hold New

Mexico and Mexico together. They have been almost separate countries since the Revolution. And you know that your army is in no condition to fight a prolonged war. I am no stranger to this country, Don Manuel. I know there is in all the world no soldier braver than the Mexican, particularly when he is defending his land. And he is led by officers of courage and skill. But your army is no match for the army now on its way to Santa Fe."

"We are no less powerful!" Archuleta said. "And we outnumber the gringos. And we have Apache Canyon fighting with us."

"You may outnumber them, Don Diego," Magoffin agreed softly, "but their rifles and cannon are superior to yours and their men are better trained. And unfortunately for you, señores, passion and valor are not quite enough in modern battle. Gallantry is no armor against hot lead." A shadow passed over his face. "I speak in your behalf, excelencia. I am almost half Mexican. My wife, who was related to your excellency by marriage, was of your nationality, and in the veins of my children American blood mixes with Mexican. Perhaps they symbolize the future here in which both our peoples will merge in peace." He looked away for a moment. Then he continued with suppressed passion: "I believe with all my heart that Kearny can win the day against you. But at what cost! The earth will stream with blood, American blood and Mexican blood. Perhaps that will salve Mexican honor, but it also will leave Mexican families bereft."

"That is war," Archuleta said indifferently.

"The death of a soldier should serve some useful end," Magoffin replied. "If defeat is predestined, the battle may be honorable but it also will be useless—so useless."

"It is your opinion that the war will terminate with victory for your side," Archuleta said. "I do not grant that for a moment, por Dios!"

"I know the quality of the troops Kearny has with him and the equipment they bear," Magoffin said.

"And I know that Kearny and his men are even now short of food and that he pleads with our people to sell him cattle and sheep," Archuleta said. "You have seen Apache Canyon, Don Santiago. A few hundred men can stand off an army there. And Kearny cannot afford to be delayed for the shortest time. There is not enough food where he is to fill the bellies of his soldiers. And neither can he march around the mountains to Galisteo. The earth is parched. The streams are dry. I do not agree with you that our cause is hopeless. And even if I did, I would oppose surrender."

"Perhaps you are right, Don Diego," Magoffin said. "You might win victory now, but in the end you would still suffer defeat. I believe Kearny can do it, but if he fails there are thousands behind him and behind those thousands there are thousands more. My government considers New Mexico east of the Rio Grande as part of the United States and it never will consider it otherwise. I do not know how much you have learned of the history of my country, Don Diego, but we have not yet lost a war and we take possession of what we believe to be our own. You speak of honor, señores, and I respect you both for it. But I also ask you to remember that the lives of men depend on the answer you give to me."

"You have not yet made your offer, Don Santiago," Don Manuel said somnolently.

"I am authorized, excelencia, to place at your disposal the sum of thirty thousand dollars if you dismiss your soldiers and remove yourself from Santa Fe."

Cooke held his breath.

"It is not an unattractive sum," Don Manuel said.

"It will be delivered to your account either in Albuquerque or Chihuahua or any other place you specify."

"Except Santa Fe."

"Except Santa Fe, excelencia."

Don Manuel got to his feet. "I will leave now, señores." He turned to Cooke. "My answer to Coronel Kearny remains unchanged, capitán." He shook hands with Cooke and then with Magoffin. "Undoubtedly there are still some things you desire to discuss with Don Diego," he said. "Good night, señores." He limped from the room.

Magoffin's manner became brusque. "Don Diego, there is but one additional thing I wish to point out to you. You have heard the message Coronel Kearny sent to General Armijo?"

"I have."

"Then I desire to recall to you that the United States regards the land *east* of the Rio Grande as territory of the United States.

There is a vast area west of the river that always has been claimed by Mexico. It will still be considered as such after the Americans occupy the land east of the river." Magoffin looked at the colonel meaningfully. "After Don Manuel you are the most powerful man in your country. When he is gone, there will be none greater. There is the situation, Don Diego: a land that will be without a leader, and a leader who will be without a land. It appears to me to suggest an obvious partnership. And I will add that if you take control of the country between the Rio Grande and the Californias you will find yourself among friends when you visist across the river."

Archuleta's obdurate expression remain unchanged. He bowed with stiff courtesy. "Good night, Don Santiago, señor capitán."

"May God give you many of them, Don Diego," Magoffin said.

Archuleta marched out of the room. When the front door opened and closed, Magoffin breathed deeply and wiped his face with a kerchief. "Would you be good enough to pour another drink for me and for yourself, captain?" he said, his suave voice suddenly hoarse. He looked at Cooke's perplexed face and smiled. "It was very confusing, wasn't it?"

"Sir, I have never been so bewildered in my life!"

Magoffin swallowed the whisky and then laughed tiredly. "I don't blame you, son."

"But we both spoke about the same thing, capitulation. To me he said no, definitely no, we fight! To you he said nothing, but his silence means perhaps. Archuleta, hard as brass, and yet he listened to you and did not refuse either. My God, colonel, what kind of people are these?"

Magoffin took another swallow. His eyes became reflective. "Inside, no different from anybody else, captain. But I will agree with you. Outwardly they are very strange. I have lived with them for years and they still can puzzle me. I think perhaps they may be better understood by both of us—and by the others who are coming here—if we all realize they are living an anachronism." He closed his eyes for a moment and his face showed his strain. "You must understand, captain, that except for the traders New Mexico has been cut off from the world for a long time. And in its way it's been rather lovely. To come here has always been like stepping back through time to the Middle Ages. It's one of the things I shall regret to see disappear."

"I still don't understand those men."

"I guess not, son. You see, Armijo and I understand each other so well, and we both know that the end of his time has come and with it a manner of life. I have played the part of gravedigger tonight and I weep a little inside for what I am burying. My roots have gone deep into this beautiful land." For a moment his face softened and his eyes became tender. He finished the whisky in the glass. Then he said musingly: "With the Mexicans what is done is not so important as the manner in which it is done. The style is everything. Anything may be done if it is done in the proper style. And the style is part of the honor, and the honor must be served before all else."

He smiled wanly. "Now, you know all about honor. You are an officer. But this is a different kind of honor. I see it in my own sons. There is certain face that has to be maintained, like that of the orientals. Of all the things I said tonight to Don Manuel, only one thing carried any weight, and that was the amount of money he was being offered to get out. But it was necessary to prefix it with the argument that resistance was useless, which is debatable, as Archuleta proved. I had to save Don Manuel's face for him, to himself, even as I offered a bribe. On his part Don Manuel upheld his honor when he officially rejected Kearny's demand. And then he went away and permitted me to speak to Archuleta alone so the colonel's face might be saved. Don Diego served his honor in his own fashion and all of this was necessary, and if you fail to see it also was sincere, you miss the point entirely. Colonel Kearny understood this even better than I did. That is why we were sent jointly, with identical demands but with separate weapons, and that is why I planned it so you would see Armijo first, and alone. Don Manuel was able to make the required chivalrous reply to you. And he also was able to listen to me."

After a fitful few hours Cooke was wakened at sunrise with a request from Don Manuel to join him at breakfast. He found the Governor freshly groomed and apparently rested, and very cheerful. The invitation was one of pure courtesy. Don Manuel said nothing of the business of a few hours before. Chocolate was served in silver goblets, and bread and cakes on silver plates. Cooke remarked, with the greatest sincerity, that he had never before tasted such delicious chocolate, and Don Manuel accepted the compliment with delight.

The Governor accompanied Cooke to the door of the palace. Magoffin, Connelly, and the dragoons were mounted and waiting. Don Manuel squeezed Cooke's hand. "*Vaya con Dios, mi capitán.*"

As the party crossed the plaza the morning quiet was shattered by the blast of a bugle and the beat of drums. Soldiers entered the square and formed ranks. Insults were shouted at the Americans. At the edge of the plaza Cooke stood up in his stirrups and shook his fist. "I'll call again in a week!" he cried.

All that morning they passed soldiers marching toward Apache Canyon.

THE TIME OF THE GRINGO PART XXV

1

O<small>N THE SAME DAY</small> that Cooke and Magoffin left Santa Fe, August 13, the Army of the West crossed the Sapello River and encountered a company of Mexican dragoons bearing a message from Don Manuel to Colonel Kearny.

"You have notified me that you intend to take possession of the country I govern," the Governor had written. "The people of the country have risen en masse in my defense. If you take the country it will be because you prove strongest in battle. I suggest to you that you stop at the Sapello and I will march to Las Vegas. We will meet and negotiate on the plains between."

"What the devil does he mean by negotiate?" Kearny asked Robideaux. "Does he mean talk or fight?"

The interpreter read the sentence again. "It can be taken either way, sir," he said.

Kearny asked the Mexican dragoons to remain with him and he ordered the march resumed. Camp was made a mile from the village of Las Vegas, and Kearny summoned the officer in command of the dragoons to his tent. "I have considered the words of your Governor," he said. "The road to Santa Fe is as free to you as it is to myself. Say to my friend General Armijo, I shall soon meet him, and I hope it will be as friends." He repeated avowal of friendship for the New Mexican people, but warned again he would treat as enemies all who resisted. Then he said impulsively: "I swear to you, lieutenant, that not an onion or a pepper will be taken from your people without a full equivalent in cash!"

When the words were translated, the Mexican officer threw his arms around Kearny and held him tightly. He went to each American officer in the tent and repeated the gesture. He stepped back and saluted magnificently, and a half-hour later the Mexican dragoons galloped off for Apache Canyon.

Kearny watched them depart. "I don't know how many of you are in the habit of saying your prayers at night, gentlemen," he said to his officers, "but I suggest that all of us might go on our knees this night and pray that we do not have to deal with these people as enemies."

Later in the evening, as Kearny was finishing his meager meal, he heard shouting and cheers outside and he stepped to the flap of the tent. He asked a soldier what was the matter. The man was so excited he began to speak before saluting. He recovered himself and then said: "Some Mexicans are bringing cattle and sheep into camp, sir, a load of them. The boys say there is going to be food for us. Is that right, sir?"

"Yes," Kearny said.

The soldier threw his hat into the air. "Wheee!" he said. "I beg your pardon, sir."

Kearny smiled. "Would you mind doing it once again, for me?"

He felt encouraged as he went to sleep that night, despite the continuing reports he was receiving on the fortification of Apache Canyon, but he was not to sleep the night through. It was just after midnight when he was wakened by his aide. "Three officers have just arrived with dispatches from Bent's Fort, sir," the soldier said.

"Won't it wait until morning?" Kearny grumbled.

"I think you'd better read them at once, sir. The officers have traveled from Fort Leavenworth at the greatest possible speed, and when they discovered you had already left Bent's Fort they continued after you without resting."

The aide lit a lamp on Kearny's field desk, and the colonel got up. He pulled on his trousers. The three officers entered the tent and the foremost handed Kearny a leather envelope. The colonel took out a sheet of paper. It was his commission as brigadier general.

"Congratulations, sir," the officer said. He placed a pair of starred shoulder tabs on the desk.

"It was very good of you gentlemen to hurry to me with this," Kearny said at length.

"Well, general, we wanted to get this to you as soon as possible, of course. . . ." The officer's voice trailed off.

557

Kearny cocked his head. "But that was not the only reason you broke your necks to get here."

"Well, general, they told us at Bent's Fort that there was going to be a fight."

"And you were afraid you might miss it?"

"Yes, sir."

"I see," Kearny said. "We enter Las Vegas tomorrow at eight o'clock in the morning. This is the first New Mexican community of any size that we have thus far come to. I have given orders to the men to clean themselves up and shine up their gear. We will go through Las Vegas as though on parade."

"We'll be ready, general," the officer said.

"As they were leaving the tent Kearny said: "You have come here spoiling for a fight. I hope you will be disappointed."

He looked at the stars and then tried again to sleep.

2

KEARNY stepped outside the tent as Esquipulas Caballero and his men rode up to it. The air was still crisp with the early morning. Caballero dismounted and Kearny shook his hand warmly. "I wish you success," the general said. "What happens in Las Vegas this morning will be reported to Armijo's soldiers in Apache Canyon before nightfall. It will be repeated to Armijo himself. It must go off well."

"We shall do our best, mi general."

"I shall enter Las Vegas at eight o'clock precisely."

Caballero hesitated for a moment. "General Kearny, I will talk to my people and they will listen to me, but in the end it will be only what you will say that will be important. May I speak openly, sir?"

"Of course, Don Esquipulas."

"General, speak to them about small things," Caballero said earnestly. "The people are plain and they will suspect big promises. Words like 'liberty' and 'freedom' and 'justice' are very beautiful, but they also are the same words that Don Manuel uses and the people do not have faith in them. I spoke to the New Mexican dragoons after you spoke to the lieutenant last night and the words that made the most impression on them were your promise not to take a single onion or pepper without paying for it. The people understand what it is to have their food taken from them. If you make them believe you will not rob them, it will mean more than anything you can say about rights and liberties. Remember, sir, that Armijo speaks about rights and liberties. But he dares not talk about onions or peppers—or about cattle or sheep or corn or wheat."

"Thank you, señor," Kearny said.

Caballero looked at the stars on Kearny's shoulders. He widened his eyes and said with great seriousness: "It should be much easier for you now, mi general. Now you have exactly the same rank as Don Manuel. Although he probably will promote himself when he hears about it!"

The natives of Las Vegas had been in a state of excitement from the time the American troops made camp outside the village the evening before. Now, despite the early hour, the plaza was filled. Caballero reined in his horse in the center of the square and looked at the anxious faces that surrounded him. Then he said clearly: "People of Las Vegas, I have something to say to you. You know me. You have listened to me before. I have never lied to you. I do not lie to you now. Listen to what I have to tell you. . . ."

The villagers in one corner of the square parted to make way for the alcalde, Don Juan Dios de Maes, a short, fat man with many chins who marched up to Caballero followed by twenty men of the Las Vegas militia. The official thrust a pudgy finger at Caballero and shouted: "This man is a traitor! He is wanted by Governor Armijo. Arrest him!"

In the silence that followed there could be distinctly heard the clicking sounds as Caballero's men cocked their rifles. The villagers between Caballero and his men fled, screaming. Don Juan Dios de Maes stamped his foot. His tiny black eyes, lost in the folds of his cheeks, snapped furiously. "This man is an enemy of the state! Arrest him!"

The captain of the Rurales looked uncomfortably at Caballero's men. Caballero asked the alcalde quietly: "Are you afraid for your people to hear what I have to say, señor?"

"You are a traitor!"

"Perhaps, señor, as you define the word. And yet I will speak."

A man shouted: "Let him speak!" The cry was repeated by others. A woman said loudly: "This one has been good to us! Let him be heard!"

Don Juan Dios de Maes looked in all directions, his button eyes trying to identify the persons calling out. The captain of the Rurales said something to him. The alcalde shook his head and stamped his foot again. The captain spoke again and shrugged his shoulders. The alcalde flung up his hands and stalked out of the plaza.

Caballero held up his hand. "Thousand thanks, friends. This morning an American general will enter your village at the head of a powerful army. I have come here before him so that I might talk to you first. When he gets here he will speak for himself. He does not speak our language and his words will have to be translated to you, so that perhaps he will not reach to your hearts as directly as he would if you could understand the words as they came from his lips.

"This American general is a good man. He has not come to hurt you. He will not hurt you. He will not rob you. His army is very strong and it lies within his power to destroy anything that may oppose him. He hopes he will never have to use this army. He bears with him a command from the President of the United States not to injure New Mexicans who do not resist him, and to respect them in all ways. He does not look upon you as his enemy. He looks upon none of our people as enemy. He hopes that he may persuade Governor Armijo to abdicate peacefully. But that is between General Kearny and Governor Armijo and does not concern any of you.

"You have heard terrible things about the American soldiers and what they will do when they are among you. These things are not true. Not one of you who does not raise his hand against the Americans—not a man, not a woman, not a child, I say again, not a woman—will be harmed in any way, and if any American soldier forgets the orders of his general he will be punished to the degree of his offense. I swear this to you on the name of the Blessed Virgin of Guadalupe, who is Holy Mother to us all!

"You know me well. I have never broken faith with you. My men and I have stood between you and the Rurales who stole from you. My men and I have fought and some of us have died in your behalf. And now you must believe me when I say that the Americans come to do for you what I with my small band tried to do. Only the Americans will do it once and for all, and when they are here the hand of the tyrant will be lifted."

He stood up in his stirrups and turned his head slowly. "People of Las Vegas! I have been with this American general for many weeks. He is a good man. He is your friend. He will not injure you. None of his soldiers will injure you. They come now to your village. Welcome them!"

He led his men from the plaza, and then to the golden notes of a bugle General Kearny rode into the village in the forefront of his First Dragoons.

3

Don Manuel watched Magoffin and Cooke and their escort cross the plaza and then he returned directly to his apartment. He slumped heavily into a chair. His cheerfulness fell from him like used-up skin. The muscles sagged in his face. His body felt like lead. His wound ached. He felt old and tired and the fear was around him.

The need to appear confident to Cooke and Magoffin had imposed an overwhelming strain. He had not closed his eyes for a moment between the time he left Magoffin's office and the time Cooke had come to breakfast. It had required monumental endeavor to seem fresh and relaxed at the final meeting with the American officer. Now the play was over and the curtain was down.

His head fell back against the chair and he closed his eyes. He struck the arm of the chair with his fist. "I am Manuel Armijo," he whispered. He forced himself to sit upright and held out his arm and stared at it until the shaking stopped. "I am General Armijo," he said, repeating the words again and again as though he were uttering an incantation, "I am General Armijo," saying the words slowly, so that his ears could listen distinctly to each word. "I will resist the Americans and I will defeat them. I am tired and it is natural to be tense, but I have no fear." He said again: "*No tengo miedo, no tengo miedo.*"

He heard footsteps and his eyes widened with surprise at the sight of Doña María Trinidad. His wife had avoided him since the episode of the Haitian dancer and he had not spoken half a dozen words to her in as many days. He crouched warily in his chair as she walked across the wide room with a decorum that sat curiously on her dumpy figure. She touched the silver pitcher of chocolate and then shook a little bell. When a servant appeared she said: "This is cold. Make some fresh and bring it here." She remained standing until the servant left the room and then she took a seat across from her husband. "*Buenas días, le de Dios, Manuel,*" she said.

"*Que Dios se los de buenos á usted,*" he said.

She made a cigarette with fingers that were covered as always with rings. Her fleshy face was without cosmetics, and the mark of her appetites was stamped on it.

"She is an ugly woman," he thought with disgust. "Santa Madre, but she is an old and ugly woman!" He remembered when they had been friends and he wondered where that had gone.

"Word of your reply to the gringo officer has spread through the city, Manuel," she said. "It was a statement of honor."

"Many thanks, señora."

"Don Santiago Magoffin arrived with the American officer. Why did he come?"

"To bribe me to surrender without fight."

"What did you reply to him?"

"I gave him no final answer."

She flicked ash from the cigarette. "You must reject it. Honor demands that you defend your country."

His lips turned down. "Honor! Honor!" he said loudly. "I defecate on honor!" They were all alike! How easy to talk of honor when they ran no danger!

"It is what your people expect of you," she said quietly. "You must go to Apache Canyon and take your place at the head of your troops."

"And die, perhaps?" he snarled.

"If that is necessary."

"I will do whatever it pleases me to do!"

The servant entered the sala with a steaming pitcher of chocolate, and Don Manuel subsided. At a gesture from Doña María Trinidad the servant set the pitcher on the table and left the room. She poured the hot drink into two cups and gave one to her husband. "You have had all the good, Manuel," she said, "and now you must accept this as well. You will be adjudged a great leader or villain. But no one ever must be able to call you coward. You have no choice."

"I have no desire to die—not for history or anything else!"

"You must take that risk." She sipped the chocolate and then placed the cup on the table and took his hand. "I am an old woman, Manuel, and I am without beauty. You have never considered me as wife or even as woman. And during all the time I have loved you."

He pulled his hand from hers and turned his head.

"I love you first as a man and then as legend," she continued. "You have become legend to your people but you were first legend to me. We have each followed our own course so that people have said we were not truly married. We were married, Manuel. We were much married! The things that we did with others were unconnected with those things we owned between us." Her magnificent eyes glowed. "There have been those occasions when it has been difficult for me to remember that and I have been consumed with jealousy. That was foolish because what you were giving was not taken from our mutual treasure. We have been friends, Manuelito, and we are friends now. *Somos amigos!* There are no more beautiful words in our language! And now at this time when I love you more than I have ever loved you, I say there is no choice. You must go forth as leader of your people and stand between them and the enemy who comes to do them harm, and if God in His wisdom so wills it, you must die. You were born to greatness and you have fulfilled your greatness and now you must take the path that lies before you with that greatness in your soul, in courage and pride and honor."

He raised his eyes finally and asked: "Have you done, woman?"

"But for one thing, mi excelencia. The path that I urge upon you is lonely. My body has done you no service for many years. Let it serve you now."

"What do you mean?"

"I would go with you and stand at your side, and if it is intended that a gringo ball seek out your heart, then perhaps its twin will do a similar favor for me."

She stood up and her fingers stroked his cheek. He took them and kissed them and then she walked from the room.

Don Manuel gave himself no rest that day. He plunged into the papers that were piled on his desk and disposed of them with such bewildering speed that Don Juan Bautista Vigil, who now also styled himself Secretary of State, found it necessary to ask the secretary of the adjourned Junta to give him assistance.

Don Manuel's decisions were never surer. His mind was never more incisive. The right answer came to him instantaneously for each problem he tackled. His collectors were returning now with the funds they had gathered for the emergency tax. He set up a plan, earmarking so much of the money for food for the troops, so much for pay, so much to operate the government. He was scrupulously honest about this money, putting into his pocket only the five hundred dollars that Don Mariano Martínez had taken from him.

Volunteers continued to arrive in the capital in droves, some of them armed with muskets and scatter-guns of various ages, others bearing bows and arrows, knives, or just spears with fire-sharpened points. Many had nothing to offer but themselves. The volunteers were formed into companies as rapidly as they arrived and those without weapons were supplied from the stock in the armory.

He worked out the disposition of these volunteer companies with Don Diego Archuleta, who spent two hours with him that morning. The bulk of the troops was sent to Apache Canyon to take their place there with the other soldiers. At the suggestion of Don Diego, other units were dispatched to Galisteo to set up defensive positions there in the event Kearny elected to forgo an

564

attack on the pass and swing around to Santa Fe by way of the village.

Using a military map that he spread open on the Governor's desk, Don Diego explained how he planned to establish liaison points between Apache Canyon and Galisteo on the west side of the mountains, stationing waiting couriers with fast horses at these points, so that the troops could be moved from one place to the other, depending on Kearny's tactics.

Neither Don Manuel nor Don Diego said anything of the meeting with Magoffin.

Archuleta completed outlining his plans and rolled up the map. "If your excellency has no further need of me in Santa Fe, I will leave for Apache Canyon and see to the final preparations," he said. "I will take command of the army until you arrive, excelencia."

"*Bueno*, Don Diego," Don Manuel said. "Today is the 13th. The gringos cannot reach Apache Canyon earlier than the 17th or 18th. I will come to the pass on the 16th." He embraced Archuleta. "*Vaya con Dios, mi coronel*," he said. "I will see you three days hence."

The dark, square face set inflexibly. "*Adiós, mi general*," Archuleta said.

In the evening Don Manuel dined quietly with his wife and afterward they sat together in the sala and spoke of old days, recalling many things they had forgotten during the years, and then they went to their bedchambers and presently Don Manuel came to her bed and took her in his arms and that night she was not old and she was not ugly.

When he woke in the morning he discovered he was holding her hand. In her sleep the lines of old lusts were obliterated and her face was content. She wakened at last and smiled with a strange girlishness and he saw that her eyes were truly beautiful.

"I have ordered a carriage to take you to Alburquerque this morning," he said.

"You will not allow me to go with you?"

"No."

"But you go?"

"Yes, my wife, I go."

565

4

AFTER Doña María Trinidad was packed and gone, Don Manuel summoned to his office Don Gaspar Ortiz, another brother of the vicar, whom he had appointed alcalde of Santa Fe. He spoke at considerable length with Don Gaspar and then he wrote the following lines:

Let it appear by these presents that I authorize with sufficient general power Don Gaspar Ortiz, in case of death or during my absence, to settle all private affairs with as much power as if my affairs were his own. He is authorized to deal and contract in my affairs, and in the event of the death of my wife before me, he shall remain in charge of all my interests, without there being anyone to hinder him in the exercise of his duties until he disposes of the same, as my last will. . . .

He reread what he had written and presented the paper to the alcalde. Don Gaspar said: "This is a very great honor, excelencia. I pray only that I shall not have reason to obey its instructions."

Don Manuel sent out for someone to witness the covenant and a few minutes later Donanciano Vigil entered the office. Don Manuel repressed a smile. Donanciano Vigil, of all persons! It was, he thought wryly, in keeping.

Don Donanciano's eyes sparkled as they scanned the lines. "Then you go to Apache Canyon, excelencia."

Don Manuel raised his brows. "Are there those who doubt it then, señor?"

Don Donanciano became flustered. "Pardon, excelencia. It is just that there is talk that Don Santiago Magoffin came here to make some arrangement with you."

Without answering, Don Manuel added to the document the words: "To this frank manifestation of my sentiments, as witness, Don Donanciano Vigil, Santa Fe, August 14, 1846." He signed his name and surrounded it with his rubric, and then Don Donanciano affixed his own signature and rubric.

"Permit me to say that I am proud of you, excelencia," Don Donanciano said as he laid down the pen.

"Are you?" Don Manuel asked. "That is very kind of you."

Don Manuel continued to work energetically through the day, disposing of affairs of state and his own personal affairs as well. He was finishing the last of the business of the day when Damasio Salazar was announced. Salazar, whom he had restored to the rank of major, had rushed to Taos when word had come that Caballero was up there spreading propaganda among the peasants. A glance at Salazar as he burst into the room informed Don Manuel he had failed again. "You were unable to put your finger on him," the Governor said with mild sarcasm.

"I almost had him, excelencia," Salazar whined.

"That is no progress, Don Damasio. You have almost had him for years."

"I will still get him, excelencia!"

"It is too late, Don Damasio," the Governor said. "You have achieved your final almost. By now he is back with his gringo friends, and the next sight of him will be outside the opening to Apache Canyon."

"I will get him!" Salazar said vehemently.

Don Manuel smiled. "How, Don Damasio? Do you suggest you will cross over when the battle begins and snatch him from the gringos?"

Salazar, covered with the dust of the road, his face streaked with dried sweat, clenched his sword. "I will watch out for him, excelencia, during the fighting. I swear it! Before the smoke fades away I will have put a ball in his heart."

"I doubt it," Don Manuel said.

"I will be in the forefront of battle, excelencia! He will not escape me!"

Don Manuel sat back in the chair and clasped his hands placidly over his belly. "I think you will not, Don Damasio," he said. "You have failed, and you have failed for all time."

"You will see, excelencia!"

"For three years, Don Damasio, you have had a single assignment from me," Don Manuel said with annihilating calm. "The world has moved on. Governments have come and gone. Better men than you have been slain fighting wild Indians. A great war has started. None of these things has been permitted to interfere. With all this change taking place around you, you were given soldiers and a simple task: to kill or capture one man. One man who has never had more than a fifth of your forces. And this one man has outwitted you at every turn. He has eluded you when it suited his purpose to elude you and he has outfought you when he has had to fight. In his person he has constituted the great single disturbance to my government and you have not succeeded in doing the smallest thing to stop him. And now it is at last too late. He has succeeded in his work and you have failed in yours. He is better than you are. He has beaten you."

Salazar was livid under the grime. "Your excellency speaks as though you were secretly happy that the traitor has evaded me!"

A strange expression appeared on Don Manuel's face. "Do I? Perhaps I am, Don Damasio."

"Excelencia!"

"If the gringos occupy this country it will be largely because of him," Don Manuel said. "I hate him more than I do any living man. And yet perhaps I am happy that he has managed to keep out of your fingers." His eyes got cold. "He is a man, Don Damasio. I am surrounded by pygmies and I look over their heads and in the distance there I see a man. You are not his size, señor, and I believe it would have been unfit for you to have had the honor to take him captive."

The Governor's lips turned down with disdain. "And now you promise me that you will kill him in battle. You will not. There is such a thing as justice, Don Damasio, a very high justice, and before it we must all of us kneel and obey. Don Esquipulas Caballero was not saved from you for these years to succumb to you now. He may die in the fighting because he is brave and he will fight among those in the front, but he will not die to you. The ball that kills him must come from a clean gun."

"Excelencia—" Salazar choked.

Don Manuel raised his hand. "Say nothing, señor, for there is nothing to say. You once made to me the observation that there are differences among men, and you have yourself proved this to be true, only you have demonstrated inadvertently that the difference may not be due alone to the name to which a man is born. There are one or two other factors involved." He stood up and sauntered to a window. "As soon as your men and horses are fed and rested, go to Apache Canyon. There will be ample opportunity there to correct old errors and to atone for old sins, for yourself as well as for others."

"Excelencia—"

"Go now," Don Manuel said with ineffable boredom. "You have talked too much and for too long and you nauseate me. I would be tempted to break you and send you to fight among the lowest soldiers, only the disgrace would be more upon me than upon you."

Governor Armijo dined alone that night at the great table of state, and the palace was empty without his wife.

5

Damasio Salazar left the palace feeling that an iron band had been tightened around his skull. He gave orders to his next in command, Captain Jesús Alpuente, to look after the men and to pick him up at La Fonda at midnight. He lurched across the plaza and found a small table in the darkest corner of the inn. He ordered that a bottle of brandy and a glass be put on his table and that he be left alone.

He drank two glasses of the Taos Lightning, and in the agony of his head the searing liquid was without taste. He remembered coming years before upon the body of a man who had been tortured to death by Apaches. A wet rawhide had been tied around the man's skull and he had been set in the sun so that the rawhide dried and tightened, and when Salazar had found him, his brains had burst from his head. It was how Don Damasio now felt.

The cool, darkened room swam around him and there were many faces, but he could see nothing but the face of the Governor, poisonous with contempt. He knew there was the murmur of conversation around him, but all he could hear were the words of the Governor. They fell again and again into his ears like drops of molten lead and he pressed the palms of his hands against his head and closed his eyes to shut out the words, but they were not outside him to be shut out.

It was not the fault of Don Manuel. Don Manuel had always been good to him. Don Manuel had always loved him. Don Manuel had always known that nowhere in New Mexico was there a man more devoted to him than Damasio Salazar. It was not even the fault of Caballero. He had done what he had done to save his skin, and Salazar could not blame him for that. It was the bitch! He emptied the glass and banged it on the table. It was the fault of the bitch! She had driven Don Manuel crazy for years so that now he did not know what he was saying when he spoke to those who served him. It was her fault from the beginning. It was because of her that Don Manuel had fallen out with Caballero. It was because of her that Caballero had become an outlaw. It was because of her that Don Manuel had kept his most faithful officer in the hunt for Caballero. Don Manuel wanted Caballero out of the way not because of his traitorous activities but because he wanted a clear field to the bitch. She alone was to blame for everything, she alone, the bitch!

He drank the brandy, and the torment in his head lessened and then disappeared because now he had found the reason and it was not that Don Manuel had truly turned on him but that he was enamorado and not responsible. What man was responsible when the witch got her claws on his heart? Don Manuel was diseased with desire and for that his most devoted officer had to listen to words that no man should be required to hear, for that he had to stand in silence while insults were heaped on his head like excrement, and he drank and his eyes got tiny and sharp and baleful, and his fingers fondled the brandy glass as though it were the throat of a woman, and his mouth hung open like a wound that would not heal.

It was the Abreu, the rica, who thought her thighs were too good for Manuel Armijo. It was the Abreu, the rica, who without doubt whored nightly with men of her own class but who disdained the Governor of New Mexico. He whispered the words: "Abreu, rica, Abreu, rica," and when he said them he did not hear the words of the Governor. Sweat gathered in clusters around his lips and his spittle soaked his cigarette, and he breathed the words "Abreu, rica, Abreu, rica," until they ceased to be words with meaning and became cabalistic sounds uttered to exorcise demons, used as some Indian ancestor had used other mystic mutterings to drive away the black spirits that hovered in the night.

Don Manuel said it was too late for Caballero, and that might be, but it was not too late for her. Only it would have to be something fitting, more than simple death, something uniquely suitable, something that belonged to her, the Abreu, the rica, not just the extinguishing of life, something that was designed for no person but her, for her name, for her heritage. It would come to him, he knew, if he said the sounds enough, the right thing for the Abreu, the rica, and he said the sounds and he drank the brandy and then the pinpoints of his eyes came to glittering triumph. When Captain Alpuente stood before him and said it was midnight, he ordered him to take the soldiers to Apache Canyon and said he would join him there.

When he left the tavern, the night was clear and cool and the ache was gone altogether from his head, and the brandy gave him lightness and ease. He vaulted into the saddle as though he were winged and he touched his fingers in courtesy to the dark bulk of the palace, rode across the plaza, deserted in the early morning, and turned into the Calle de la Muralla. Somewhere he heard the soft sounds of a guitar and he thought how sweet was the music of Mexico, and the horse stopped, of its own volition, it seemed, in front of Number 23. Don Damasio patted him affectionately on the neck and said: "You are intelligent, mi caballo."

He entered the house, and when he left a few minutes later he carried in his arms the bound and gagged and unconscious figure of Doña Soledad, the Abreu, the rica. He threw the limp body over the horse and, still winged, he leaped into the saddle and rode out of Santa Fe on the Chihuahua Trail to the southwest.

6

DON MANUEL rattled around in the empty palace. Doña María Trinidad had gone away before, but the palace had never seemed so abandoned. It was depressing to stay in his apartment and he went to his office, though by now there was little left to do.

He listened to the noises in the plaza and thought that when he returned from Apache Canyon he would order a fiesta. There would be reason enough to celebrate. He would repeat it each year and establish a tradition as had the victorious Spanish captains of the past. Each year, long after he had passed on, the people would gather in the plaza and celebrate the victory of Manuel Armijo. The priests would march with the holy images and voices would rise in song, and the story of Don Manuel Armijo, El Caudillo Victorioso, would be repeated so that the smallest child would be familiar with it.

He was in a glow of pleasant rumination on his immortality when Padre Martínez came in to visit him. He was surprised at how pleased he was to see the priest. "What passes, padre?" he boomed. "What brings you down from Taos?"

"Curiosity, excelencia," Martínez said.

"And what are you curious about, Don Antonio?"

"Your intentions, excelencia."

Don Manuel sighed and shook his head. "Are you too worried about my honor? It appears people talk of nothing else."

"Believe me, Don Manuel, that is a subject that does not perplex me. I am interested only in knowing whether you plan to fight the Americans or not."

Don Manuel looked at him with exaggerated wonderment. "Can you doubt that?"

The priest wrapped his skirt around his legs and sat down. "I have heard gossip that you have been asked by Don Santiago Magoffin to surrender the country for a price."

"The gossip is true. I have been so asked, and by Don Santiago, and a price was mentioned."

"And what will you do?"

Don Manuel selected a cigar and lit it with elaborate care. "You know, padre, there is an old saying that history never changes but merely repeats itself. We sat together at the beginning, in the dark of your little office in Taos. How long ago was that? Ten years! And here we sit together again and you ask me again what are my intentions. What do you believe I will do, padre?"

572

The priest looked at him piercingly. "I think that you do not know yourself."

"So?" Don Manuel pushed the will he had executed across his desk. "Read that."

"This could apply in either event," Martínez said.

Don Manuel grinned appreciatively. "Your mind has lost none of its subtlety, Don Antonio. Others read in it only guaranteed proof of my intention to make a heroic defense and perhaps to die in so doing."

"What will you do, Don Manuel?"

"Fight."

The priest stiffened and his eyes blazed. "Is that true?"

"The simple truth." Don Manuel held up a finger lazily. "It is unnecessary to say it. I know you are proud of me."

"I am more surprised," the priest said.

For a moment Don Manuel's face was unpleasant. "Tact was hardly ever one of your virtues, padre," he said. He contemplated the end of his cigar. "Why do you not come with me and see for yourself."

"Is that an order?"

"An invitation. On one side are less than two thousand half-starved gringos. On the other more than six thousand brave and loyal New Mexicans. Between them is a granite wall with only the smallest of openings. It should be something to see."

"I thought the American army was larger."

"You were supposed to think so. We were all supposed to think so. I know better. The number is as I have said and the men and their animals suffer from lack of food and water. We will destroy them. The outcome is forgone."

"In that event, Don Manuel, may I be permitted to decline your invitation? It hardly seems worth the effort."

Don Manuel shrugged. "As you wish, padre. But you will dine with me this evening? Doña María Trinidad is gone and I am alone."

After dinner they sat in the sala and Don Manuel spoke of ideas he had to eliminate the American influence in New Mexico when the war was ended. He stopped in mid-sentence and smiled.

573

"Here we are again, padre, the two old warhorses, with our cigars and brandy, talking about the future of our country."

"You are making the plans, as before," the priest said.

"The difference is that my hair is grayer and the lines on your face are deeper and this room is somewhat larger than the other room."

Martínez swirled the brandy in the glass. "Do you believe you can rid New Mexico of the ascendancy of the Americans? Can one turn back the clock?"

"You imply that the infiltration of gringos is part of historical process, padre," the Governor said. "I do not agree with you. The gringos have infected our life, but it has been done because of our carelessness. That can be corrected."

"Can it, excelencia? I wonder." The priest looked at him intently. "It appears to me that this is the time of the gringo. They are strong and we are weak. They are young and we are old."

"I am stronger than they are," Don Manuel said.

"Your army is stronger than their army, Don Manuel. That is true. But I do not speak of armies and battles. I speak of the imprint one people makes on another. You may defeat the gringo army, but this other fight will be the more difficult one. Soldiers may be beaten, but ideas are elusive things. One cannot turn muskets and cannon on them. For almost twenty-five years the gringos have brought in their ideas along with their merchandise. Those ideas in big ways and in little ways have taken hold. The time of the gringo truly began when the first wagon rolled in from the prairie. The merchants have been more dangerous than the soldiers who come today. Today the soldiers come only to take formal possession of what the gringos have been nibbling on since the Spaniards were kicked out of Mexico."

"And I will remove their food and send them from the table!"

"I pray with all my soul that you do so, excelencia!"

Don Manuel looked at him curiously. "Why, padre? I have listened to you for many years. You have had liberal ideas, almost revolutionary ideas, too liberal for a country controlled by Mexicans. The thoughts you hold on education, on freedom, on treatment of the wild Indians, your desire for newspapers and periodicals such as the one you yourself published, all these things are closer to the thinking of the gringos than to the thinking of your own people. In a sense you have been an alien among Mexicans, padre, a lonely and discontented alien. I should not have been surprised to hear that you would welcome the gringos."

The priest stared moodily at the floor. "In some ways I do, Don Manuel," he said in a low voice.

Don Manuel gave a short laugh. "You believe that *I* am torn by doubts and am undecided, padre, and yet compared with you I am a man of single purpose. You would hail the gringos because they would bring with them laws and practices of which you approve. But you also know your stature as a priest would be lessened in a land of heretics and that your political powers would be taken away forever. I grieve for you, padre. I would not exchange my problems for yours."

"We know each other too well, Don Manuel," Martínez said harshly. "To each of us the mind of the other is clearer than his own."

"It is true, padre, and it should make us friends," Don Manuel said. "Or perhaps it is the reason we cannot be friends."

"We have left both friendship and enmity long behind us, Don Manuel. A new word would have to be invented to define what we are to each other."

Don Manuel puffed quietly on his cigar. "I have not used you properly, Don Antonio. It is late to find that out, but I have failed to avail myself of all the power that lies behind your eyes. I have come a long way from Taos of '37, but I have not kept you close enough to me. It may offer you some little consolation to know that it was my honest intention to give you Taos for a country of your own."

"Thank you."

"I know it means nothing now."

The priest looked at him shrewdly. "It means only that you are not as confident as you would have me believe that you will rout the gringo army."

"There is always the risk of death in battle, padre," Don Manuel said. "It is only that at this time I desire to make the ledger as neat as possible."

"If you are killed, excelencia, your assurances will provide comfort in my old age," Martínez said.

"If I am killed, padre, your old age will be in consummate

575

need of comfort," Don Manuel said. He picked up the brandy bottle. "I hesitate to think of Padre Martínez in a land of gringos."

A servant entered the room. "Excelencia, an officer has arrived from Apache Canyon. He requests an immediate audience with your excellency."

"Tell him to wait until morning."

"It is your nephew, excelencia. He says it is a matter of the greatest importance."

Don Manuel put down the bottle. "Bring him in."

Captain Martínez strode into the room, showing signs of a hard ride. "Excelencia, soldiers in Apache Canyon are at the point of insurrection!"

Don Manuel leaped to his feet. The brandy glass shattered on the floor. "Explain yourself!"

"The dragoons you sent to intercept General Kearny returned to the pass with word that the general treated them as friends and that he swore to them he was coming as comrade and not enemy. They brought with them proclamations signed by the general in which he said he would regard all New Mexicans who laid down their arms and returned to their homes as citizens of the United States who would not be harmed in any way. I brought one of the circulars with me. You may read it yourself. They were read out loud to the soldiers and many of them believe what the general is saying."

Don Manuel took the paper but he did not look at it. "General Kearny? Do you not mean Coronel Kearny?"

"He is general now, excelencia."

"Do you mean to tell me that my soldiers believe the lies this gringo spreads? I will order the dragoons executed as traitors!"

"It is more than the dragoons," Don Tomás said. "Las Vegas has surrendered to the gringo army."

Don Manuel sat down slowly.

"Esquipulas Caballero spoke first to the people there and then Kearny entered with his army and spoke to the people and promised that no one would be harmed and that not a single thing would be taken from them without their permission and without payment," Don Tomás continued heatedly. "The alcalde and the officers of the militia swore allegiance to the United States. General Kearny continued them in office as *his* deputies and then he left, and no one was injured and nothing was taken. The soldiers have all heard about this and there are many who now say it is proof that the Americans do not come to make war on them. Many soldiers asked why they should be killed fighting Americans who have no desire to fight with them, and they have abandoned their posts. They have been supported by many officers and they talk about leaving Apache Canyon as General Kearny has requested and returning to their homes. You must come there immediately, excelencia! They will listen only to you!"

"What of Archuleta?" Don Manuel asked. "Why did he permit this condition to develop?"

"Coronel Archuleta? He is not there, excelencia."

"Not there! Why did he leave?"

Don Tomás shook his head. "He did not leave, excelencia. He has not been there."

An unholy smile crossed Don Manuel's face, illuminating each feature. "That Don Santiago," he whispered. "That Don Santiago." He crushed the unread proclamation and threw it to the floor. "Go to the barracks, Don Tomás. Alert the captain of my guard. Tell him we leave for Apache Canyon at once. Order my horse saddled."

"Two horses," Padre Martínez said.

1

A FEW MILES beyond Las Vegas an outrider for the Army of the West galloped back to General Kearny. "Sir, we met some natives who told us there were some six hundred of Armijo's soldiers dug in at a gorge in the hills a couple of miles ahead!"

"Ride on and verify it, if possible," Kearny said quickly.

He gave the order for his army to make ready for battle. The banners and guidons that had been unfurled in Las Vegas for the first time since the troops had crossed the Missouri River were put away. Excitement rippled through the lines. Men checked their gear. Officers inspected the cannon. Eyes brightened. Aching muscles and blistered feet were forgotten. Sick men got out of ambulance wagons.

The outrider returned. The information had been erroneous. The gorge was empty. Kearny countermanded the battle order. The tenseness slackened, the weariness returned. The men dragged on.

Kearny watched them plodding along, his brow creased with concern. The men were tired and they were hungry. The livestock brought down by the peasants of Mora had provided one good meal and the men had been on half rations for more than two weeks. The water shortage was acute. No food had come from Las Vegas. The stock owned by the natives of that village had been driven into the hills long before the Americans got there and it would have taken two or three days for the animals to be rounded up and brought down. Kearny had not dared to wait. To delay his advance at this time would serve only to emphasize the weakness of his commissary.

Kearny knew he was not fighting a simple war. He was committed to an attitude of peace. He had been cast in the role of liberator, not conqueror. He had pledged his word to buy food, not confiscate it, and to buy only that which was offered freely.

The pledge was one of his strongest weapons and he could not violate it.

More than the hunger and the thirst was the uncertainty. When the men thought they were going to have a scrap on their hands they forgot everything else. When the scrap was not forthcoming it was a kind of defeat. His troops, in the main, were not professionals. They had enlisted for adventure and for a fight. So far there had been nothing but marching and dysentery and bleeding feet and inflamed eyes.

He himself was sick. The fever had never wholly left him. Despite his weakness he had refused to take more food or water than was rationed to any other man.

At the tiny hamlet of Tecolote he was met by Magoffin and Captain Cooke. He hoped that the uncertainties might now be settled, but the reports of his envoys to Armijo only increased the confusion.

Cooke told him how Armijo had proclaimed his resolute intention to fight, and that his stand was supported by his second in command, Colonel Archuleta, and, as far as Cooke could determine, by the soldiers and the people. He reported in detail how powerfully Apache Canyon had been fortified and how at least five thousand men were in position there. The breaching of the pass, in his opinion, would be a military task of the first magnitude.

For his part, Magoffin could say no more than that he had made his offer to Don Manuel and that Don Manuel had listened, and that he had made a supplementary offer to Archuleta and that he too had listened. "I dangled the bait, sir," he said. "Whether or not they will take it I cannot say."

Henry Connelly then was brought before the general, but he contributed very little. The American emissary from Don Manuel was bewildered by the unexpected mission thrust on him. The Governor, he said, had instructed him only to investigate Kearny's intentions. He did supply the intelligence that Don Manuel was not staking everything on a showdown at Apache Canyon. "Armijo has sent a sizable army to Galisteo to make a stand there if you decide to avoid the pass, general," he said.

Kearny decided that Connelly had been sent out by Armijo only to delay matters while he further strengthened his positions. He made a short address in Tecolote, where the allegiance cere-

579

mony performed in Las Vegas was repeated, and he pressed on.

With each mile the reports increased on the activities in the canyon. At San Miguel, after Caballero had preceded him, he made his speech for the third time and accepted the oath from the alcalde and Rurale officers stationed there. The officials substantiated the reports on the size of the army in Apache Canyon. Kearny learned too, to his dismay, that, two days before, soldiers had come out of the pass and had taken all the livestock in the vicinity. Apart from a small supply of corn, there was no food to be obtained in San Miguel. Kearny gave orders to reduce rations by one half again and to march on.

In his tent that evening he considered his position. He faced battle against forces that outnumbered his more than three to one, dug into a natural fortress which Cooke had said was all but unassailable, and for the job he had an army of starving men. A shadow fell across the open vent. Caballero stood in the opening. "Yes, señor," Kearny said.

"May I have a little moment, mi general?"

"Come in," Kearny said.

Caballero removed his hat and entered. For a moment he gazed silently at the sick general, at his sunken cheeks and shadowed eyes. "I should like to have the general's permission to take two men and go into Apache Canyon," he said.

Kearny frowned. "What could you accomplish by that?"

"Who knows?" Caballero shrugged. "Perhaps nothing. But I know the pass well. If Don Manuel is serious about resisting, you will have a difficult time. Perhaps there is some small thing that may be done."

Kearny looked at him bleakly. "You would quite probably be delivering yourselves to a firing squad."

"I have not failed to consider that, sir."

Kearny shook his head. "It is a gallant offer, Don Esquipulas, but I cannot permit it. You have been very effective speaking to the villagers, but this is another thing. General Armijo would give you no opportunity to talk to his soldiers. He would have you shot before you opened your mouth and he would be within his rights."

Caballero gripped the brim of his hat. "General, your soldiers are almost at the end of their rope. They have put up with hardships as though they were made of iron. But they are not made of iron, por Dios! They are men and there is only so much men may demand of themselves, and it may be said your men have already reached that point if they have not more truly passed it. In the state they are in, it will take them at least two days, possibly three days, to reach the canyon and there is no food between here and there and very little water. The men are hardly in condition for a long fight now and they will be less so when they reach the pass. I do not know if it is possible to change anything by going there, but if there is the smallest chance to do anything it should be attempted."

"Even though you would face almost certain death?"

"I have been both soldier and outlaw, mi general," Caballero said. "I have examined the dark face before and the stake was always less than this."

"You had a fighting chance always. You would have none now."

"I have something of more value. I have belief in what you have come here to do. If Don Manuel defeats you at Apache Canyon he will again eat of the flesh of my people and drink of their blood, only he will be stronger than ever and he may never be defeated." He leaned on Kearny's desk. His eyes went cold and flat. "That is the big thing, but there is something else."

"What is that?"

Caballero's face was austere. "There is war between our countries and there are armies involved, but here the thing belongs to two men, Don Manuel and me." His voice got hard. "You must not deny me this."

2

THE BLAZING SUMMER SUN was more than two hours above the peaks of the Sangre de Cristos and the sky had already turned the color of blue, against which the Navajo Indians tested their turquoise for holiness when Don Manuel and Padre Martínez reached Apache Canyon.

During the night ride from Santa Fe, Don Manuel had

thought of little but the defection of Colonel Archuleta. How typical it was of him to complete the defenses to the last detail before he disappeared! He had sold out and he had known from the time of his meeting with Magoffin that he was going to sell out, and yet the adamant pride he had had in his soldier's craft had required that he finish his work first. What had El Don offered that had corrupted the incorruptible?

When Don Manuel reached the canyon and saw the disorganization of the soldiers and heard the angry clamor of their voices the fear hit him and he thought no more of Colonel Archuleta.

As he rode into the canyon a few scattered cheers went up. Most of the soldiers merely stared at him, and as he passed he left behind him a wake of silence. He sat upright in his saddle and acknowledged the few cries of welcome with the familiar wave of his hand. His eyes roamed sharply in all directions and he listened to the conflicting noises. There were violent arguments everywhere. Some men still wanted to fight. The fear was in his belly and he knew he must remain calm. He set a smile on his lips to stop the twitching. He had to have all of himself. He had to reach out and connect with the faces. They were children. They were sheep. Some of them had started to run in one direction. They could be turned, but he had to be all together. It would be his will against their will. They had numbers. He had the voice. He was Manuel Armijo. "I am Don Manuel, Governor of New Mexico!"

He rode slowly to the tent that had been erected for his headquarters and he ordered his bodyguard, which had been enlarged since the beginning of the war until it now numbered eighty men, to post itself around the tent. He ordered his nephew to summon to him the officers who still desired to resist the Americans. He entered the tent and sat down and laid his fists on the field desk. "I am Manuel Armijo," he said.

"Will that be enough?"

He looked up with a start. Padre Martínez had come into the tent. There was question on the priest's face. "It has always been enough," Don Manuel said. "It will be enough now."

"God so grant!" the priest said. He folded his arms, slipping his hands into his sleeves, and he took a place in a far corner.

The officers came into the tent one by one and Don Manuel questioned them crisply. Kearny's propaganda had reached all of them. The phrase "not a pepper, not an onion," had been repeated everywhere among the soldiers and it had caught on. It was a battle cry in reverse, the motto of the House of Kearny. "Nombre de Dios!" Don Manuel said. "How can the fools believe such lies!"

One of the officers hunched his shoulders. "Then men talk a great deal of the fact that Don Esquipulas Caballero is with the Americans, excelencia. They say that he has helped the peasants for many years and that a Caballero could not be false to his country. They say the gringo general must speak the truth or Don Esquipulas would not remain with him and make speeches in his behalf."

"Caballero!" Don Manuel's eyes shot to Padre Martínez. The priest's face was inscrutable.

Another officer reported that approximately three hundred men from the Rio Abajo had left quietly during the night with six of their officers. Don Manuel felt the fear. "The vessel is cracked," he thought, "and already is leaking." He collected himself. He could stop the leak. Alone he could stop the leak and he alone could do it. It was necessary only for him to remember who he was and to make the men remember.

When the last officer was gone he evaluated the intelligence they had brought to him. About a quarter of the troops wanted to lay down their arms. Half of the others wavered and the rest still wanted to fight. The situation was bad but it was not hopeless. Even if all who wanted to quit deserted he would still be stronger than the gringos and he was still secure behind the slit of the pass. It could still be done.

The priest left the tent to give comfort to men who needed it and then the entrance darkened again. Damasio Salazar lurched in. "I have been wondering where you were," Don Manuel said. "I believed your absence might have indicated you joined the rebels."

Salazar was unkempt and unshaved. A loosely filled cigarette dangled from his lips and there were shreds on his tunic. He saluted elaborately. He lost his balance and caught himself on the desk. The air filled with the smell of brandy.

Don Manuel slapped the cigarette from his mouth. "You are

drunk! How dare you appear before me in this condition!"

Salazar gripped the desk to steady himself. He raised a grimy black-nailed hand to his mouth. "I have not joined with the insurrectos, excelencia," he said with studied gravity. "As always I am at the disposition of your excellency." His tongue wrestled with the words. "How do you find things here?"

Don Manuel opened his mouth to shout for the guard when something in Salazar's face stopped him. "Bad enough, but I shall correct them."

"Of course, excelencia," Salazar said heartily. "You will correct everything. The cowards wait only to hear your voice, and then rabbits will fight like lions. But things are bad, very bad, very bad." He shook his head dolefully. "And do you know why, excelencia?"

Don Manuel gritted his teeth. "Tell me why."

Salazar's eyes were holes of rheumy hatred. "Caballero! Agreed?"

"Agreed," Don Manuel said through closed teeth.

A smile broadened until it bisected Salazar's face, until the upper and lower parts appeared to have no relation to each other. "It was too late," Salazar said, wagging a filthy finger under the Governor's nose. "You said that yourself, excelencia. It was too late to catch the fox. The fox escaped the trap. But there was still time for the vixen."

Don Manuel did not understand him at first and it was in the chilling of his blood that the meaning came to him.

Salazar preened. "It was too late for el zorro but I took good care of la zorra."

"*Doña Soledad.*"

Salazar waved his hand. "She will trouble you no more."

The chair spun half across the tent. Don Manuel seized Salazar by the throat and dragged him across the desk. "What have you done with her!"

"She who tried to make an insurrection in the Rio Abajo will trouble you no more, excelencia."

Don Manuel tightened his fingers. "Chingado! What have you done with her!"

It came suddenly to Salazar that Don Manuel did not ap-

584

prove. He tore at the Governor's fingers, and when he could not loosen them he clawed at the Governor's face.

"*What have you done with her!*"

Salazar twisted like a wildcat. "You will never know if you strangle me!" he gasped.

Don Manuel flung him across the dirt floor of the tent. Salazar sprang instantly to his feet, his knife in his hand.

"And now you bare steel at me," Don Manuel said.

Salazar sidled cautiously toward the opening of the tent, the brandy glow gone from him now. His free hand kneaded his throat. "Come no closer, excelencia," he said painfully. "Come no closer. As you value life, come no closer."

Don Manuel drew his sword and then through his mind flashed a picture of Salazar seated languidly in a chair in the palace, his blade quivering in the door through which Captain José Caballero had just passed. He hesitated and Salazar's lips curled as he took another step toward the opening, his arm poised to cast the knife.

"Tell me what you did with her," Don Manuel said from where he stood, his sword lowered. "You will not be punished, Don Damasio. I give you my word."

"Your word!" Salazar spat.

"You will leave here a free man. Tell me what you did with her."

The voices of men rolled into the tent like sudden wind. Salazar twisted his head. Then he sheathed his blade and his eyes gleamed diabolically. "Concern yourself with whether *you* will leave here a free man," he said.

Don Manuel looked through the vent. A group of officers was approaching the tent, those who had not responded to his call and who were leading the revolt. The fear was in him again and he said silently: "Dulce Virgen, help me, dulce Madre de Dios, cause them to listen." He clapped his plumed hat upon his head and walked toward the opening.

Salazar bowed mockingly. "Remember, excelencia, it is better to be thought a brave man than to be brave."

Without anger Don Manuel whipped him across the face with the flat of his sword. "You are a dead man, Don Damasio."

3

OUTSIDE NOW in the high, clear light, the light in which nothing could be hidden, the troops were gathered in their thousands, and in the center of the mass, directly in front of the tent, were grouped the officers who wanted no battle with the Americans. They were the branches and the others were the leaves and he looked swiftly at their faces and saw hostility there, but it was negative hostility and there was no disrespect. The officers were not in rebellion against him. Their revolt was against the battle and not the commander. The distinction was important, he told himself.

Now as he strode from the tent the murmuring stopped and he faced the men and with great care slipped the shining sword into the scabbard. The metallic sound of the handguard striking the scabbard rang clearly in the still air and men stiffened involuntarily to attention. Don Manuel called for his horse. He gave the order calmly. It had begun now, and everything from now on, every act and every sound, would be counted. He knew, as no other man in New Mexico could know, that he was involved with a mob, the most delicate thing in the world. It no longer was an army he had in Apache Canyon. He could give no military order that would be obeyed.

His horse was led up to him. "Your hand," he said. The soldier made a stirrup of his hands and Don Manuel lifted himself into the saddle. The soldier could have done it, he thought. If he had refused his hand and had walked away he would have done it. He settled himself in his saddle and raised his head. His face was composed. "Remember," he said silently as he looked at the faces, "remember that you are Don Manuel Armijo and that you are the Jefe Político y Militar and that these men are your subjects and that they have learned to obey you, and that if you do not permit it they will not disobey you now."

He needed no more than everything he had ever had. No more than that, just everything that was in him, but he needed it all.

"Soldiers of New Mexico! Friends! Brothers! Hear me!" He
bent his ears to the sounds. He was the duelist, flexing his blade.
What he heard was good. The voice never was more sonorous. It
was not necessary for him to shout. Except for his voice the world
was in silence. He was strong and large and much of everything,
and nothing was in his way. "Marching upon us today across the
holy soil of New Mexico is an army of gringo invaders. They have
come like wolves in the night. They speak words of friendship, but
behind those words they come with guns and cannon, with hatred
and with lust, they come like a disease, like a plague, destroying
everything they find in their path. . . ."

He sensed a stirring and shifting around him, as a forest stirs
and shifts in the wind. *I am Manuel Armijo, the master of mobs.
I can produce music from it as though it were a guitar under my
fingers.* He jutted his chin and placed his hands upon his hips.
"They are heretics! They come to destroy the true religion! They
come to murder the holy padres! They come to defile our churches,
to turn them into places of assignation with whores! They come to
rape our women and to brand them on their cheeks so that other
gringos will rape them! Who says gringos says plunder, rape, kill,
steal, burn, destroy. . . ."

"That is a lie, Don Manuel."

". . . And to protect your women and your children and your
priests and your churches and your houses, to annihilate this army
of evil men, you, soldiers and children of New Mexico, have been
called together in your greatness and your might. . . ."

"That is a lie."

He lowered his head and a shadow was on the canyon. The
officers in front of him separated and three men rode up, and the
first of the three was Caballero and his throat dried and the fear
was in him again, balling like a spiked fist in his belly, and the
smell of it was in his nose. "Don Esquipulas, you have returned to
your people at last," he said, working hard on it. The timbre was
gone.

"You lie, Don Manuel," Caballero said. His own voice was
flat and without tone, and now the soldiers strained to hear him
and he remembered Ramón Baca in the plaza before the palace
calling upon these same officers. "You have lied from the beginning, and your lie now is greater than before. The Americans do

not come as enemies. They have committed no crimes. They have passed through villages of New Mexico and they have harmed no one. They are not all heretics. There are Catholics among them, many Catholics, good Catholics, as good and as devout as any here. They have injured no priests. They have burned no churches. They have raped no women and they carry no branding irons. You lie, Don Manuel!"

The agitation started again and Don Manuel knew it was changing. The wind was altering its course and the trees were beginning to bend in a new direction and the fire that he had kindled was beginning to blow in his face. The fear was tying knots in him and the smell would soon escape and other men would smell it. If only he could stop the pushing long enough to look again on himself. "Do you believe that any loyal soldier of New Mexico will believe the word of a traitor?" he demanded, and this time he got scorn into his voice. All he needed was a little time. *I am Don Manuel Armijo,* he shouted to himself, *I am the Governor,* and he felt the sweat on his face and he smelled the fear.

"I am no traitor," Caballero said in the same pitiless voice, remembering how Baca had cried out and how men who had given him their word had refused him. "I have never been traitor to my country. My word is more honest than yours."

"You were traitor from the beginning!"

"I supported you when you journeyed to Taos to start the revolution that loosed the Indian Gonzales upon your own people. Was I traitor to you then, Don Manuel?"

"You speak falsely!" Don Manuel shouted, and now he had to shout. The vibrancy was gone and noise had to substitute.

"I guarded your life on that journey, Don Manuel, may God forgive me, and I helped the revolution you made by bringing to the Indian the guns that killed New Mexicans, and I was at his side when those guns were fired for the first time."

"Lies! Lies! All lies!"

Caballero pointed with his rifle. "There stands Padre Martínez. Ask the priest if I lie."

Don Manuel turned his head to Padre Martínez. The camp was empty of sound as though no living thing were there. The eyes of the Governor and the priest locked and then on the eroded face

588

the mark of fatality settled and the priest lowered his head and the fear roiled. They were back to the beginning of all things, the three, the intriguer and the priest and the rico.

"He speaks true," Padre Martínez said.

"I have lived with these Americans," Caballero said. "They are men of decency. Their leader has dignity and truth. Half of the land to the north has gone over to him. Las Vegas, Tecolote, San Miguel, all are now pledged in allegiance to the United States. The Americans are stronger than you are, Don Manuel, and with their guns they have truth and liberty on their side. You speak from a well of lies, and when you go from the land a stench will go with you."

The agitation erupted into shouting and Don Manuel knew it now was gone. His hand had been opened and his fingers had been spread apart and it had trickled through them like grains of sand. He turned again to look at the priest and he heard a snarl of rage and an oath and then a shot and he whirled to see a musket spinning from the hands of a soldier and blood spreading on his wrist and smoke curling from the mouth of Caballero's rifle. And then, in that time of his peril and his abandonment, he knew he no longer had the fear.

"You will not make him into a martyr," Caballero said. "It will not be said in the time to come that Manuel Armijo was assassinated on the field of battle by a treacherous soldier. The name of Armijo will not become legend and weapon to rally other evil men." He moved his eyes to Fernando, seated immobile on his horse, next to Carlos Gutiérrez. "It is not Manuel Armijo alone who must be removed from New Mexico. It is the idea of Armijo."

"Lies! All treachery and lies!" Don Manuel shouted automatically, sounds in an empty hall.

"There sits Carlos Gutiérrez," Caballero said. "You engaged him to misguide Texans five years ago and then pretended to the world that you defeated them honorably. Ask this man if he was traitor then or is now."

It was ended now, everything was ended, the pattern had been woven to its close. And the fear, the old fear, the great and consuming fear that had lived with him always as an obscene odor, was ended with it and now all that remained was the style. He gestured carelessly with his hand and said with pure indifference:

"Thousand thanks, Don Esquipulas, for saving my life even though it is only that I may be the more fully destroyed."

"For nothing," Caballero said, and, recognizing the style and responding to it, added: "Excelencia."

Now Don Manuel raised his arms and filled his lungs. "Soldiers! Hear me! Until I go I am your Governor and your commanding general! You will obey me to the last, as soldiers!" The voice rose powerfully over the clamor. The sonority was there again and the words rolled out like thunderclaps. His face was transfixed with triumphant exaltation and his eyes blazed with his new victory. "Cannoneers, spike your cannon!" he commanded. "Officers, form your companies and lead them from the canyon in order!" He looked upon his soldiers for the last time and he gave his final command. "Army of New Mexico! Return to your houses. You are dismissed."

He sat in his saddle with the true arrogance, the arrogance that he had sought all his life and that had eluded him always and had come to him now unbidden, and he watched the men march away with precision as soldiers, in obedience, and then he thought of that which he had had no time to think of since he had stepped forth from his tent. "Salazar! Where is Salazar?"

Captain Tomás Martínez pointed across the flatland to a rider galloping toward Santa Fe. "He has gone, excelencia."

"Don Esquipulas!" Don Manuel said.

"Yes, excelencia."

"Catch him! He has done some evil with your wife."

Caballero spun around to Carlos Gutiérrez. "Return to General Kearny and give him word of what has occurred here!" He faced Don Manuel. "You make up for much, excelencia."

Don Manuel knew peace. "It balances, Don Esquipulas, it balances always," he said tranquilly. "Now hurry, friend, and may the Blessed Virgin give your horse speed."

He watched with untroubled eyes as Caballero and Fernando flew off to the west, and then he turned his gaze on the columns of soldiers marching out of the canyon and he shrugged his shoulders with the manner and he signaled to the captain of his guard. "Ready the men, señor capitán, he said. "We leave."

The captain touched his hat. "I obey, excelencia."

Don Manuel looked down at Padre Martínez. "Ea, padre, the

time of Armijo is finished and now the time of the gringo officially
begins. Adiós, padre."

"Adiós, Don Manuel." The priest's fingers touched his cross.
Don Manuel waved his hand and rode away to the south.

1

Iᴛ ᴡᴀѕ ᴍᴏʀᴇ than five miles east of Apache Canyon on the road to Santa Fe before the two men came close enough to Damasio Salazar for Fernando to loosen the coils of his lazo. For more than half an hour Salazar had been within rifleshot and he had fired twice at his pursuers, and Caballero's hand had twitched at his gun and he knew he could not use it and risk killing Salazar. He had thought even of shooting the horse, but he had been afraid that Salazar might be thrown and knocked unconscious or even killed. As Fernando opened the noose, Salazar fired again and then the lazo was cast and the noose circled and dropped over Salazar's shoulders. As he squirmed to slip it off, Fernando's horse came to automatic stop and Salazar was jerked from the saddle and the lazo had not slackened its tension before Caballero was astride him, his knife at his throat.

"Speak quickly," Caballero said.

Salazar's eyes glazed with panic. He struggled. Caballero flicked a tiny triangle of flesh from his throat. "Speak! I have not the strength in my arm to keep the steel too long from your throat. En el nombre de Dios, where is she before I skewer you to the ground!"

Salazar stopped his struggling. "I tell you what I told Don Manuel. You will not kill me. If I am dead you will never find where she is."

"I will ask you once again," Caballero said. "Where is she?" He touched the throat with the knife point.

"And you will never know!"

"Santo Dios!" Caballero's face tightened and it was the moment before death.

"He is right," Fernando said. "You cannot kill him."

"Get off me!" Salazar screamed suddenly. For another moment the death remained in Caballero's face and then he got slowly to his feet. Salazar scrambled up. He slipped the lazo from his arms and straightened his tunic and pushed back his hair. He kicked the lazo. "I alone know where she is!" he taunted. "Kill me! Kill me! Without me you are blind!" He spat at Caballero's feet. "Kill me! Kill me! And when you find her you will find nothing but bones drying in the sun!" He pounded his chest with his fists. "I am the only one who can lead you to her! I!" He danced back and forth.

"Cut a small twig from a tree, Fernando," Caballero said.

Puzzled, Fernando drew his knife and hacked off a sprig. Salazar stopped his capering and looked at one and then the other.

"Cut me some slivers," Caballero said. "Ten of them. One for each finger."

Salazar threw his hands behind his back. "No!"

"Don Ramón suffered all ten," Caballero said remotely. "This scum will not, but if he should surprise me we will cut another ten for the feet."

Salazar backed away. "No!"

Caballero picked up the noose and dropped it over Salazar's shoulders again and tightened it, securing his arms to his sides, and he kicked Salazar's feet from under him. He sat on his chest and took his right hand and straightened the fingers. "Give me the first sliver, Fernando. And then take out your flint. We need fire as well."

"I will tell you where she is!" Salazar screamed.

Caballero paused with the sliver half an inch from Salazar's forefinger.

"I will tell you where she is. Swear to me that you will not kill me afterward."

Caballero inserted the sliver under the nail and took out his knife, and holding it by the blade, he raised the haft.

"You have no time to lose, believe me," Salazar panted. "Swear to me that you will not lay hands on me later and I will tell you where she is."

"He will faint with the first sliver and it will take half a day to revive him," Fernando said.

The knife handle remained poised. "I swear it," Caballero said.

"Nor that you will permit him to slay me for you."

593

"I swear it."

"Nor engage any other man."

"Cuerpo de Cristo!" Fernando roared. "This filth should have been a lawyer!"

"I swear it." Caballero's voice was without shadow of life.

"Repeat it, word for word," Salazar said.

Caballero closed his eyes. "I swear that I will not harm you nor permit Fernando to harm you nor hire anyone else to harm you. Now speak or I kill you before the words can come from your mouth."

"On your honor."

"On my honor as a Caballero." The haft shook.

Still Salazar hesitated and then the words spewed forth. "I brought her to the pueblo of Santo Domingo."

"Where her father was butchered." Caballero reversed the knife in his hand. "And you told them she was born Abreu."

"*Remember your oath!*"

"You are wasting minutes," Fernando said gruffly. He took Caballero by the shoulder. "*Vamanos!* There may still be time."

Caballero stood up with the stiff, aching, angular motions of a rheumatic. "We will take this thing with us."

"You gave your word," Salazar wept.

"If we are late, I will reclaim it."

2

FERNANDO pointed to the lurid glow in the night sky. "There is a ceremony going on."

"The ceremony is a long one," Caballero said. He crossed himself. "If they have started, Nuestro Señor, then take her to You quickly. Do not allow her to linger, I beseech You." He whipped his horse.

Then in the night they heard the Teguan chanting. "Can you tell anything from the sounds, Fernando?" Caballero asked.

"No."

"It is different before and during and afterward." He prayed:

"Nuestro Señor, bring me there before it has begun, or after it is ended. If it has started, take her to You quickly."

"They are all unfamiliar to me," Fernando said.

Caballero's horse stumbled. He pulled back on the reins and kicked his spurs into the animal's heaving sides.

"Easy," Fernando said. "The horses are almost done in."

The hoofs sparked on the stones and the gully widened and the glow became brighter and the chanting drifted across the night.

"What is your plan?" Fernando asked.

"What plan can there be? I will go to her."

"And then?"

"I do not know. At the least I can give her the death faster than they will."

They climbed out of the gully and rode across an open field, and before them was the great fire. They saw figures dancing, and the chanting swelled until the night held nothing but that; and then one of the dancing figures threw something into the fire and a great orange flame soared, and in that light they saw the stock and the figure that was locked in the stock.

"Remain just outside the light, Fernando," Caballero said. "Do not allow this thing to get away from you."

He whipped the horse again and was in the plaza and then at her side. He slid from the horse and looked at her, and he saw she was alive and not yet mutilated. "*Gracias, Nuestro Señor,*" he whispered. He stepped behind her and put his hand around her shoulder and under her chin, and he held her tightly, feeling the trembling in her. And now the dancing stopped, as though time had stopped, and the chanting died and the plaza was quiet except for the crackling of the fire.

He felt her nails dig into his wrist. "You know what they mean to do," she said.

"Yes."

"Do not let them, Esquipulas."

"I will not," he said.

"Use the steel."

"There is time for that."

"There is no time," she said fiercely. "They will rush you. Use the steel now!"

595

"There is time."

"Unsheathe it and hold it against me. Let me feel that it is there. Hombre, do not let them touch me."

"I will not. I swear it, Soledad."

"The death is nothing. Do not let them touch me."

"They will not."

No one had moved. From everywhere they stared at him. He knew that the shock had stunned them and that if he would speak, it must be now. "Indios del pueblo de Santo Domingo, hear me!" His voice went out into the night and echoed on the walls of the pueblo and he heard the words repeated as though from a great way away.

"Where is it?" she asked. "Where is the steel?"

He drew his knife and held the point at her back behind her heart, and with his other hand he took his revolver from its holster and cocked it and held it at his side. The Indians still were silent. "You are about to do an evil thing to this woman who is my wife," he said. The words repeated themselves mockingly. "You do not know this woman and you cannot hate her and yet you would kill her because of the memory of her father, who you believe committed wrongs against you. This woman no longer is Abreu. She is Caballero, and no one of that name has ever injured you." The words came back to him and they were the wrongest words.

The cracked voice of an old man rose in answer. "She was born Abreu. It is enough. Death to the Abreu!" A great shout acclaimed the pronouncement. The words echoed with lunatic insistence.

"You revenged yourself on the judge," Caballero said. "He died here in this plaza in this stock and he died bravely and you received your vengeance in full measure. You drew from him what you might have drawn from six lesser men. He died as a warrior and he fed your vengeance and it needs no more. You are a brave people and you have warriors among you and it does no honor to your pueblo to take vengeance on a woman."

"Kill the Abreu!" The words sang back: Kill the Abreu, kill the Abreu. . . .

"Kill her husband with her!" . . . her husband with her, her husband with her. . . .

She struggled at the bonds that held her hands and feet and

he felt a light blow on the knife. He looked down and saw she had impinged herself on the tip of the blade. He pulled the knife away. "Wait!"

"There is no time, hombre, do it now!" She flung back her shoulders.

"When the time comes, wife, it will take but a little moment."

"*Now, now, now!*" She fought with her bonds. "Someone may shoot you from a distance. Now, now, while there is yet time. Ah, Santa Madre, do not be a coward, hombre. The death is nothing. *Do it now!*"

A breeze stirred and he felt sweat chill on his body. "Indios! Heed me before you do what may not be undone. The time of Judge Abreu is long passed. The time that has followed the judge has passed. A new time has come on the land today. We are a new country. Governor Armijo has fled and an American army has come here. New Mexico now belongs to the Americans. Your legend is that men with yellow hair and blue eyes will come from the east and deliver you. That day is today. The Americans are here. Do not couple with murder the fulfillment of your holy legend!"

Now many voices were raised in shouting and then a figure stepped forth from among the Indians. He said, in Spanish: "I am a warrior. I will speak." He walked slowly toward the stock.

"Los dulces Nombres," she whispered. "Before he gets here, Esquipulas, quickly. Nuestro Señor Jesucristo, forgive me my sins. *Now, hombre, now!*" She writhed on the bench and tried again to impale herself on the knife.

"He spoke in Spanish for a reason," Caballero said swiftly. "It was so we would understand him."

"They have seen your pistol. The steel, husband, or the ball!"

The man now was almost on them and there was something about him that tugged at Caballero's memory, and yet there was nothing about the powerful figure in the buffalo robe or the face marked with yellow and red that he recognized.

"If I do it, Soledad, it will be without warning."

"Yes, yes," she said. "Hombre, you I love! Now, quickly, deeply, do not miss the mark!"

The man stopped five paces from them and he turned and faced his people. He raised his muscular arms for silence and there were angry protests. He began to speak in Teguan in a voice that was not loud. He was interrupted now and again by more shouting, but each time it seemed to Caballero, waiting with the knife and the revolver, looking down at the dark hair, at the neck, at the arms, at the swell of the breasts, at the trembling in the belly, remembering all of the flesh that was under the blouse and under the skirt, each time, it seemed, there were fewer voices to oppose the speaker. And then he was interrupted no longer and his voice ceased to explain and it got hard and he no longer was asking. He was telling, with tones of command, and no one defied him and his voice became stronger with each word, and Caballero saw the shuddering lessen in the shoulders that were pressed against his thighs and he felt the old and lost aching.

The Indian stopped and waited, and when the plaza remained silent for a full minute, he turned toward the stock and struck out the pegs that held the clamps locked. He lifted the bar that covered her legs and lifted the bar that held down her arms, and he said, in Spanish: "You are free, Señora Caballero. Forgive my people. Many of the old ones still live with their forefathers." He turned his painted face to Caballero. "My gods have favored me, Don Esquipulas. They have privileged me to return favor and there is no greater gift. I would have come to you as soon as you pronounced your name, but as you began to speak I knew it would be good for my people to listen to what you had to say." Then he looked down at the revolver and the knife with the blood dark on its point. "I might have been too late."

"Who are you?" Caballero asked.

"Have you rescued so many pueblo Indians from Navajos that you have forgotten, Don Esquipulas?"

Caballero's eyes opened wide. "Teniente Angel! I had forgotten you were of this pueblo!" He held the Indian to his heart.

"We were twenty, Don Esquipulas," Lieutenant Hernandez Angel said. "We are still in your debt." Then he asked: "Has Don Manuel truly fled?"

"This morning."

"And the Americans are here?"

"Yes, friend."

"Then my people will have greater reason for celebration tonight than even the old men could have foretold. Come, I will give you fresh horses. You may walk among my people in safety. I have told them that because of you twenty of their sons are alive."

"There are two others waiting outside the plaza," Caballero said.

"I will order horses for all."

They walked past the people, who now gazed at them in silence, and then an old woman ran to Caballero and took his hand and kissed it.

"She is the mother of one of the men you saved from Navajo knives," Angel said.

Four horses were led out and the saddles were changed and Fernando lifted Salazar and placed him on one of the fresh horses. Angel glanced curiously at the fettered man but he said nothing. "Return again, Don Esquipulas," he said. "Let my people make up to you their inhospitality to your name. You should know that the debate ran for two days in the kiva and that it was only the old men who desired your wife to be slain." He stepped back. "*Hasta luego, amigos.*"

3

WHEN THEY WERE AWAY from the pueblo, Soledad reached out and squeezed Fernando's hand and then she asked: "Who is the other?"

"A friend named Salazar," Caballero said.

"You keep exquisite company, hombre. What do you do with him?"

"I have not yet decided."

"We keep him to frighten snakes," Fernando grunted.

"You swore to free me," Salazar snarled. "You have the woman back. Why do you not keep your word?"

"I swore only to do you no harm," Caballero said. "I am not harming you. To ride on a horse is healthful."

"You gave your oath!"

"Fernando, if he opens his mouth again, stuff something into it."

"Such as a fist?"

"No permita Dios!" Soledad said. "You would poison yourself."

"I forgot about that," Fernando said.

"Could he be kept to the rear?" Soledad asked. "I spent one night bound and gagged across the back of his horse and I have grown to dislike him."

The chanting in the pueblo started again.

"Esquipulas, my husband," Soledad said in another voice.

"There is no need to say anything," he said swiftly.

She was silent for a moment. "I was going to say only that I cannot ride much longer. I was frightened there in the pueblo, hombre, and I am tired."

"We will make camp soon."

"I am very tired. May I ride with you?"

He moved his horse next to hers and lifted her into the saddle in front of him.

"Thank you, Don Esquipulas," she said.

"For favor."

"Esquipulas."

"Yes."

"Don Manuel is gone?"

"Yes, señora."

"For good?"

"Yes."

"Did he run from Santa Fe?"

"He went first to Apache Canyon."

"But there was no battle with the gringos?"

"No."

"He left his troops in the canyon and fled?"

"He dismissed them."

"So that after all in the end he did badly."

"Not too badly, señora. He did it well."

"To give up without a fight? To flee?"

"There were circumstances. He did not do too badly."

"Did he have anything to do with Salazar abducting me, Esquipulas?"

"It was he who told me of it. If he had not, I would not have found out until it was too late."

She said in a low, distant voice: "It is typical. He was small in great things and great in small things." Her voice petered out. "May I close my eyes for a little moment?"

"Please."

"If your arm tires, waken me."

"We will make camp in a little while and then you can sleep in more comfort."

She settled in the saddle and pressed his arm against her breast. "I am comfortable," she said, and was asleep.

The glow behind them was dim in the night. The chanting was remote and without meaning.

"What do we do with this filth?" Fernando asked.

"I have been thinking about him," Caballero said.

"It would be pleasant to kill him."

"It would be."

"You swore," Salazar sobbed.

"You should have given him to the Indians in exchange for Doña Soledad," Fernando said.

He felt her breast on his arm. "I thought of that too. But then we would have had to stay and watch and I was getting bored."

"It is true. It was a dull sight. And it would not have been proper after that speech. Por Dios, hombre, but that was a speech! It was very moving."

"Thanks, for nothing."

"Two in the same day. You are becoming the great talker. When the gringos make their new government you should become a politician. Perhaps you can persuade Don Manuel to return to Santa Fe and give you advice."

"I will consider it."

"But what *of* this thing?"

"I do not know, amigo."

"But you have been thinking."

"Yes."

"Fruitfully?"

"Who knows?"

"It would be pleasant to kill him, even quickly."

"Would it not?"

Salazar groaned. Soledad stirred and Caballero tightened his arm around her.

1

THE ARMY OF THE WEST reached the east approach to
Apache Canyon on the morning of August 18, forty-eight hours
after General Armijo dismissed his troops. Carlos Gutiérrez had re-
joined Kearny the day before and had given him a full report on
what had taken place in the canyon. Other natives encountered
on the route verified that the pass was undefended, but, wary of
possible trickery, Kearny dispatched a reconnaisance party under
Captain Cooke to explore the stronghold.

Cooke found the pass abandoned. He left some soldiers to
take apart enough of the abatis for the army to pass by freely and
returned to Kearny with the word that there now was apparently
nothing between him and the capital of New Mexico.

Kearny entered the pass a few minutes before noon. He took
in the position rapidly. "They were well prepared for us," he said.

An officer rode up. "There is a horseman waiting on the plains
beyond, general."

"Bring him to me." Kearny lifted his glasses. Then he lowered
them. "I thought it might have been Caballero. Colonel Magoffin,
take these glasses and see if you recognize that man."

Magoffin said: "It is Donanciano Vigil."

"Who is he?"

"He was a loyal supporter of Governor Pérez."

Vigil rode up behind the officer and bowed low in his saddle.
"General Kearny, I come to you in the name of Don Juan Bautista
Vigil, who is Acting Governor of New Mexico. Don Juan Bautista
presents his compliments and sends you this letter."

Magoffin translated the communication: "Don Manuel
Armijo has fled from New Mexico. I serve in his place. I welcome
you to Santa Fe and offer you the hospitality and friendship of the
people of New Mexico." The note was signed: "Don Juan Bautista
Vigil y Alarid, Lieutenant Governor of New Mexico." Magoffin

smiled to himself, thinking how the magnificently protean post-master had adapted himself to this completest of all changes in government with his usual flawless skill.

"We will continue on to the capital immediately," Kearny said.

"We can get there before nightfall if we push, general," Magoffin said.

A note of excitement crept into Kearny's voice. "Then by God, we'll push, colonel! Tell this gentleman I'll be in Santa Fe before the day is out."

Don Donanciano's teeth flashed. He waved his sombrero and took off.

Again Kearny glanced around the canyon. "It would have been quite a fight, Colonel Magoffin," he said. "I wonder what did the trick. Captain Cooke, was it you? Or you, Colonel Magoffin? Or was it Caballero?"

"Perhaps it was a combination of all three," Magoffin said.

"The important thing is that it has worked," Kearny said, "although I understand the boys are disappointed because they have been denied a fight. They seem to feel I have let them down." He breathed deeply. "I have no regret."

Kearny ordered spare horses and mules for the artillery carriages, and the army moved on. The men forgot their hunger and weariness with magical speed. The animals possessed no such imagination. A half-dozen times on the way to Santa Fe the infantry was forced to halt to give the animals rest. Kearny was determined the Army of the West would enter the capital intact.

At three o'clock in the afternoon the first units marched into the city. The last soldier was in Santa Fe by six o'clock. The Army of the West had traveled from the Missouri River to the capital of New Mexico, a distance of eight hundred and twenty-one miles, in less than sixty days.

The natives lined the streets, and though women did not run in terror with their children, there were many who wept and it could not be said which tears were shed in sorrow and which in relief.

Don Juan Bautista Vigil and a number of prominent citizens, including many men just released from the prison cells where they had been detained by Don Manuel, awaited the American general in front of the Palace of the Governors. And there from the aged postmaster General Kearny accepted the surrender of New Mexico.

The August sun slipped toward the rim of the Jemez Mountains and the adobe buildings took on their rosy color and the red pool rose slowly on the Sangre de Cristos. "The conquistadores called those mountains the Blood of Christ, señor general," Don Juan Bautista said. "The blood rises, as you can see."

Kearny lifted his eyes to the sun-stained mountains. He said quietly: "Let us give our thanks to Him that no other blood has flowed in New Mexico today."

At that moment the hush in the plaza was rent by a thirteen-gun salute from the cannon that had been dragged up the hill to the south. They were the first shots fired by the Americans in New Mexico. The reverberation still shivered the air as the Mexican flag was lowered from its staff in front of the palace and for the first time the Stars and Stripes were raised over the ancient Royal City of the Holy Faith of St. Francis.

General Kearny was escorted to the governor's apartment in the palace, and before he made himself ready for the reception that was to be given in his honor that evening he wrote a short dispatch to the Secretary of War in which he reported that the conquest of New Mexico had been accomplished "without firing a shot, or spilling a drop of blood."

2

La Fonda was filled with American soldiers. The air was almost opaque with smoke, and the low vigas shook with the singing and shouting. Caballero stepped into the room and looked around and then he walked from table to table, peering down at the revelers. His face brightened and he pushed his way through the crowd. "Don Cornelio," he said.

Cornelius Fitzgerald looked up and then jumped to his feet with a yell and threw his arms around Caballero. "Where the hell have you been, laddie?"

"So you have reached Santa Fe at last," Caballero smiled.

"Five years late, but, by the saints, I made it! Sit down and have a drink."

"Are you happy, amigo?"

"For the moment."

"Only for the moment?"

The joy left Fitzgerald's face. "I have a little business to take care of."

"You have not forgotten?"

"I'll never forget!"

"You have not cast thoughts of revenge from your mind?"

Fitzgerald's blue eyes turned icy. "It *is* my mind."

Caballero shook his head reprovingly. "And what do you do?"

"Drink, laddie, drink. Sit down and join me."

"Would it be possible for you to spare a moment or two?"

"For what?"

"You remember Don Ramón Baca."

"I'm not in the habit of forgetting people who save my life."

"Perhaps you would not mind it too much if I asked you to pay a short visit to his old house here."

Fitzgerald scratched his red hair. "Now?"

"Now, for favor."

"Of course, laddie, if you say so." He finished what was left in his glass and followed Caballero out of the tavern.

During the short walk through the crowded plaza and up the narrow street Caballero was silent. They entered the Casa Baca. Fitzgerald looked around. "Looks like nobody lived here for quite a while."

"It is true," Caballero said in a low voice.

The furniture was covered with dust. The cloth around the walls hung in tatters. The house smelled unused.

"No one lives here now," Caballero said. "Once this was a very happy house, Don Cornelio. You could not tell it now, but there was much happiness here. There were children and there was noise and there was laughter, and Don Ramón and Doña Guadalupe teased each other and they loved each other very much."

"Where is she now?"

"She lives with relatives in the country. She could not bear to remain here. She is like an old woman now, I have been told. It is difficult for me to think of Lupe as an old woman." Caballero went to a cabinet and took out a bottle. He held it up. It was a third full. "This must be how Don Ramón left it," he said. "Lupe did not like to drink alone. I do not believe it would be wrong to swallow a little brandy to Don Ramón. I believe he would have been quite happy on this day."

He poured the brandy and when they drank it he said: "That one liked his brandy very much. With no more than two drinks he used to make unkind remarks about Don Manuel. Lupe worried about him all the time." Then Caballero said: "You know, Don Cornelio, this Baca was a great fencer. He had a special room to practice in. He had not the length of arm to be among the best, but he made up for it with activity. Would you like to see his fencing-room?"

"Yes," Fitzgerald said.

"Follow me." They walked down a corridor and turned a corner. In front of a closed door stood Fernando, his arms folded on his chest. "Don Ramón had many swords, some from Spain and others from France," Caballero said musingly. "He prized them. He had this room built with thick walls and he had the windows barred. Of course, none of the weapons are in the room now, but I believe it will hold interest for you." Fernando stepped aside and Caballero pushed open the door. "Go in, Don Cornelio."

Fitzgerald stepped into the room. His body became rigid. A look of pure rapture settled on his face.

Caballero closed the door behind him quietly. "You removed the bonds, of course," he said.

"Of course," Fernando said.

"Long enough ago for the arms to lose their stiffness?"

"Yes."

"Bueno. I do not believe Don Cornelio would want it too easy and yet I also do not believe he could wait." He shrugged. "We had better go, Fernando. I have heard that the Irish have bad tempers."

606

3

In the street Caballero asked: "What do you do now?"

"I return to Bent's Fort."

"Of course. Give my affections to Morena and the children."

"I have been told that Don Carlos will leave there shortly to come to Santa Fe to begin his service as governor. I hope to get there in time to return with my family with him."

"Don Ramón's house will remain empty. Why do you not all move in there?"

"Perhaps we will."

"I believe it would please Doña Guadalupe very much."

"And you, Esquipulas? What do you do now?"

They reached the corner of the plaza. "Who knows?"

Fernando took his arm. "Go to her."

"You had better get started."

"You said it yourself. All things are now begun anew."

"Go with God, Fernando," Caballero said.

Alone, Caballero walked slowly under the portal opposite the palace. From the time he had brought Soledad to the house on the Calle de la Muralla the day before, he had felt a stranger in the city he had not seen in four years. He had visited the grave of his father and he still felt he no longer belonged to Santa Fe.

He was about to enter La Fonda when he heard himself hailed. He turned his head. His eyes lighted. "Capitán Cooke," he said. "It is good to see you again. I was just going in to have a little drink. I would be honored if you would join me."

"I should like nothing better, Don Esquipulas, but I am on duty," Cooke said. "I was sent by the general to find you. There is going to be a reception in the palace, and the general wants very much for you to attend."

"He is kind," Caballero said.

Cooke looked at him keenly. "You do not seem happy, señor. Is this not what you wanted?"

"I am happy, mi capitán. In a way I am happier than I have ever been happy before. It is good that you all are here at last,

607

and it pleases me that I was of some help. But it is also strange and a little sad."

"I understand, Don Esquipulas," Cooke said quietly. "But you will come to the official reception?"

"If that is what the general desires."

"He requested that you put on your old uniform."

Caballero looked up quickly. He said: "I will do so."

"The general will expect you as soon as you have changed."

"I will be there," Caballero said.

He crossed the plaza and walked up the Calle de la Muralla. He paused for a moment outside the house and then he entered. He went directly to his room and opened a chest. He took out his uniform and his father was very close to him and for a moment he was unable to move. Then he laid the uniform on his bed and washed and shaved and dressed himself. He looked on the wall for his sword and remembered it had been taken from him the last time he had gone to see Don Manuel in the palace.

He went to his father's room and took his father's sword from its place on the wall and buckled it on. He looked at the bed in which his father had died and he knelt and crossed himself, and then he walked from the room.

The sala was almost in darkness. "Don Esquipulas."

He stopped and did not turn toward the voice. "Pardon, señora, I did not intend to disturb you. General Kearny has asked that I attend the reception given in his honor in the palace and he specified that I appear in uniform, else I would not have come here."

"And now you go to drink Don Manuel's wine and smoke Don Manuel's cigars."

"Would you prefer that Don Manuel was there to serve as host, señora?"

"I would not. But neither am I overjoyed to see gringos there in triumph."

"It needed to be the one or the other."

"Perhaps. And yet I am less than happy."

"You may go to the Rio Abajo. It still will take time before the Americans penetrate to the haciendas."

"Is it your desire that I remove myself from your house?"

"This no longer is my house, señora. I will not disturb you again."

"Don Esquipulas."

"Yes, señora."

"It is strange to see you again in uniform."

"It feels no less strange."

"I remember the day you wore another, just like it."

"That was a long time ago, señora. I will keep you no longer."

"Give your eyes to me once before you depart."

He turned and looked at her in the twilight of the room. The ache was there and he knew it would never leave.

"I spoke some words at the pueblo, señor," she said.

"You said many things in your distress, Doña Soledad. It is understandable. I have forgotten them all."

"Is there another woman, husband?"

"No."

"Is there anything left of us?"

His fingers trembled against his sword. "You are still distraught, señora."

"Don Esquipulas."

"Yes, señora."

"This house and everything in it are yours."

He stood silent in the shadows of the room and then he went to her.

4

EARLY THE NEXT MORNING at General Kearny's order the people of Santa Fe were summoned to the plaza. Kearny and his staff, and Don Juan Bautista Vigil, who had culminated a quarter of century of service in the New Mexican government by becoming, at the end, the New Mexican government itself, climbed to the roof of the palace. Kearny, his emaciated face flushed with fever, stood at the rampart and looked down at the massed people.

"New Mexicans, we have come amongst you to take possession of New Mexico, which we do in the name of the government of the United States," the general said. "We have come with peaceable intentions and kind feelings to you all. We come to better your conditions and make you part of the Republic of the United States."

In a corner of the plaza Soledad held tightly to the hand of her husband and she held her head in the manner he had come to know as belonging to her alone.

"We do not mean to murder you or rob you of your property," Kearny continued. "Your families shall be free from molestation, your women secure from violence. My soldiers shall take nothing but what they pay for. In taking possession of New Mexico we do not mean to take away from you your religion. Religion and government have no connection in our country. There all religions are equal. One has no preference over the other, the Catholic and the Protestant are esteemed alike. Every man has the right to serve God according to his heart. When a man dies he must render to God an account of his acts here on earth, whether they be good or bad. In our government all men are equal. We esteem the most peaceable man, the best man. I advise you to attend to your domestic pursuits, cultivate industry, be peaceable and obedient to the laws. Do not resort to violent means to correct abuses."

He paused and then said: "I do hereby proclaim that being in possession of Santa Fe I am therefore virtually in possession of all New Mexico. Armijo no longer is your governor. His power is departed, but he will return and be as one of you. When he shall return you are not to molest him. You are no longer Mexican subjects. You are now become American citizens, subject only to the laws of the United States. A change of government has taken place and you no longer owe allegiance to the Mexican government. I do hereby proclaim my intention to establish in this department a civil government, on a republican basis, similar to those in our own states. It is my intention also to continue in office those by whom you have been governed, except the Governor, and such other persons as I shall appoint to office by virtue of authority vested in me.

"I am your Governor! Henceforth look to me for protection!"

There was no response from the people as Robideaux translated the last of the words, and now Don Juan Bautista Vigil stepped forward and cleared his throat and blinked his eyes. He said: "General, the address you have just delivered, in which you announce that you have taken possession of this great country in the name of the United States of America, gives us some idea of the wonderful future that awaits us. It is not for us to determine the boundaries of nations. The cabinets of Mexico and Washington will arrange these differences. It is for us to obey and respect the established authorities, no matter what may be our private opinions."

He pulled an enormous kerchief from his pocket and blew his nose. With dignity he said: "The inhabitants of this department humbly and honorably present their loyalty to the government of North America. No one in this world can successfully resist the power of him who is stronger. Do not find it strange if there has been no manifestation of joy and enthusiasm in seeing this city occupied by your military forces. To us the power of the Mexican Republic is dead. What child shall not shed abundant tears at the tomb of his parents?"

He raised his face and now his voice rang with pride: "I might indicate some of the causes for her misfortunes, but domestic troubles shall not be made public. It is sufficient to say that civil war is the cursed source of the deadly poison that has spread over one of the grandest and greatest countries ever created! Today we belong to a great and powerful nation. Its flag, with its stars and stripes, covers the horizon of New Mexico, and its brilliant light shall grow like a good seed, well cultivated."

Soledad's fingers grew rigid as it appeared Don Juan Bautista would not be able to finish. Then the old man turned to Kearny and said: "We are cognizant of your kindness, of your courtesy, and of your accommodating officers and of the strict discipline of your troops. We know we belong to the republic that owes its origin to the immortal Washington, whom all civilized nations admire and respect. How different would be our situation had we been invaded by European nations! We are aware of the unfortunate condition of the Poles." He lifted a shaking hand. "In the name then of the entire department, I swear obedience to the Northern Republic, and I render my respect to its laws and authority."

Caballero and Soledad left the plaza and walked up the street to their house. She bit her lip to hold back the tears. "He did it well," she said. "He was the last one I would have thought could have done it, and yet he did it well."

"Each in his way did it well," Caballero said.

5

ON A BRISK SEPTEMBER DAY, some three weeks from the time the Americans took possession of Santa Fe, a group of boys streamed from morning worship in the church in Taos and gathered around their priest.

"Boys," Padre Martínez said, "you have come to this school with the purpose of studying for the priesthood, and in this matter I have done what I could that you might attain that desired end. But with the present change of government a change of ideas may be necessary."

The boys looked puzzled. Padre Martínez smiled. "The genius of the American government travels in complete harmony with tolerance of worship and an entire separation of church and state. From this, logically, you will be able to gather that for the clergy the foot-of-the-knife has been broken."

"Padre, what do you mean by the foot-of-the-knife," a boy named Inocencia asked.

Padre Martínez sighed. "Did you never own a gamecock, my son?"

"No, padre."

"The knife-leg of the cock is armed with a spur, or knife."

"And now, for the priests, that is gone?" Inocencia asked.

"Yes, my son."

"What then is the form of the American government, padre?"

"Republican," the priest said. He turned his face toward the Taos Mountains. "You might say, my son, that the American government is like a burro, but on this burro jog along lawyers and not the clergy."

AFTERWARD

Don Manuel's flight carried him into Mexico, where he faced charges of desertion and cowardice. He defended his honor by maintaining that it was his army which deserted *him*, that in Apache Canyon that day only seventy-five of his troops remained loyal, referring evidently to his own elite guard, which stayed with him to the end.

Eventually he returned to the Rio Abajo and lived the life of a private and wealthy merchant for the rest of his days. It is quite possible that he never again revisited Santa Fe. He was not molested and in time he was forgotten by his contemporaries, though he became the favorite of the children near his estate for his custom of tossing handfuls of shining American copper pennies to them when he passed in his carriage. He kept a supply of the coppers in his pocket at all times for this purpose.

On the 13th day of December in 1853, during the session of the Territorial Legislature in Santa Fe, Don Manuel's old friend Henry Connelly, then a member of the Council and destined himself to serve as Governor of New Mexico during the Civil War, rose to his feet and said: "Gentlemen, I have just received word of the death of Manuel Armijo."

He offered the following resolution:

Resolved, That this Council offer the most sincere condolence to the family and friends of General Armijo, and to the Territory for the loss of one of its greatest benefactors.

Resolved, That in respect to the memory and distinguished services of General Armijo, this Council now adjourns until ten o'clock tomorrow morning.

The resolution was passed unanimously.

A NOTE ON THE TYPE

This book was set on the Linotype in ELECTRA, *designed by W. A. Dwiggins. The Electra face is a simple and readable type suitable for printing books by present-day processes. It is not based on any historical model, and hence does not echo any particular time or fashion. It is without eccentricities to catch the eye and interfere with reading—in general, its aim is to perform the function of a good book printing-type: to be read, and not seen.*

The book was composed, printed, and bound by Kingsport Press, Inc., Kingsport, Tennessee. Typography based on designs by W. A. Dwiggins. Binding design by Charles E. Skaggs.